Part III.
A Crisis on Both Worlds
Volume 3

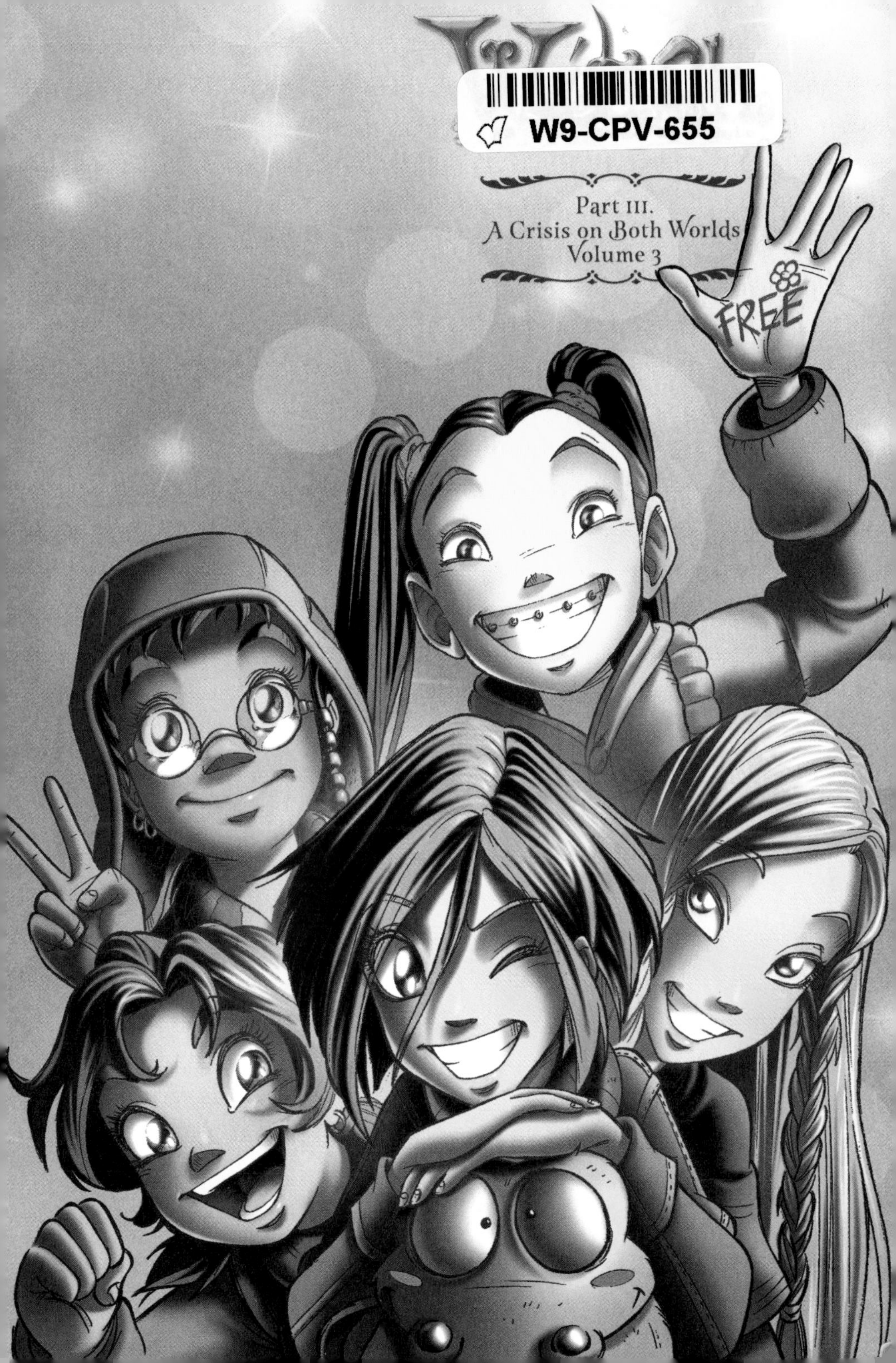
FREE

W.i.t.c.h.

Will   Irma   Taranee   Cornelia   Hay Lin

Part III.
A Crisis on Both Worlds
Volume 3

CONTENTS

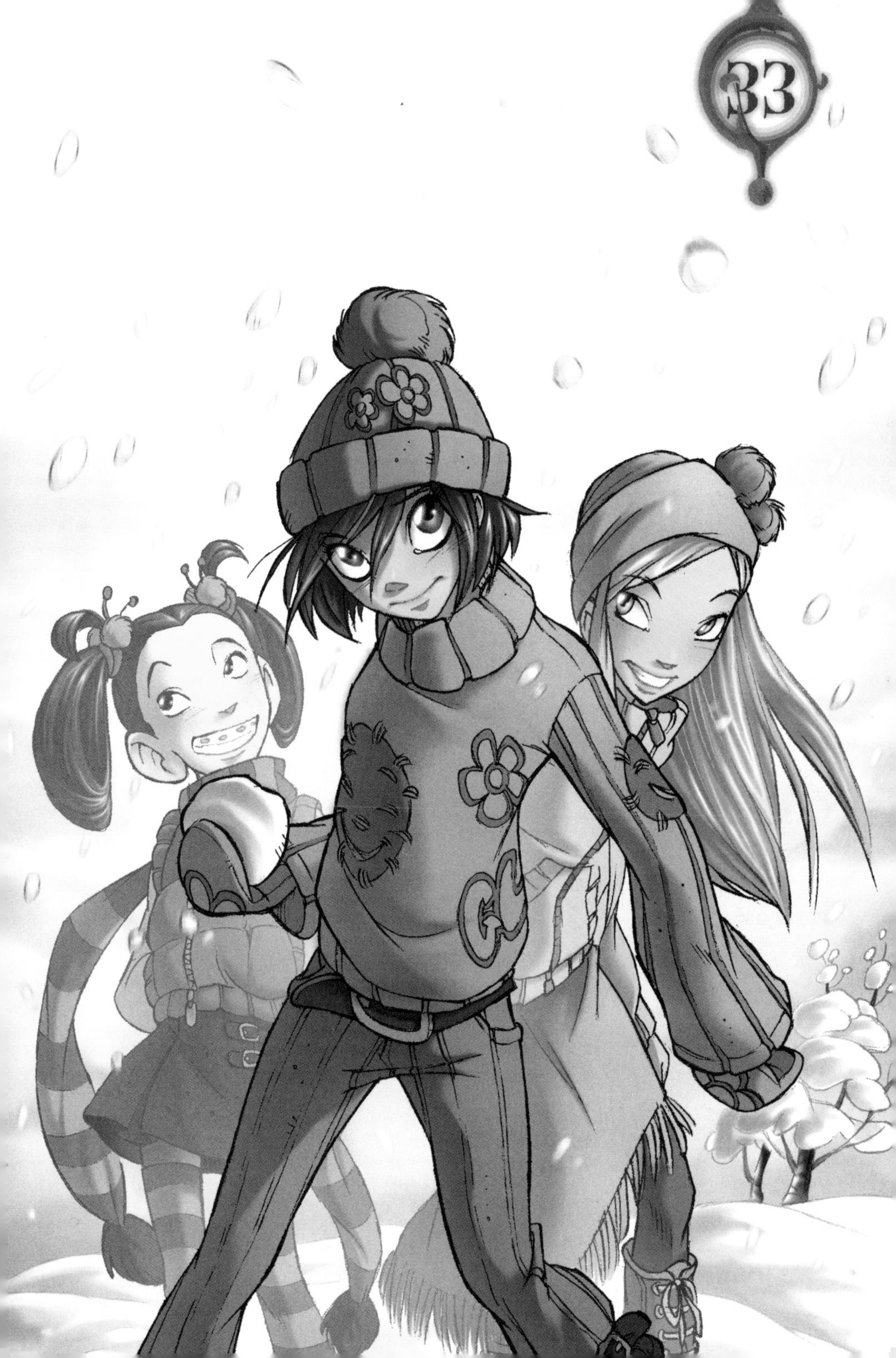
33

The Greatest Gift

"Then we'll do what needs to be done..."

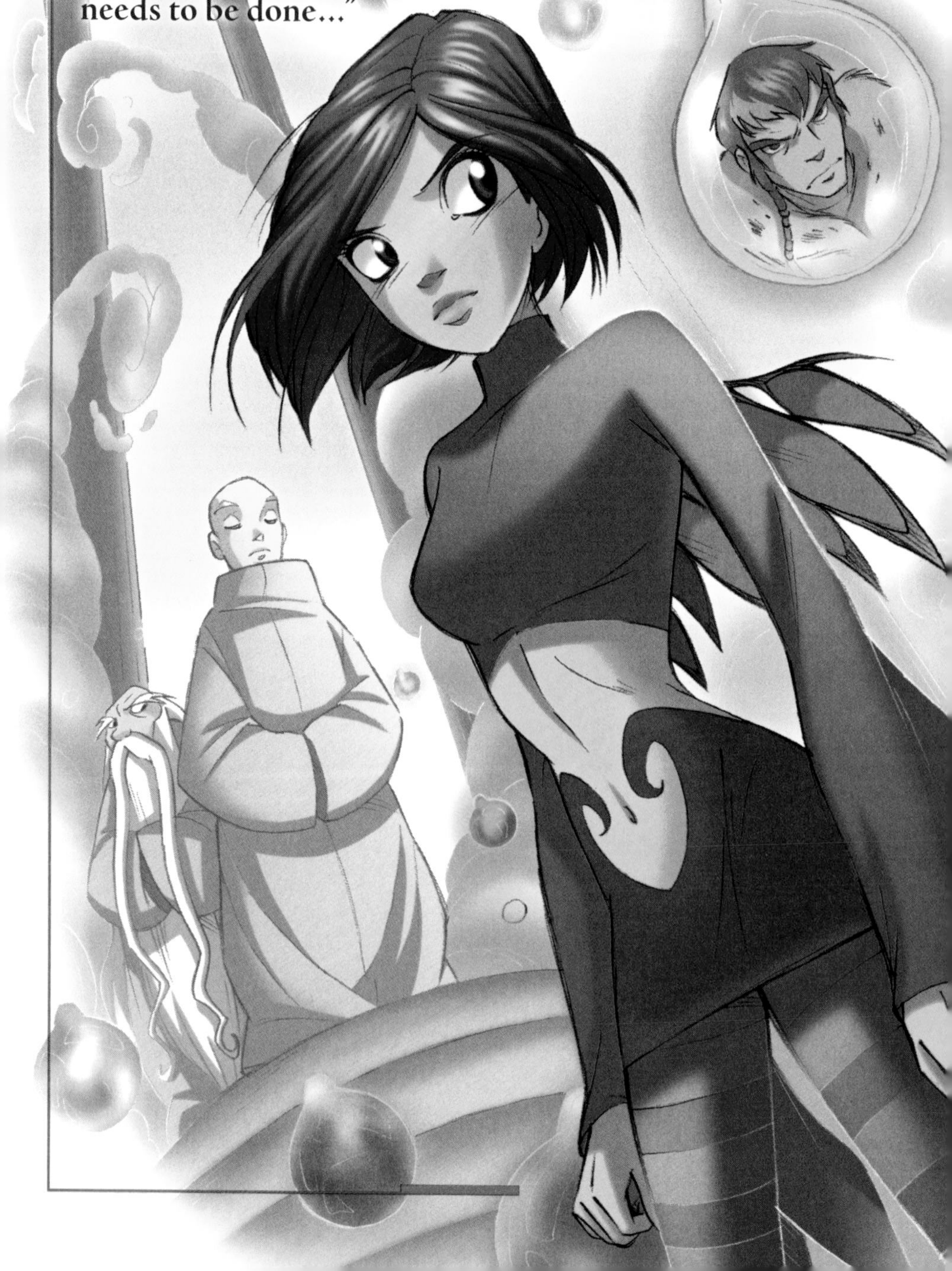

W.i.t.c.h.

Will Irma Taranee Cornelia Hay Lin

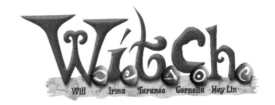

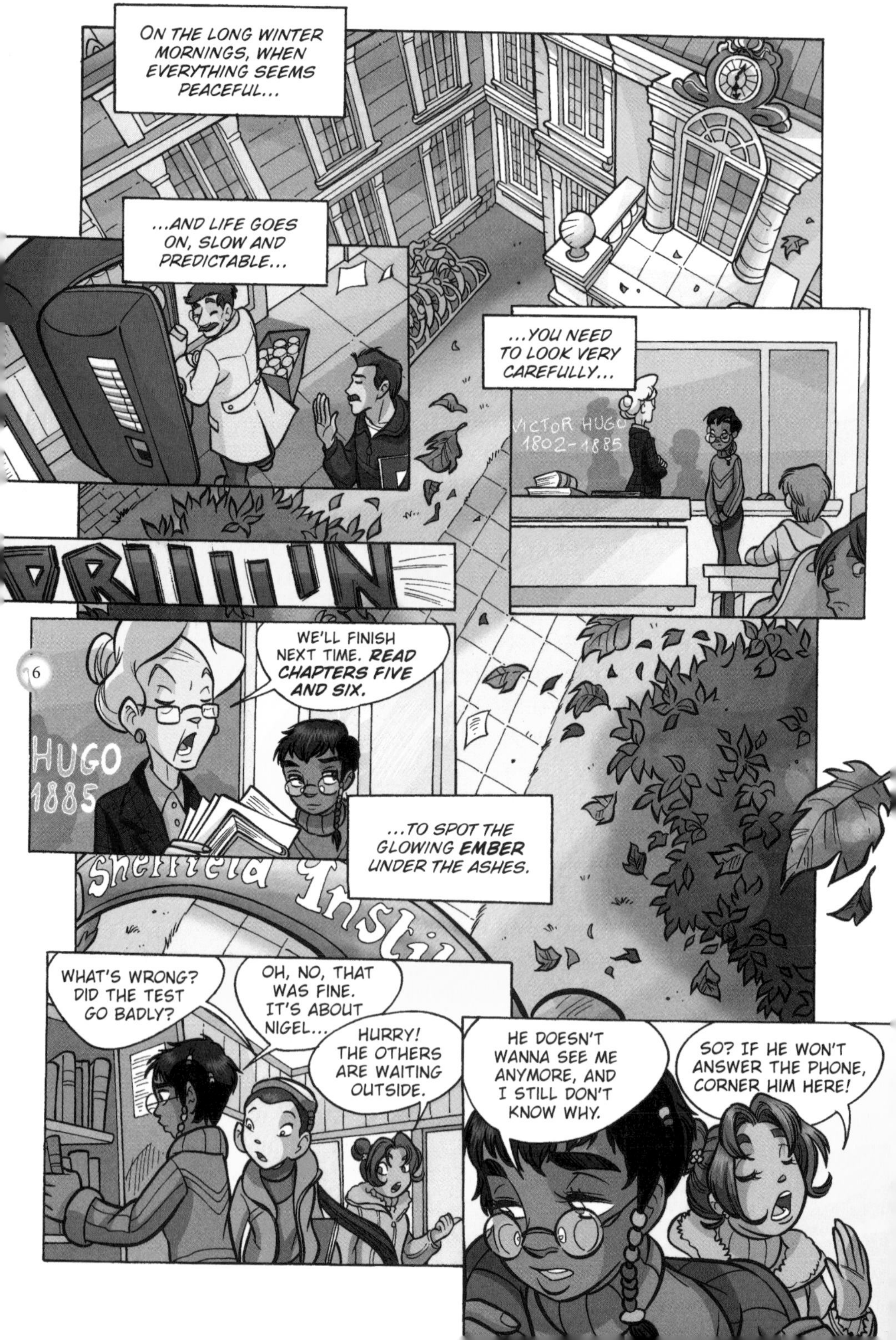

ON THE LONG WINTER MORNINGS, WHEN EVERYTHING SEEMS PEACEFUL...
...AND LIFE GOES ON, SLOW AND PREDICTABLE...
...YOU NEED TO LOOK VERY CAREFULLY...
VICTOR HUGO 1802-1885
DRIIIIN
WE'LL FINISH NEXT TIME. READ CHAPTERS FIVE AND SIX.
HUGO 1885
...TO SPOT THE GLOWING EMBER UNDER THE ASHES.
Sheffield Insti
WHAT'S WRONG? DID THE TEST GO BADLY?
OH, NO, THAT WAS FINE. IT'S ABOUT NIGEL...
HURRY! THE OTHERS ARE WAITING OUTSIDE.
HE DOESN'T WANNA SEE ME ANYMORE, AND I STILL DON'T KNOW WHY.
SO? IF HE WON'T ANSWER THE PHONE, CORNER HIM HERE!

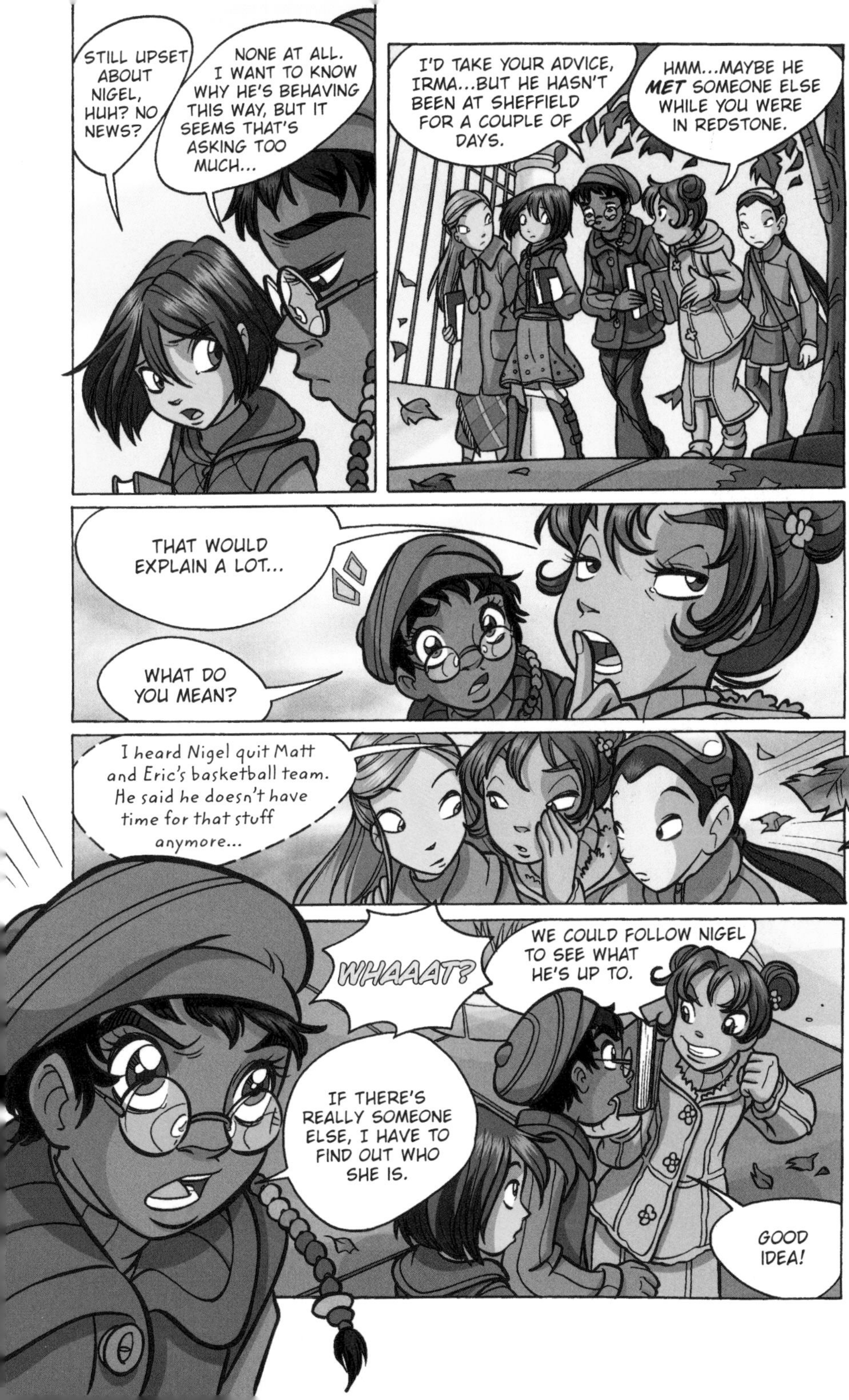
STILL UPSET ABOUT NIGEL, HUH? NO NEWS?
NONE AT ALL. I WANT TO KNOW WHY HE'S BEHAVING THIS WAY, BUT IT SEEMS THAT'S ASKING TOO MUCH...
I'D TAKE YOUR ADVICE, IRMA...BUT HE HASN'T BEEN AT SHEFFIELD FOR A COUPLE OF DAYS.
HMM...MAYBE HE MET SOMEONE ELSE WHILE YOU WERE IN REDSTONE.
THAT WOULD EXPLAIN A LOT...
WHAT DO YOU MEAN?
I heard Nigel quit Matt and Eric's basketball team. He said he doesn't have time for that stuff anymore...
WHAAAT?
WE COULD FOLLOW NIGEL TO SEE WHAT HE'S UP TO.
IF THERE'S REALLY SOMEONE ELSE, I HAVE TO FIND OUT WHO SHE IS.
GOOD IDEA!

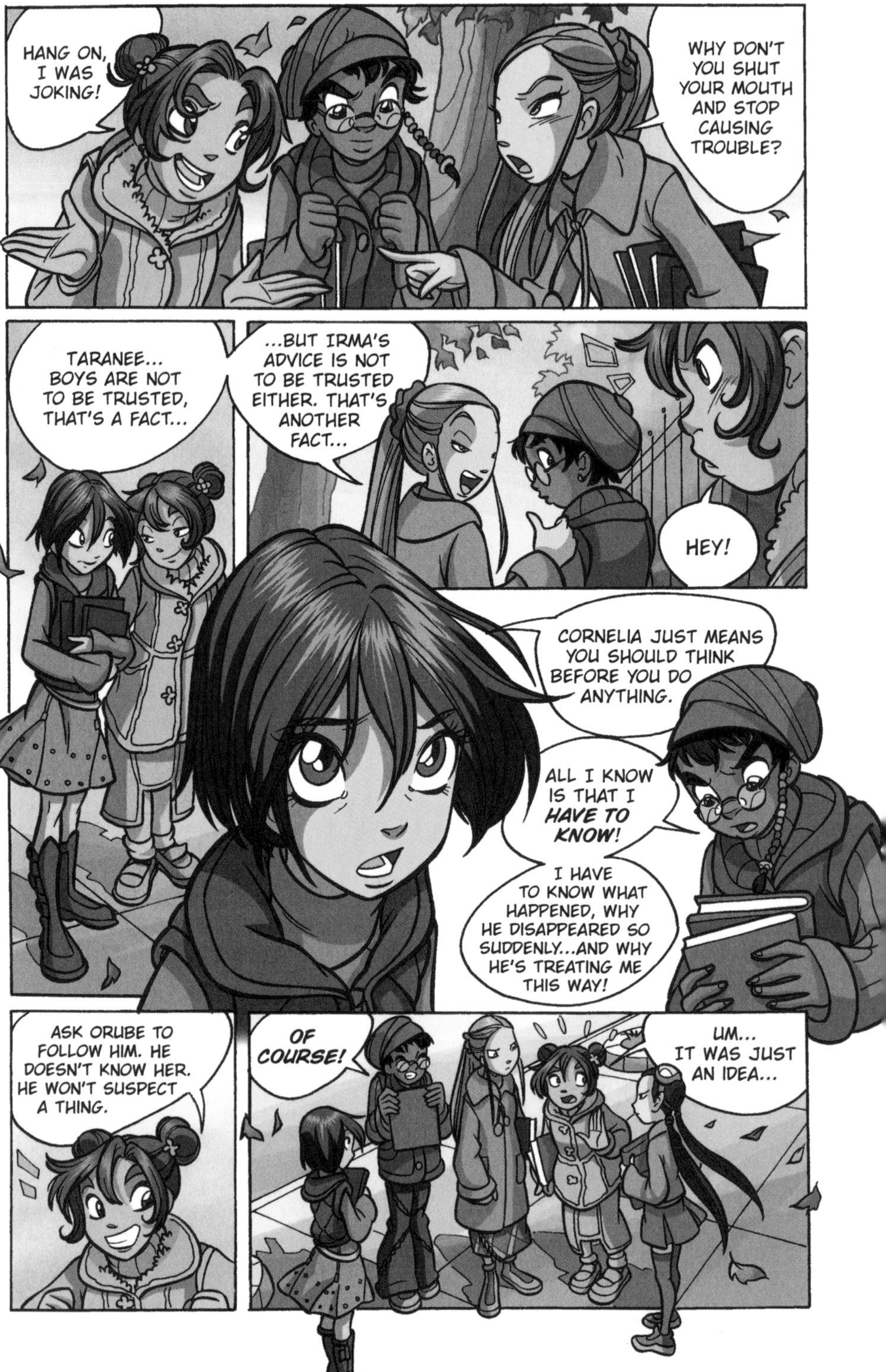

HANG ON, I WAS JOKING!
WHY DON'T YOU SHUT YOUR MOUTH AND STOP CAUSING TROUBLE?
TARANEE... BOYS ARE NOT TO BE TRUSTED, THAT'S A FACT...
...BUT IRMA'S ADVICE IS NOT TO BE TRUSTED EITHER. THAT'S ANOTHER FACT...
HEY!
CORNELIA JUST MEANS YOU SHOULD THINK BEFORE YOU DO ANYTHING.
ALL I KNOW IS THAT I *HAVE TO KNOW!*
I HAVE TO KNOW WHAT HAPPENED, WHY HE DISAPPEARED SO SUDDENLY...AND WHY HE'S TREATING ME THIS WAY!
ASK ORUBE TO FOLLOW HIM. HE DOESN'T KNOW HER. HE WON'T SUSPECT A THING.
OF COURSE!
UM... IT WAS JUST AN IDEA...

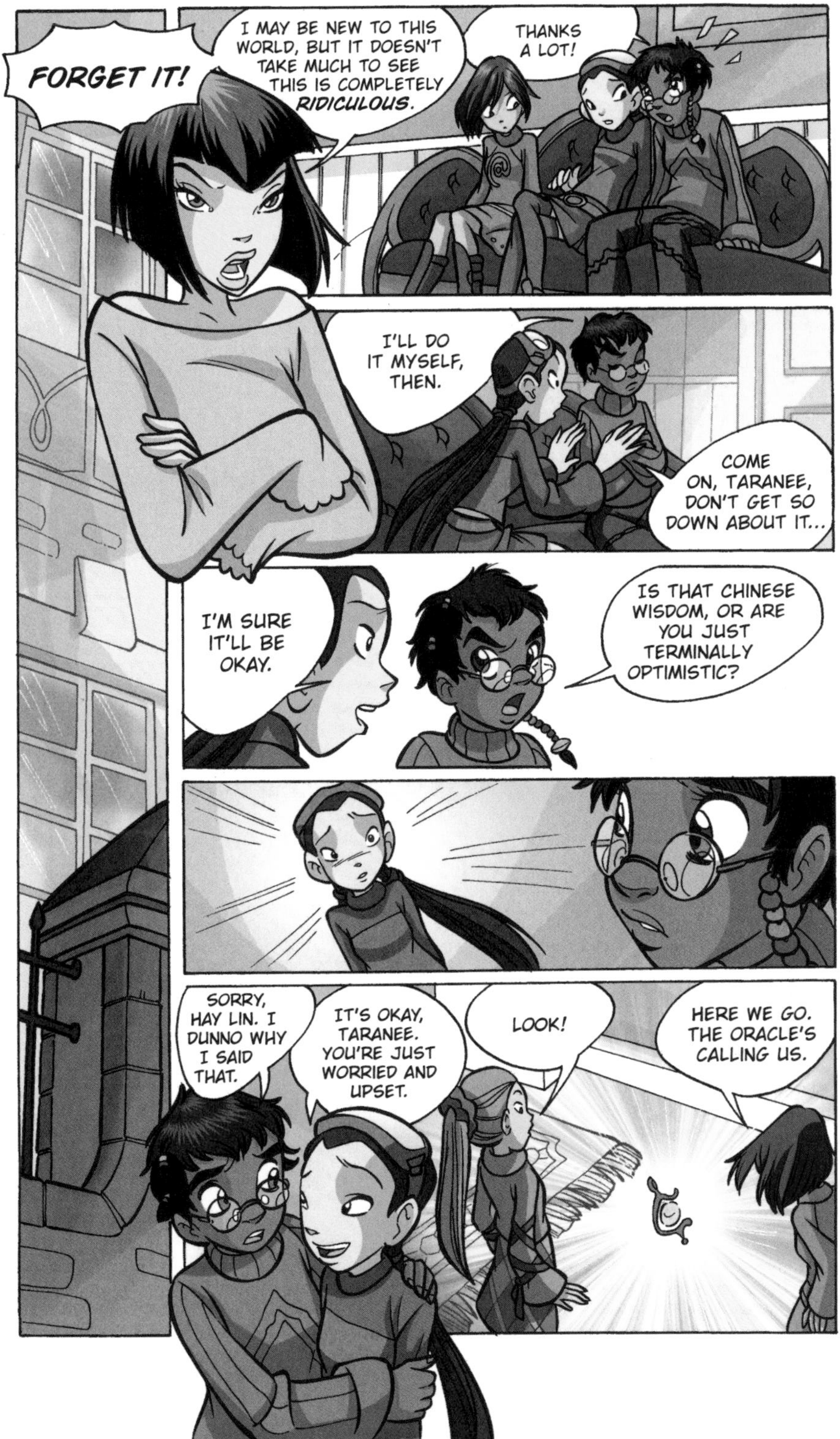
FORGET IT!
I MAY BE NEW TO THIS WORLD, BUT IT DOESN'T TAKE MUCH TO SEE THIS IS COMPLETELY RIDICULOUS.
THANKS A LOT!
I'LL DO IT MYSELF, THEN.
COME ON, TARANEE, DON'T GET SO DOWN ABOUT IT...
I'M SURE IT'LL BE OKAY.
IS THAT CHINESE WISDOM, OR ARE YOU JUST TERMINALLY OPTIMISTIC?
SORRY, HAY LIN. I DUNNO WHY I SAID THAT.
IT'S OKAY, TARANEE. YOU'RE JUST WORRIED AND UPSET.
LOOK!
HERE WE GO. THE ORACLE'S CALLING US.

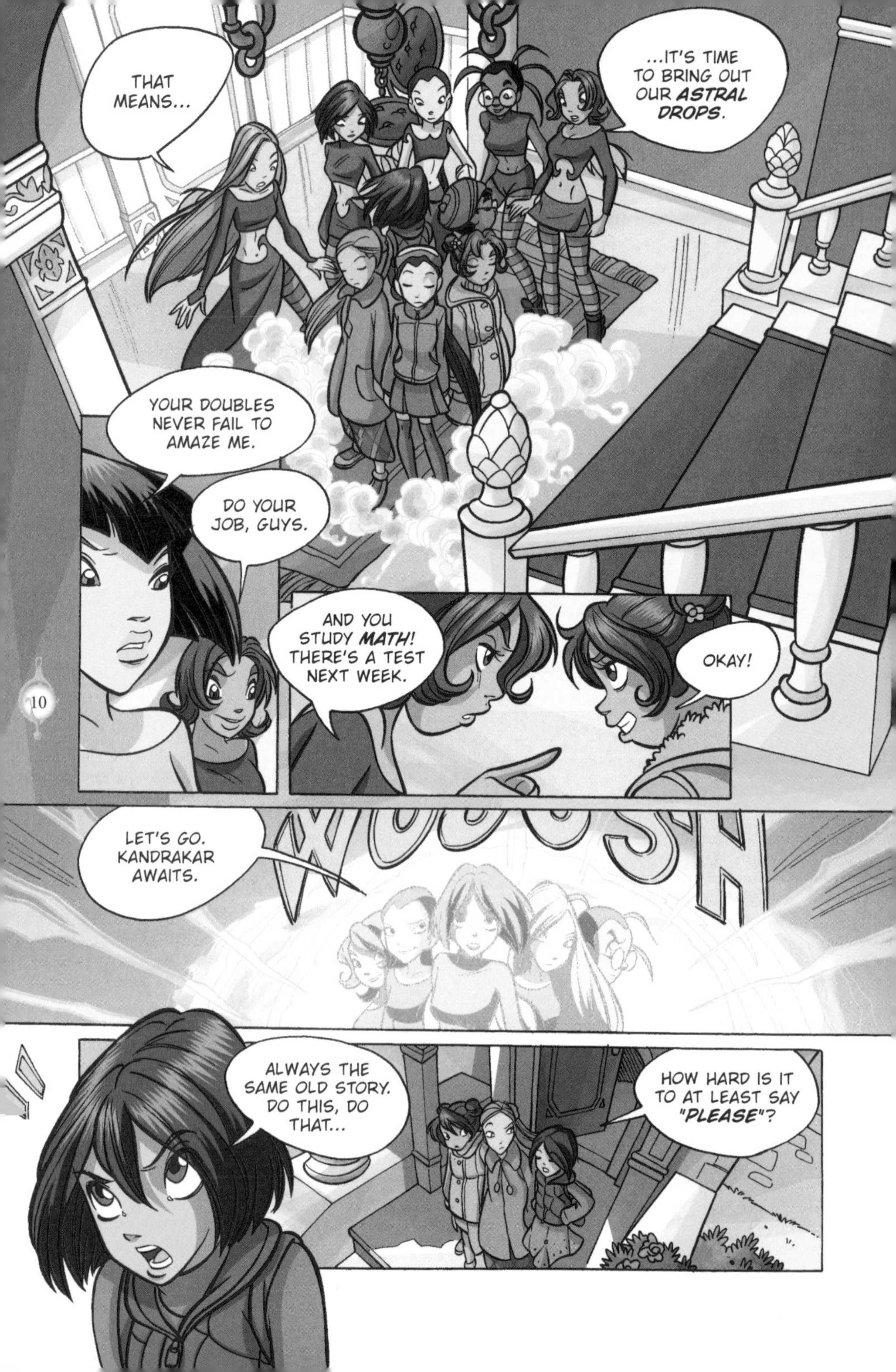
THAT MEANS...
...IT'S TIME TO BRING OUT OUR ASTRAL DROPS.
YOUR DOUBLES NEVER FAIL TO AMAZE ME.
DO YOUR JOB, GUYS.
AND YOU STUDY MATH! THERE'S A TEST NEXT WEEK.
OKAY!
LET'S GO. KANDRAKAR AWAITS.
WOOOOSH
ALWAYS THE SAME OLD STORY. DO THIS, DO THAT...
HOW HARD IS IT TO AT LEAST SAY "PLEASE"?

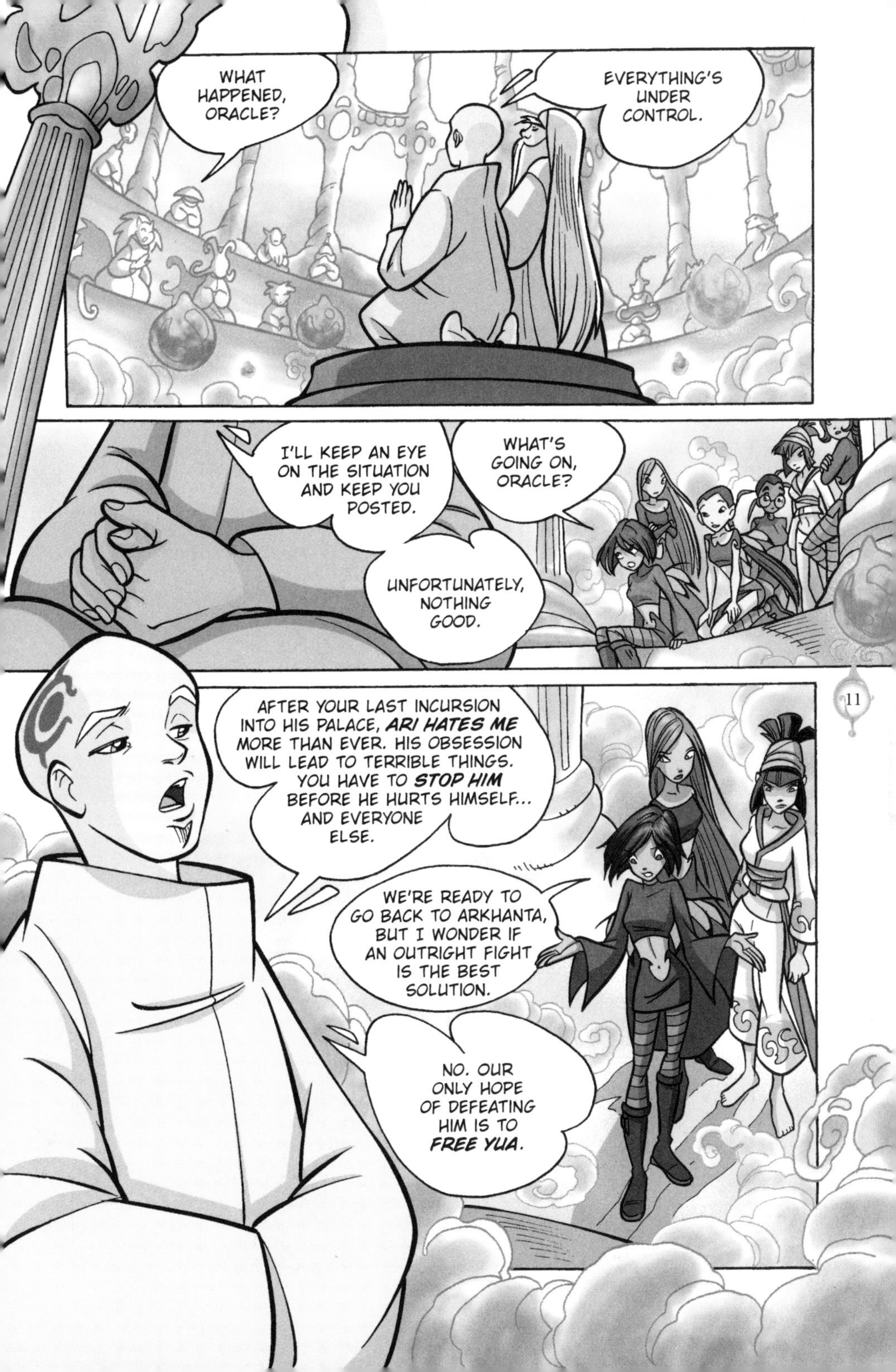
WHAT HAPPENED, ORACLE?
EVERYTHING'S UNDER CONTROL.
I'LL KEEP AN EYE ON THE SITUATION AND KEEP YOU POSTED.
WHAT'S GOING ON, ORACLE?
UNFORTUNATELY, NOTHING GOOD.
AFTER YOUR LAST INCURSION INTO HIS PALACE, **ARI HATES ME** MORE THAN EVER. HIS OBSESSION WILL LEAD TO TERRIBLE THINGS. YOU HAVE TO **STOP HIM** BEFORE HE HURTS HIMSELF... AND EVERYONE ELSE.
WE'RE READY TO GO BACK TO ARKHANTA, BUT I WONDER IF AN OUTRIGHT FIGHT IS THE BEST SOLUTION.
NO. OUR ONLY HOPE OF DEFEATING HIM IS TO **FREE YUA**.

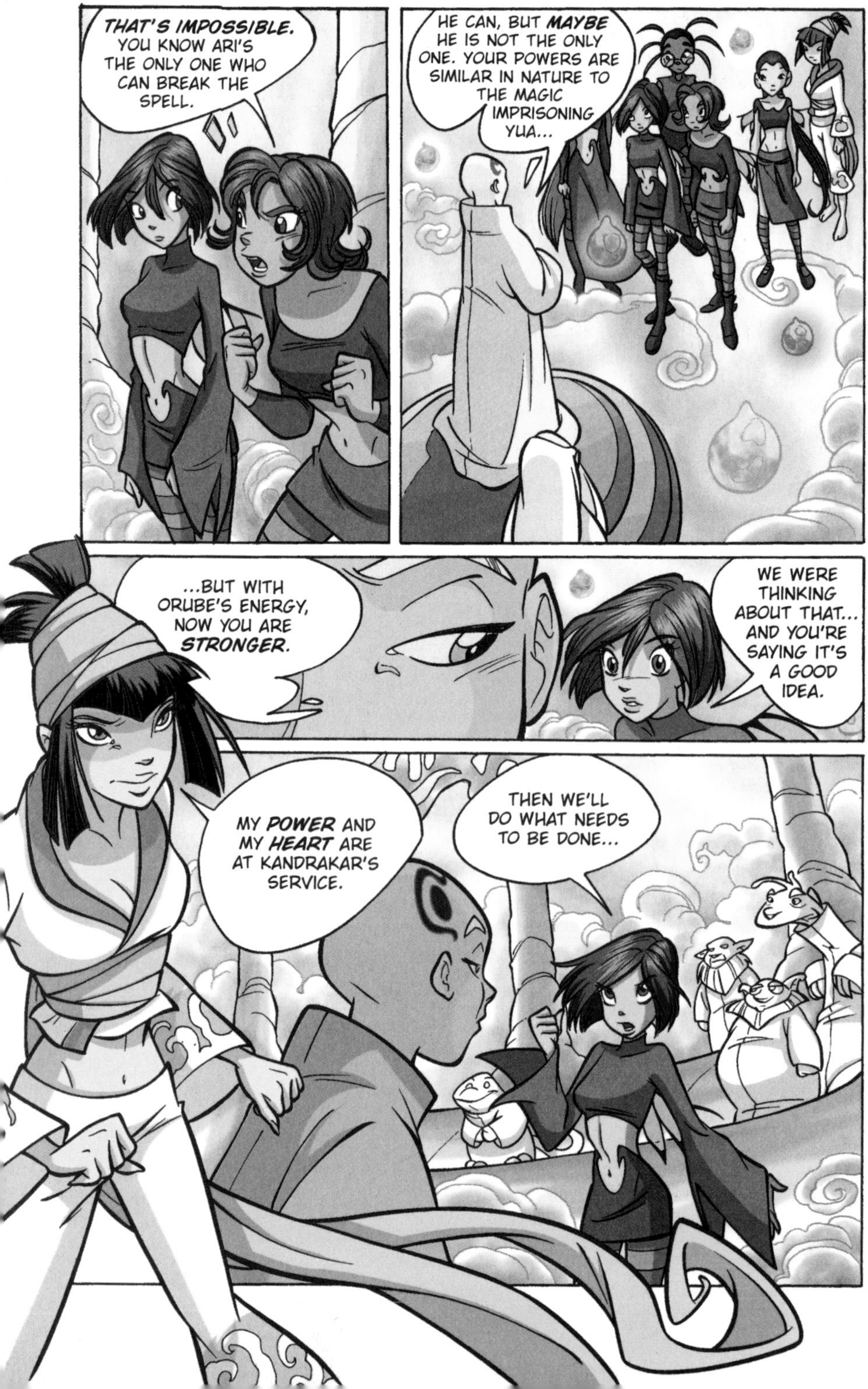
THAT'S IMPOSSIBLE. YOU KNOW ARI'S THE ONLY ONE WHO CAN BREAK THE SPELL.
HE CAN, BUT MAYBE HE IS NOT THE ONLY ONE. YOUR POWERS ARE SIMILAR IN NATURE TO THE MAGIC IMPRISONING YUA...
...BUT WITH ORUBE'S ENERGY, NOW YOU ARE STRONGER.
WE WERE THINKING ABOUT THAT... AND YOU'RE SAYING IT'S A GOOD IDEA.
MY POWER AND MY HEART ARE AT KANDRAKAR'S SERVICE.
THEN WE'LL DO WHAT NEEDS TO BE DONE...

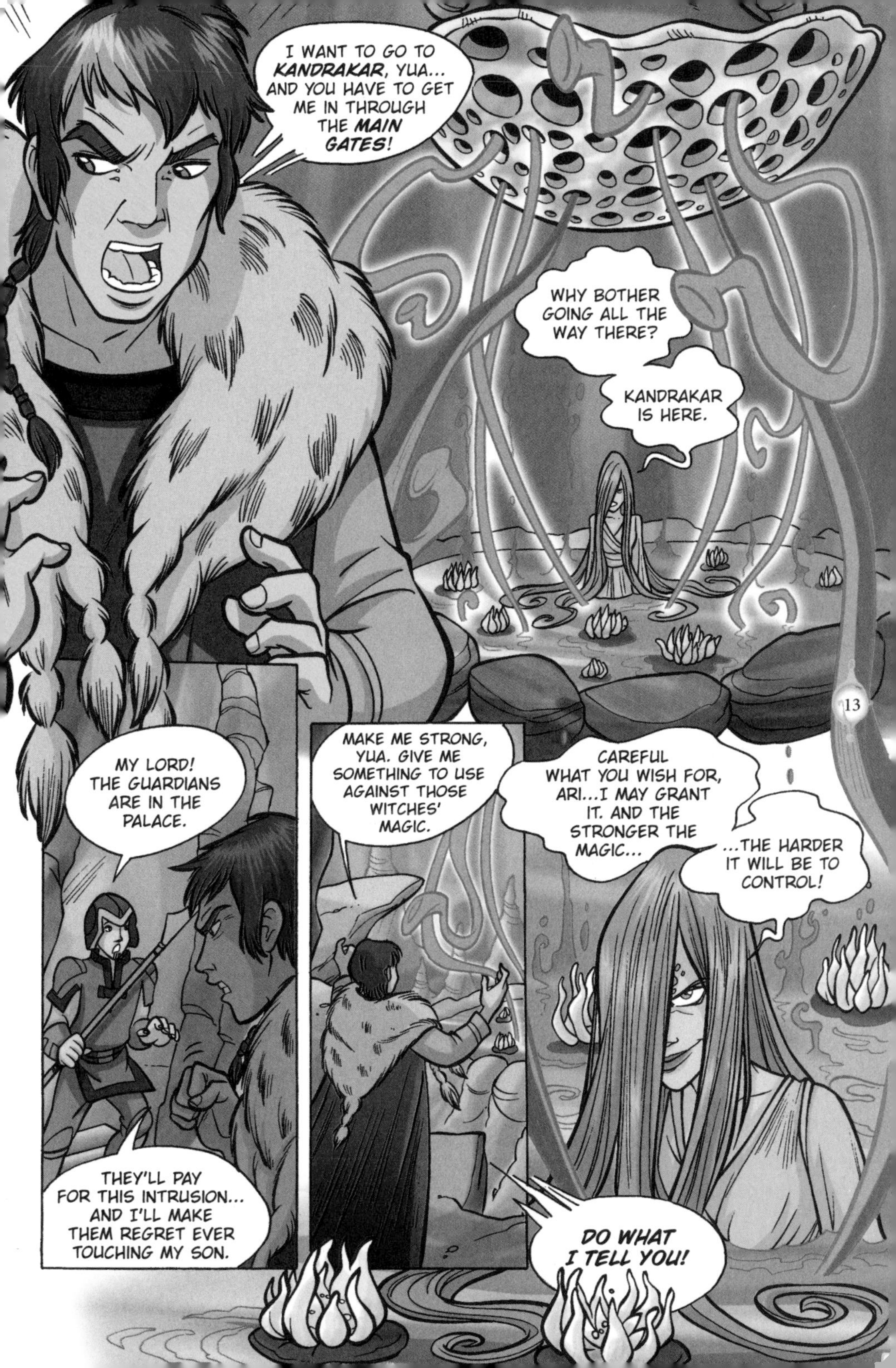
I WANT TO GO TO KANDRAKAR, YUA... AND YOU HAVE TO GET ME IN THROUGH THE MAIN GATES!
WHY BOTHER GOING ALL THE WAY THERE?
KANDRAKAR IS HERE.
MY LORD! THE GUARDIANS ARE IN THE PALACE.
THEY'LL PAY FOR THIS INTRUSION... AND I'LL MAKE THEM REGRET EVER TOUCHING MY SON.
MAKE ME STRONG, YUA. GIVE ME SOMETHING TO USE AGAINST THOSE WITCHES' MAGIC.
CAREFUL WHAT YOU WISH FOR, ARI...I MAY GRANT IT. AND THE STRONGER THE MAGIC...
...THE HARDER IT WILL BE TO CONTROL!
DO WHAT I TELL YOU!

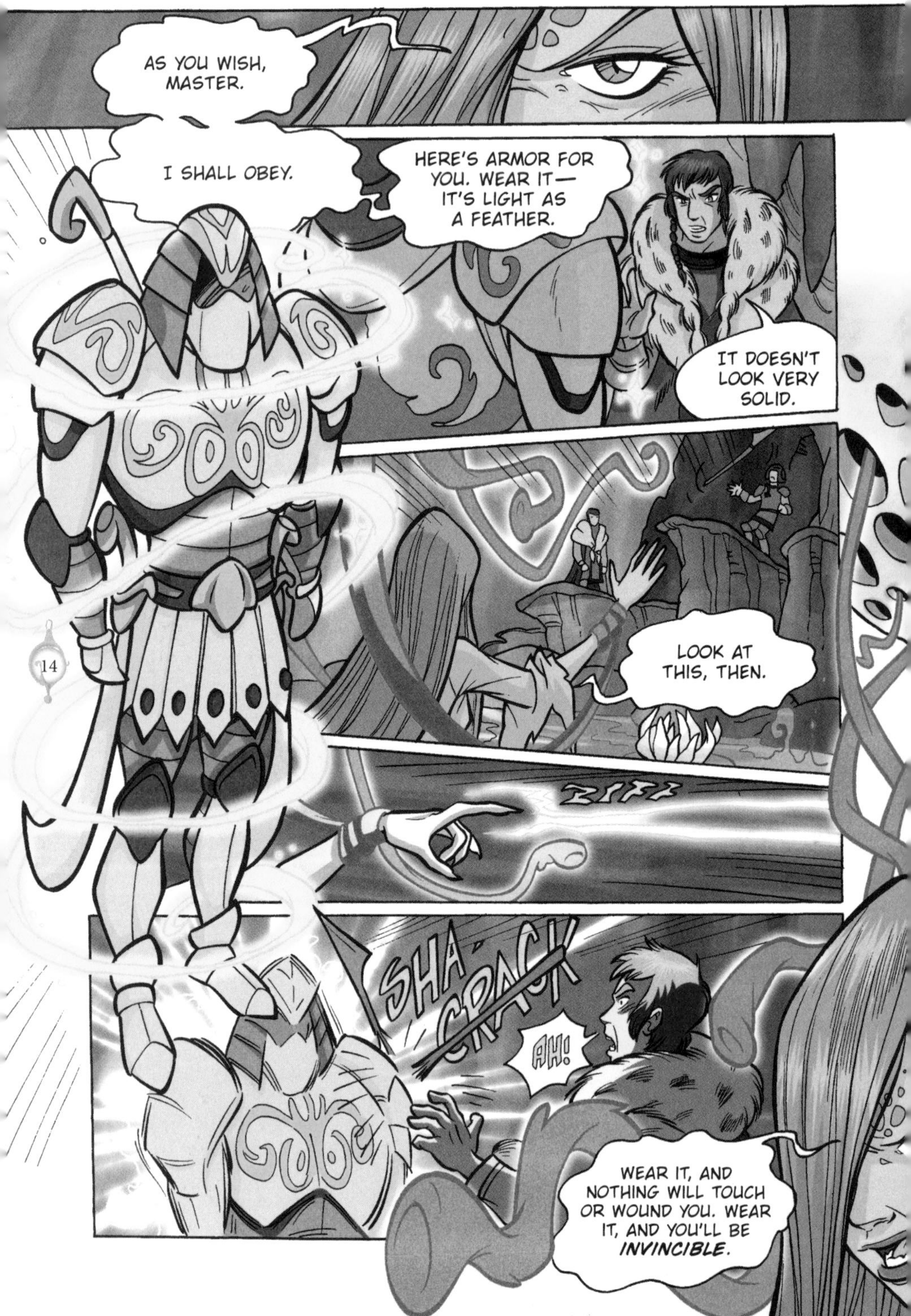
AS YOU WISH, MASTER.
I SHALL OBEY.
HERE'S ARMOR FOR YOU. WEAR IT—IT'S LIGHT AS A FEATHER.
IT DOESN'T LOOK VERY SOLID.
LOOK AT THIS, THEN.
ZIFF
SHA-CRACK
AH!
WEAR IT, AND NOTHING WILL TOUCH OR WOUND YOU. WEAR IT, AND YOU'LL BE *INVINCIBLE*.

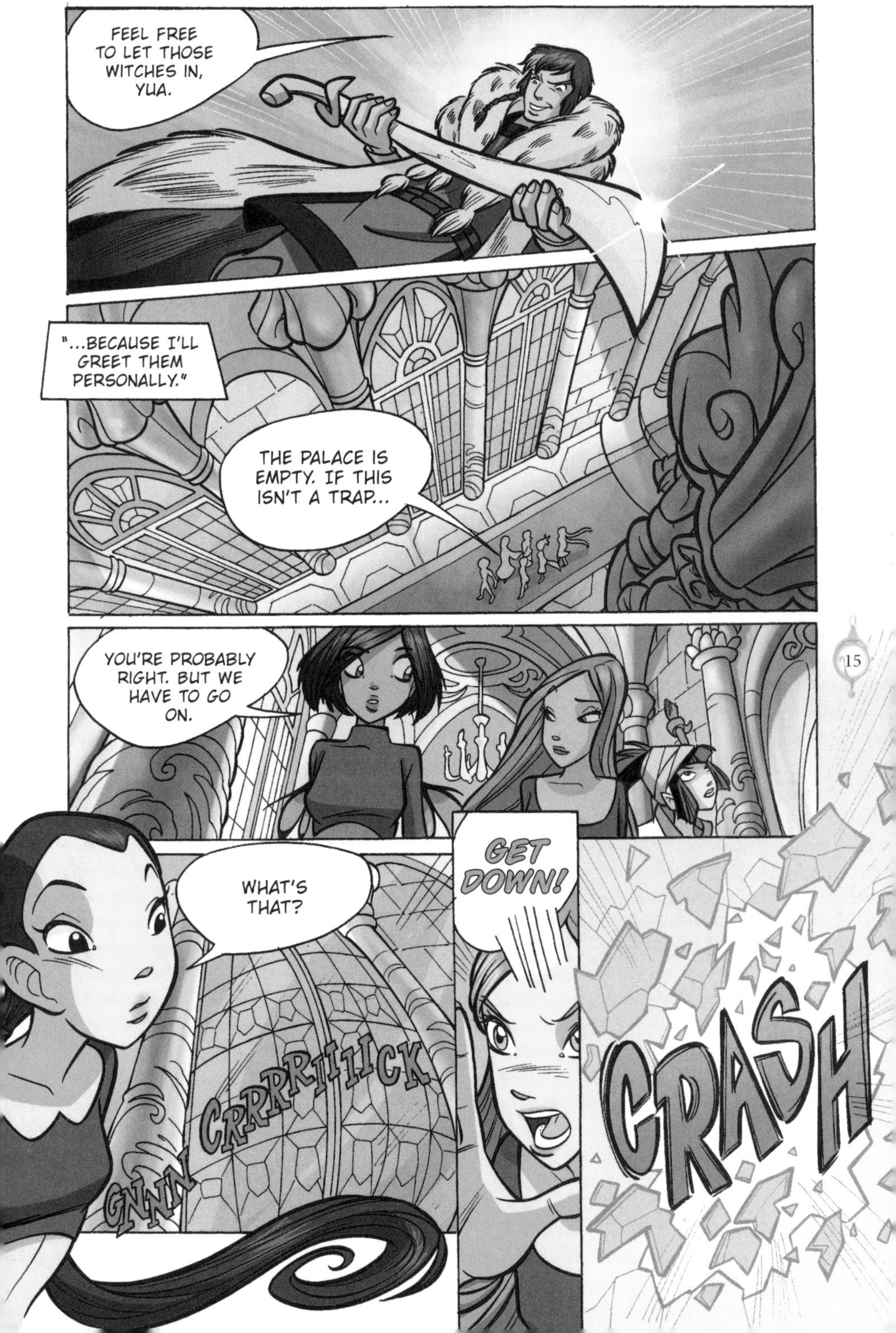
FEEL FREE TO LET THOSE WITCHES IN, YUA.
"...BECAUSE I'LL GREET THEM PERSONALLY."
THE PALACE IS EMPTY. IF THIS ISN'T A TRAP...
YOU'RE PROBABLY RIGHT. BUT WE HAVE TO GO ON.
WHAT'S THAT?
CRRRRIIIICK
GNNN
GET DOWN!
CRASH

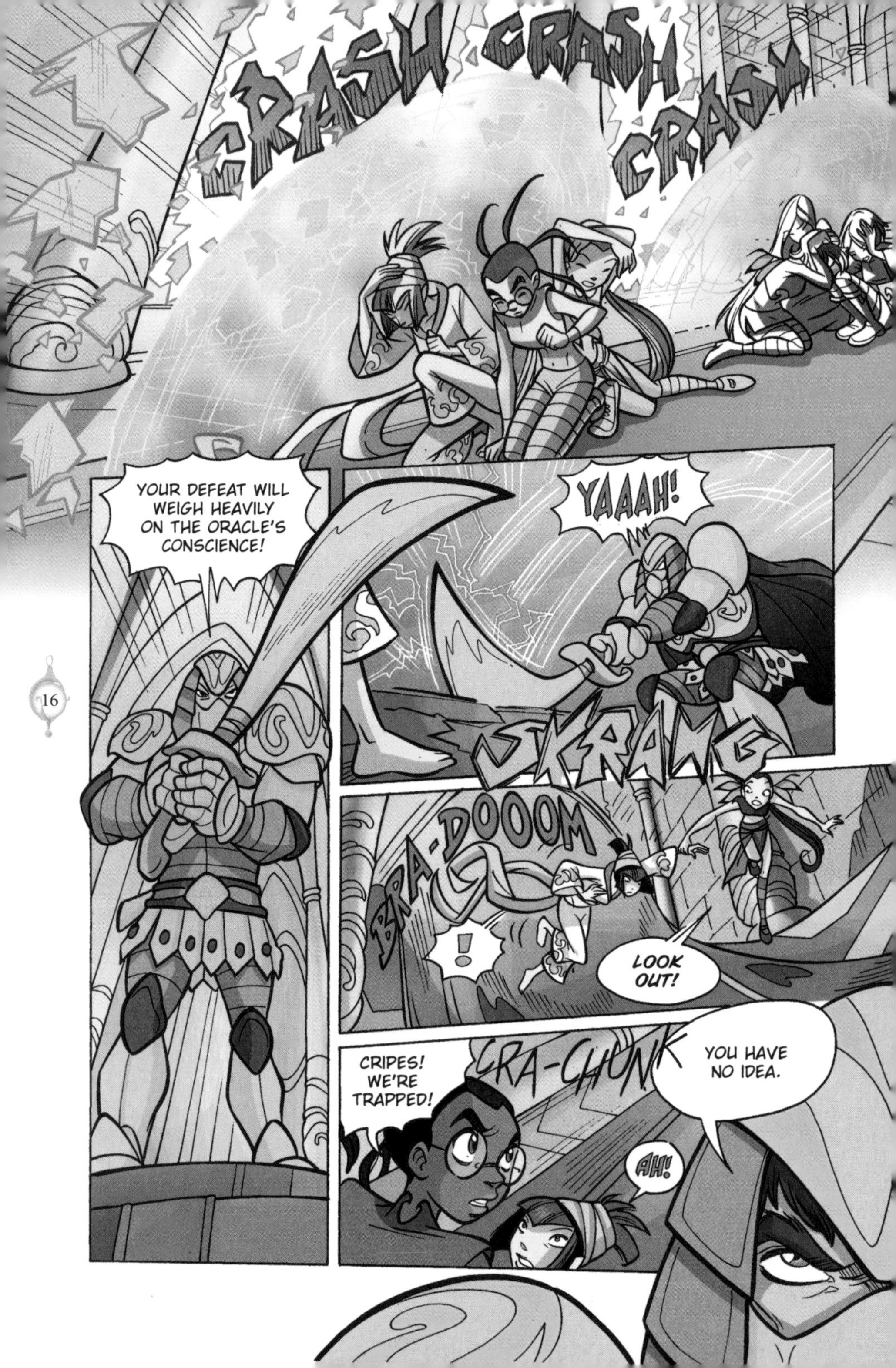
CRASH
CRASH
CRASH
YOUR DEFEAT WILL WEIGH HEAVILY ON THE ORACLE'S CONSCIENCE!
YAAAH!
SKRANG
BRA-DOOOM
!
LOOK OUT!
CRIPES! WE'RE TRAPPED!
CRA-CHUNK
YOU HAVE NO IDEA.
AH!

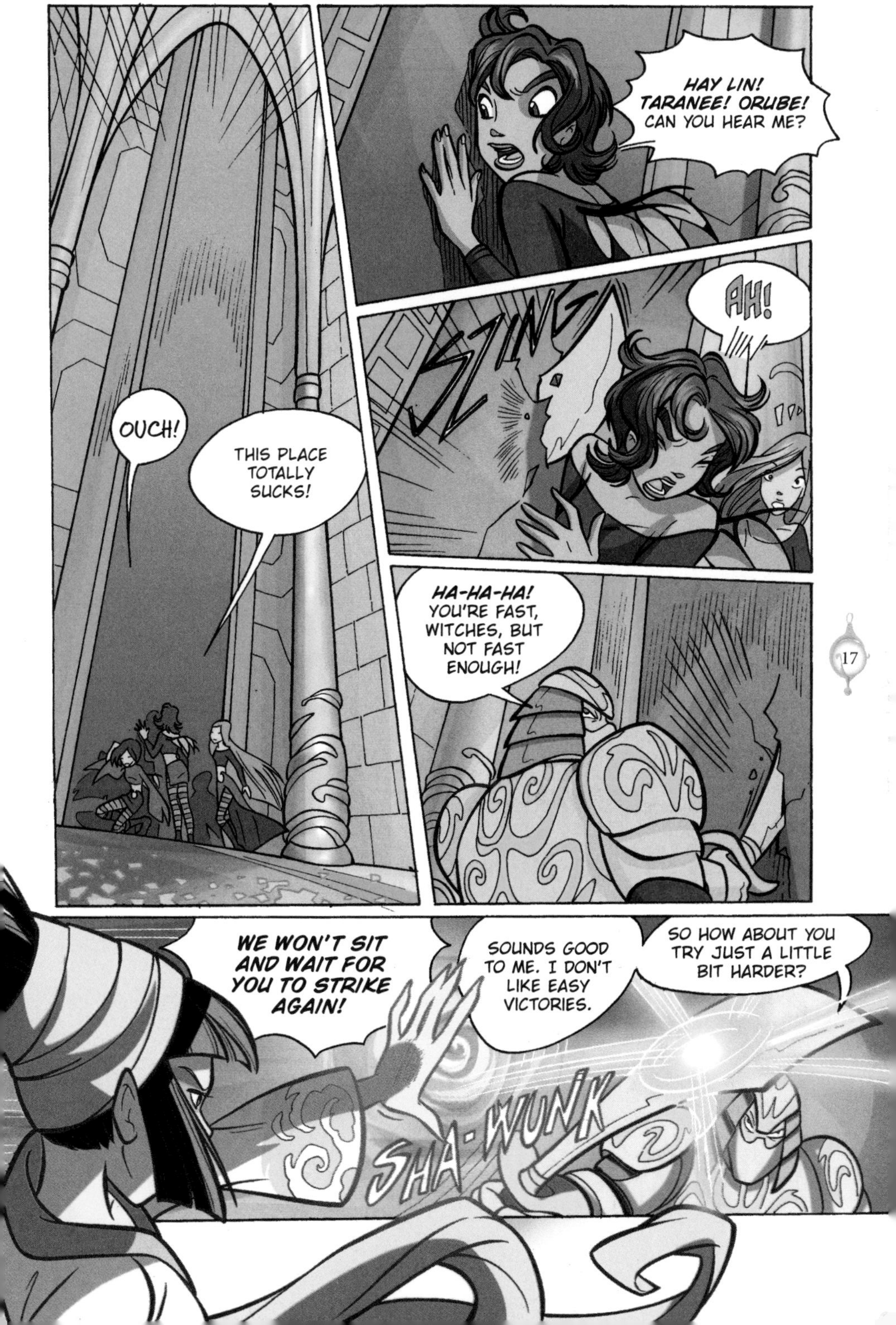
HAY LIN! TARANEE! ORUBE! CAN YOU HEAR ME?
OUCH!
THIS PLACE TOTALLY SUCKS!
SZING
AH!
HA-HA-HA! YOU'RE FAST, WITCHES, BUT NOT FAST ENOUGH!
WE WON'T SIT AND WAIT FOR YOU TO STRIKE AGAIN!
SOUNDS GOOD TO ME. I DON'T LIKE EASY VICTORIES.
SO HOW ABOUT YOU TRY JUST A LITTLE BIT HARDER?
SHA-WUNK

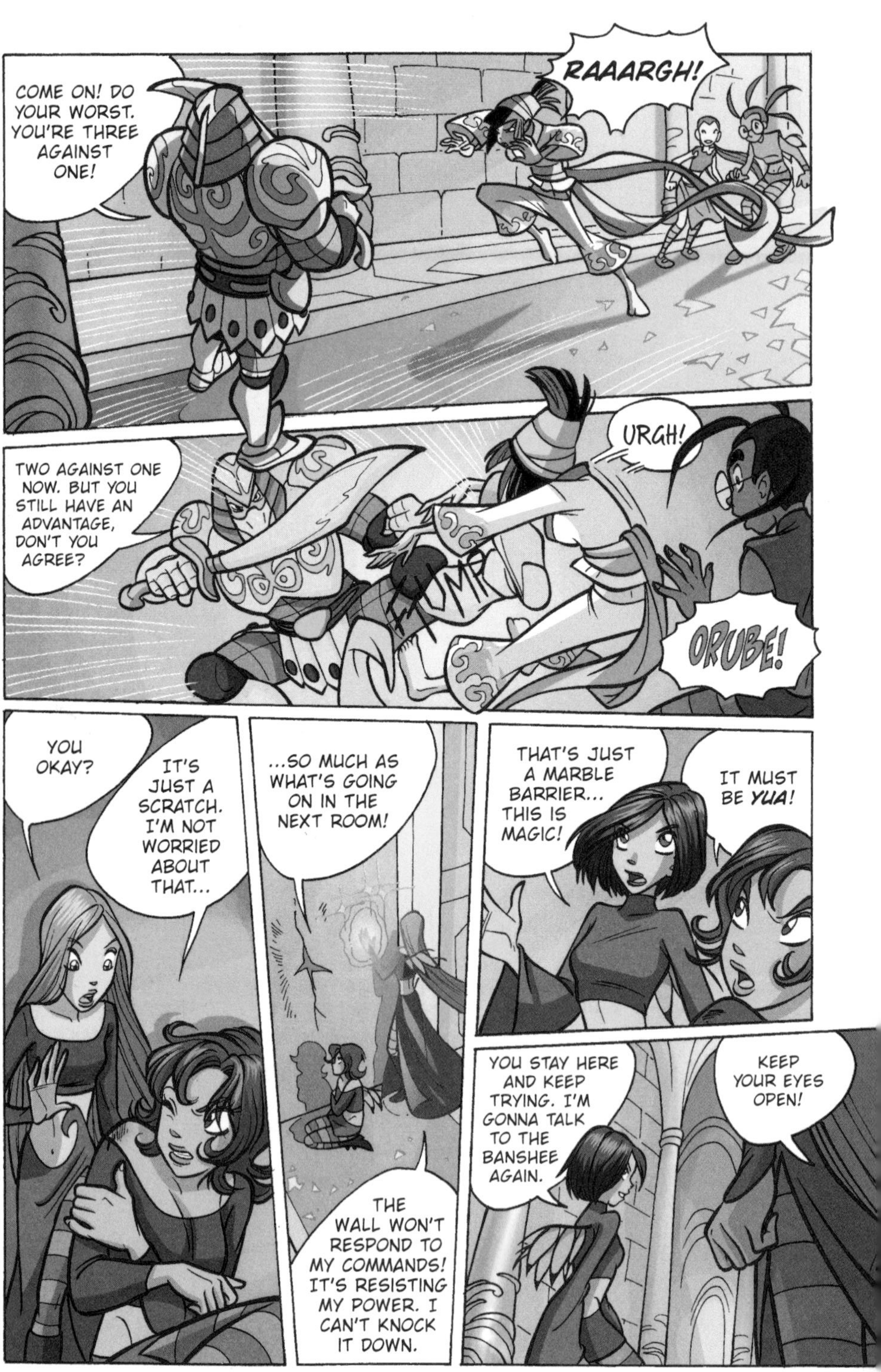
COME ON! DO YOUR WORST. YOU'RE THREE AGAINST ONE!
RAAARGH!
TWO AGAINST ONE NOW. BUT YOU STILL HAVE AN ADVANTAGE, DON'T YOU AGREE?
URGH!
THUMP
ORUBE!
YOU OKAY?
IT'S JUST A SCRATCH. I'M NOT WORRIED ABOUT THAT...
...SO MUCH AS WHAT'S GOING ON IN THE NEXT ROOM!
THE WALL WON'T RESPOND TO MY COMMANDS! IT'S RESISTING MY POWER. I CAN'T KNOCK IT DOWN.
THAT'S JUST A MARBLE BARRIER... THIS IS MAGIC!
IT MUST BE *YUA*!
YOU STAY HERE AND KEEP TRYING. I'M GONNA TALK TO THE BANSHEE AGAIN.
KEEP YOUR EYES OPEN!

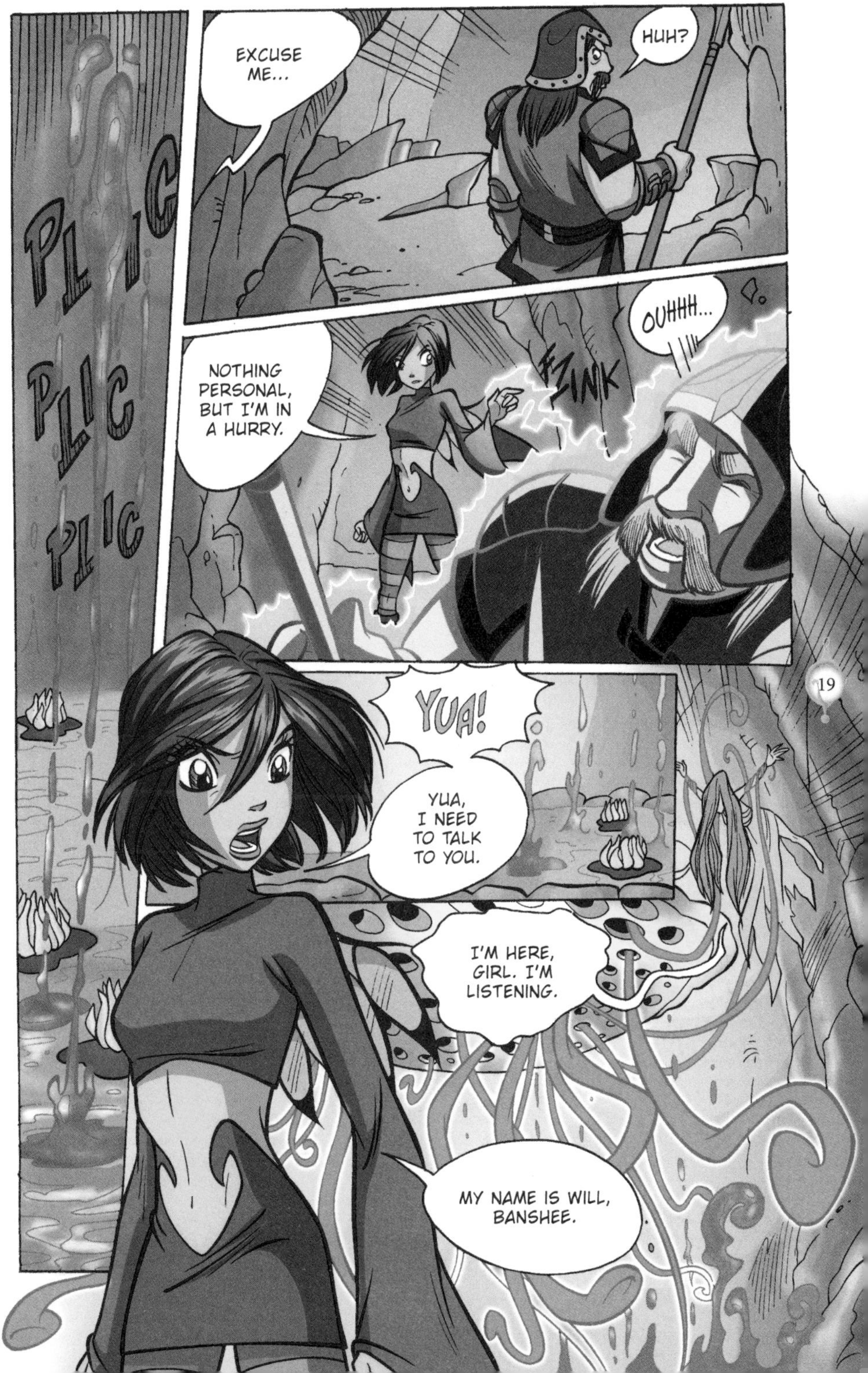
PLIC
PLIC
PLIC
EXCUSE ME...
HUH?
NOTHING PERSONAL, BUT I'M IN A HURRY.
OUHHH...
ZINK
YUA!
YUA, I NEED TO TALK TO YOU.
I'M HERE, GIRL. I'M LISTENING.
MY NAME IS WILL, BANSHEE.

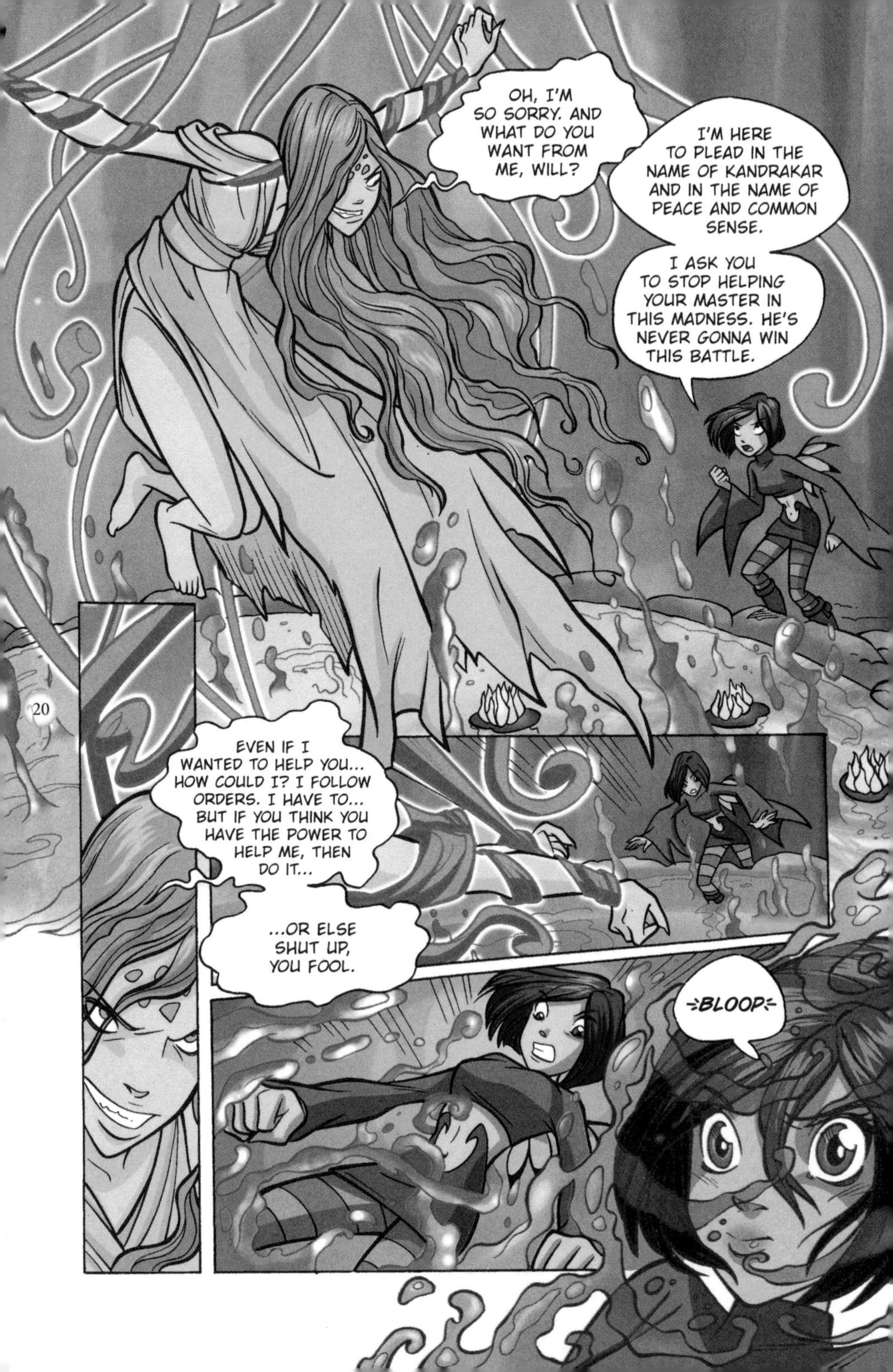

OH, I'M SO SORRY. AND WHAT DO YOU WANT FROM ME, WILL?
I'M HERE TO PLEAD IN THE NAME OF KANDRAKAR AND IN THE NAME OF PEACE AND COMMON SENSE.
I ASK YOU TO STOP HELPING YOUR MASTER IN THIS MADNESS. HE'S NEVER GONNA WIN THIS BATTLE.
EVEN IF I WANTED TO HELP YOU... HOW COULD I? I FOLLOW ORDERS. I HAVE TO... BUT IF YOU THINK YOU HAVE THE POWER TO HELP ME, THEN DO IT...
...OR ELSE SHUT UP, YOU FOOL.
BLOOP

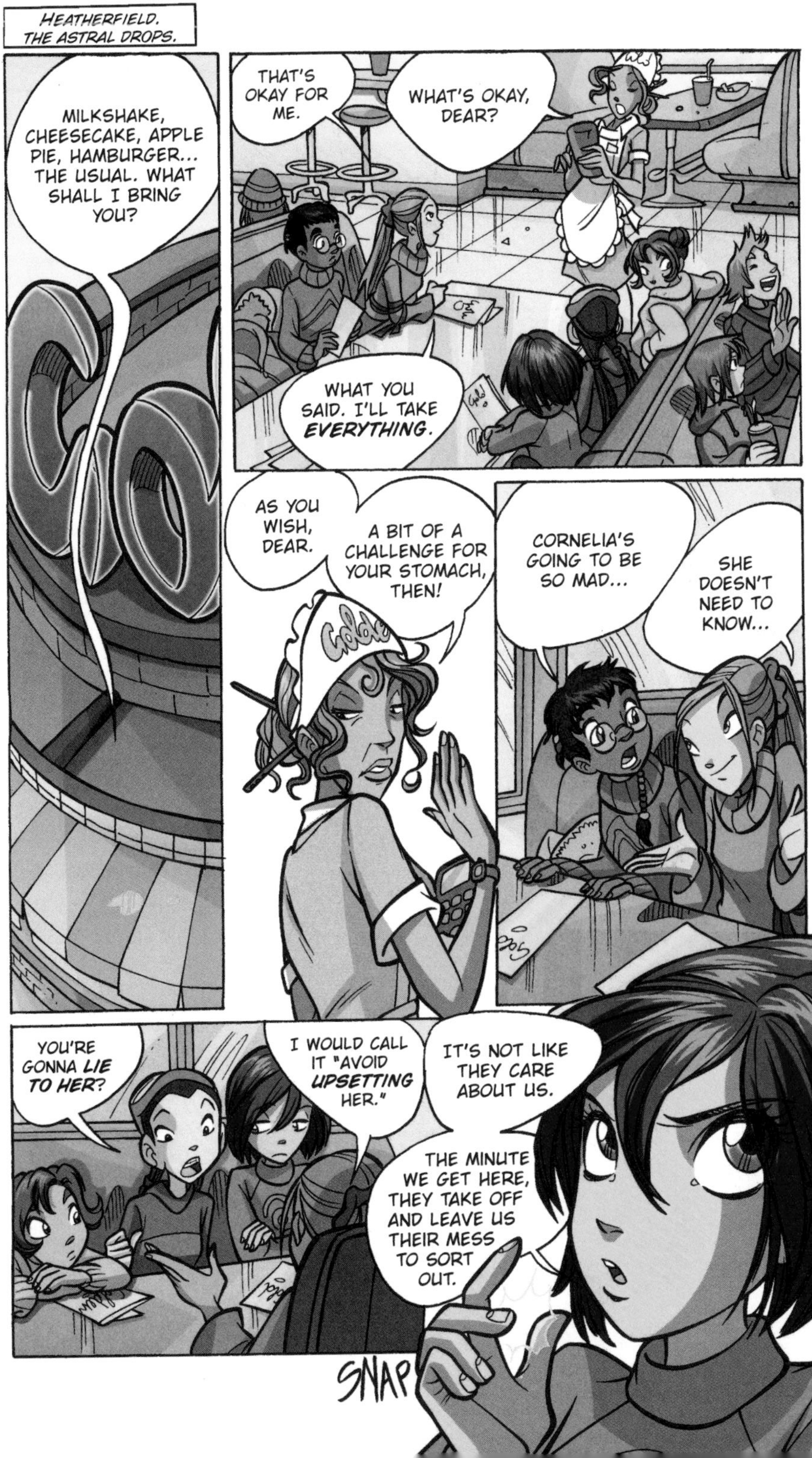
HEATHERFIELD. THE ASTRAL DROPS.
MILKSHAKE, CHEESECAKE, APPLE PIE, HAMBURGER... THE USUAL. WHAT SHALL I BRING YOU?
THAT'S OKAY FOR ME.
WHAT'S OKAY, DEAR?
WHAT YOU SAID. I'LL TAKE EVERYTHING.
AS YOU WISH, DEAR.
A BIT OF A CHALLENGE FOR YOUR STOMACH, THEN!
CORNELIA'S GOING TO BE SO MAD...
SHE DOESN'T NEED TO KNOW...
YOU'RE GONNA LIE TO HER?
I WOULD CALL IT "AVOID UPSETTING HER."
IT'S NOT LIKE THEY CARE ABOUT US.
THE MINUTE WE GET HERE, THEY TAKE OFF AND LEAVE US THEIR MESS TO SORT OUT.
SNAP

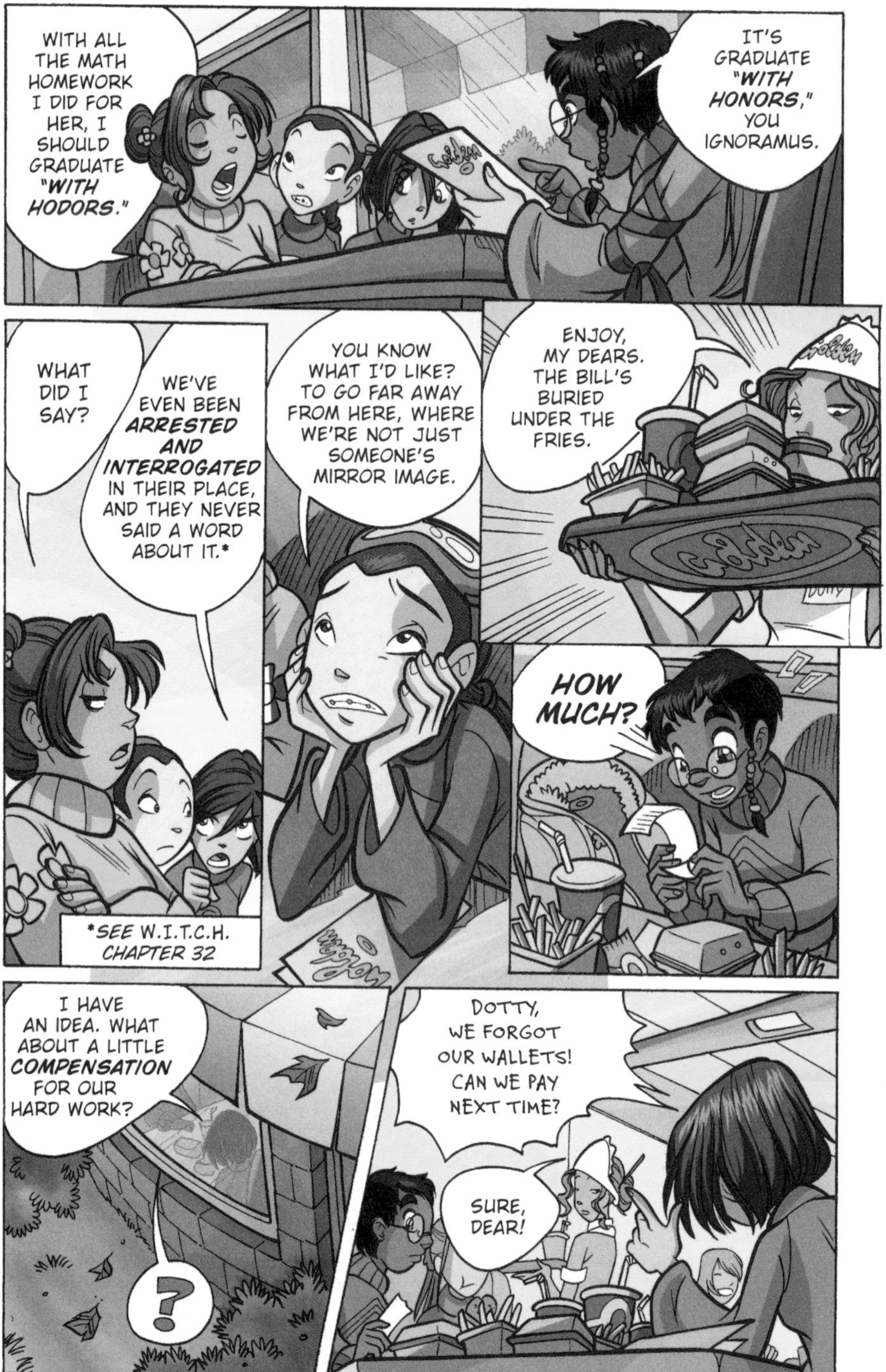

WITH ALL THE MATH HOMEWORK I DID FOR HER, I SHOULD GRADUATE "WITH HODORS."
IT'S GRADUATE "WITH HONORS," YOU IGNORAMUS.
WHAT DID I SAY?
WE'VE EVEN BEEN ARRESTED AND INTERROGATED IN THEIR PLACE, AND THEY NEVER SAID A WORD ABOUT IT.*
*SEE W.I.T.C.H. CHAPTER 32
YOU KNOW WHAT I'D LIKE? TO GO FAR AWAY FROM HERE, WHERE WE'RE NOT JUST SOMEONE'S MIRROR IMAGE.
ENJOY, MY DEARS. THE BILL'S BURIED UNDER THE FRIES.
HOW MUCH?
I HAVE AN IDEA. WHAT ABOUT A LITTLE COMPENSATION FOR OUR HARD WORK?
?
DOTTY, WE FORGOT OUR WALLETS! CAN WE PAY NEXT TIME?
SURE, DEAR!

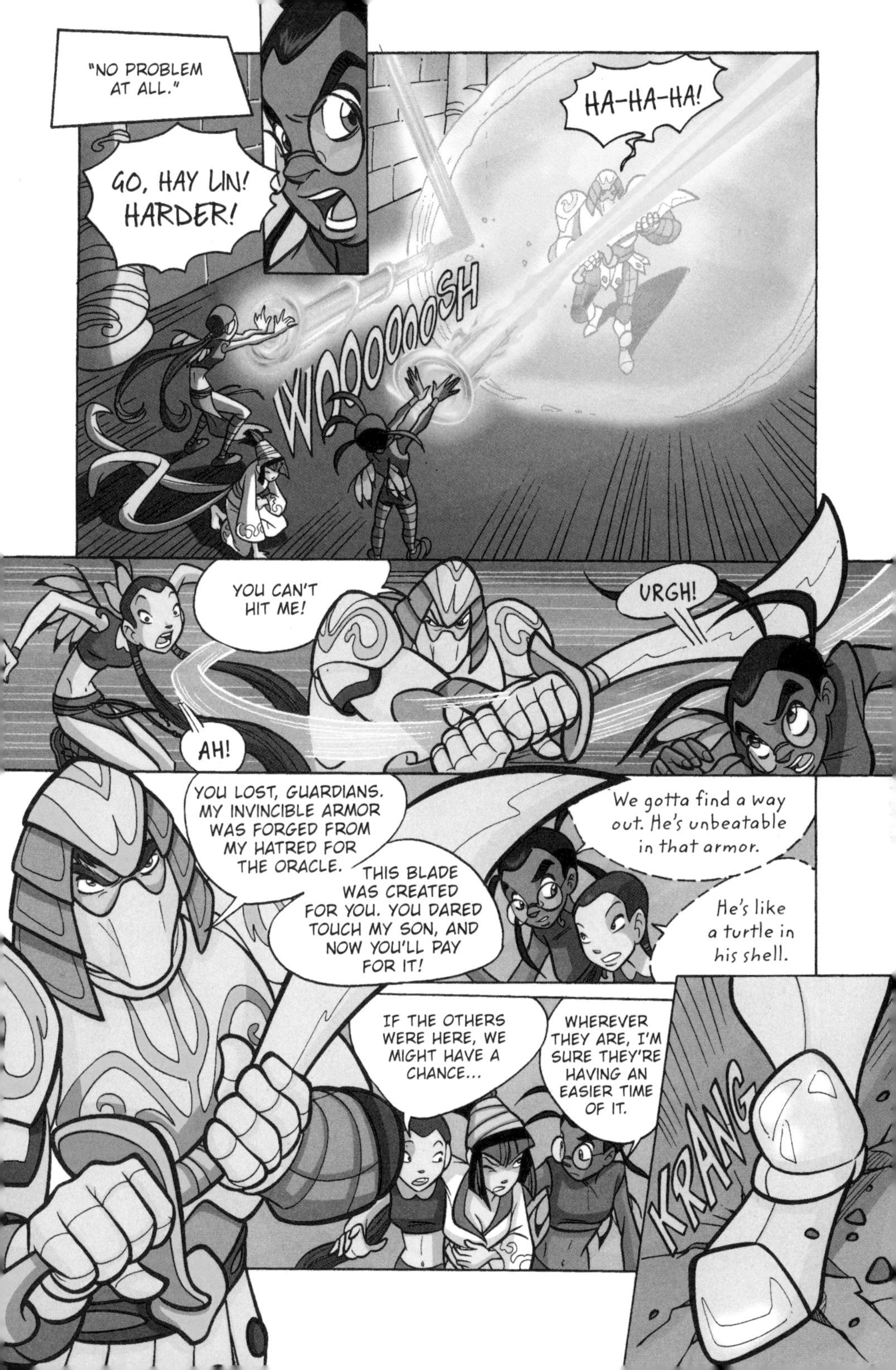
"NO PROBLEM AT ALL."
GO, HAY LIN! HARDER!
HA-HA-HA!
WOOOOOOOSH
YOU CAN'T HIT ME!
URGH!
AH!
YOU LOST, GUARDIANS. MY INVINCIBLE ARMOR WAS FORGED FROM MY HATRED FOR THE ORACLE.
THIS BLADE WAS CREATED FOR YOU. YOU DARED TOUCH MY SON, AND NOW YOU'LL PAY FOR IT!
We gotta find a way out. He's unbeatable in that armor.
He's like a turtle in his shell.
IF THE OTHERS WERE HERE, WE MIGHT HAVE A CHANCE...
WHEREVER THEY ARE, I'M SURE THEY'RE HAVING AN EASIER TIME OF IT.
KRANG

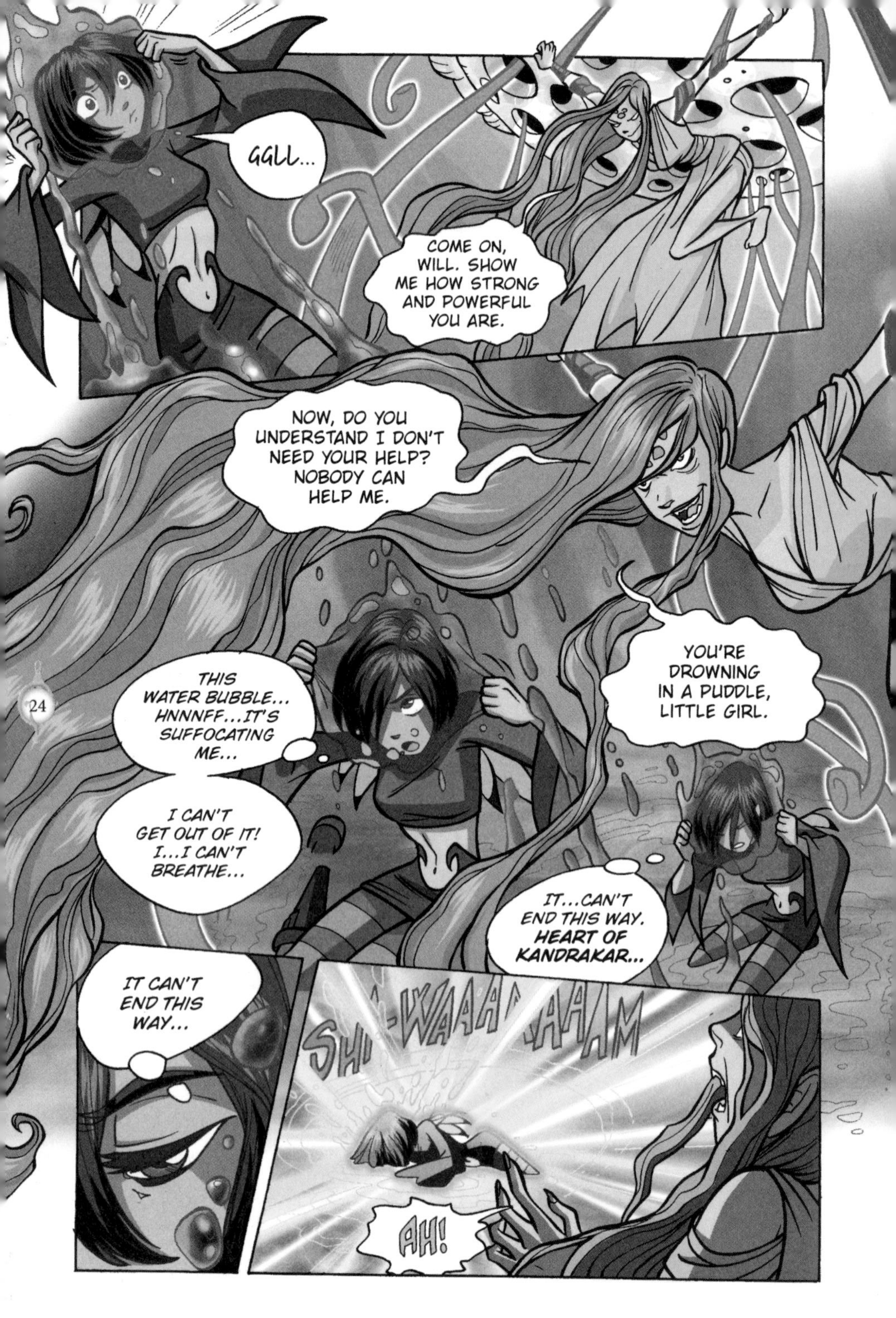
GGLL...
COME ON, WILL. SHOW ME HOW STRONG AND POWERFUL YOU ARE.
NOW, DO YOU UNDERSTAND I DON'T NEED YOUR HELP? NOBODY CAN HELP ME.
THIS WATER BUBBLE... HNNNFF...IT'S SUFFOCATING ME...
I CAN'T GET OUT OF IT! I...I CAN'T BREATHE...
YOU'RE DROWNING IN A PUDDLE, LITTLE GIRL.
IT...CAN'T END THIS WAY. HEART OF KANDRAKAR...
IT CAN'T END THIS WAY...
AH!

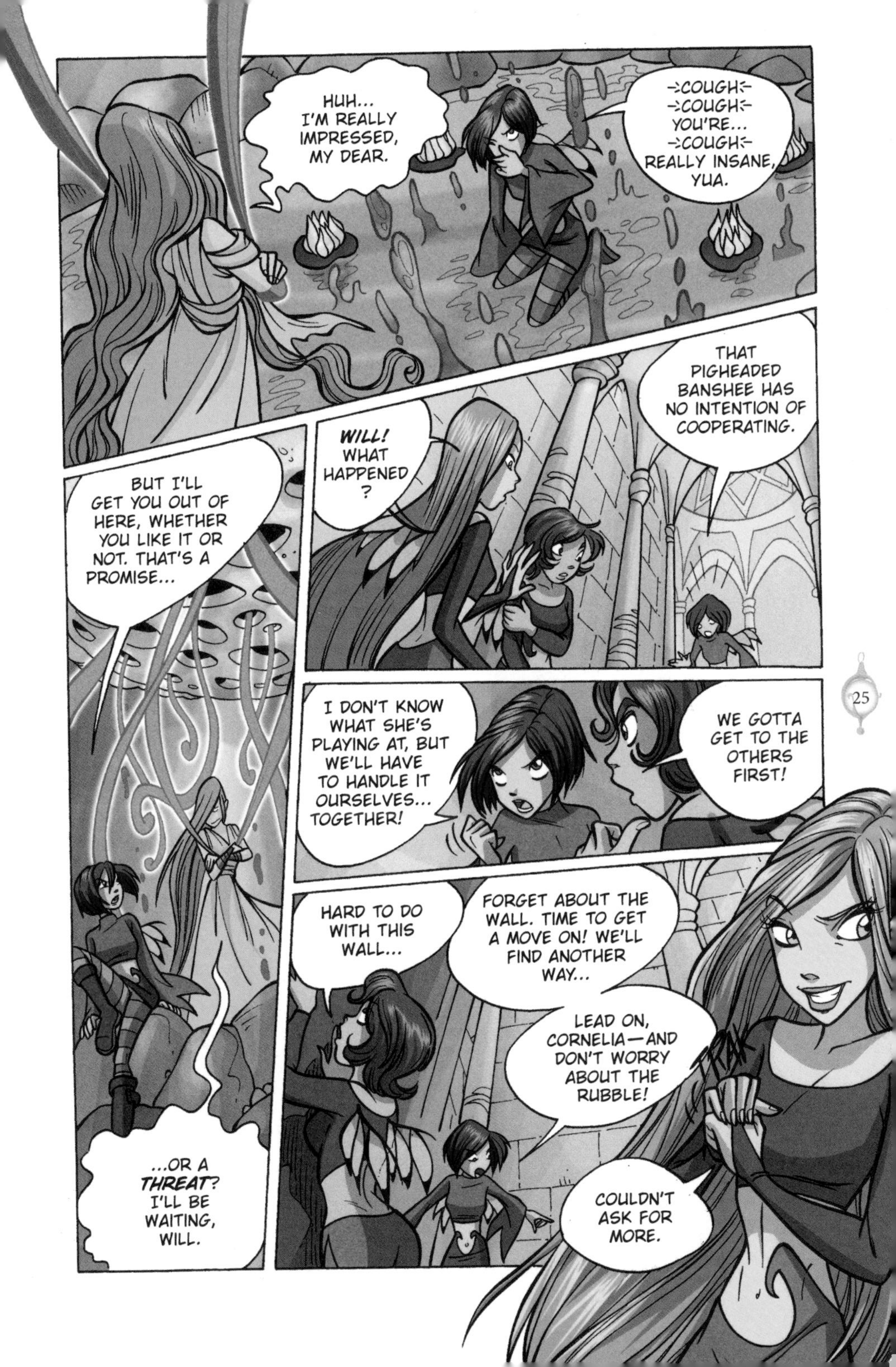
HUH... I'M REALLY IMPRESSED, MY DEAR.
-COUGH- -COUGH- YOU'RE... -COUGH- REALLY INSANE, YUA.
WILL! WHAT HAPPENED?
THAT PIGHEADED BANSHEE HAS NO INTENTION OF COOPERATING.
BUT I'LL GET YOU OUT OF HERE, WHETHER YOU LIKE IT OR NOT. THAT'S A PROMISE...
I DON'T KNOW WHAT SHE'S PLAYING AT, BUT WE'LL HAVE TO HANDLE IT OURSELVES... TOGETHER!
WE GOTTA GET TO THE OTHERS FIRST!
HARD TO DO WITH THIS WALL...
FORGET ABOUT THE WALL. TIME TO GET A MOVE ON! WE'LL FIND ANOTHER WAY...
LEAD ON, CORNELIA—AND DON'T WORRY ABOUT THE RUBBLE!
...OR A THREAT? I'LL BE WAITING, WILL.
COULDN'T ASK FOR MORE.

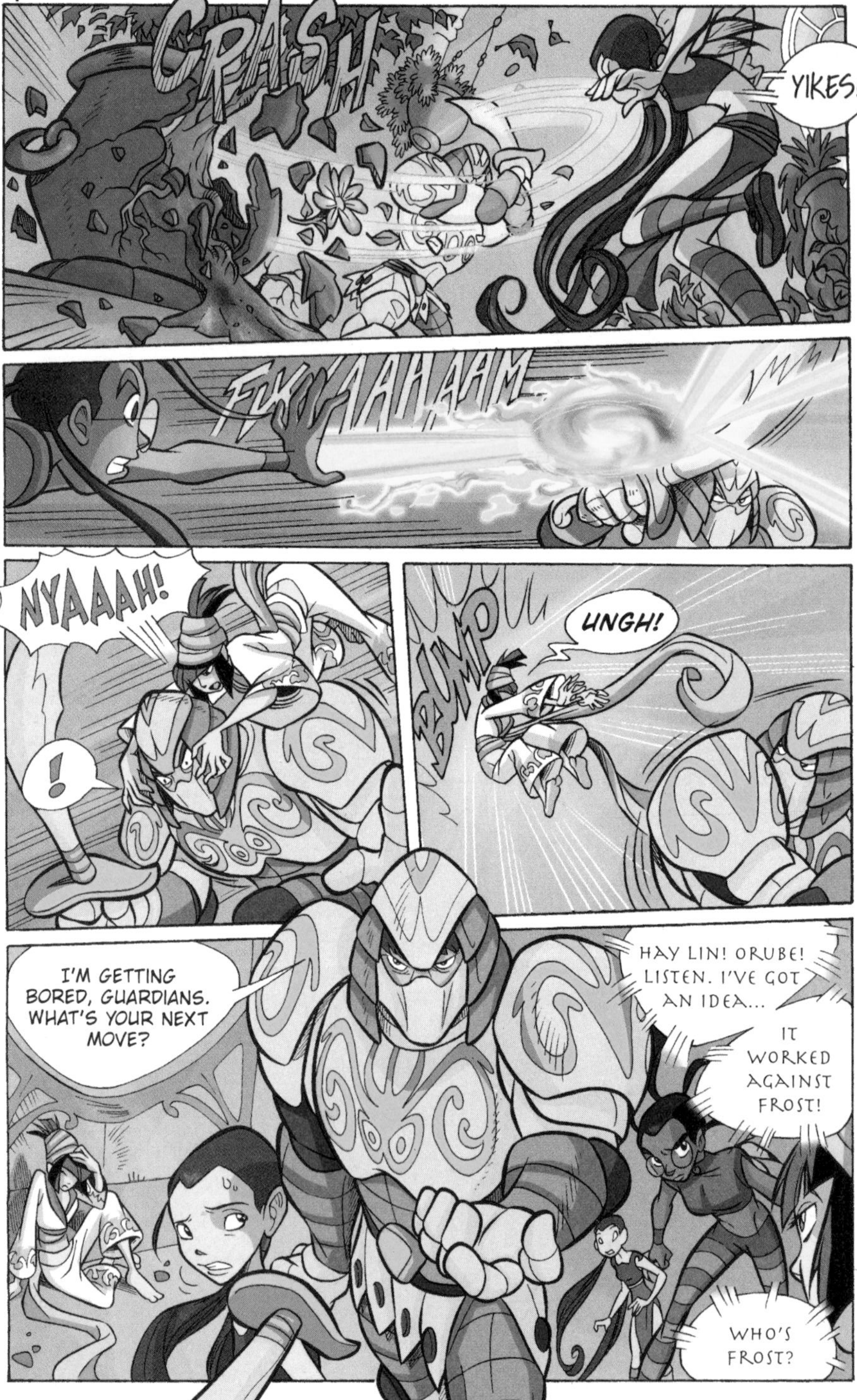
CRASH
YIKES!
FZKAAAHAAM
NYAAAH!
!
BUMP
UNGH!
I'M GETTING BORED, GUARDIANS. WHAT'S YOUR NEXT MOVE?
HAY LIN! ORUBE! LISTEN. I'VE GOT AN IDEA...
IT WORKED AGAINST FROST!
WHO'S FROST?

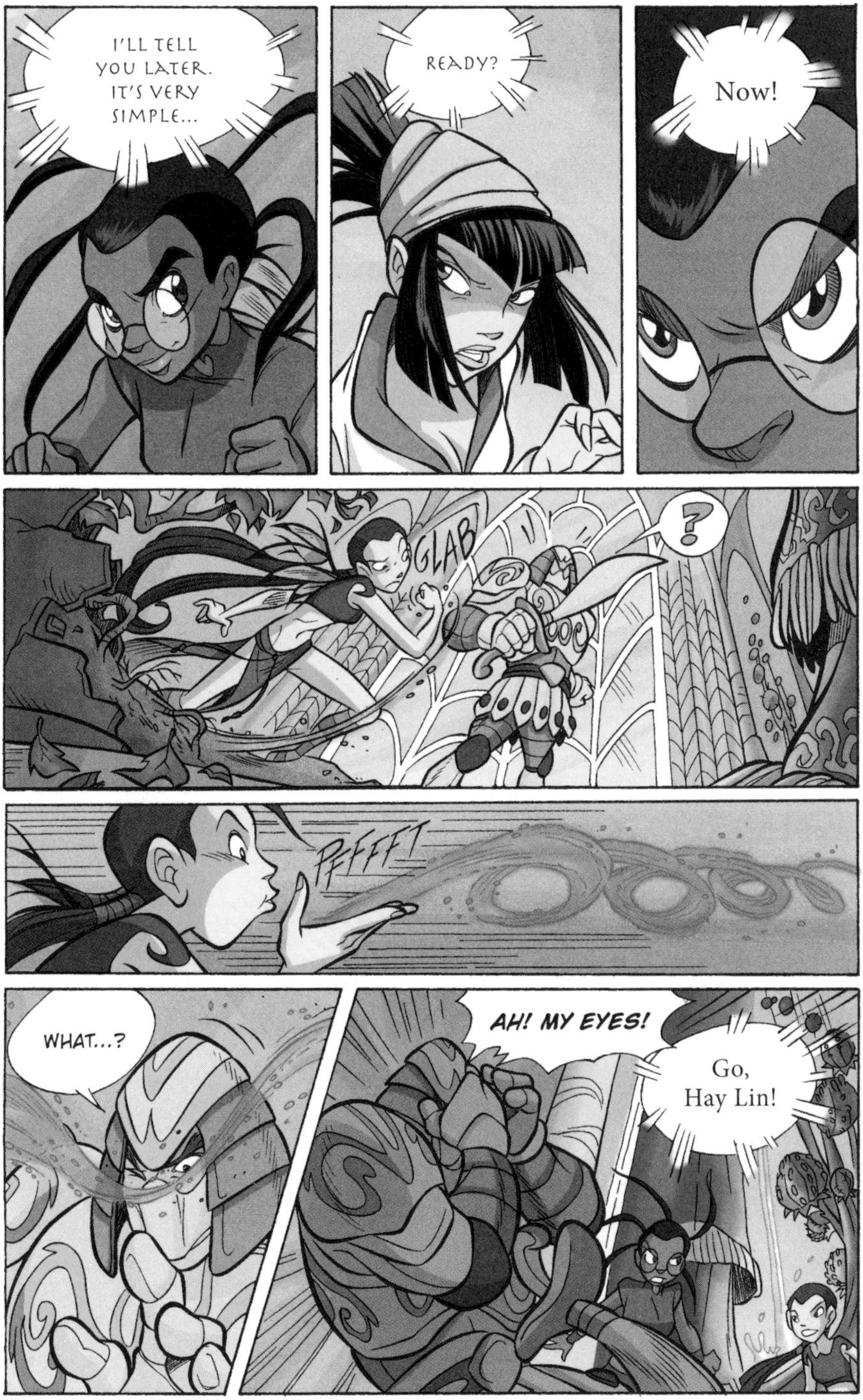
I'LL TELL YOU LATER. IT'S VERY SIMPLE...
READY?
Now!
GLAB
?
PFFFFT
WHAT...?
AH! MY EYES!
Go, Hay Lin!

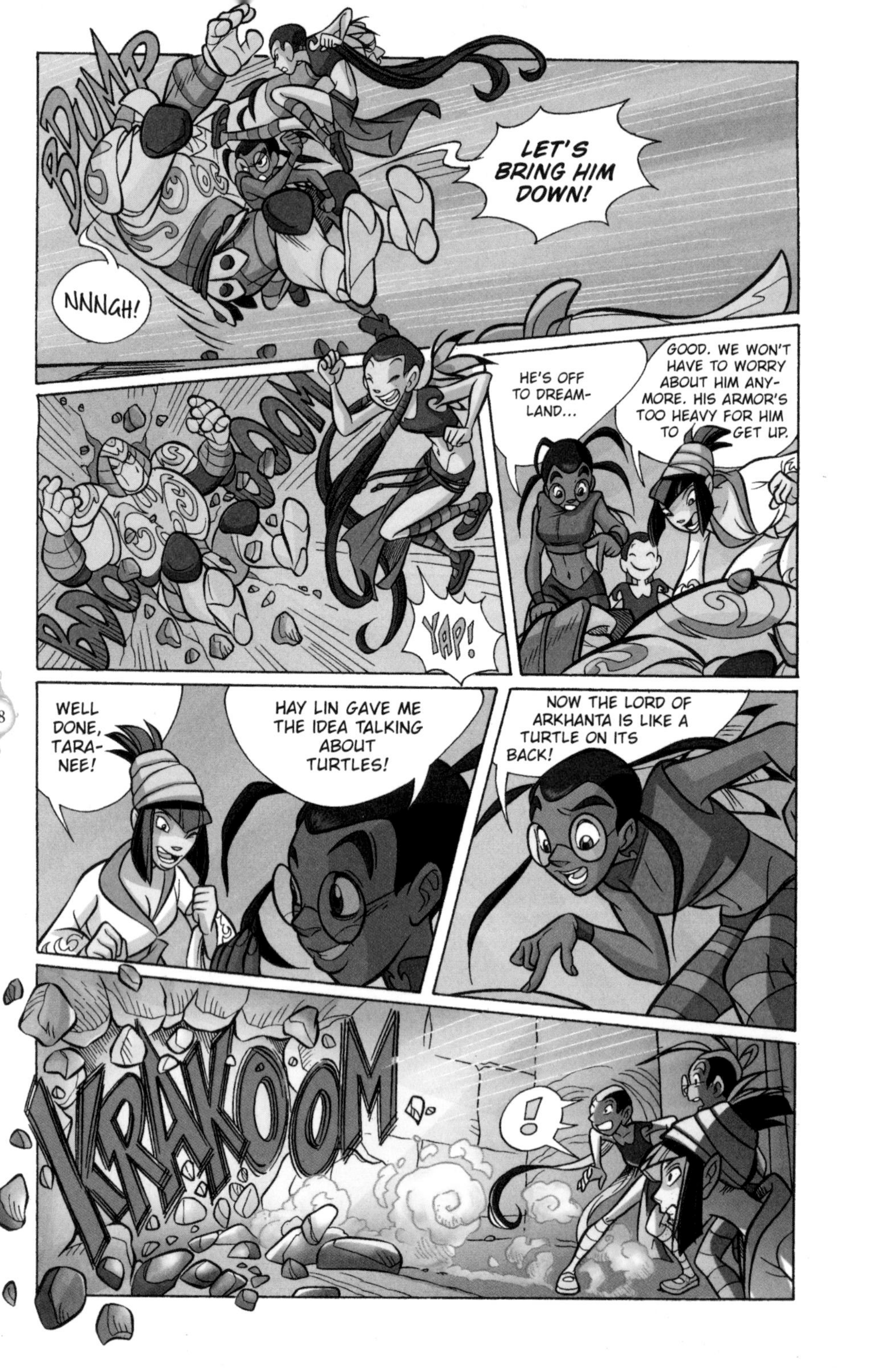
BDUMP
LET'S BRING HIM DOWN!
NNNGH!
BOOOOOM
YAP!
HE'S OFF TO DREAM-LAND...
GOOD. WE WON'T HAVE TO WORRY ABOUT HIM ANY-MORE. HIS ARMOR'S TOO HEAVY FOR HIM TO GET UP.
WELL DONE, TARA-NEE!
HAY LIN GAVE ME THE IDEA TALKING ABOUT TURTLES!
NOW THE LORD OF ARKHANTA IS LIKE A TURTLE ON ITS BACK!
KRAKOOM
!

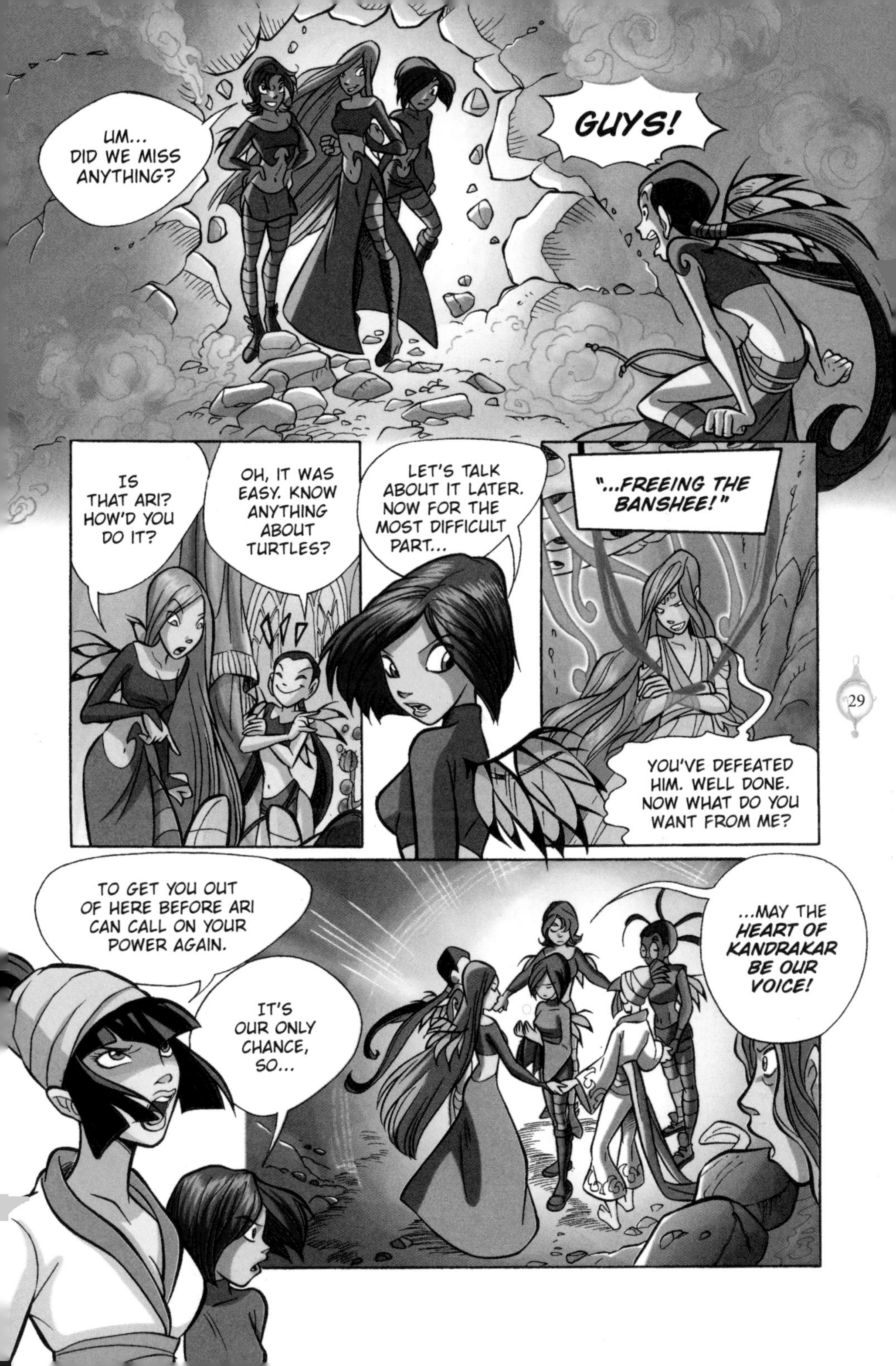

UM... DID WE MISS ANYTHING?
GUYS!
IS THAT ARI? HOW'D YOU DO IT?
OH, IT WAS EASY. KNOW ANYTHING ABOUT TURTLES?
LET'S TALK ABOUT IT LATER. NOW FOR THE MOST DIFFICULT PART...
"...FREEING THE BANSHEE!"
YOU'VE DEFEATED HIM. WELL DONE. NOW WHAT DO YOU WANT FROM ME?
TO GET YOU OUT OF HERE BEFORE ARI CAN CALL ON YOUR POWER AGAIN.
IT'S OUR ONLY CHANCE, SO...
...MAY THE HEART OF KANDRAKAR BE OUR VOICE!

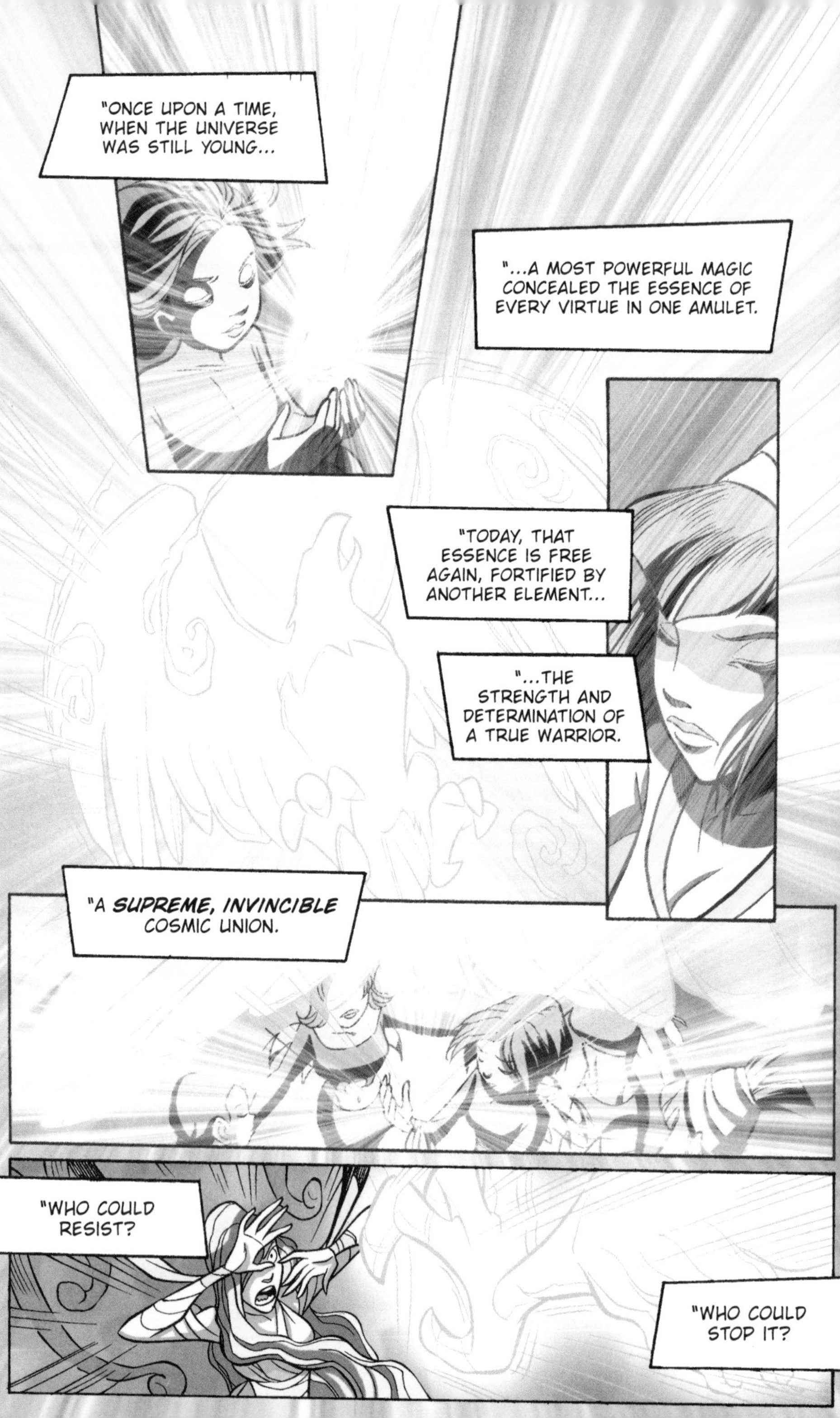
"ONCE UPON A TIME, WHEN THE UNIVERSE WAS STILL YOUNG...
"...A MOST POWERFUL MAGIC CONCEALED THE ESSENCE OF EVERY VIRTUE IN ONE AMULET.
"TODAY, THAT ESSENCE IS FREE AGAIN, FORTIFIED BY ANOTHER ELEMENT...
"...THE STRENGTH AND DETERMINATION OF A TRUE WARRIOR.
"A SUPREME, INVINCIBLE COSMIC UNION.
"WHO COULD RESIST?
"WHO COULD STOP IT?

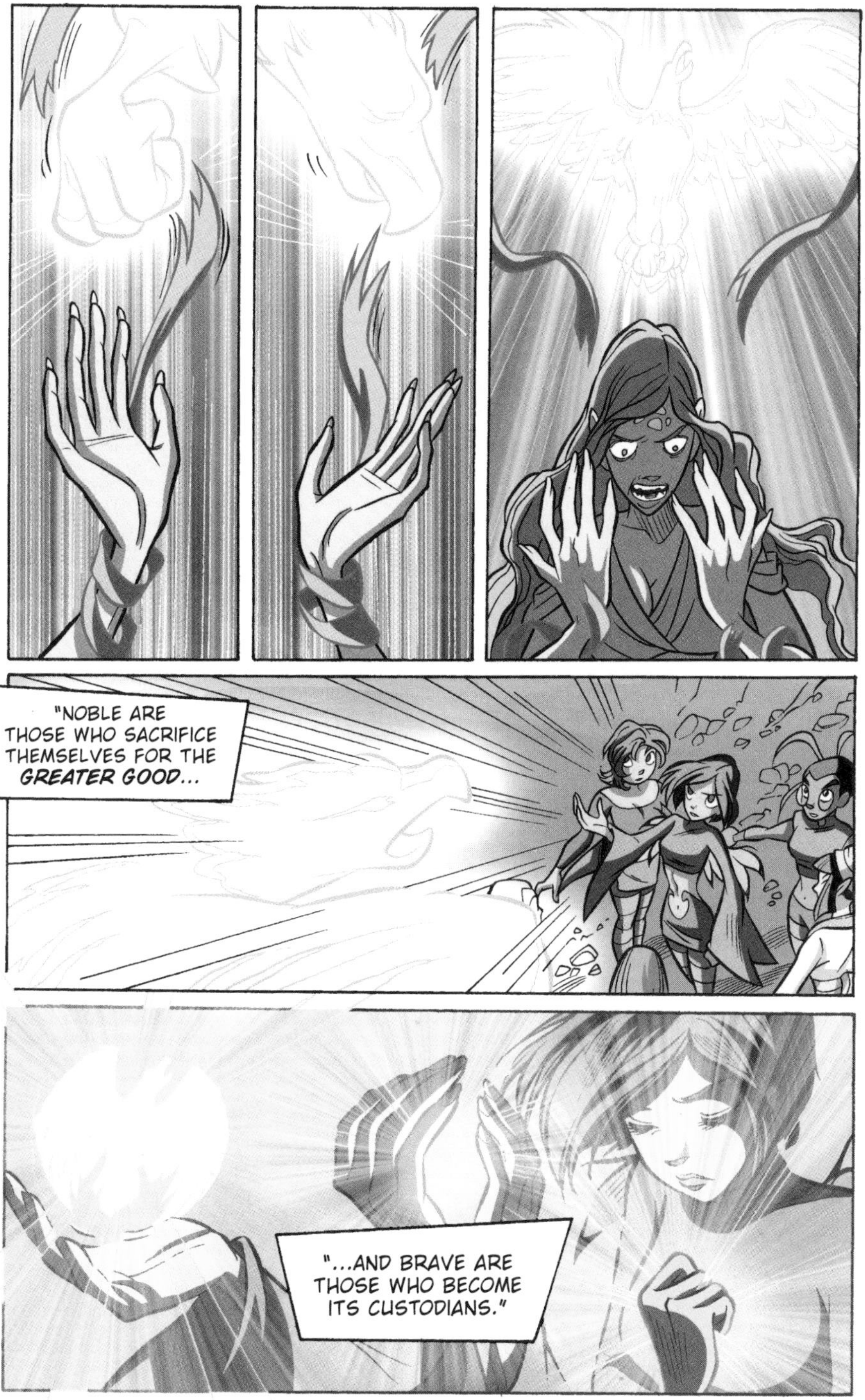
"NOBLE ARE THOSE WHO SACRIFICE THEMSELVES FOR THE **GREATER GOOD...**
"...AND BRAVE ARE THOSE WHO BECOME ITS CUSTODIANS."

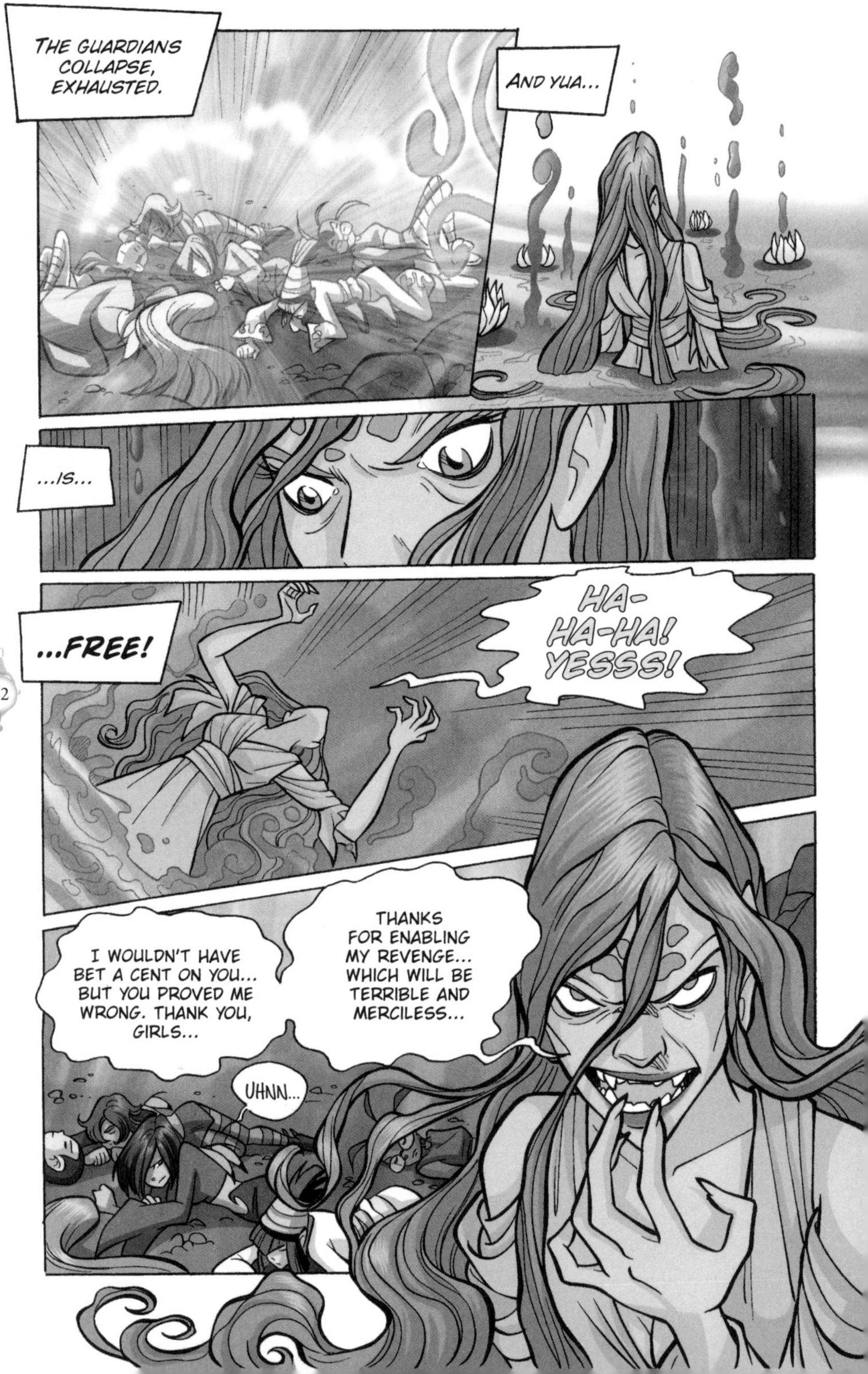
THE GUARDIANS COLLAPSE, EXHAUSTED.
AND YUA...
...IS...
...FREE!
HA-HA-HA! YESSS!
I WOULDN'T HAVE BET A CENT ON YOU... BUT YOU PROVED ME WRONG. THANK YOU, GIRLS...
THANKS FOR ENABLING MY REVENGE... WHICH WILL BE TERRIBLE AND MERCILESS...
UHNN...

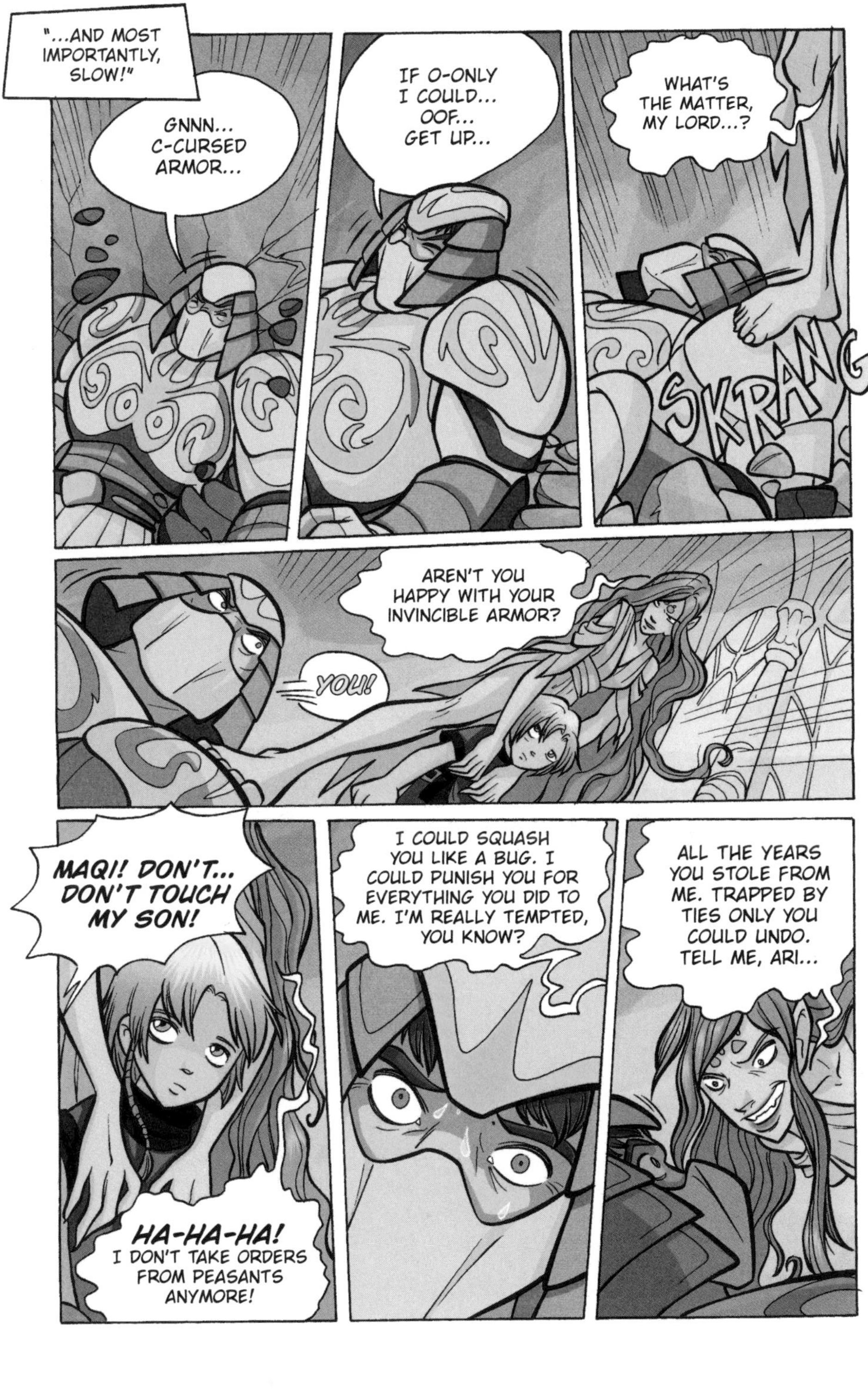
"...AND MOST IMPORTANTLY, SLOW!"
GNNN... C-CURSED ARMOR...
IF O-ONLY I COULD... OOF... GET UP...
WHAT'S THE MATTER, MY LORD...?
SKRANG
AREN'T YOU HAPPY WITH YOUR INVINCIBLE ARMOR?
YOU!
MAQI! DON'T... DON'T TOUCH MY SON!
HA-HA-HA! I DON'T TAKE ORDERS FROM PEASANTS ANYMORE!
I COULD SQUASH YOU LIKE A BUG. I COULD PUNISH YOU FOR EVERYTHING YOU DID TO ME. I'M REALLY TEMPTED, YOU KNOW?
ALL THE YEARS YOU STOLE FROM ME. TRAPPED BY TIES ONLY YOU COULD UNDO. TELL ME, ARI...

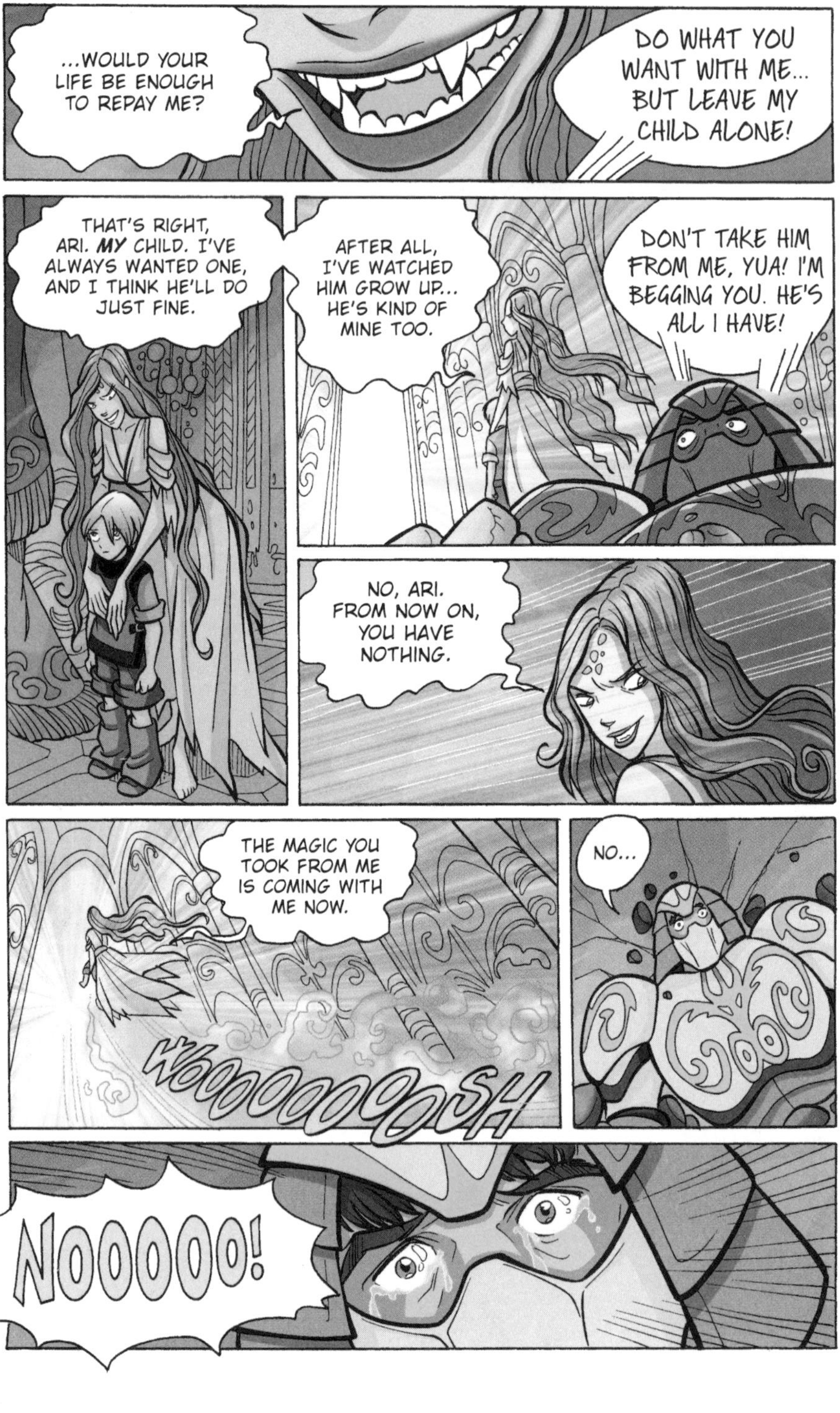
...WOULD YOUR LIFE BE ENOUGH TO REPAY ME?
DO WHAT YOU WANT WITH ME... BUT LEAVE MY CHILD ALONE!
THAT'S RIGHT, ARI. *MY* CHILD. I'VE ALWAYS WANTED ONE, AND I THINK HE'LL DO JUST FINE.
AFTER ALL, I'VE WATCHED HIM GROW UP... HE'S KIND OF MINE TOO.
DON'T TAKE HIM FROM ME, YUA! I'M BEGGING YOU. HE'S ALL I HAVE!
NO, ARI. FROM NOW ON, YOU HAVE NOTHING.
THE MAGIC YOU TOOK FROM ME IS COMING WITH ME NOW.
WOOOOOOOOSH
NO...
NOOOOO!

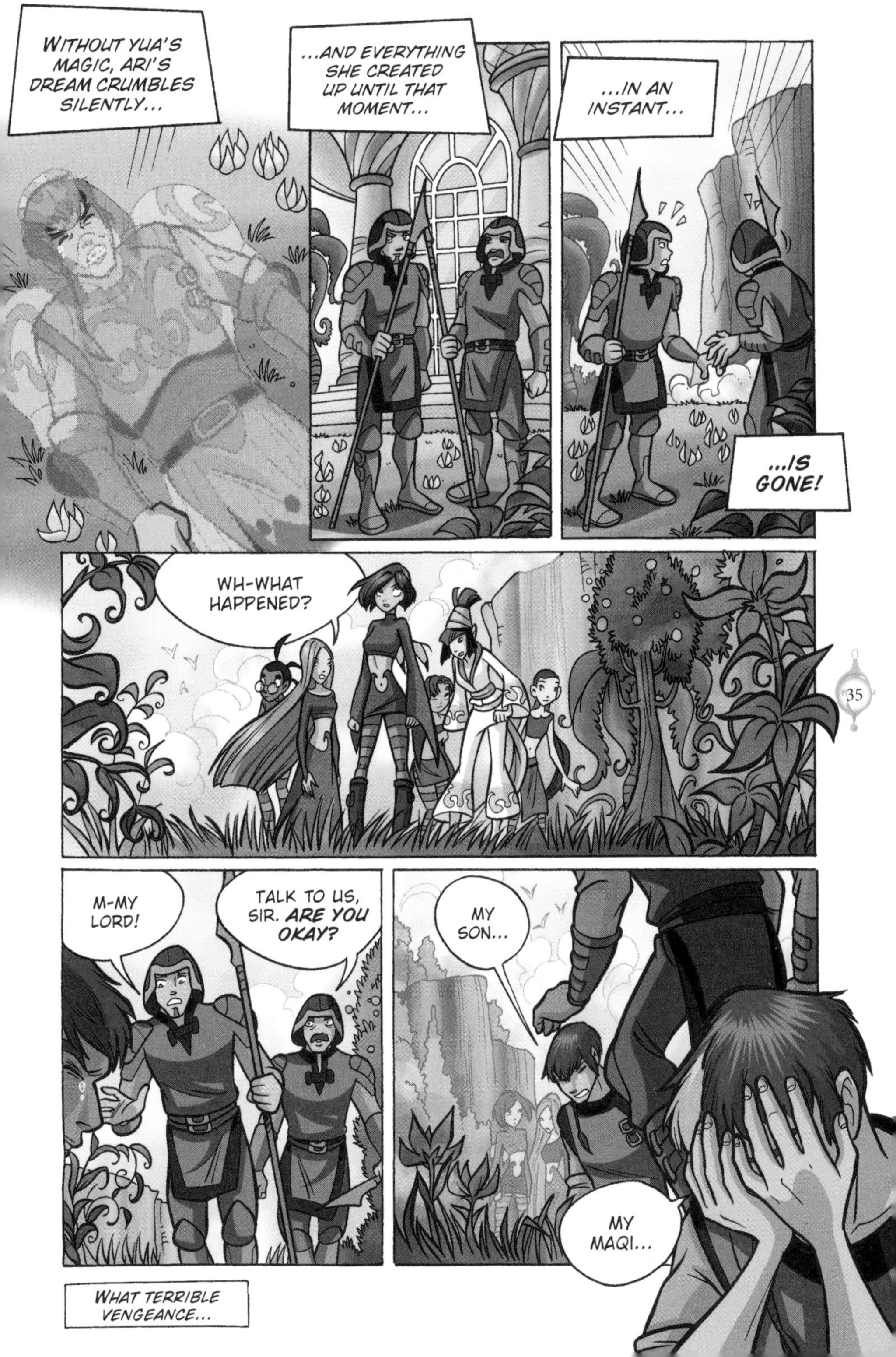
WITHOUT YUA'S MAGIC, ARI'S DREAM CRUMBLES SILENTLY...
...AND EVERYTHING SHE CREATED UP UNTIL THAT MOMENT...
...IN AN INSTANT...
...IS GONE!
WH-WHAT HAPPENED?
M-MY LORD!
TALK TO US, SIR. ARE YOU OKAY?
MY SON...
MY MAQI...
WHAT TERRIBLE VENGEANCE...

W.i.t.c.h.

Will Irma Taranee Cornelia Hay Lin

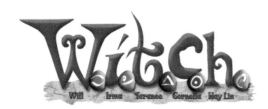

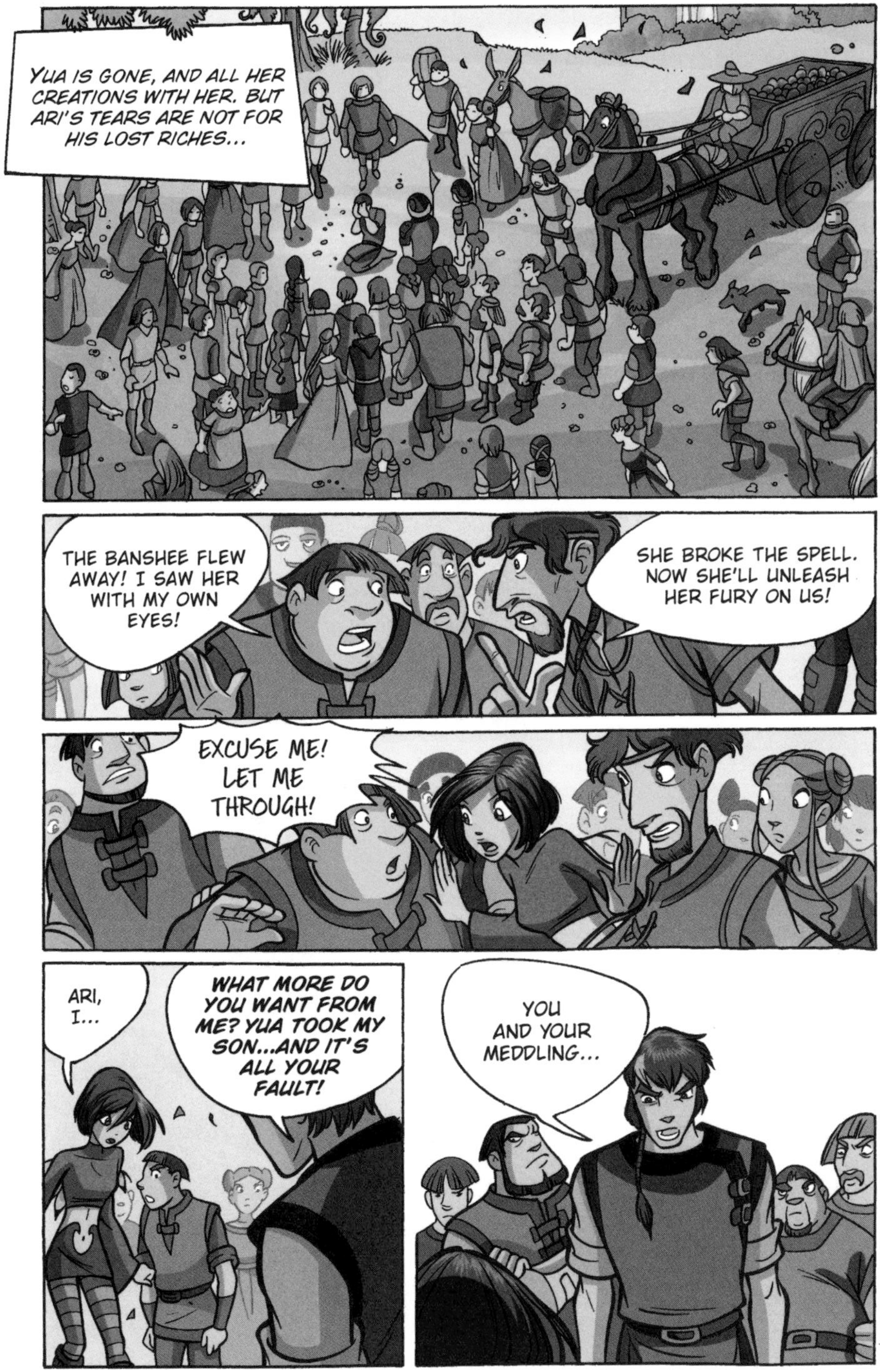

YUA IS GONE, AND ALL HER CREATIONS WITH HER. BUT ARI'S TEARS ARE NOT FOR HIS LOST RICHES...
THE BANSHEE FLEW AWAY! I SAW HER WITH MY OWN EYES!
SHE BROKE THE SPELL. NOW SHE'LL UNLEASH HER FURY ON US!
EXCUSE ME! LET ME THROUGH!
ARI, I...
WHAT MORE DO YOU WANT FROM ME? YUA TOOK MY SON...AND IT'S ALL YOUR FAULT!
YOU AND YOUR MEDDLING...

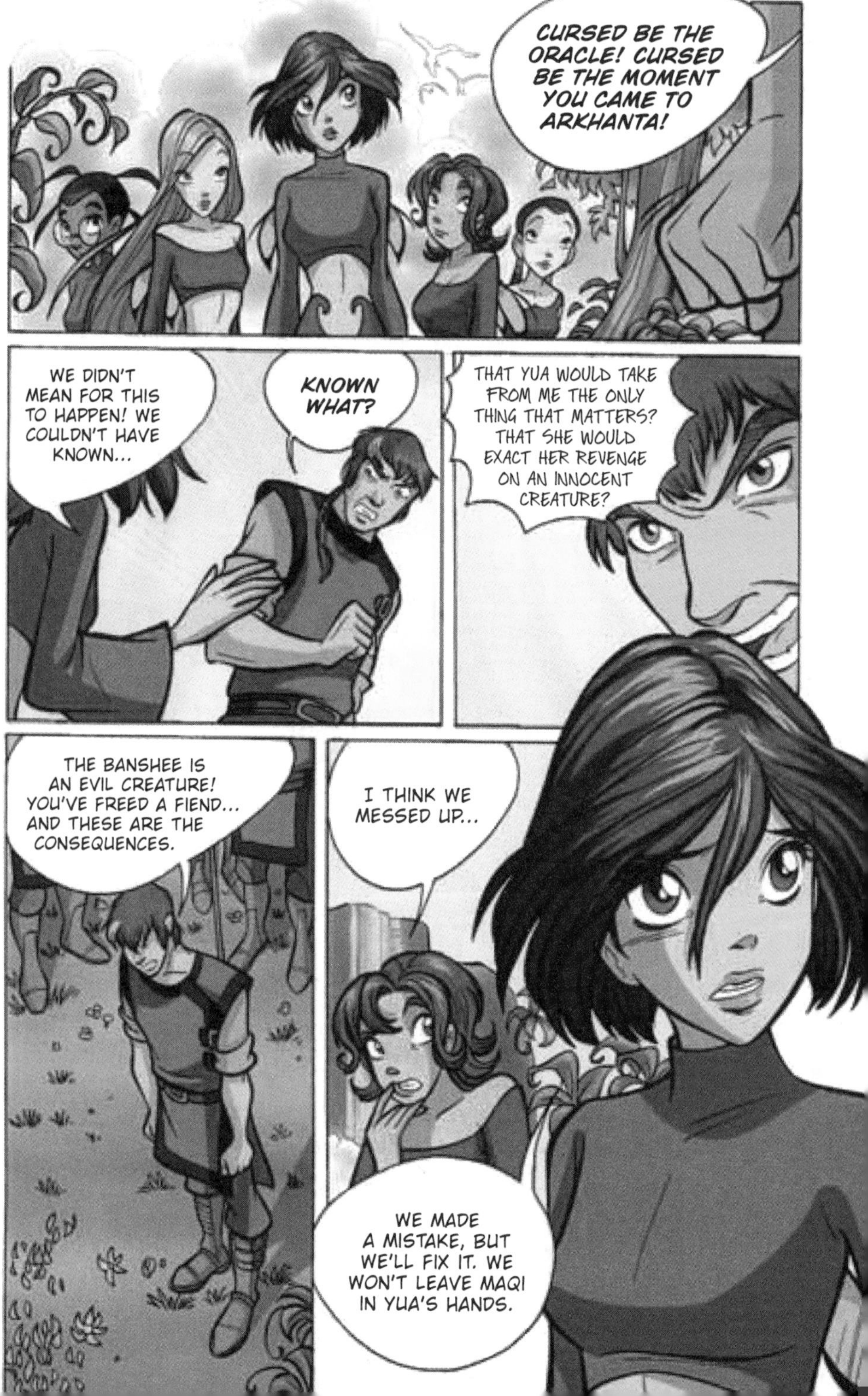
CURSED BE THE ORACLE! CURSED BE THE MOMENT YOU CAME TO ARKHANTA!
WE DIDN'T MEAN FOR THIS TO HAPPEN! WE COULDN'T HAVE KNOWN...
KNOWN WHAT?
THAT YUA WOULD TAKE FROM ME THE ONLY THING THAT MATTERS? THAT SHE WOULD EXACT HER REVENGE ON AN INNOCENT CREATURE?
THE BANSHEE IS AN EVIL CREATURE! YOU'VE FREED A FIEND... AND THESE ARE THE CONSEQUENCES.
I THINK WE MESSED UP...
WE MADE A MISTAKE, BUT WE'LL FIX IT. WE WON'T LEAVE MAQI IN YUA'S HANDS.

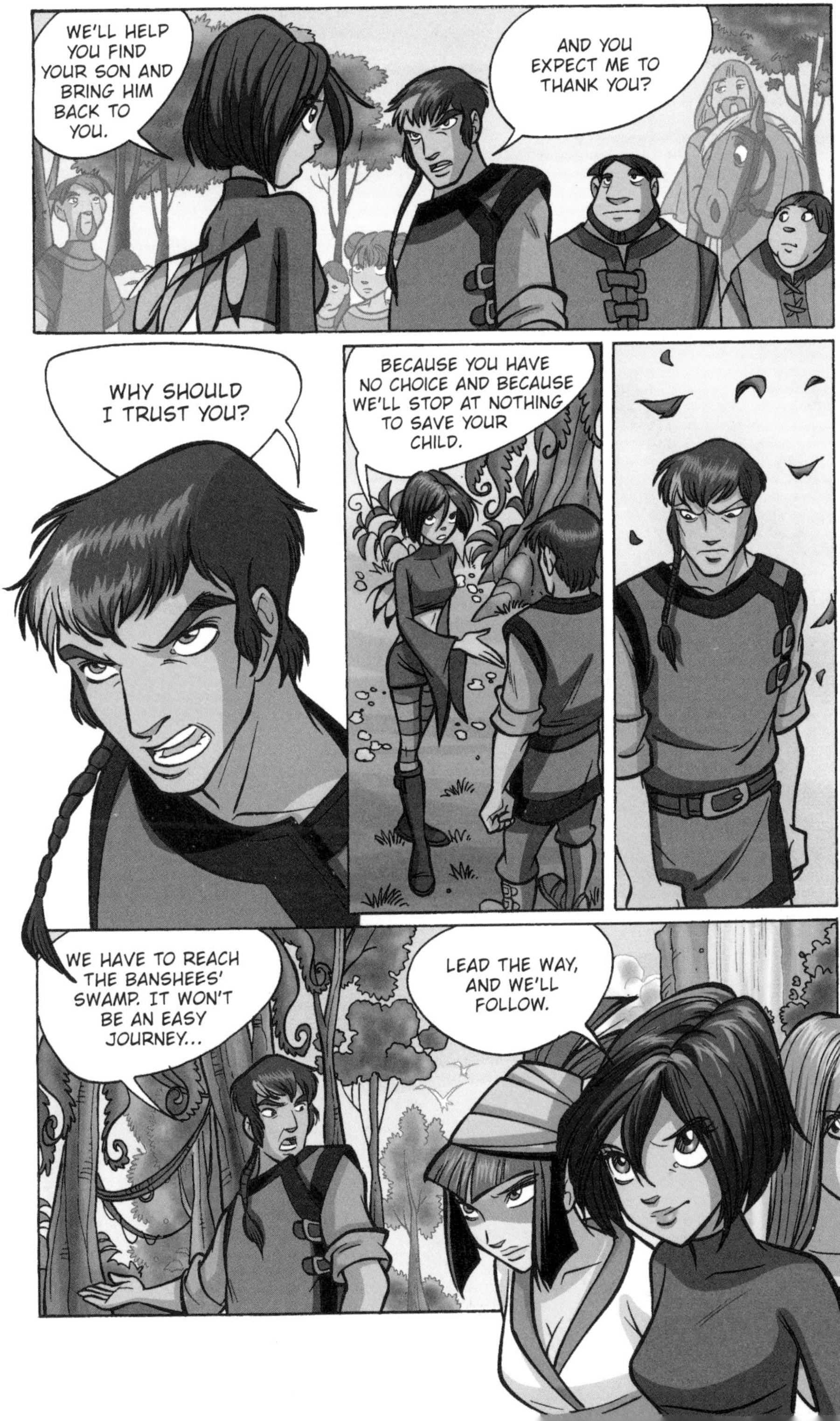
WE'LL HELP YOU FIND YOUR SON AND BRING HIM BACK TO YOU.
AND YOU EXPECT ME TO THANK YOU?
WHY SHOULD I TRUST YOU?
BECAUSE YOU HAVE NO CHOICE AND BECAUSE WE'LL STOP AT NOTHING TO SAVE YOUR CHILD.
WE HAVE TO REACH THE BANSHEES' SWAMP. IT WON'T BE AN EASY JOURNEY...
LEAD THE WAY, AND WE'LL FOLLOW.

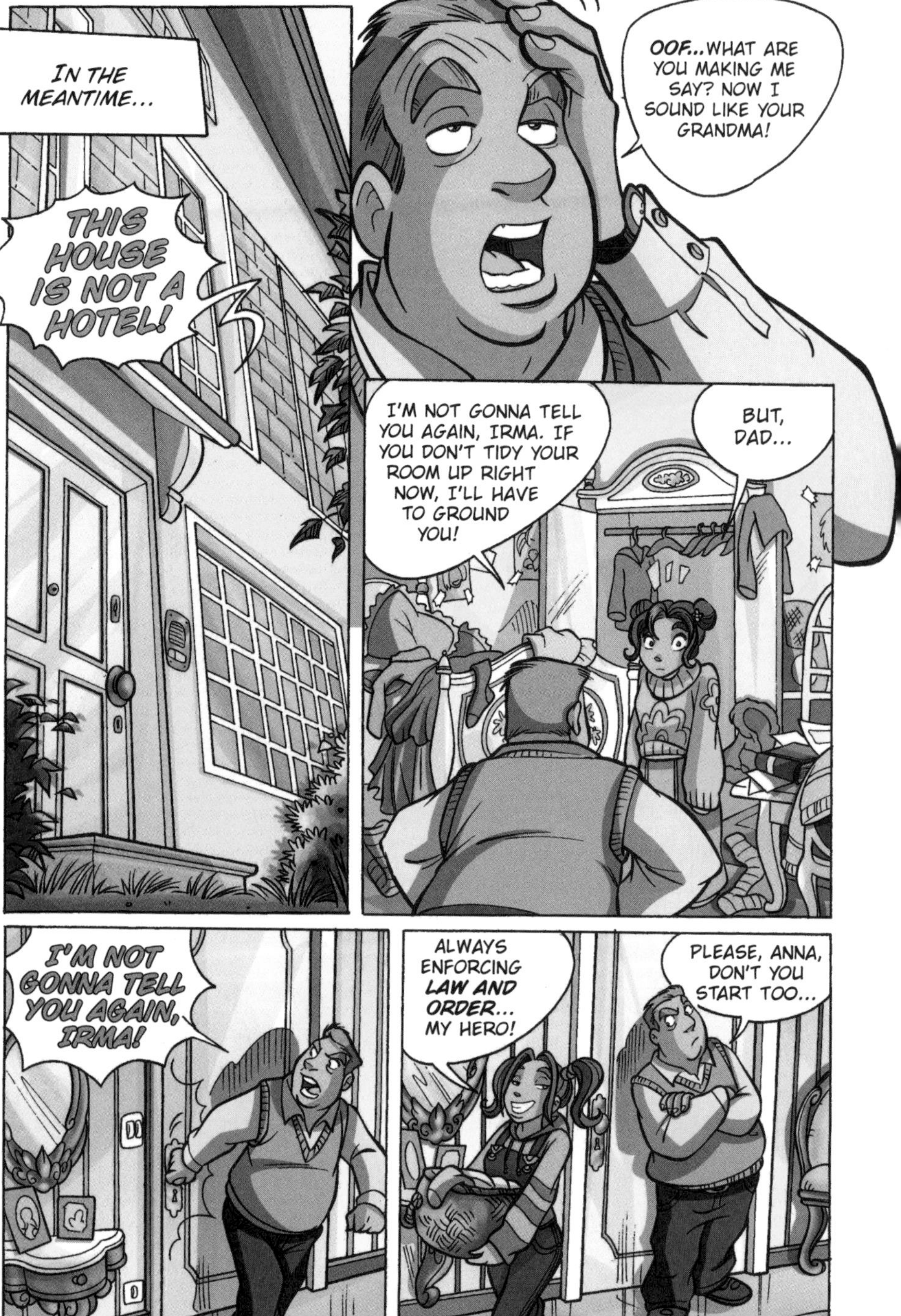
IN THE MEANTIME...
THIS HOUSE IS NOT A HOTEL!
OOF...WHAT ARE YOU MAKING ME SAY? NOW I SOUND LIKE YOUR GRANDMA!
I'M NOT GONNA TELL YOU AGAIN, IRMA. IF YOU DON'T TIDY YOUR ROOM UP RIGHT NOW, I'LL HAVE TO GROUND YOU!
BUT, DAD...
I'M NOT GONNA TELL YOU AGAIN, IRMA!
ALWAYS ENFORCING LAW AND ORDER... MY HERO!
PLEASE, ANNA, DON'T YOU START TOO...

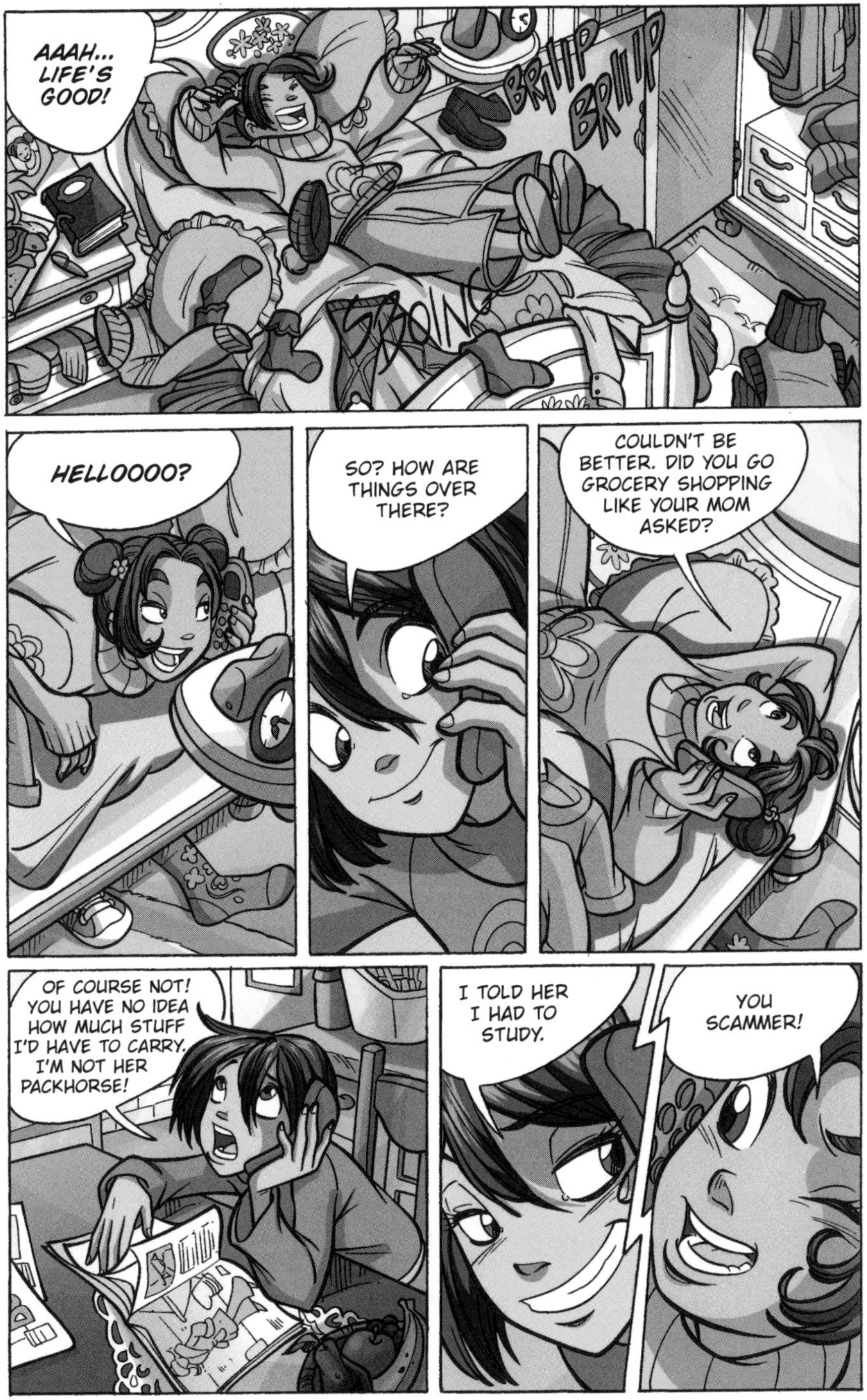
AAAH... LIFE'S GOOD!
BRIIIP BRIIIP
SBOING
HELLOOOO?
SO? HOW ARE THINGS OVER THERE?
COULDN'T BE BETTER. DID YOU GO GROCERY SHOPPING LIKE YOUR MOM ASKED?
OF COURSE NOT! YOU HAVE NO IDEA HOW MUCH STUFF I'D HAVE TO CARRY. I'M NOT HER PACKHORSE!
I TOLD HER I HAD TO STUDY.
YOU SCAMMER!

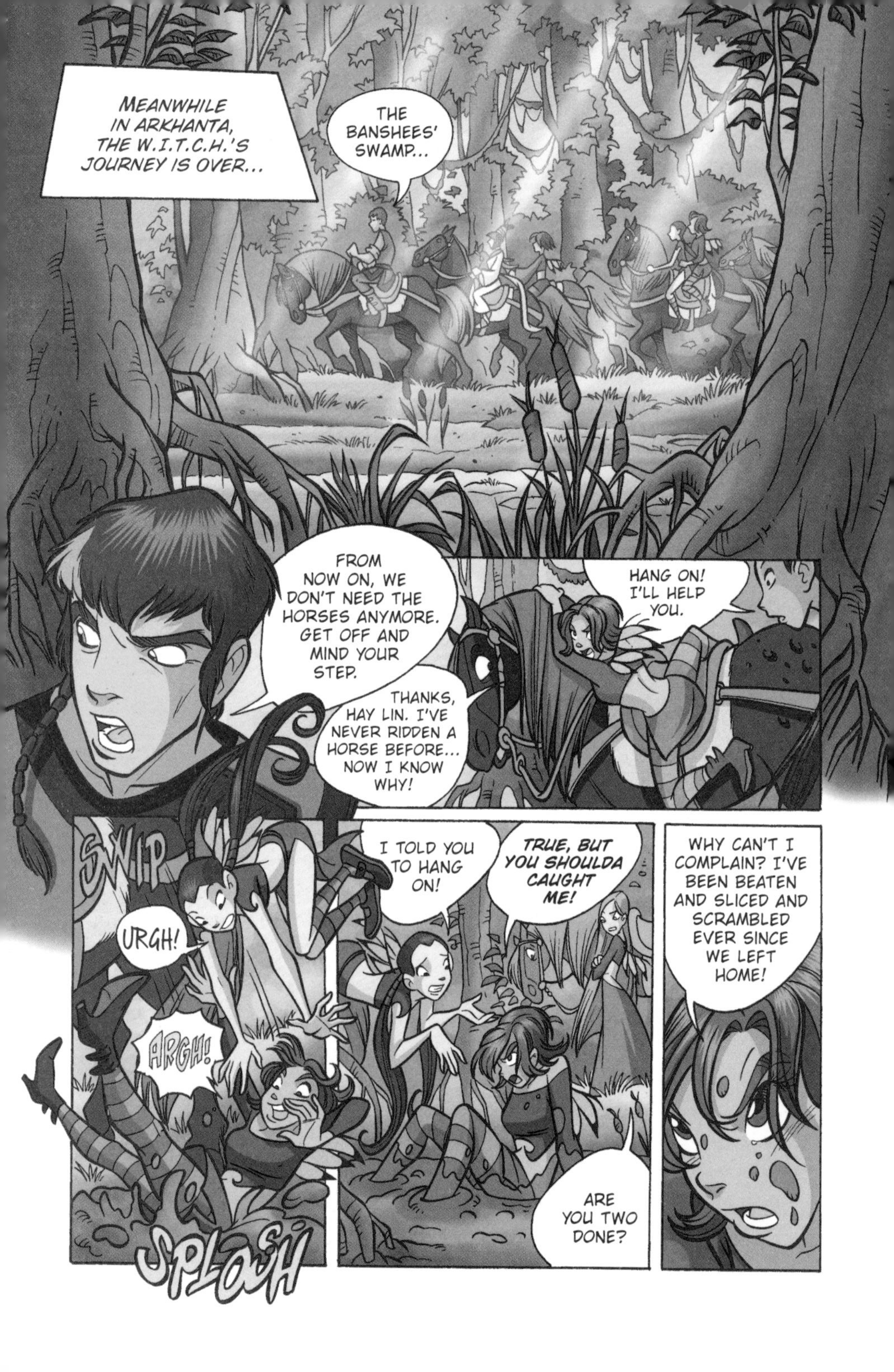
MEANWHILE IN ARKHANTA, THE W.I.T.C.H.'S JOURNEY IS OVER...
THE BANSHEES' SWAMP...
FROM NOW ON, WE DON'T NEED THE HORSES ANYMORE. GET OFF AND MIND YOUR STEP.
HANG ON! I'LL HELP YOU.
THANKS, HAY LIN. I'VE NEVER RIDDEN A HORSE BEFORE... NOW I KNOW WHY!
SWIP
URGH!
ARGH!
SPLOSH
I TOLD YOU TO HANG ON!
TRUE, BUT YOU SHOULDA CAUGHT ME!
ARE YOU TWO DONE?
WHY CAN'T I COMPLAIN? I'VE BEEN BEATEN AND SLICED AND SCRAMBLED EVER SINCE WE LEFT HOME!

HEY! THE WOUND IS *GONE!*

THAT'S BECAUSE OF THE *GIFT...*

FIRST TARANEE'S EYES, NOW IRMA'S ARM! IT'S THE EFFECTS OF *XIN JING'S GIFT.*

I DON'T UNDERSTAND YOUR WORDS, GIRLS... BUT I DIDN'T COME HERE TO LISTEN TO YOU TALK.

ARI'S RIGHT. *LET'S GO...*

43

FRUUUSH

BURLLSIKUUUURLEAKKAR

YUCK! WHAT'S THIS STENCH?

LISTEN...

IT'S THE BANSHEES TRYING TO KEEP US AWAY FROM THEIR HOME.

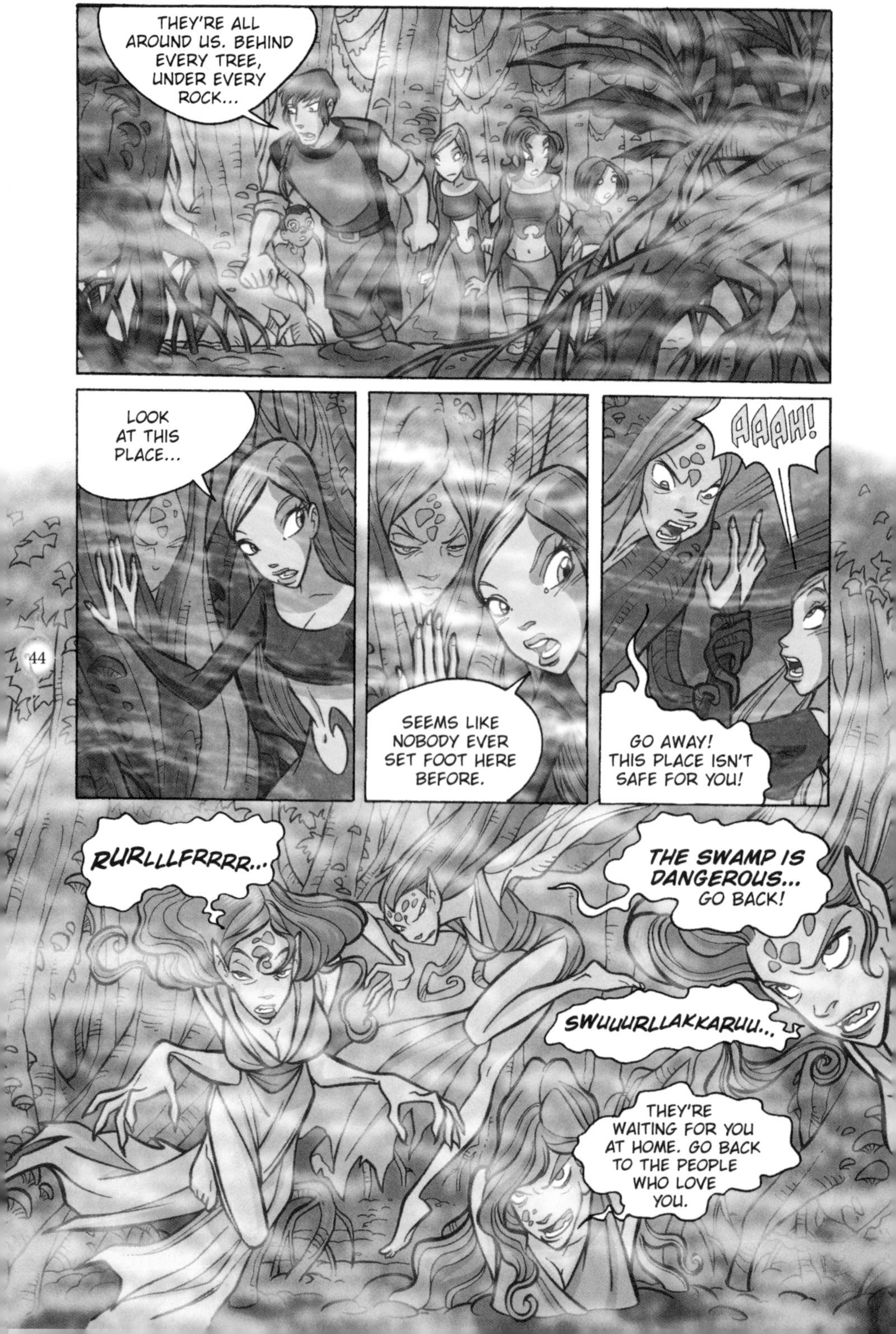
THEY'RE ALL AROUND US. BEHIND EVERY TREE, UNDER EVERY ROCK...
LOOK AT THIS PLACE...
SEEMS LIKE NOBODY EVER SET FOOT HERE BEFORE.
AAAH!
GO AWAY! THIS PLACE ISN'T SAFE FOR YOU!
RURLLLFRRRR...
THE SWAMP IS DANGEROUS... GO BACK!
SWUUURLLAKKARUU...
THEY'RE WAITING FOR YOU AT HOME. GO BACK TO THE PEOPLE WHO LOVE YOU.

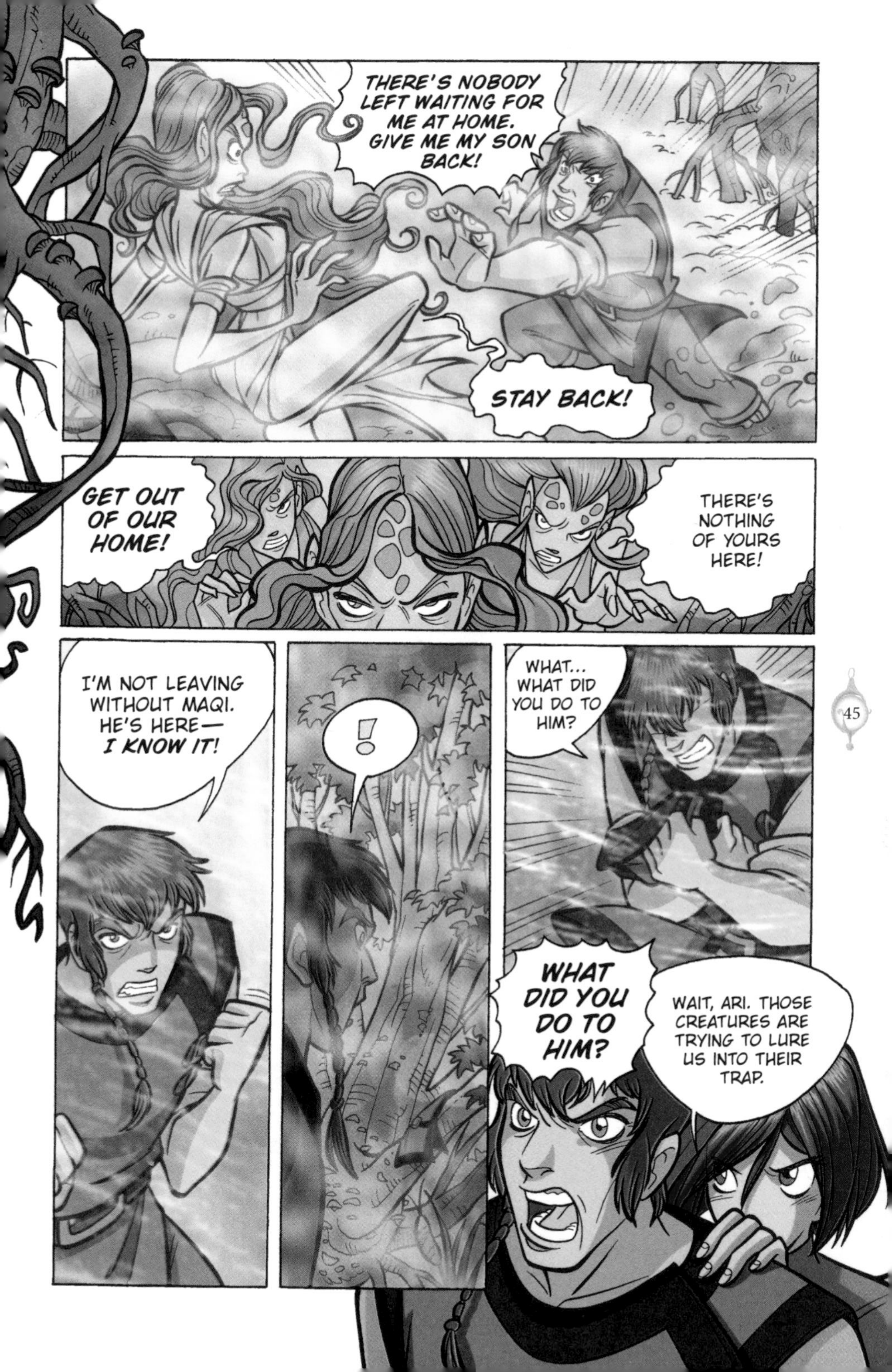
THERE'S NOBODY LEFT WAITING FOR ME AT HOME. GIVE ME MY SON BACK!
STAY BACK!
GET OUT OF OUR HOME!
THERE'S NOTHING OF YOURS HERE!
I'M NOT LEAVING WITHOUT MAQI. HE'S HERE— I KNOW IT!
!
WHAT... WHAT DID YOU DO TO HIM?
WHAT DID YOU DO TO HIM?
WAIT, ARI. THOSE CREATURES ARE TRYING TO LURE US INTO THEIR TRAP.

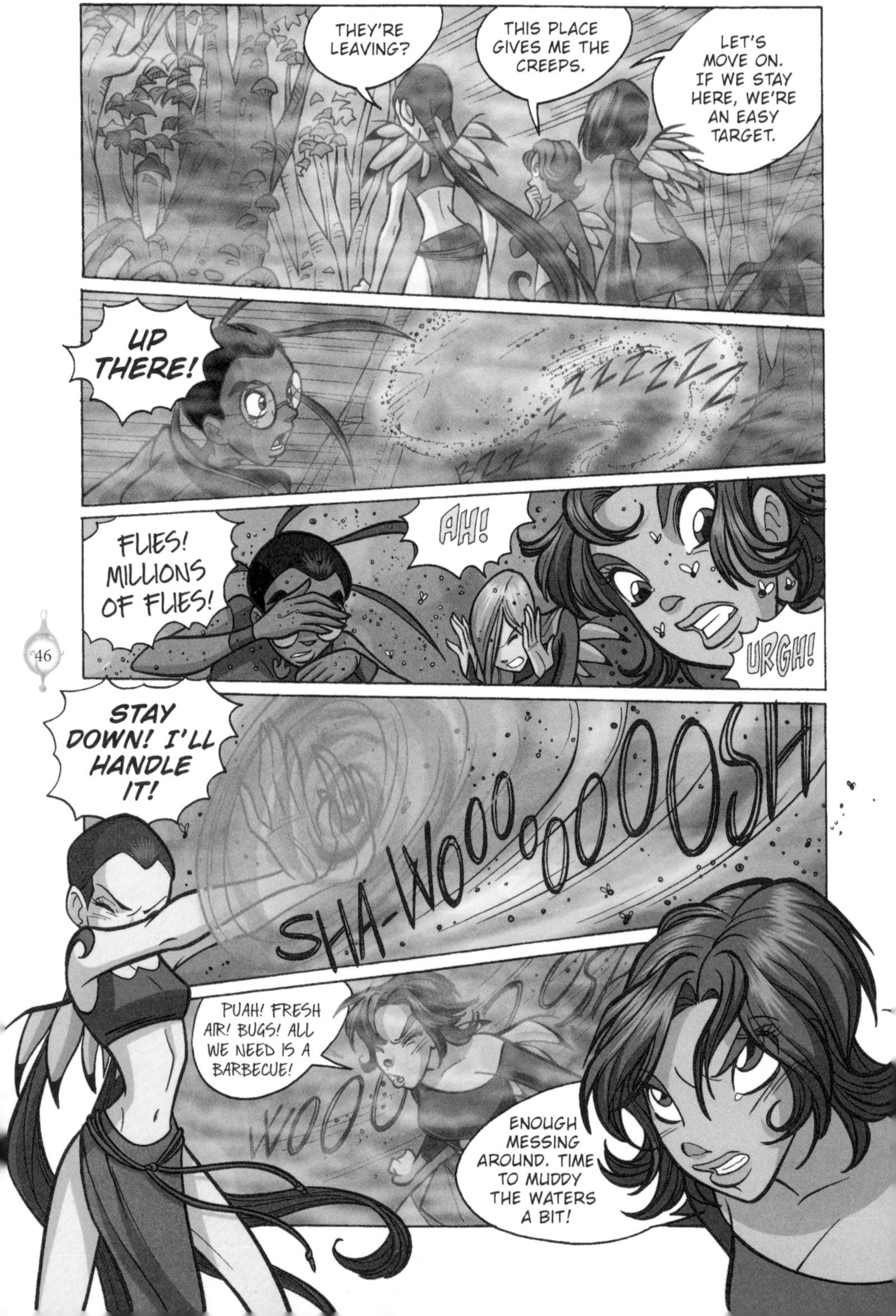
THEY'RE LEAVING?
THIS PLACE GIVES ME THE CREEPS.
LET'S MOVE ON. IF WE STAY HERE, WE'RE AN EASY TARGET.
UP THERE!
ZZZZZZZZ
FLIES! MILLIONS OF FLIES!
AH!
URGH!
STAY DOWN! I'LL HANDLE IT!
SHA-WOOOOOOOOSH!
PUAH! FRESH AIR! BUGS! ALL WE NEED IS A BARBECUE!
ENOUGH MESSING AROUND. TIME TO MUDDY THE WATERS A BIT!

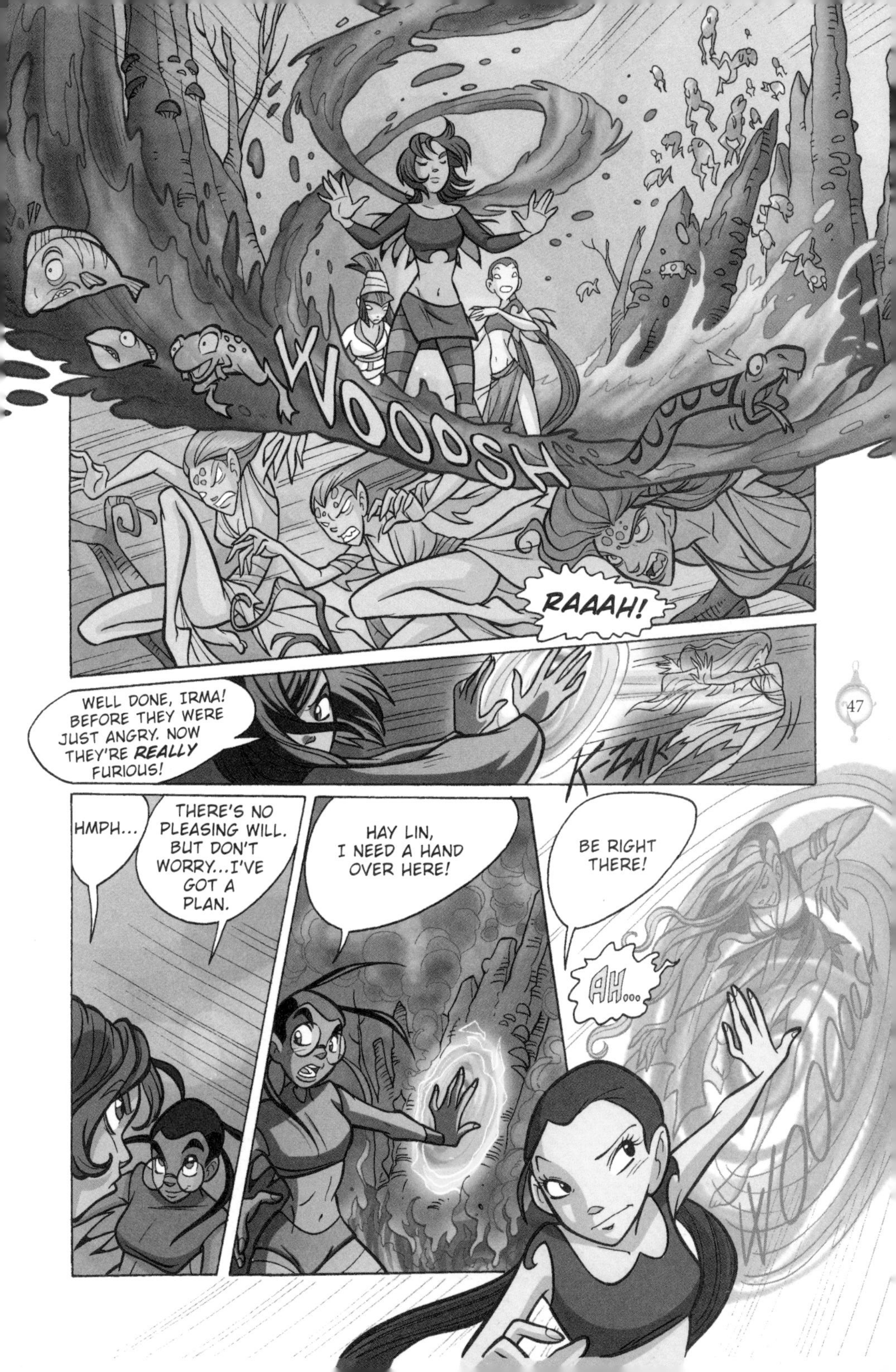
WOOOSH
RAAAH!
WELL DONE, IRMA! BEFORE THEY WERE JUST ANGRY. NOW THEY'RE REALLY FURIOUS!
K-ZAK
HMPH...
THERE'S NO PLEASING WILL. BUT DON'T WORRY...I'VE GOT A PLAN.
HAY LIN, I NEED A HAND OVER HERE!
BE RIGHT THERE!
AH...

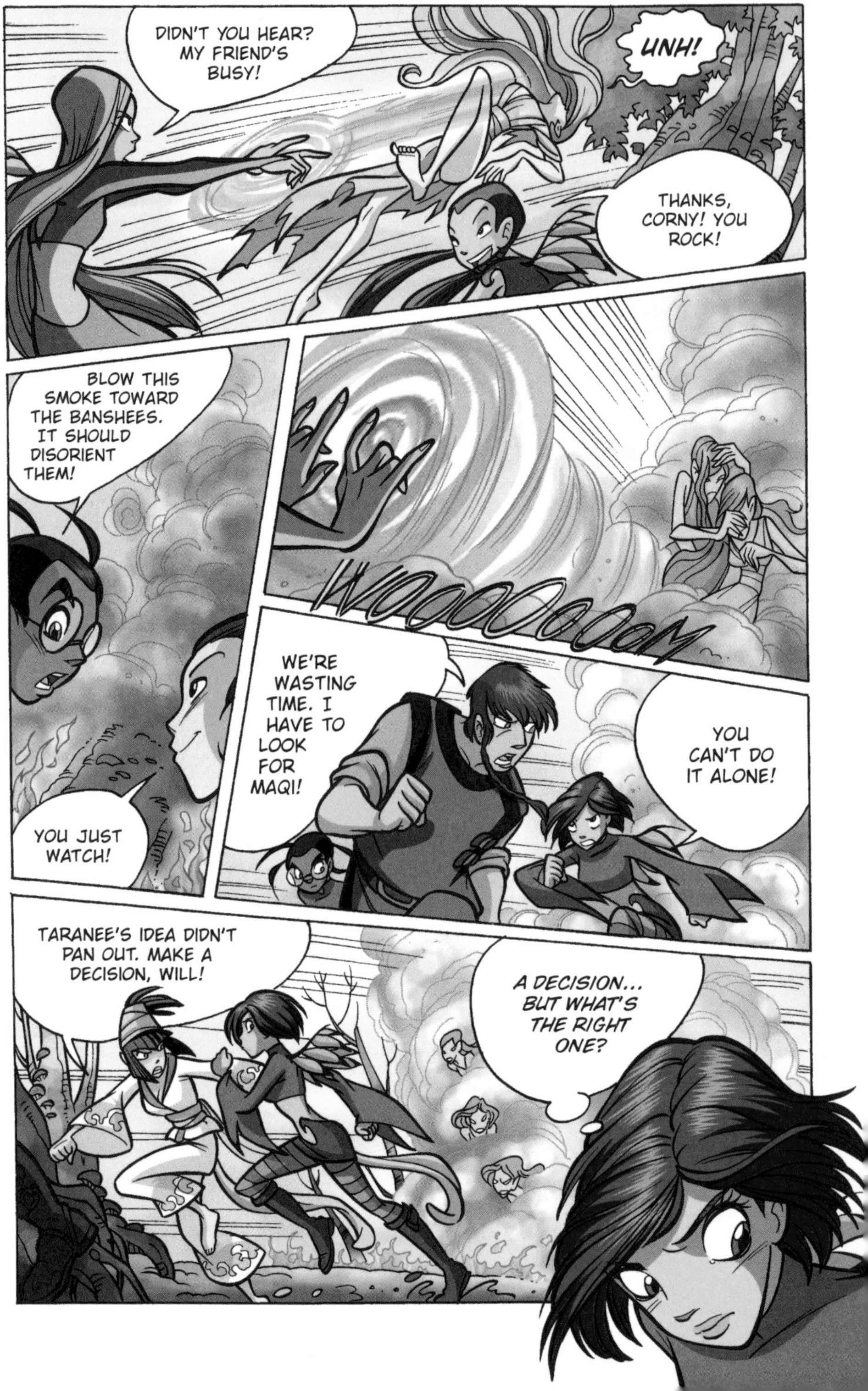
DIDN'T YOU HEAR? MY FRIEND'S BUSY!
UNH!
THANKS, CORNY! YOU ROCK!
BLOW THIS SMOKE TOWARD THE BANSHEES. IT SHOULD DISORIENT THEM!
YOU JUST WATCH!
WOOOOOOOOM
WE'RE WASTING TIME. I HAVE TO LOOK FOR MAQI!
YOU CAN'T DO IT ALONE!
TARANEE'S IDEA DIDN'T PAN OUT. MAKE A DECISION, WILL!
A DECISION... BUT WHAT'S THE RIGHT ONE?

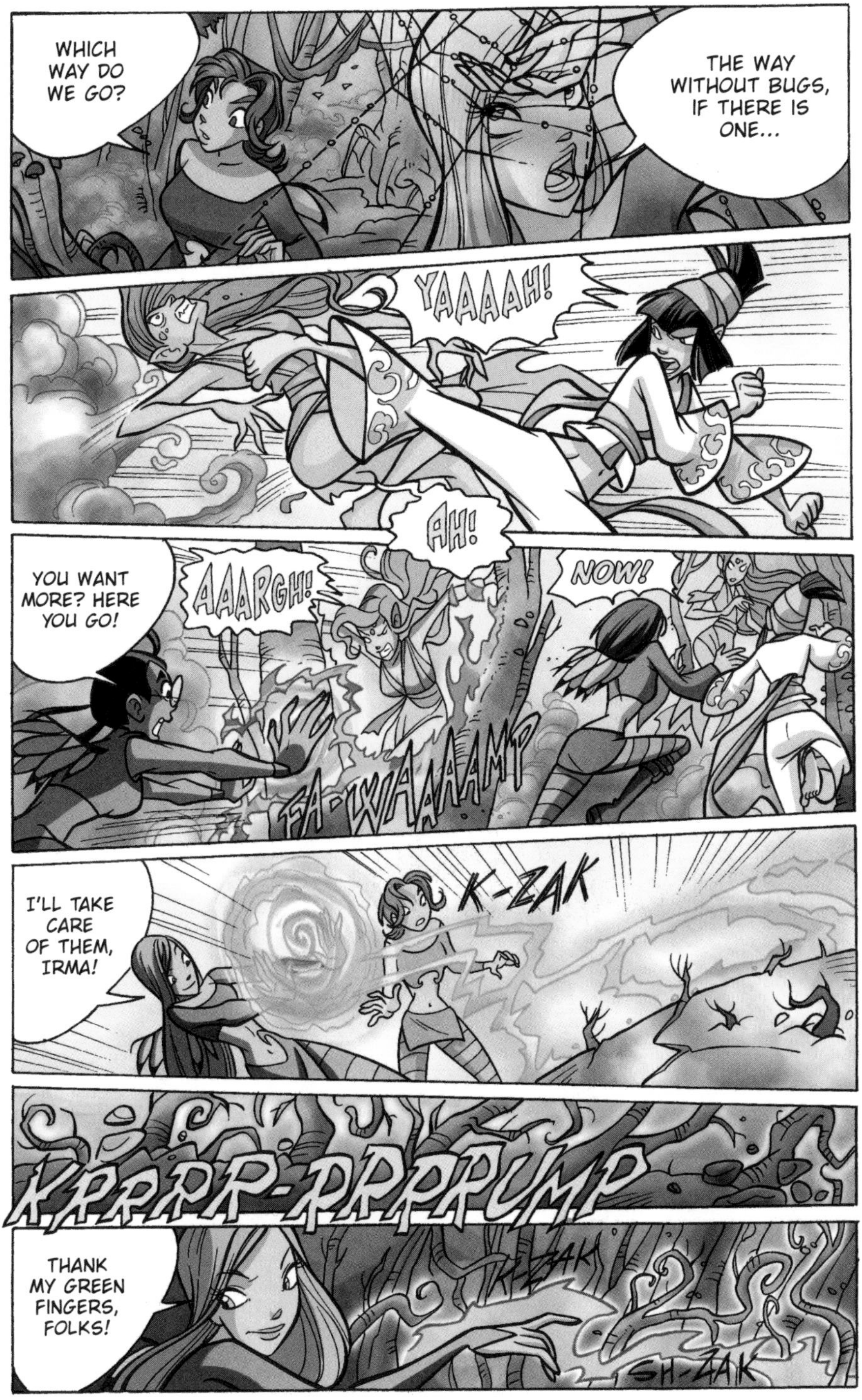
WHICH WAY DO WE GO?
THE WAY WITHOUT BUGS, IF THERE IS ONE...
YAAAAH!
AH!
YOU WANT MORE? HERE YOU GO!
AAARGH!
NOW!
FA-WAAAAAMP
I'LL TAKE CARE OF THEM, IRMA!
K-ZAK
KRRRR-RRRRUMP
THANK MY GREEN FINGERS, FOLKS!
K-ZAK
SH-ZAK

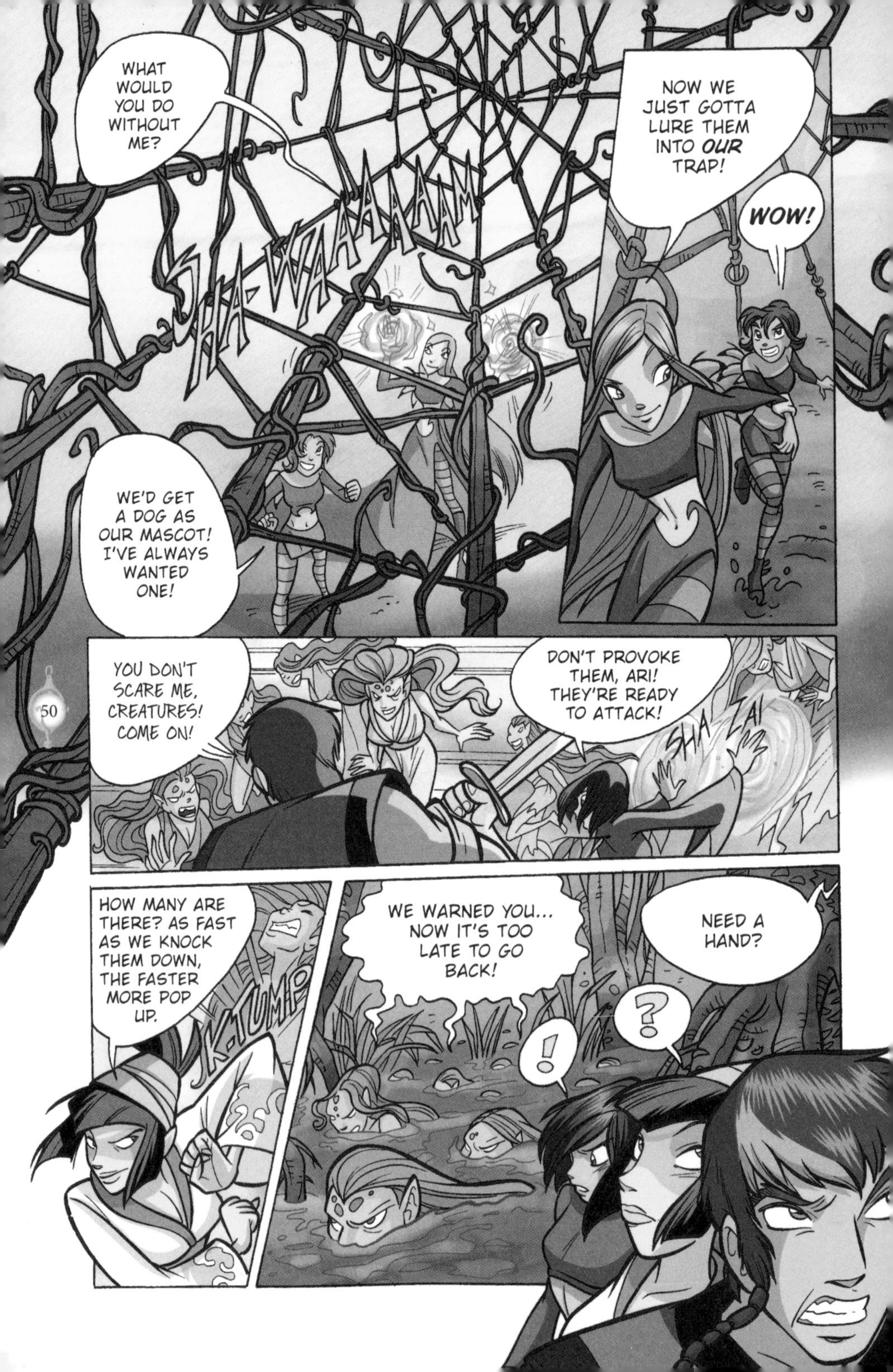
WHAT WOULD YOU DO WITHOUT ME?
SHA-WAAAAAAM
NOW WE JUST GOTTA LURE THEM INTO OUR TRAP!
WOW!
WE'D GET A DOG AS OUR MASCOT! I'VE ALWAYS WANTED ONE!
YOU DON'T SCARE ME, CREATURES! COME ON!
DON'T PROVOKE THEM, ARI! THEY'RE READY TO ATTACK!
SHA ZAI
HOW MANY ARE THERE? AS FAST AS WE KNOCK THEM DOWN, THE FASTER MORE POP UP.
K-TUMP
WE WARNED YOU... NOW IT'S TOO LATE TO GO BACK!
NEED A HAND?
!
?

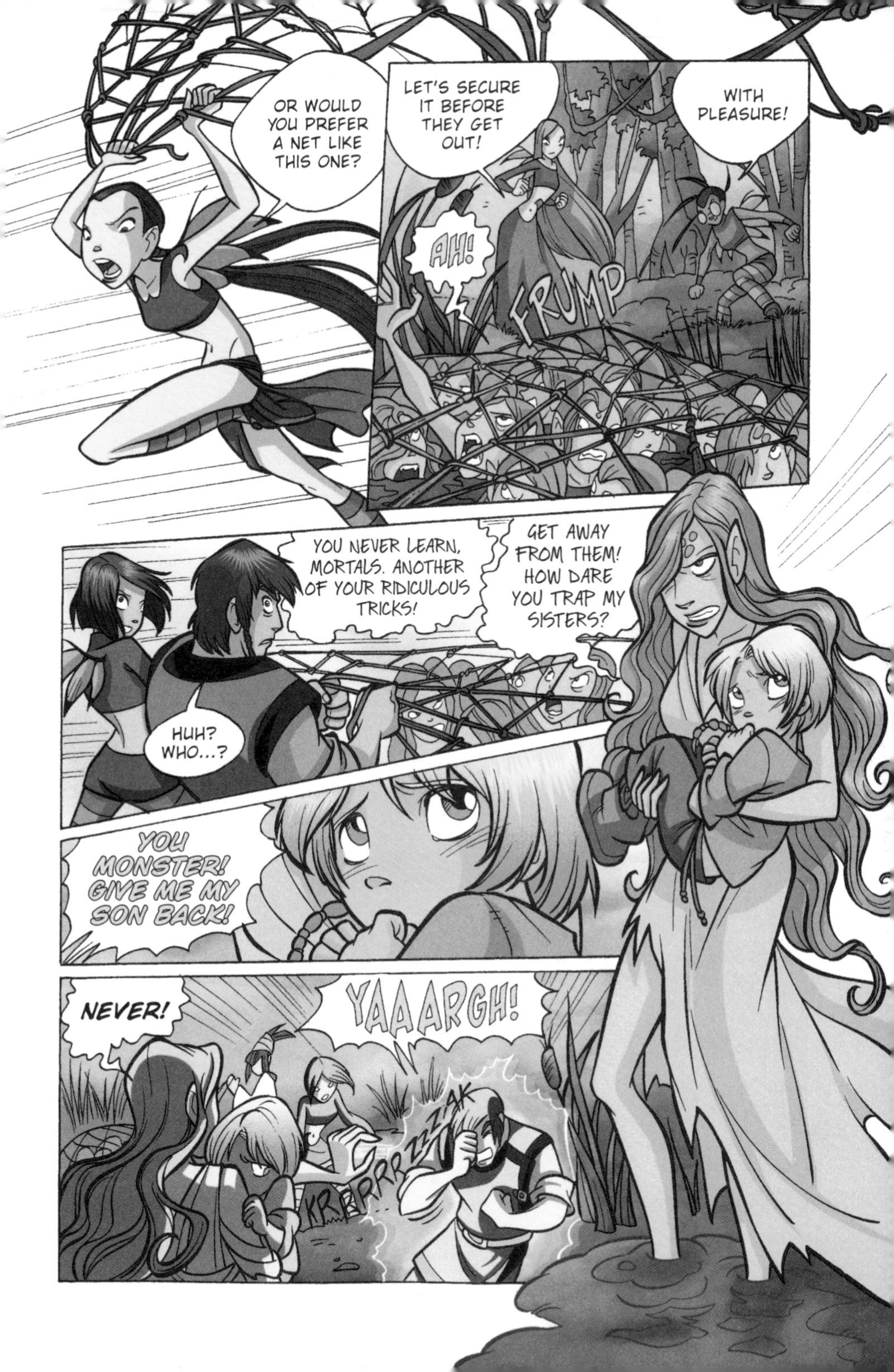
OR WOULD YOU PREFER A NET LIKE THIS ONE?
LET'S SECURE IT BEFORE THEY GET OUT!
WITH PLEASURE!
AH!
FRUMP
YOU NEVER LEARN, MORTALS. ANOTHER OF YOUR RIDICULOUS TRICKS!
GET AWAY FROM THEM! HOW DARE YOU TRAP MY SISTERS?
HUH? WHO...?
YOU MONSTER! GIVE ME MY SON BACK!
NEVER!
YAAARGH!
KRRRRRZZZZAK

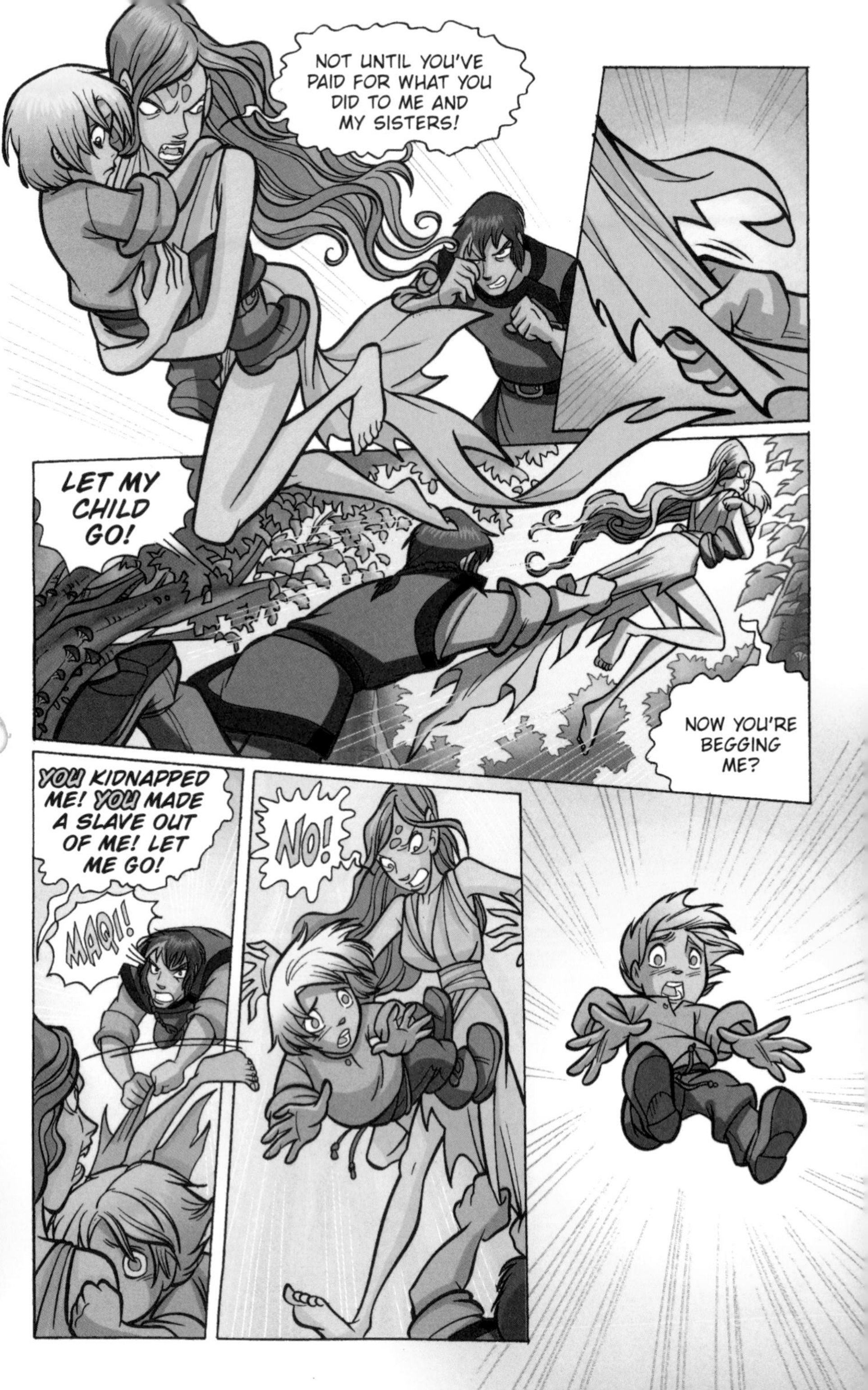
NOT UNTIL YOU'VE PAID FOR WHAT YOU DID TO ME AND MY SISTERS!
LET MY CHILD GO!
NOW YOU'RE BEGGING ME?
YOU KIDNAPPED ME! YOU MADE A SLAVE OUT OF ME! LET ME GO!
MAQI!
NO!

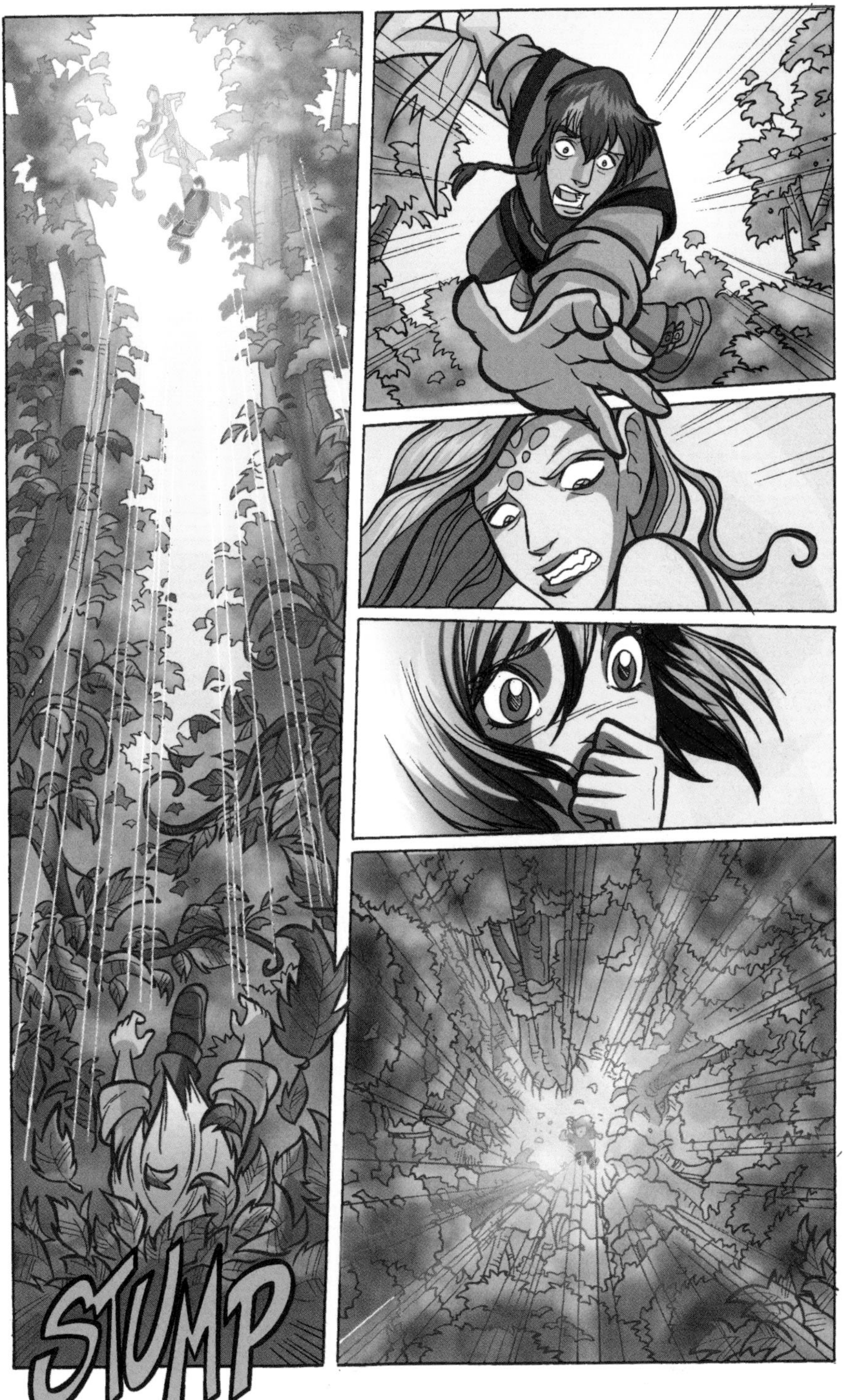
STUMP

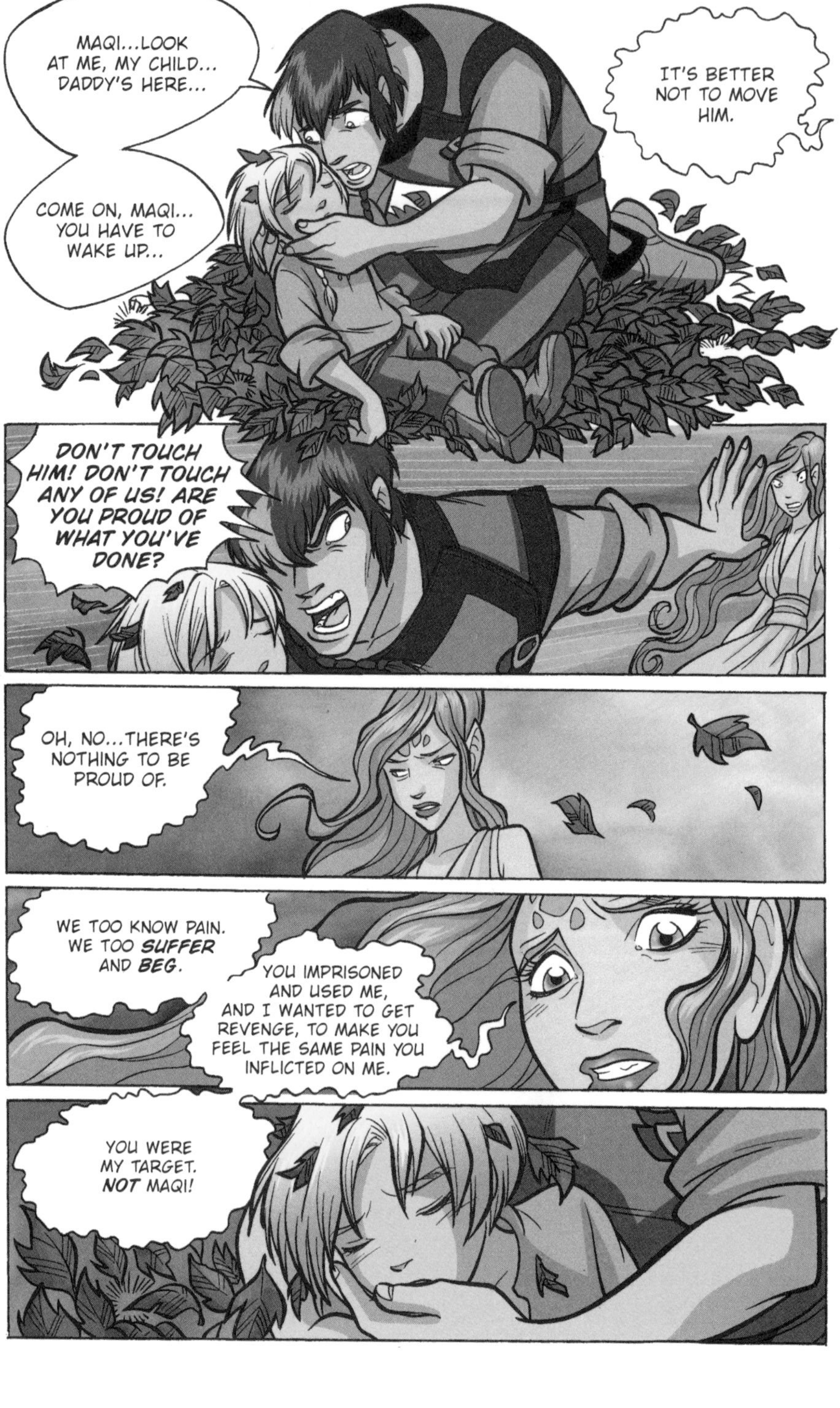
MAQI...LOOK AT ME, MY CHILD... DADDY'S HERE...
COME ON, MAQI... YOU HAVE TO WAKE UP...
IT'S BETTER NOT TO MOVE HIM.
DON'T TOUCH HIM! DON'T TOUCH ANY OF US! ARE YOU PROUD OF WHAT YOU'VE DONE?
OH, NO...THERE'S NOTHING TO BE PROUD OF.
WE TOO KNOW PAIN. WE TOO SUFFER AND BEG.
YOU IMPRISONED AND USED ME, AND I WANTED TO GET REVENGE, TO MAKE YOU FEEL THE SAME PAIN YOU INFLICTED ON ME.
YOU WERE MY TARGET. NOT MAQI!

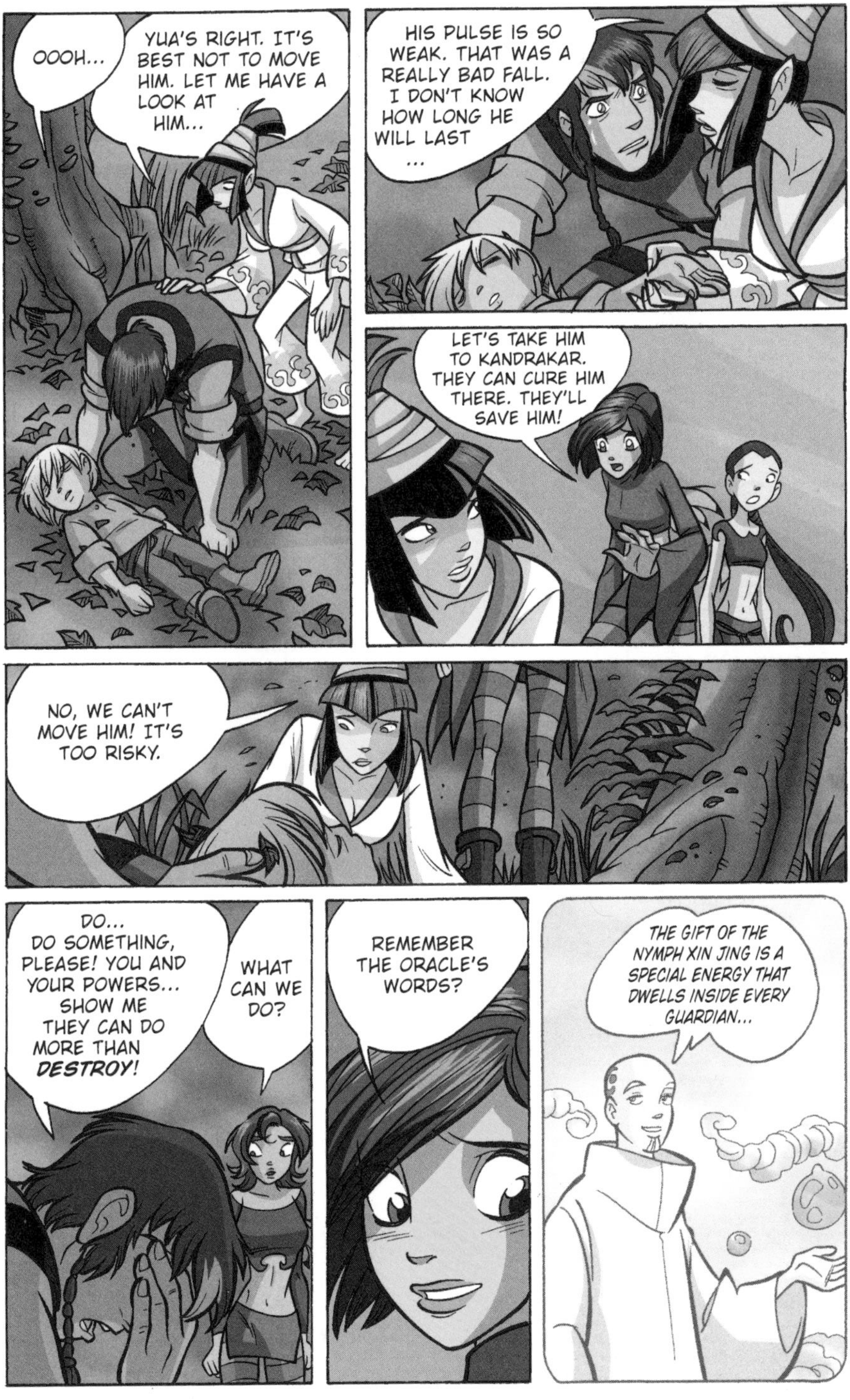
OOOH...
YUA'S RIGHT. IT'S BEST NOT TO MOVE HIM. LET ME HAVE A LOOK AT HIM...
HIS PULSE IS SO WEAK. THAT WAS A REALLY BAD FALL. I DON'T KNOW HOW LONG HE WILL LAST ...
LET'S TAKE HIM TO KANDRAKAR. THEY CAN CURE HIM THERE. THEY'LL SAVE HIM!
NO, WE CAN'T MOVE HIM! IT'S TOO RISKY.
DO... DO SOMETHING, PLEASE! YOU AND YOUR POWERS... SHOW ME THEY CAN DO MORE THAN DESTROY!
WHAT CAN WE DO?
REMEMBER THE ORACLE'S WORDS?
THE GIFT OF THE NYMPH XIN JING IS A SPECIAL ENERGY THAT DWELLS INSIDE EVERY GUARDIAN...

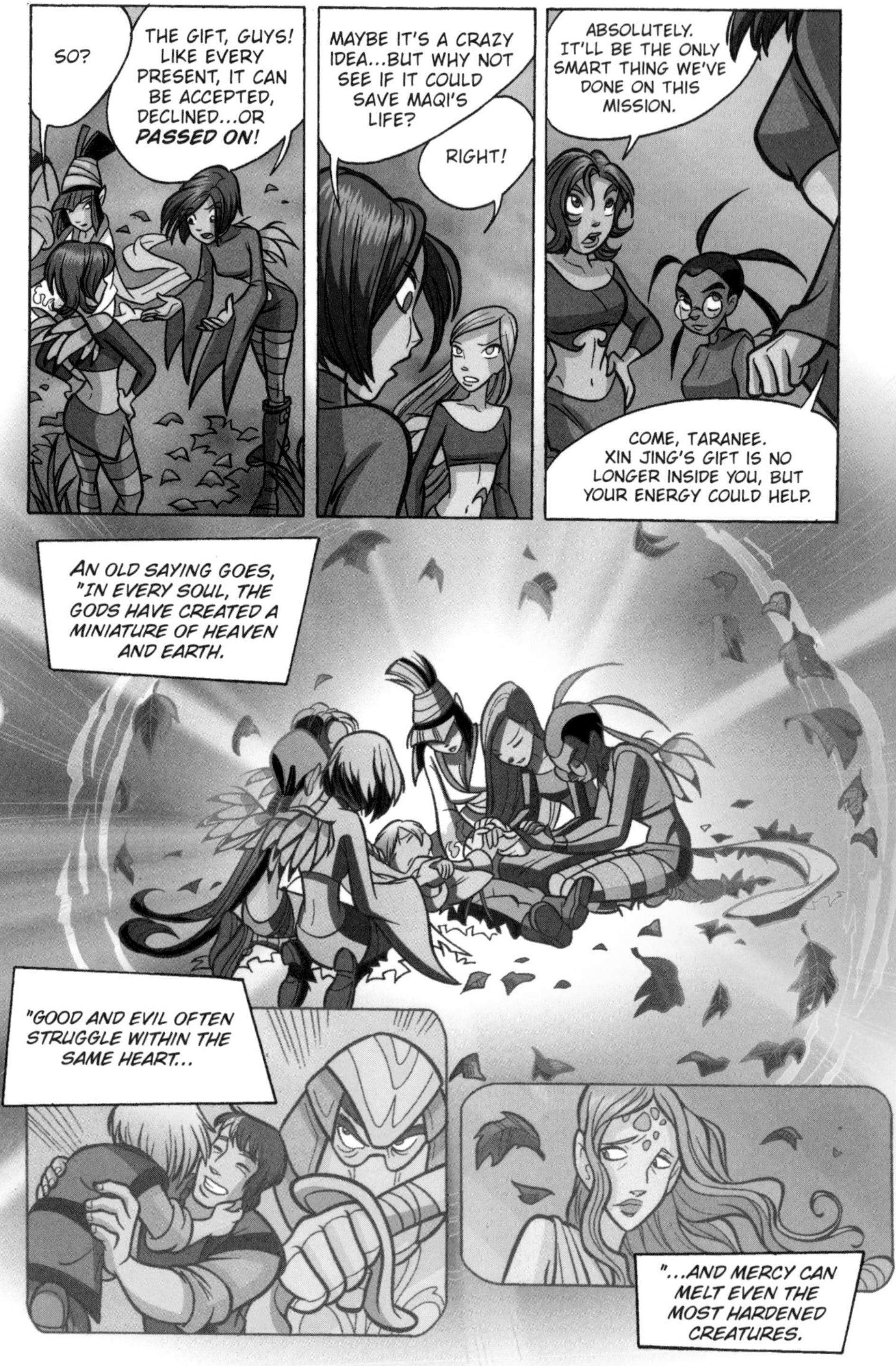

SO?
THE GIFT, GUYS! LIKE EVERY PRESENT, IT CAN BE ACCEPTED, DECLINED...OR **PASSED ON**!
MAYBE IT'S A CRAZY IDEA...BUT WHY NOT SEE IF IT COULD SAVE MAQI'S LIFE?
RIGHT!
ABSOLUTELY. IT'LL BE THE ONLY SMART THING WE'VE DONE ON THIS MISSION.
COME, TARANEE. XIN JING'S GIFT IS NO LONGER INSIDE YOU, BUT YOUR ENERGY COULD HELP.
AN OLD SAYING GOES, "IN EVERY SOUL, THE GODS HAVE CREATED A MINIATURE OF HEAVEN AND EARTH.
"GOOD AND EVIL OFTEN STRUGGLE WITHIN THE SAME HEART...
"...AND MERCY CAN MELT EVEN THE MOST HARDENED CREATURES.

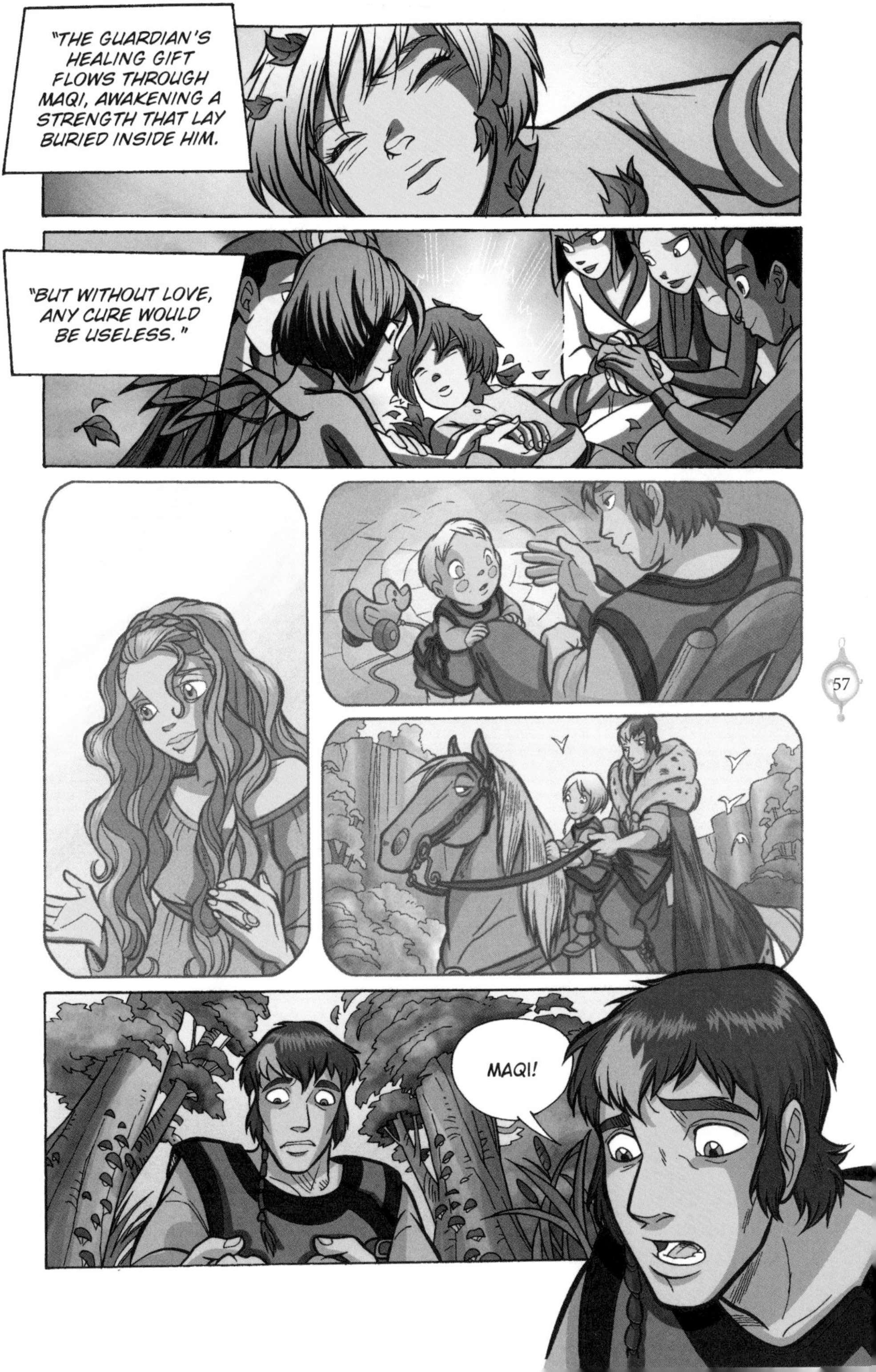
"THE GUARDIAN'S HEALING GIFT FLOWS THROUGH MAQI, AWAKENING A STRENGTH THAT LAY BURIED INSIDE HIM.
"BUT WITHOUT LOVE, ANY CURE WOULD BE USELESS."
MAQI!

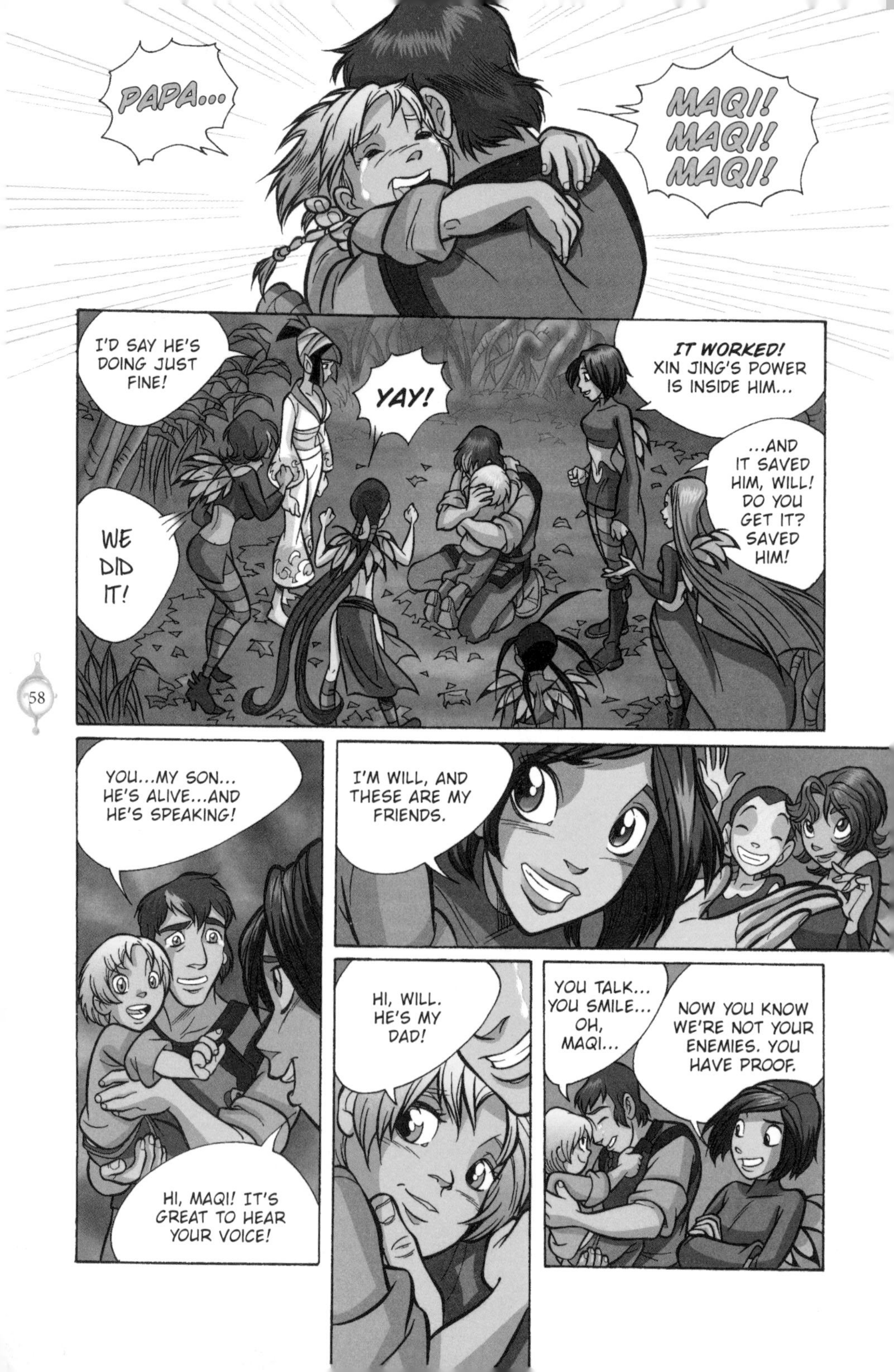
PAPA...
MAQI! MAQI! MAQI!
I'D SAY HE'S DOING JUST FINE!
YAY!
WE DID IT!
IT WORKED! XIN JING'S POWER IS INSIDE HIM...
...AND IT SAVED HIM, WILL! DO YOU GET IT? SAVED HIM!
YOU...MY SON... HE'S ALIVE...AND HE'S SPEAKING!
HI, MAQI! IT'S GREAT TO HEAR YOUR VOICE!
I'M WILL, AND THESE ARE MY FRIENDS.
HI, WILL. HE'S MY DAD!
YOU TALK... YOU SMILE... OH, MAQI...
NOW YOU KNOW WE'RE NOT YOUR ENEMIES. YOU HAVE PROOF.

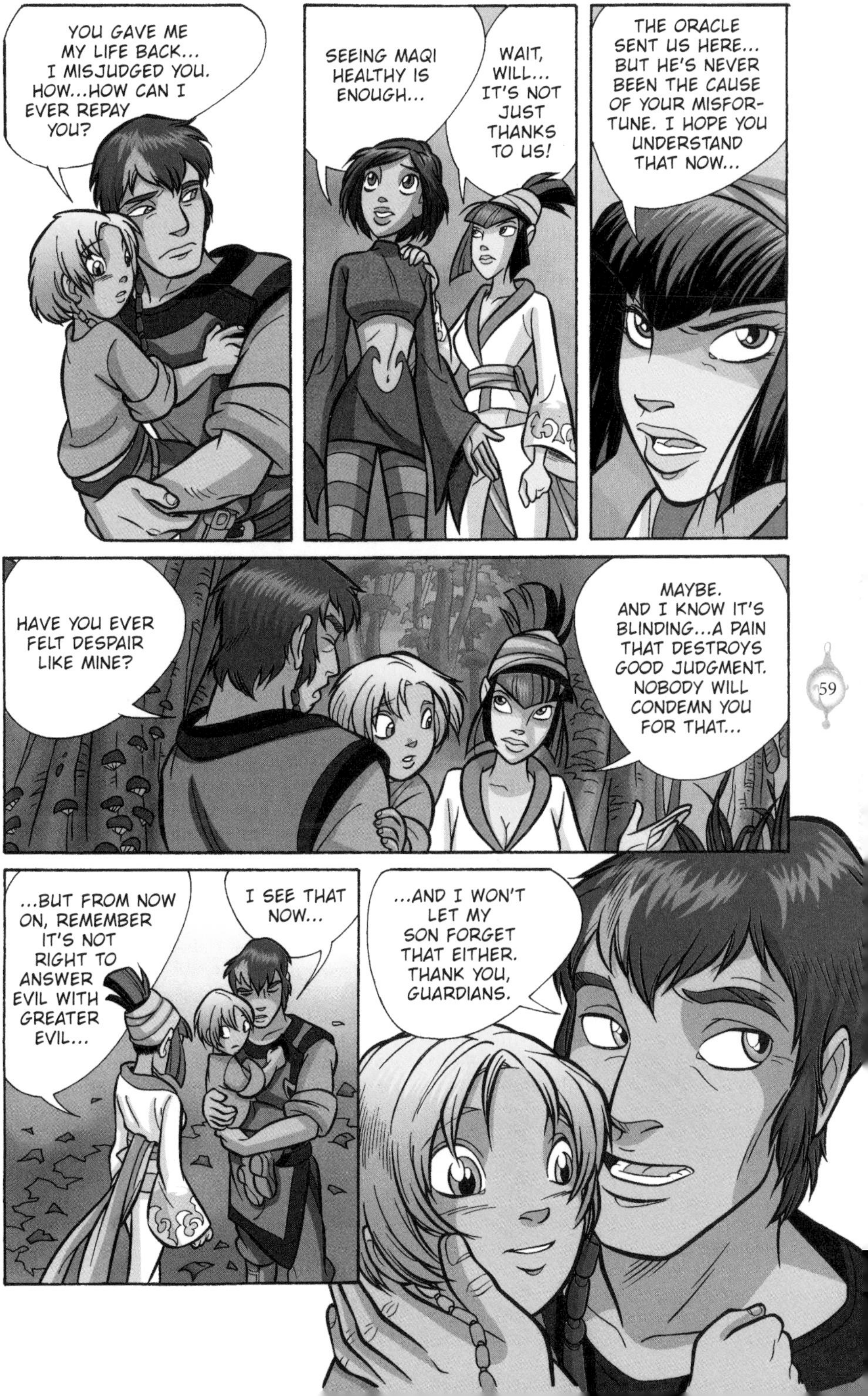
YOU GAVE ME MY LIFE BACK... I MISJUDGED YOU. HOW...HOW CAN I EVER REPAY YOU?
SEEING MAQI HEALTHY IS ENOUGH...
WAIT, WILL... IT'S NOT JUST THANKS TO US!
THE ORACLE SENT US HERE... BUT HE'S NEVER BEEN THE CAUSE OF YOUR MISFOR-TUNE. I HOPE YOU UNDERSTAND THAT NOW...
HAVE YOU EVER FELT DESPAIR LIKE MINE?
MAYBE. AND I KNOW IT'S BLINDING...A PAIN THAT DESTROYS GOOD JUDGMENT. NOBODY WILL CONDEMN YOU FOR THAT...
...BUT FROM NOW ON, REMEMBER IT'S NOT RIGHT TO ANSWER EVIL WITH GREATER EVIL...
I SEE THAT NOW...
...AND I WON'T LET MY SON FORGET THAT EITHER. THANK YOU, GUARDIANS.

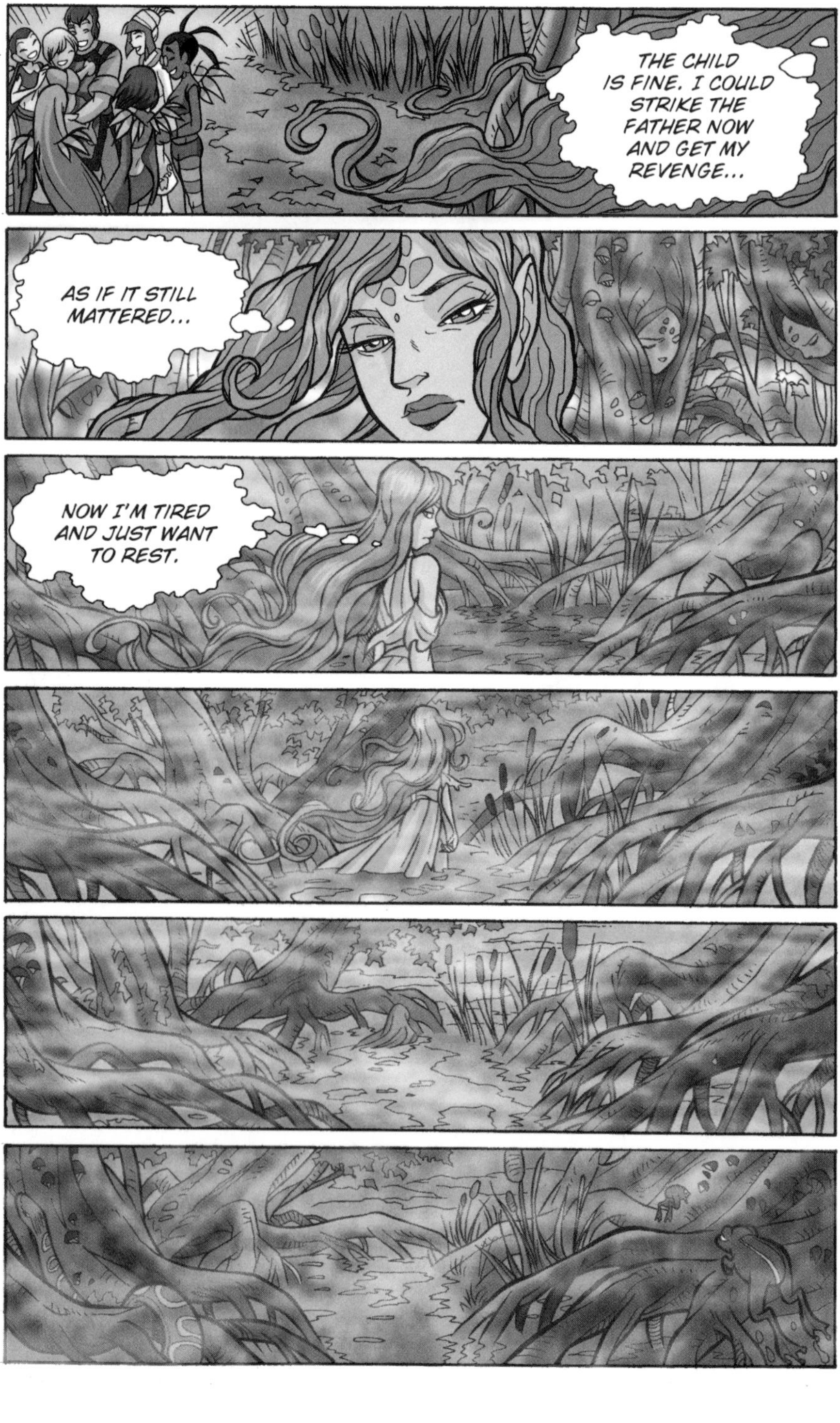
THE CHILD IS FINE. I COULD STRIKE THE FATHER NOW AND GET MY REVENGE...
AS IF IT STILL MATTERED...
NOW I'M TIRED AND JUST WANT TO REST.

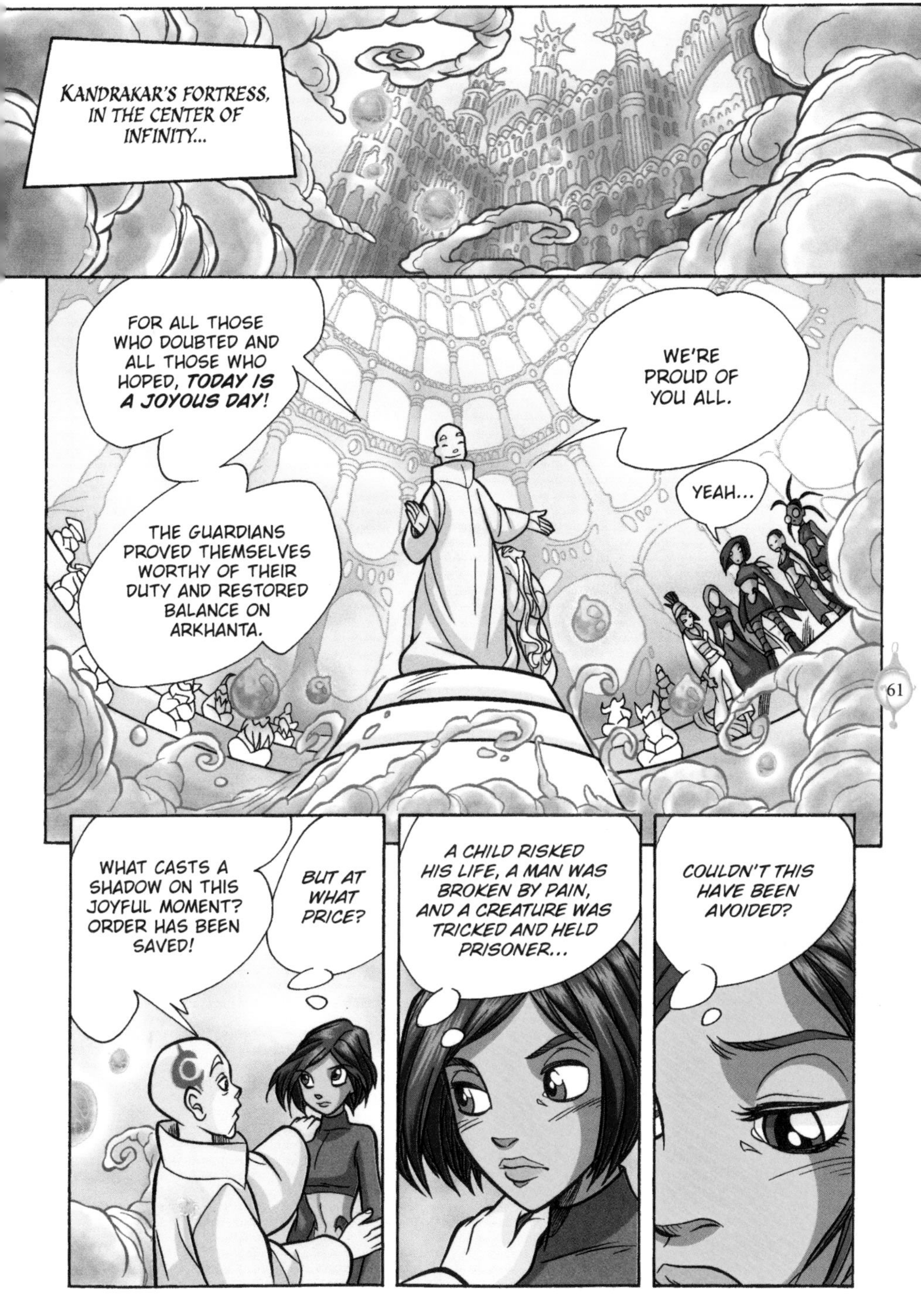
KANDRAKAR'S FORTRESS, IN THE CENTER OF INFINITY...
FOR ALL THOSE WHO DOUBTED AND ALL THOSE WHO HOPED, TODAY IS A JOYOUS DAY!
THE GUARDIANS PROVED THEMSELVES WORTHY OF THEIR DUTY AND RESTORED BALANCE ON ARKHANTA.
WE'RE PROUD OF YOU ALL.
YEAH...
WHAT CASTS A SHADOW ON THIS JOYFUL MOMENT? ORDER HAS BEEN SAVED!
BUT AT WHAT PRICE?
A CHILD RISKED HIS LIFE, A MAN WAS BROKEN BY PAIN, AND A CREATURE WAS TRICKED AND HELD PRISONER...
COULDN'T THIS HAVE BEEN AVOIDED?

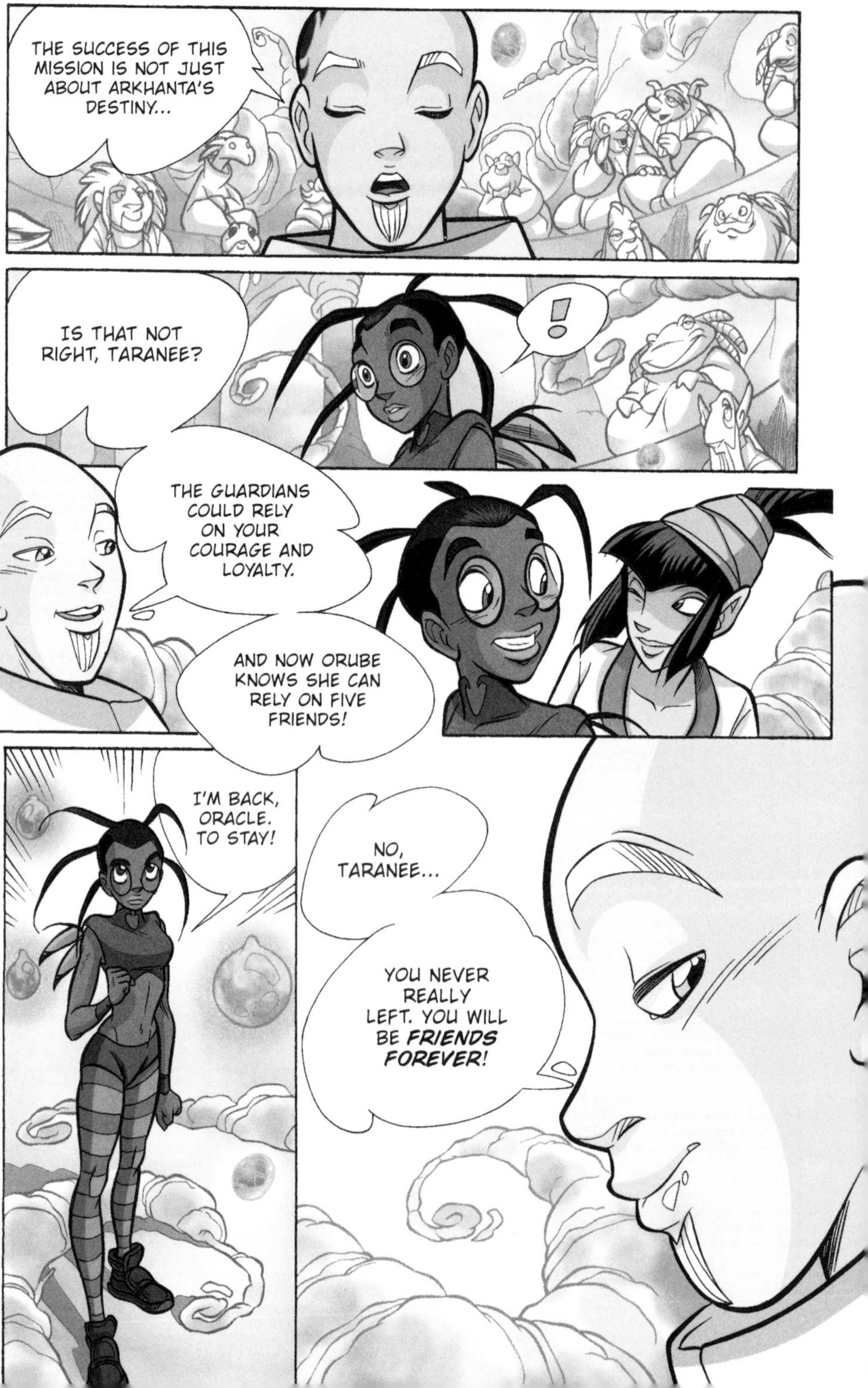
THE SUCCESS OF THIS MISSION IS NOT JUST ABOUT ARKHANTA'S DESTINY...
IS THAT NOT RIGHT, TARANEE?
!
THE GUARDIANS COULD RELY ON YOUR COURAGE AND LOYALTY.
AND NOW ORUBE KNOWS SHE CAN RELY ON FIVE FRIENDS!
I'M BACK, ORACLE. TO STAY!
NO, TARANEE...
YOU NEVER REALLY LEFT. YOU WILL BE ***FRIENDS FOREVER***!

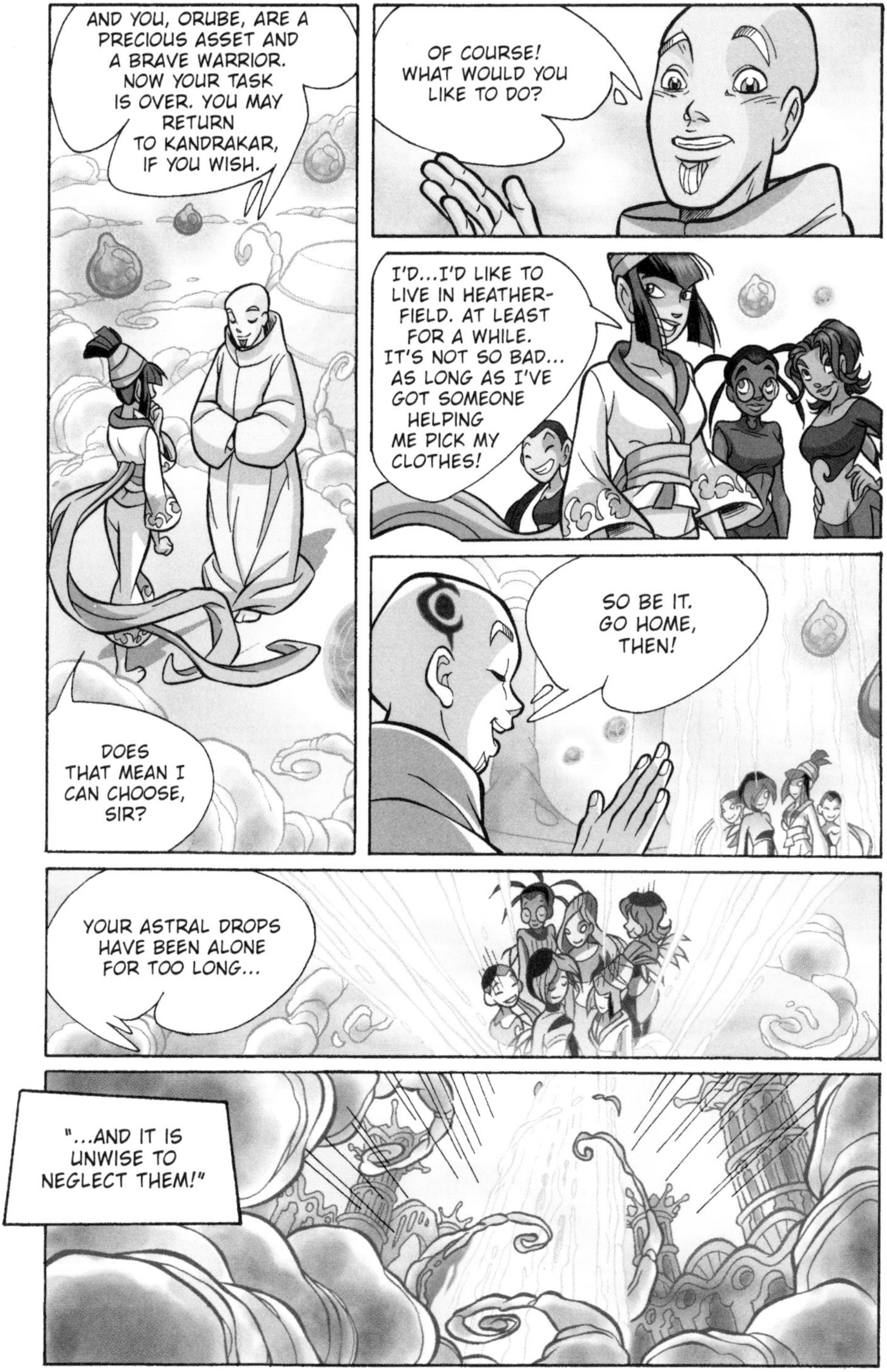
AND YOU, ORUBE, ARE A PRECIOUS ASSET AND A BRAVE WARRIOR. NOW YOUR TASK IS OVER. YOU MAY RETURN TO KANDRAKAR, IF YOU WISH.
DOES THAT MEAN I CAN CHOOSE, SIR?
OF COURSE! WHAT WOULD YOU LIKE TO DO?
I'D...I'D LIKE TO LIVE IN HEATHER-FIELD. AT LEAST FOR A WHILE. IT'S NOT SO BAD... AS LONG AS I'VE GOT SOMEONE HELPING ME PICK MY CLOTHES!
SO BE IT. GO HOME, THEN!
YOUR ASTRAL DROPS HAVE BEEN ALONE FOR TOO LONG...
"...AND IT IS UNWISE TO NEGLECT THEM!"

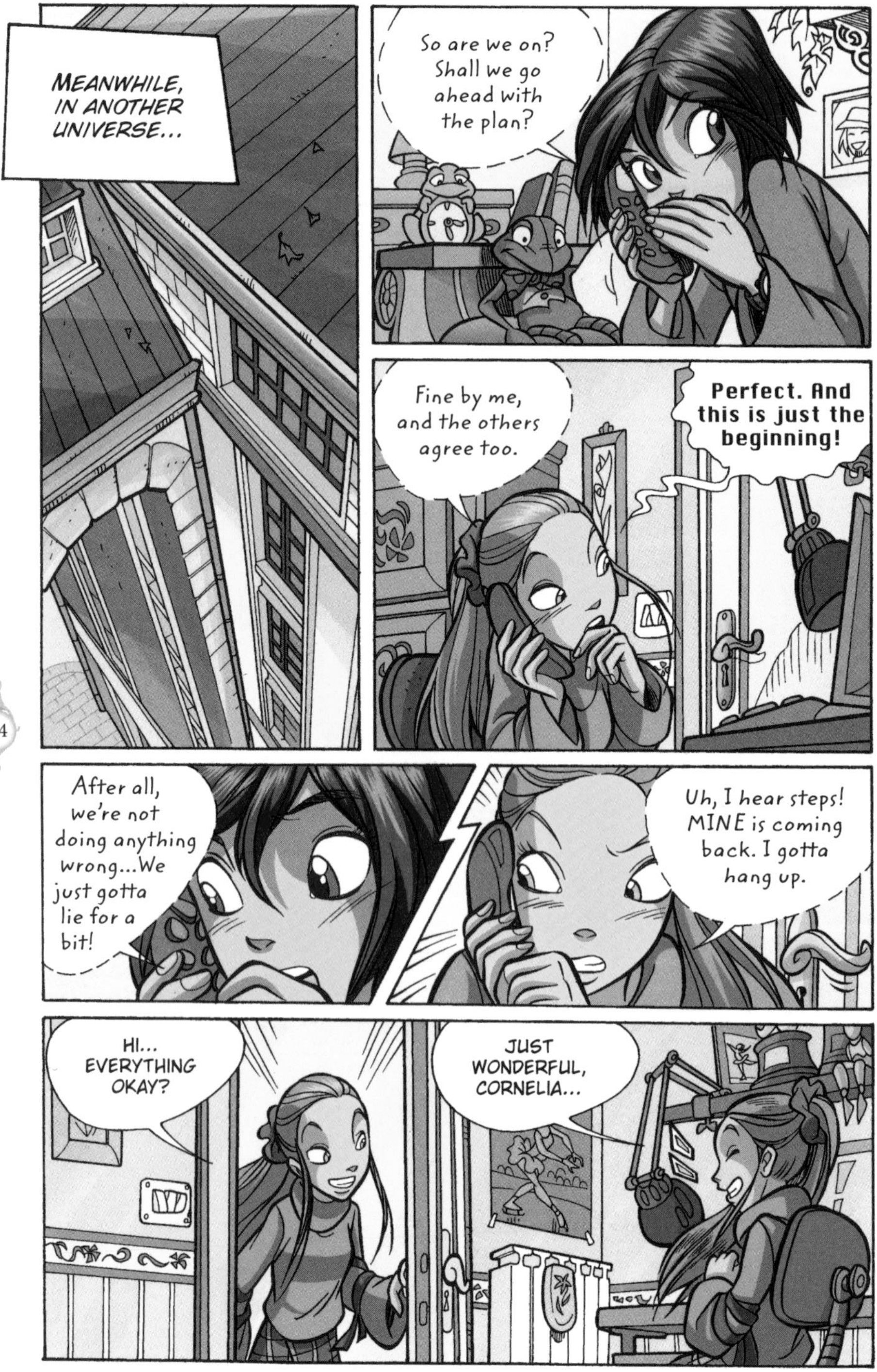
MEANWHILE, IN ANOTHER UNIVERSE...
So are we on? Shall we go ahead with the plan?
Fine by me, and the others agree too.
Perfect. And this is just the beginning!
After all, we're not doing anything wrong...We just gotta lie for a bit!
Uh, I hear steps! MINE is coming back. I gotta hang up.
HI... EVERYTHING OKAY?
JUST WONDERFUL, CORNELIA...

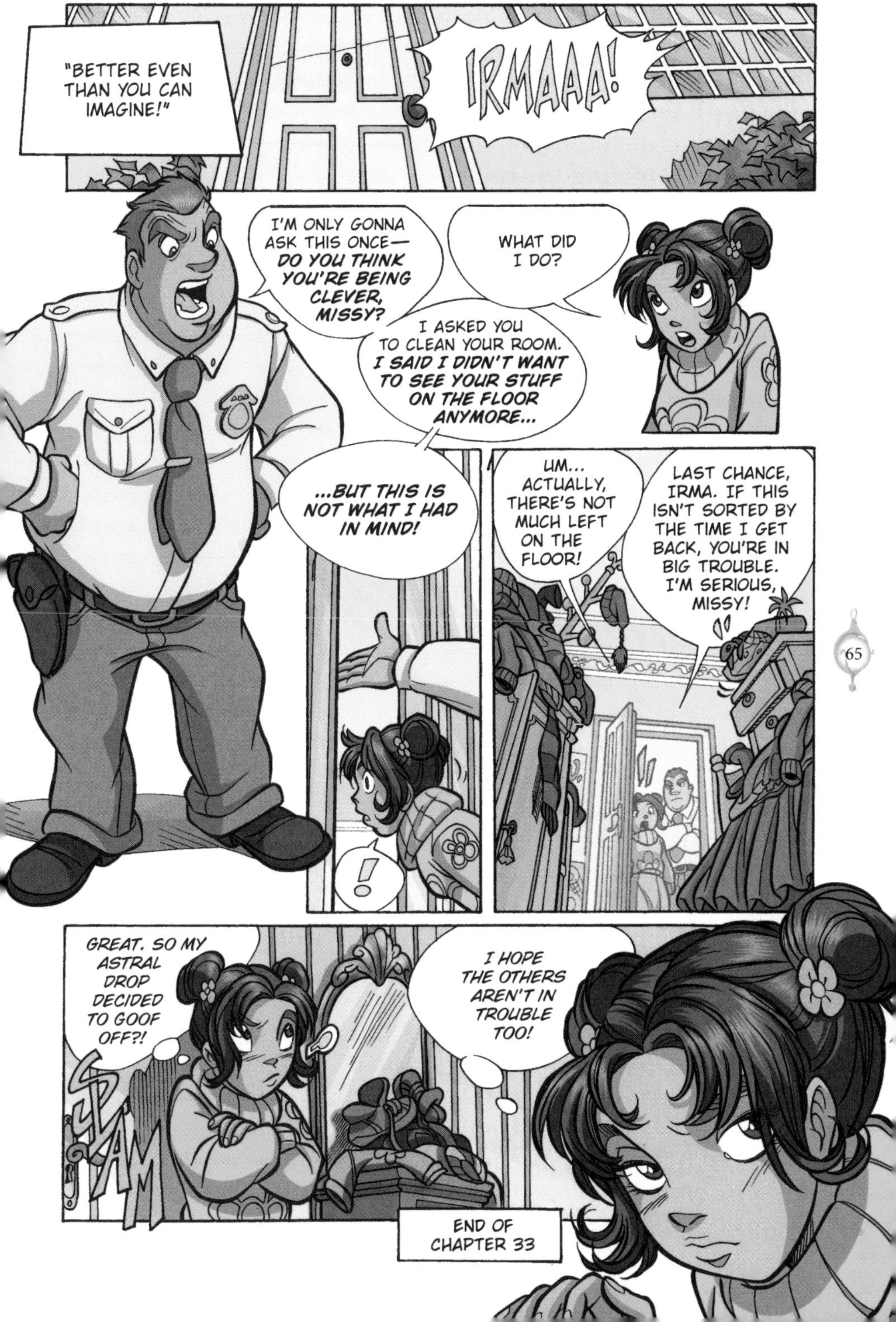

"BETTER EVEN THAN YOU CAN IMAGINE!"
IRMAAA!
I'M ONLY GONNA ASK THIS ONCE— DO YOU THINK YOU'RE BEING CLEVER, MISSY?
WHAT DID I DO?
I ASKED YOU TO CLEAN YOUR ROOM. I SAID I DIDN'T WANT TO SEE YOUR STUFF ON THE FLOOR ANYMORE...
...BUT THIS IS NOT WHAT I HAD IN MIND!
!
UM... ACTUALLY, THERE'S NOT MUCH LEFT ON THE FLOOR!
LAST CHANCE, IRMA. IF THIS ISN'T SORTED BY THE TIME I GET BACK, YOU'RE IN BIG TROUBLE. I'M SERIOUS, MISSY!
GREAT. SO MY ASTRAL DROP DECIDED TO GOOF OFF?!
SLAM
I HOPE THE OTHERS AREN'T IN TROUBLE TOO!
END OF CHAPTER 33

W.i.t.c.h.

Will Irma Taranee Cornelia Hay Lin

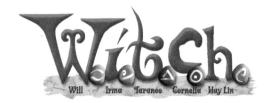

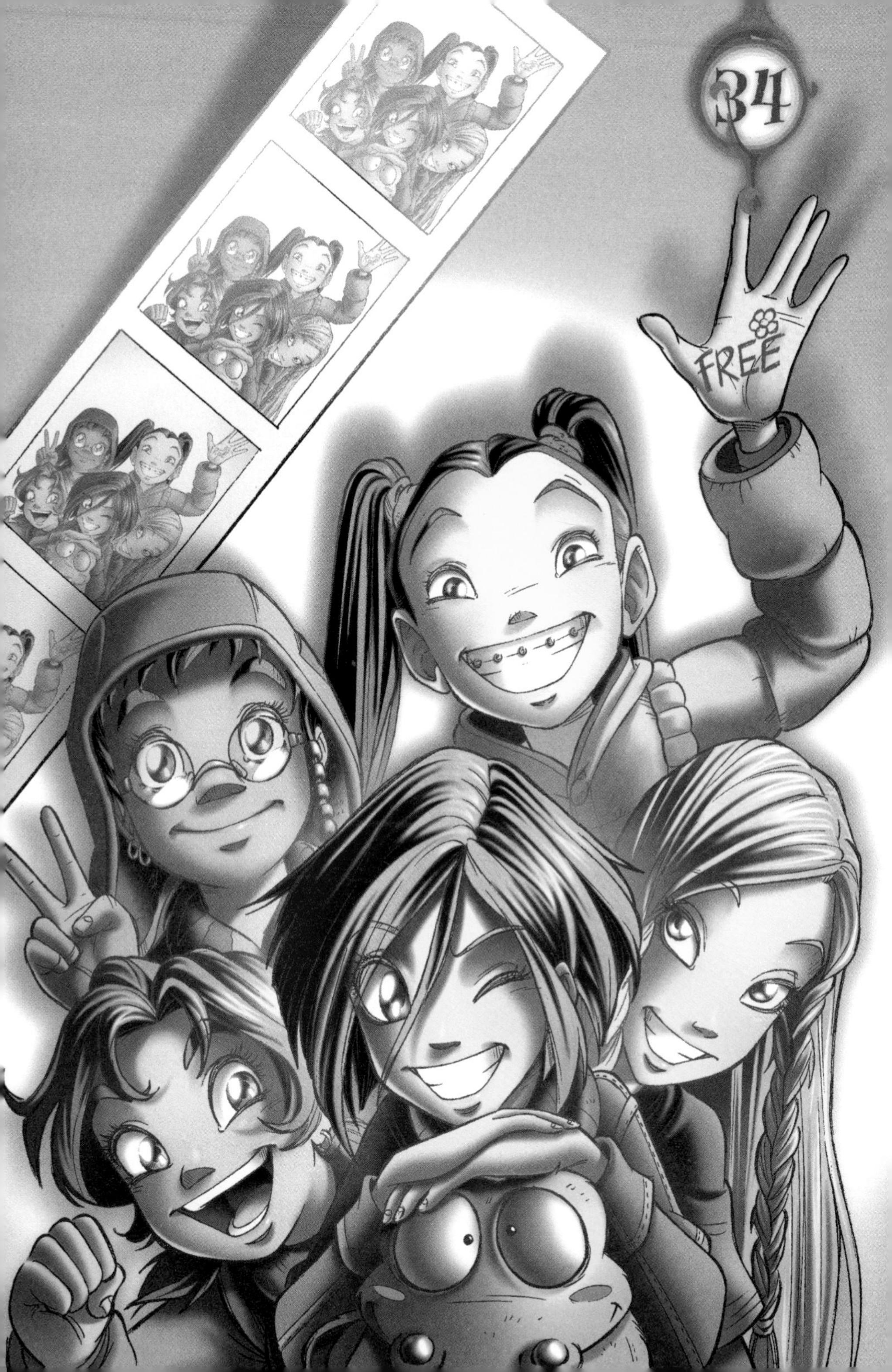
34
FREE

Drops of Freedom

"It takes a lot of courage to make a decision."

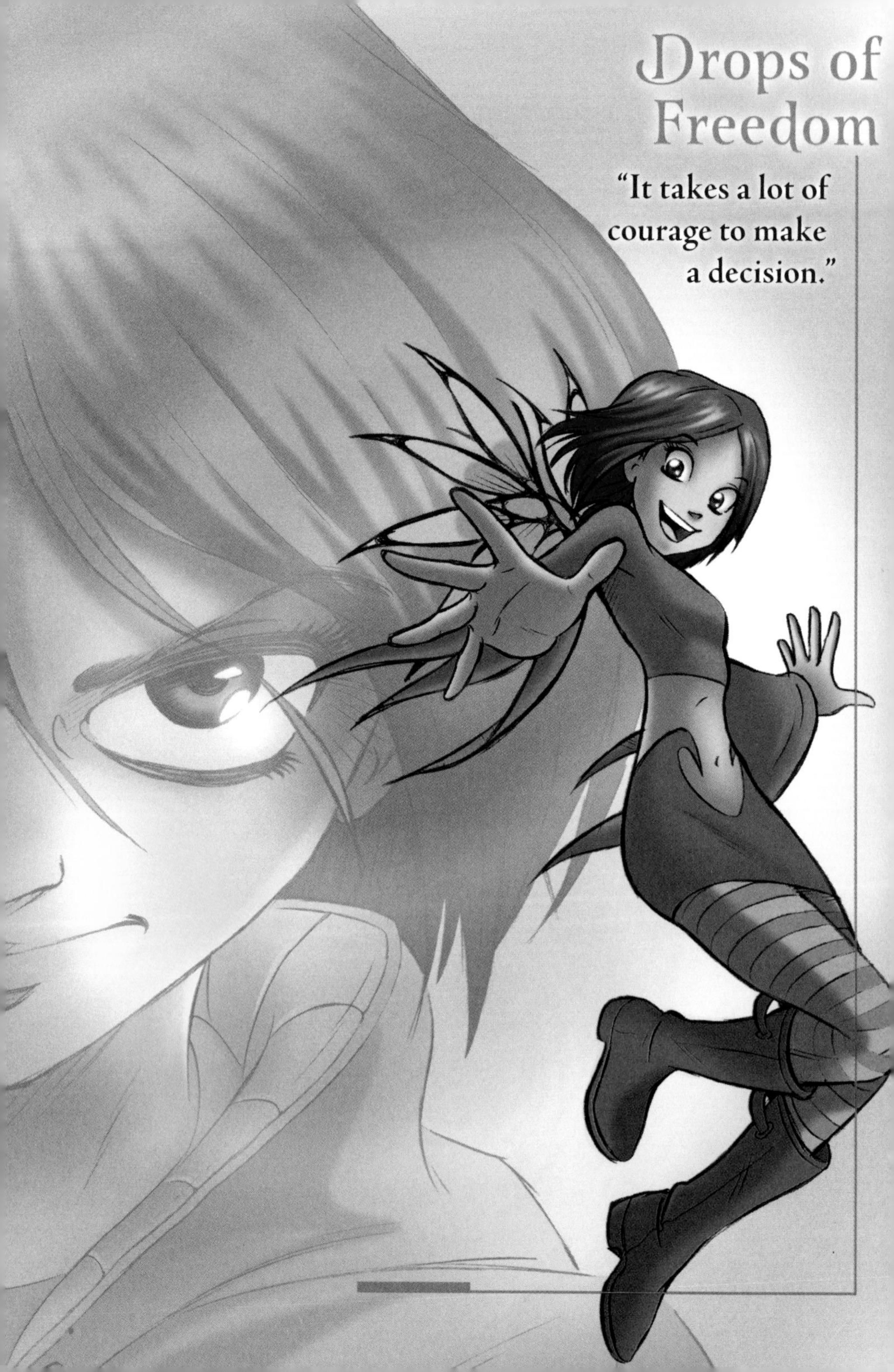

W.i.t.c.h.

Will Irma Taranee Cornelia Hay Lin

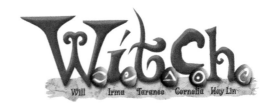

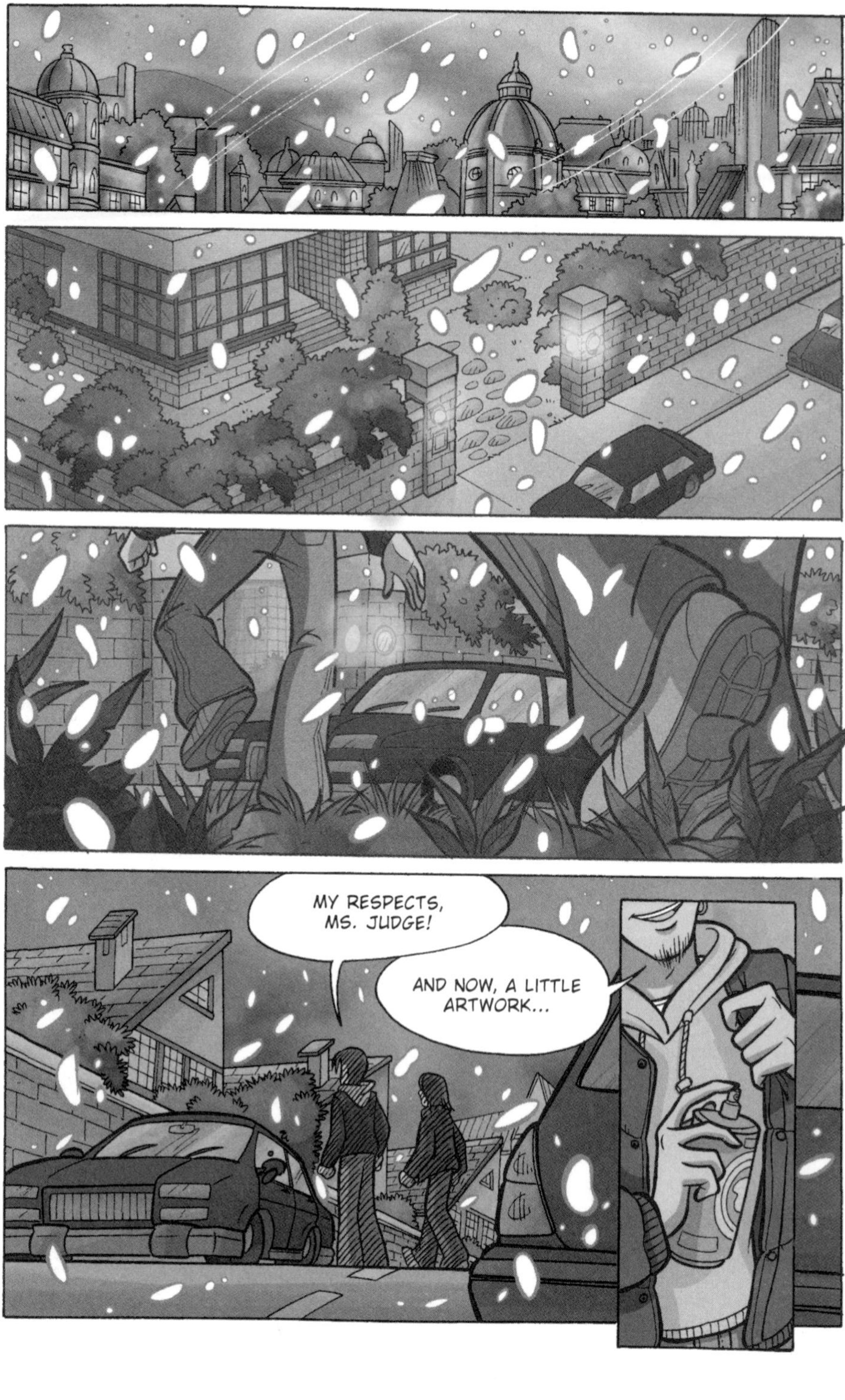
MY RESPECTS, MS. JUDGE!
AND NOW, A LITTLE ARTWORK...

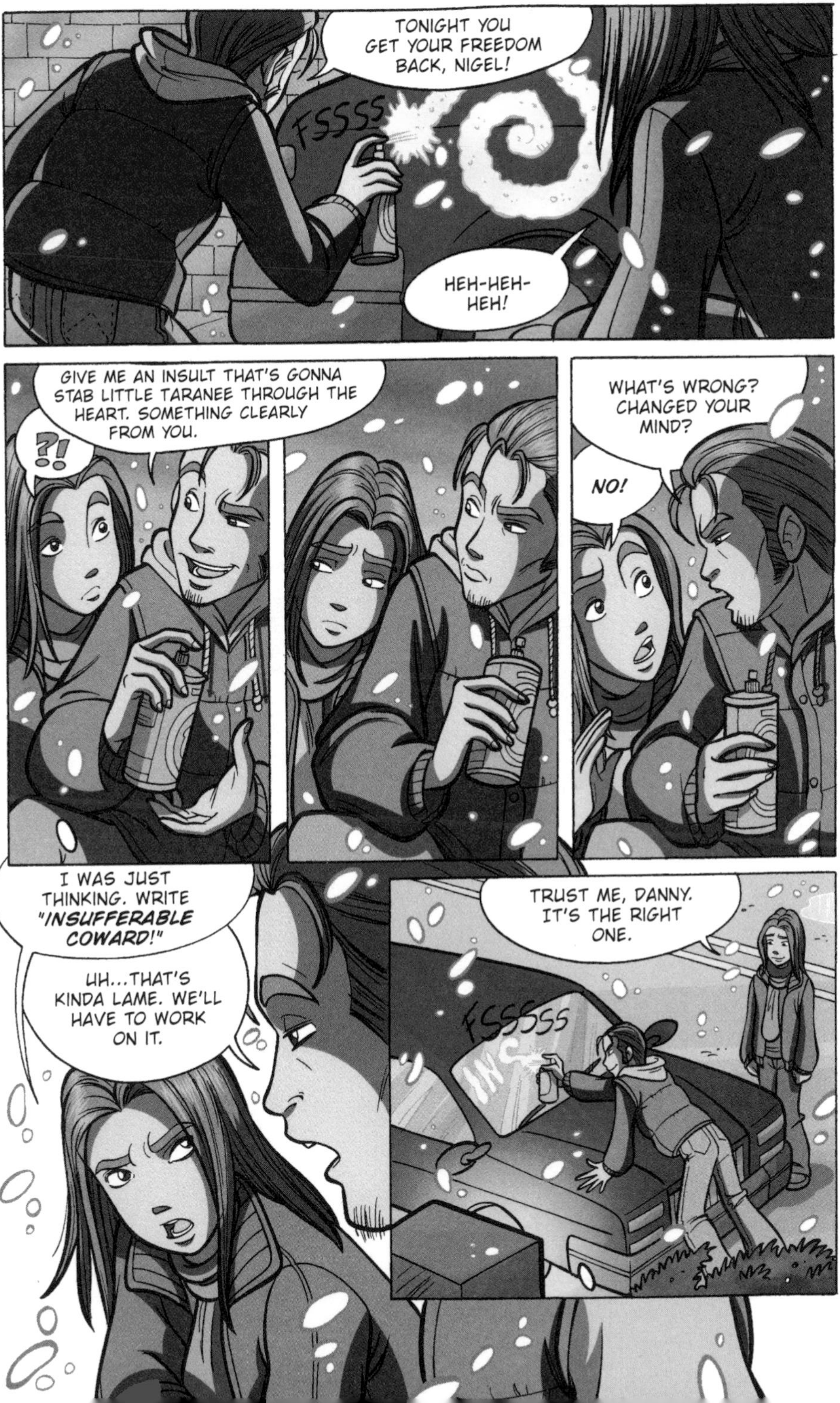
TONIGHT YOU GET YOUR FREEDOM BACK, NIGEL!
FSSSS
HEH-HEH-HEH!
GIVE ME AN INSULT THAT'S GONNA STAB LITTLE TARANEE THROUGH THE HEART. SOMETHING CLEARLY FROM YOU.
?!
WHAT'S WRONG? CHANGED YOUR MIND?
NO!
I WAS JUST THINKING. WRITE "INSUFFERABLE COWARD!"
UH...THAT'S KINDA LAME. WE'LL HAVE TO WORK ON IT.
TRUST ME, DANNY. IT'S THE RIGHT ONE.
FSSSSS

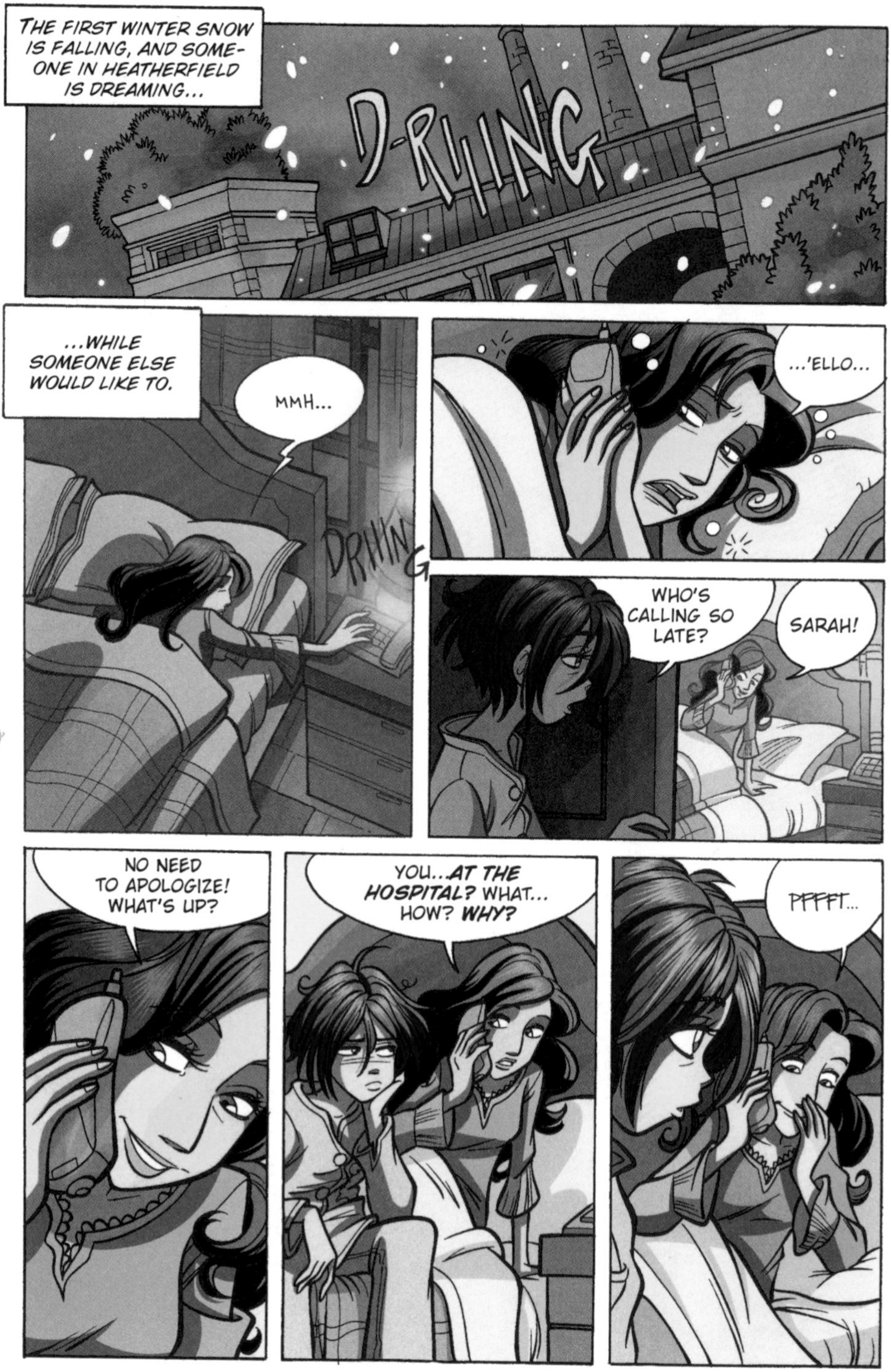
THE FIRST WINTER SNOW IS FALLING, AND SOMEONE IN HEATHERFIELD IS DREAMING...
D-RIING
...WHILE SOMEONE ELSE WOULD LIKE TO.
MMH...
DRIIING
...'ELLO...
WHO'S CALLING SO LATE?
SARAH!
NO NEED TO APOLOGIZE! WHAT'S UP?
YOU...AT THE HOSPITAL? WHAT... HOW? WHY?
PFFFT...

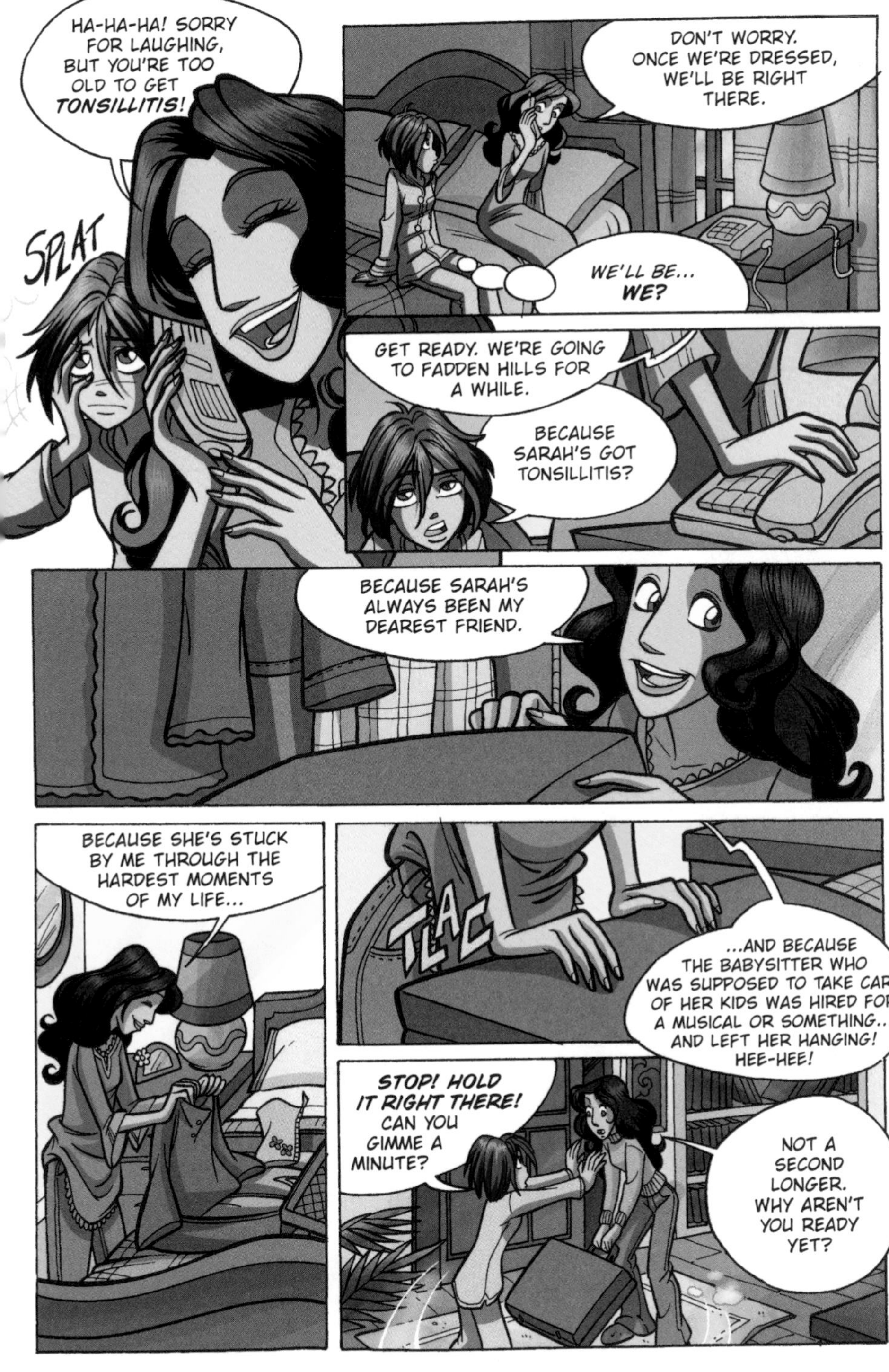

HA-HA-HA! SORRY FOR LAUGHING, BUT YOU'RE TOO OLD TO GET TONSILLITIS!
SPLAT
DON'T WORRY. ONCE WE'RE DRESSED, WE'LL BE RIGHT THERE.
WE'LL BE... WE?
GET READY. WE'RE GOING TO FADDEN HILLS FOR A WHILE.
BECAUSE SARAH'S GOT TONSILLITIS?
BECAUSE SARAH'S ALWAYS BEEN MY DEAREST FRIEND.
BECAUSE SHE'S STUCK BY ME THROUGH THE HARDEST MOMENTS OF MY LIFE...
TLAC
...AND BECAUSE THE BABYSITTER WHO WAS SUPPOSED TO TAKE CARE OF HER KIDS WAS HIRED FOR A MUSICAL OR SOMETHING... AND LEFT HER HANGING! HEE-HEE!
STOP! HOLD IT RIGHT THERE! CAN YOU GIMME A MINUTE?
NOT A SECOND LONGER. WHY AREN'T YOU READY YET?

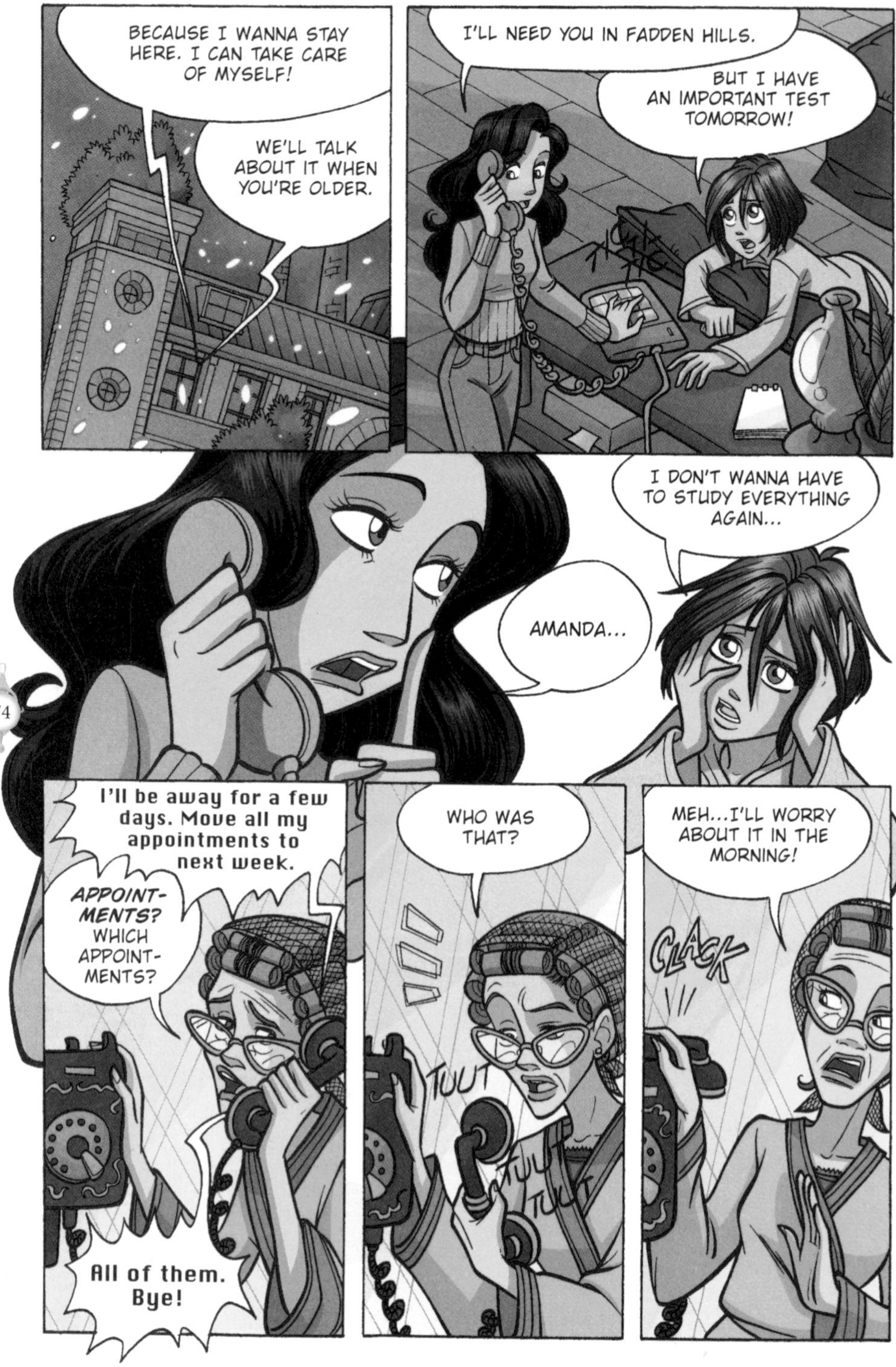
BECAUSE I WANNA STAY HERE. I CAN TAKE CARE OF MYSELF!
WE'LL TALK ABOUT IT WHEN YOU'RE OLDER.
I'LL NEED YOU IN FADDEN HILLS.
BUT I HAVE AN IMPORTANT TEST TOMORROW!
I DON'T WANNA HAVE TO STUDY EVERYTHING AGAIN...
AMANDA...
I'll be away for a few days. Move all my appointments to next week.
APPOINTMENTS? WHICH APPOINTMENTS?
All of them. Bye!
WHO WAS THAT?
TUUT
TUUT
TUUT
CLACK
MEH...I'LL WORRY ABOUT IT IN THE MORNING!

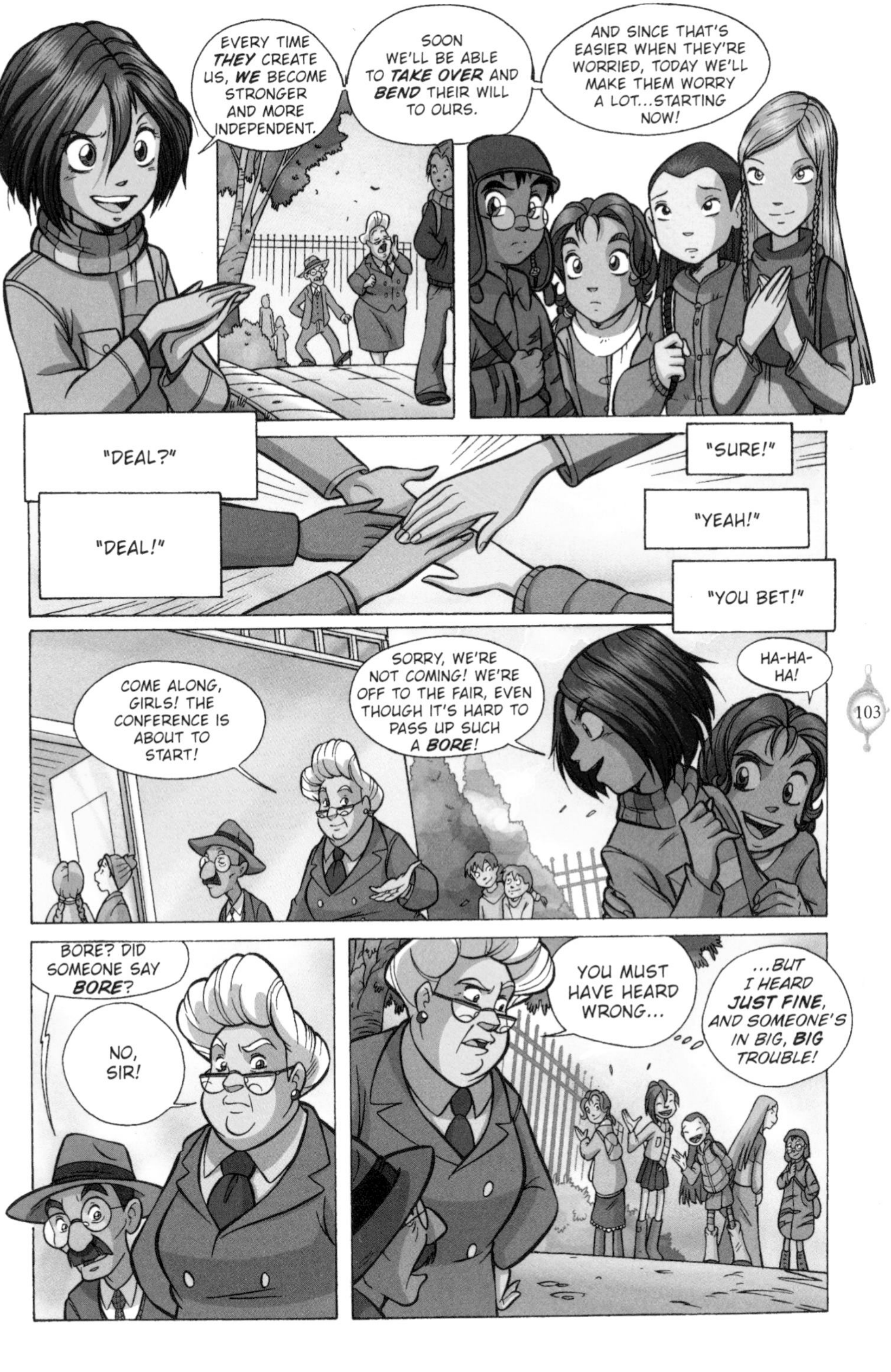
EVERY TIME THEY CREATE US, WE BECOME STRONGER AND MORE INDEPENDENT.
SOON WE'LL BE ABLE TO TAKE OVER AND BEND THEIR WILL TO OURS.
AND SINCE THAT'S EASIER WHEN THEY'RE WORRIED, TODAY WE'LL MAKE THEM WORRY A LOT...STARTING NOW!
"DEAL?"
"DEAL!"
"SURE!"
"YEAH!"
"YOU BET!"
COME ALONG, GIRLS! THE CONFERENCE IS ABOUT TO START!
SORRY, WE'RE NOT COMING! WE'RE OFF TO THE FAIR, EVEN THOUGH IT'S HARD TO PASS UP SUCH A BORE!
HA-HA-HA!
BORE? DID SOMEONE SAY BORE?
NO, SIR!
YOU MUST HAVE HEARD WRONG...
...BUT I HEARD JUST FINE, AND SOMEONE'S IN BIG, BIG TROUBLE!

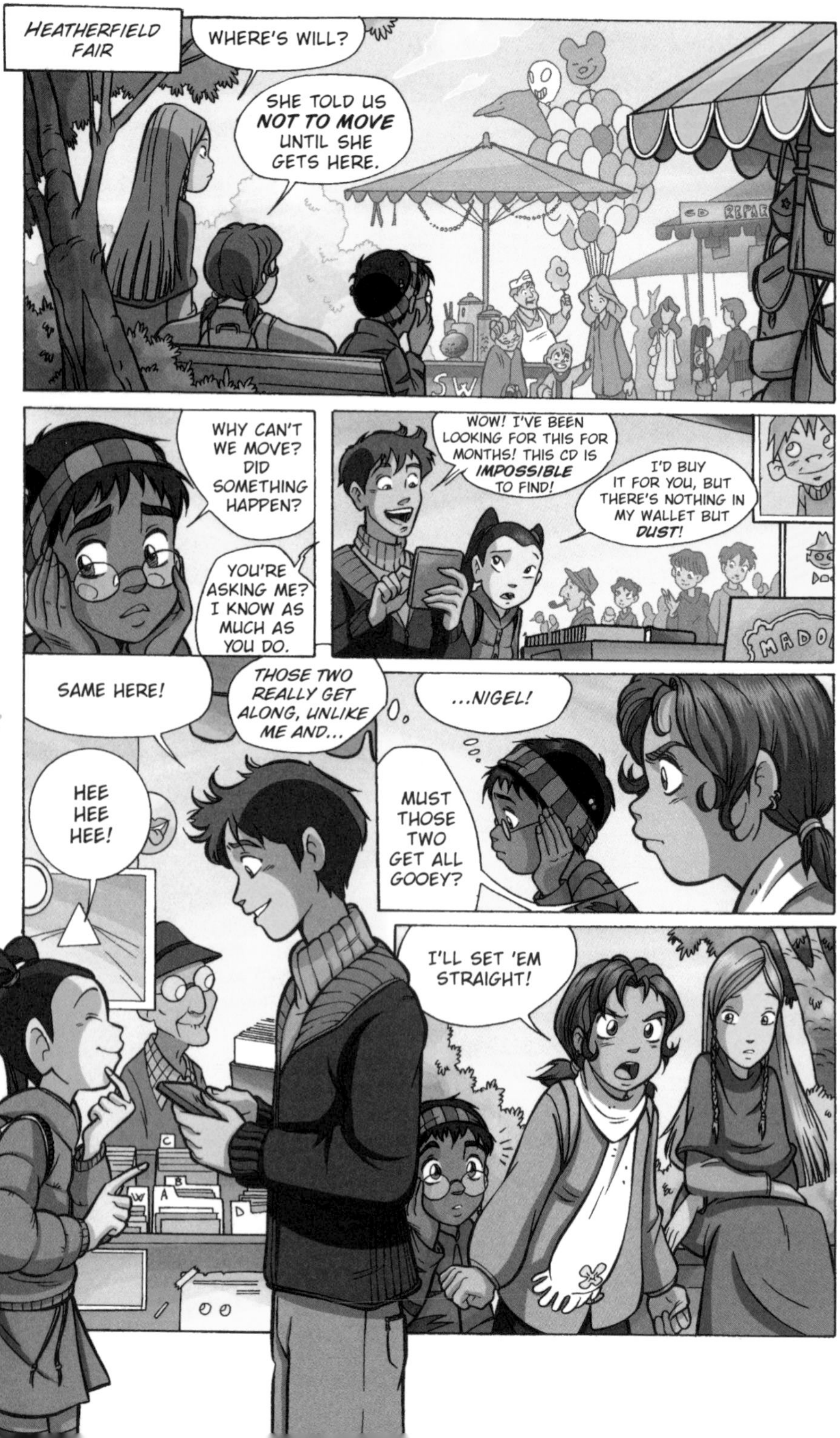
HEATHERFIELD FAIR
WHERE'S WILL?
SHE TOLD US **NOT TO MOVE** UNTIL SHE GETS HERE.
WHY CAN'T WE MOVE? DID SOMETHING HAPPEN?
YOU'RE ASKING ME? I KNOW AS MUCH AS YOU DO.
WOW! I'VE BEEN LOOKING FOR THIS FOR MONTHS! THIS CD IS **IMPOSSIBLE** TO FIND!
I'D BUY IT FOR YOU, BUT THERE'S NOTHING IN MY WALLET BUT **DUST**!
SAME HERE!
HEE HEE HEE!
THOSE TWO REALLY GET ALONG, UNLIKE ME AND...
...NIGEL!
MUST THOSE TWO GET ALL GOOEY?
I'LL SET 'EM STRAIGHT!

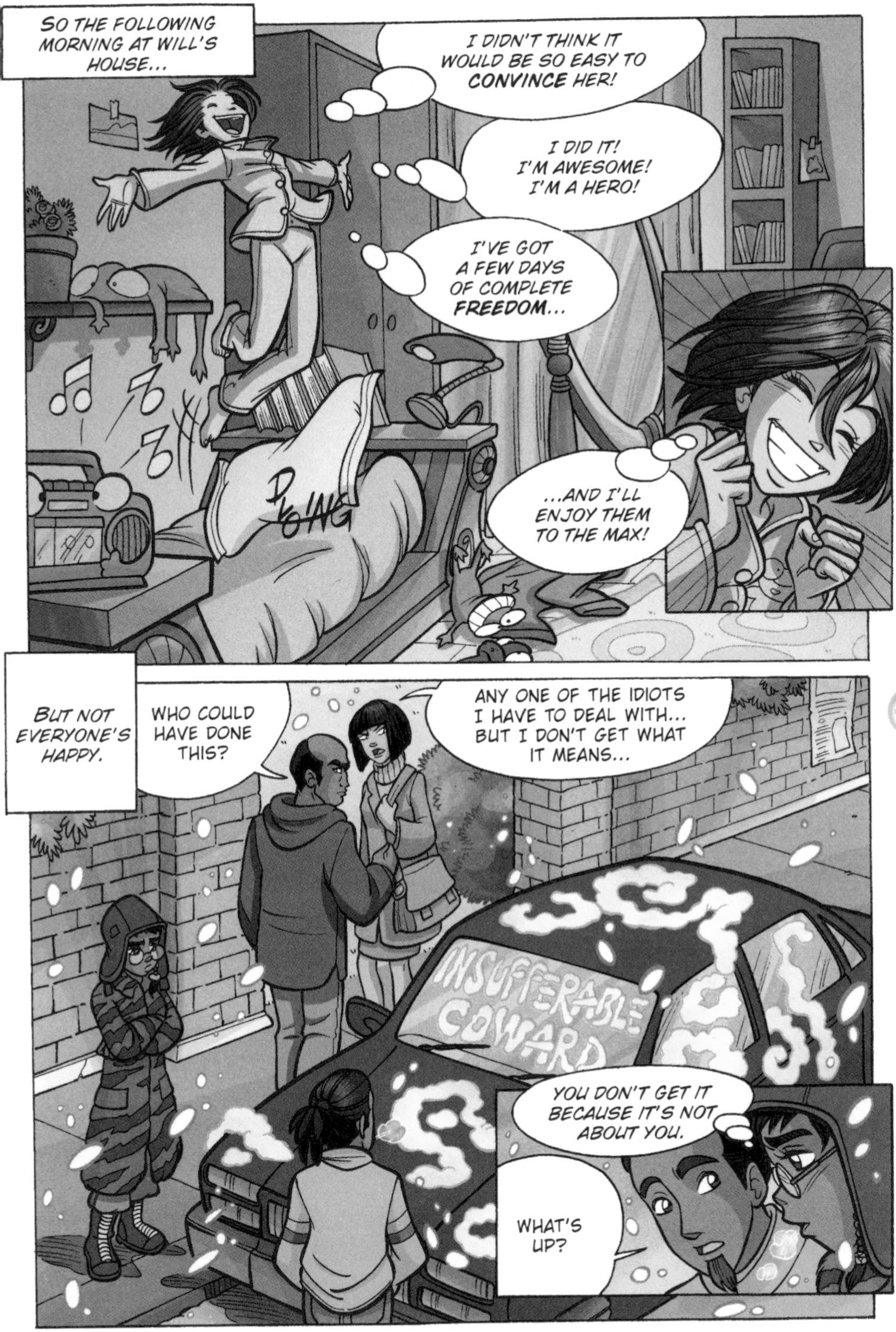

SO THE FOLLOWING MORNING AT WILL'S HOUSE...
I DIDN'T THINK IT WOULD BE SO EASY TO CONVINCE HER!
I DID IT! I'M AWESOME! I'M A HERO!
I'VE GOT A FEW DAYS OF COMPLETE FREEDOM...
DOING
...AND I'LL ENJOY THEM TO THE MAX!
BUT NOT EVERYONE'S HAPPY.
WHO COULD HAVE DONE THIS?
ANY ONE OF THE IDIOTS I HAVE TO DEAL WITH... BUT I DON'T GET WHAT IT MEANS...
INSUFFERABLE COWARD
YOU DON'T GET IT BECAUSE IT'S NOT ABOUT YOU.
WHAT'S UP?

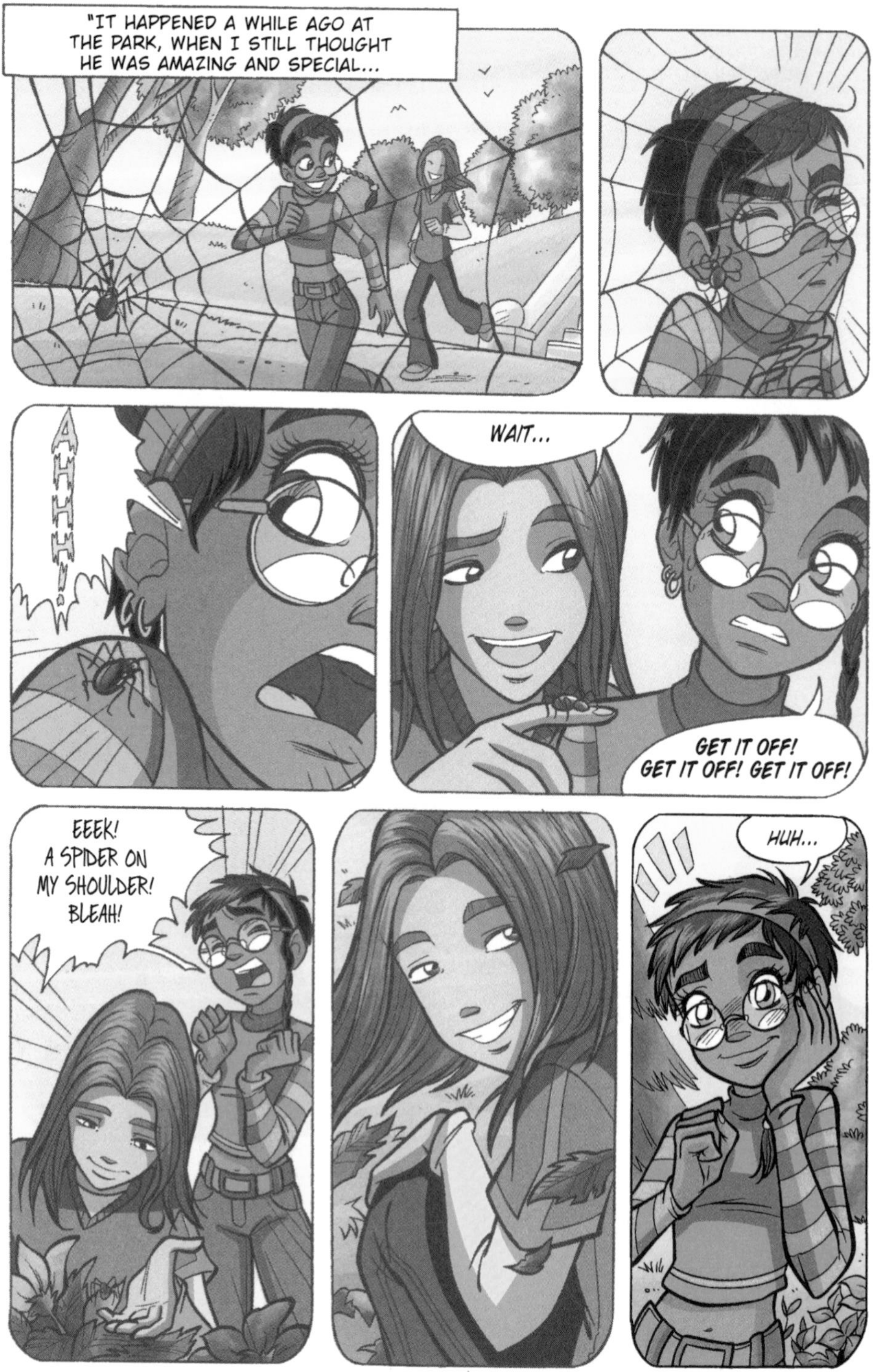
"IT HAPPENED A WHILE AGO AT THE PARK, WHEN I STILL THOUGHT HE WAS AMAZING AND SPECIAL...
AHHH!
WAIT...
GET IT OFF! GET IT OFF! GET IT OFF!
EEEK! A SPIDER ON MY SHOULDER! BLEAH!
HUH...

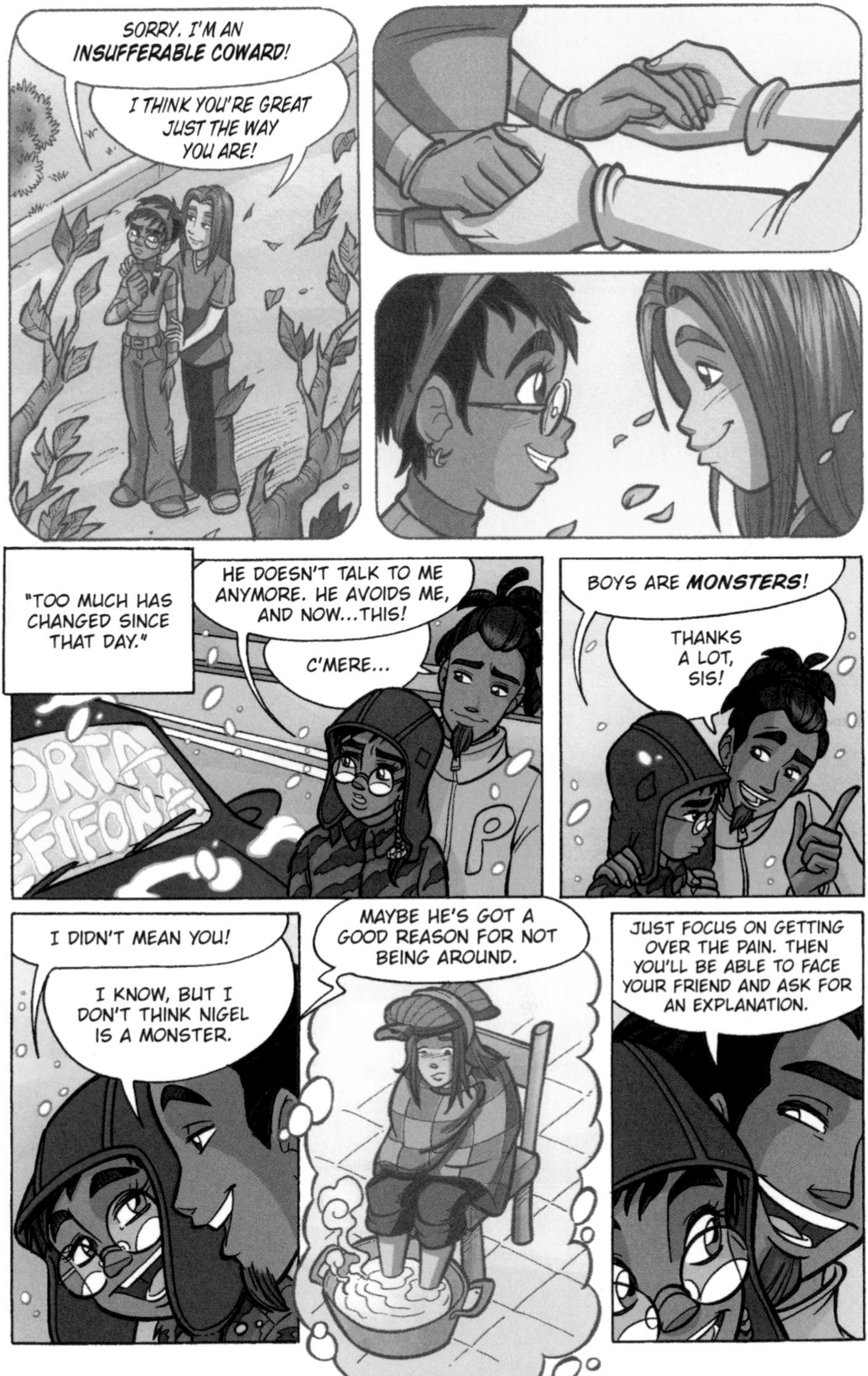
SORRY. I'M AN **INSUFFERABLE COWARD!**
I THINK YOU'RE GREAT JUST THE WAY YOU ARE!
"TOO MUCH HAS CHANGED SINCE THAT DAY."
HE DOESN'T TALK TO ME ANYMORE. HE AVOIDS ME, AND NOW...THIS!
C'MERE...
BOYS ARE **MONSTERS!**
THANKS A LOT, SIS!
I DIDN'T MEAN YOU!
I KNOW, BUT I DON'T THINK NIGEL IS A MONSTER.
MAYBE HE'S GOT A GOOD REASON FOR NOT BEING AROUND.
JUST FOCUS ON GETTING OVER THE PAIN. THEN YOU'LL BE ABLE TO FACE YOUR FRIEND AND ASK FOR AN EXPLANATION.

WELL DONE, EVERYONE. THE TEST WENT REALLY WELL.

ADMIT IT, TEACH. WE'RE GENIUSES!

DON'T SPEAK TOO SOON, IRMA.

EVERYONE DID WELL ON THEIR TEST... EXCEPT YOU!

HUH?!

NOW TELL ME WHAT THIS MEANS...*LANG BUMP BUMP BOOO IRMA?*

A *SECRET CODE?*

ISN'T IT TIME TO *GROW UP* AND STOP WITH THIS SILLINESS?

AND DO YOU KNOW THAT WHEN YOU'RE ANNOYED YOU LOOK LIKE AN *OWL?*

WHAT THE HECK DID I JUST SAY?

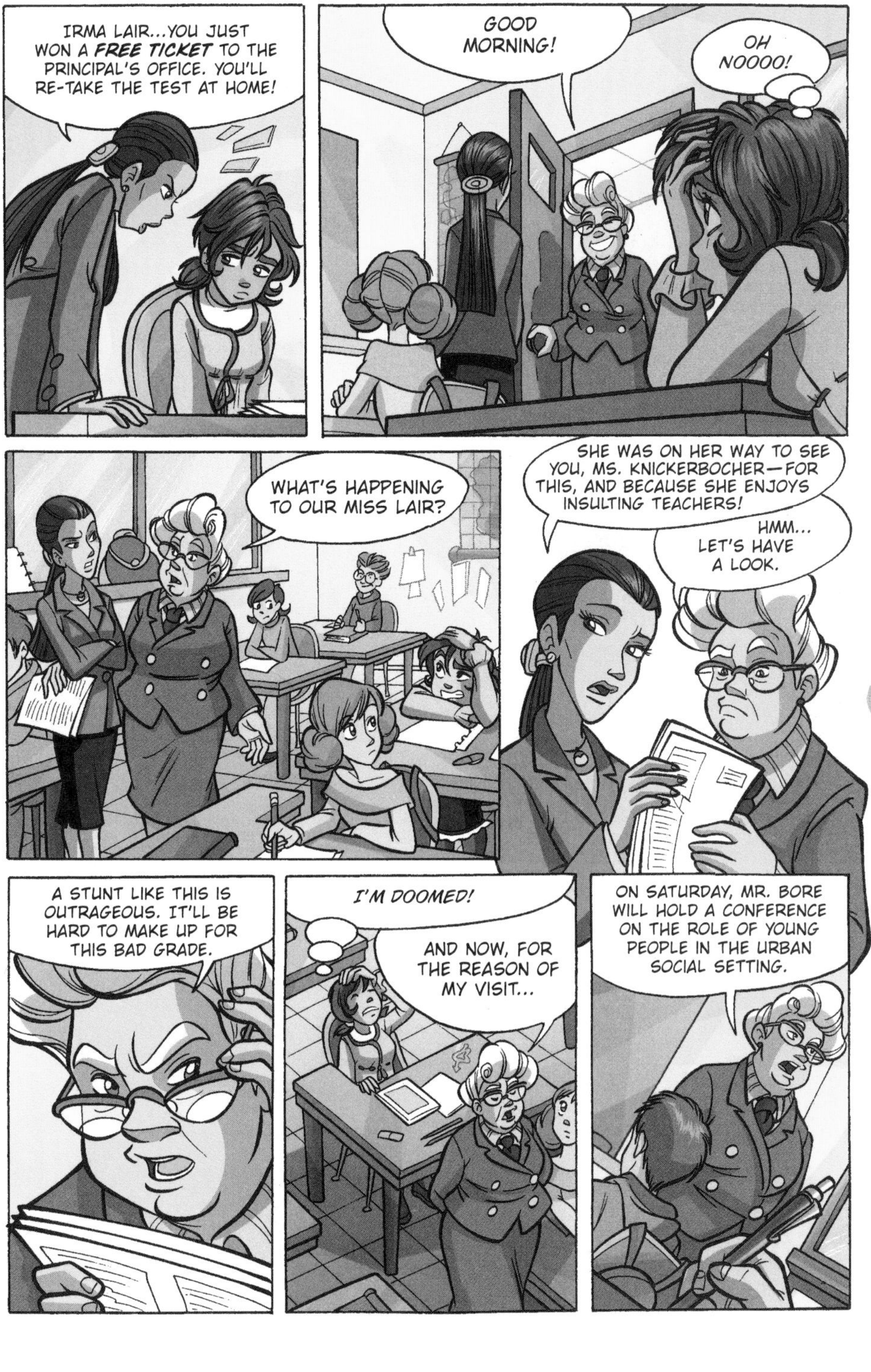
IRMA LAIR...YOU JUST WON A **FREE TICKET** TO THE PRINCIPAL'S OFFICE. YOU'LL RE-TAKE THE TEST AT HOME!
GOOD MORNING!
OH NOOOO!
WHAT'S HAPPENING TO OUR MISS LAIR?
SHE WAS ON HER WAY TO SEE YOU, MS. KNICKERBOCHER—FOR THIS, AND BECAUSE SHE ENJOYS INSULTING TEACHERS!
HMM... LET'S HAVE A LOOK.
A STUNT LIKE THIS IS OUTRAGEOUS. IT'LL BE HARD TO MAKE UP FOR THIS BAD GRADE.
I'M DOOMED!
AND NOW, FOR THE REASON OF MY VISIT...
ON SATURDAY, MR. BORE WILL HOLD A CONFERENCE ON THE ROLE OF YOUNG PEOPLE IN THE URBAN SOCIAL SETTING.

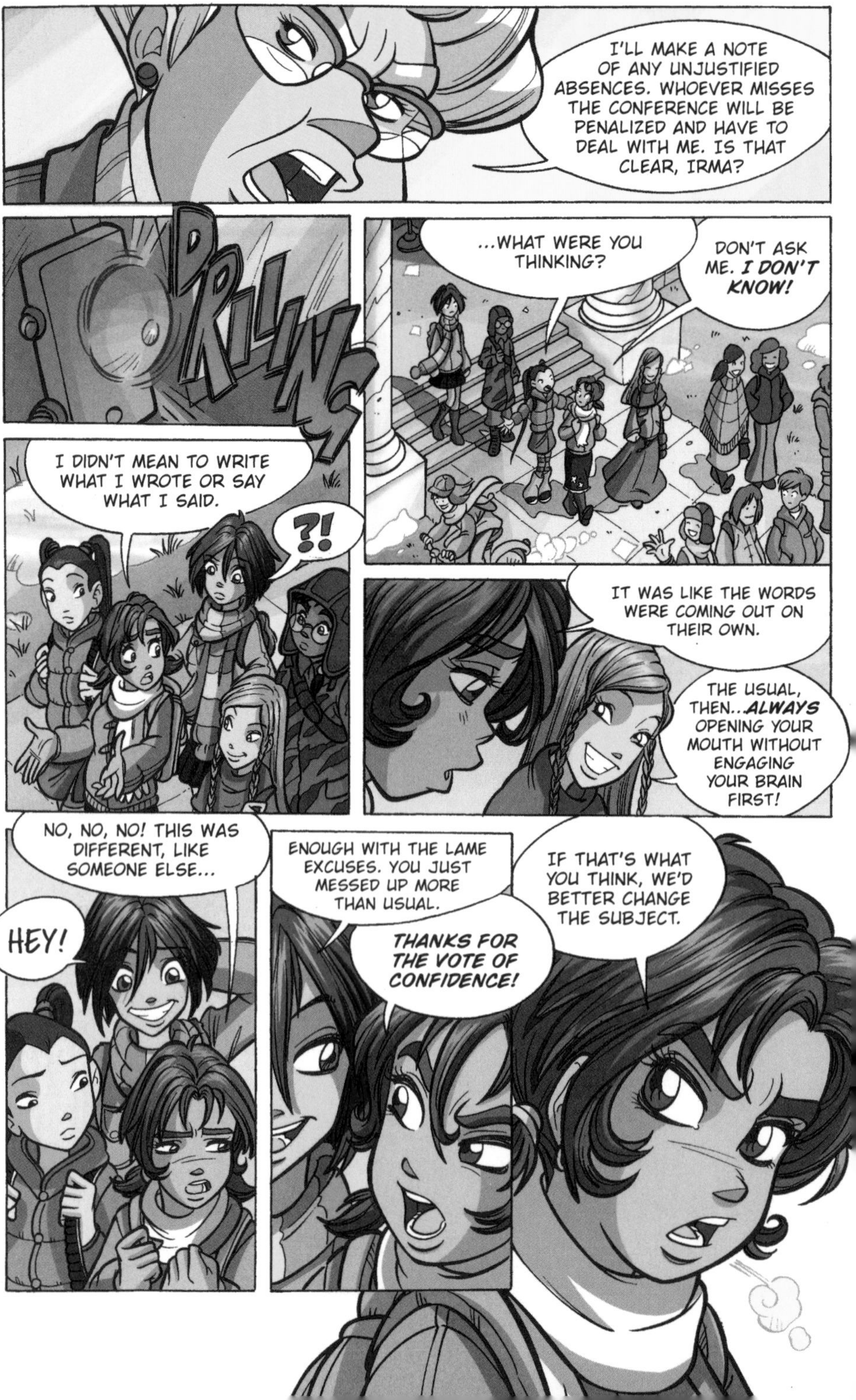
I'LL MAKE A NOTE OF ANY UNJUSTIFIED ABSENCES. WHOEVER MISSES THE CONFERENCE WILL BE PENALIZED AND HAVE TO DEAL WITH ME. IS THAT CLEAR, IRMA?
DRRIIINNG
...WHAT WERE YOU THINKING?
DON'T ASK ME. *I DON'T KNOW!*
I DIDN'T MEAN TO WRITE WHAT I WROTE OR SAY WHAT I SAID.
?!
IT WAS LIKE THE WORDS WERE COMING OUT ON THEIR OWN.
THE USUAL, THEN...*ALWAYS* OPENING YOUR MOUTH WITHOUT ENGAGING YOUR BRAIN FIRST!
NO, NO, NO! THIS WAS DIFFERENT, LIKE SOMEONE ELSE...
HEY!
ENOUGH WITH THE LAME EXCUSES. YOU JUST MESSED UP MORE THAN USUAL.
THANKS FOR THE VOTE OF CONFIDENCE!
IF THAT'S WHAT YOU THINK, WE'D BETTER CHANGE THE SUBJECT.

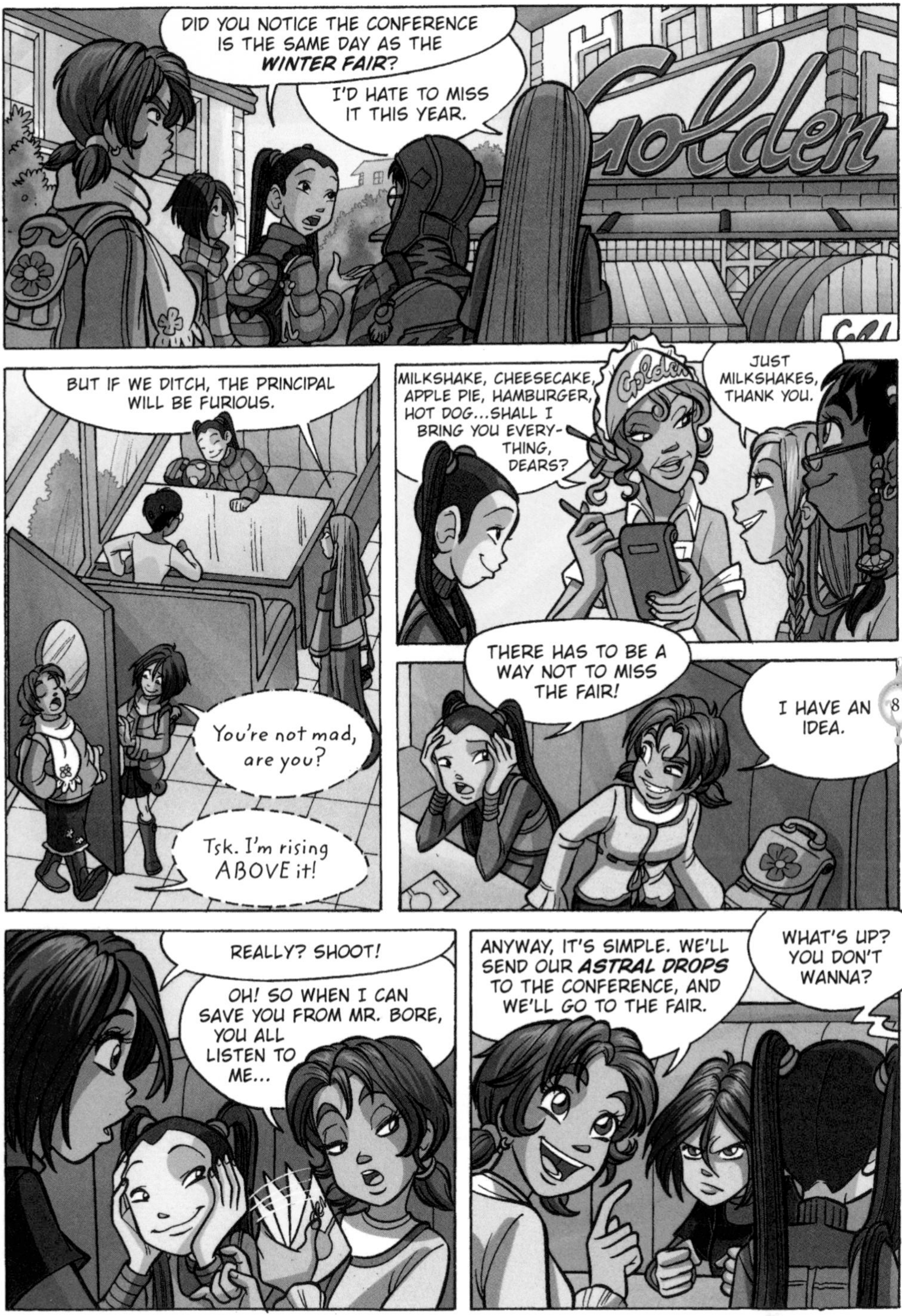
DID YOU NOTICE THE CONFERENCE IS THE SAME DAY AS THE WINTER FAIR?
I'D HATE TO MISS IT THIS YEAR.
Golden
BUT IF WE DITCH, THE PRINCIPAL WILL BE FURIOUS.
You're not mad, are you?
Tsk. I'm rising ABOVE it!
MILKSHAKE, CHEESECAKE, APPLE PIE, HAMBURGER, HOT DOG...SHALL I BRING YOU EVERYTHING, DEARS?
JUST MILKSHAKES, THANK YOU.
THERE HAS TO BE A WAY NOT TO MISS THE FAIR!
I HAVE AN IDEA.
REALLY? SHOOT!
OH! SO WHEN I CAN SAVE YOU FROM MR. BORE, YOU ALL LISTEN TO ME...
ANYWAY, IT'S SIMPLE. WE'LL SEND OUR ASTRAL DROPS TO THE CONFERENCE, AND WE'LL GO TO THE FAIR.
WHAT'S UP? YOU DON'T WANNA?

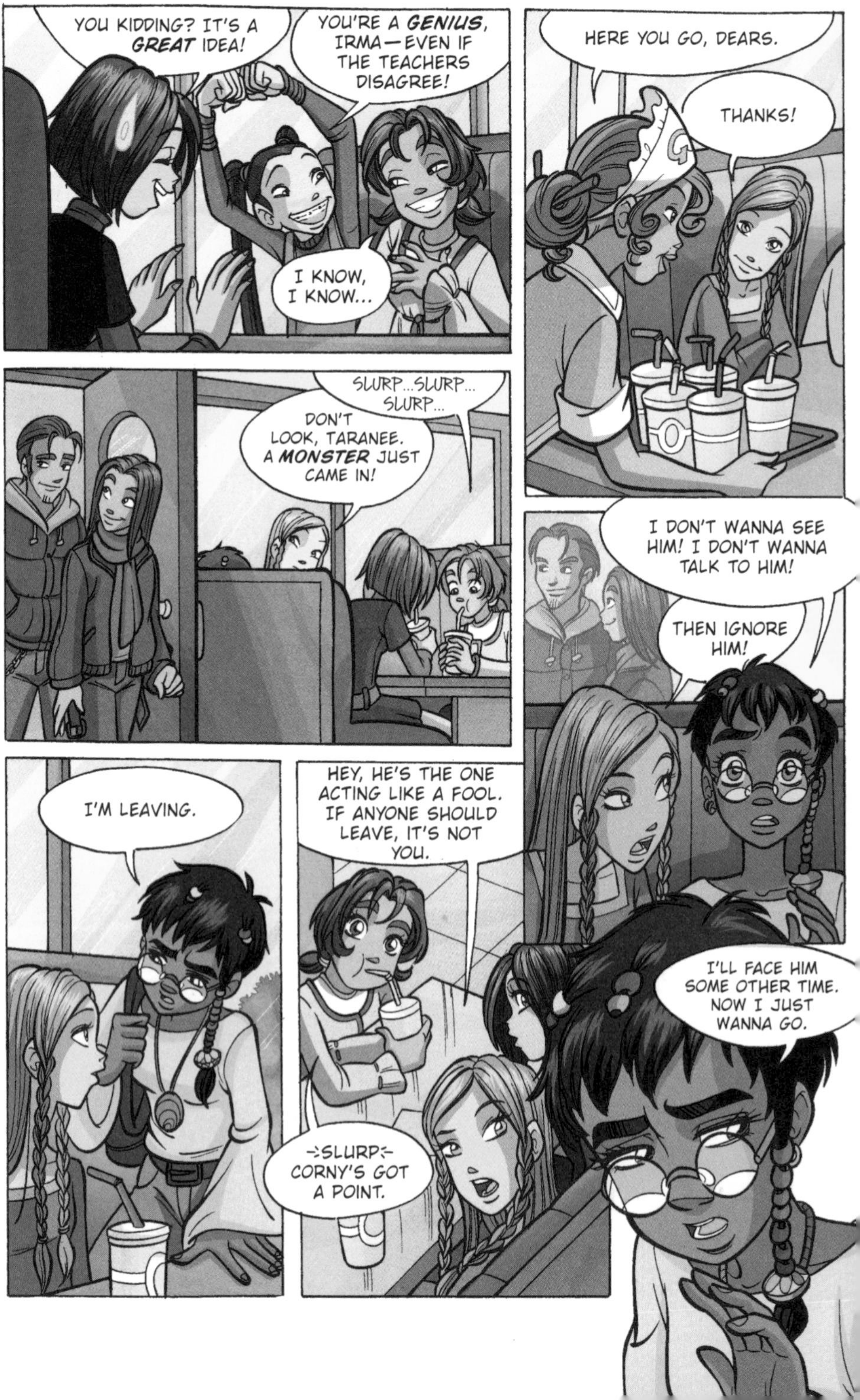
YOU KIDDING? IT'S A GREAT IDEA!
YOU'RE A GENIUS, IRMA—EVEN IF THE TEACHERS DISAGREE!
I KNOW, I KNOW...
HERE YOU GO, DEARS.
THANKS!
SLURP...SLURP... SLURP...
DON'T LOOK, TARANEE. A MONSTER JUST CAME IN!
I DON'T WANNA SEE HIM! I DON'T WANNA TALK TO HIM!
THEN IGNORE HIM!
I'M LEAVING.
HEY, HE'S THE ONE ACTING LIKE A FOOL. IF ANYONE SHOULD LEAVE, IT'S NOT YOU.
SLURP CORNY'S GOT A POINT.
I'LL FACE HIM SOME OTHER TIME. NOW I JUST WANNA GO.

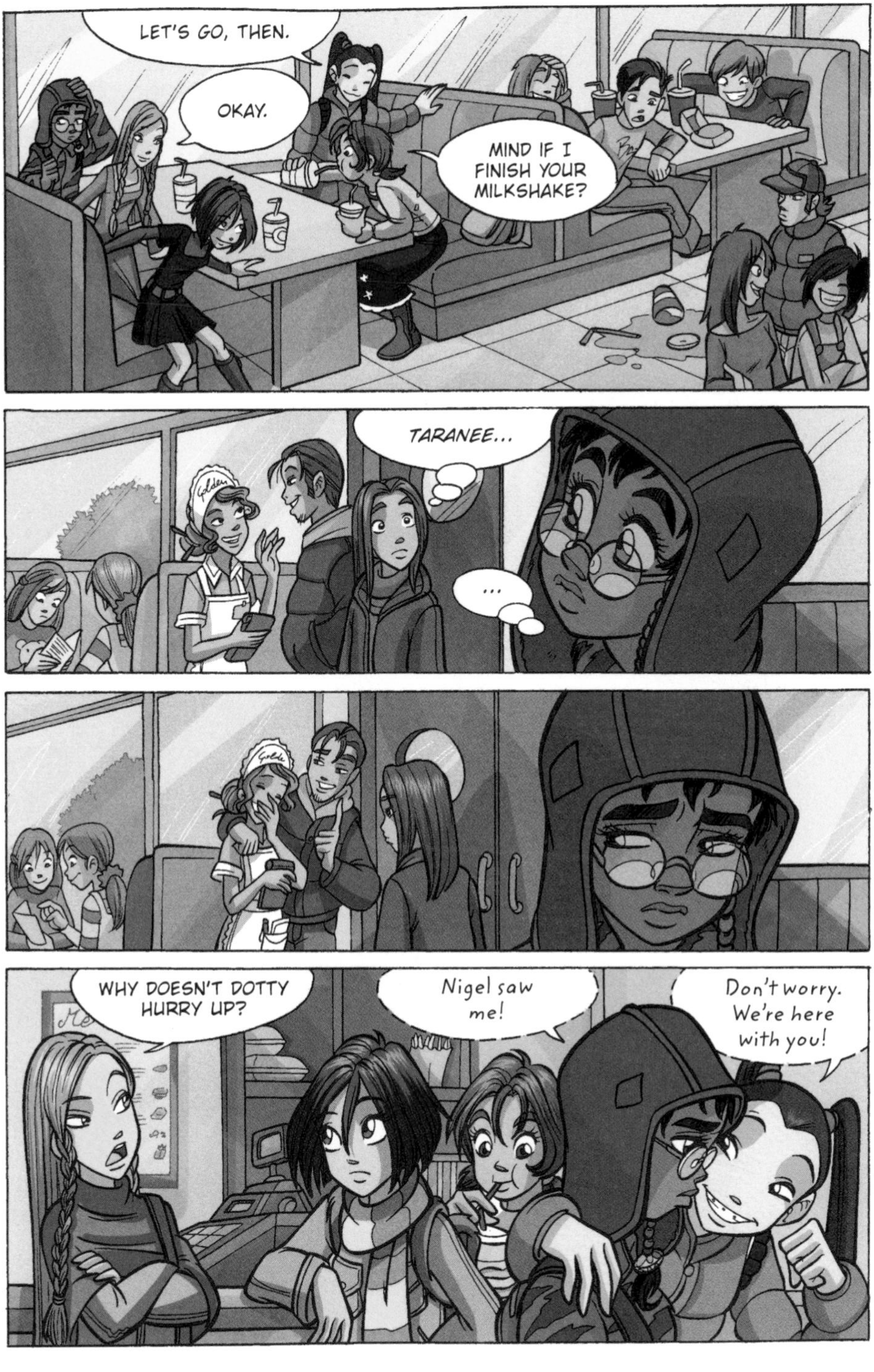
LET'S GO, THEN.
OKAY.
MIND IF I FINISH YOUR MILKSHAKE?
TARANEE...
...
WHY DOESN'T DOTTY HURRY UP?
Nigel saw me!
Don't worry. We're here with you!

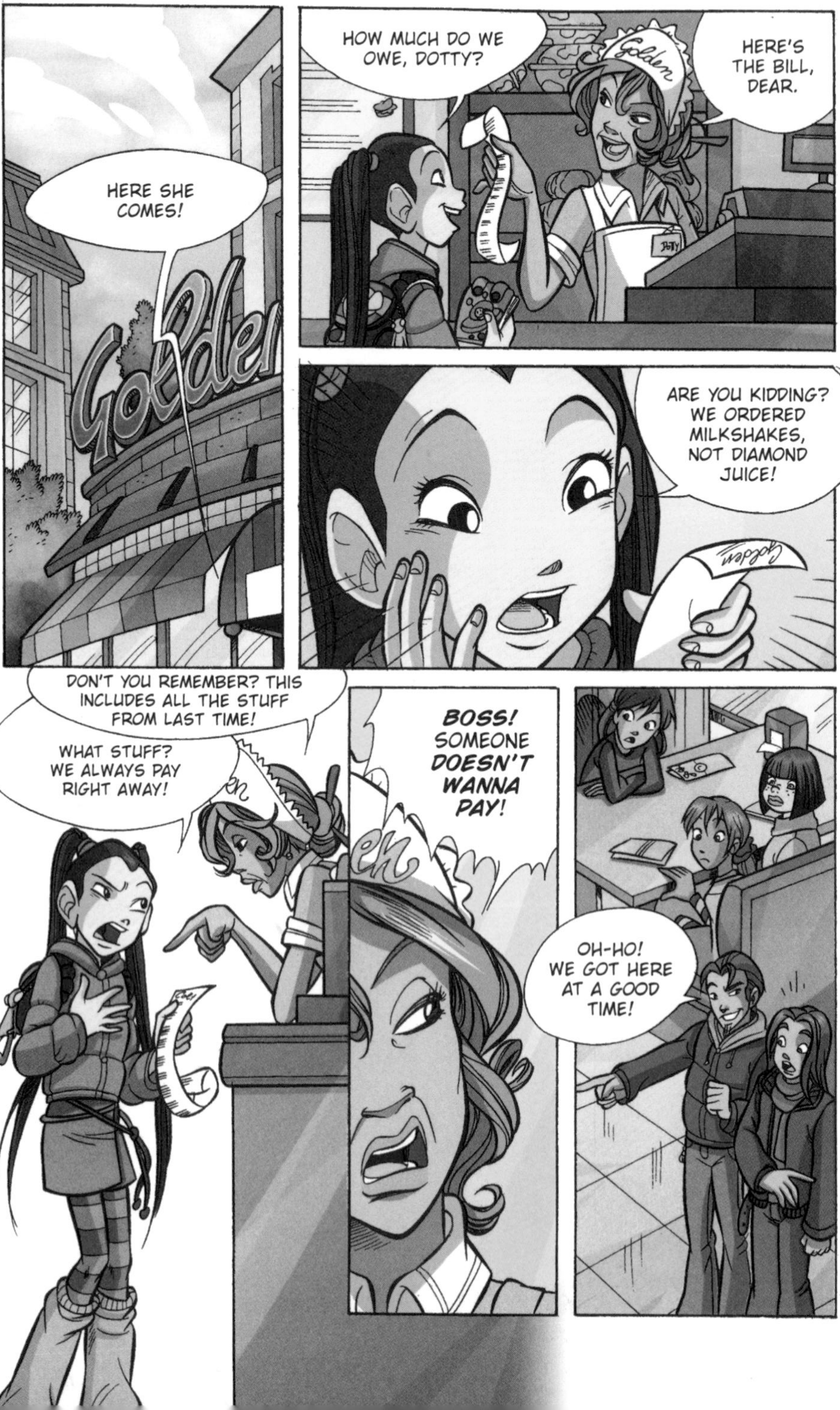
HERE SHE COMES!
Golden
HOW MUCH DO WE OWE, DOTTY?
HERE'S THE BILL, DEAR.
ARE YOU KIDDING? WE ORDERED MILKSHAKES, NOT DIAMOND JUICE!
DON'T YOU REMEMBER? THIS INCLUDES ALL THE STUFF FROM LAST TIME!
WHAT STUFF? WE ALWAYS PAY RIGHT AWAY!
BOSS! SOMEONE DOESN'T WANNA PAY!
OH-HO! WE GOT HERE AT A GOOD TIME!

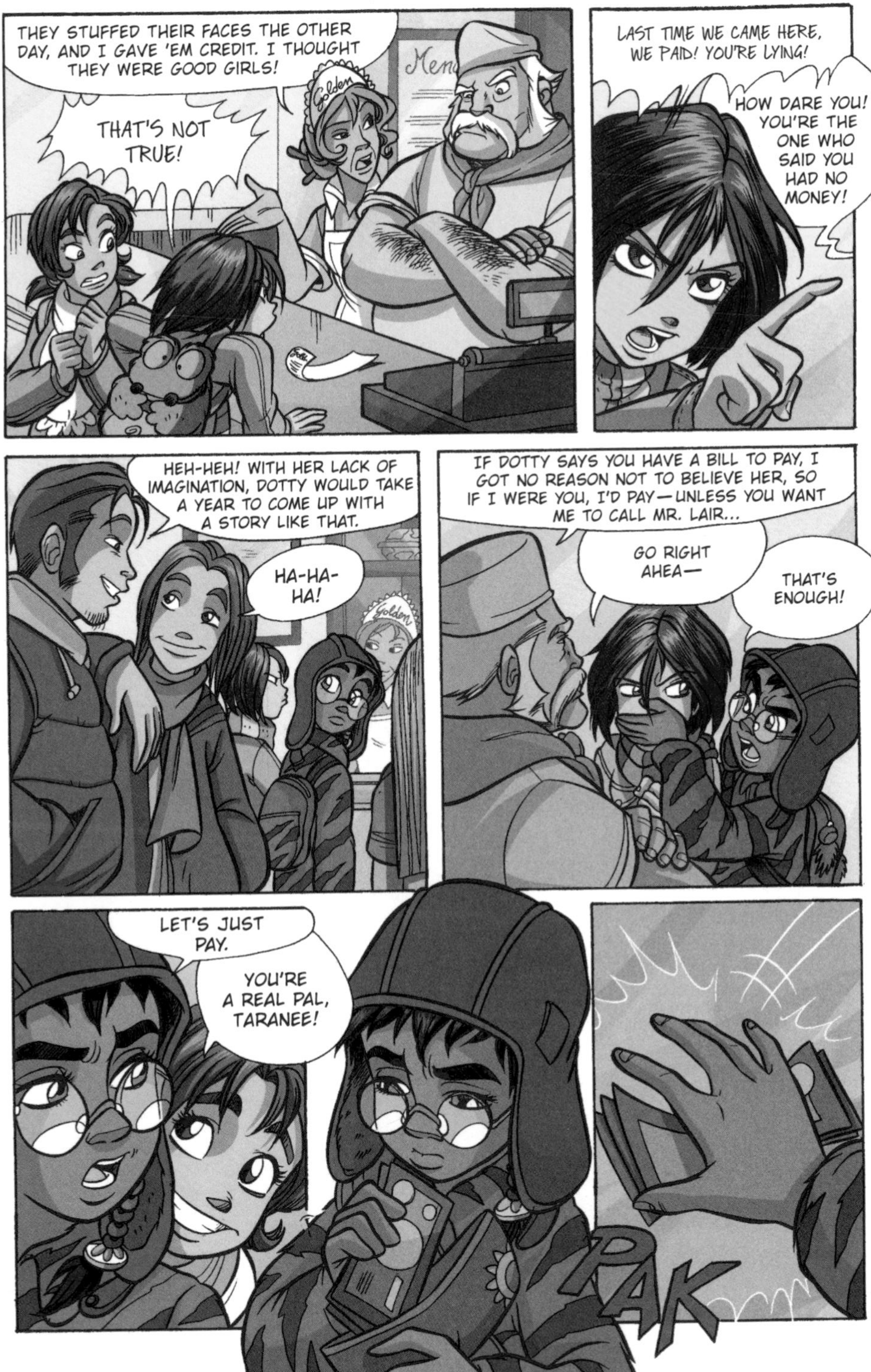
THEY STUFFED THEIR FACES THE OTHER DAY, AND I GAVE 'EM CREDIT. I THOUGHT THEY WERE GOOD GIRLS!
THAT'S NOT TRUE!
LAST TIME WE CAME HERE, WE PAID! YOU'RE LYING!
HOW DARE YOU! YOU'RE THE ONE WHO SAID YOU HAD NO MONEY!
HEH-HEH! WITH HER LACK OF IMAGINATION, DOTTY WOULD TAKE A YEAR TO COME UP WITH A STORY LIKE THAT.
HA-HA-HA!
IF DOTTY SAYS YOU HAVE A BILL TO PAY, I GOT NO REASON NOT TO BELIEVE HER, SO IF I WERE YOU, I'D PAY—UNLESS YOU WANT ME TO CALL MR. LAIR...
GO RIGHT AHEA—
THAT'S ENOUGH!
LET'S JUST PAY.
YOU'RE A REAL PAL, TARANEE!
PAK

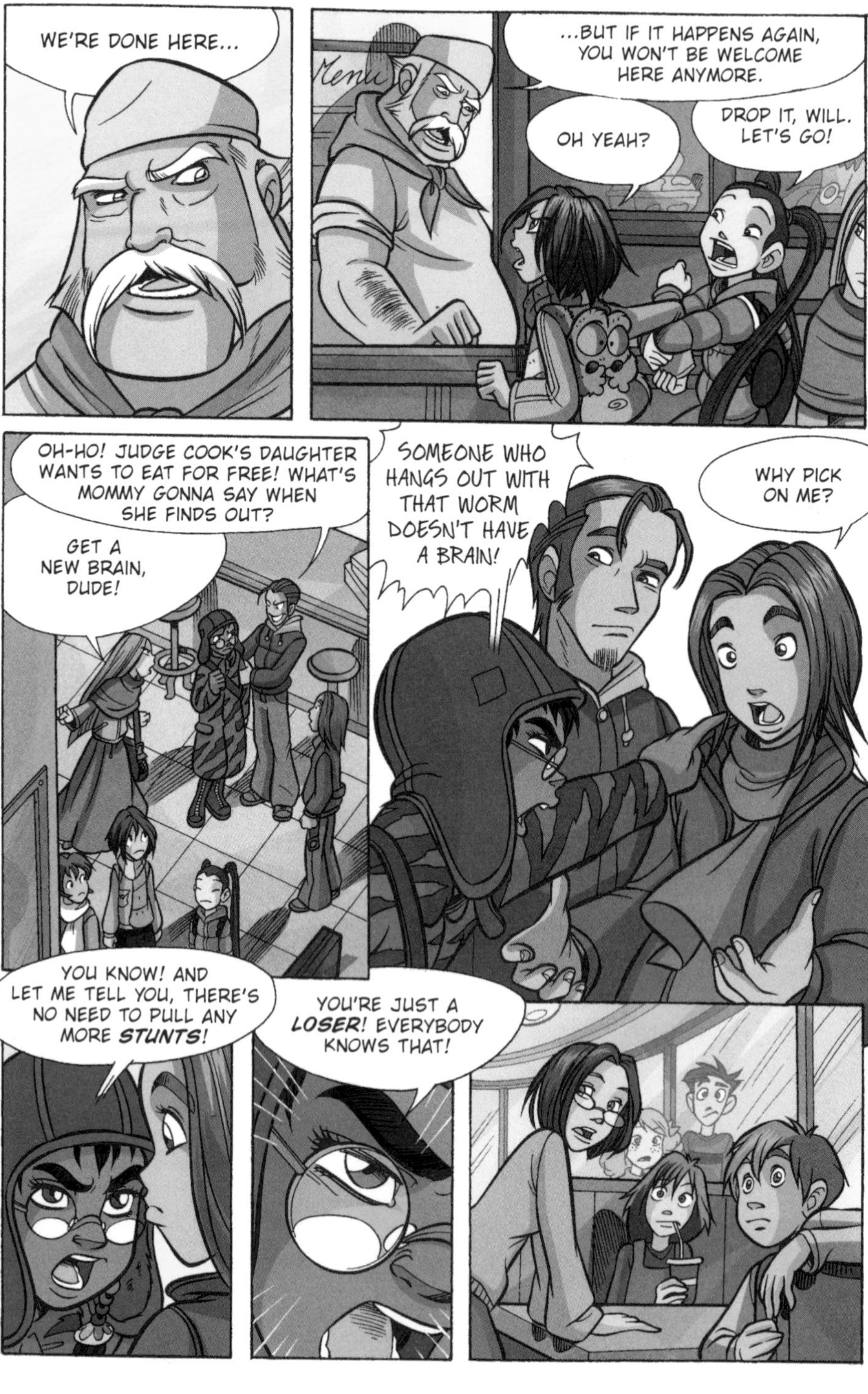
WE'RE DONE HERE...
Menu
...BUT IF IT HAPPENS AGAIN, YOU WON'T BE WELCOME HERE ANYMORE.
OH YEAH?
DROP IT, WILL. LET'S GO!
OH-HO! JUDGE COOK'S DAUGHTER WANTS TO EAT FOR FREE! WHAT'S MOMMY GONNA SAY WHEN SHE FINDS OUT?
GET A NEW BRAIN, DUDE!
SOMEONE WHO HANGS OUT WITH THAT WORM DOESN'T HAVE A BRAIN!
WHY PICK ON ME?
YOU KNOW! AND LET ME TELL YOU, THERE'S NO NEED TO PULL ANY MORE STUNTS!
YOU'RE JUST A LOSER! EVERYBODY KNOWS THAT!

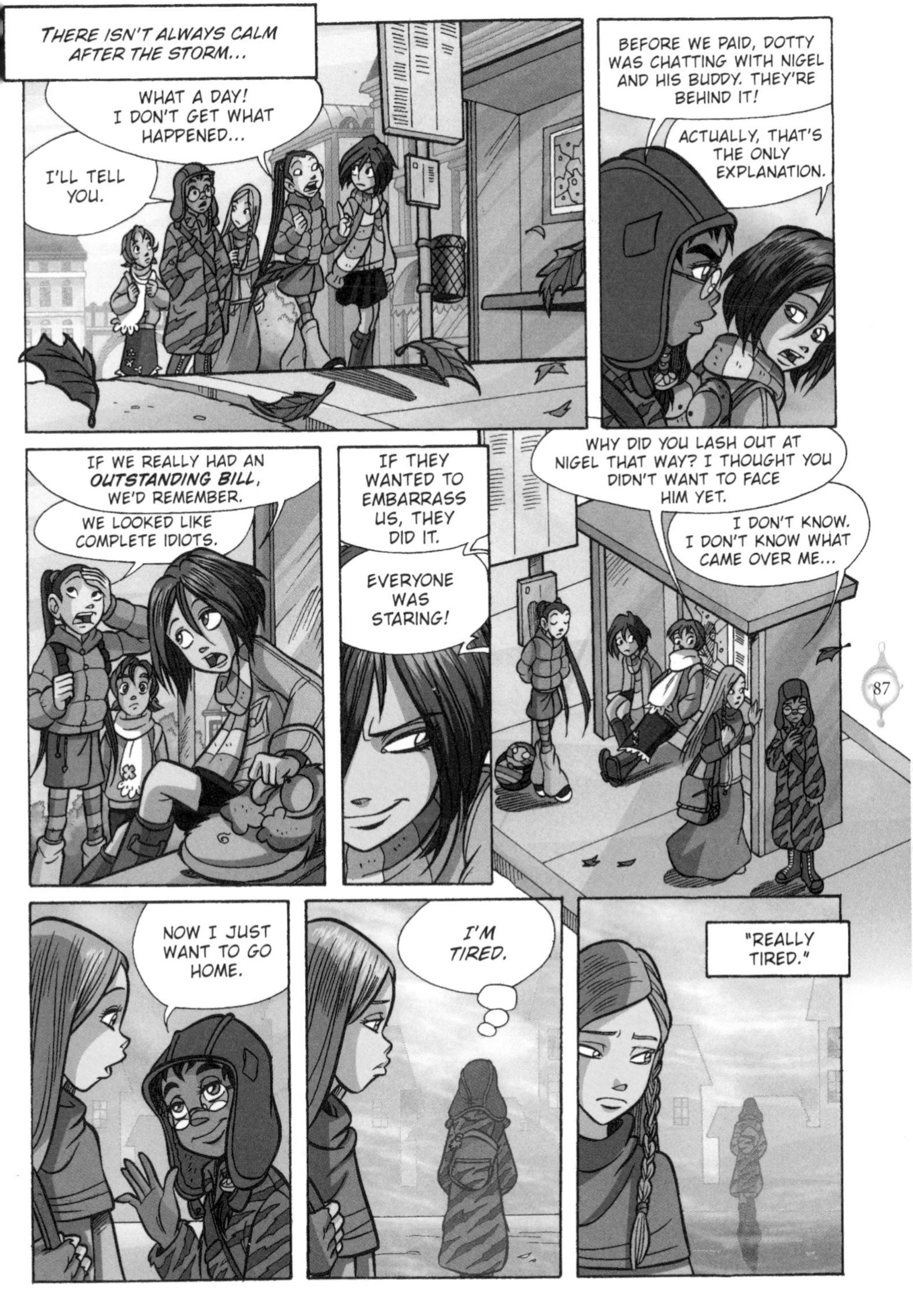
THERE ISN'T ALWAYS CALM AFTER THE STORM...
WHAT A DAY! I DON'T GET WHAT HAPPENED...
I'LL TELL YOU.
BEFORE WE PAID, DOTTY WAS CHATTING WITH NIGEL AND HIS BUDDY. THEY'RE BEHIND IT!
ACTUALLY, THAT'S THE ONLY EXPLANATION.
IF WE REALLY HAD AN OUTSTANDING BILL, WE'D REMEMBER.
WE LOOKED LIKE COMPLETE IDIOTS.
IF THEY WANTED TO EMBARRASS US, THEY DID IT.
EVERYONE WAS STARING!
WHY DID YOU LASH OUT AT NIGEL THAT WAY? I THOUGHT YOU DIDN'T WANT TO FACE HIM YET.
I DON'T KNOW. I DON'T KNOW WHAT CAME OVER ME...
NOW I JUST WANT TO GO HOME.
I'M TIRED.
"REALLY TIRED."

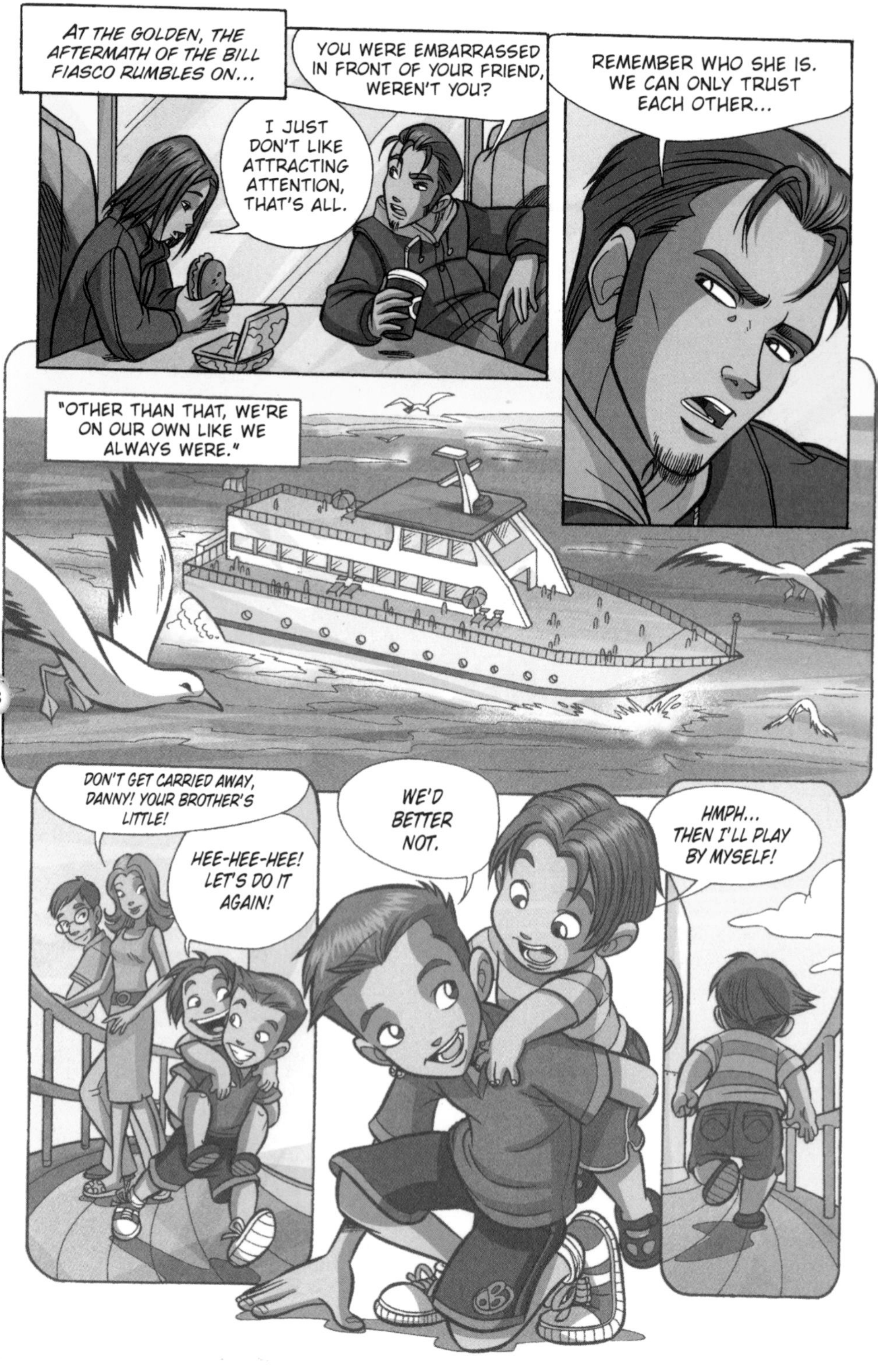

AT THE GOLDEN, THE AFTERMATH OF THE BILL FIASCO RUMBLES ON...
YOU WERE EMBARRASSED IN FRONT OF YOUR FRIEND, WEREN'T YOU?
I JUST DON'T LIKE ATTRACTING ATTENTION, THAT'S ALL.
REMEMBER WHO SHE IS. WE CAN ONLY TRUST EACH OTHER...
"OTHER THAN THAT, WE'RE ON OUR OWN LIKE WE ALWAYS WERE."
DON'T GET CARRIED AWAY, DANNY! YOUR BROTHER'S LITTLE!
HEE-HEE-HEE! LET'S DO IT AGAIN!
WE'D BETTER NOT.
HMPH... THEN I'LL PLAY BY MYSELF!

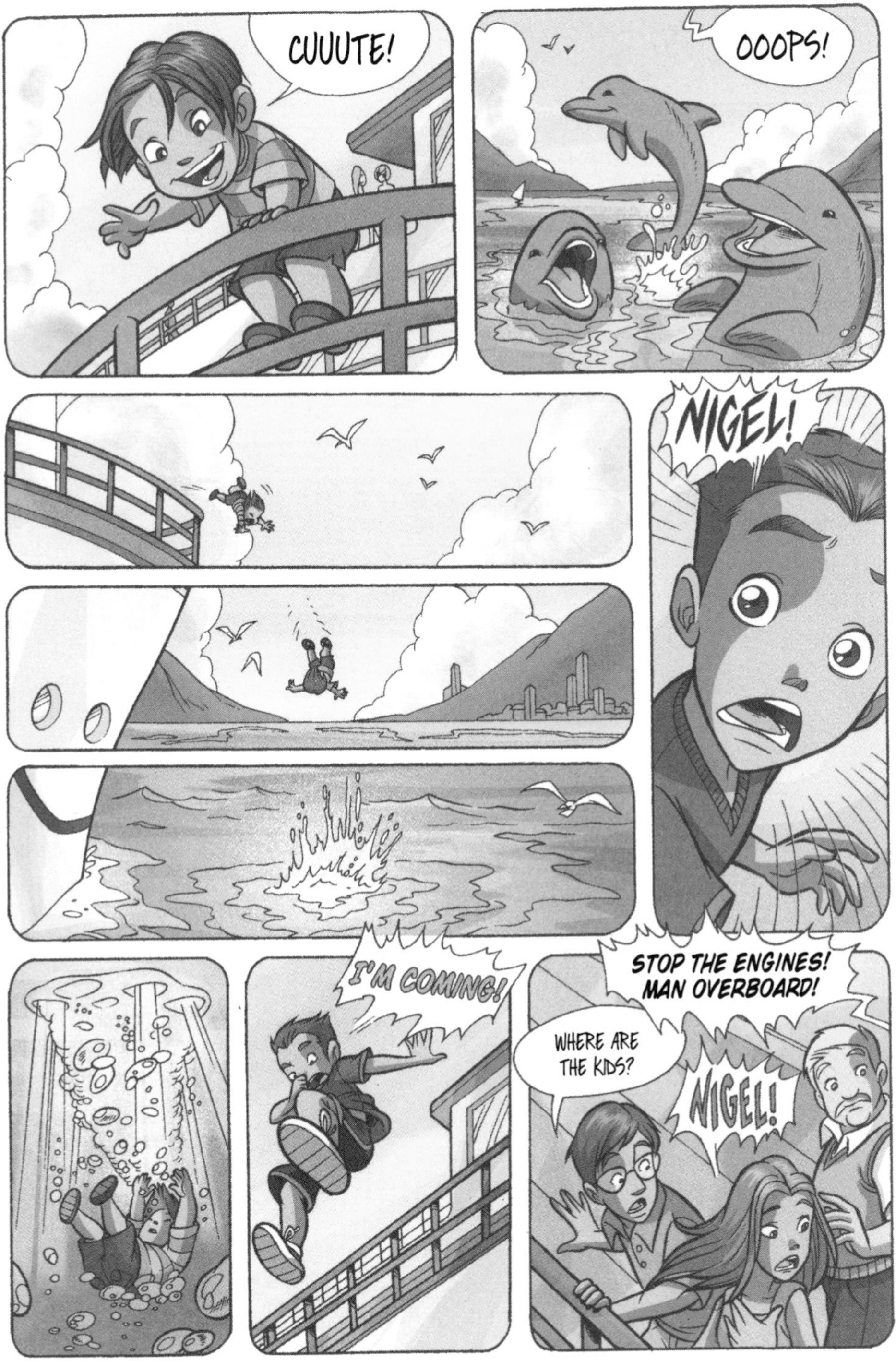
CUUUTE!
OOOPS!
NIGEL!
I'M COMING!
STOP THE ENGINES! MAN OVERBOARD!
WHERE ARE THE KIDS?
NIGEL!

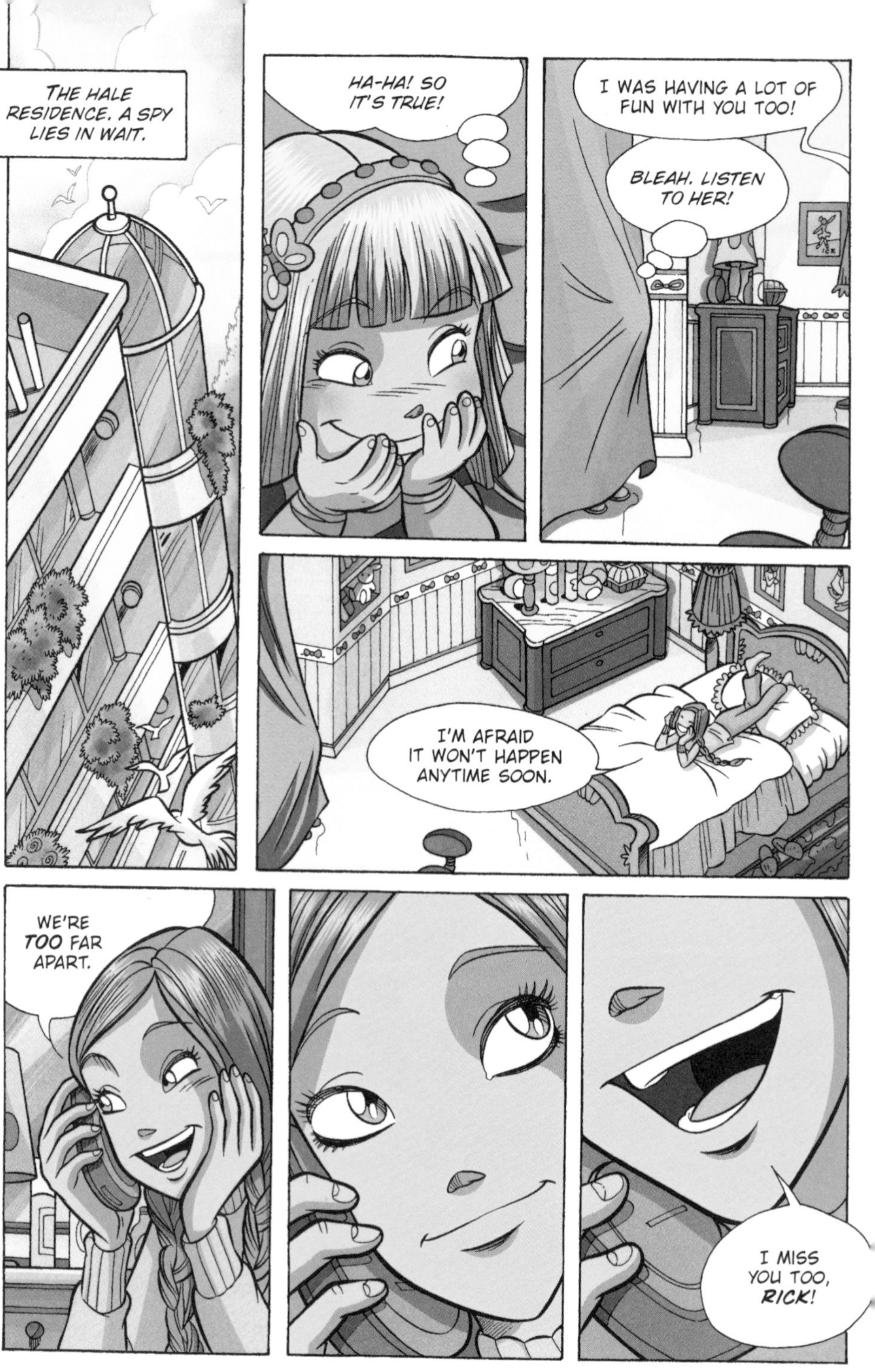

THE HALE RESIDENCE. A SPY LIES IN WAIT.
HA-HA! SO IT'S TRUE!
I WAS HAVING A LOT OF FUN WITH YOU TOO!
BLEAH. LISTEN TO HER!
I'M AFRAID IT WON'T HAPPEN ANYTIME SOON.
WE'RE **TOO** FAR APART.
I MISS YOU TOO, **RICK**!

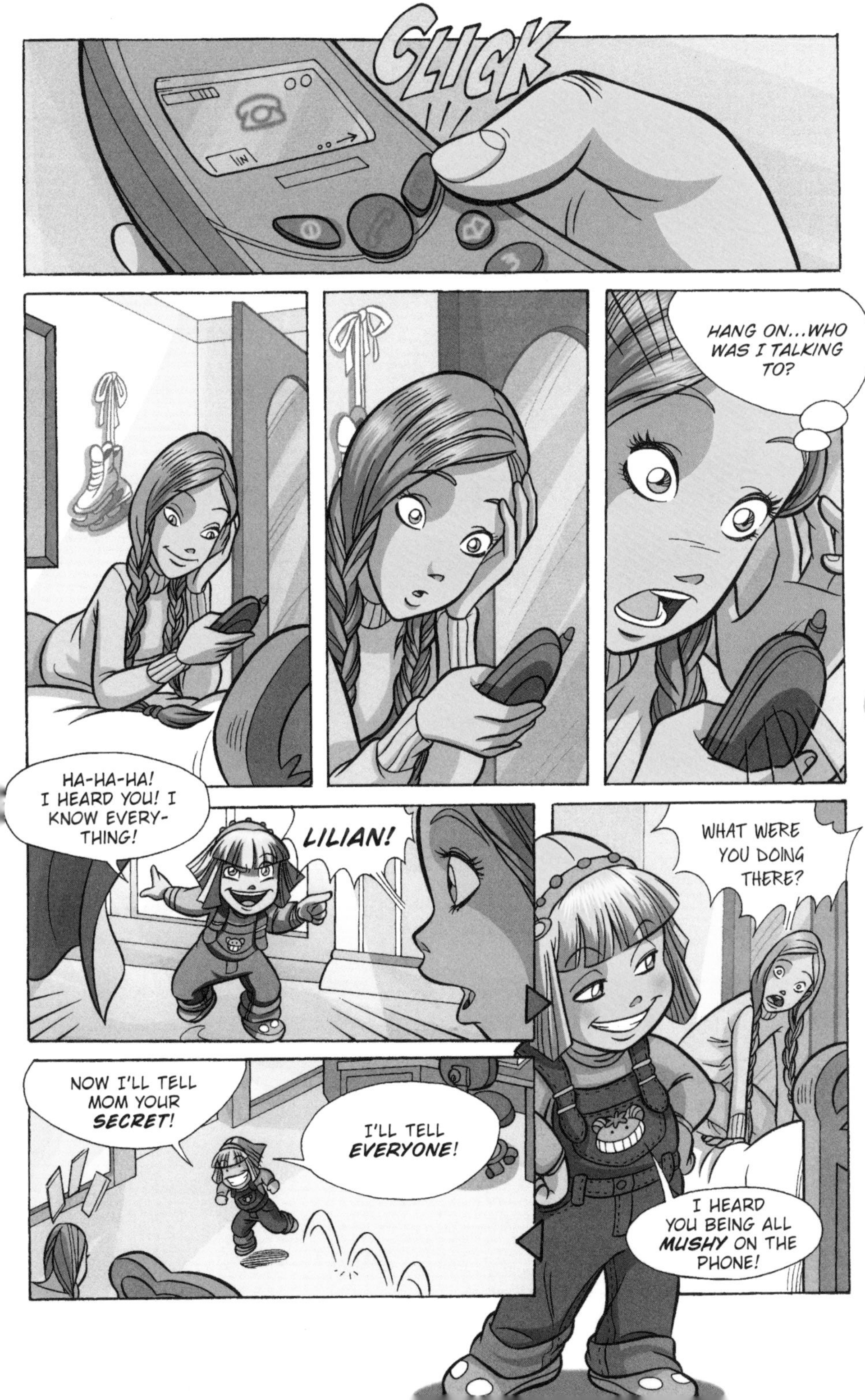
CLICK
HANG ON...WHO WAS I TALKING TO?
HA-HA-HA! I HEARD YOU! I KNOW EVERY-THING!
LILIAN!
WHAT WERE YOU DOING THERE?
NOW I'LL TELL MOM YOUR **SECRET**!
I'LL TELL **EVERYONE**!
I HEARD YOU BEING ALL **MUSHY** ON THE PHONE!

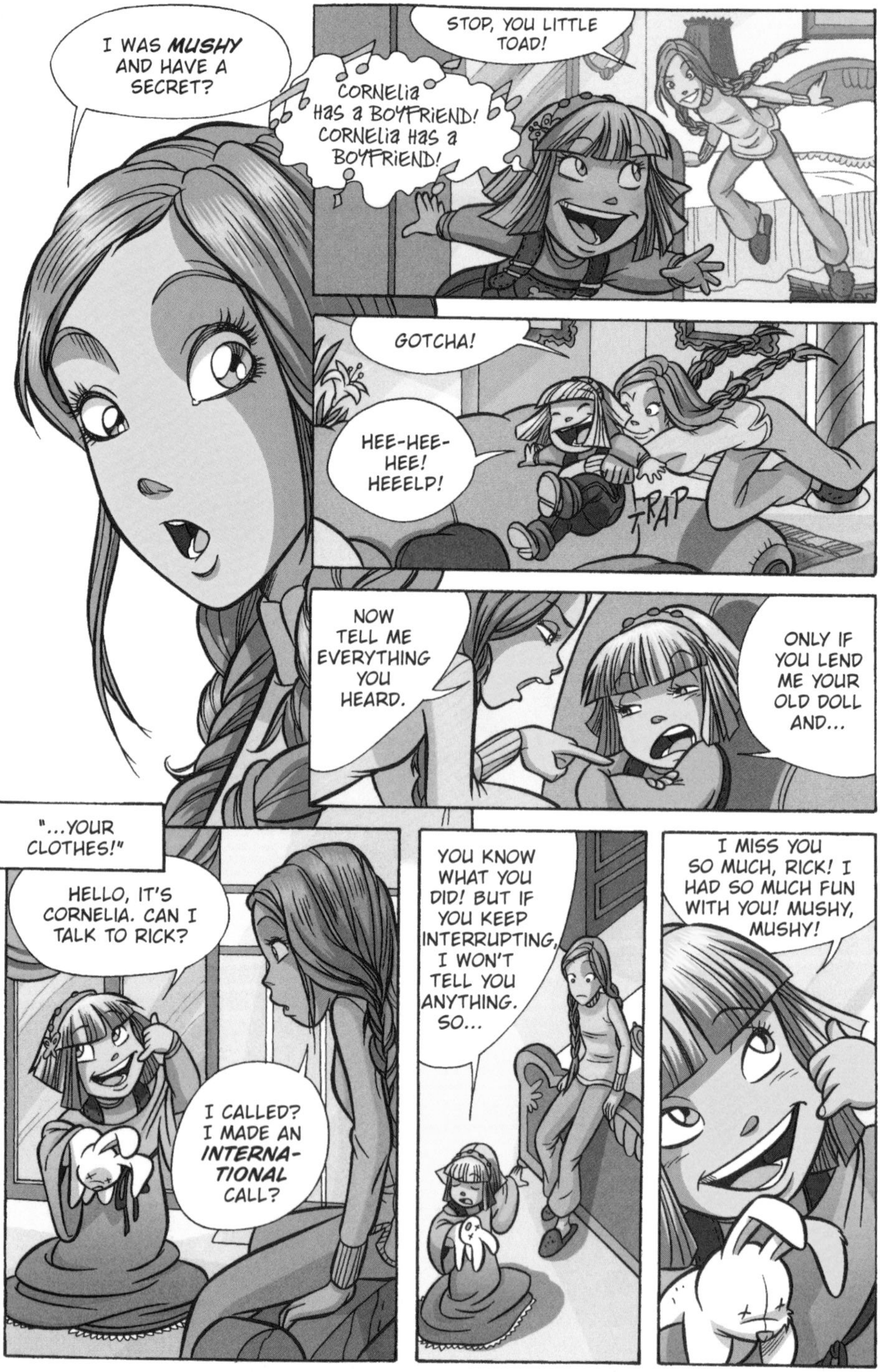
I WAS MUSHY AND HAVE A SECRET?
STOP, YOU LITTLE TOAD!
CORNELia HaS a BOYFRIEND! CORNELia HaS a BOYFRIEND!
GOTCHA!
HEE-HEE-HEE! HEEELP!
TRAP
NOW TELL ME EVERYTHING YOU HEARD.
ONLY IF YOU LEND ME YOUR OLD DOLL AND...
"...YOUR CLOTHES!"
HELLO, IT'S CORNELIA. CAN I TALK TO RICK?
I CALLED? I MADE AN INTERNATIONAL CALL?
YOU KNOW WHAT YOU DID! BUT IF YOU KEEP INTERRUPTING, I WON'T TELL YOU ANYTHING. SO...
I MISS YOU SO MUCH, RICK! I HAD SO MUCH FUN WITH YOU! MUSHY, MUSHY!

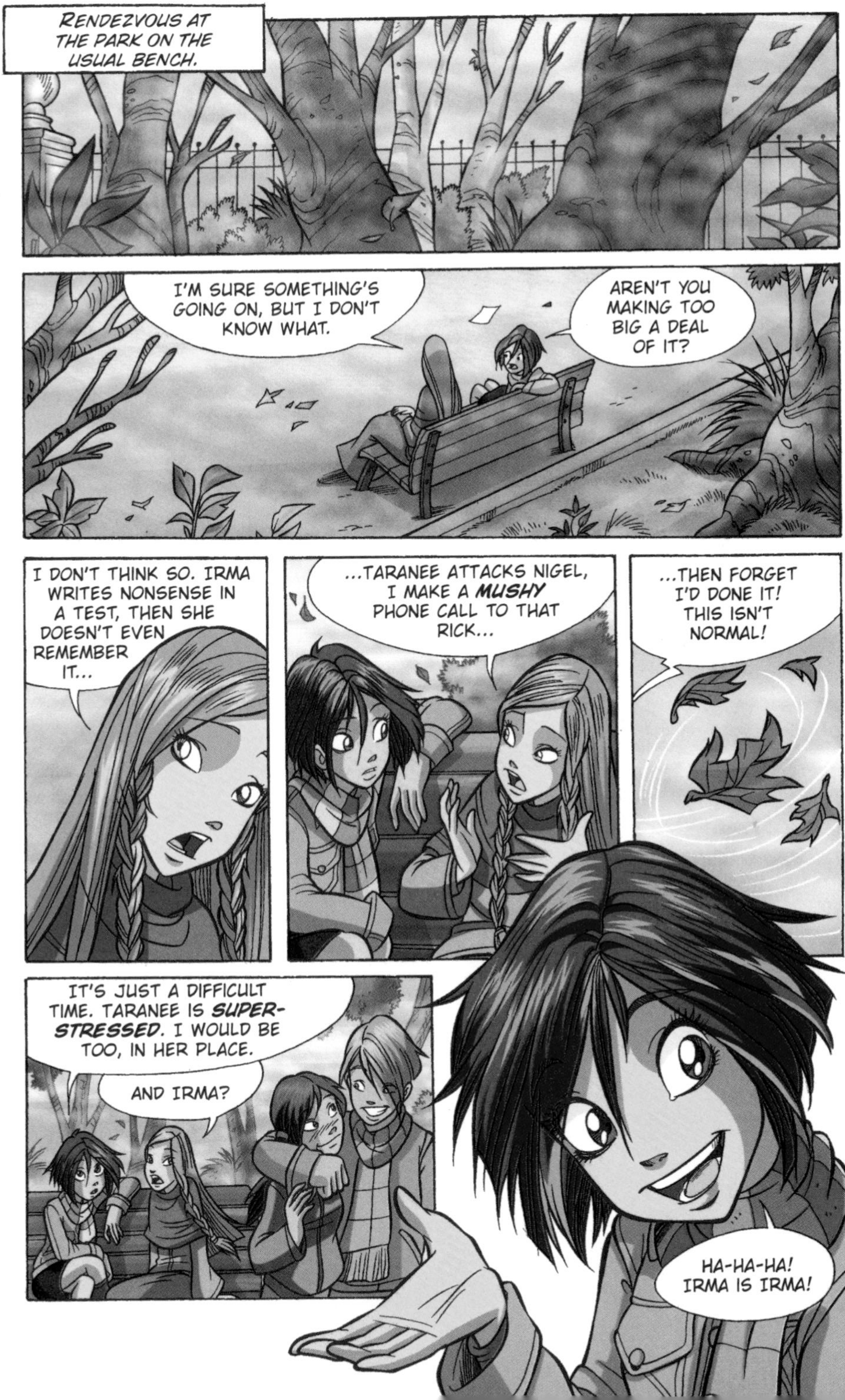
RENDEZVOUS AT THE PARK ON THE USUAL BENCH.
I'M SURE SOMETHING'S GOING ON, BUT I DON'T KNOW WHAT.
AREN'T YOU MAKING TOO BIG A DEAL OF IT?
I DON'T THINK SO. IRMA WRITES NONSENSE IN A TEST, THEN SHE DOESN'T EVEN REMEMBER IT...
...TARANEE ATTACKS NIGEL, I MAKE A MUSHY PHONE CALL TO THAT RICK...
...THEN FORGET I'D DONE IT! THIS ISN'T NORMAL!
IT'S JUST A DIFFICULT TIME. TARANEE IS SUPER-STRESSED. I WOULD BE TOO, IN HER PLACE.
AND IRMA?
HA-HA-HA! IRMA IS IRMA!

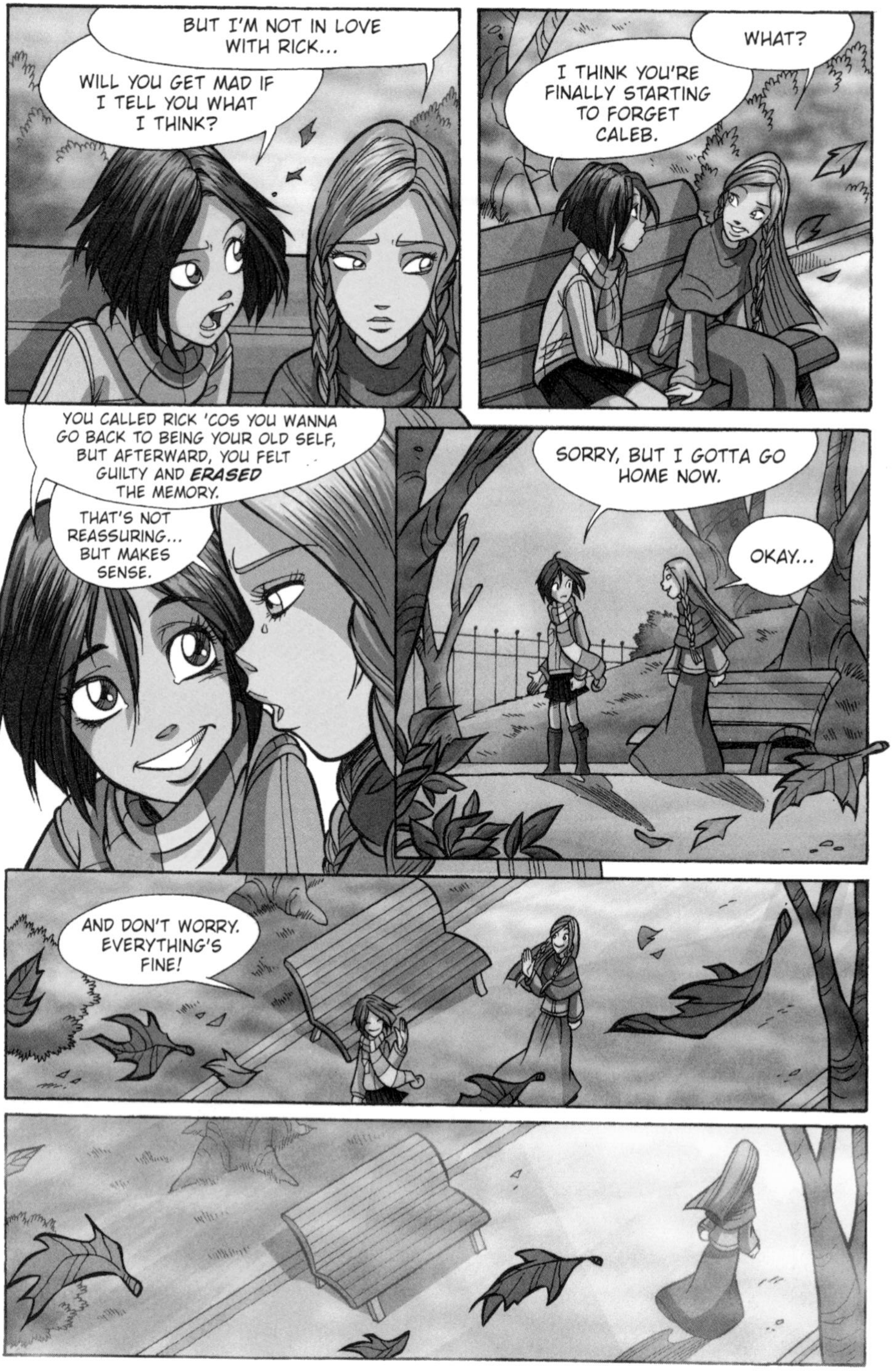

BUT I'M NOT IN LOVE WITH RICK...
WILL YOU GET MAD IF I TELL YOU WHAT I THINK?
WHAT?
I THINK YOU'RE FINALLY STARTING TO FORGET CALEB.
YOU CALLED RICK 'COS YOU WANNA GO BACK TO BEING YOUR OLD SELF, BUT AFTERWARD, YOU FELT GUILTY AND ***ERASED*** THE MEMORY.
THAT'S NOT REASSURING... BUT MAKES SENSE.
SORRY, BUT I GOTTA GO HOME NOW.
OKAY...
AND DON'T WORRY. EVERYTHING'S FINE!

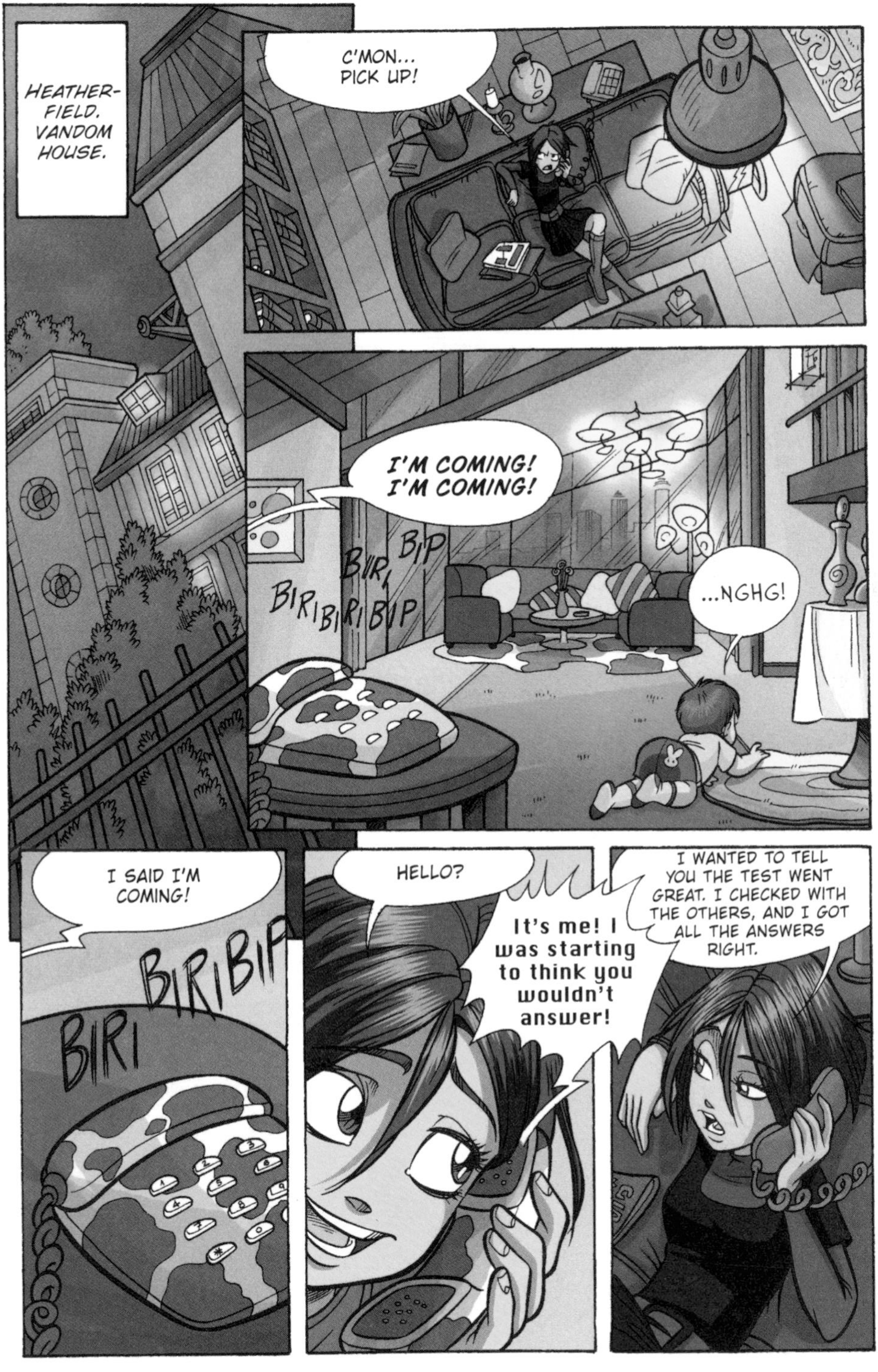
HEATHER-
FIELD.
VANDOM
HOUSE.
C'MON...
PICK UP!
I'M COMING!
I'M COMING!
BIRI BIP
BIRIBIRIBIP
...NGHG!
I SAID I'M
COMING!
BIRIBIP
BIRI
HELLO?
It's me! I
was starting
to think you
wouldn't
answer!
I WANTED TO TELL
YOU THE TEST WENT
GREAT. I CHECKED WITH
THE OTHERS, AND I GOT
ALL THE ANSWERS
RIGHT.

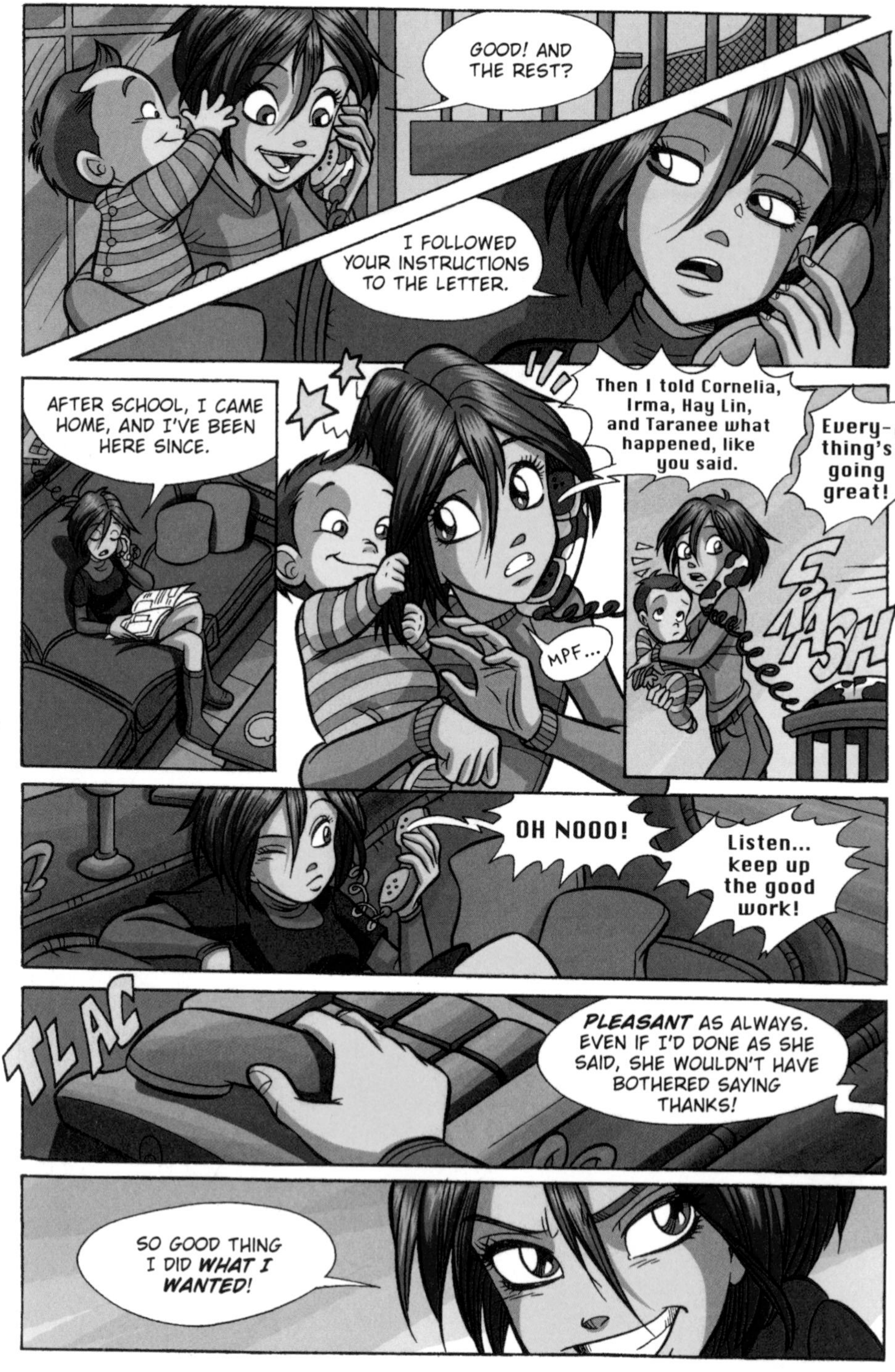
GOOD! AND THE REST?
I FOLLOWED YOUR INSTRUCTIONS TO THE LETTER.
AFTER SCHOOL, I CAME HOME, AND I'VE BEEN HERE SINCE.
Then I told Cornelia, Irma, Hay Lin, and Taranee what happened, like you said.
MPF...
Every-thing's going great!
CRASH
OH NOOO!
Listen... keep up the good work!
TLAC
PLEASANT AS ALWAYS. EVEN IF I'D DONE AS SHE SAID, SHE WOULDN'T HAVE BOTHERED SAYING THANKS!
SO GOOD THING I DID WHAT I WANTED!

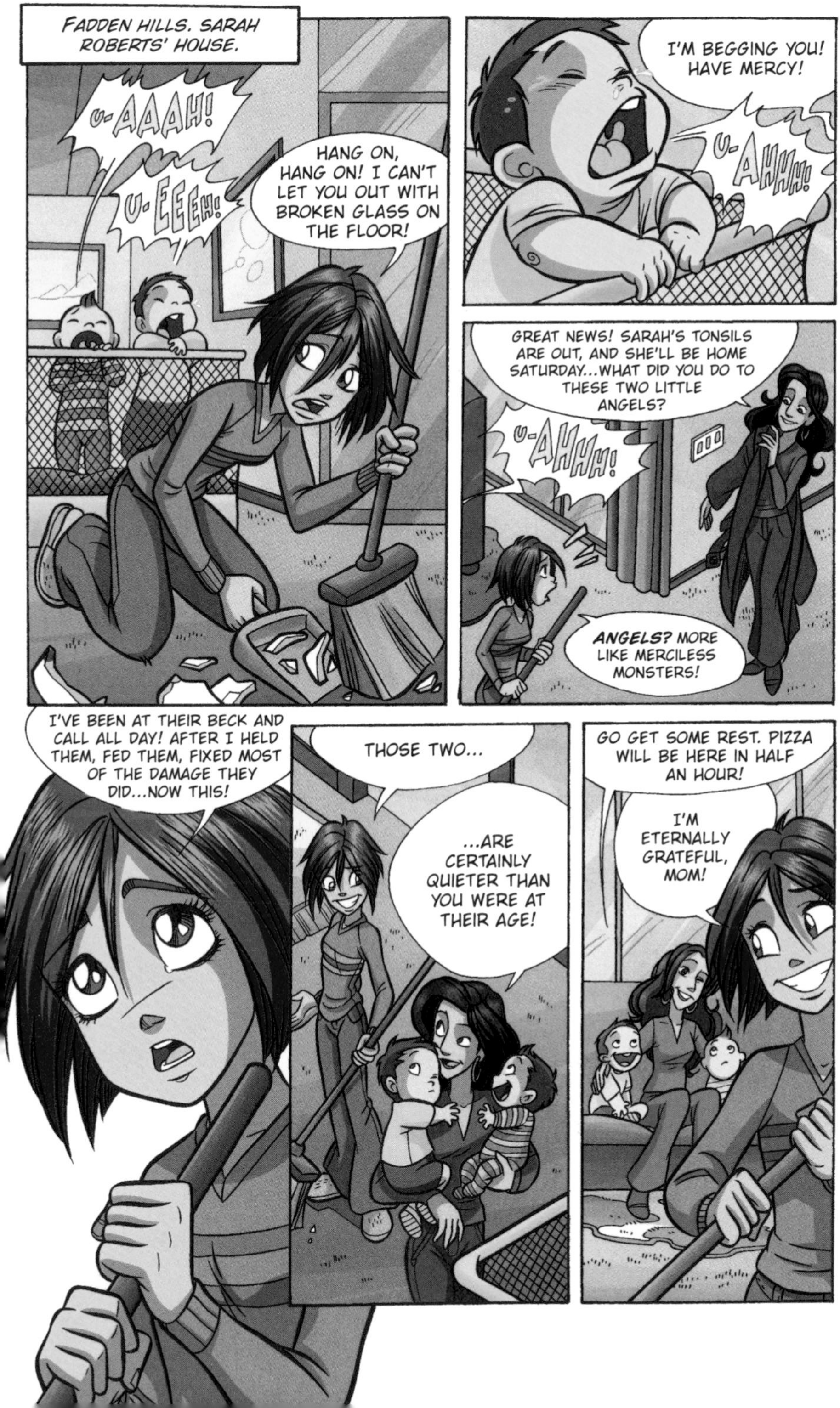

FADDEN HILLS. SARAH ROBERTS' HOUSE.
U-AAAH!
U-EEEH!
HANG ON, HANG ON! I CAN'T LET YOU OUT WITH BROKEN GLASS ON THE FLOOR!
I'M BEGGING YOU! HAVE MERCY!
U-AHHH!
GREAT NEWS! SARAH'S TONSILS ARE OUT, AND SHE'LL BE HOME SATURDAY...WHAT DID YOU DO TO THESE TWO LITTLE ANGELS?
U-AHHH!
ANGELS? MORE LIKE MERCILESS MONSTERS!
I'VE BEEN AT THEIR BECK AND CALL ALL DAY! AFTER I HELD THEM, FED THEM, FIXED MOST OF THE DAMAGE THEY DID...NOW THIS!
THOSE TWO...
...ARE CERTAINLY QUIETER THAN YOU WERE AT THEIR AGE!
GO GET SOME REST. PIZZA WILL BE HERE IN HALF AN HOUR!
I'M ETERNALLY GRATEFUL, MOM!

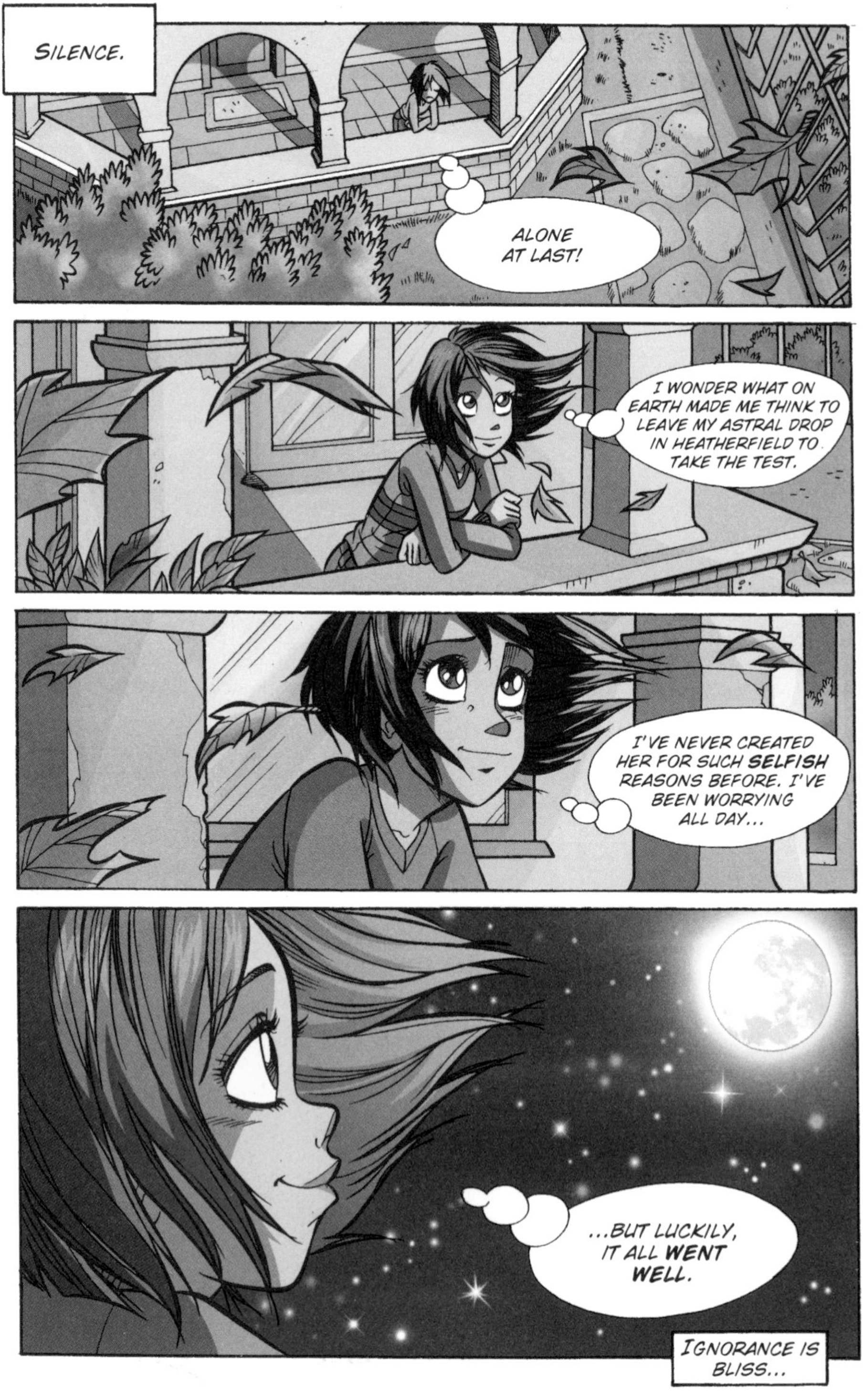
SILENCE.
ALONE AT LAST!
I WONDER WHAT ON EARTH MADE ME THINK TO LEAVE MY ASTRAL DROP IN HEATHERFIELD TO TAKE THE TEST.
I'VE NEVER CREATED HER FOR SUCH SELFISH REASONS BEFORE. I'VE BEEN WORRYING ALL DAY...
...BUT LUCKILY, IT ALL WENT WELL.
IGNORANCE IS BLISS...

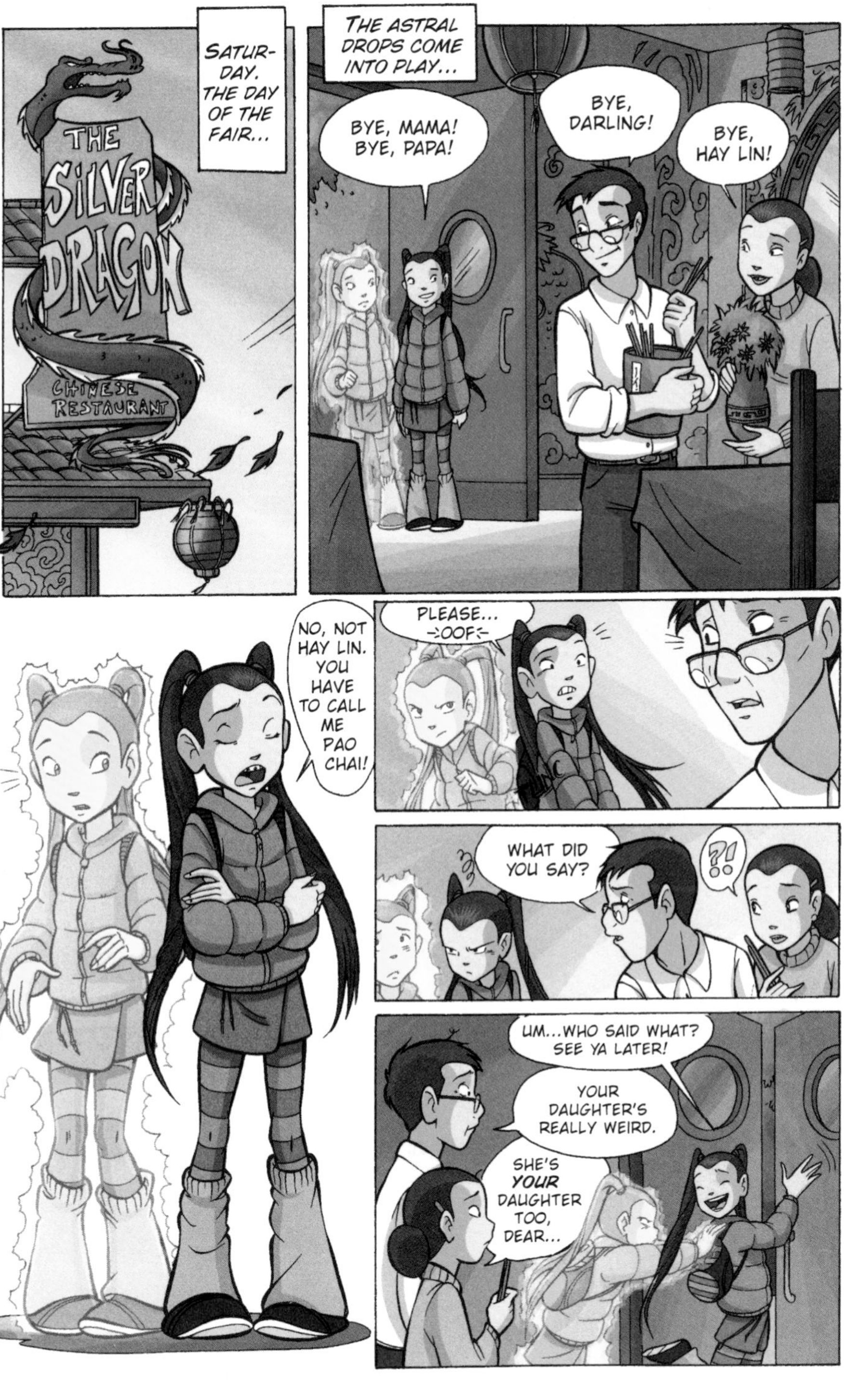
THE SILVER DRAGON
CHINESE RESTAURANT
SATURDAY. THE DAY OF THE FAIR...
THE ASTRAL DROPS COME INTO PLAY...
BYE, MAMA! BYE, PAPA!
BYE, DARLING!
BYE, HAY LIN!
NO, NOT HAY LIN. YOU HAVE TO CALL ME PAO CHAI!
PLEASE... OOF
WHAT DID YOU SAY?
?!
UM...WHO SAID WHAT? SEE YA LATER!
YOUR DAUGHTER'S REALLY WEIRD.
SHE'S *YOUR* DAUGHTER TOO, DEAR...

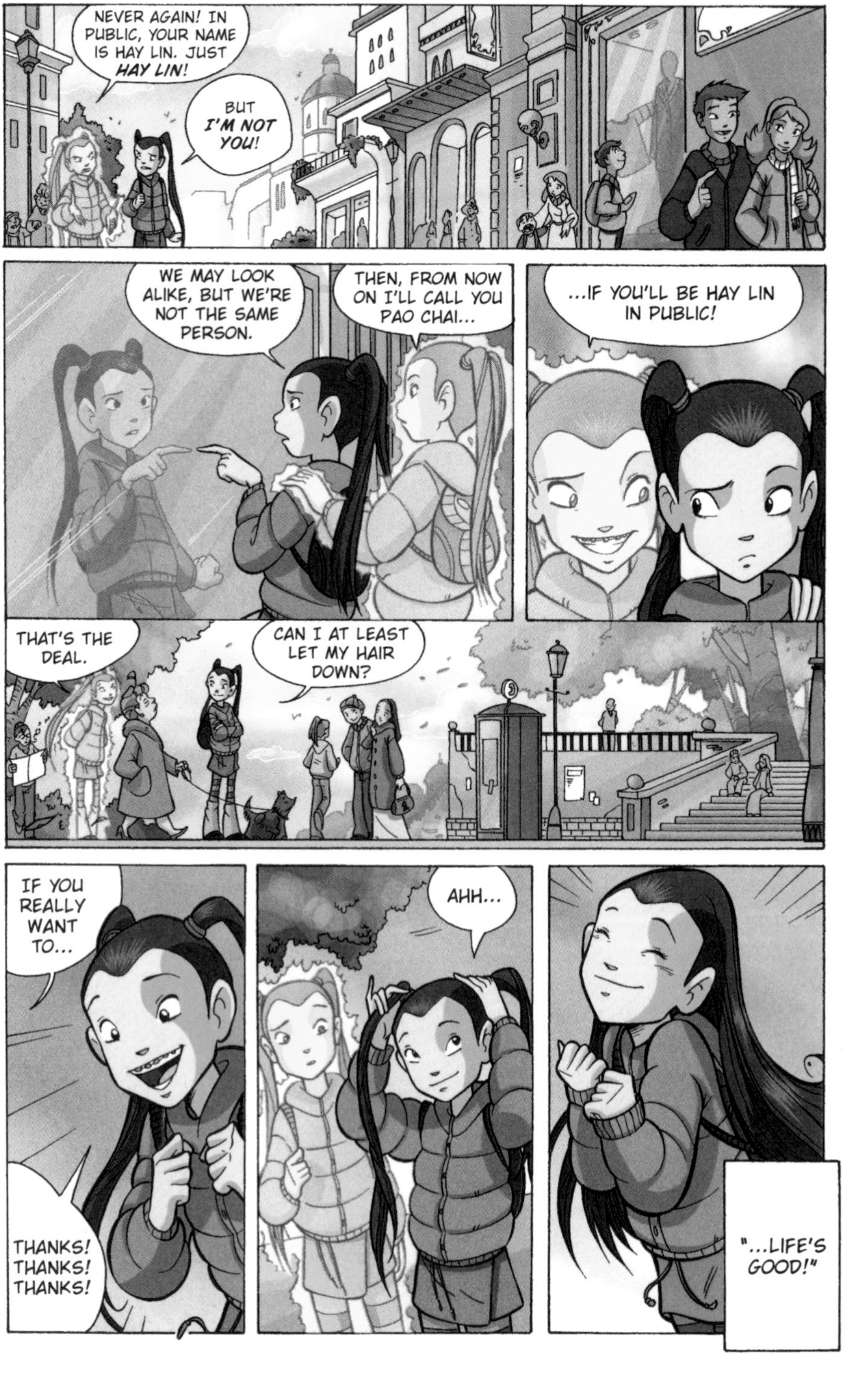
NEVER AGAIN! IN PUBLIC, YOUR NAME IS HAY LIN. JUST HAY LIN!
BUT I'M NOT YOU!
WE MAY LOOK ALIKE, BUT WE'RE NOT THE SAME PERSON.
THEN, FROM NOW ON I'LL CALL YOU PAO CHAI...
...IF YOU'LL BE HAY LIN IN PUBLIC!
THAT'S THE DEAL.
CAN I AT LEAST LET MY HAIR DOWN?
IF YOU REALLY WANT TO...
THANKS! THANKS! THANKS!
AHH...
"...LIFE'S GOOD!"

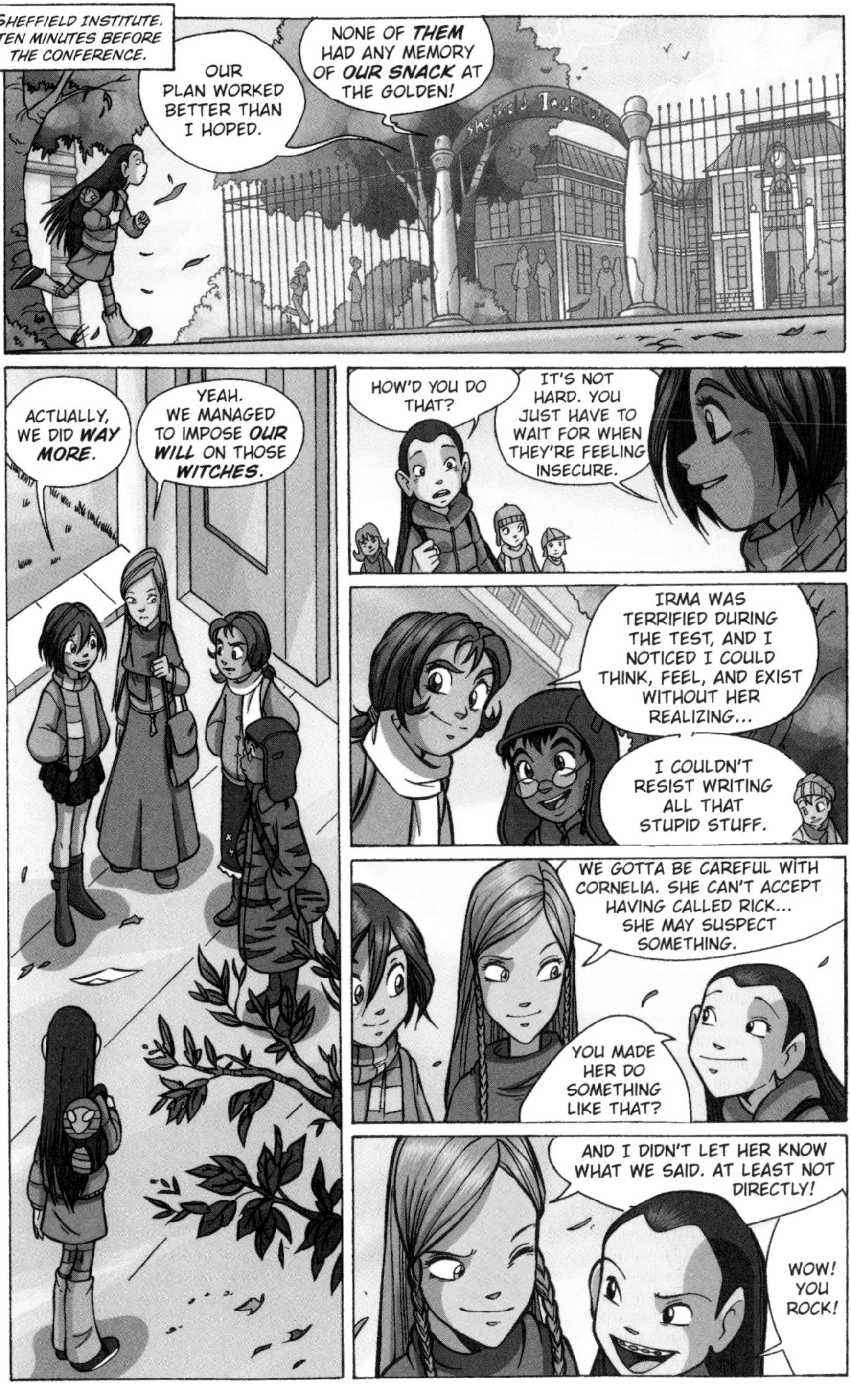
SHEFFIELD INSTITUTE. TEN MINUTES BEFORE THE CONFERENCE.
OUR PLAN WORKED BETTER THAN I HOPED.
NONE OF **THEM** HAD ANY MEMORY OF **OUR SNACK** AT THE GOLDEN!
ACTUALLY, WE DID **WAY MORE**.
YEAH. WE MANAGED TO IMPOSE **OUR WILL** ON THOSE **WITCHES**.
HOW'D YOU DO THAT?
IT'S NOT HARD. YOU JUST HAVE TO WAIT FOR WHEN THEY'RE FEELING INSECURE.
IRMA WAS TERRIFIED DURING THE TEST, AND I NOTICED I COULD THINK, FEEL, AND EXIST WITHOUT HER REALIZING...
I COULDN'T RESIST WRITING ALL THAT STUPID STUFF.
WE GOTTA BE CAREFUL WITH CORNELIA. SHE CAN'T ACCEPT HAVING CALLED RICK... SHE MAY SUSPECT SOMETHING.
YOU MADE HER DO SOMETHING LIKE THAT?
AND I DIDN'T LET HER KNOW WHAT WE SAID. AT LEAST NOT DIRECTLY!
WOW! YOU ROCK!

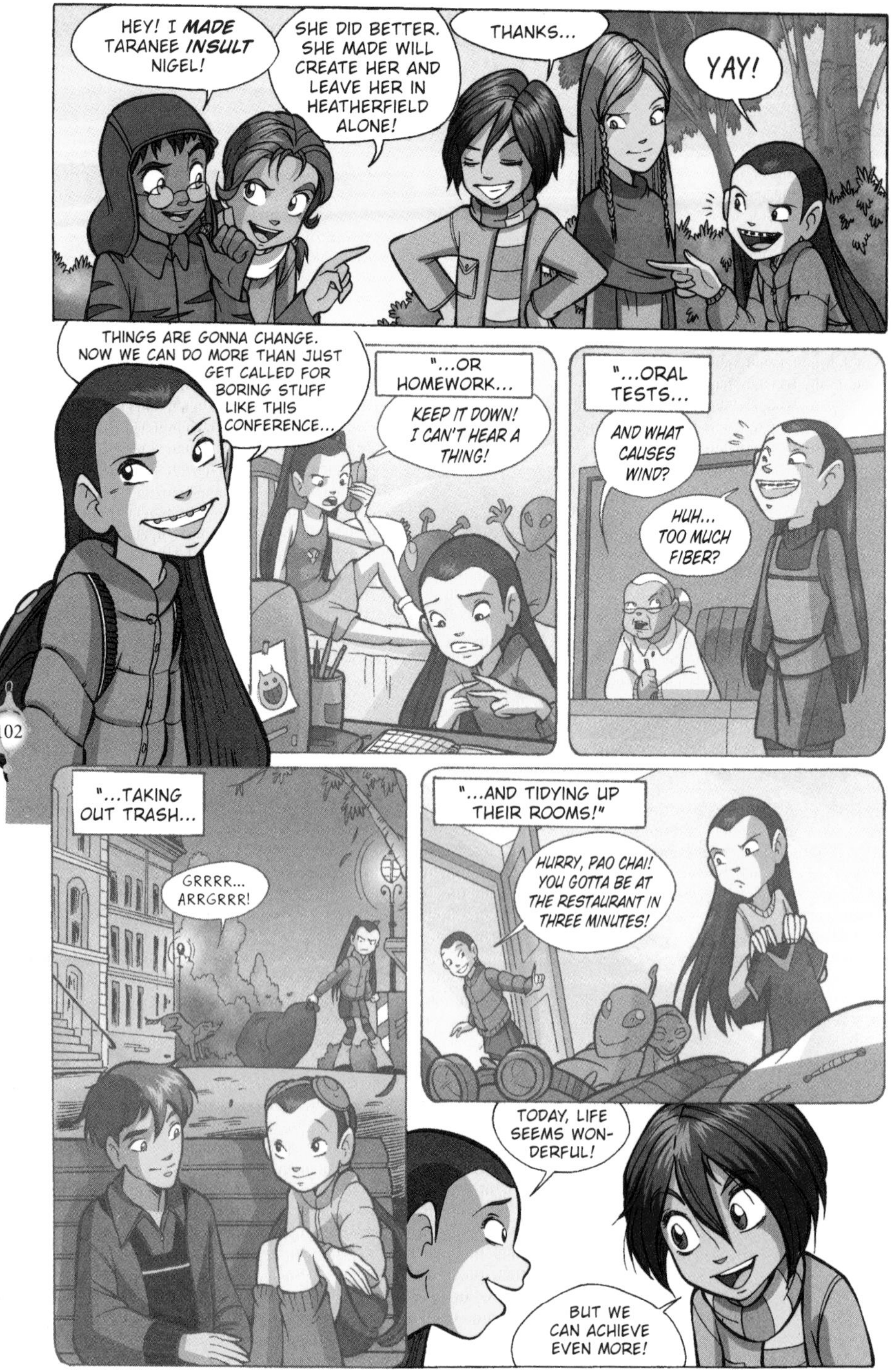

HEY! I MADE TARANEE INSULT NIGEL!
SHE DID BETTER. SHE MADE WILL CREATE HER AND LEAVE HER IN HEATHERFIELD ALONE!
THANKS...
YAY!
THINGS ARE GONNA CHANGE. NOW WE CAN DO MORE THAN JUST GET CALLED FOR BORING STUFF LIKE THIS CONFERENCE...
"...OR HOMEWORK...
KEEP IT DOWN! I CAN'T HEAR A THING!
"...ORAL TESTS...
AND WHAT CAUSES WIND?
HUH... TOO MUCH FIBER?
"...TAKING OUT TRASH...
GRRRR... ARRGRRR!
"...AND TIDYING UP THEIR ROOMS!"
HURRY, PAO CHAI! YOU GOTTA BE AT THE RESTAURANT IN THREE MINUTES!
TODAY, LIFE SEEMS WON-DERFUL!
BUT WE CAN ACHIEVE EVEN MORE!

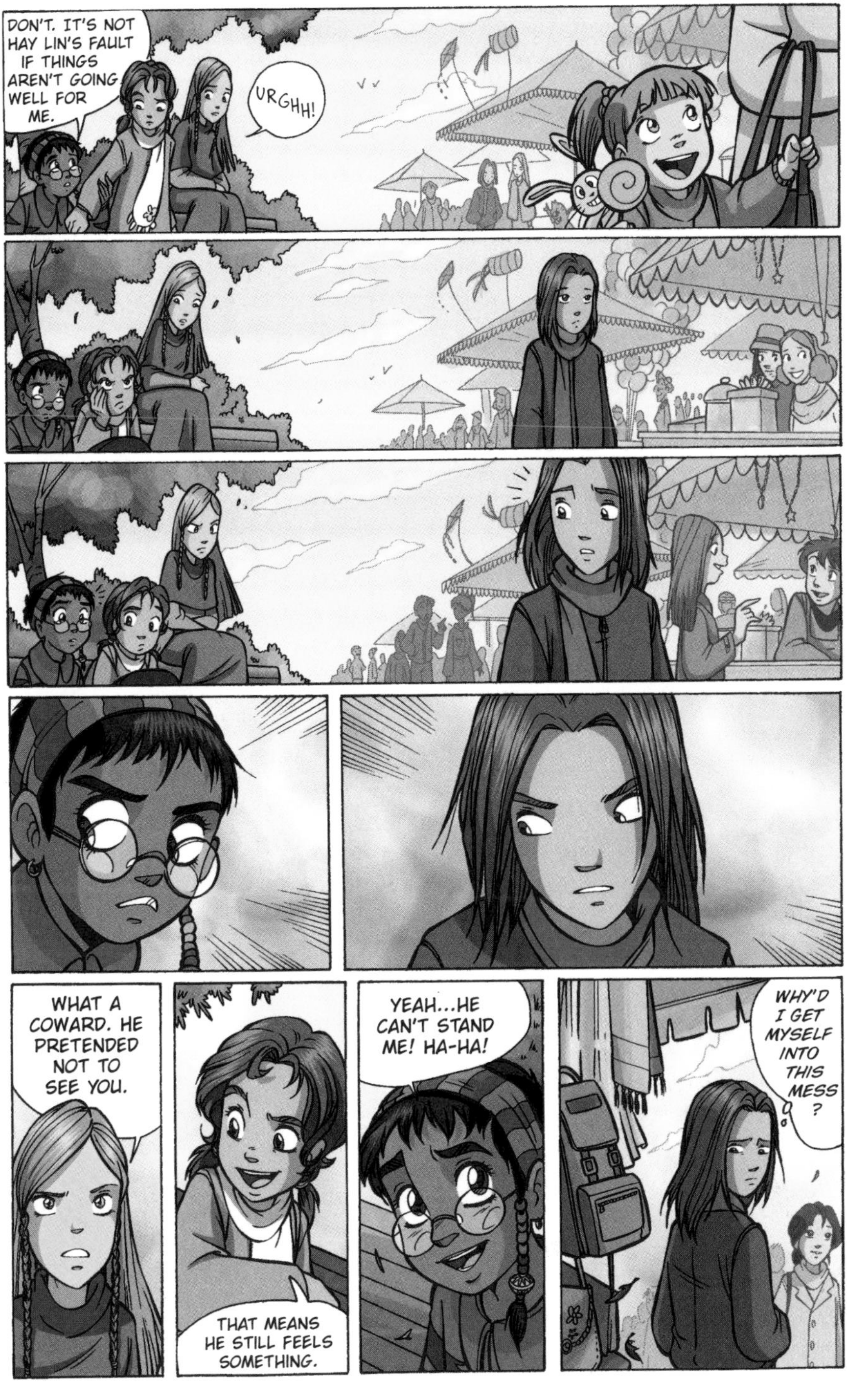
DON'T. IT'S NOT HAY LIN'S FAULT IF THINGS AREN'T GOING WELL FOR ME.
URGHH!
WHAT A COWARD. HE PRETENDED NOT TO SEE YOU.
THAT MEANS HE STILL FEELS SOMETHING.
YEAH...HE CAN'T STAND ME! HA-HA!
WHY'D I GET MYSELF INTO THIS MESS?

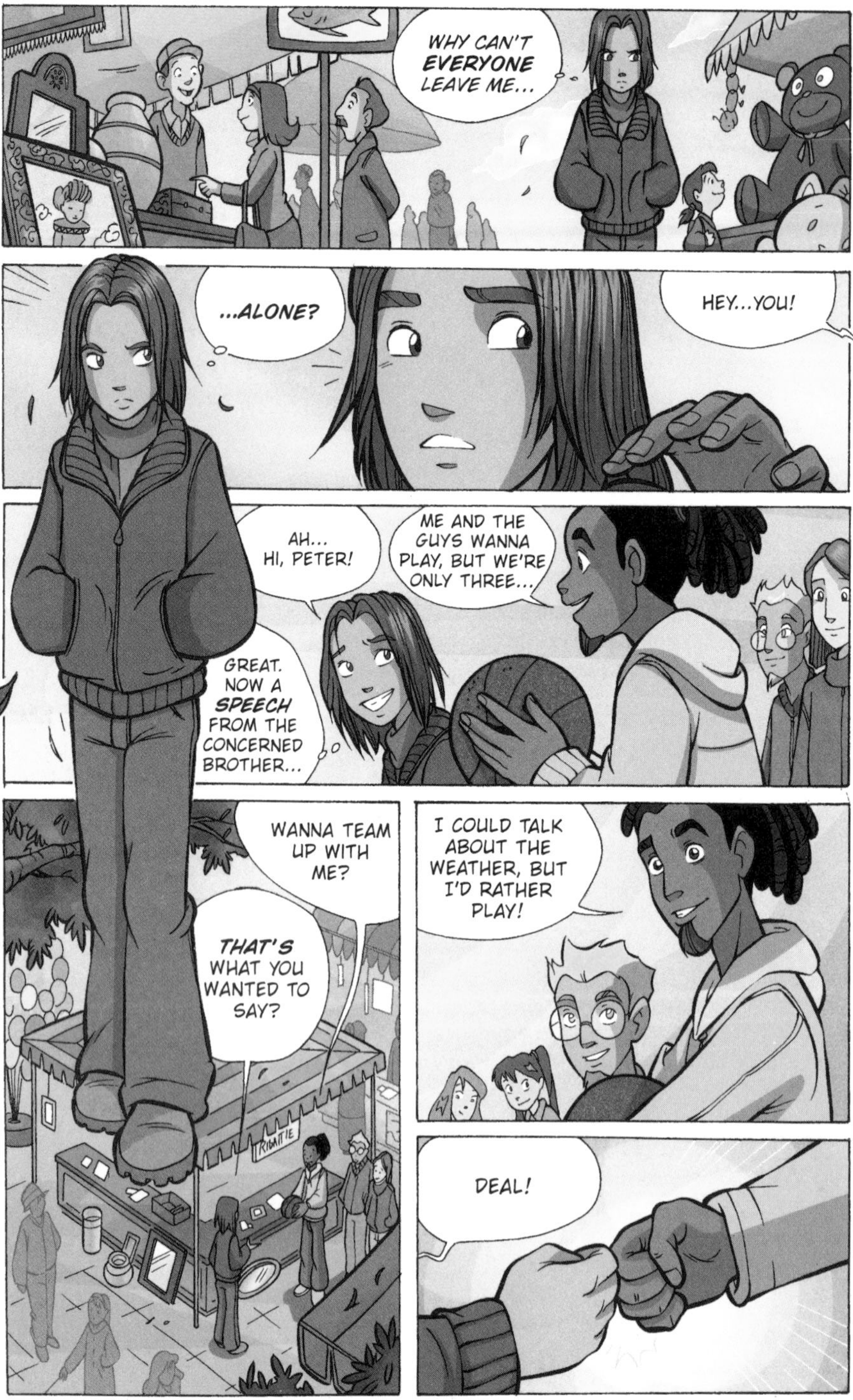
WHY CAN'T EVERYONE LEAVE ME...
...ALONE?
HEY...YOU!
AH... HI, PETER!
ME AND THE GUYS WANNA PLAY, BUT WE'RE ONLY THREE...
GREAT. NOW A SPEECH FROM THE CONCERNED BROTHER...
WANNA TEAM UP WITH ME?
THAT'S WHAT YOU WANTED TO SAY?
I COULD TALK ABOUT THE WEATHER, BUT I'D RATHER PLAY!
DEAL!

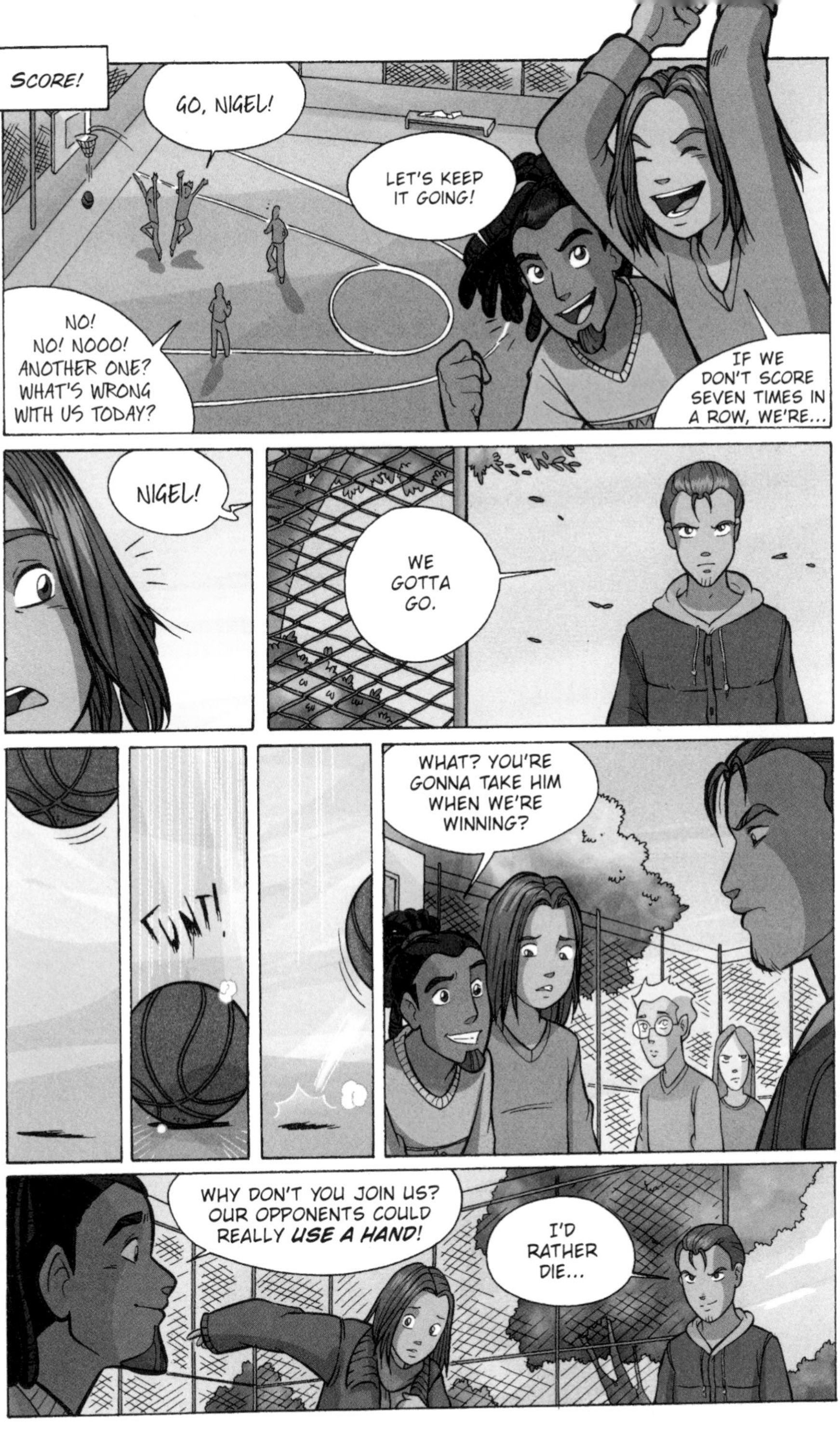
SCORE!
GO, NIGEL!
LET'S KEEP IT GOING!
NO! NO! NOOO! ANOTHER ONE? WHAT'S WRONG WITH US TODAY?
IF WE DON'T SCORE SEVEN TIMES IN A ROW, WE'RE...
NIGEL!
WE GOTTA GO.
TUNK!
WHAT? YOU'RE GONNA TAKE HIM WHEN WE'RE WINNING?
WHY DON'T YOU JOIN US? OUR OPPONENTS COULD REALLY USE A HAND!
I'D RATHER DIE...

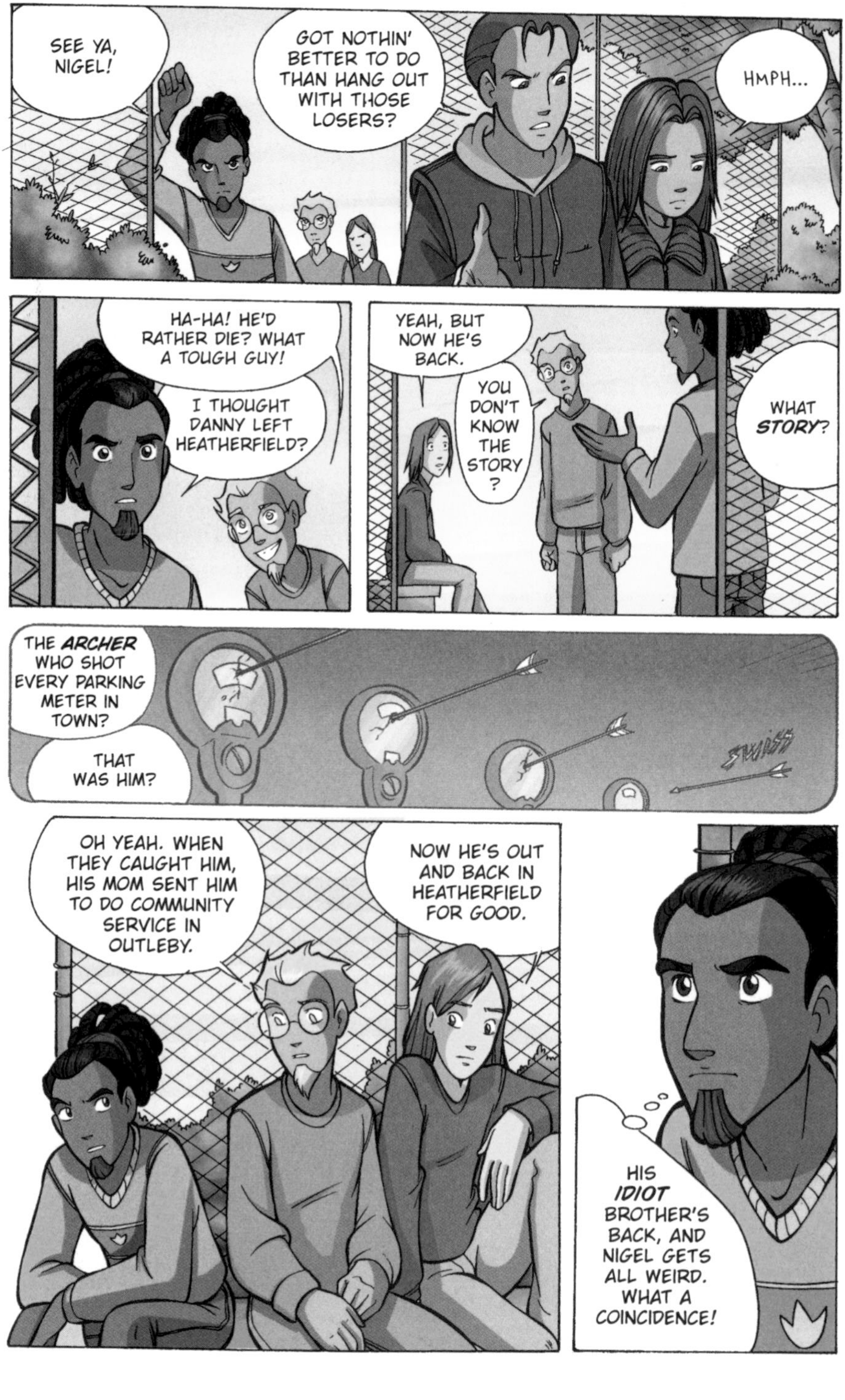
SEE YA, NIGEL!
GOT NOTHIN' BETTER TO DO THAN HANG OUT WITH THOSE LOSERS?
HMPH...
HA-HA! HE'D RATHER DIE? WHAT A TOUGH GUY!
I THOUGHT DANNY LEFT HEATHERFIELD?
YEAH, BUT NOW HE'S BACK.
YOU DON'T KNOW THE STORY?
WHAT STORY?
THE ARCHER WHO SHOT EVERY PARKING METER IN TOWN?
THAT WAS HIM?
OH YEAH. WHEN THEY CAUGHT HIM, HIS MOM SENT HIM TO DO COMMUNITY SERVICE IN OUTLEBY.
NOW HE'S OUT AND BACK IN HEATHERFIELD FOR GOOD.
HIS IDIOT BROTHER'S BACK, AND NIGEL GETS ALL WEIRD. WHAT A COINCIDENCE!

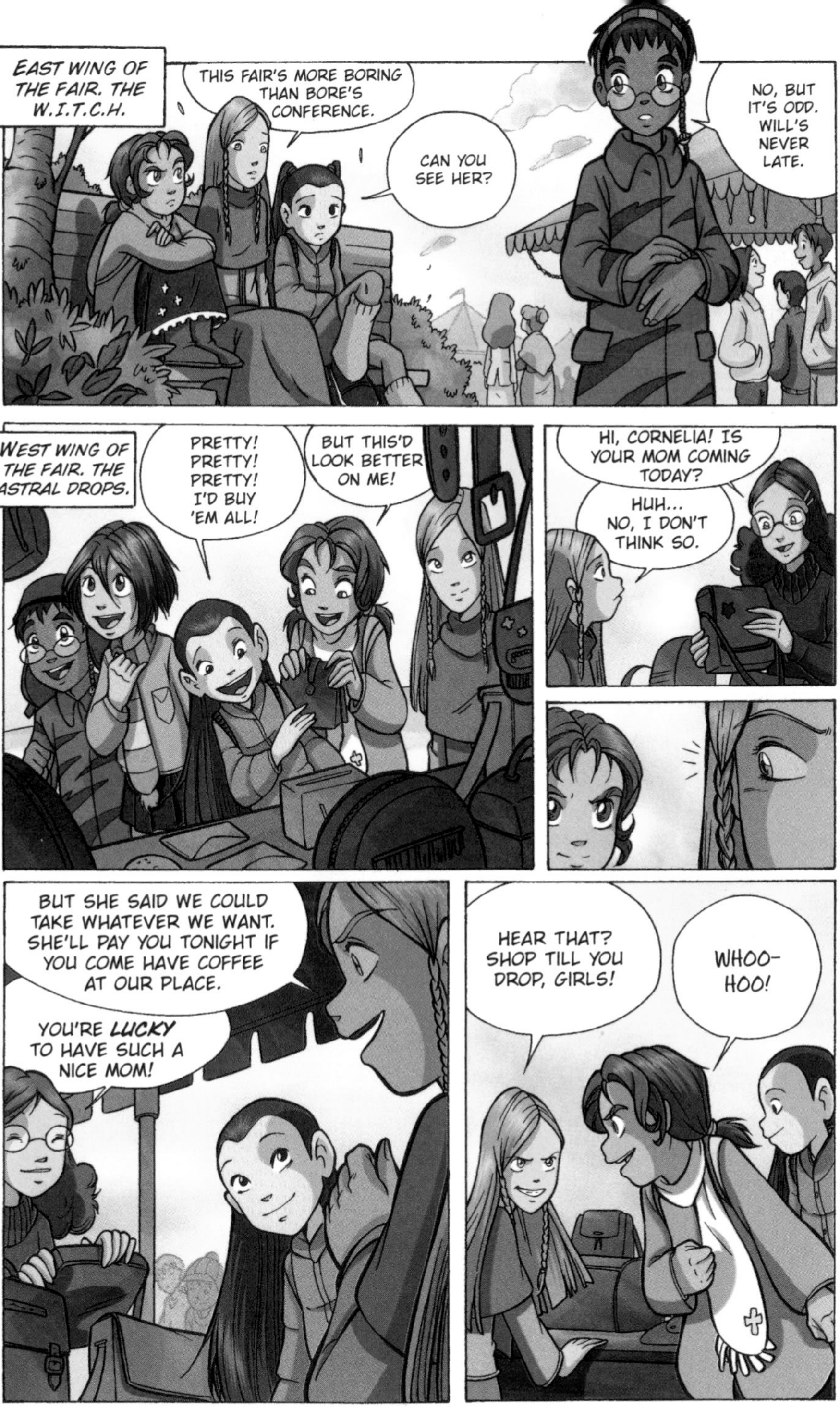
EAST WING OF THE FAIR. THE W.I.T.C.H.
THIS FAIR'S MORE BORING THAN BORE'S CONFERENCE.
CAN YOU SEE HER?
NO, BUT IT'S ODD. WILL'S NEVER LATE.
WEST WING OF THE FAIR. THE ASTRAL DROPS.
PRETTY! PRETTY! PRETTY! I'D BUY 'EM ALL!
BUT THIS'D LOOK BETTER ON ME!
HI, CORNELIA! IS YOUR MOM COMING TODAY?
HUH... NO, I DON'T THINK SO.
BUT SHE SAID WE COULD TAKE WHATEVER WE WANT. SHE'LL PAY YOU TONIGHT IF YOU COME HAVE COFFEE AT OUR PLACE.
YOU'RE LUCKY TO HAVE SUCH A NICE MOM!
HEAR THAT? SHOP TILL YOU DROP, GIRLS!
WHOO-HOO!

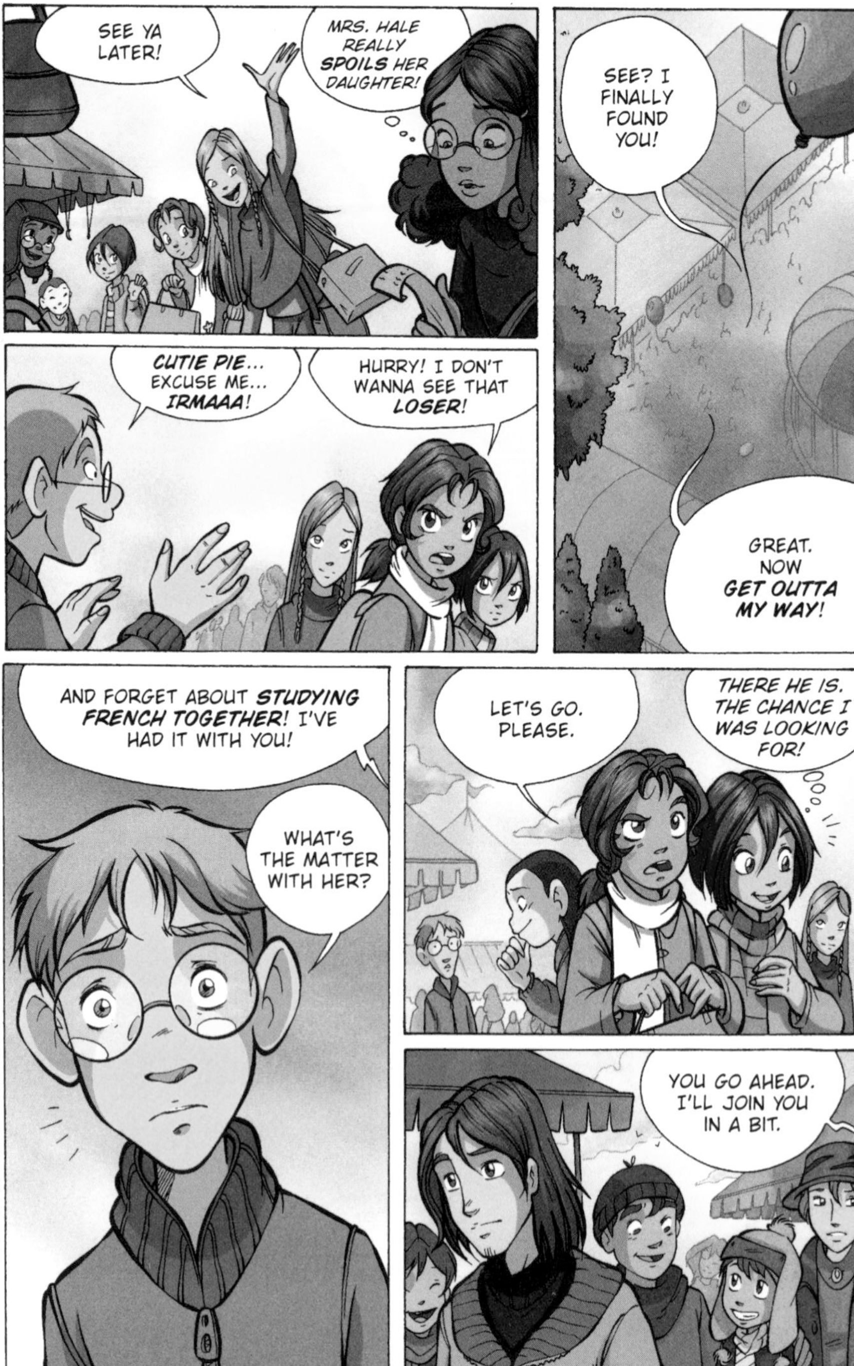
SEE YA LATER!
MRS. HALE REALLY **SPOILS** HER DAUGHTER!
SEE? I FINALLY FOUND YOU!
GREAT. NOW ***GET OUTTA MY WAY!***
CUTIE PIE... EXCUSE ME... ***IRMAAA!***
HURRY! I DON'T WANNA SEE THAT ***LOSER!***
AND FORGET ABOUT ***STUDYING FRENCH TOGETHER!*** I'VE HAD IT WITH YOU!
WHAT'S THE MATTER WITH HER?
LET'S GO. PLEASE.
THERE HE IS. THE CHANCE I WAS LOOKING FOR!
YOU GO AHEAD. I'LL JOIN YOU IN A BIT.

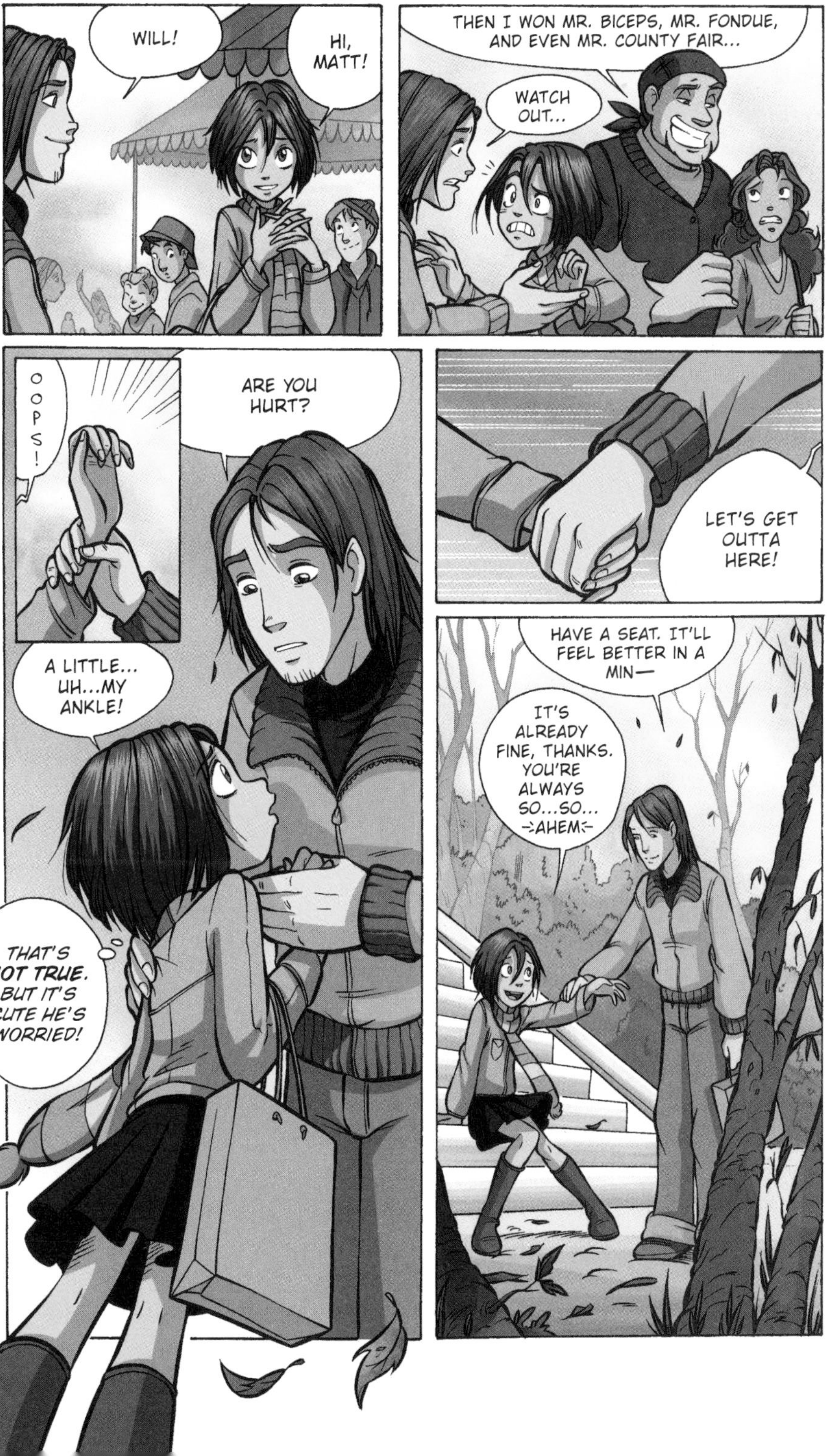
WILL!
HI, MATT!
THEN I WON MR. BICEPS, MR. FONDUE, AND EVEN MR. COUNTY FAIR...
WATCH OUT...
OOPS!
ARE YOU HURT?
A LITTLE... UH...MY ANKLE!
THAT'S **NOT TRUE.** BUT IT'S CUTE HE'S WORRIED!
LET'S GET OUTTA HERE!
HAVE A SEAT. IT'LL FEEL BETTER IN A MIN—
IT'S ALREADY FINE, THANKS. YOU'RE ALWAYS SO...SO... AHEM

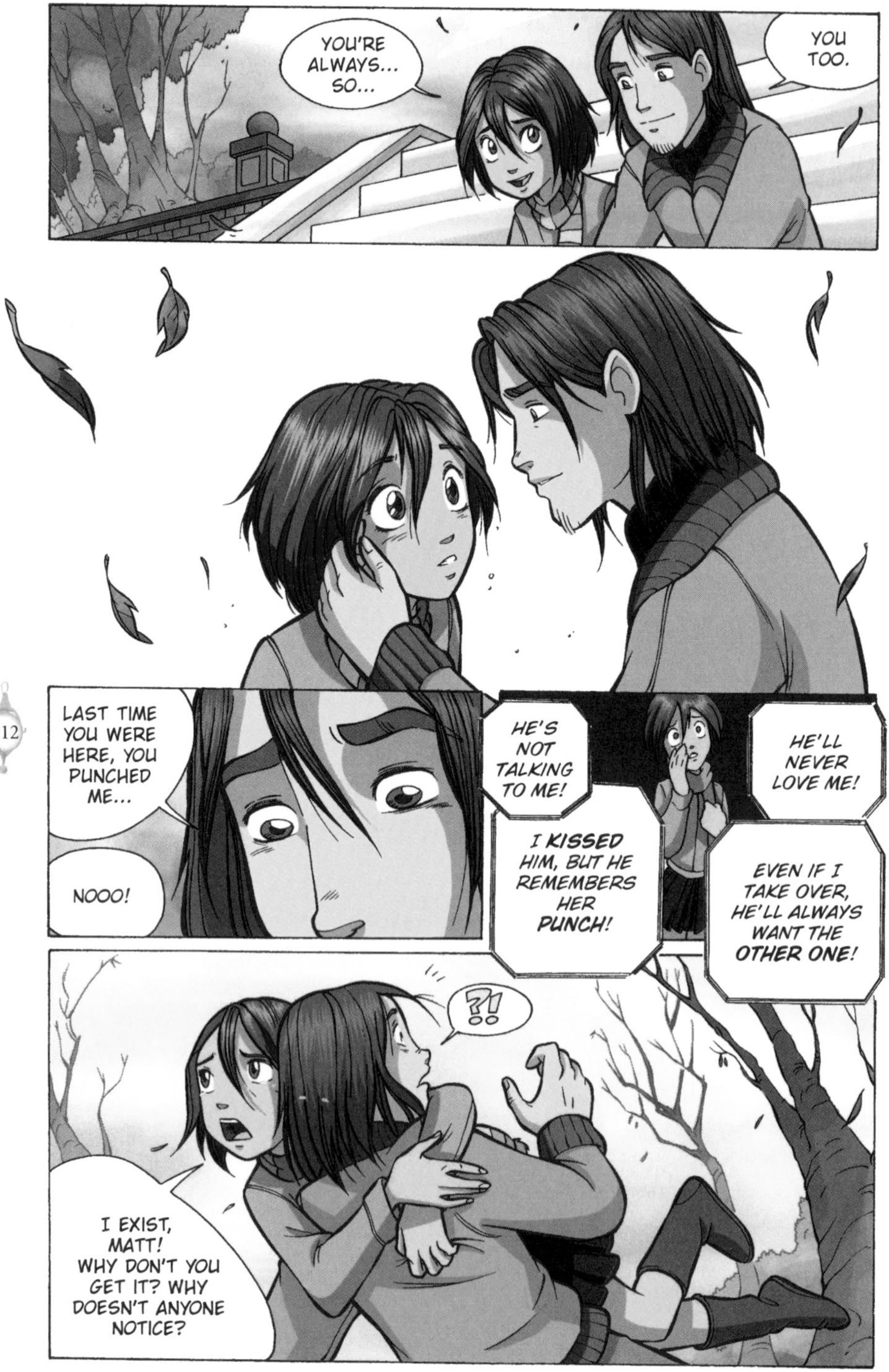
YOU'RE ALWAYS... SO...
YOU TOO.
LAST TIME YOU WERE HERE, YOU PUNCHED ME...
NOOO!
HE'S NOT TALKING TO ME!
I KISSED HIM, BUT HE REMEMBERS HER PUNCH!
HE'LL NEVER LOVE ME!
EVEN IF I TAKE OVER, HE'LL ALWAYS WANT THE OTHER ONE!
?!
I EXIST, MATT! WHY DON'T YOU GET IT? WHY DOESN'T ANYONE NOTICE?

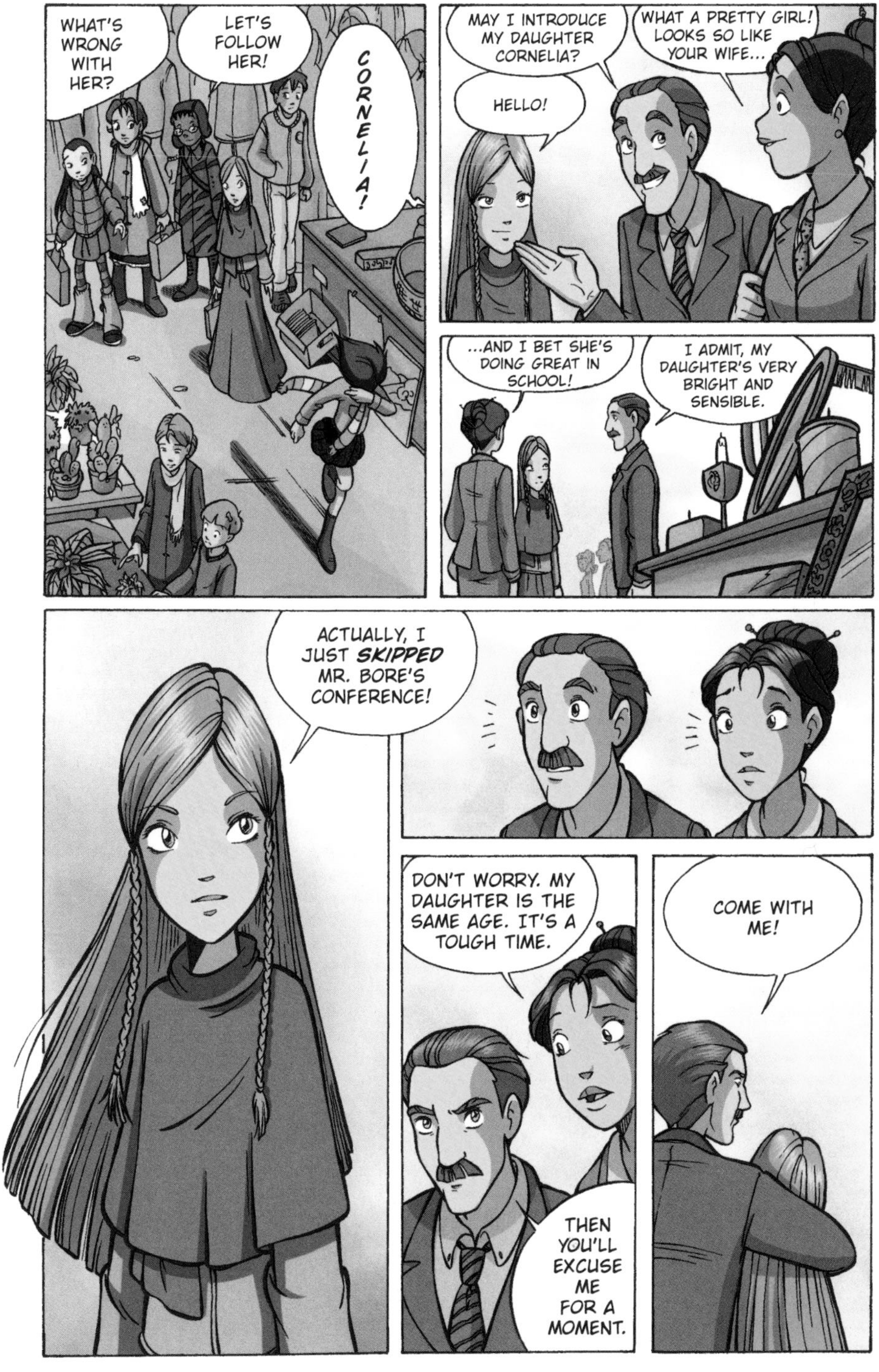
WHAT'S WRONG WITH HER?
LET'S FOLLOW HER!
CORNELIA!
MAY I INTRODUCE MY DAUGHTER CORNELIA?
HELLO!
WHAT A PRETTY GIRL! LOOKS SO LIKE YOUR WIFE...
...AND I BET SHE'S DOING GREAT IN SCHOOL!
I ADMIT, MY DAUGHTER'S VERY BRIGHT AND SENSIBLE.
ACTUALLY, I JUST SKIPPED MR. BORE'S CONFERENCE!
DON'T WORRY. MY DAUGHTER IS THE SAME AGE. IT'S A TOUGH TIME.
THEN YOU'LL EXCUSE ME FOR A MOMENT.
COME WITH ME!

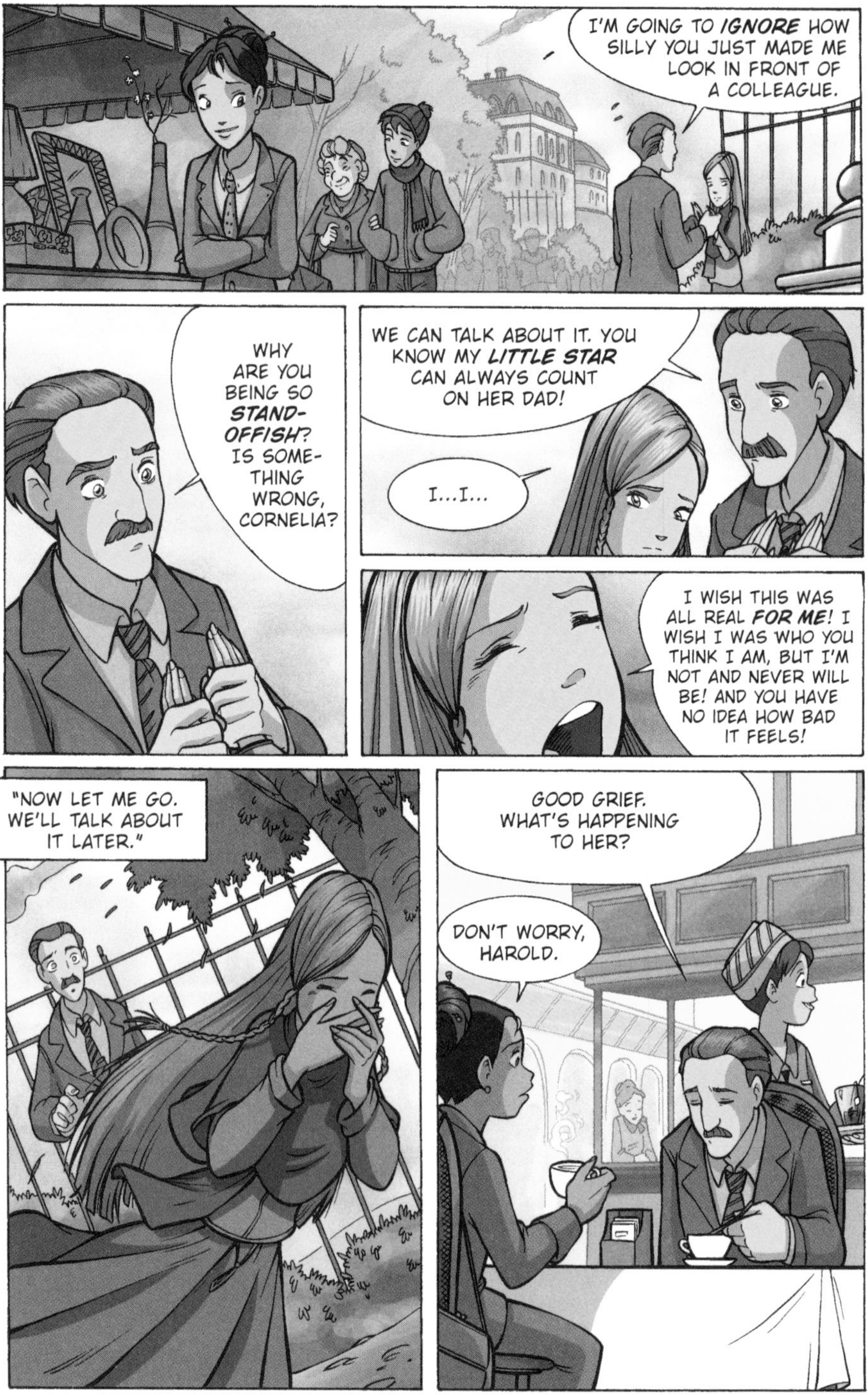
I'M GOING TO ***IGNORE*** HOW SILLY YOU JUST MADE ME LOOK IN FRONT OF A COLLEAGUE.
WHY ARE YOU BEING SO ***STAND-OFFISH***? IS SOMETHING WRONG, CORNELIA?
WE CAN TALK ABOUT IT. YOU KNOW MY ***LITTLE STAR*** CAN ALWAYS COUNT ON HER DAD!
I...I...
I WISH THIS WAS ALL REAL ***FOR ME!*** I WISH I WAS WHO YOU THINK I AM, BUT I'M NOT AND NEVER WILL BE! AND YOU HAVE NO IDEA HOW BAD IT FEELS!
"NOW LET ME GO. WE'LL TALK ABOUT IT LATER."
GOOD GRIEF. WHAT'S HAPPENING TO HER?
DON'T WORRY, HAROLD.

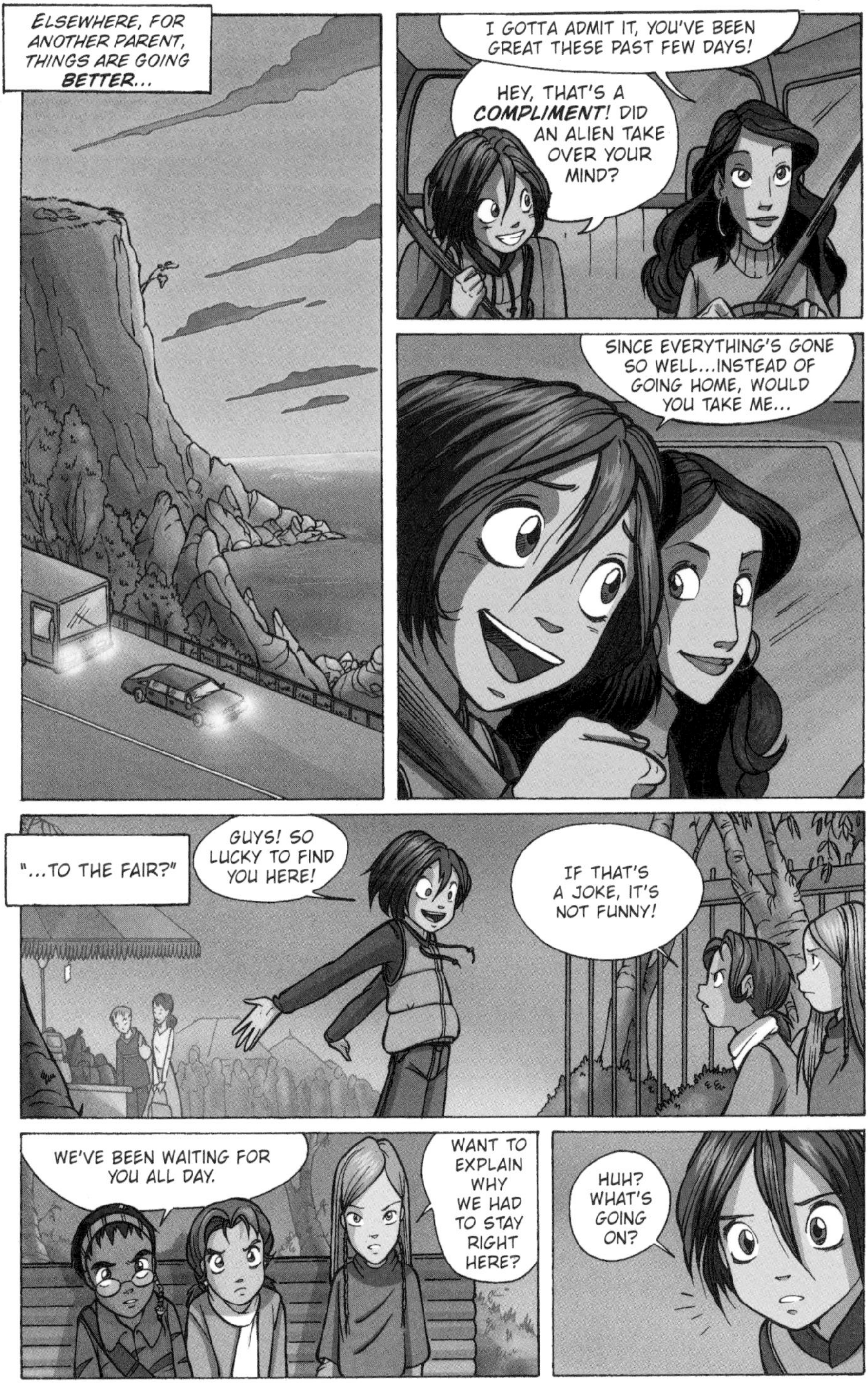
ELSEWHERE, FOR ANOTHER PARENT, THINGS ARE GOING **BETTER**...
I GOTTA ADMIT IT, YOU'VE BEEN GREAT THESE PAST FEW DAYS!
HEY, THAT'S A **COMPLIMENT**! DID AN ALIEN TAKE OVER YOUR MIND?
SINCE EVERYTHING'S GONE SO WELL...INSTEAD OF GOING HOME, WOULD YOU TAKE ME...
"...TO THE FAIR?"
GUYS! SO LUCKY TO FIND YOU HERE!
IF THAT'S A JOKE, IT'S NOT FUNNY!
WE'VE BEEN WAITING FOR YOU ALL DAY.
WANT TO EXPLAIN WHY WE HAD TO STAY RIGHT HERE?
HUH? WHAT'S GOING ON?

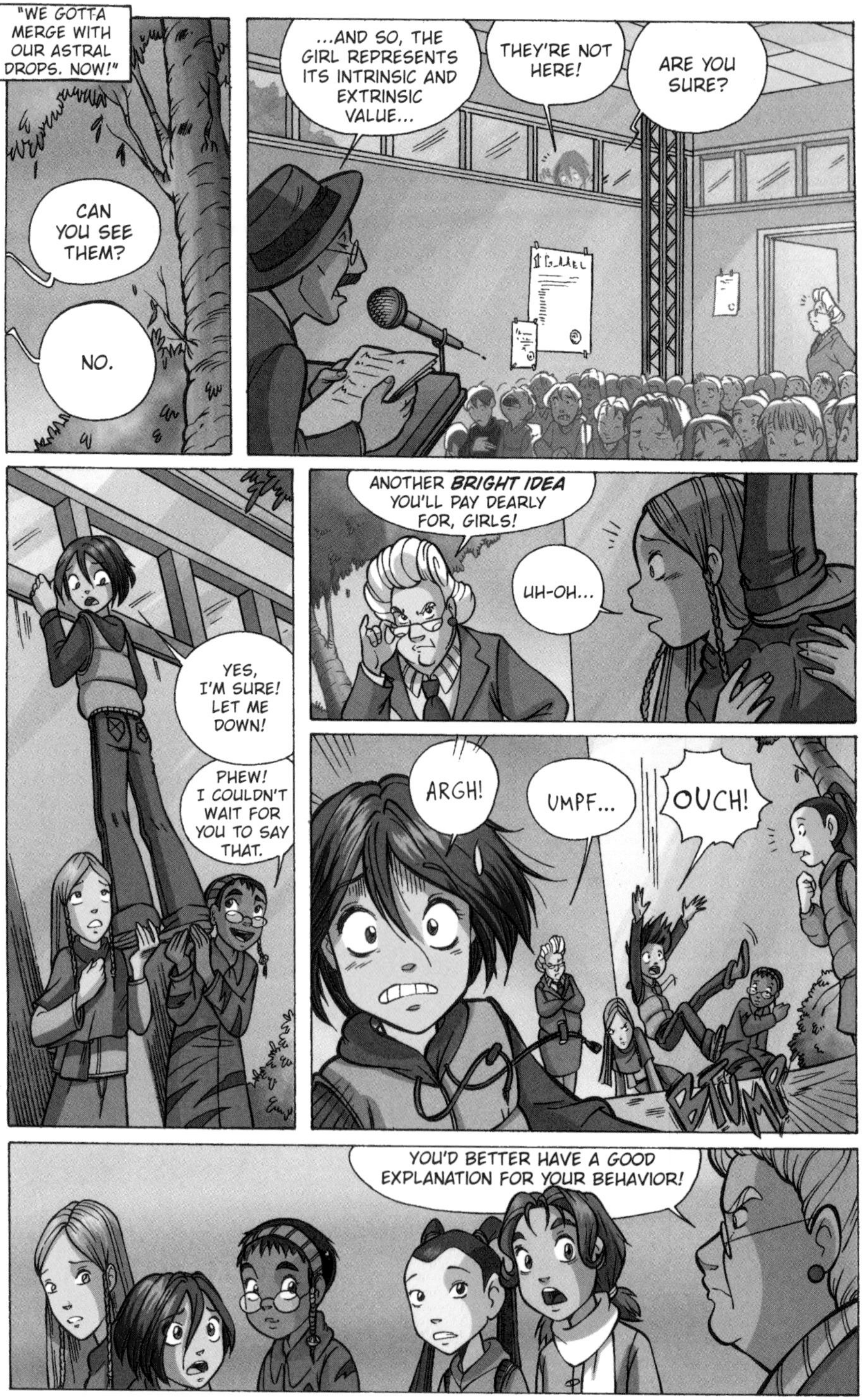
"WE GOTTA MERGE WITH OUR ASTRAL DROPS. NOW!"
CAN YOU SEE THEM?
NO.
...AND SO, THE GIRL REPRESENTS ITS INTRINSIC AND EXTRINSIC VALUE...
THEY'RE NOT HERE!
ARE YOU SURE?
YES, I'M SURE! LET ME DOWN!
PHEW! I COULDN'T WAIT FOR YOU TO SAY THAT.
ANOTHER BRIGHT IDEA YOU'LL PAY DEARLY FOR, GIRLS!
UH-OH...
ARGH!
UMPF...
OUCH!
BATUMP
YOU'D BETTER HAVE A GOOD EXPLANATION FOR YOUR BEHAVIOR!

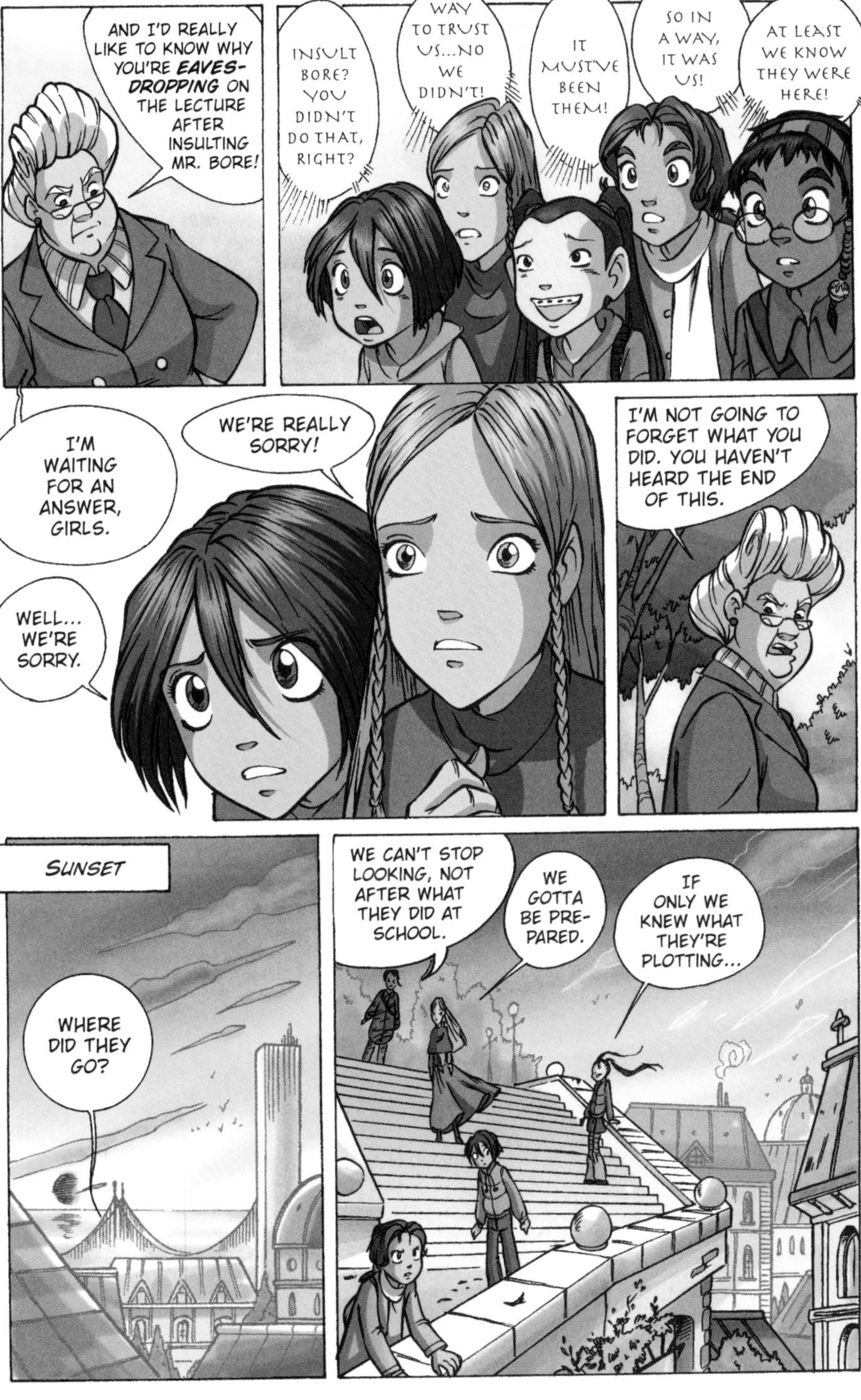
AND I'D REALLY LIKE TO KNOW WHY YOU'RE **EAVES-DROPPING** ON THE LECTURE AFTER INSULTING MR. BORE!
INSULT BORE? YOU DIDN'T DO THAT, RIGHT?
WAY TO TRUST US...NO WE DIDN'T!
IT MUST'VE BEEN THEM!
SO IN A WAY, IT WAS US!
AT LEAST WE KNOW THEY WERE HERE!
I'M WAITING FOR AN ANSWER, GIRLS.
WE'RE REALLY SORRY!
WELL... WE'RE SORRY.
I'M NOT GOING TO FORGET WHAT YOU DID. YOU HAVEN'T HEARD THE END OF THIS.
SUNSET
WHERE DID THEY GO?
WE CAN'T STOP LOOKING, NOT AFTER WHAT THEY DID AT SCHOOL.
WE GOTTA BE PRE-PARED.
IF ONLY WE KNEW WHAT THEY'RE PLOTTING...

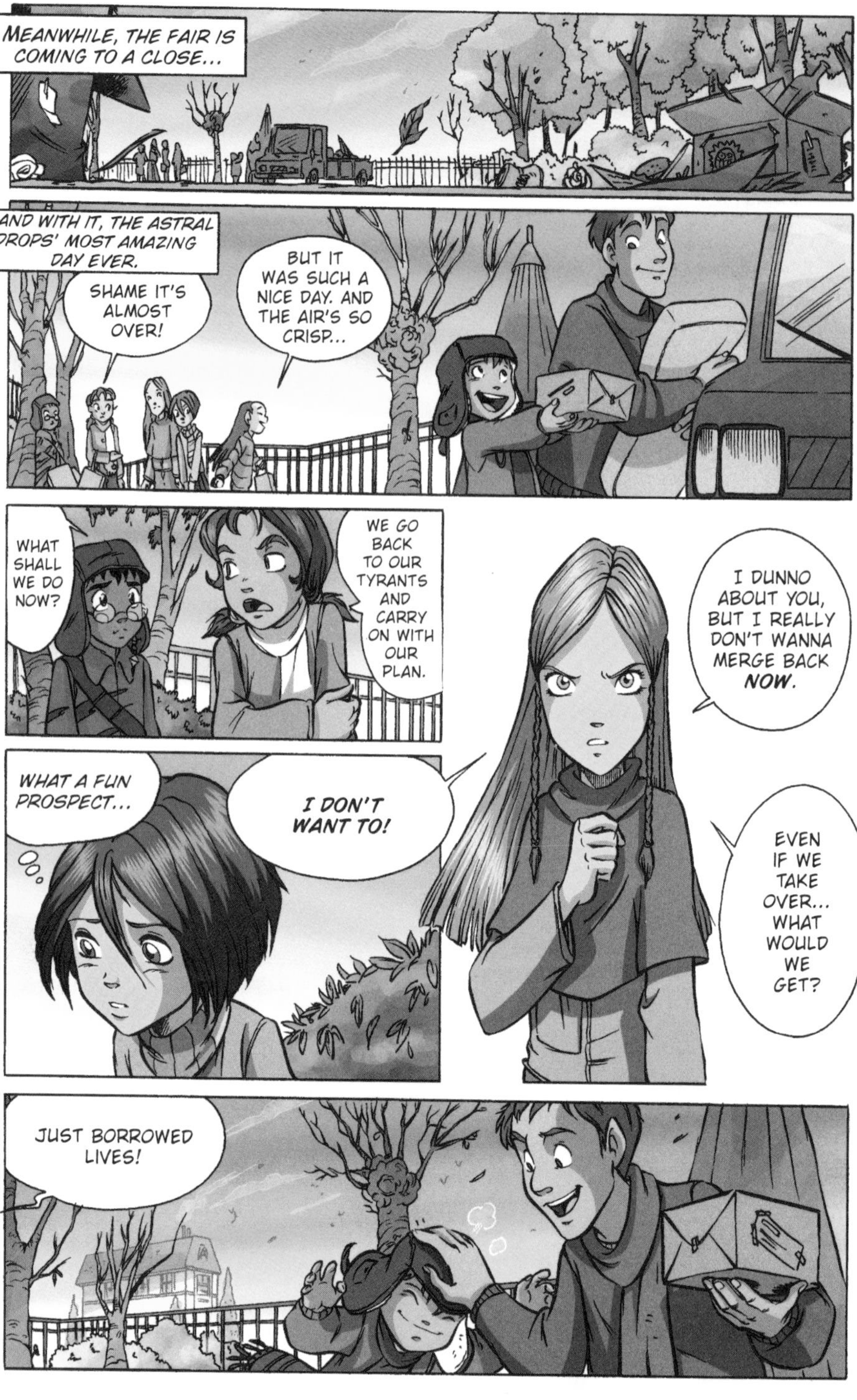
MEANWHILE, THE FAIR IS COMING TO A CLOSE...
...AND WITH IT, THE ASTRAL DROPS' MOST AMAZING DAY EVER.
SHAME IT'S ALMOST OVER!
BUT IT WAS SUCH A NICE DAY. AND THE AIR'S SO CRISP...
WHAT SHALL WE DO NOW?
WE GO BACK TO OUR TYRANTS AND CARRY ON WITH OUR PLAN.
I DUNNO ABOUT YOU, BUT I REALLY DON'T WANNA MERGE BACK NOW.
WHAT A FUN PROSPECT...
I DON'T WANT TO!
EVEN IF WE TAKE OVER... WHAT WOULD WE GET?
JUST BORROWED LIVES!

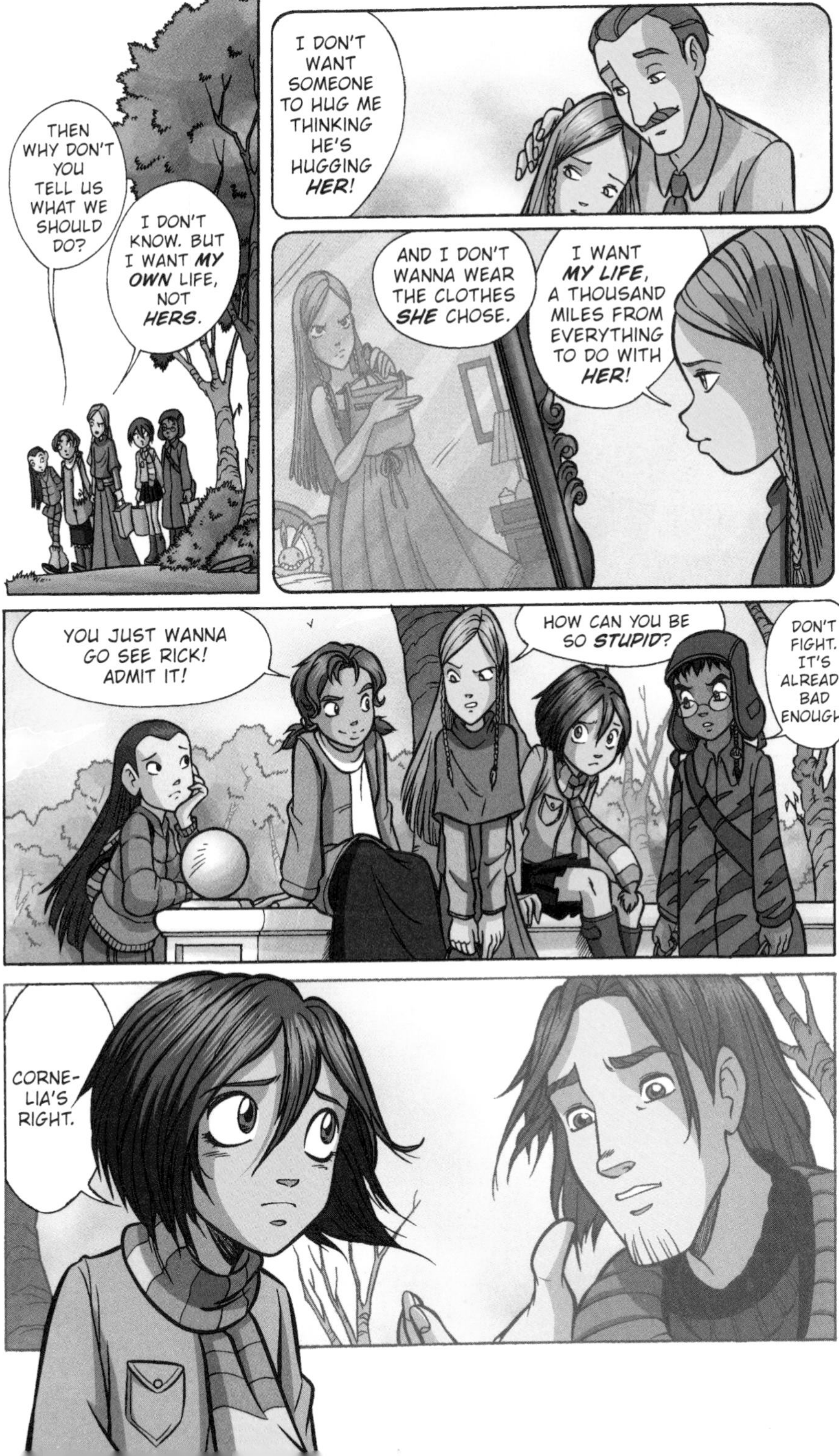
THEN WHY DON'T YOU TELL US WHAT WE SHOULD DO?
I DON'T KNOW. BUT I WANT MY OWN LIFE, NOT HERS.
I DON'T WANT SOMEONE TO HUG ME THINKING HE'S HUGGING HER!
AND I DON'T WANNA WEAR THE CLOTHES SHE CHOSE.
I WANT MY LIFE, A THOUSAND MILES FROM EVERYTHING TO DO WITH HER!
YOU JUST WANNA GO SEE RICK! ADMIT IT!
HOW CAN YOU BE SO STUPID?
DON'T FIGHT. IT'S ALREADY BAD ENOUGH.
CORNE-LIA'S RIGHT.

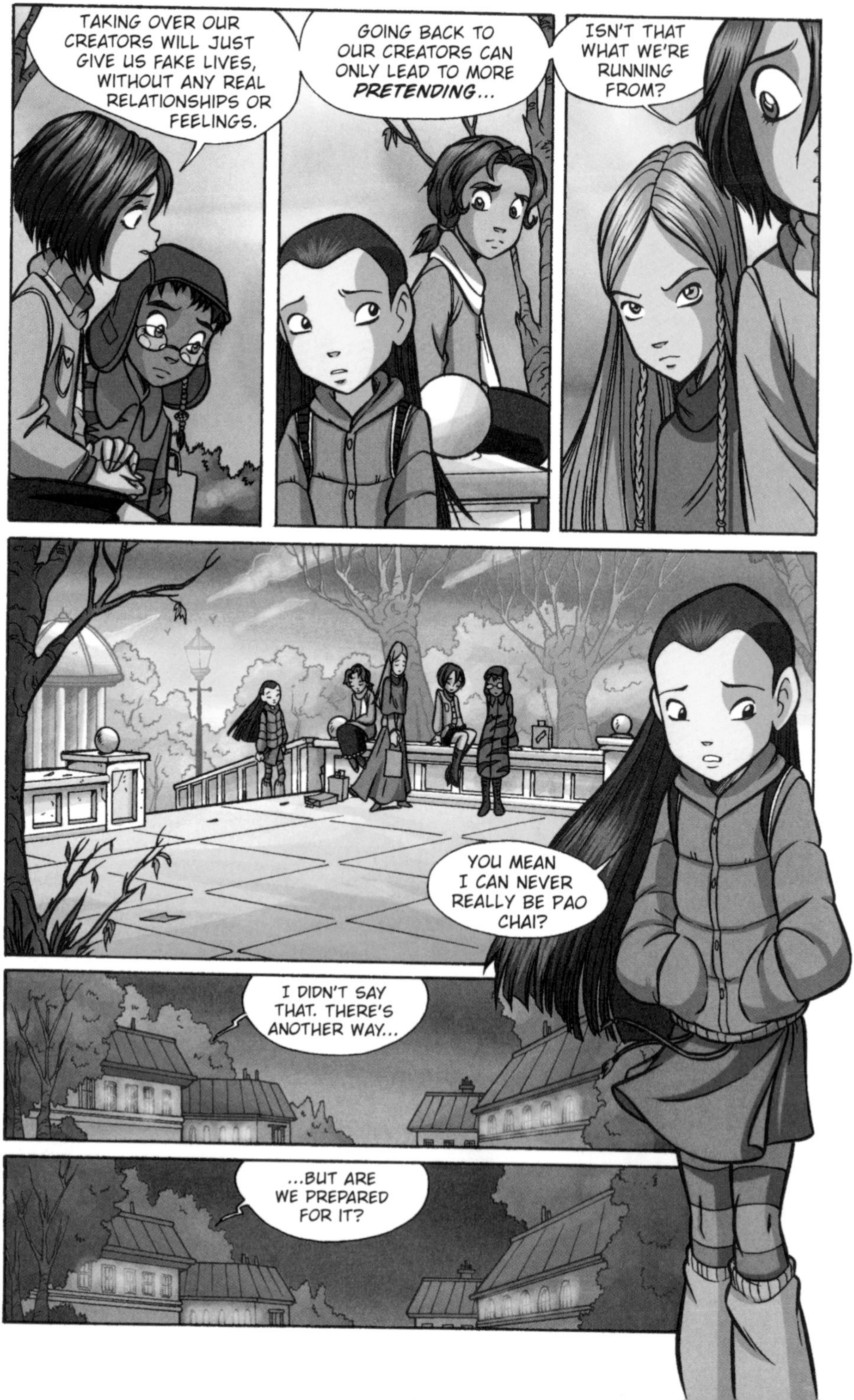
TAKING OVER OUR CREATORS WILL JUST GIVE US FAKE LIVES, WITHOUT ANY REAL RELATIONSHIPS OR FEELINGS.
GOING BACK TO OUR CREATORS CAN ONLY LEAD TO MORE *PRETENDING*...
ISN'T THAT WHAT WE'RE RUNNING FROM?
YOU MEAN I CAN NEVER REALLY BE PAO CHAI?
I DIDN'T SAY THAT. THERE'S ANOTHER WAY...
...BUT ARE WE PREPARED FOR IT?

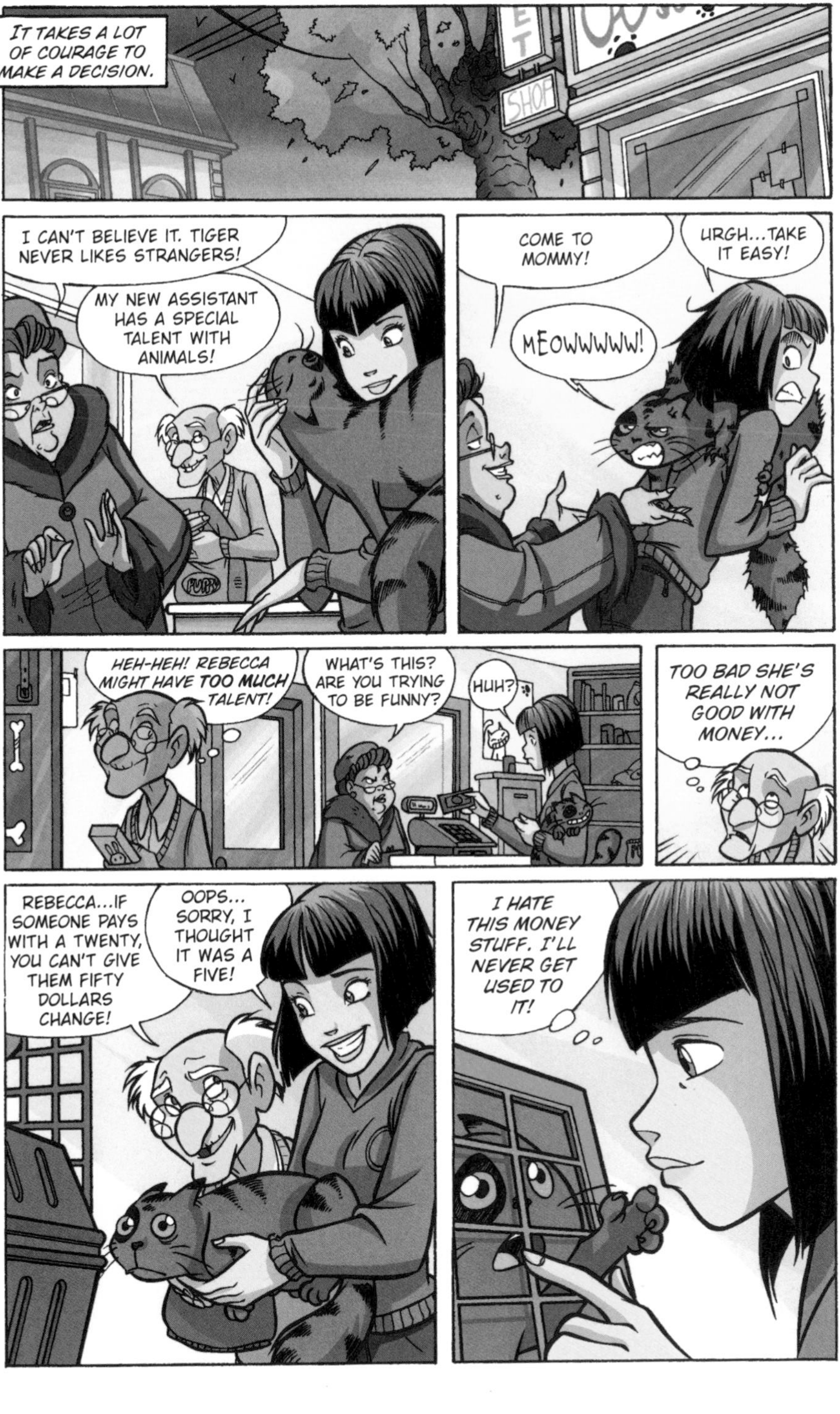

IT TAKES A LOT OF COURAGE TO MAKE A DECISION.
SHOP
I CAN'T BELIEVE IT. TIGER NEVER LIKES STRANGERS!
MY NEW ASSISTANT HAS A SPECIAL TALENT WITH ANIMALS!
PUPPY
COME TO MOMMY!
URGH...TAKE IT EASY!
MEOWWWWW!
HEH-HEH! REBECCA MIGHT HAVE TOO MUCH TALENT!
WHAT'S THIS? ARE YOU TRYING TO BE FUNNY?
HUH?
TOO BAD SHE'S REALLY NOT GOOD WITH MONEY...
REBECCA...IF SOMEONE PAYS WITH A TWENTY, YOU CAN'T GIVE THEM FIFTY DOLLARS CHANGE!
OOPS... SORRY, I THOUGHT IT WAS A FIVE!
I HATE THIS MONEY STUFF. I'LL NEVER GET USED TO IT!

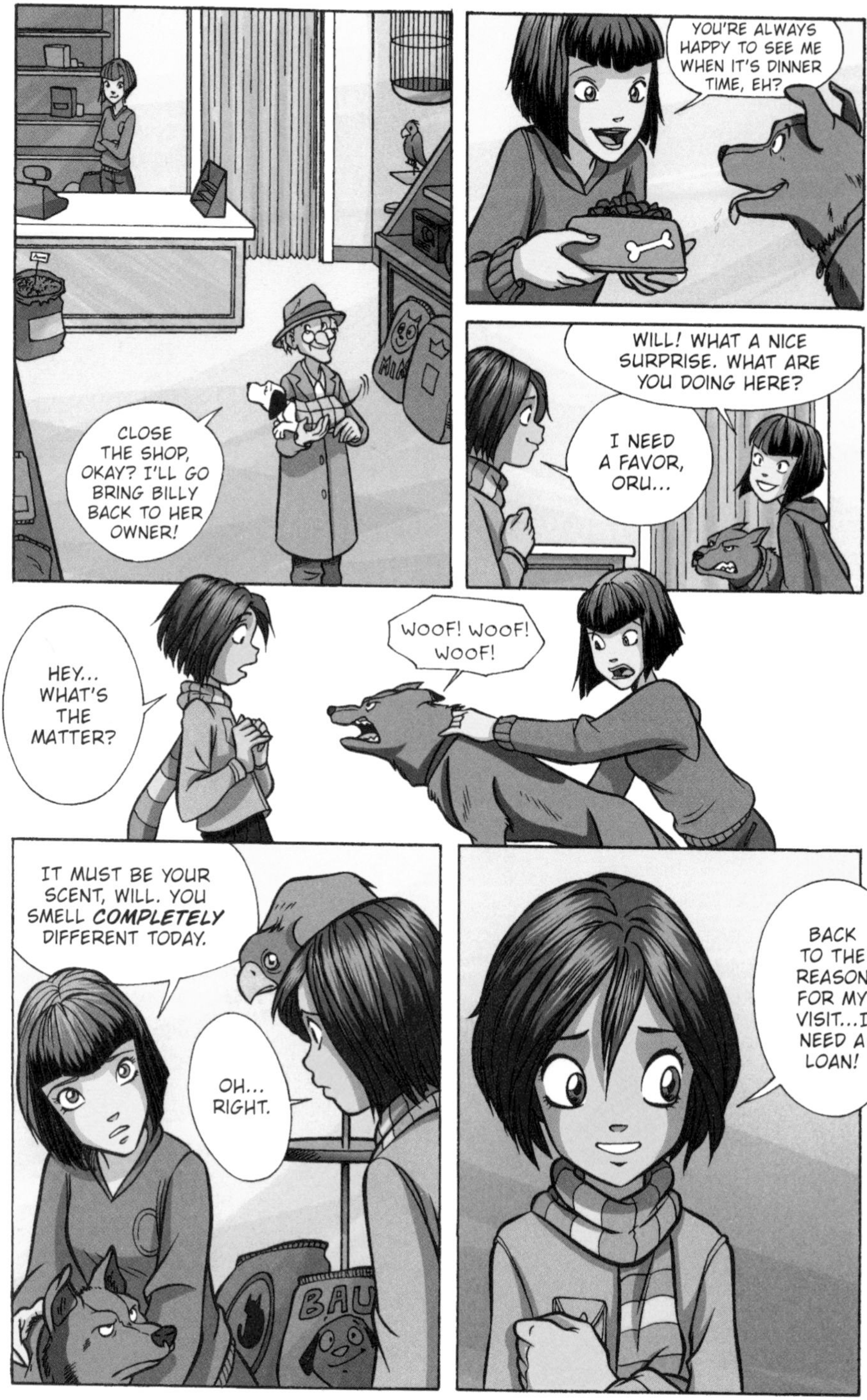

CLOSE THE SHOP, OKAY? I'LL GO BRING BILLY BACK TO HER OWNER!
YOU'RE ALWAYS HAPPY TO SEE ME WHEN IT'S DINNER TIME, EH?
WILL! WHAT A NICE SURPRISE. WHAT ARE YOU DOING HERE?
I NEED A FAVOR, ORU...
HEY... WHAT'S THE MATTER?
WOOF! WOOF! WOOF!
IT MUST BE YOUR SCENT, WILL. YOU SMELL **COMPLETELY** DIFFERENT TODAY.
OH... RIGHT.
BACK TO THE REASON FOR MY VISIT...I NEED A LOAN!

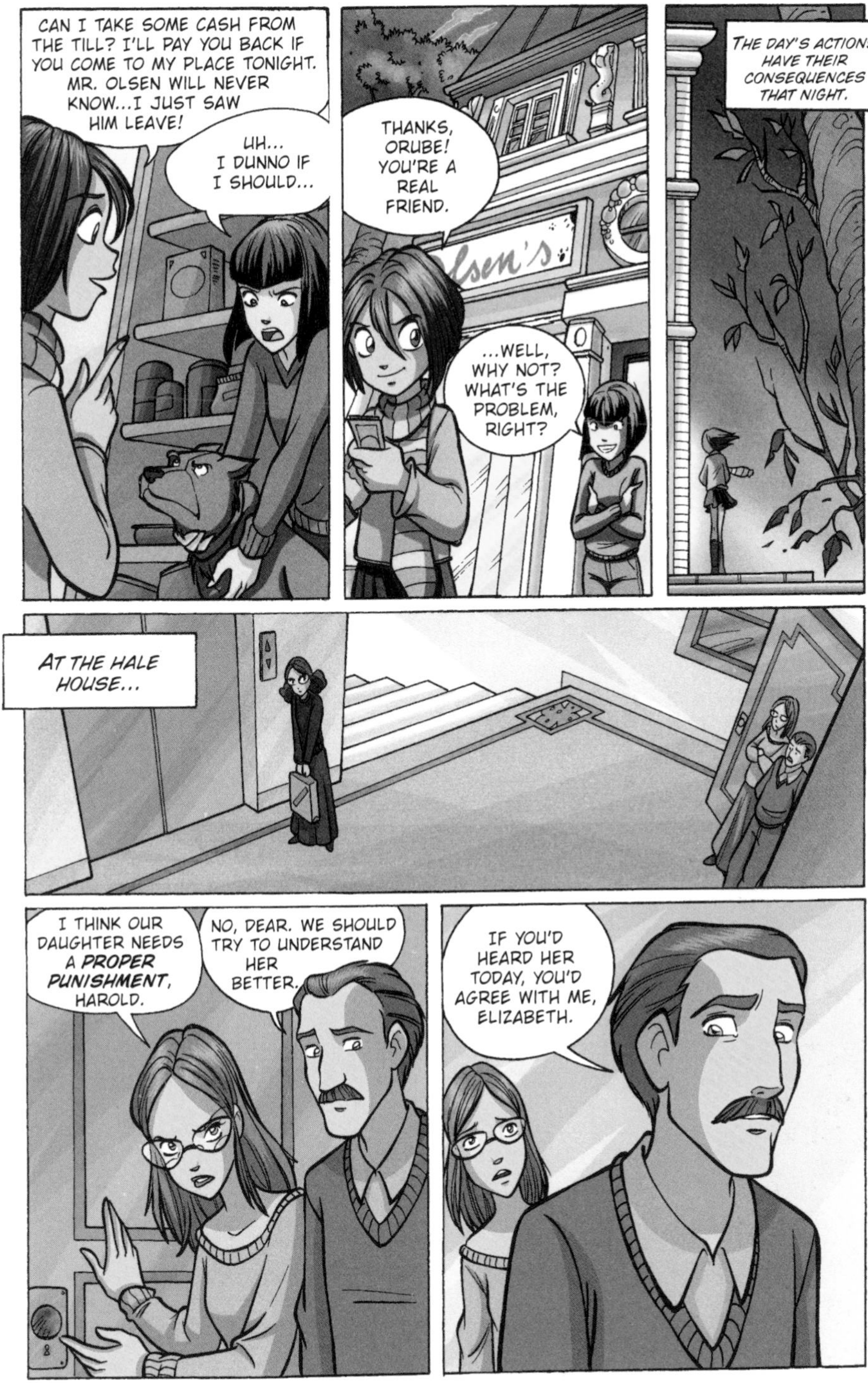
CAN I TAKE SOME CASH FROM THE TILL? I'LL PAY YOU BACK IF YOU COME TO MY PLACE TONIGHT. MR. OLSEN WILL NEVER KNOW...I JUST SAW HIM LEAVE!
UH... I DUNNO IF I SHOULD...
THANKS, ORUBE! YOU'RE A REAL FRIEND.
...WELL, WHY NOT? WHAT'S THE PROBLEM, RIGHT?
THE DAY'S ACTIONS HAVE THEIR CONSEQUENCES THAT NIGHT.
AT THE HALE HOUSE...
I THINK OUR DAUGHTER NEEDS A PROPER PUNISHMENT, HAROLD.
NO, DEAR. WE SHOULD TRY TO UNDERSTAND HER BETTER.
IF YOU'D HEARD HER TODAY, YOU'D AGREE WITH ME, ELIZABETH.

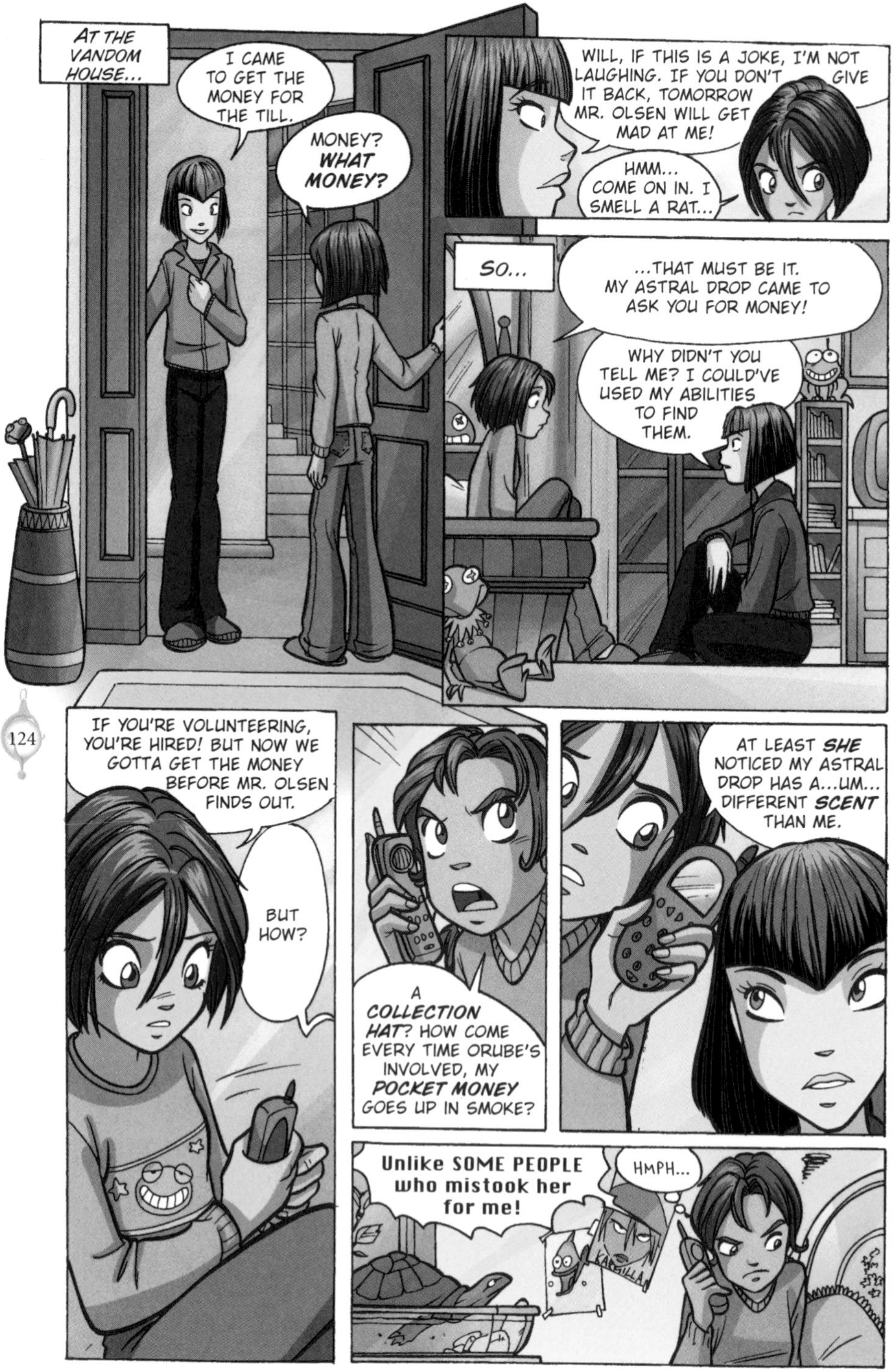
AT THE VANDOM HOUSE...
I CAME TO GET THE MONEY FOR THE TILL.
MONEY? WHAT MONEY?
WILL, IF THIS IS A JOKE, I'M NOT LAUGHING. IF YOU DON'T GIVE IT BACK, TOMORROW MR. OLSEN WILL GET MAD AT ME!
HMM... COME ON IN. I SMELL A RAT...
SO...
...THAT MUST BE IT. MY ASTRAL DROP CAME TO ASK YOU FOR MONEY!
WHY DIDN'T YOU TELL ME? I COULD'VE USED MY ABILITIES TO FIND THEM.
IF YOU'RE VOLUNTEERING, YOU'RE HIRED! BUT NOW WE GOTTA GET THE MONEY BEFORE MR. OLSEN FINDS OUT.
BUT HOW?
A COLLECTION HAT? HOW COME EVERY TIME ORUBE'S INVOLVED, MY POCKET MONEY GOES UP IN SMOKE?
AT LEAST SHE NOTICED MY ASTRAL DROP HAS A...UM... DIFFERENT SCENT THAN ME.
Unlike SOME PEOPLE who mistook her for me!
HMPH...
KARMILLA

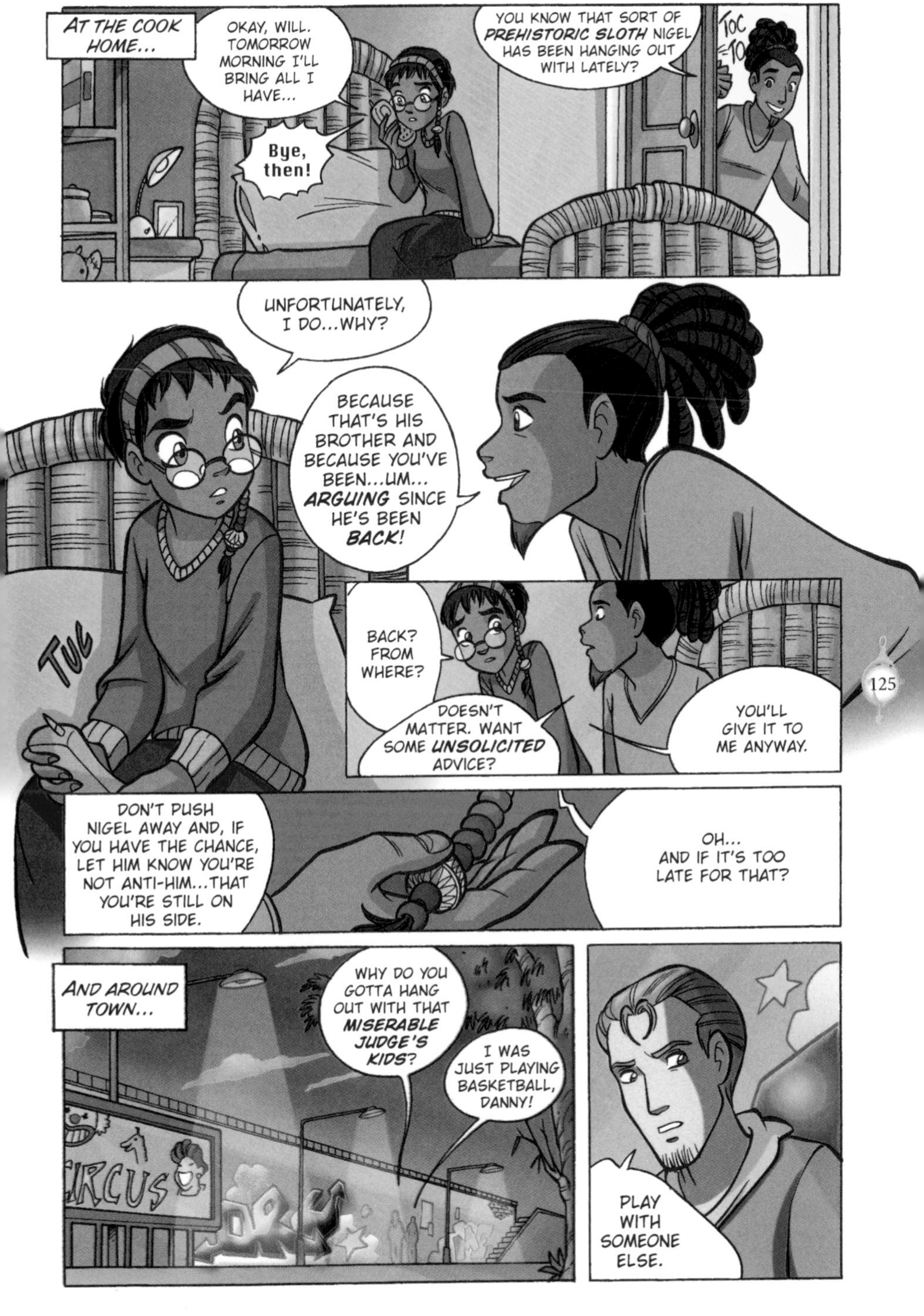
AT THE COOK HOME...
OKAY, WILL. TOMORROW MORNING I'LL BRING ALL I HAVE...
Bye, then!
YOU KNOW THAT SORT OF PREHISTORIC SLOTH NIGEL HAS BEEN HANGING OUT WITH LATELY?
TOC TOC
UNFORTUNATELY, I DO...WHY?
BECAUSE THAT'S HIS BROTHER AND BECAUSE YOU'VE BEEN...UM... ARGUING SINCE HE'S BEEN BACK!
TUC
BACK? FROM WHERE?
DOESN'T MATTER. WANT SOME UNSOLICITED ADVICE?
YOU'LL GIVE IT TO ME ANYWAY.
DON'T PUSH NIGEL AWAY AND, IF YOU HAVE THE CHANCE, LET HIM KNOW YOU'RE NOT ANTI-HIM...THAT YOU'RE STILL ON HIS SIDE.
OH... AND IF IT'S TOO LATE FOR THAT?
AND AROUND TOWN...
WHY DO YOU GOTTA HANG OUT WITH THAT MISERABLE JUDGE'S KIDS?
I WAS JUST PLAYING BASKETBALL, DANNY!
CIRCUS
PLAY WITH SOMEONE ELSE.

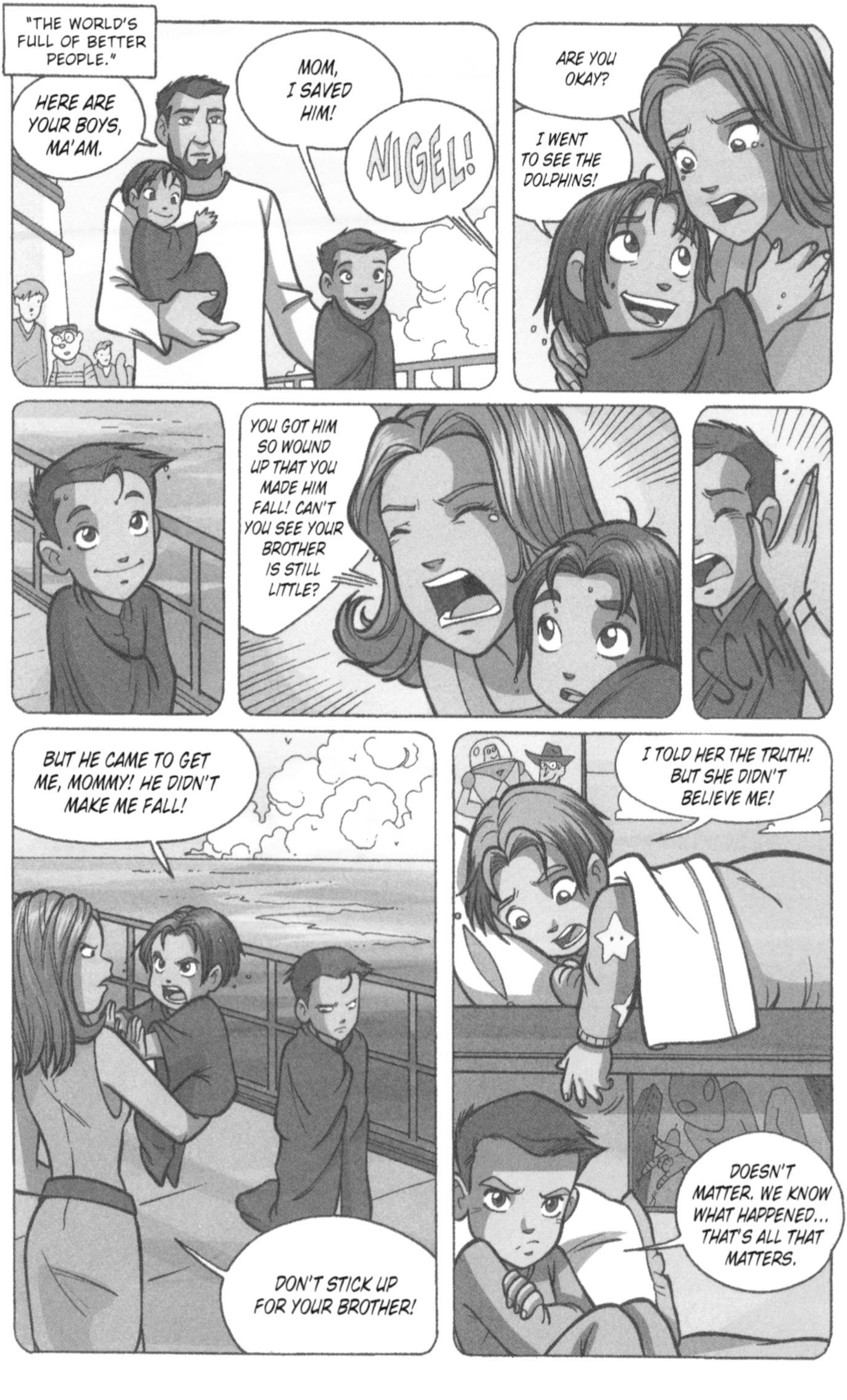

"THE WORLD'S FULL OF BETTER PEOPLE."
HERE ARE YOUR BOYS, MA'AM.
MOM, I SAVED HIM!
NIGEL!
ARE YOU OKAY?
I WENT TO SEE THE DOLPHINS!
YOU GOT HIM SO WOUND UP THAT YOU MADE HIM FALL! CAN'T YOU SEE YOUR BROTHER IS STILL LITTLE?
SCIAFF
BUT HE CAME TO GET ME, MOMMY! HE DIDN'T MAKE ME FALL!
DON'T STICK UP FOR YOUR BROTHER!
I TOLD HER THE TRUTH! BUT SHE DIDN'T BELIEVE ME!
DOESN'T MATTER. WE KNOW WHAT HAPPENED... THAT'S ALL THAT MATTERS.

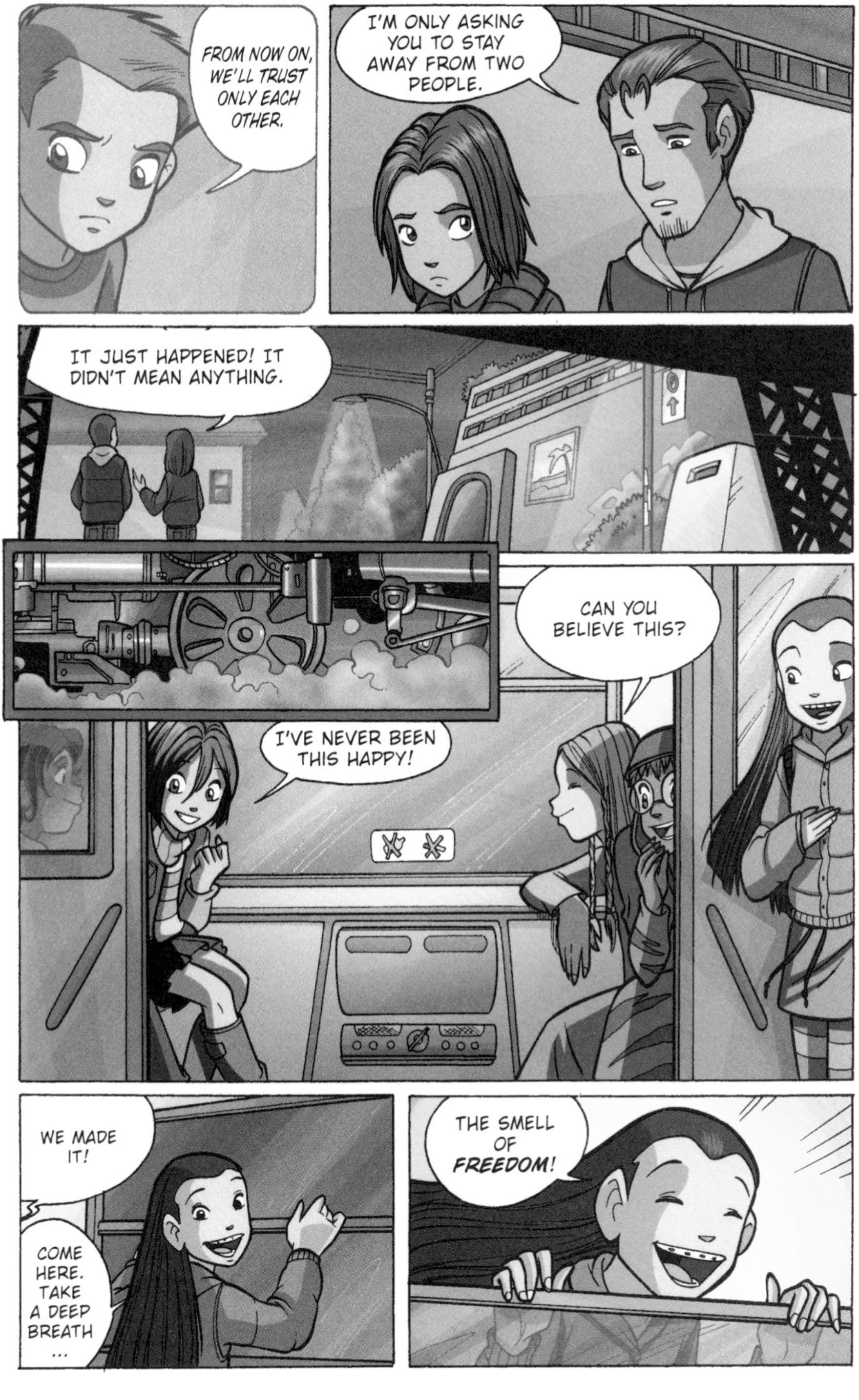
FROM NOW ON, WE'LL TRUST ONLY EACH OTHER.
I'M ONLY ASKING YOU TO STAY AWAY FROM TWO PEOPLE.
IT JUST HAPPENED! IT DIDN'T MEAN ANYTHING.
CAN YOU BELIEVE THIS?
I'VE NEVER BEEN THIS HAPPY!
WE MADE IT!
COME HERE. TAKE A DEEP BREATH ...
THE SMELL OF *FREEDOM*!

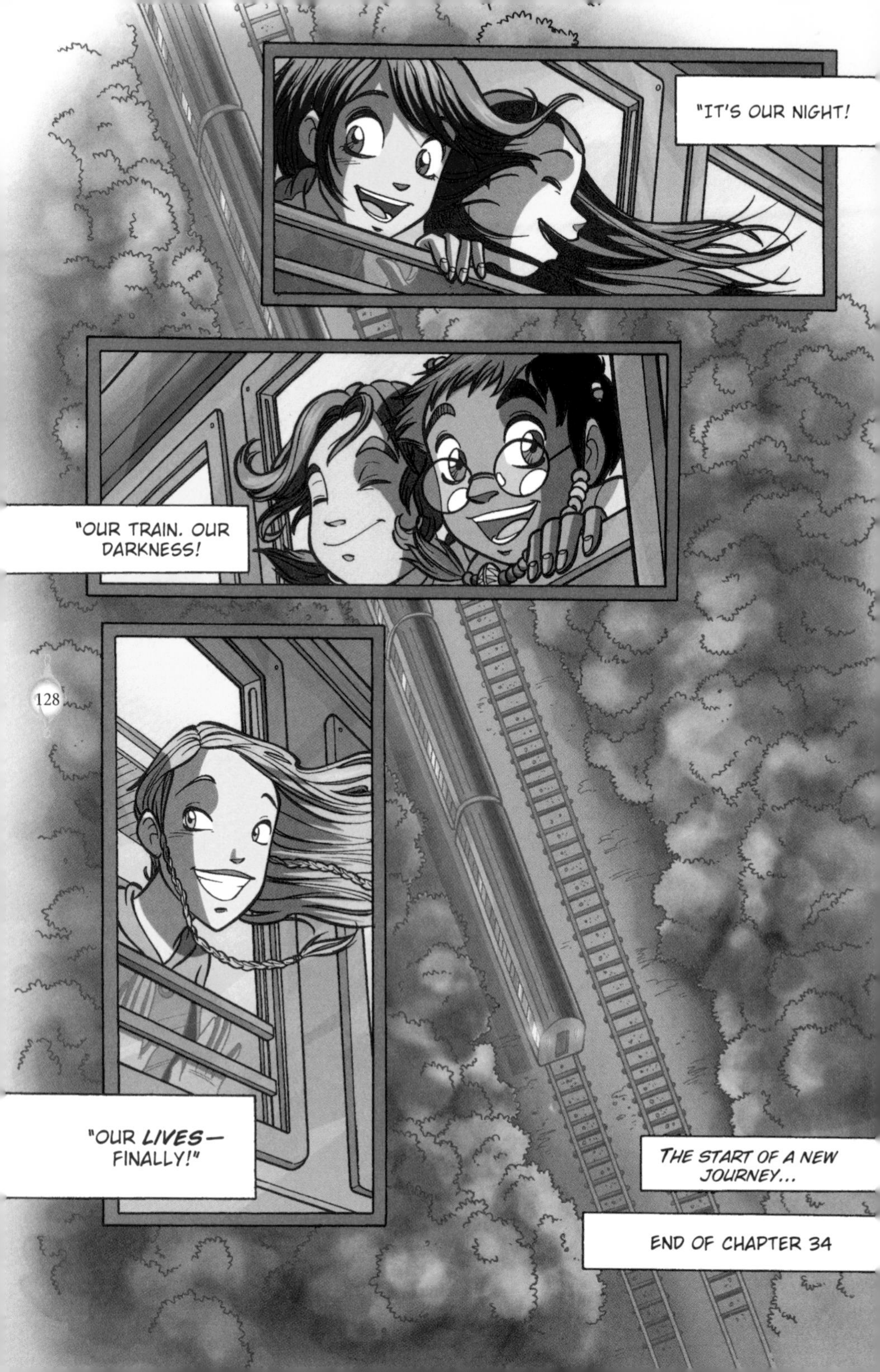

"IT'S OUR NIGHT!
"OUR TRAIN. OUR DARKNESS!
"OUR *LIVES*— FINALLY!"
THE START OF A NEW JOURNEY...
END OF CHAPTER 34

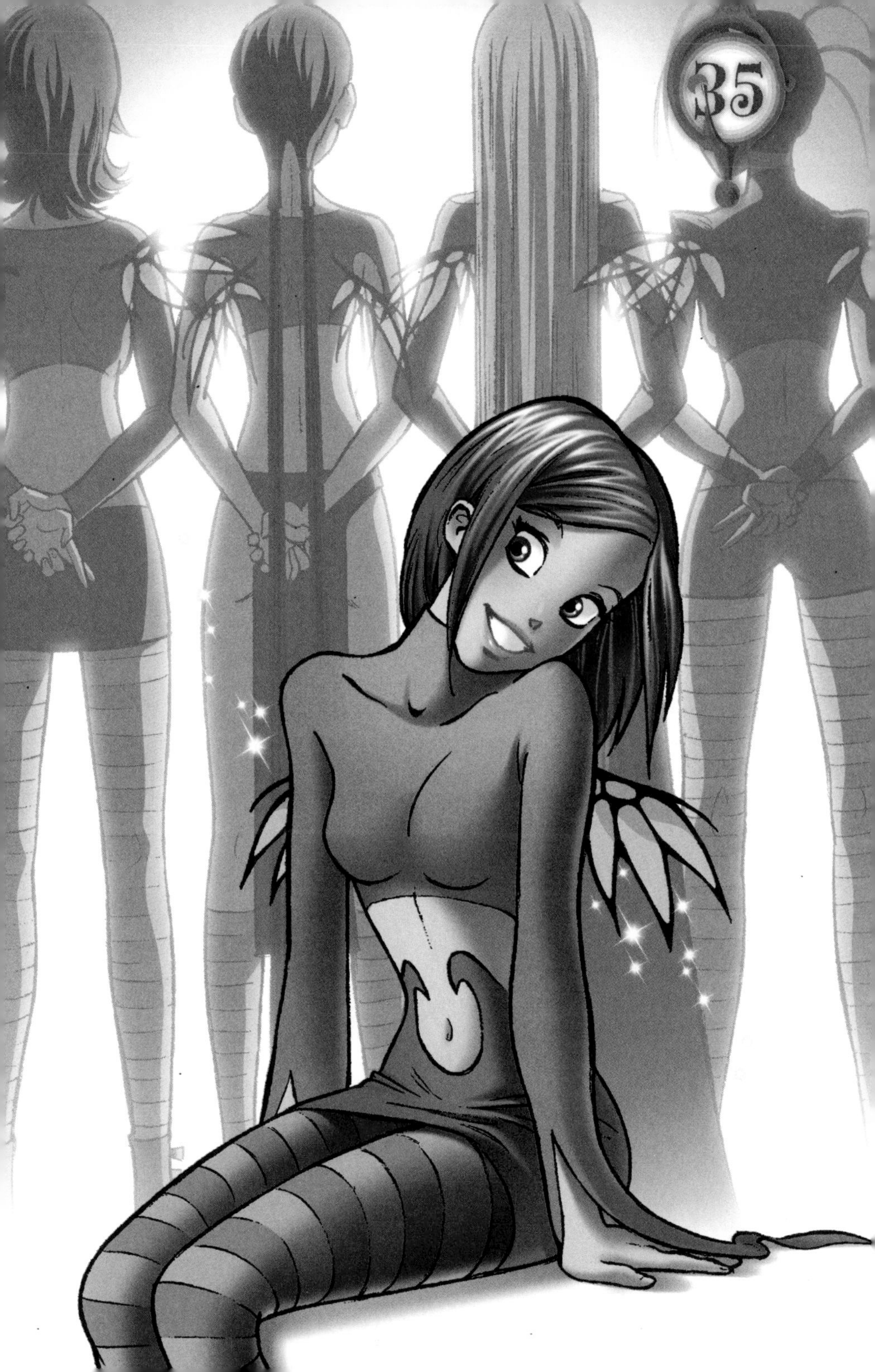
35

Reflected Lives

"My reflection told me
I was real. Authentic!"

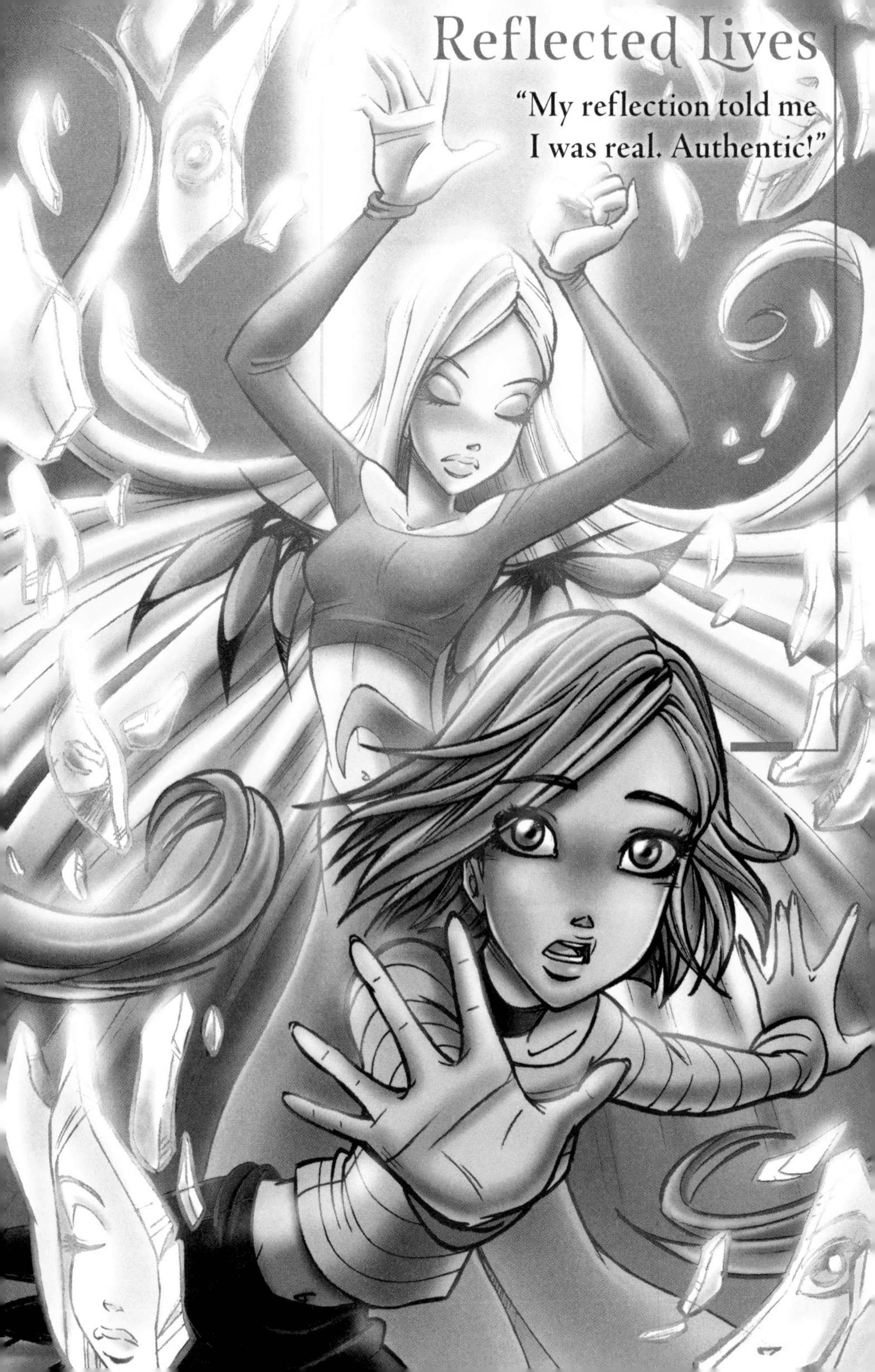

W.i.t.c.h.

Will Irma Taranee Cornelia Hay Lin

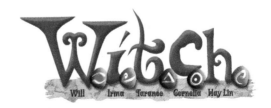

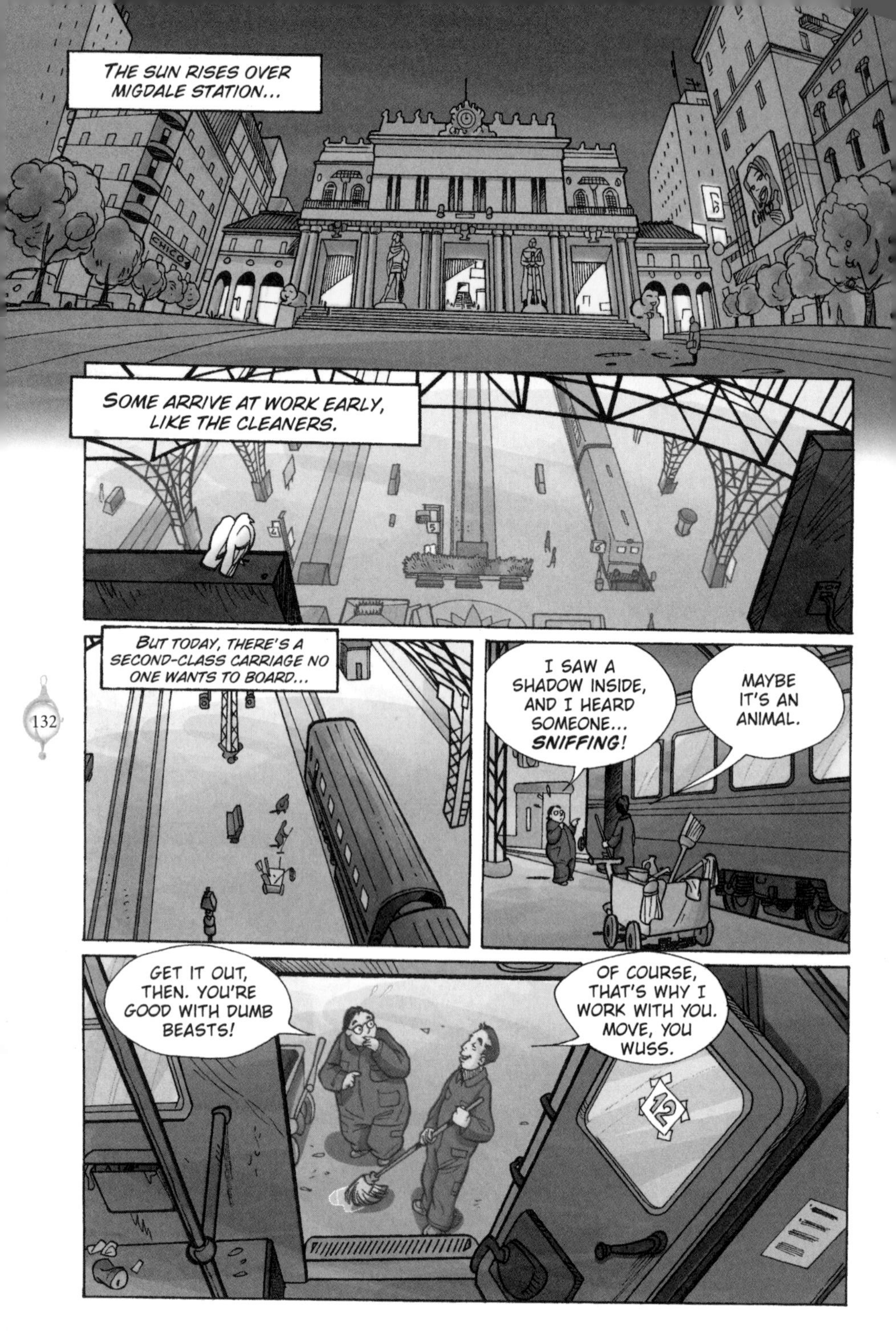
THE SUN RISES OVER MIGDALE STATION...
SOME ARRIVE AT WORK EARLY, LIKE THE CLEANERS.
BUT TODAY, THERE'S A SECOND-CLASS CARRIAGE NO ONE WANTS TO BOARD...
I SAW A SHADOW INSIDE, AND I HEARD SOMEONE... SNIFFING!
MAYBE IT'S AN ANIMAL.
GET IT OUT, THEN. YOU'RE GOOD WITH DUMB BEASTS!
OF COURSE, THAT'S WHY I WORK WITH YOU. MOVE, YOU WUSS.

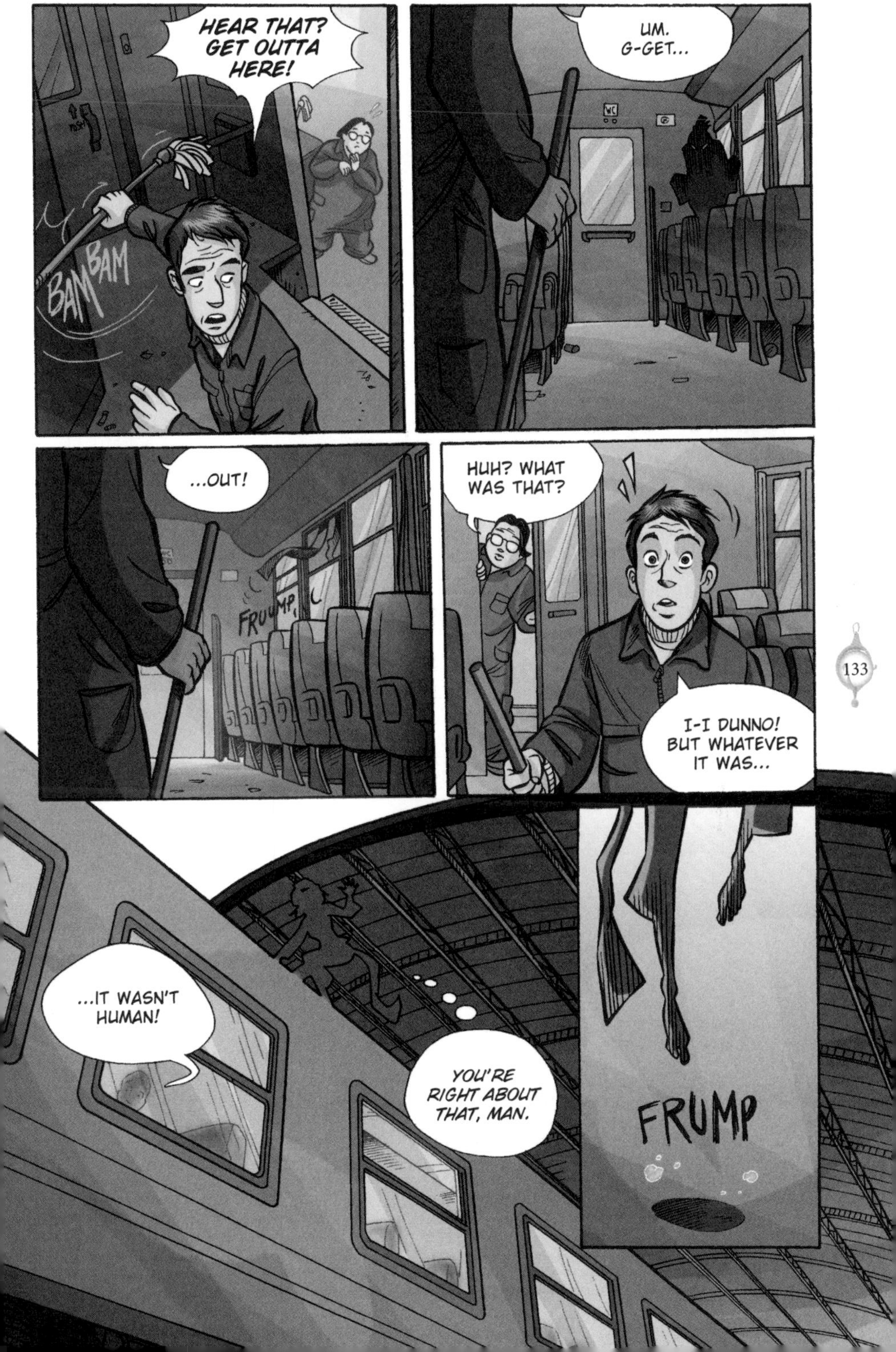
HEAR THAT? GET OUTTA HERE!
BAM BAM
UM. G-GET...
...OUT!
FRUMP
HUH? WHAT WAS THAT?
I-I DUNNO! BUT WHATEVER IT WAS...
...IT WASN'T HUMAN!
YOU'RE RIGHT ABOUT THAT, MAN.
FRUMP

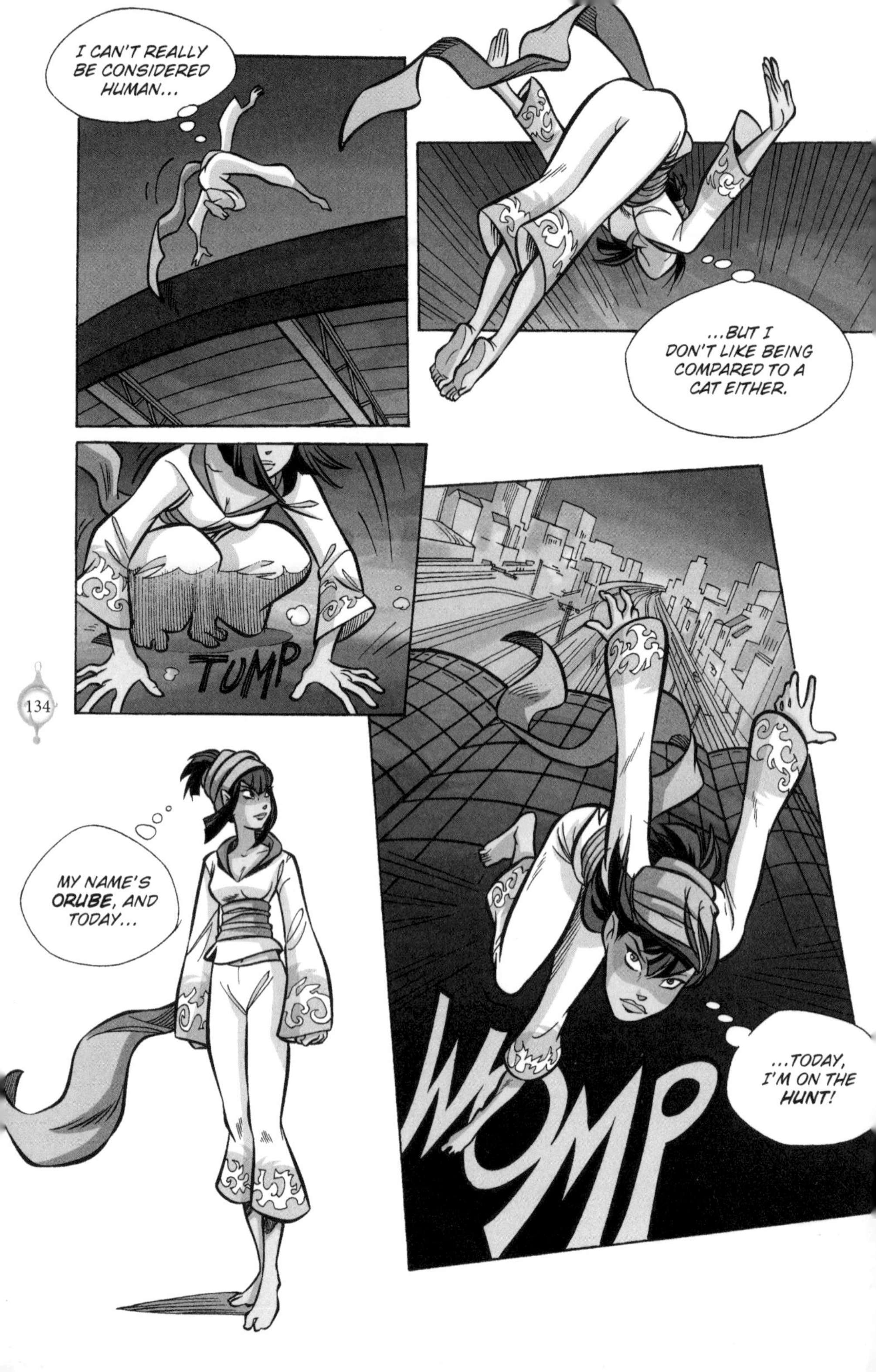
I CAN'T REALLY BE CONSIDERED HUMAN...
...BUT I DON'T LIKE BEING COMPARED TO A CAT EITHER.
TUMP
MY NAME'S ORUBE, AND TODAY...
WOMP
...TODAY, I'M ON THE HUNT!

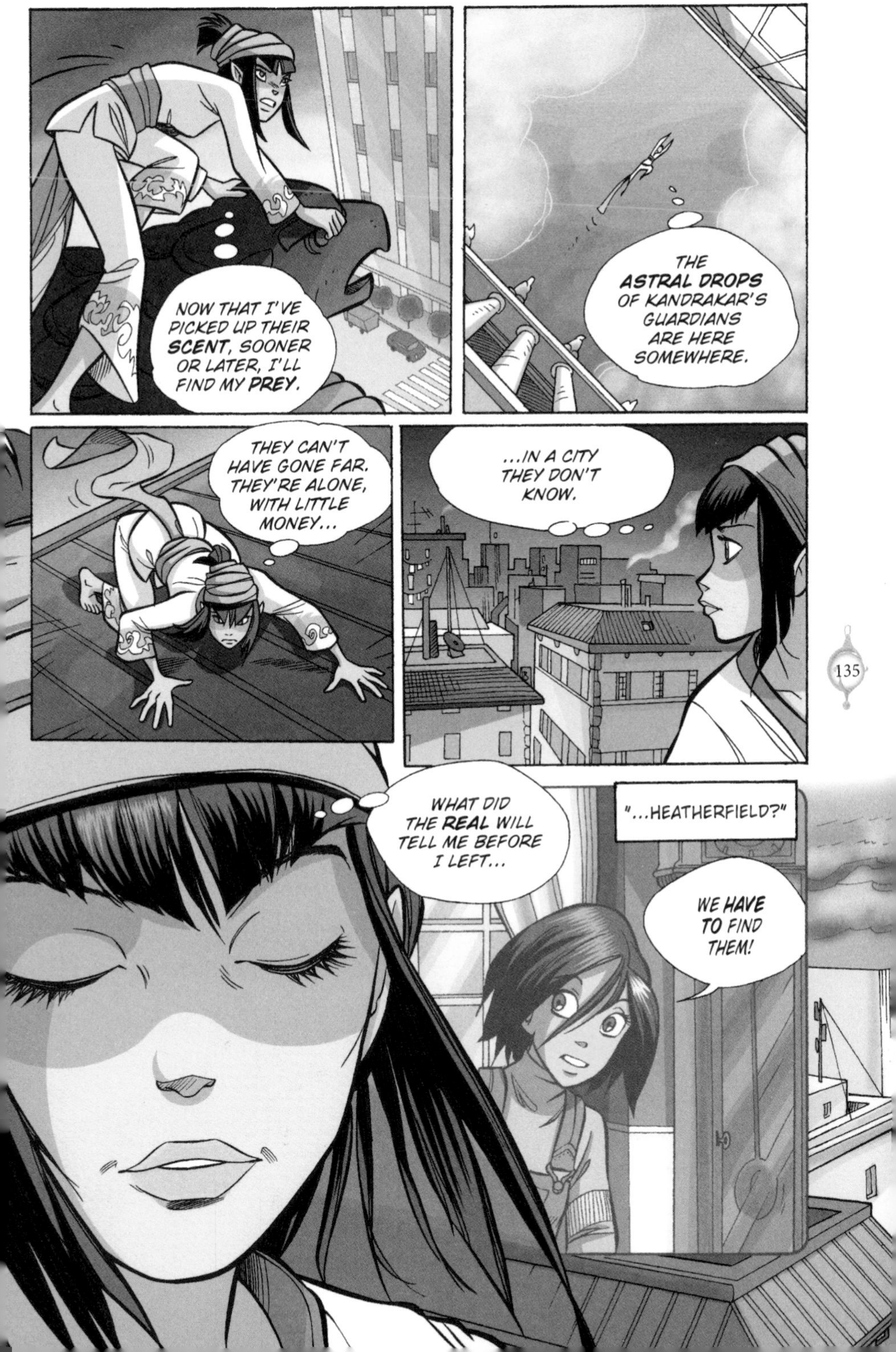
NOW THAT I'VE PICKED UP THEIR SCENT, SOONER OR LATER, I'LL FIND MY PREY.
THE ASTRAL DROPS OF KANDRAKAR'S GUARDIANS ARE HERE SOMEWHERE.
THEY CAN'T HAVE GONE FAR. THEY'RE ALONE, WITH LITTLE MONEY...
...IN A CITY THEY DON'T KNOW.
WHAT DID THE REAL WILL TELL ME BEFORE I LEFT...
"...HEATHERFIELD?"
WE HAVE TO FIND THEM!

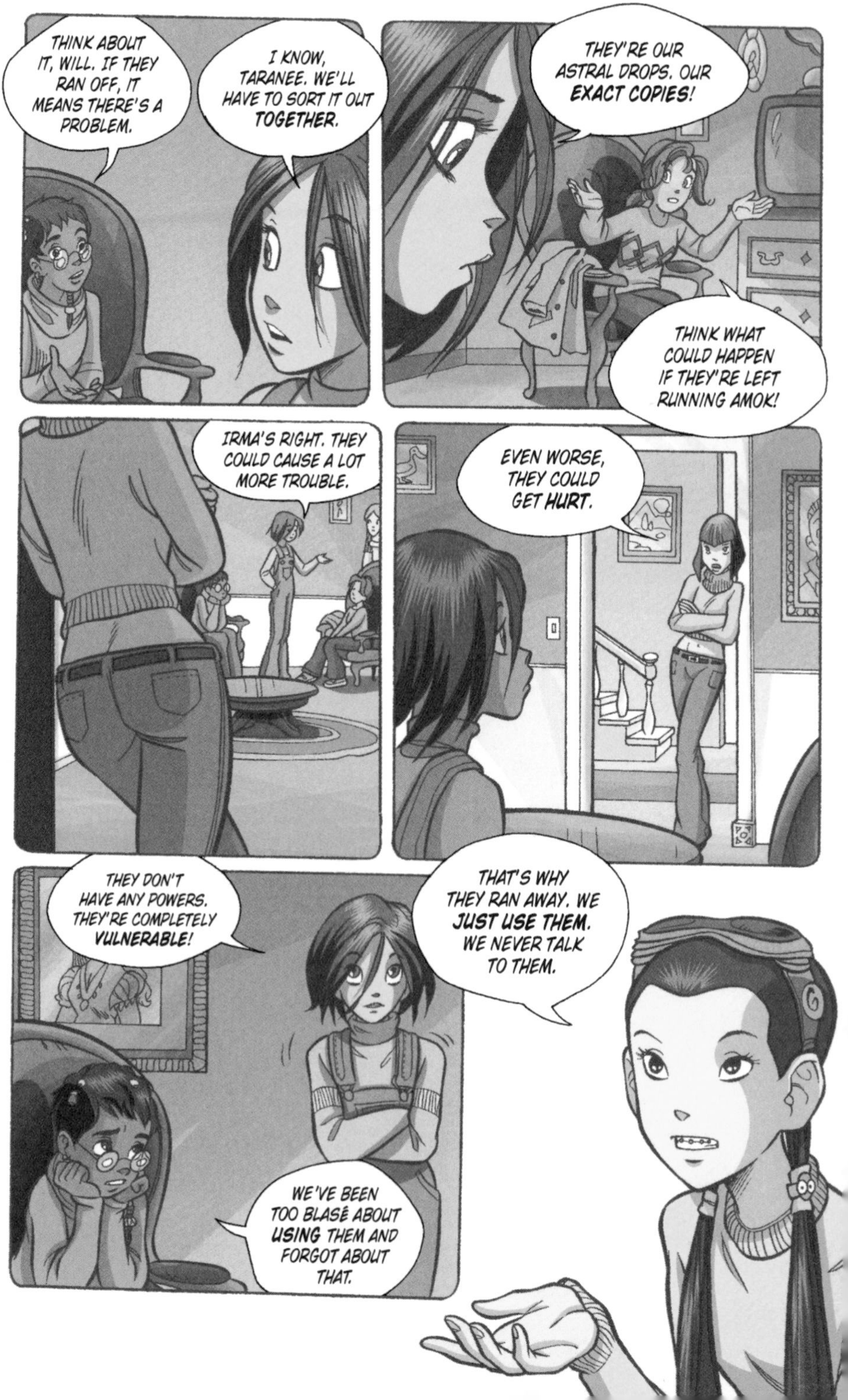
THINK ABOUT IT, WILL. IF THEY RAN OFF, IT MEANS THERE'S A PROBLEM.
I KNOW, TARANEE. WE'LL HAVE TO SORT IT OUT TOGETHER.
THEY'RE OUR ASTRAL DROPS. OUR EXACT COPIES!
THINK WHAT COULD HAPPEN IF THEY'RE LEFT RUNNING AMOK!
IRMA'S RIGHT. THEY COULD CAUSE A LOT MORE TROUBLE.
EVEN WORSE, THEY COULD GET HURT.
THEY DON'T HAVE ANY POWERS. THEY'RE COMPLETELY VULNERABLE!
THAT'S WHY THEY RAN AWAY. WE JUST USE THEM. WE NEVER TALK TO THEM.
WE'VE BEEN TOO BLASÉ ABOUT USING THEM AND FORGOT ABOUT THAT.

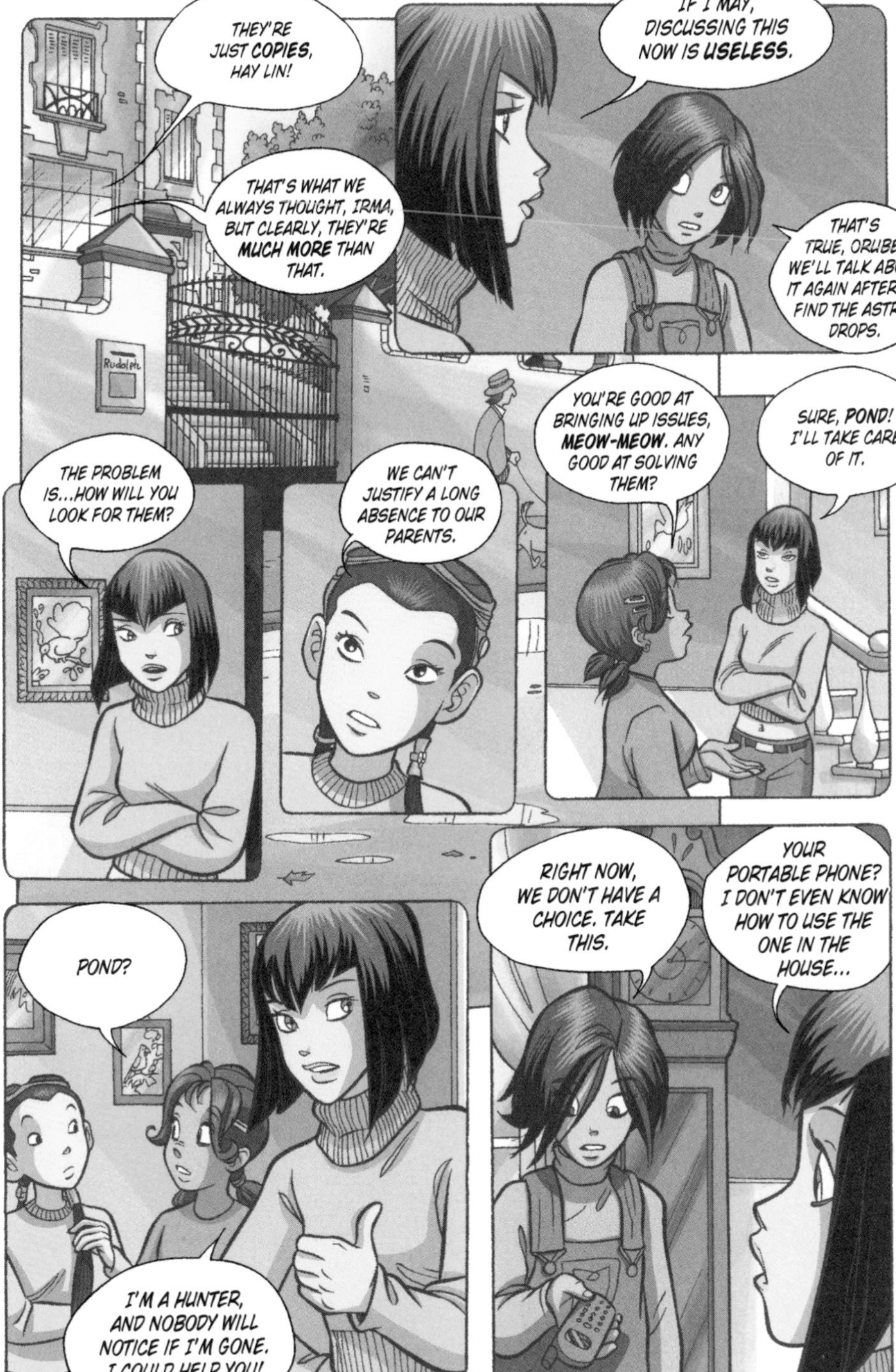

THEY'RE JUST COPIES, HAY LIN!
THAT'S WHAT WE ALWAYS THOUGHT, IRMA, BUT CLEARLY, THEY'RE MUCH MORE THAN THAT.
IF I MAY, DISCUSSING THIS NOW IS USELESS.
THAT'S TRUE, ORUBE. WE'LL TALK ABOUT IT AGAIN AFTER WE FIND THE ASTRAL DROPS.
Rudolph
THE PROBLEM IS...HOW WILL YOU LOOK FOR THEM?
WE CAN'T JUSTIFY A LONG ABSENCE TO OUR PARENTS.
YOU'RE GOOD AT BRINGING UP ISSUES, MEOW-MEOW. ANY GOOD AT SOLVING THEM?
SURE, POND! I'LL TAKE CARE OF IT.
POND?
I'M A HUNTER, AND NOBODY WILL NOTICE IF I'M GONE. I COULD HELP YOU!
RIGHT NOW, WE DON'T HAVE A CHOICE. TAKE THIS.
YOUR PORTABLE PHONE? I DON'T EVEN KNOW HOW TO USE THE ONE IN THE HOUSE...

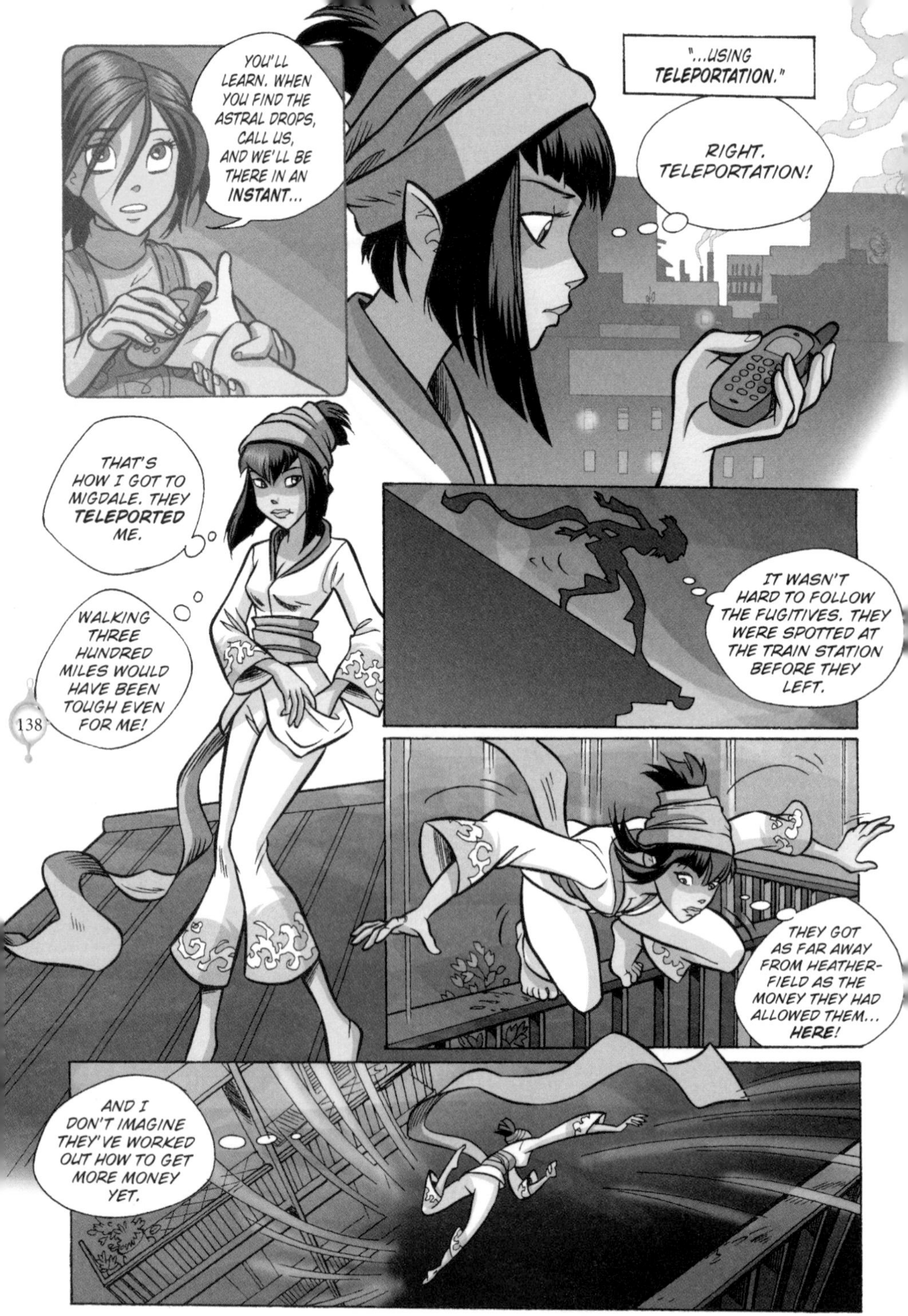

YOU'LL LEARN. WHEN YOU FIND THE ASTRAL DROPS, CALL US, AND WE'LL BE THERE IN AN INSTANT...
"...USING TELEPORTATION."
RIGHT. TELEPORTATION!
THAT'S HOW I GOT TO MIGDALE. THEY TELEPORTED ME.
WALKING THREE HUNDRED MILES WOULD HAVE BEEN TOUGH EVEN FOR ME!
IT WASN'T HARD TO FOLLOW THE FUGITIVES. THEY WERE SPOTTED AT THE TRAIN STATION BEFORE THEY LEFT.
THEY GOT AS FAR AWAY FROM HEATHER-FIELD AS THE MONEY THEY HAD ALLOWED THEM... HERE!
AND I DON'T IMAGINE THEY'VE WORKED OUT HOW TO GET MORE MONEY YET.

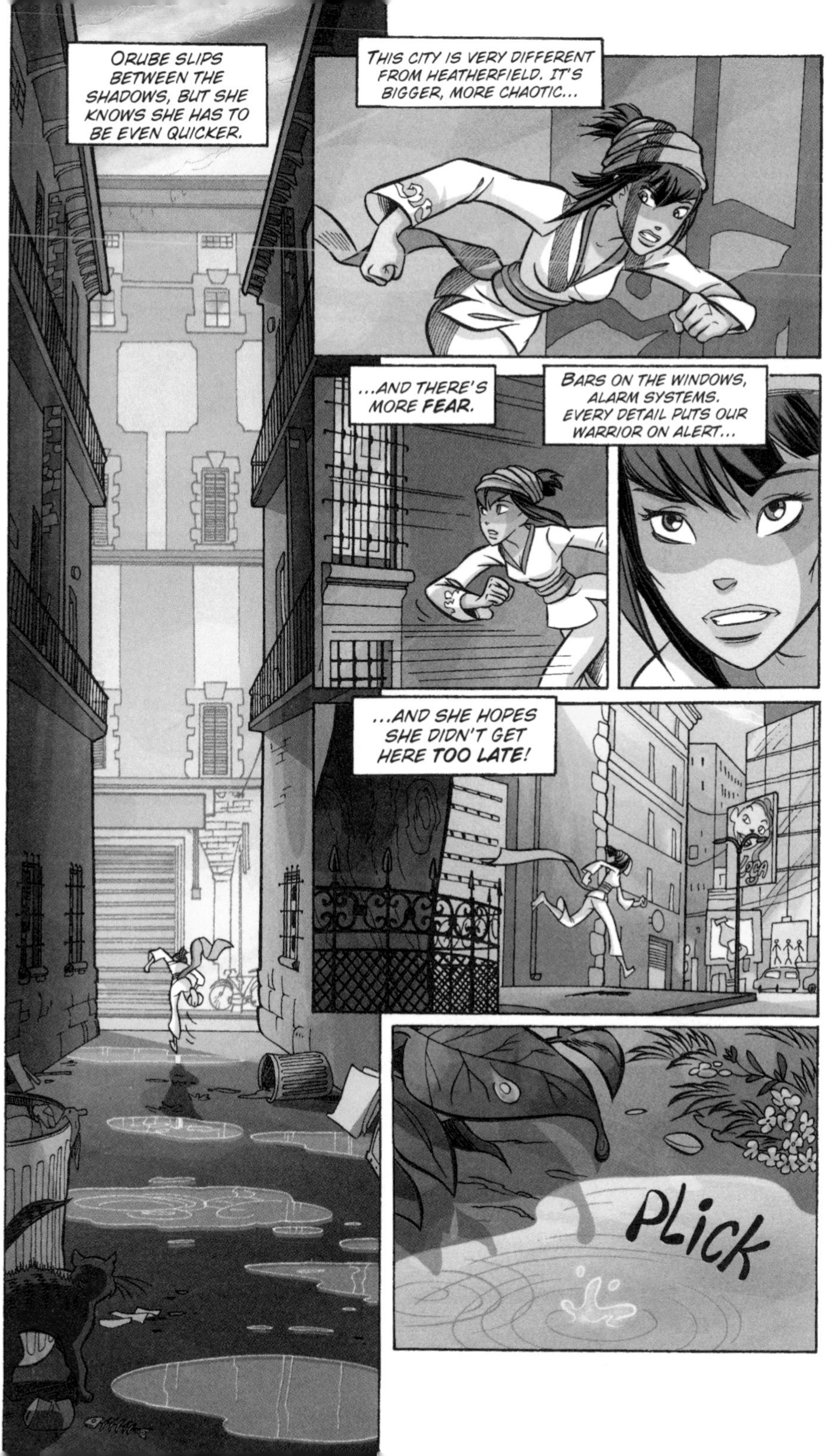
ORUBE SLIPS BETWEEN THE SHADOWS, BUT SHE KNOWS SHE HAS TO BE EVEN QUICKER.
THIS CITY IS VERY DIFFERENT FROM HEATHERFIELD. IT'S BIGGER, MORE CHAOTIC...
...AND THERE'S MORE FEAR.
BARS ON THE WINDOWS, ALARM SYSTEMS. EVERY DETAIL PUTS OUR WARRIOR ON ALERT...
...AND SHE HOPES SHE DIDN'T GET HERE TOO LATE!
PLICK

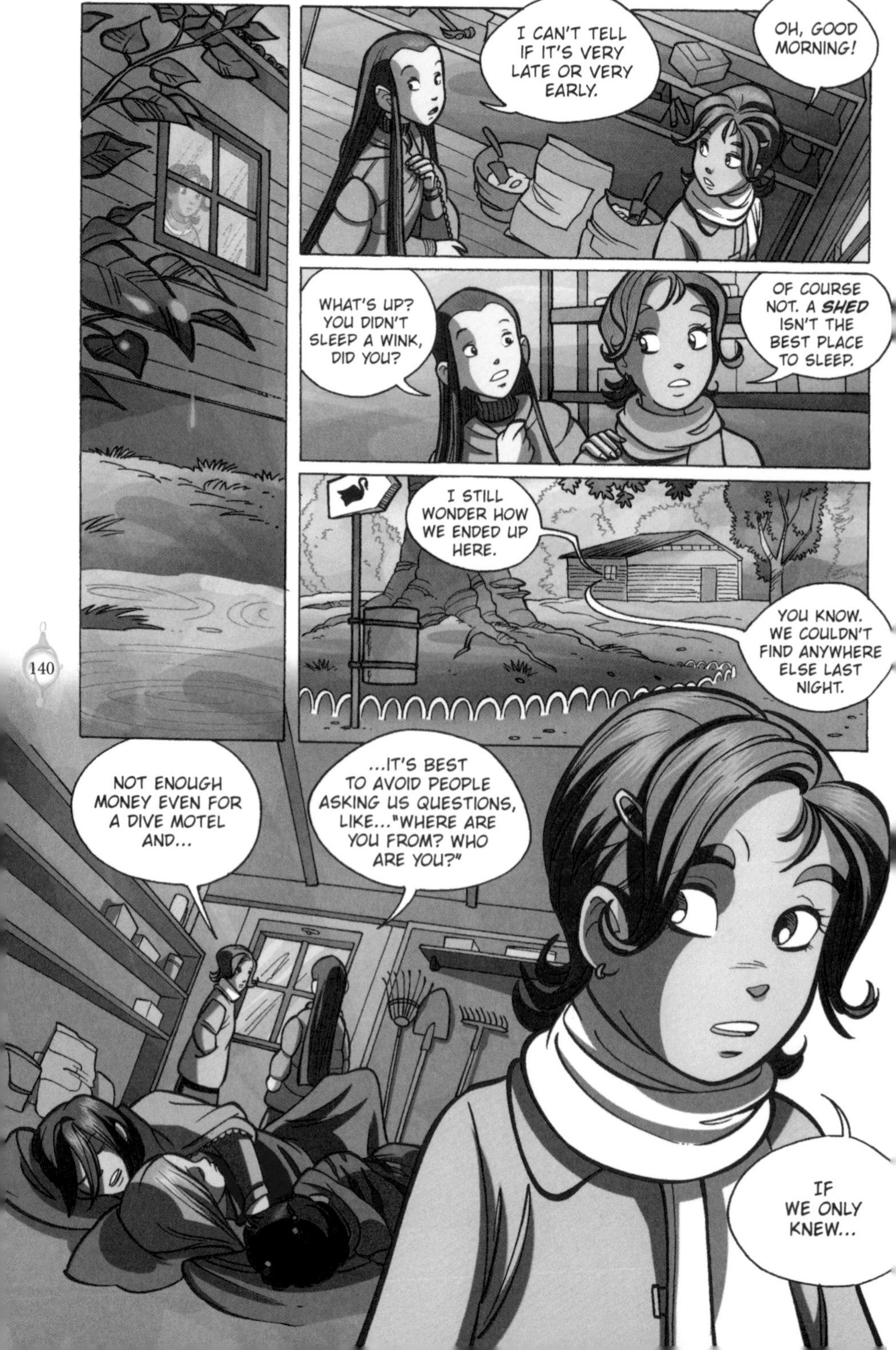
I CAN'T TELL IF IT'S VERY LATE OR VERY EARLY.
OH, GOOD MORNING!
WHAT'S UP? YOU DIDN'T SLEEP A WINK, DID YOU?
OF COURSE NOT. A SHED ISN'T THE BEST PLACE TO SLEEP.
I STILL WONDER HOW WE ENDED UP HERE.
YOU KNOW. WE COULDN'T FIND ANYWHERE ELSE LAST NIGHT.
NOT ENOUGH MONEY EVEN FOR A DIVE MOTEL AND...
...IT'S BEST TO AVOID PEOPLE ASKING US QUESTIONS, LIKE..."WHERE ARE YOU FROM? WHO ARE YOU?"
IF WE ONLY KNEW...

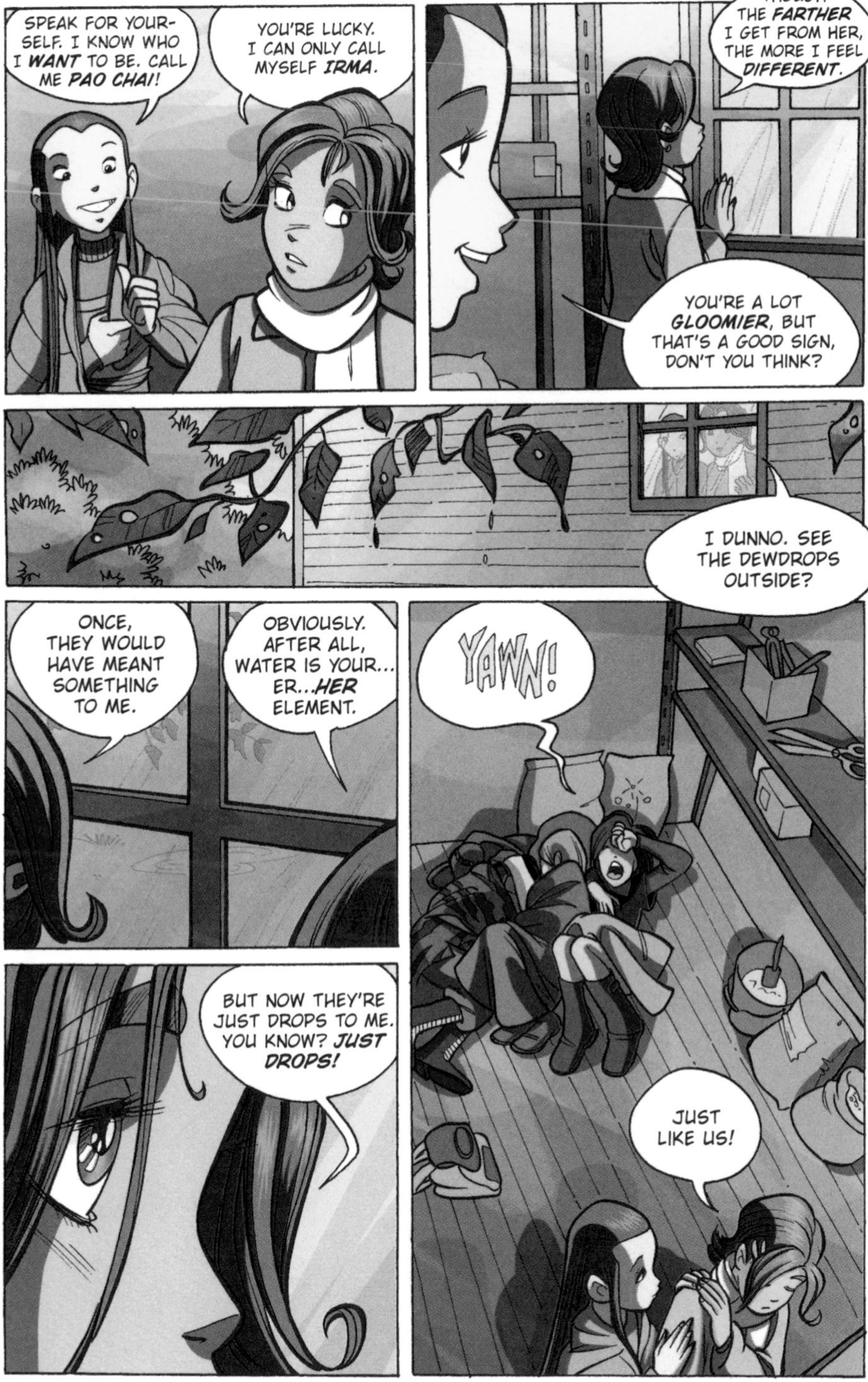
SPEAK FOR YOURSELF. I KNOW WHO I WANT TO BE. CALL ME PAO CHAI!
YOU'RE LUCKY. I CAN ONLY CALL MYSELF IRMA.
THOUGH THE FARTHER I GET FROM HER, THE MORE I FEEL DIFFERENT.
YOU'RE A LOT GLOOMIER, BUT THAT'S A GOOD SIGN, DON'T YOU THINK?
I DUNNO. SEE THE DEWDROPS OUTSIDE?
ONCE, THEY WOULD HAVE MEANT SOMETHING TO ME.
OBVIOUSLY. AFTER ALL, WATER IS YOUR... ER...HER ELEMENT.
YAWN!
BUT NOW THEY'RE JUST DROPS TO ME. YOU KNOW? JUST DROPS!
JUST LIKE US!

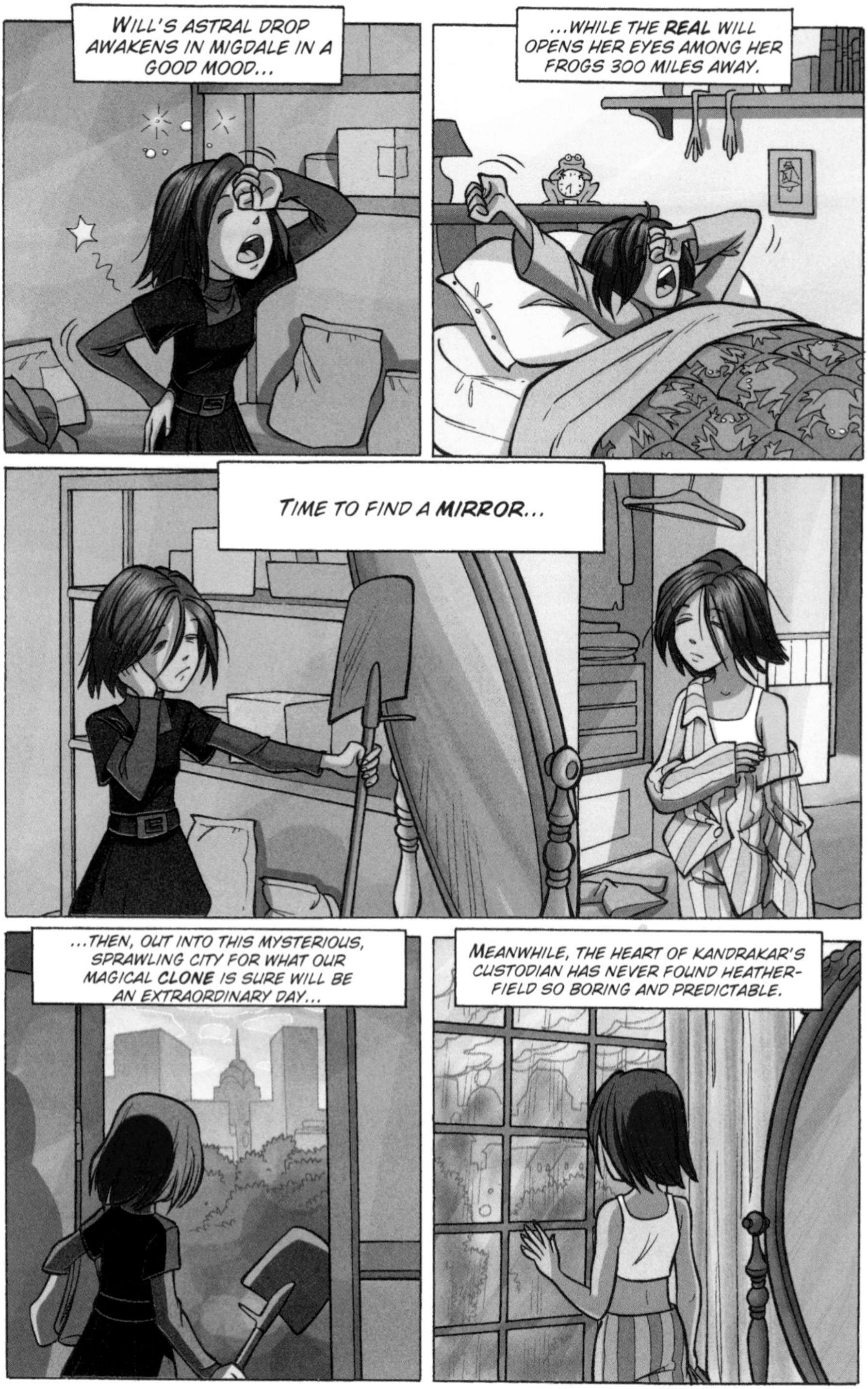
WILL'S ASTRAL DROP AWAKENS IN MIGDALE IN A GOOD MOOD...
...WHILE THE REAL WILL OPENS HER EYES AMONG HER FROGS 300 MILES AWAY.
TIME TO FIND A MIRROR...
...THEN, OUT INTO THIS MYSTERIOUS, SPRAWLING CITY FOR WHAT OUR MAGICAL CLONE IS SURE WILL BE AN EXTRAORDINARY DAY...
MEANWHILE, THE HEART OF KANDRAKAR'S CUSTODIAN HAS NEVER FOUND HEATHER-FIELD SO BORING AND PREDICTABLE.

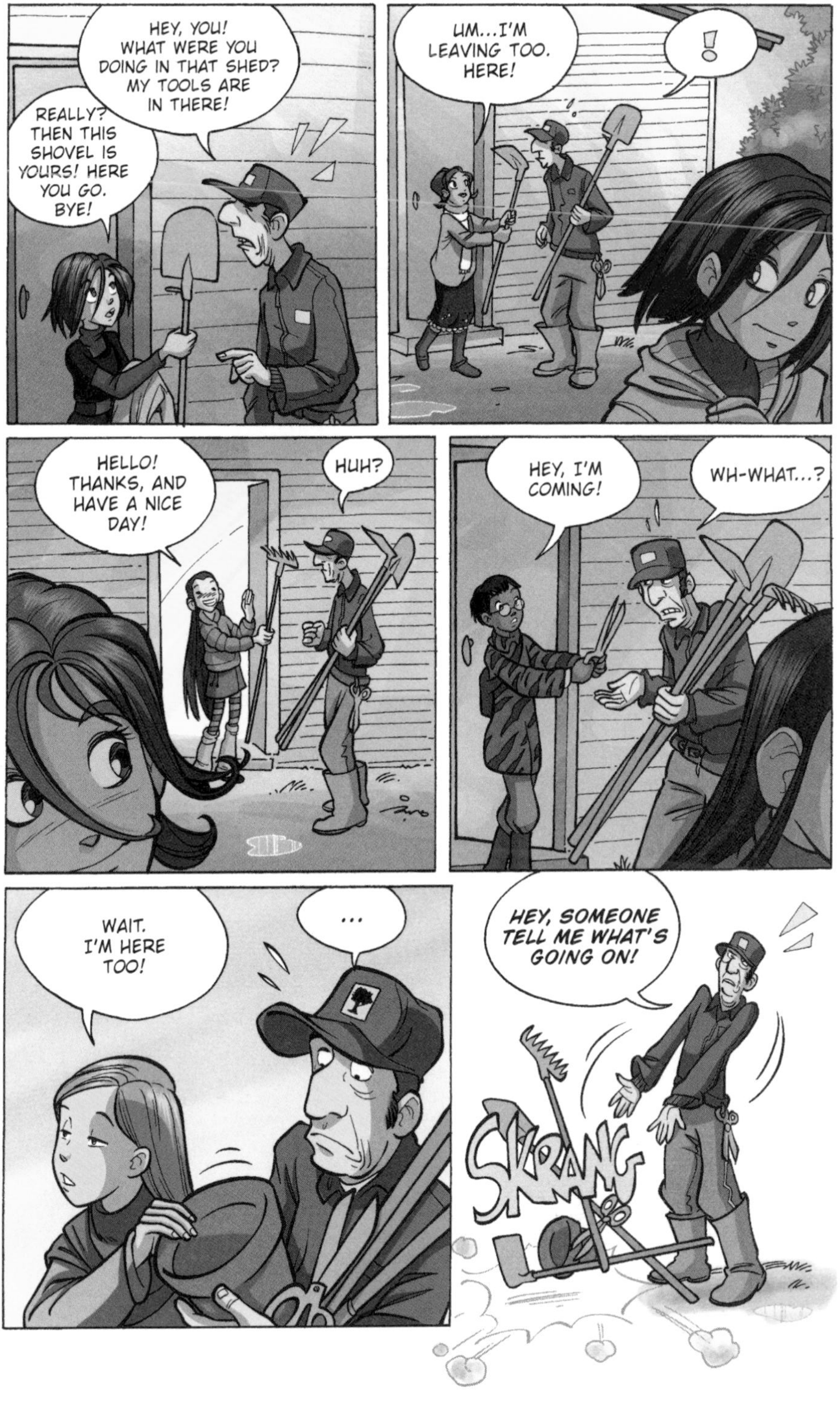
HEY, YOU!
WHAT WERE YOU DOING IN THAT SHED? MY TOOLS ARE IN THERE!
REALLY? THEN THIS SHOVEL IS YOURS! HERE YOU GO. BYE!
UM...I'M LEAVING TOO. HERE!
!
HELLO! THANKS, AND HAVE A NICE DAY!
HUH?
HEY, I'M COMING!
WH-WHAT...?
WAIT. I'M HERE TOO!
...
HEY, SOMEONE TELL ME WHAT'S GOING ON!
SKRANG

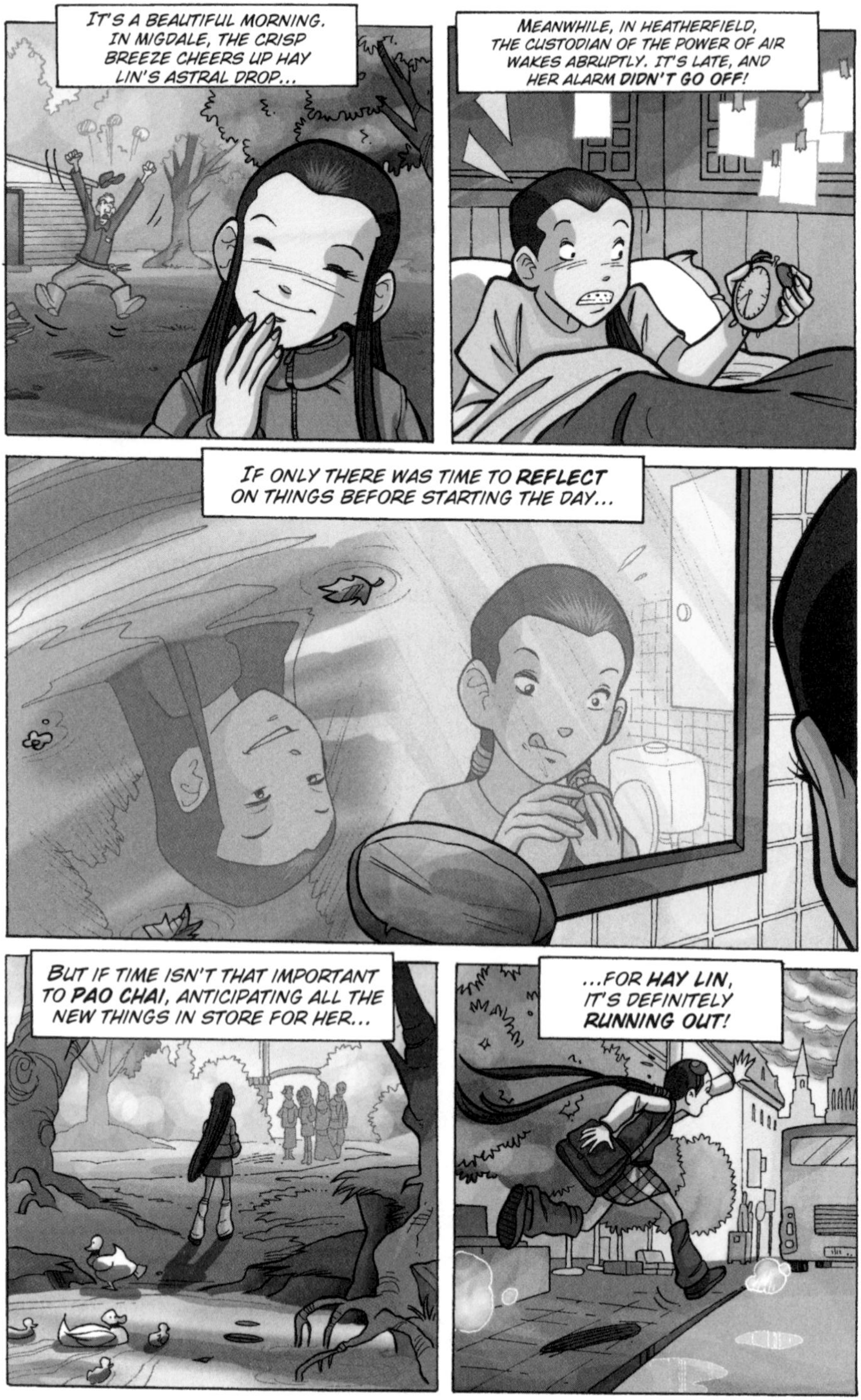
IT'S A BEAUTIFUL MORNING. IN MIGDALE, THE CRISP BREEZE CHEERS UP HAY LIN'S ASTRAL DROP...
MEANWHILE, IN HEATHERFIELD, THE CUSTODIAN OF THE POWER OF AIR WAKES ABRUPTLY. IT'S LATE, AND HER ALARM DIDN'T GO OFF!
IF ONLY THERE WAS TIME TO REFLECT ON THINGS BEFORE STARTING THE DAY...
BUT IF TIME ISN'T THAT IMPORTANT TO PAO CHAI, ANTICIPATING ALL THE NEW THINGS IN STORE FOR HER...
...FOR HAY LIN, IT'S DEFINITELY RUNNING OUT!

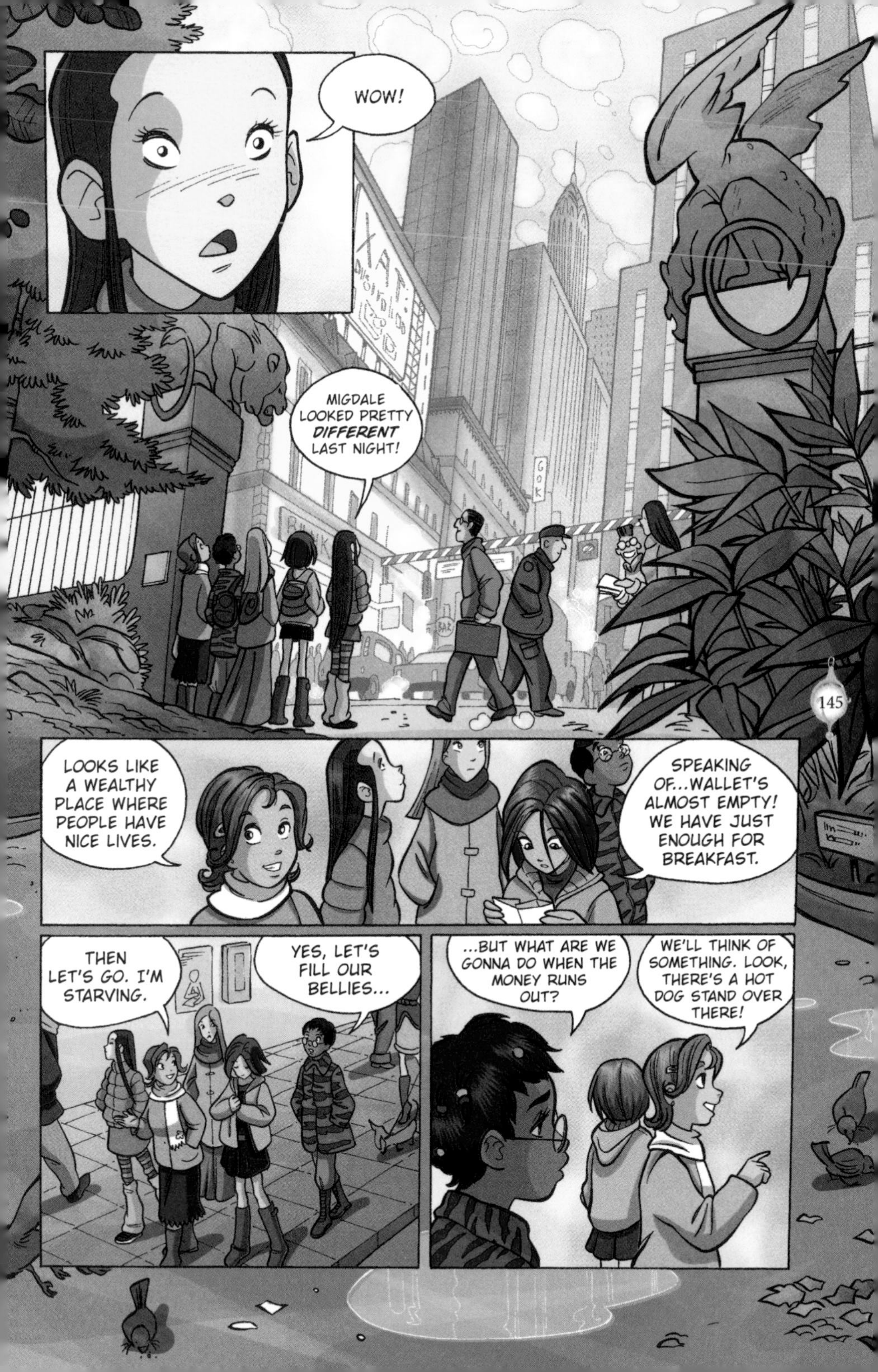
WOW!
MIGDALE LOOKED PRETTY DIFFERENT LAST NIGHT!
LOOKS LIKE A WEALTHY PLACE WHERE PEOPLE HAVE NICE LIVES.
SPEAKING OF...WALLET'S ALMOST EMPTY! WE HAVE JUST ENOUGH FOR BREAKFAST.
THEN LET'S GO. I'M STARVING.
YES, LET'S FILL OUR BELLIES...
...BUT WHAT ARE WE GONNA DO WHEN THE MONEY RUNS OUT?
WE'LL THINK OF SOMETHING. LOOK, THERE'S A HOT DOG STAND OVER THERE!

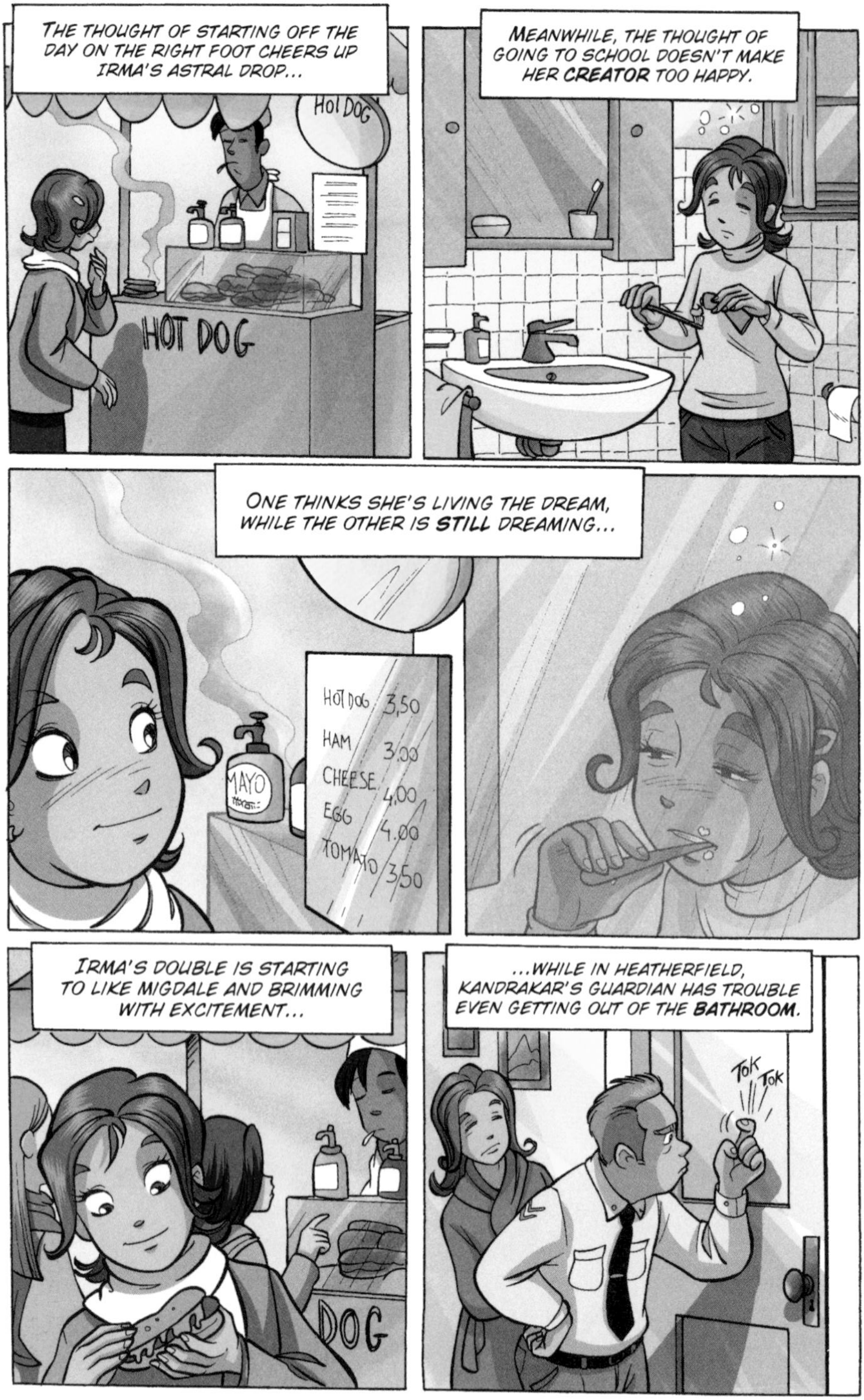
THE THOUGHT OF STARTING OFF THE DAY ON THE RIGHT FOOT CHEERS UP IRMA'S ASTRAL DROP...
HOT DOG
HOT DOG
MEANWHILE, THE THOUGHT OF GOING TO SCHOOL DOESN'T MAKE HER CREATOR TOO HAPPY.
ONE THINKS SHE'S LIVING THE DREAM, WHILE THE OTHER IS STILL DREAMING...
HOT DOG 3,50
HAM 3.00
CHEESE 4,00
EGG 4.00
TOMATO 3,50
MAYO
IRMA'S DOUBLE IS STARTING TO LIKE MIGDALE AND BRIMMING WITH EXCITEMENT...
DOG
...WHILE IN HEATHERFIELD, KANDRAKAR'S GUARDIAN HAS TROUBLE EVEN GETTING OUT OF THE BATHROOM.
TOK TOK

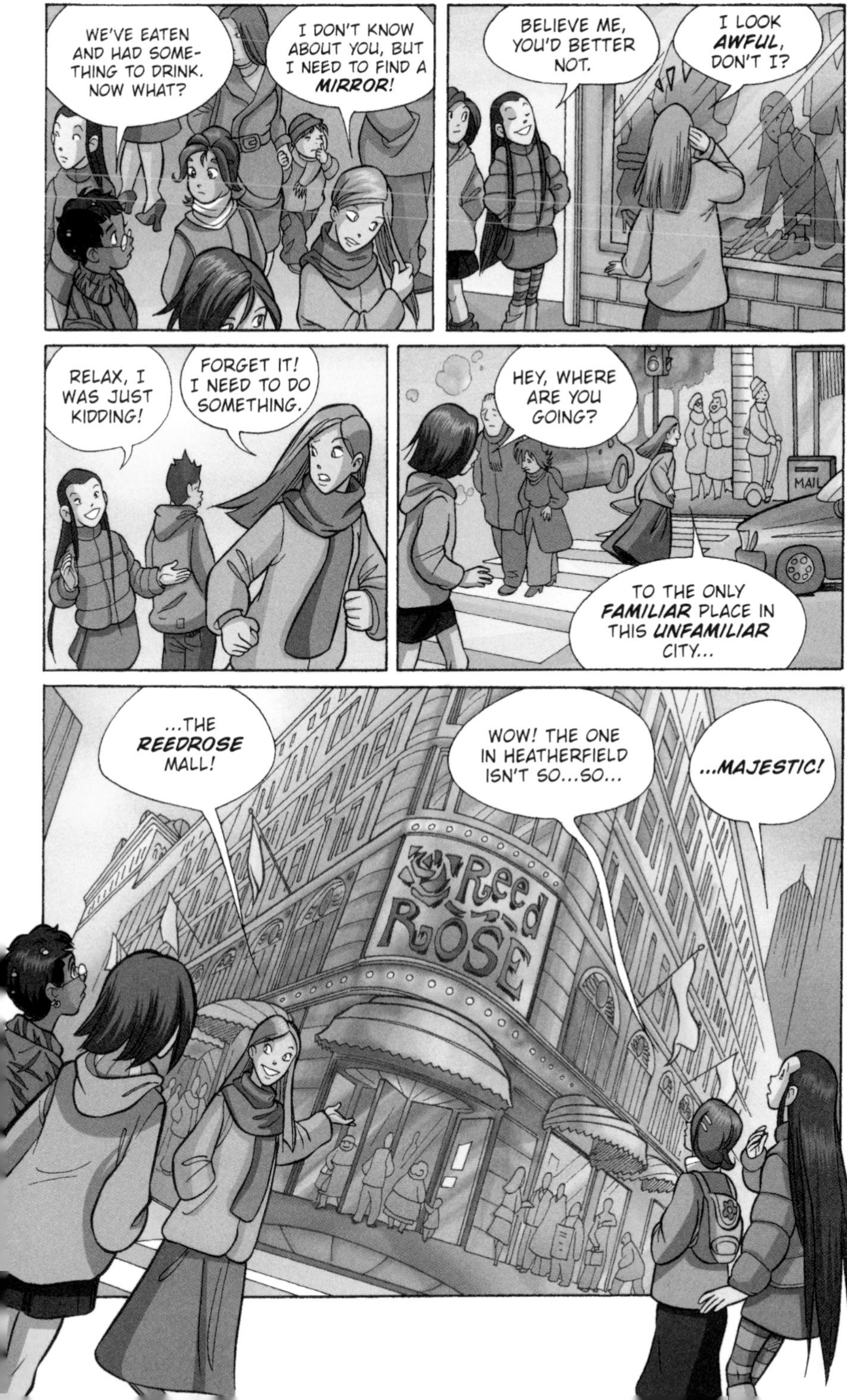
WE'VE EATEN AND HAD SOME-THING TO DRINK. NOW WHAT?
I DON'T KNOW ABOUT YOU, BUT I NEED TO FIND A **MIRROR**!
BELIEVE ME, YOU'D BETTER NOT.
I LOOK **AWFUL**, DON'T I?
RELAX, I WAS JUST KIDDING!
FORGET IT! I NEED TO DO SOMETHING.
HEY, WHERE ARE YOU GOING?
MAIL
TO THE ONLY **FAMILIAR** PLACE IN THIS **UNFAMILIAR** CITY...
...THE **REEDROSE** MALL!
Reed ROSE
WOW! THE ONE IN HEATHERFIELD ISN'T SO...SO...
...MAJESTIC!

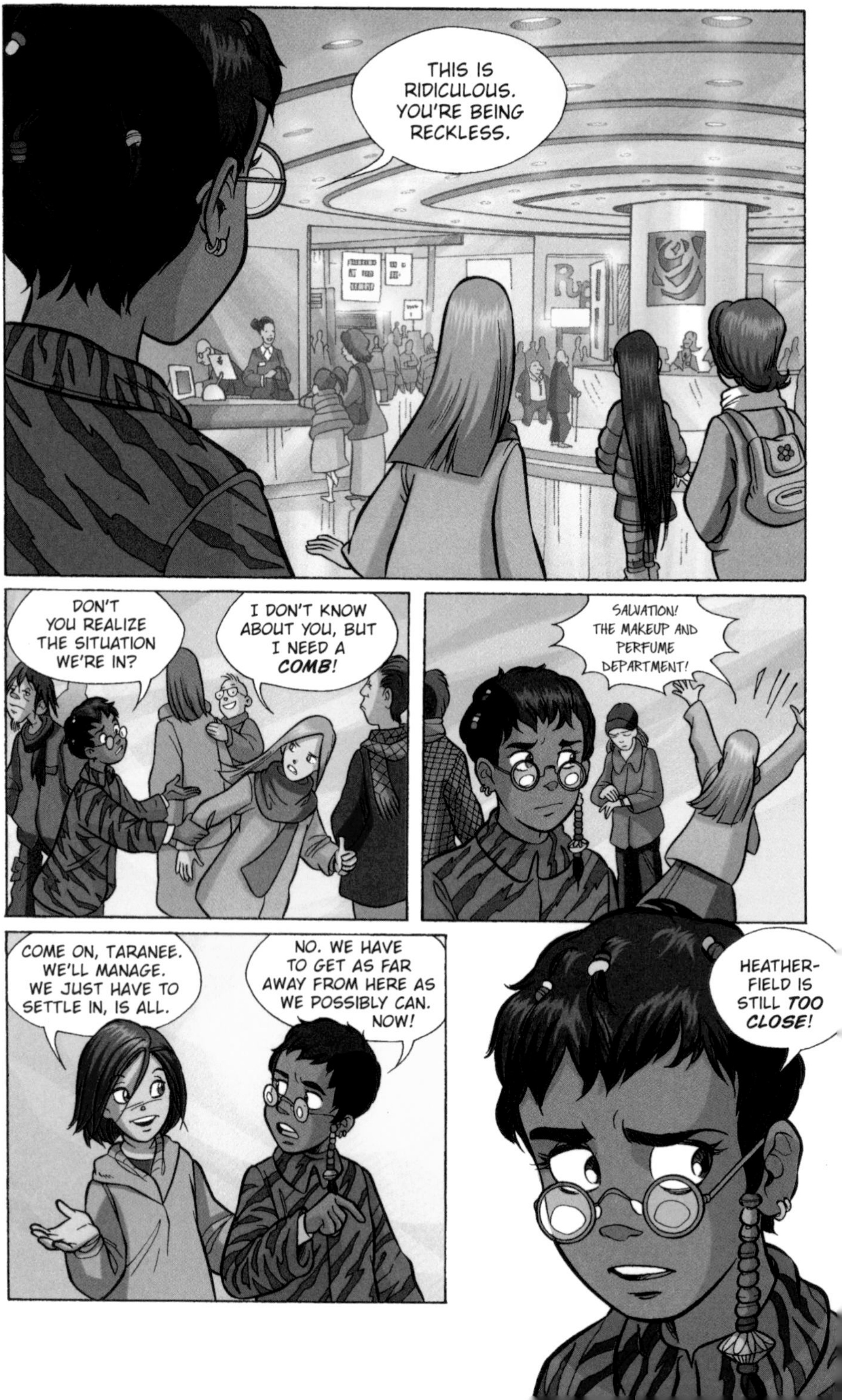
THIS IS RIDICULOUS. YOU'RE BEING RECKLESS.
DON'T YOU REALIZE THE SITUATION WE'RE IN?
I DON'T KNOW ABOUT YOU, BUT I NEED A COMB!
SALVATION! THE MAKEUP AND PERFUME DEPARTMENT!
COME ON, TARANEE. WE'LL MANAGE. WE JUST HAVE TO SETTLE IN, IS ALL.
NO. WE HAVE TO GET AS FAR AWAY FROM HERE AS WE POSSIBLY CAN. NOW!
HEATHER-FIELD IS STILL TOO CLOSE!

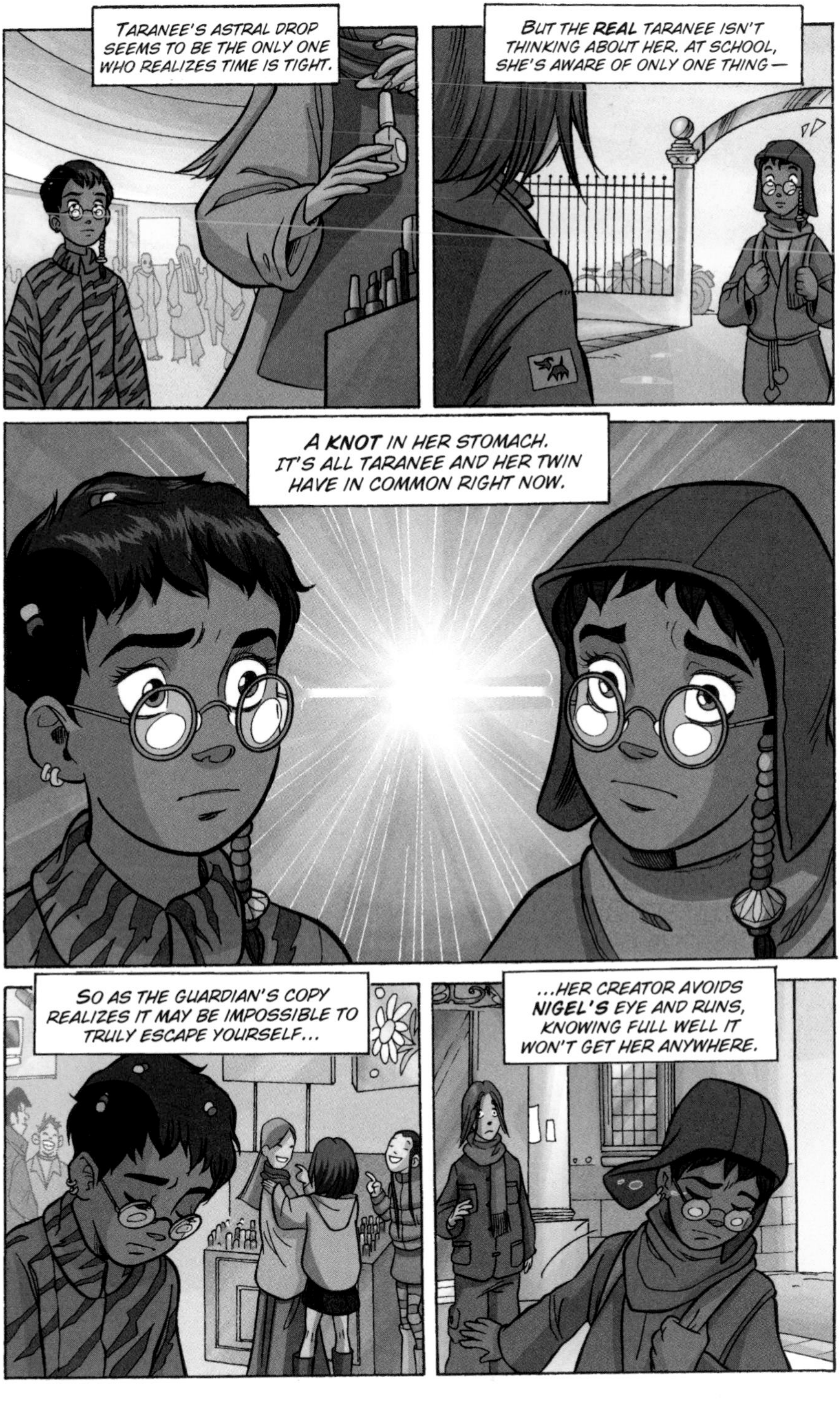
TARANEE'S ASTRAL DROP SEEMS TO BE THE ONLY ONE WHO REALIZES TIME IS TIGHT.
BUT THE **REAL** TARANEE ISN'T THINKING ABOUT HER. AT SCHOOL, SHE'S AWARE OF ONLY ONE THING —
A **KNOT** IN HER STOMACH. IT'S ALL TARANEE AND HER TWIN HAVE IN COMMON RIGHT NOW.
SO AS THE GUARDIAN'S COPY REALIZES IT MAY BE IMPOSSIBLE TO TRULY ESCAPE YOURSELF...
...HER CREATOR AVOIDS **NIGEL'S** EYE AND RUNS, KNOWING FULL WELL IT WON'T GET HER ANYWHERE.

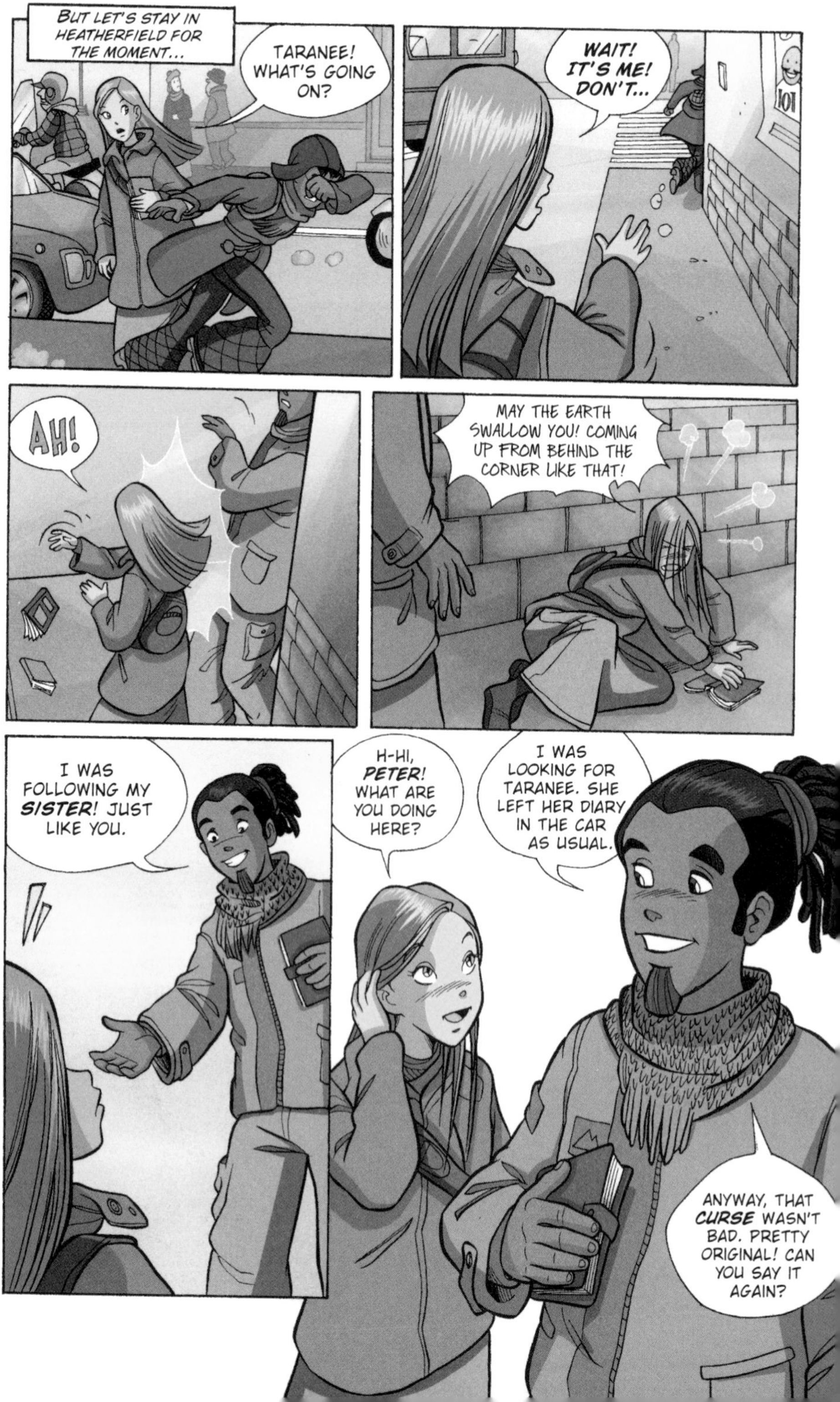

BUT LET'S STAY IN HEATHERFIELD FOR THE MOMENT...
TARANEE! WHAT'S GOING ON?
WAIT! IT'S ME! DON'T...
AH!
MAY THE EARTH SWALLOW YOU! COMING UP FROM BEHIND THE CORNER LIKE THAT!
I WAS FOLLOWING MY SISTER! JUST LIKE YOU.
H-HI, PETER! WHAT ARE YOU DOING HERE?
I WAS LOOKING FOR TARANEE. SHE LEFT HER DIARY IN THE CAR AS USUAL.
ANYWAY, THAT CURSE WASN'T BAD. PRETTY ORIGINAL! CAN YOU SAY IT AGAIN?

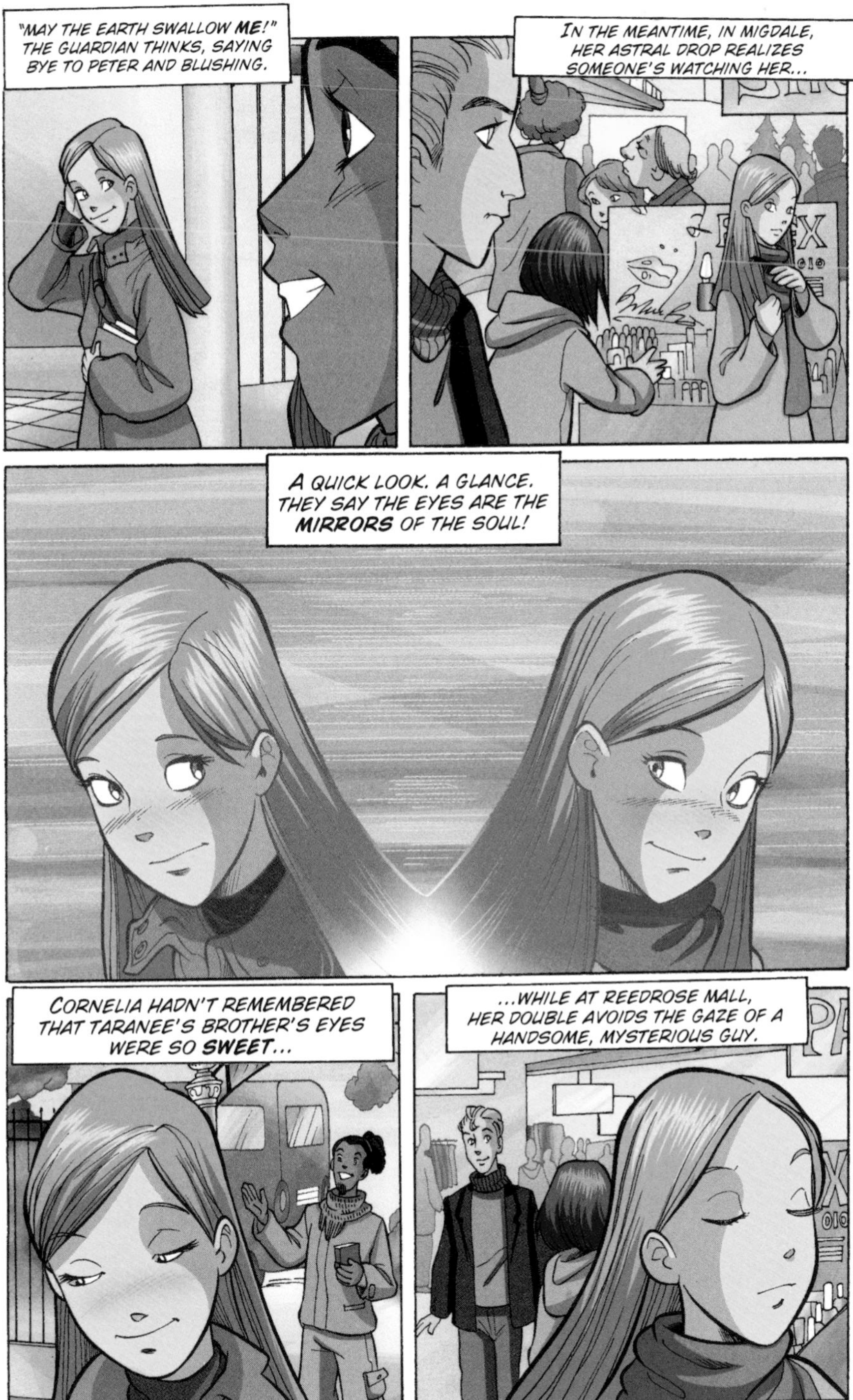
"MAY THE EARTH SWALLOW ME!" THE GUARDIAN THINKS, SAYING BYE TO PETER AND BLUSHING.
IN THE MEANTIME, IN MIGDALE, HER ASTRAL DROP REALIZES SOMEONE'S WATCHING HER...
A QUICK LOOK. A GLANCE. THEY SAY THE EYES ARE THE MIRRORS OF THE SOUL!
CORNELIA HADN'T REMEMBERED THAT TARANEE'S BROTHER'S EYES WERE SO SWEET...
...WHILE AT REEDROSE MALL, HER DOUBLE AVOIDS THE GAZE OF A HANDSOME, MYSTERIOUS GUY.

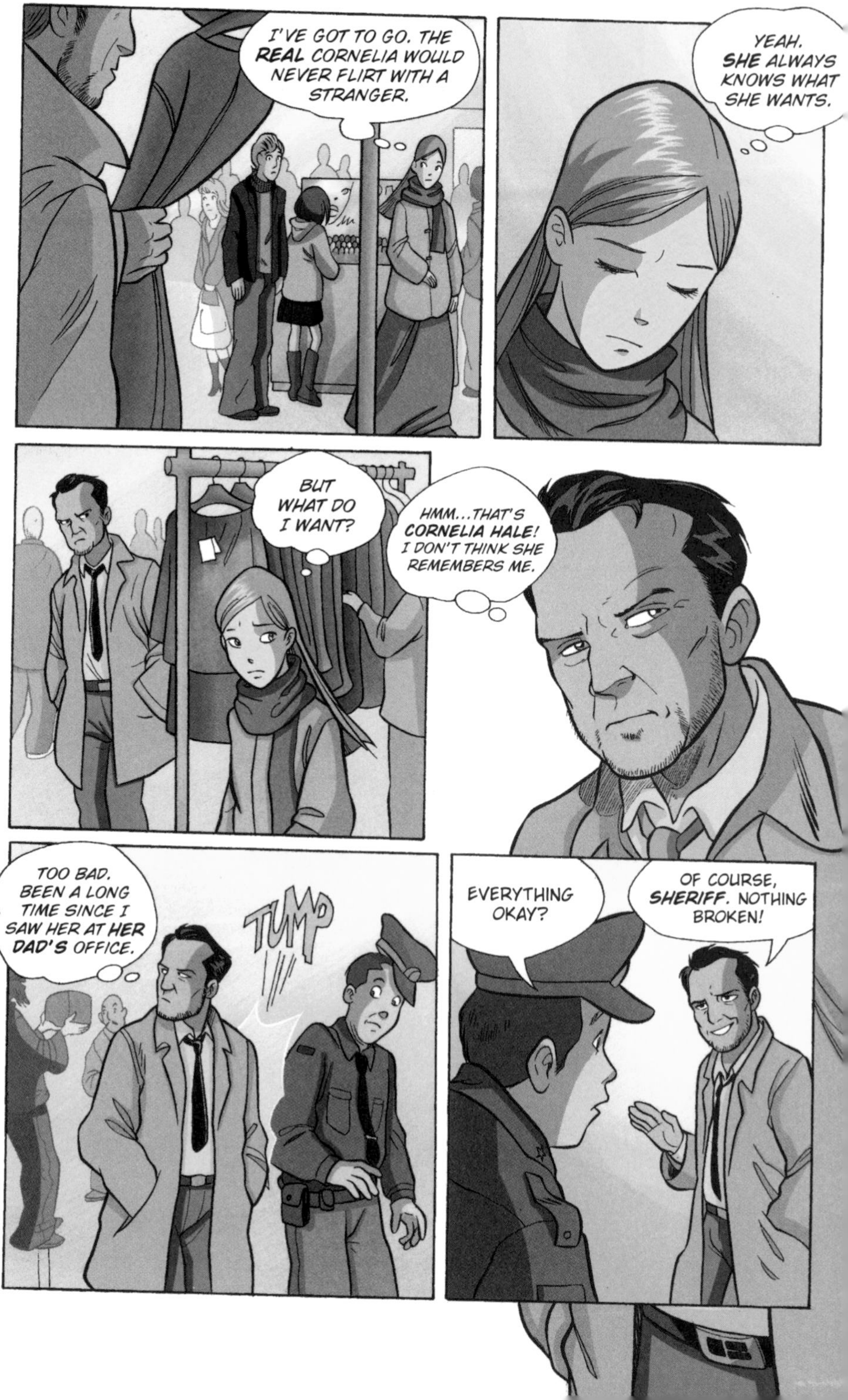
I'VE GOT TO GO. THE REAL CORNELIA WOULD NEVER FLIRT WITH A STRANGER.
YEAH. SHE ALWAYS KNOWS WHAT SHE WANTS.
BUT WHAT DO I WANT?
HMM...THAT'S CORNELIA HALE! I DON'T THINK SHE REMEMBERS ME.
TOO BAD. BEEN A LONG TIME SINCE I SAW HER AT HER DAD'S OFFICE.
TUMP
EVERYTHING OKAY?
OF COURSE, SHERIFF. NOTHING BROKEN!

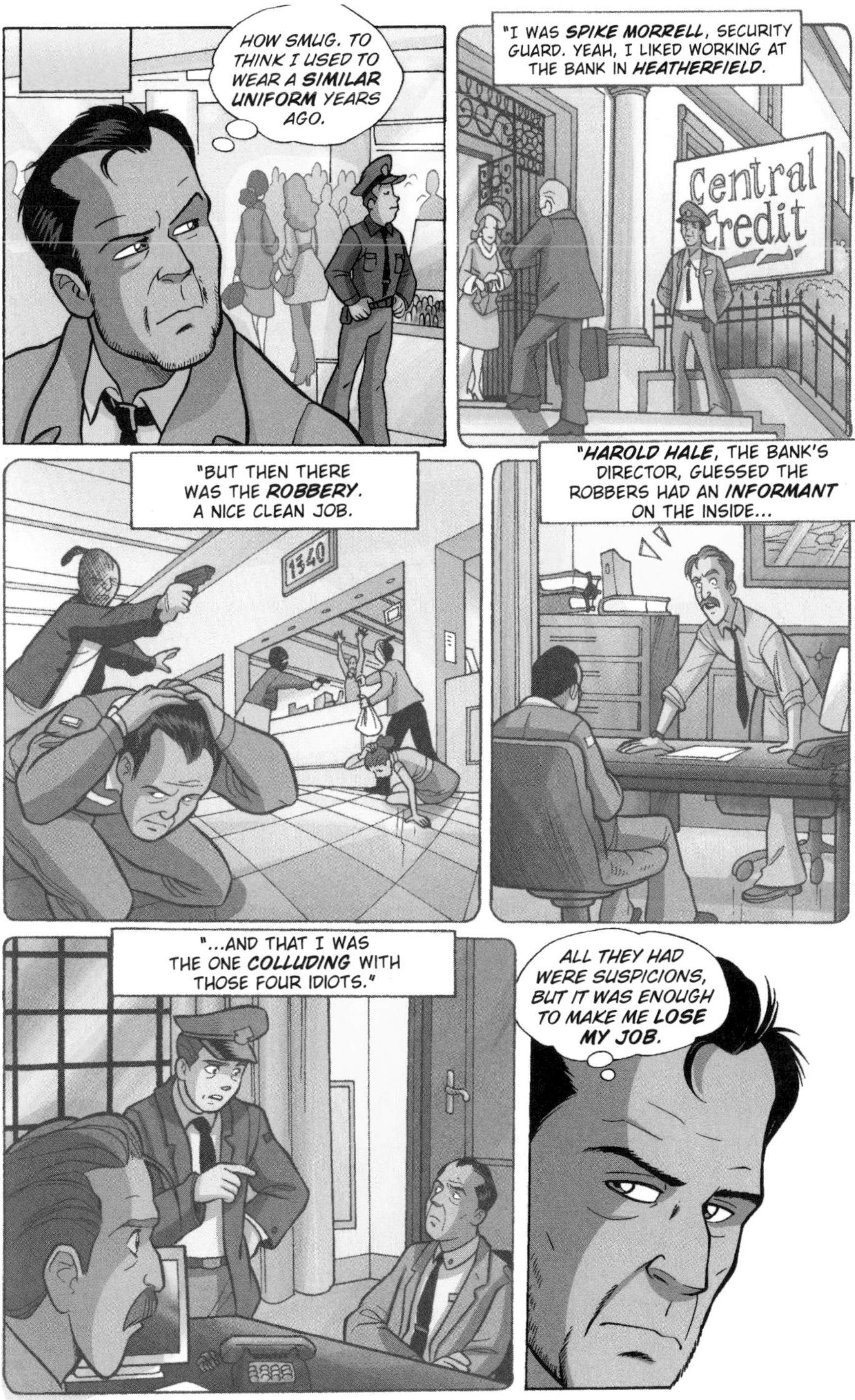
HOW SMUG. TO THINK I USED TO WEAR A SIMILAR UNIFORM YEARS AGO.
"I WAS SPIKE MORRELL, SECURITY GUARD. YEAH, I LIKED WORKING AT THE BANK IN HEATHERFIELD.
Central Credit
"BUT THEN THERE WAS THE ROBBERY. A NICE CLEAN JOB.
13:40
"HAROLD HALE, THE BANK'S DIRECTOR, GUESSED THE ROBBERS HAD AN INFORMANT ON THE INSIDE...
"...AND THAT I WAS THE ONE COLLUDING WITH THOSE FOUR IDIOTS."
ALL THEY HAD WERE SUSPICIONS, BUT IT WAS ENOUGH TO MAKE ME LOSE MY JOB.

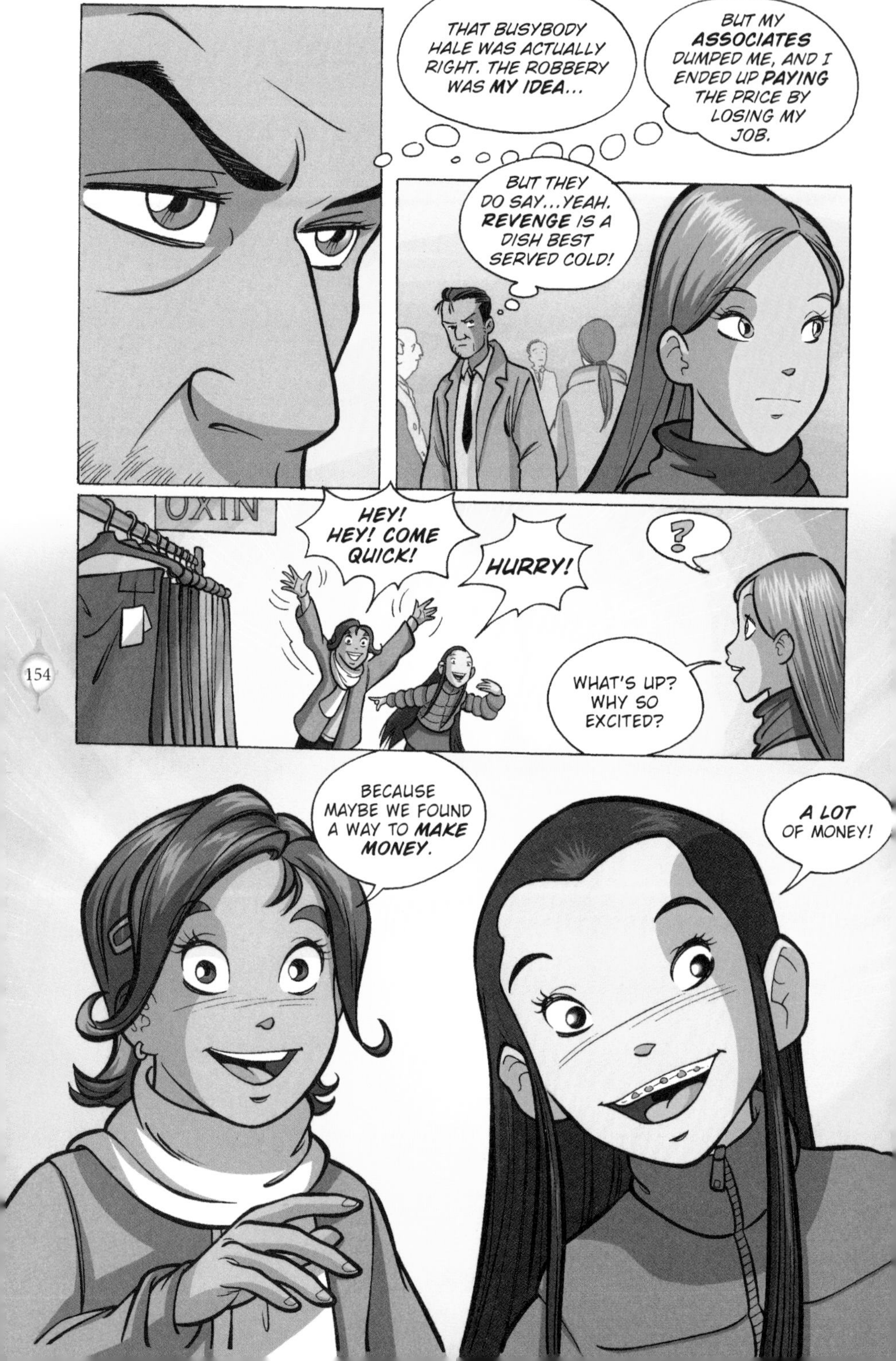
THAT BUSYBODY HALE WAS ACTUALLY RIGHT. THE ROBBERY WAS MY IDEA...
BUT MY ASSOCIATES DUMPED ME, AND I ENDED UP PAYING THE PRICE BY LOSING MY JOB.
BUT THEY DO SAY...YEAH. REVENGE IS A DISH BEST SERVED COLD!
UXIN
HEY! HEY! COME QUICK!
HURRY!
?
WHAT'S UP? WHY SO EXCITED?
BECAUSE MAYBE WE FOUND A WAY TO MAKE MONEY.
A LOT OF MONEY!

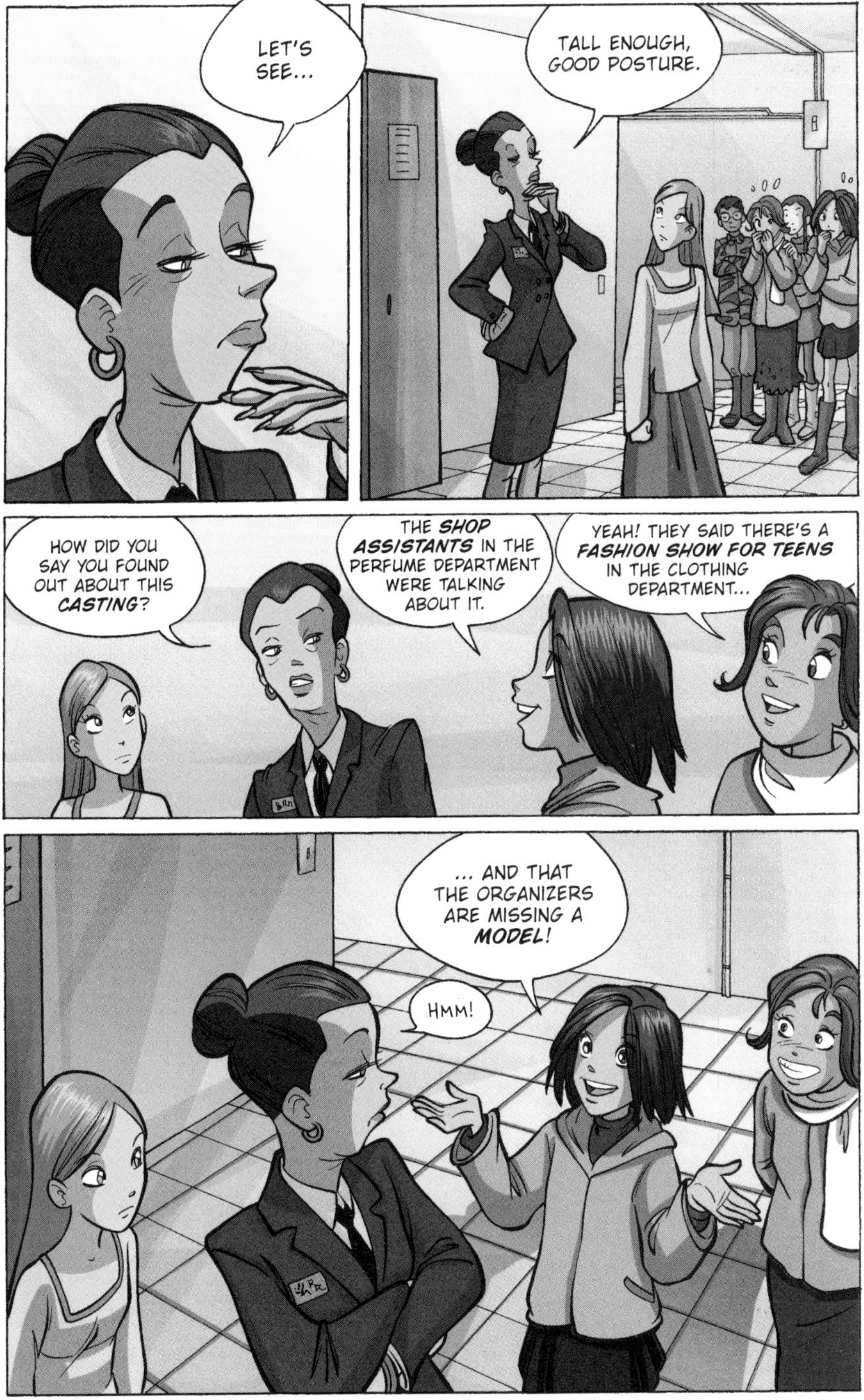
LET'S SEE...
TALL ENOUGH, GOOD POSTURE.
HOW DID YOU SAY YOU FOUND OUT ABOUT THIS CASTING?
THE SHOP ASSISTANTS IN THE PERFUME DEPARTMENT WERE TALKING ABOUT IT.
YEAH! THEY SAID THERE'S A FASHION SHOW FOR TEENS IN THE CLOTHING DEPARTMENT...
... AND THAT THE ORGANIZERS ARE MISSING A MODEL!
HMM!

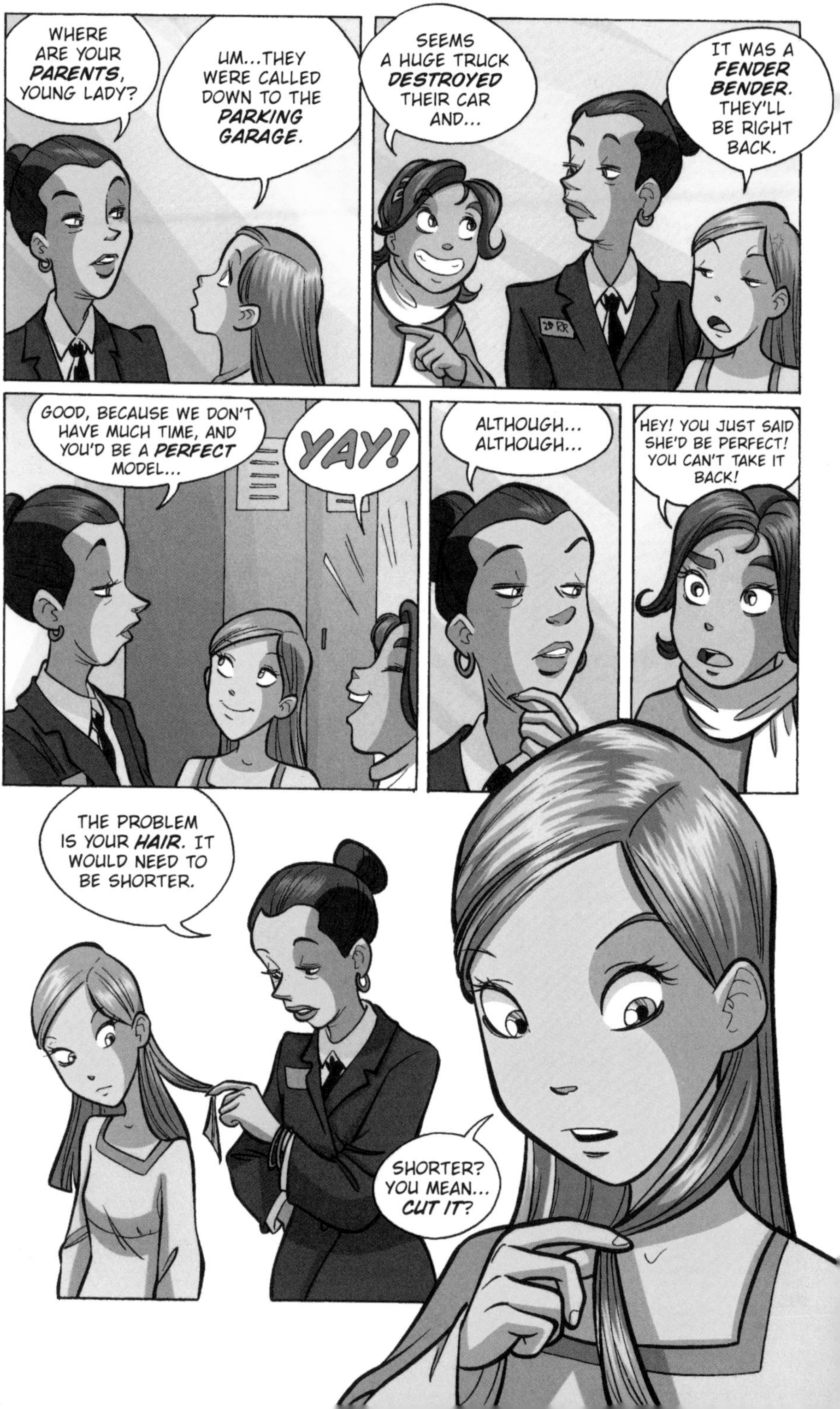
WHERE ARE YOUR PARENTS, YOUNG LADY?
UM...THEY WERE CALLED DOWN TO THE PARKING GARAGE.
SEEMS A HUGE TRUCK DESTROYED THEIR CAR AND...
IT WAS A FENDER BENDER. THEY'LL BE RIGHT BACK.
GOOD, BECAUSE WE DON'T HAVE MUCH TIME, AND YOU'D BE A PERFECT MODEL...
YAY!
ALTHOUGH... ALTHOUGH...
HEY! YOU JUST SAID SHE'D BE PERFECT! YOU CAN'T TAKE IT BACK!
THE PROBLEM IS YOUR HAIR. IT WOULD NEED TO BE SHORTER.
SHORTER? YOU MEAN... CUT IT?

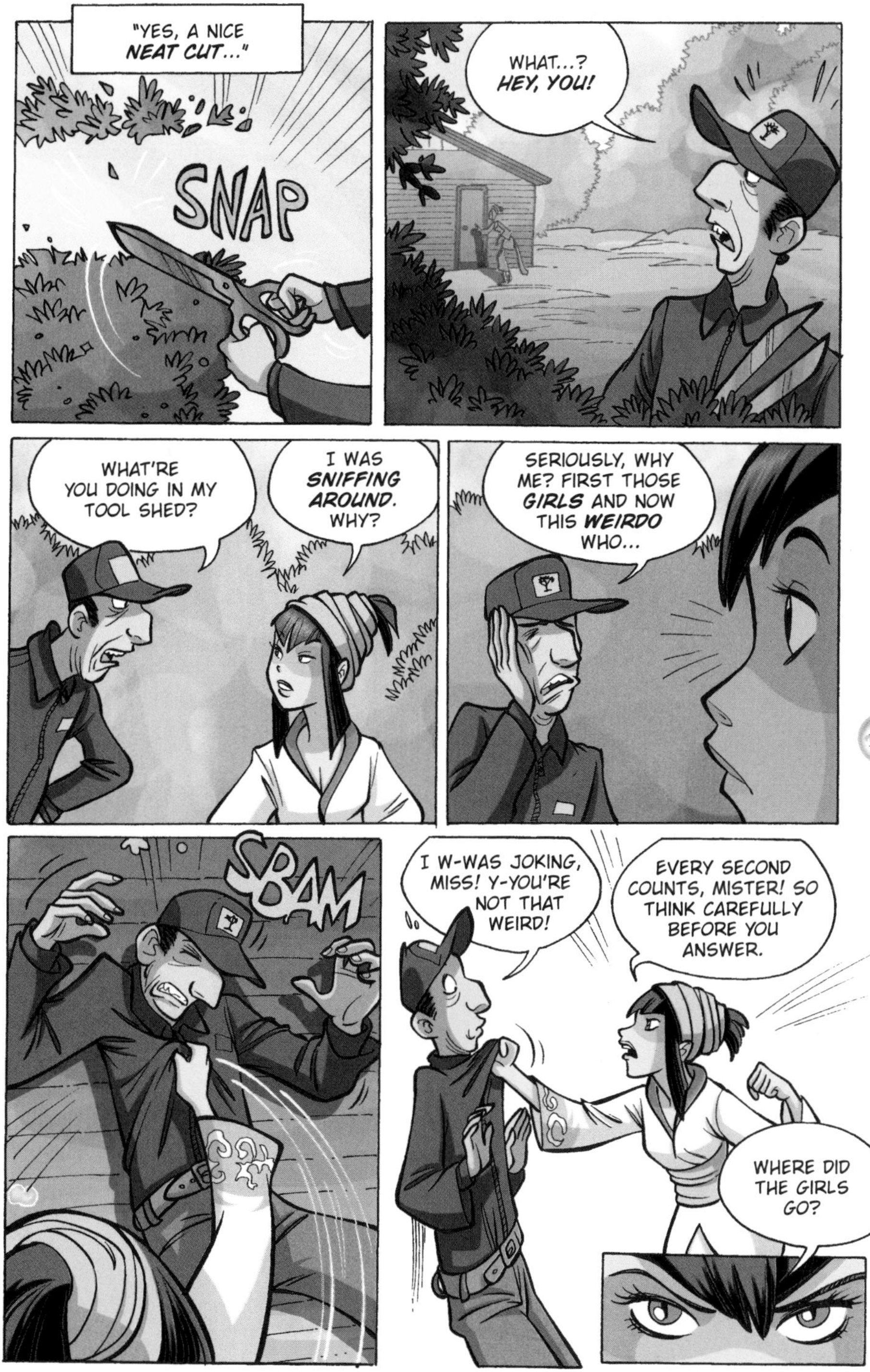
"YES, A NICE NEAT CUT..."
SNAP
WHAT...? HEY, YOU!
WHAT'RE YOU DOING IN MY TOOL SHED?
I WAS SNIFFING AROUND. WHY?
SERIOUSLY, WHY ME? FIRST THOSE GIRLS AND NOW THIS WEIRDO WHO...
SBAM
I W-WAS JOKING, MISS! Y-YOU'RE NOT THAT WEIRD!
EVERY SECOND COUNTS, MISTER! SO THINK CAREFULLY BEFORE YOU ANSWER.
WHERE DID THE GIRLS GO?

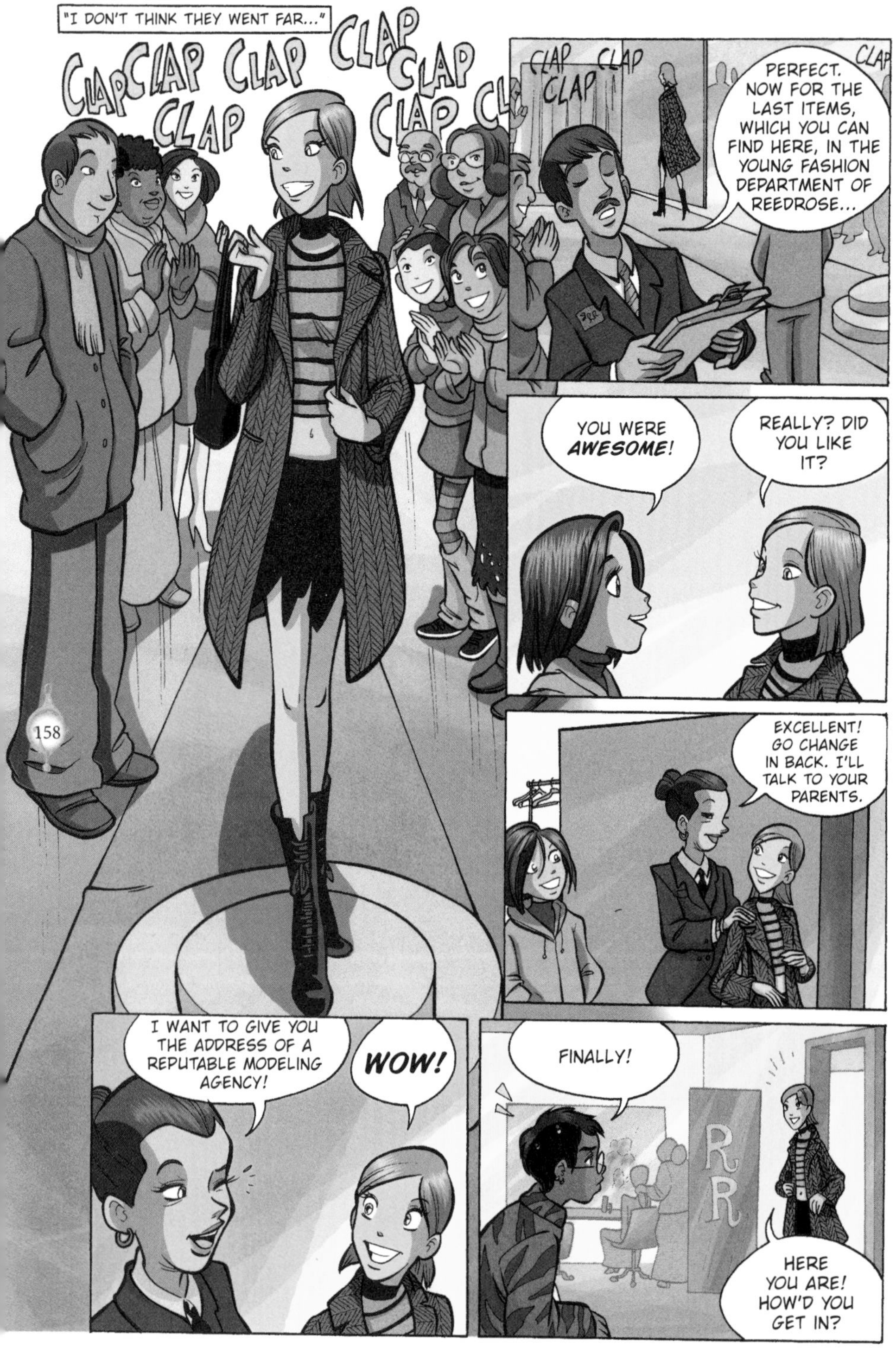
"I DON'T THINK THEY WENT FAR..."
CLAP CLAP CLAP CLAP CLAP CLAP CLAP CLAP
CLAP CLAP CLAP CLAP
PERFECT. NOW FOR THE LAST ITEMS, WHICH YOU CAN FIND HERE, IN THE YOUNG FASHION DEPARTMENT OF REEDROSE...
YOU WERE *AWESOME*!
REALLY? DID YOU LIKE IT?
EXCELLENT! GO CHANGE IN BACK. I'LL TALK TO YOUR PARENTS.
I WANT TO GIVE YOU THE ADDRESS OF A REPUTABLE MODELING AGENCY!
WOW!
FINALLY!
HERE YOU ARE! HOW'D YOU GET IN?

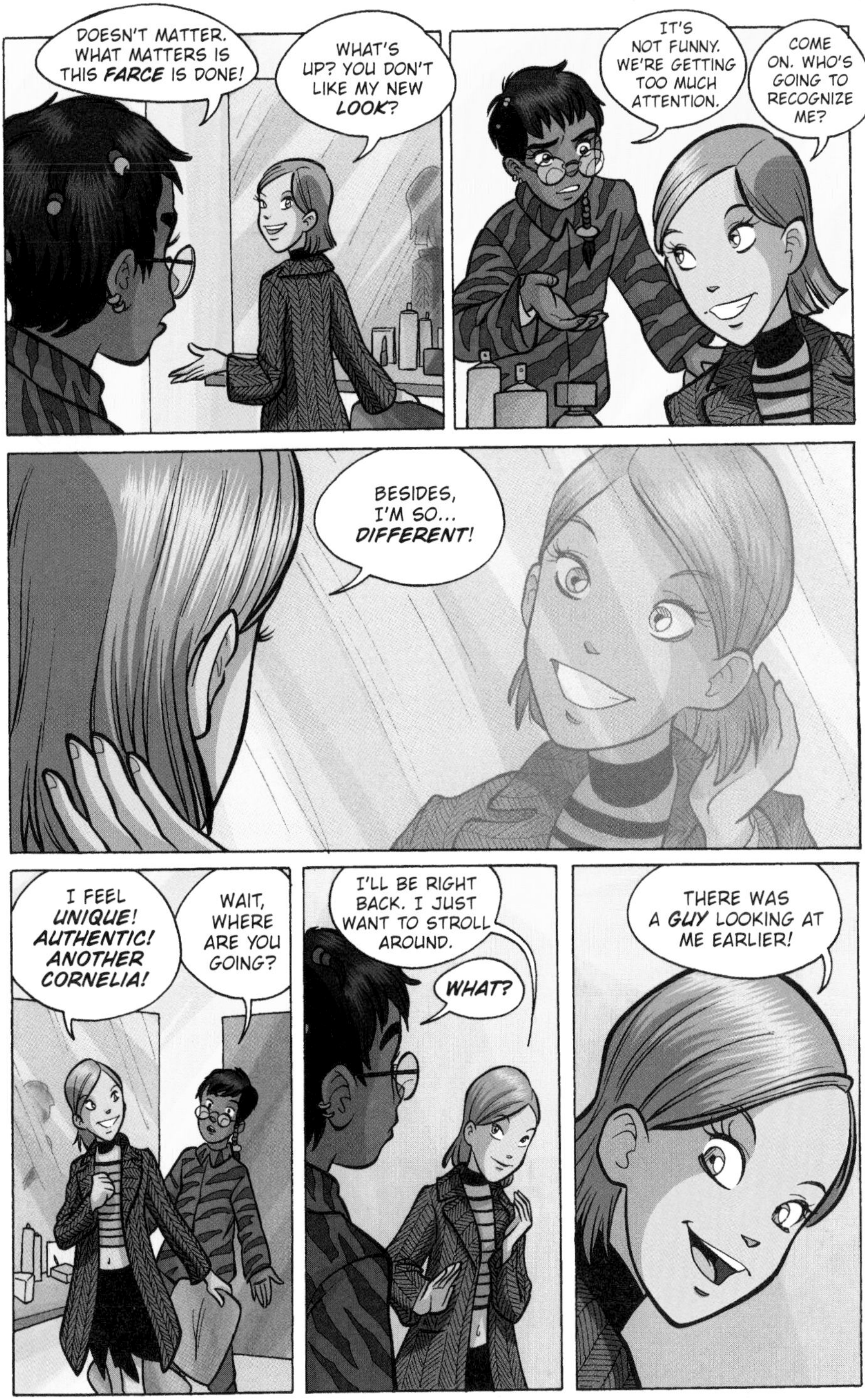
DOESN'T MATTER. WHAT MATTERS IS THIS FARCE IS DONE!
WHAT'S UP? YOU DON'T LIKE MY NEW LOOK?
IT'S NOT FUNNY. WE'RE GETTING TOO MUCH ATTENTION.
COME ON. WHO'S GOING TO RECOGNIZE ME?
BESIDES, I'M SO... DIFFERENT!
I FEEL UNIQUE! AUTHENTIC! ANOTHER CORNELIA!
WAIT, WHERE ARE YOU GOING?
I'LL BE RIGHT BACK. I JUST WANT TO STROLL AROUND.
WHAT?
THERE WAS A GUY LOOKING AT ME EARLIER!

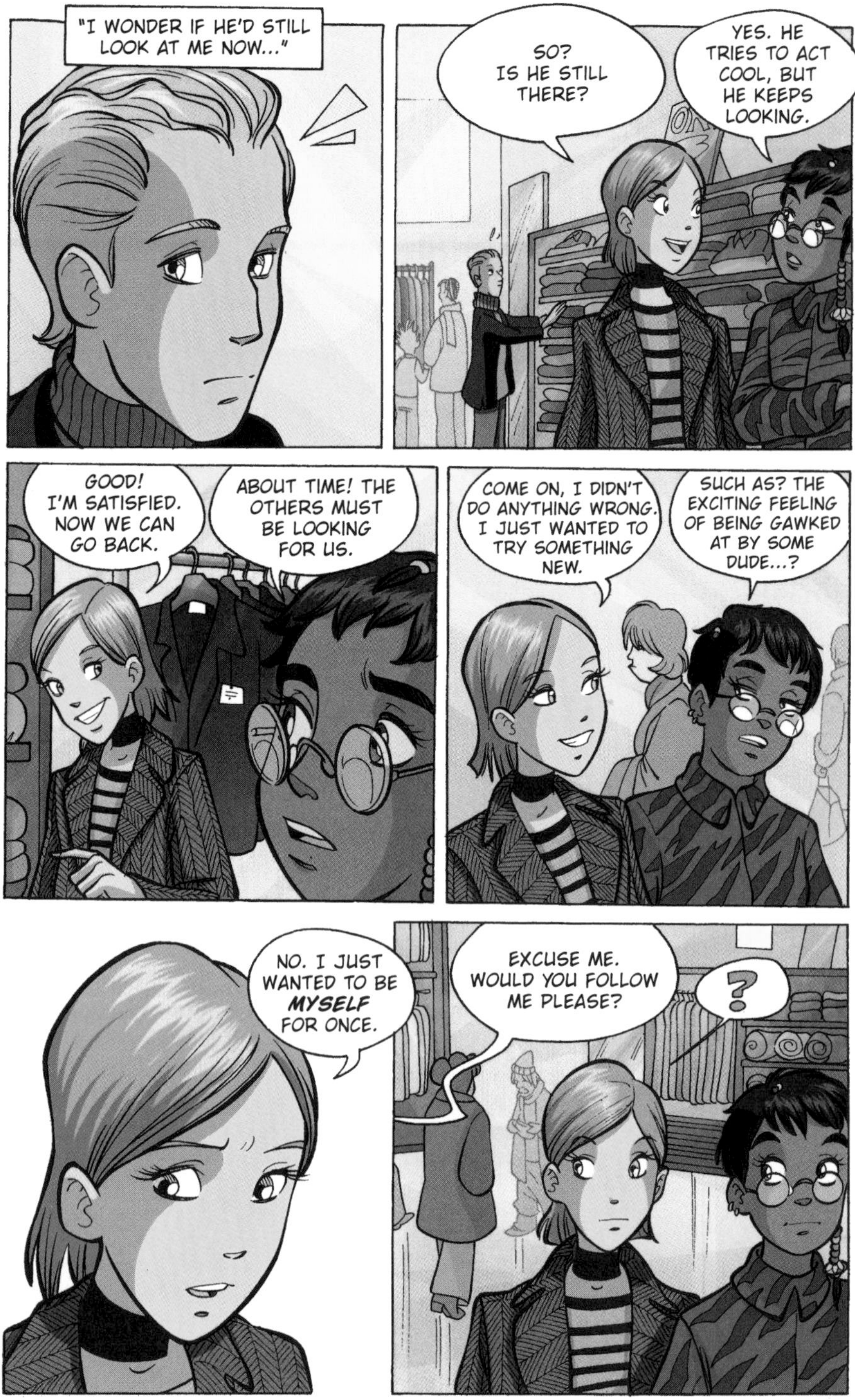

"I WONDER IF HE'D STILL LOOK AT ME NOW..."
SO? IS HE STILL THERE?
YES. HE TRIES TO ACT COOL, BUT HE KEEPS LOOKING.
GOOD! I'M SATISFIED. NOW WE CAN GO BACK.
ABOUT TIME! THE OTHERS MUST BE LOOKING FOR US.
COME ON, I DIDN'T DO ANYTHING WRONG. I JUST WANTED TO TRY SOMETHING NEW.
SUCH AS? THE EXCITING FEELING OF BEING GAWKED AT BY SOME DUDE...?
NO. I JUST WANTED TO BE ***MYSELF*** FOR ONCE.
EXCUSE ME. WOULD YOU FOLLOW ME PLEASE?
?

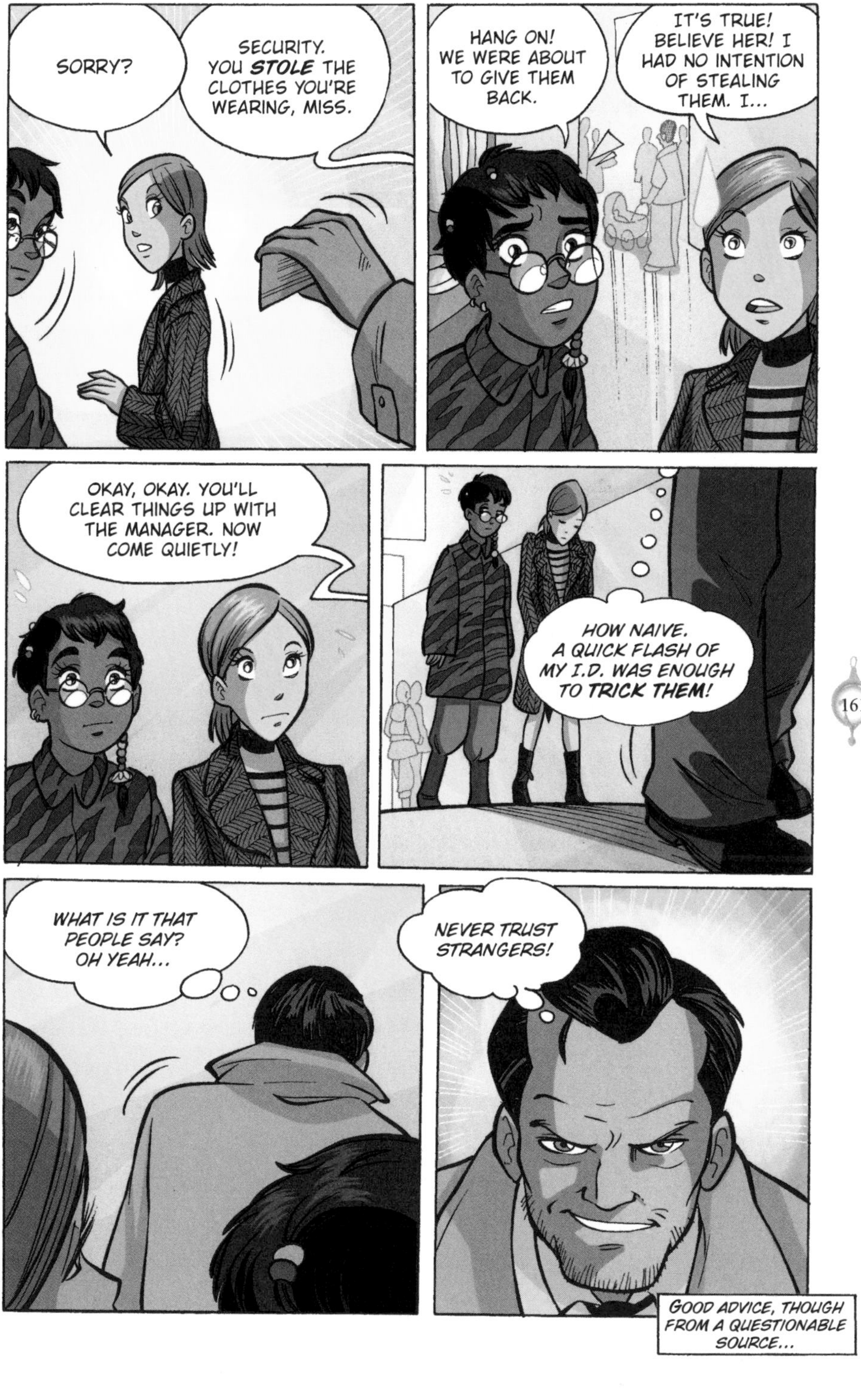
SORRY?
SECURITY. YOU STOLE THE CLOTHES YOU'RE WEARING, MISS.
HANG ON! WE WERE ABOUT TO GIVE THEM BACK.
IT'S TRUE! BELIEVE HER! I HAD NO INTENTION OF STEALING THEM. I...
OKAY, OKAY. YOU'LL CLEAR THINGS UP WITH THE MANAGER. NOW COME QUIETLY!
HOW NAIVE. A QUICK FLASH OF MY I.D. WAS ENOUGH TO TRICK THEM!
WHAT IS IT THAT PEOPLE SAY? OH YEAH...
NEVER TRUST STRANGERS!
GOOD ADVICE, THOUGH FROM A QUESTIONABLE SOURCE...

W.i.t.c.h.

Will Irma Taranee Cornelia Hay Lin

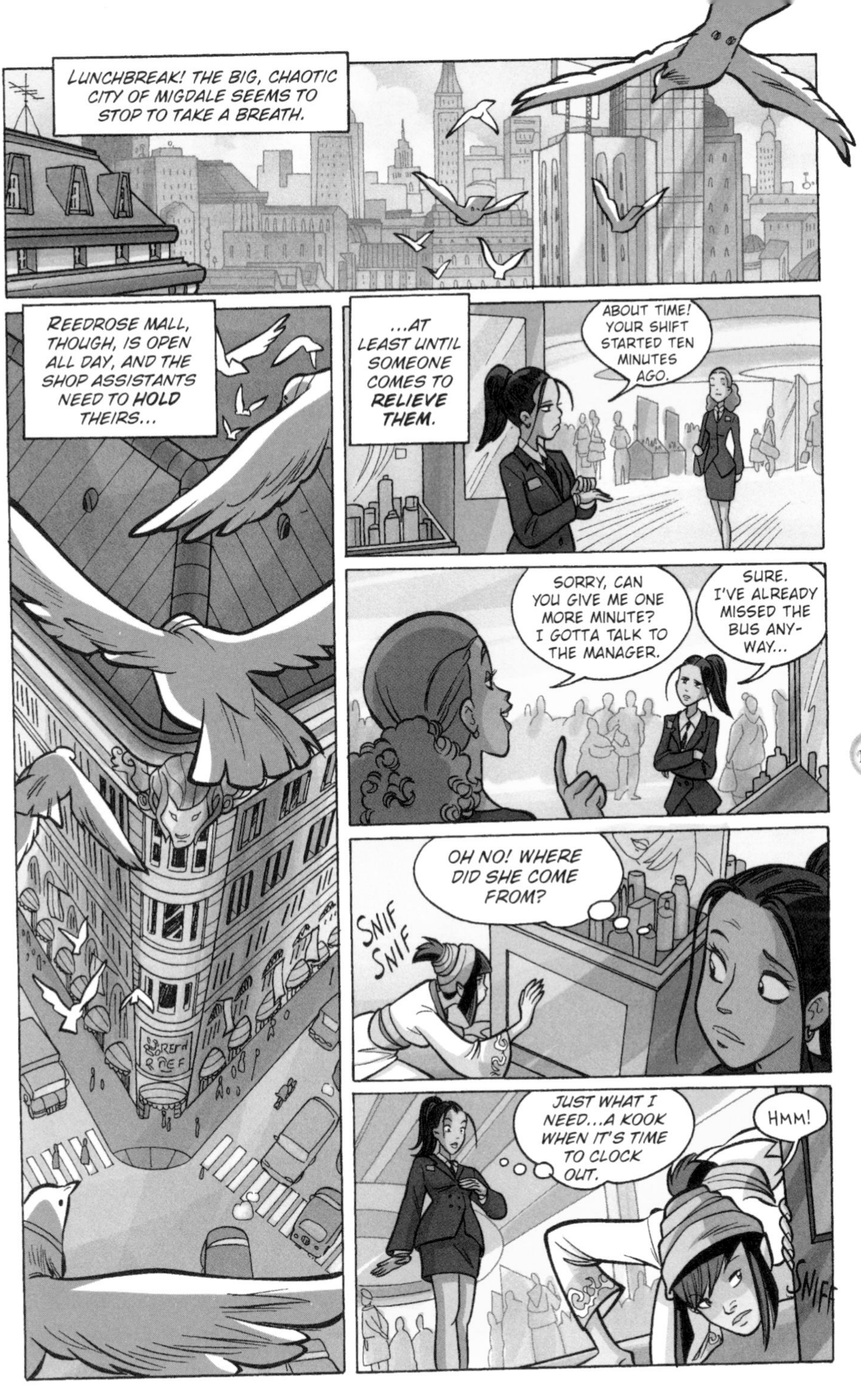

LUNCHBREAK! THE BIG, CHAOTIC CITY OF MIGDALE SEEMS TO STOP TO TAKE A BREATH.
REEDROSE MALL, THOUGH, IS OPEN ALL DAY, AND THE SHOP ASSISTANTS NEED TO HOLD THEIRS...
...AT LEAST UNTIL SOMEONE COMES TO RELIEVE THEM.
ABOUT TIME! YOUR SHIFT STARTED TEN MINUTES AGO.
SORRY, CAN YOU GIVE ME ONE MORE MINUTE? I GOTTA TALK TO THE MANAGER.
SURE. I'VE ALREADY MISSED THE BUS ANYWAY...
SNIF SNIF
OH NO! WHERE DID SHE COME FROM?
JUST WHAT I NEED...A KOOK WHEN IT'S TIME TO CLOCK OUT.
HMM!
SNIFF

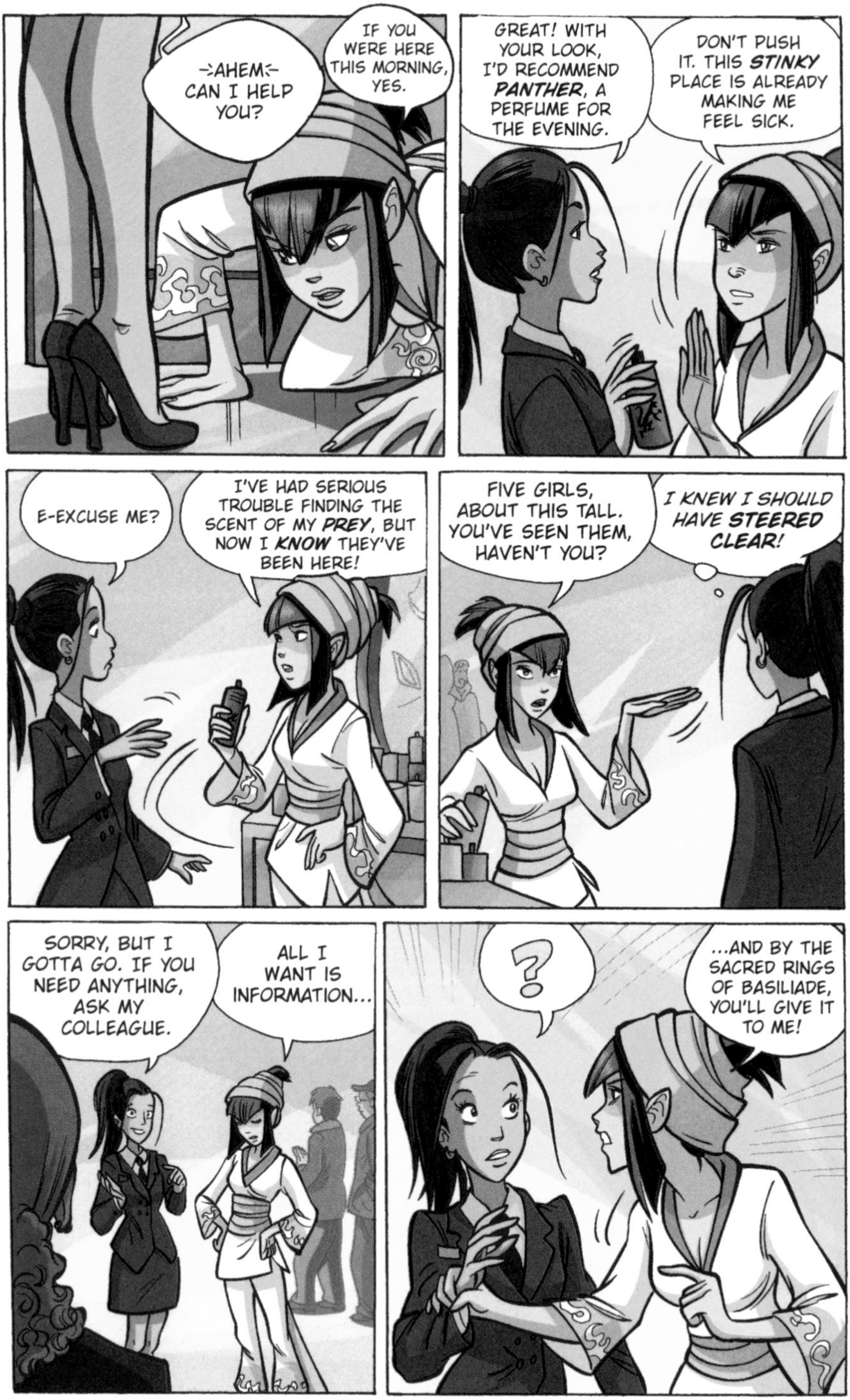

-AHEM- CAN I HELP YOU?
IF YOU WERE HERE THIS MORNING, YES.
GREAT! WITH YOUR LOOK, I'D RECOMMEND PANTHER, A PERFUME FOR THE EVENING.
DON'T PUSH IT. THIS STINKY PLACE IS ALREADY MAKING ME FEEL SICK.
E-EXCUSE ME?
I'VE HAD SERIOUS TROUBLE FINDING THE SCENT OF MY PREY, BUT NOW I KNOW THEY'VE BEEN HERE!
FIVE GIRLS, ABOUT THIS TALL. YOU'VE SEEN THEM, HAVEN'T YOU?
I KNEW I SHOULD HAVE STEERED CLEAR!
SORRY, BUT I GOTTA GO. IF YOU NEED ANYTHING, ASK MY COLLEAGUE.
ALL I WANT IS INFORMATION...
?
...AND BY THE SACRED RINGS OF BASILIADE, YOU'LL GIVE IT TO ME!

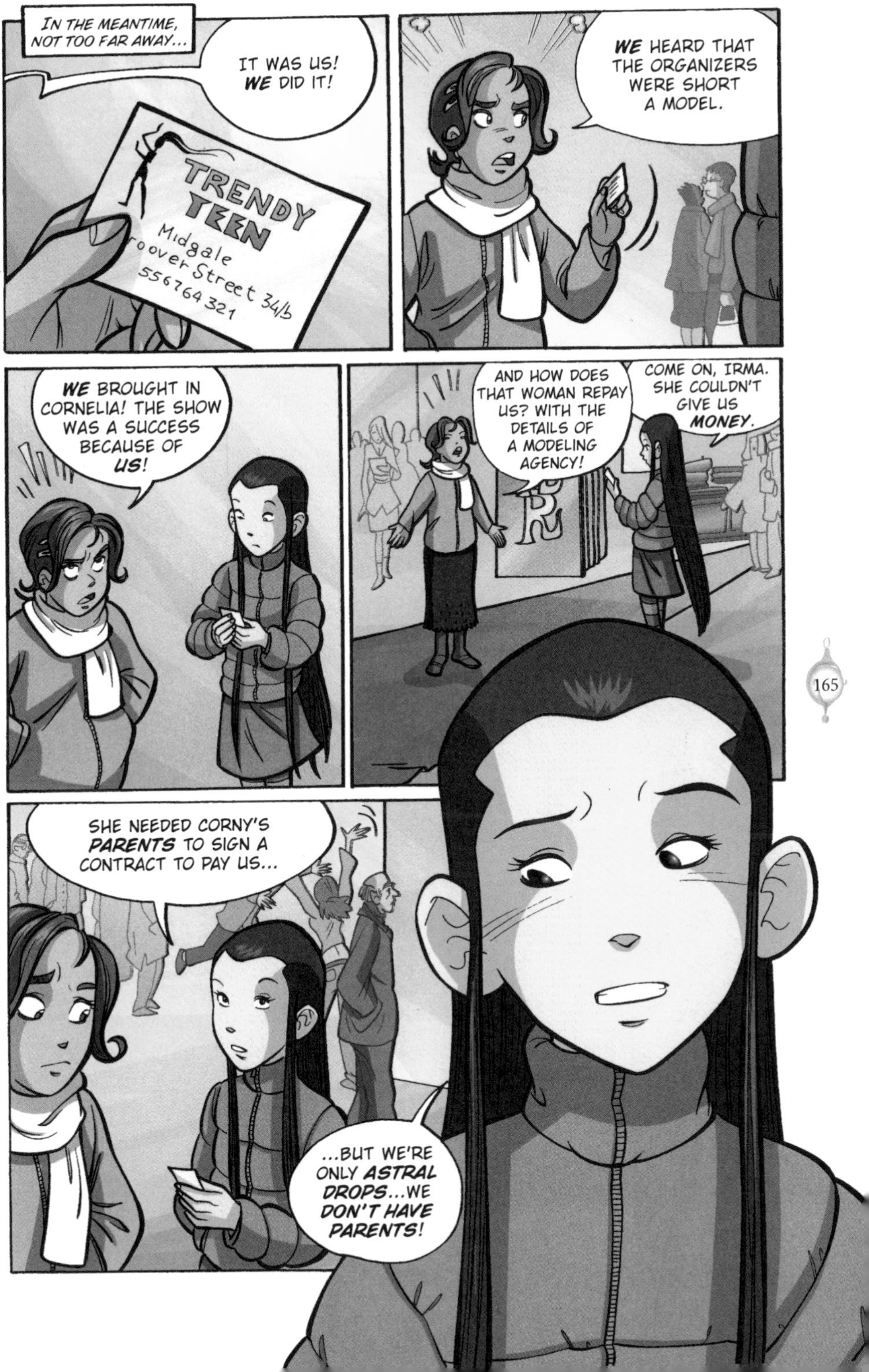
IN THE MEANTIME, NOT TOO FAR AWAY...
IT WAS US! WE DID IT!
TRENDY TEEN
Midgale
rooverStreet 34/b
556764321
WE HEARD THAT THE ORGANIZERS WERE SHORT A MODEL.
WE BROUGHT IN CORNELIA! THE SHOW WAS A SUCCESS BECAUSE OF US!
AND HOW DOES THAT WOMAN REPAY US? WITH THE DETAILS OF A MODELING AGENCY!
COME ON, IRMA. SHE COULDN'T GIVE US MONEY.
SHE NEEDED CORNY'S PARENTS TO SIGN A CONTRACT TO PAY US...
...BUT WE'RE ONLY ASTRAL DROPS...WE DON'T HAVE PARENTS!

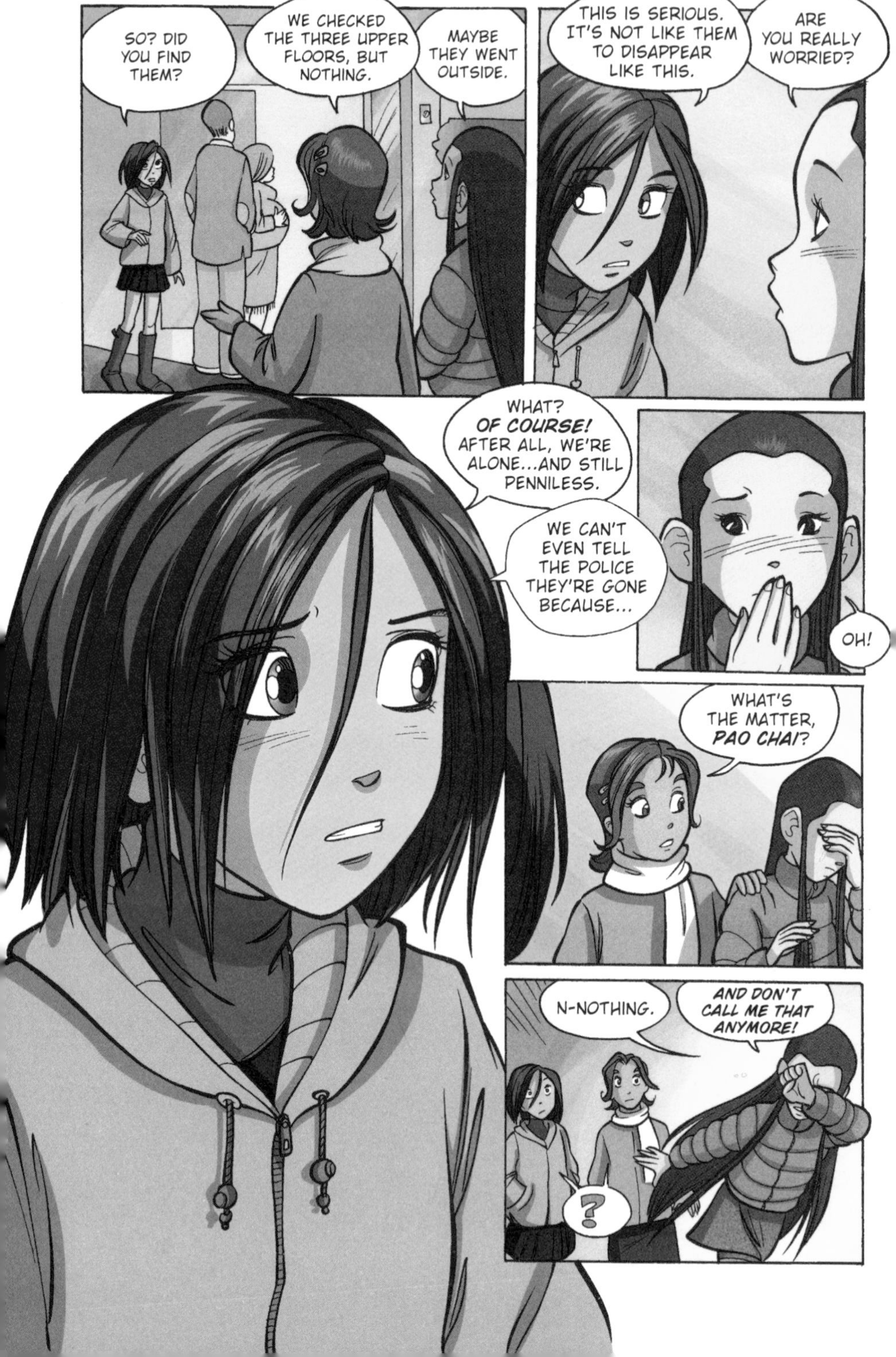
SO? DID YOU FIND THEM?
WE CHECKED THE THREE UPPER FLOORS, BUT NOTHING.
MAYBE THEY WENT OUTSIDE.
THIS IS SERIOUS. IT'S NOT LIKE THEM TO DISAPPEAR LIKE THIS.
ARE YOU REALLY WORRIED?
WHAT? OF COURSE! AFTER ALL, WE'RE ALONE...AND STILL PENNILESS.
WE CAN'T EVEN TELL THE POLICE THEY'RE GONE BECAUSE...
OH!
WHAT'S THE MATTER, PAO CHAI?
N-NOTHING.
AND DON'T CALL ME THAT ANYMORE!
?

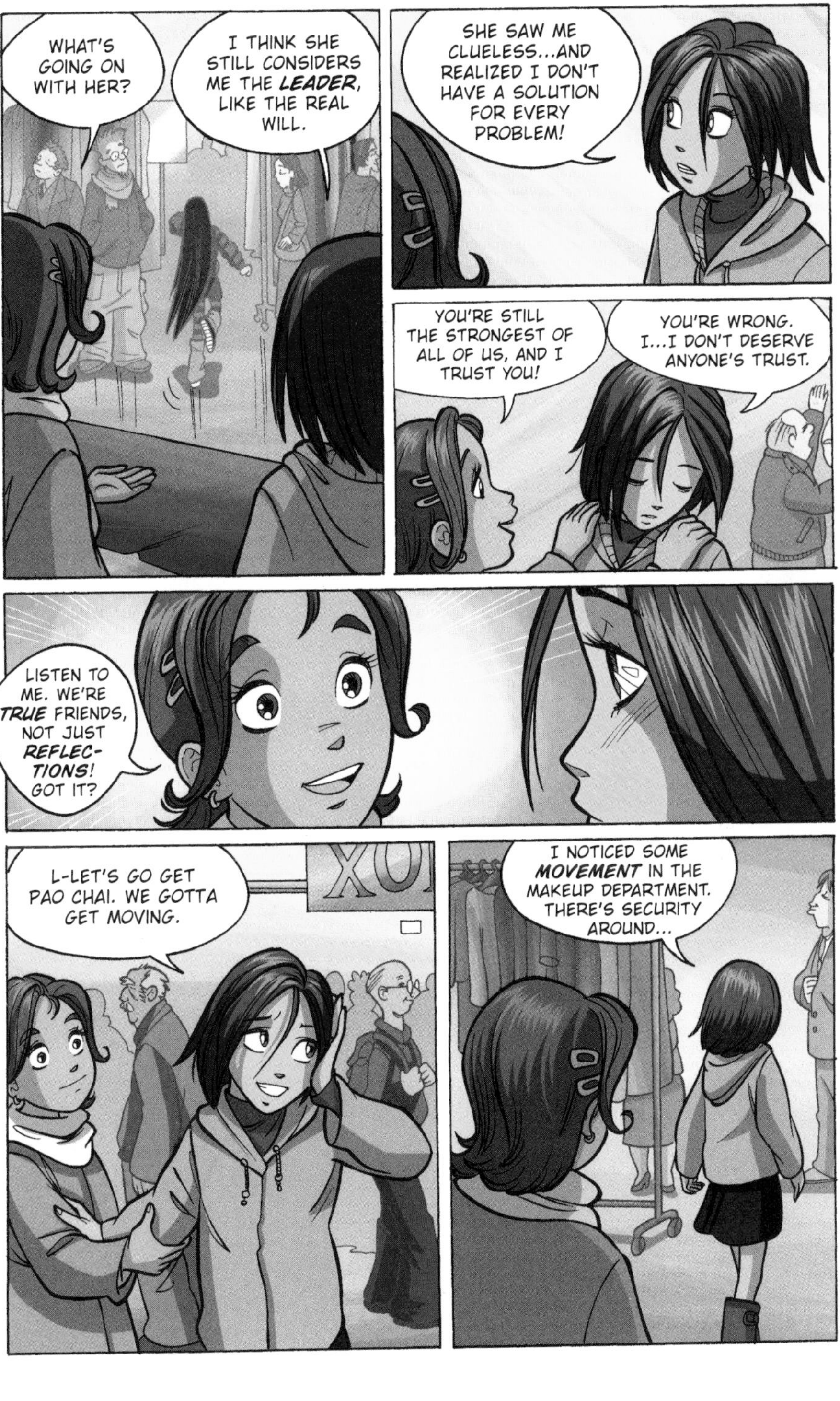

WHAT'S GOING ON WITH HER?
I THINK SHE STILL CONSIDERS ME THE LEADER, LIKE THE REAL WILL.
SHE SAW ME CLUELESS...AND REALIZED I DON'T HAVE A SOLUTION FOR EVERY PROBLEM!
YOU'RE STILL THE STRONGEST OF ALL OF US, AND I TRUST YOU!
YOU'RE WRONG. I...I DON'T DESERVE ANYONE'S TRUST.
LISTEN TO ME. WE'RE TRUE FRIENDS, NOT JUST REFLEC-TIONS! GOT IT?
L-LET'S GO GET PAO CHAI. WE GOTTA GET MOVING.
I NOTICED SOME MOVEMENT IN THE MAKEUP DEPARTMENT. THERE'S SECURITY AROUND...

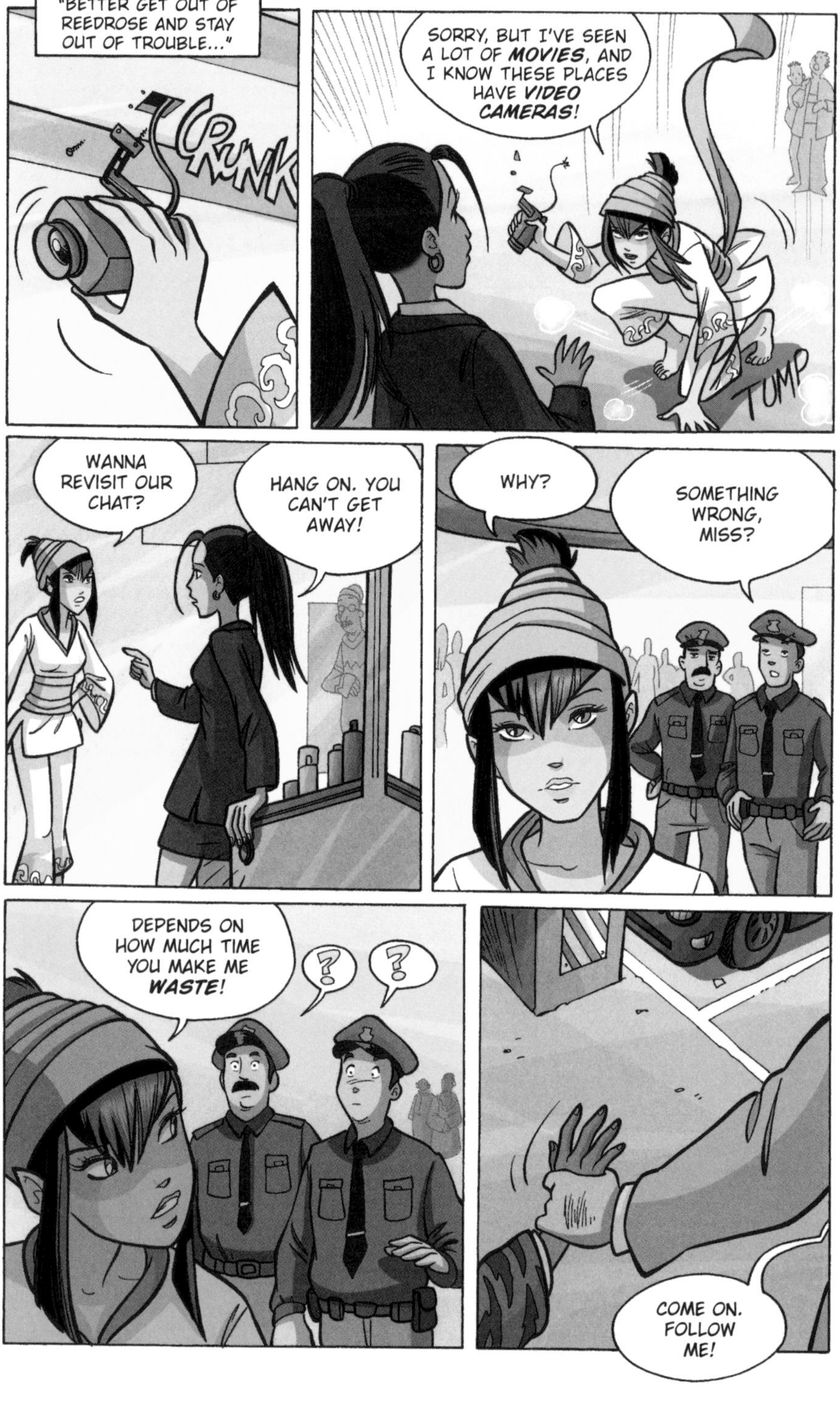

"BETTER GET OUT OF REEDROSE AND STAY OUT OF TROUBLE..."
CRUNK
SORRY, BUT I'VE SEEN A LOT OF MOVIES, AND I KNOW THESE PLACES HAVE VIDEO CAMERAS!
TUMP
WANNA REVISIT OUR CHAT?
HANG ON. YOU CAN'T GET AWAY!
WHY?
SOMETHING WRONG, MISS?
DEPENDS ON HOW MUCH TIME YOU MAKE ME WASTE!
?
?
COME ON. FOLLOW ME!

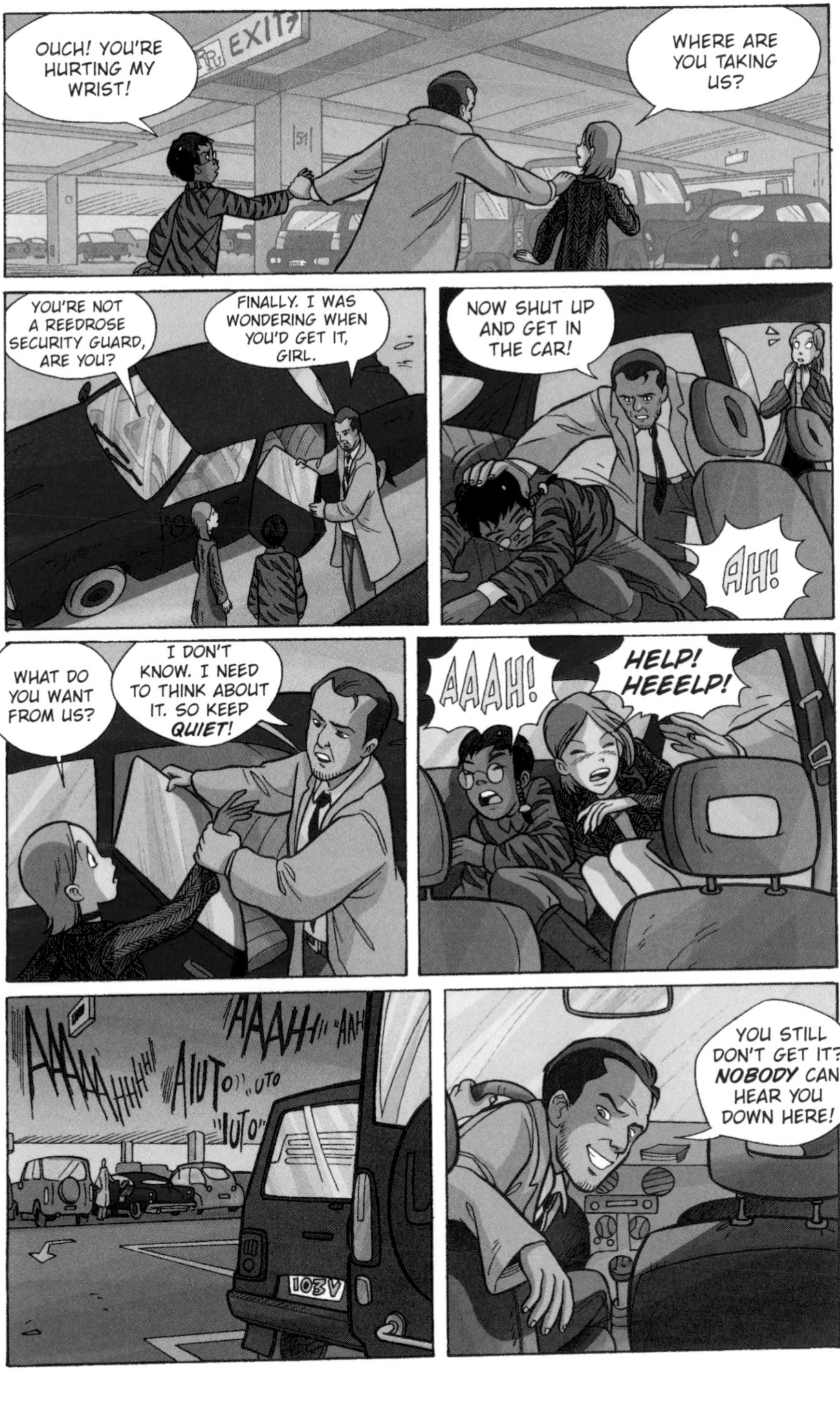
OUCH! YOU'RE HURTING MY WRIST!
EXIT
WHERE ARE YOU TAKING US?
YOU'RE NOT A REEDROSE SECURITY GUARD, ARE YOU?
FINALLY. I WAS WONDERING WHEN YOU'D GET IT, GIRL.
NOW SHUT UP AND GET IN THE CAR!
AH!
WHAT DO YOU WANT FROM US?
I DON'T KNOW. I NEED TO THINK ABOUT IT. SO KEEP *QUIET*!
AAAH!
HELP! HEEELP!
AAAAAHHH
AIUTO
AAAH
AAH
UTO
IUTO
103V
YOU STILL DON'T GET IT? *NOBODY* CAN HEAR YOU DOWN HERE!

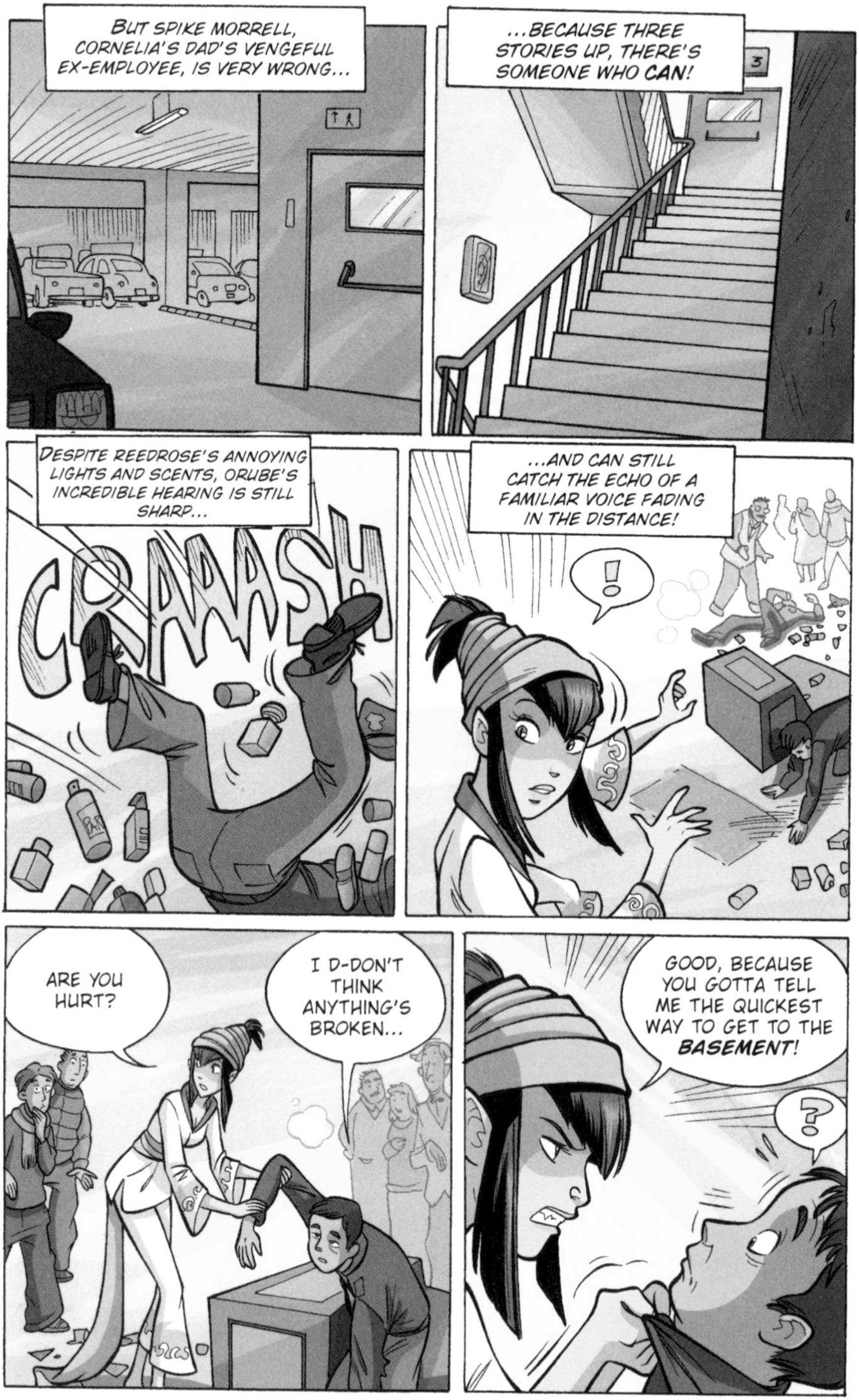

BUT SPIKE MORRELL, CORNELIA'S DAD'S VENGEFUL EX-EMPLOYEE, IS VERY WRONG...
...BECAUSE THREE STORIES UP, THERE'S SOMEONE WHO CAN!
3
DESPITE REEDROSE'S ANNOYING LIGHTS AND SCENTS, ORUBE'S INCREDIBLE HEARING IS STILL SHARP...
CRAAASH
...AND CAN STILL CATCH THE ECHO OF A FAMILIAR VOICE FADING IN THE DISTANCE!
!
ARE YOU HURT?
I D-DON'T THINK ANYTHING'S BROKEN...
GOOD, BECAUSE YOU GOTTA TELL ME THE QUICKEST WAY TO GET TO THE BASEMENT!
?

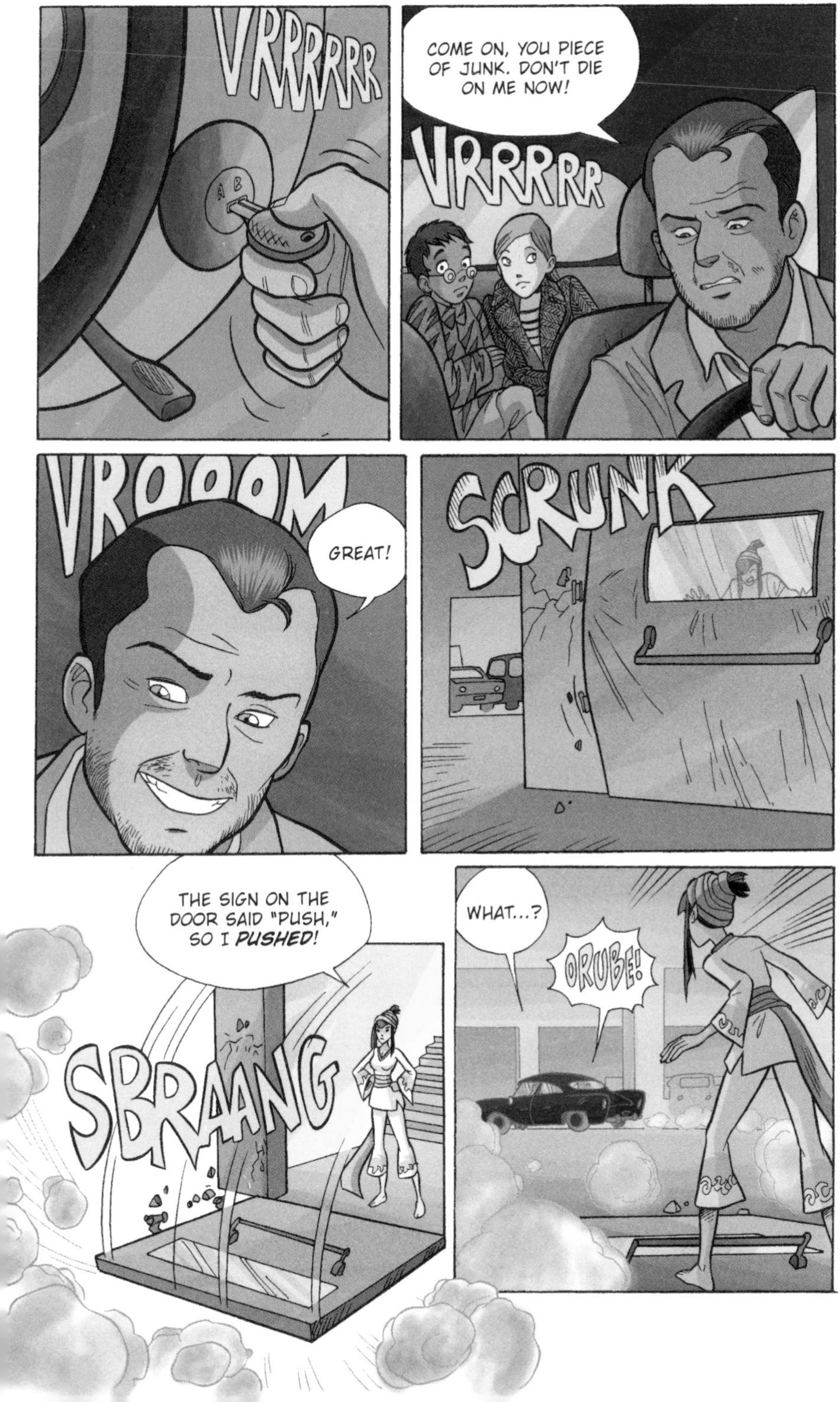
VRRRRRR
COME ON, YOU PIECE OF JUNK. DON'T DIE ON ME NOW!
VRRRRRR
VROOOM
GREAT!
SCRUNK
THE SIGN ON THE DOOR SAID "PUSH," SO I *PUSHED*!
SBRAANG
WHAT...?
ORUBE!

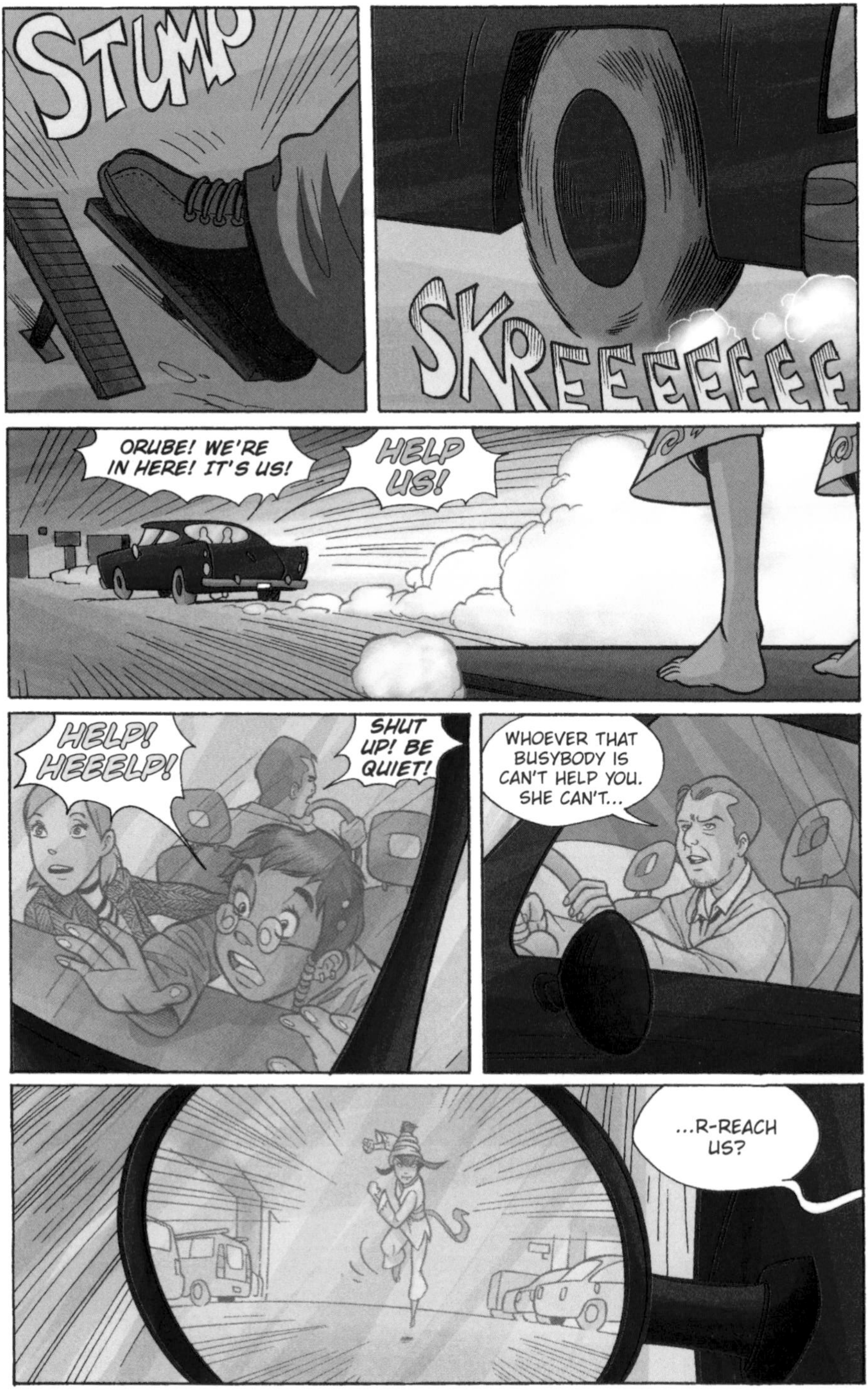
STUMP
SKREEEEEEEE
ORUBE! WE'RE IN HERE! IT'S US!
HELP US!
HELP! HEEELP!
SHUT UP! BE QUIET!
WHOEVER THAT BUSYBODY IS CAN'T HELP YOU. SHE CAN'T...
...R-REACH US?

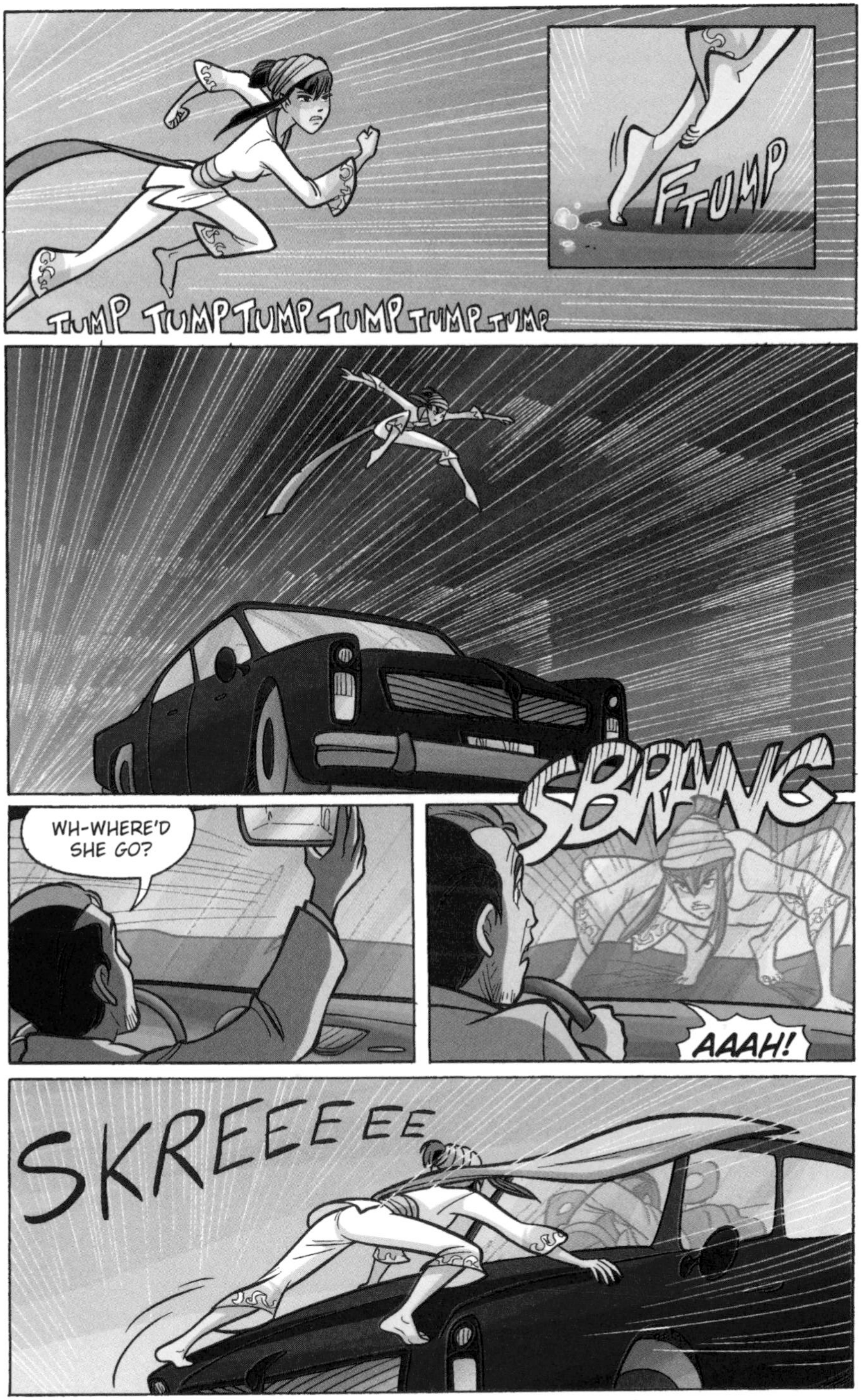
FTUMP
TUMP TUMP TUMP TUMP TUMP TUMP
SBRANG
WH-WHERE'D SHE GO?
AAAH!
SKREEEEEE

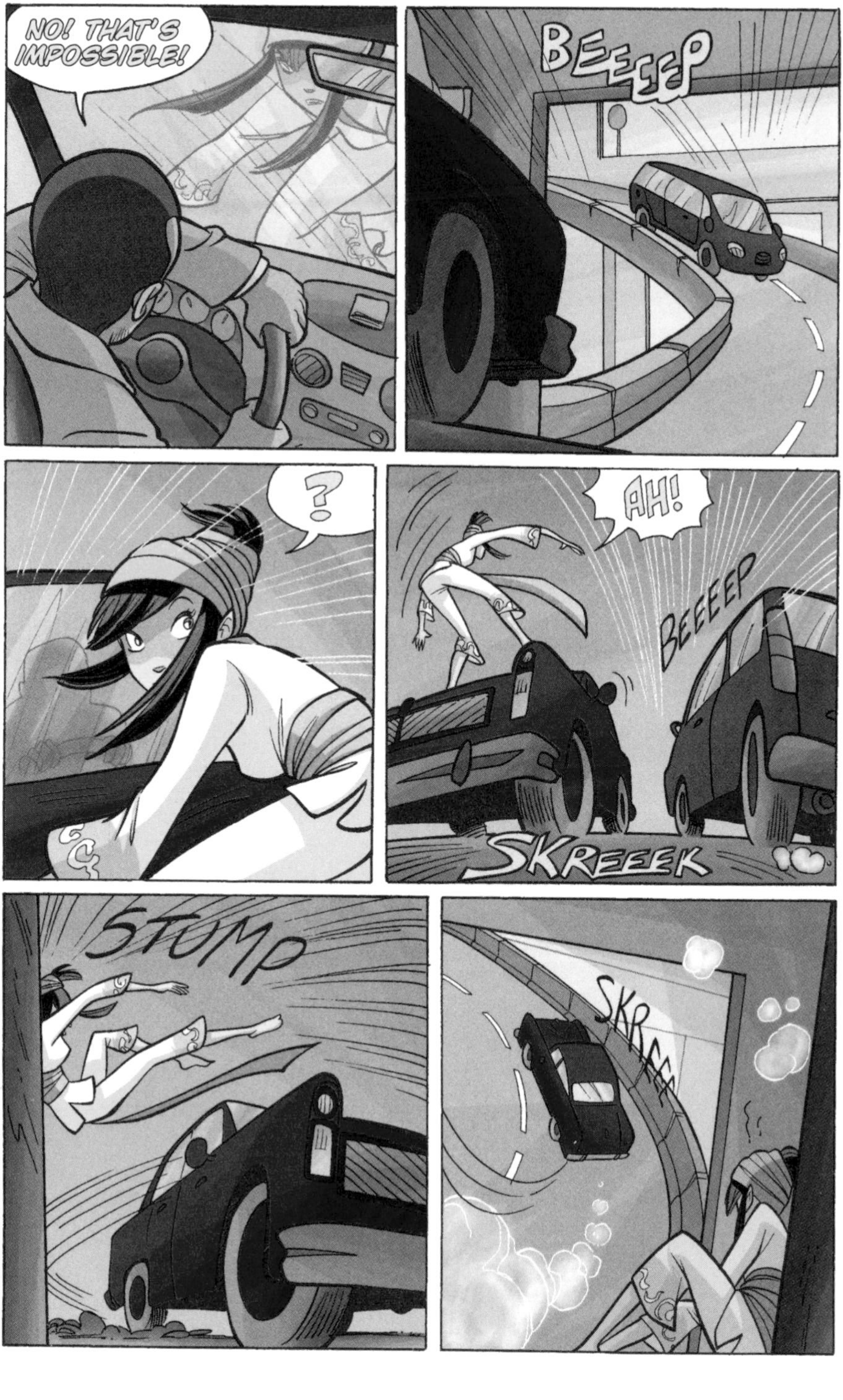
NO! THAT'S IMPOSSIBLE!
BEEEEP
?
AH!
BEEEEP
SKREEEK
STUMP
SKREEE

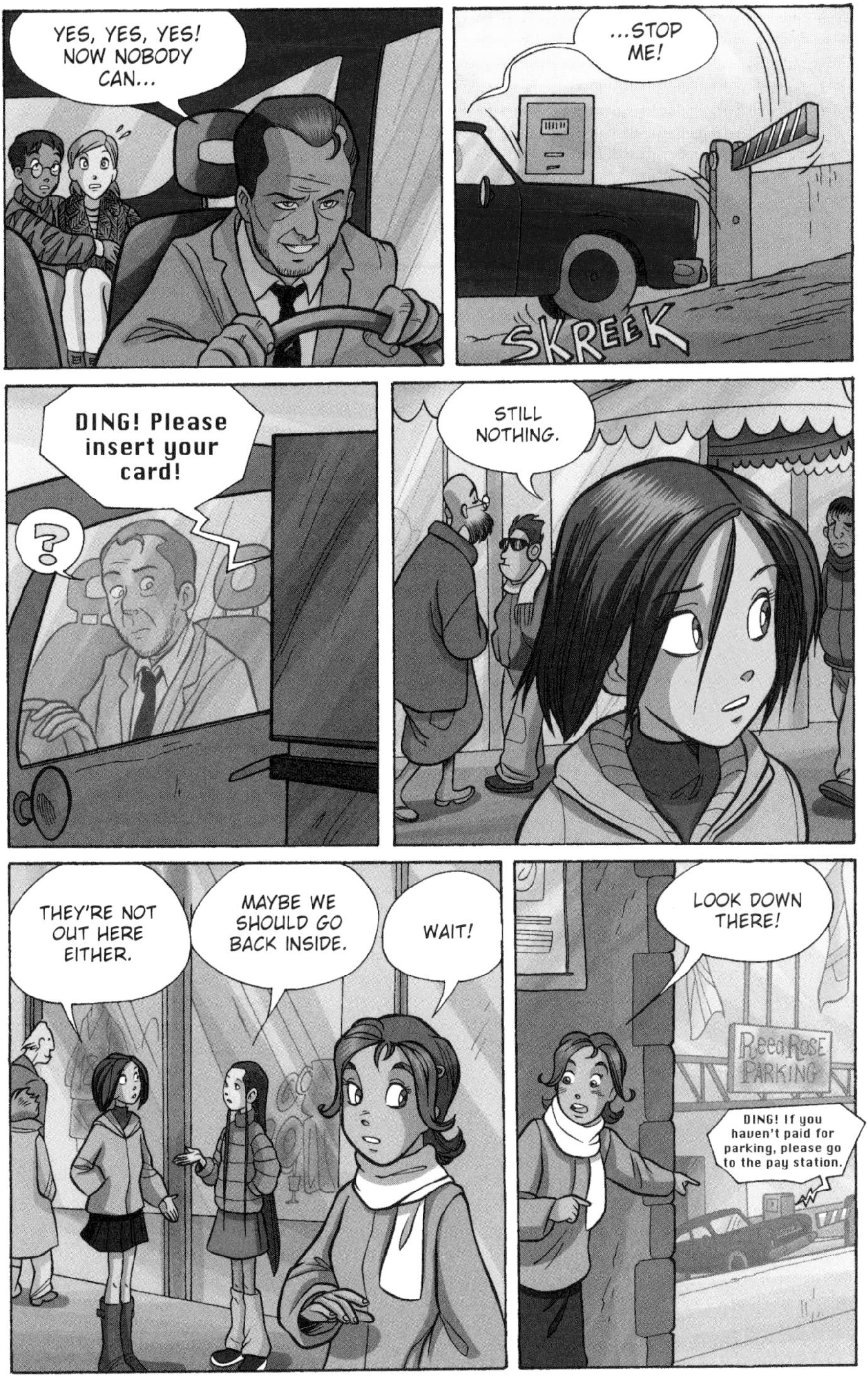
YES, YES, YES! NOW NOBODY CAN...
...STOP ME!
SKREEK
DING! Please insert your card!
?
STILL NOTHING.
THEY'RE NOT OUT HERE EITHER.
MAYBE WE SHOULD GO BACK INSIDE.
WAIT!
LOOK DOWN THERE!
Reed Rose PARKING
DING! If you haven't paid for parking, please go to the pay station.

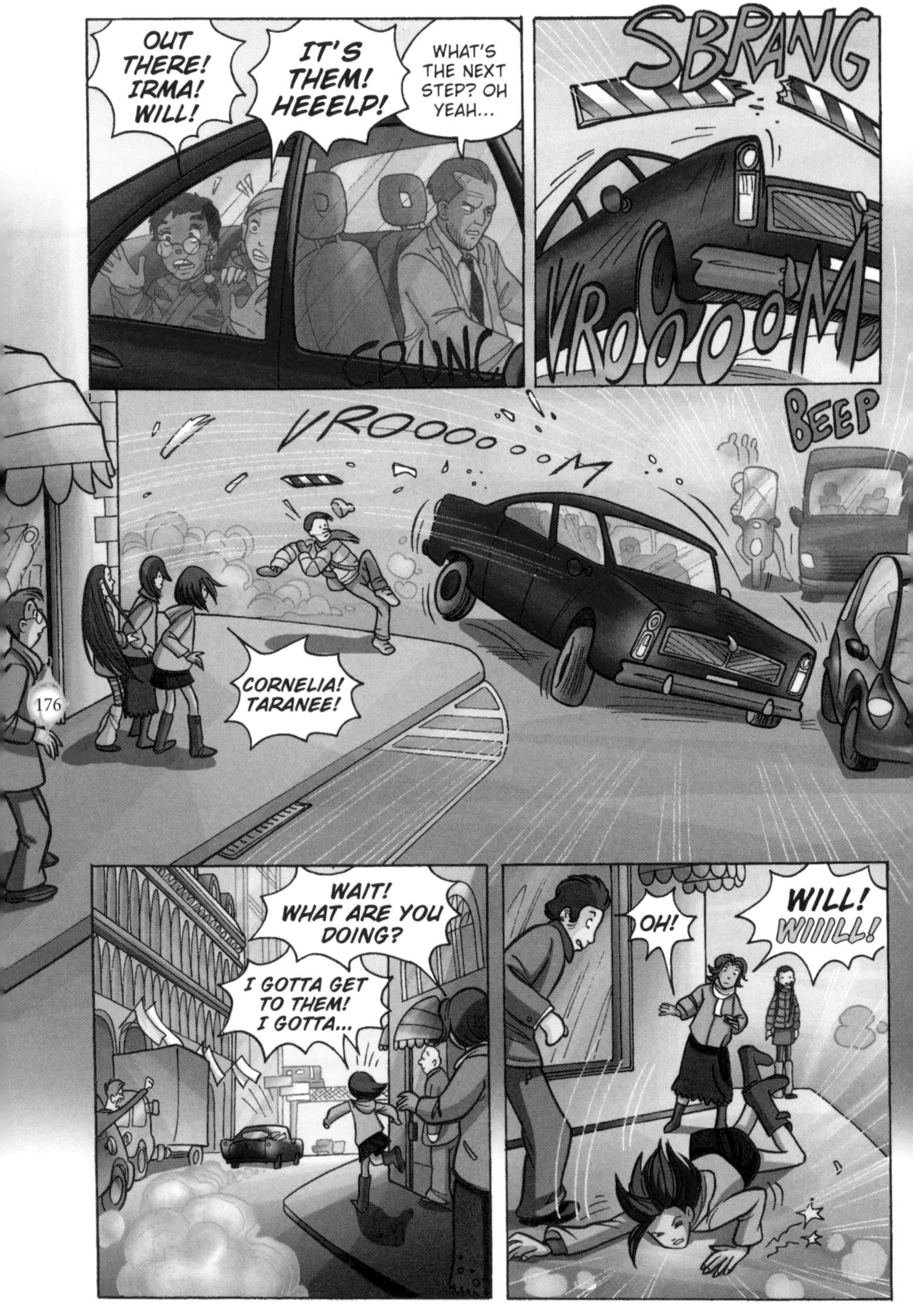
OUT THERE! IRMA! WILL!
IT'S THEM! HEEELP!
WHAT'S THE NEXT STEP? OH YEAH...
CRUNG
SBRANG
VROOOOOOM
BEEP
VROOOOOOOM
CORNELIA! TARANEE!
WAIT! WHAT ARE YOU DOING?
I GOTTA GET TO THEM! I GOTTA...
OH!
WILL! WIIILL!

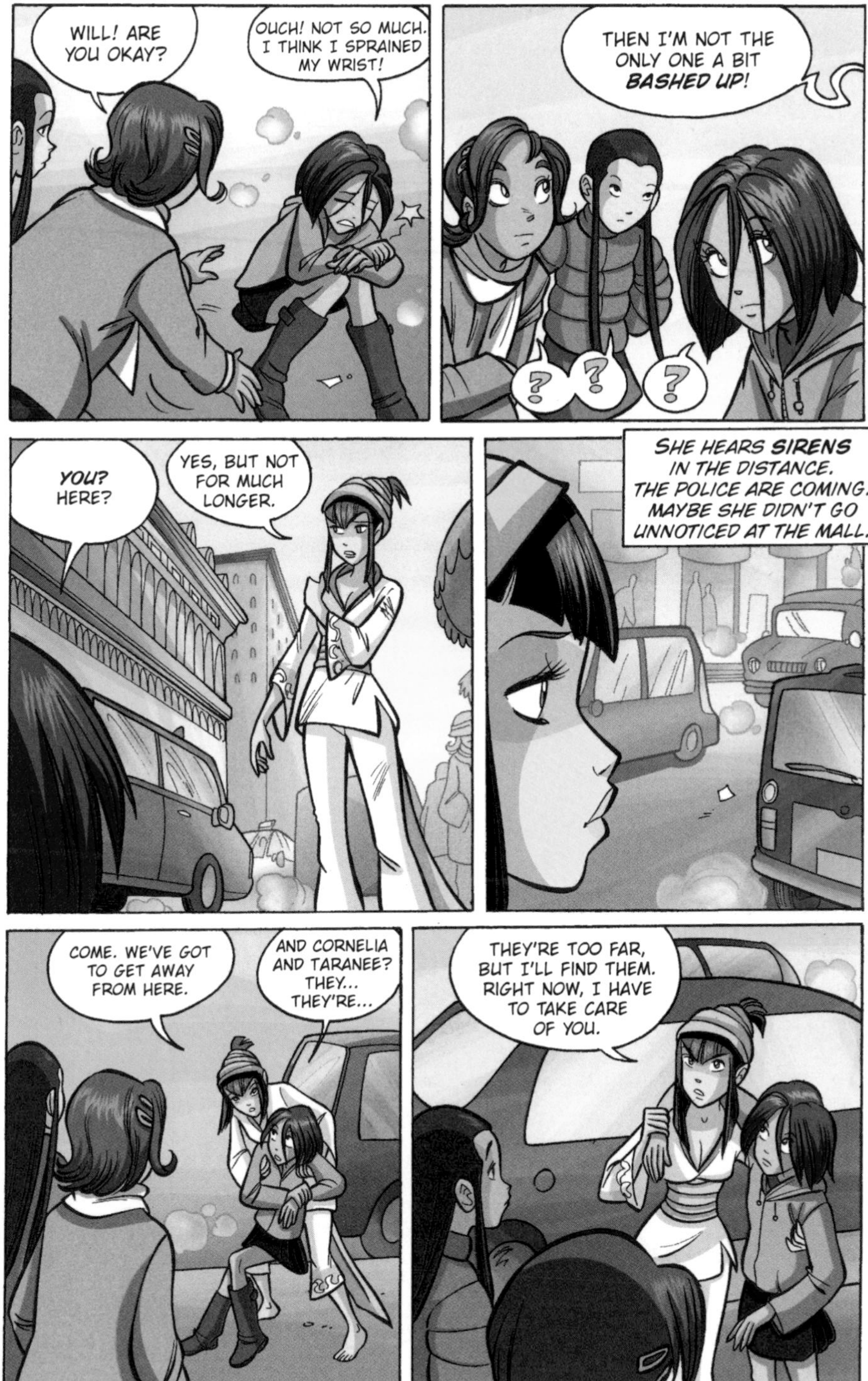
WILL! ARE YOU OKAY?
OUCH! NOT SO MUCH. I THINK I SPRAINED MY WRIST!
THEN I'M NOT THE ONLY ONE A BIT BASHED UP!
?
?
?
YOU? HERE?
YES, BUT NOT FOR MUCH LONGER.
SHE HEARS SIRENS IN THE DISTANCE. THE POLICE ARE COMING. MAYBE SHE DIDN'T GO UNNOTICED AT THE MALL.
COME. WE'VE GOT TO GET AWAY FROM HERE.
AND CORNELIA AND TARANEE? THEY... THEY'RE...
THEY'RE TOO FAR, BUT I'LL FIND THEM. RIGHT NOW, I HAVE TO TAKE CARE OF YOU.

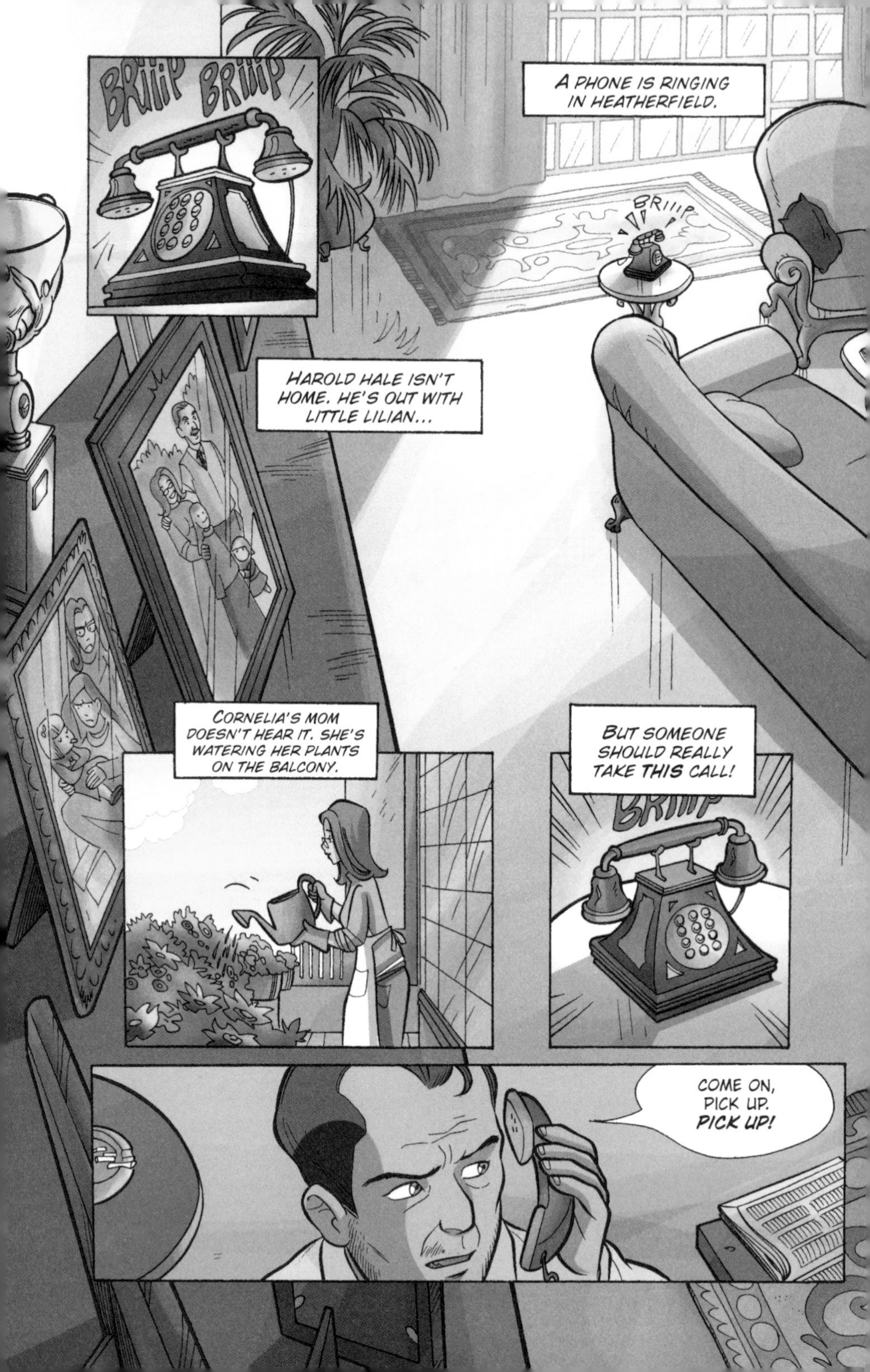

BRIIIP BRIIIP
A PHONE IS RINGING IN HEATHERFIELD.
BRIIIP
HAROLD HALE ISN'T HOME. HE'S OUT WITH LITTLE LILIAN...
CORNELIA'S MOM DOESN'T HEAR IT. SHE'S WATERING HER PLANTS ON THE BALCONY.
BUT SOMEONE SHOULD REALLY TAKE THIS CALL!
BRIIIP
COME ON, PICK UP. PICK UP!

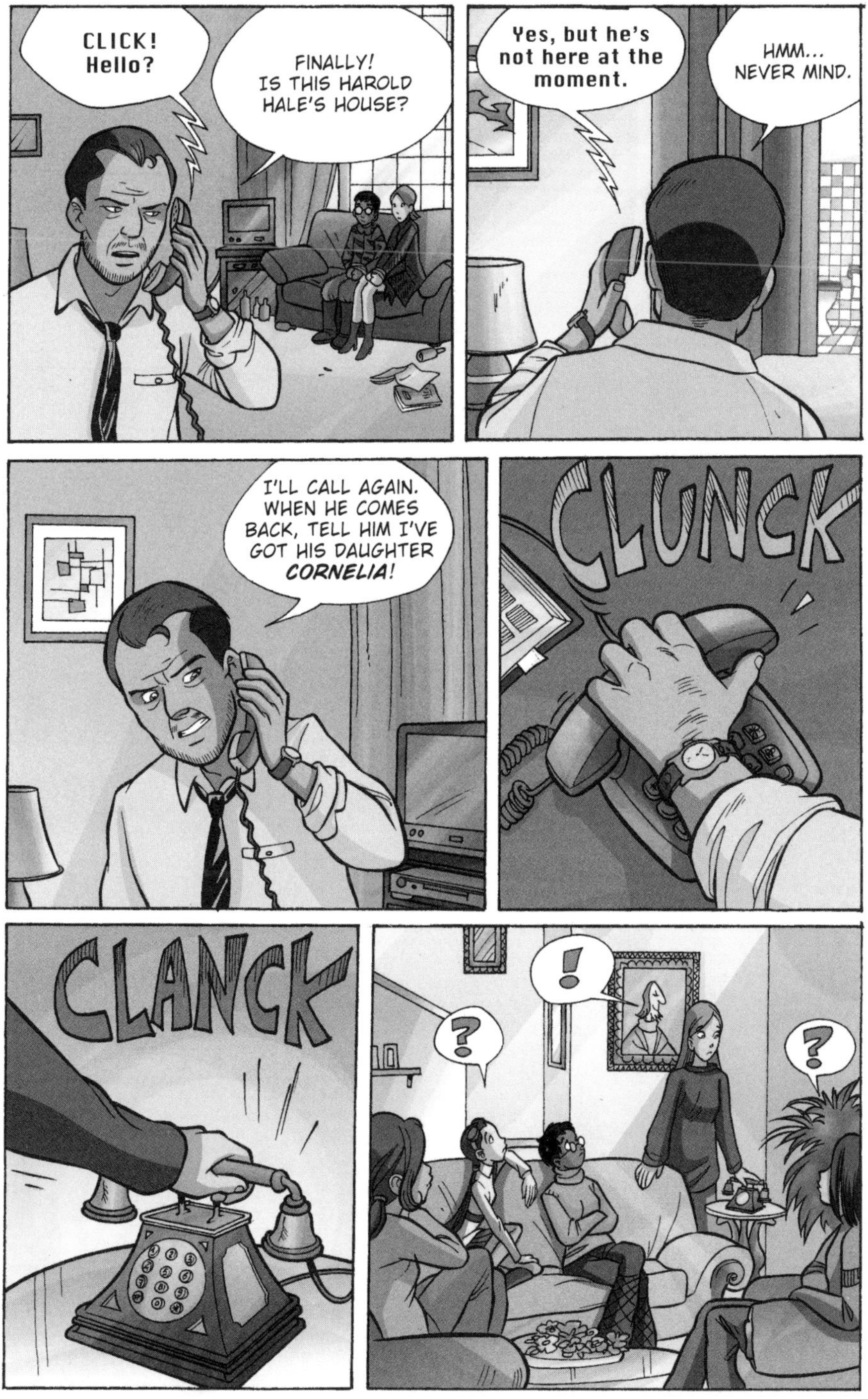
CLICK! Hello?
FINALLY! IS THIS HAROLD HALE'S HOUSE?
Yes, but he's not here at the moment.
HMM... NEVER MIND.
I'LL CALL AGAIN. WHEN HE COMES BACK, TELL HIM I'VE GOT HIS DAUGHTER CORNELIA!
CLUNCK
CLANCK
!
?
?

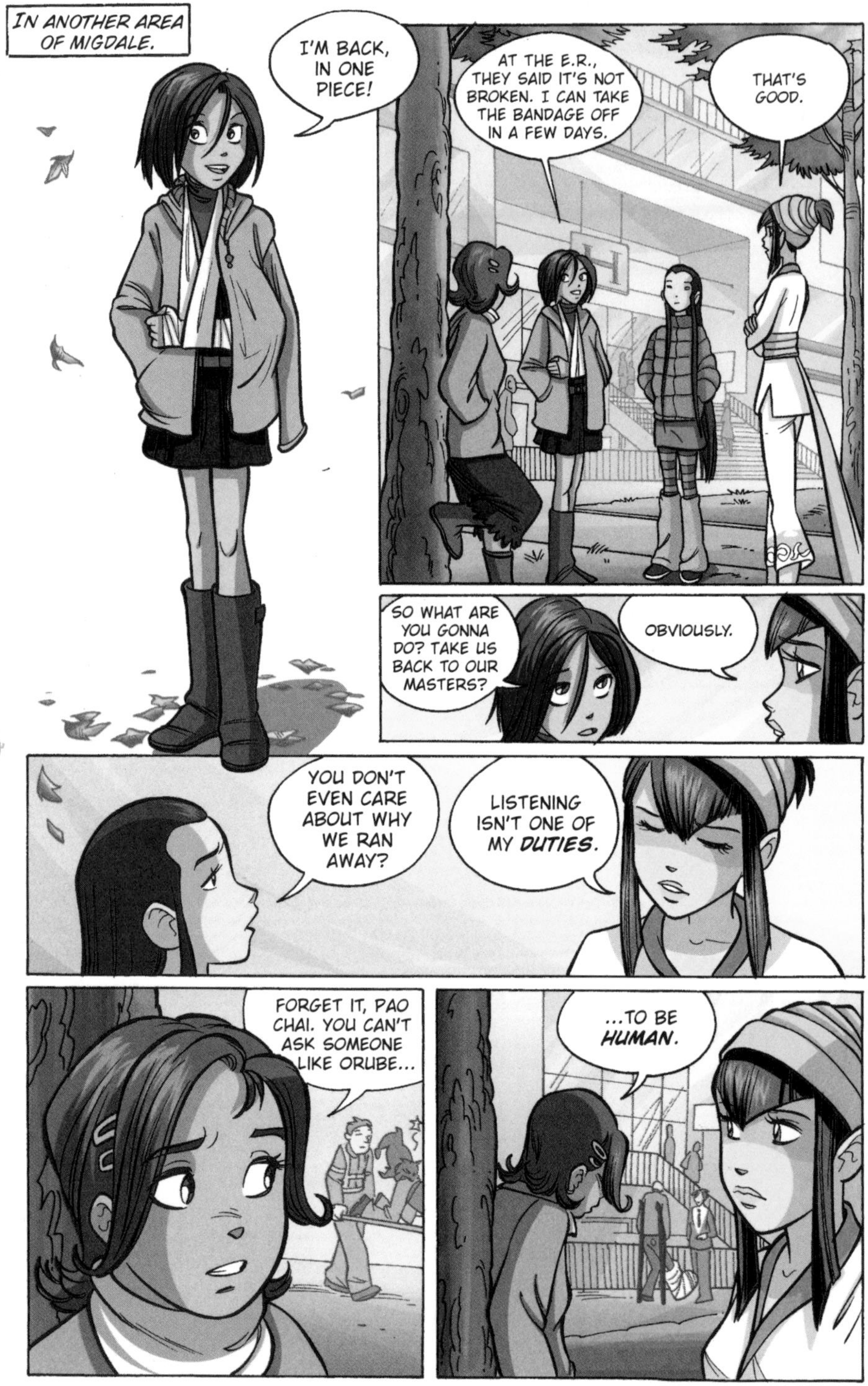
IN ANOTHER AREA OF MIGDALE.
I'M BACK, IN ONE PIECE!
AT THE E.R., THEY SAID IT'S NOT BROKEN. I CAN TAKE THE BANDAGE OFF IN A FEW DAYS.
THAT'S GOOD.
SO WHAT ARE YOU GONNA DO? TAKE US BACK TO OUR MASTERS?
OBVIOUSLY.
YOU DON'T EVEN CARE ABOUT WHY WE RAN AWAY?
LISTENING ISN'T ONE OF MY DUTIES.
FORGET IT, PAO CHAI. YOU CAN'T ASK SOMEONE LIKE ORUBE...
...TO BE HUMAN.

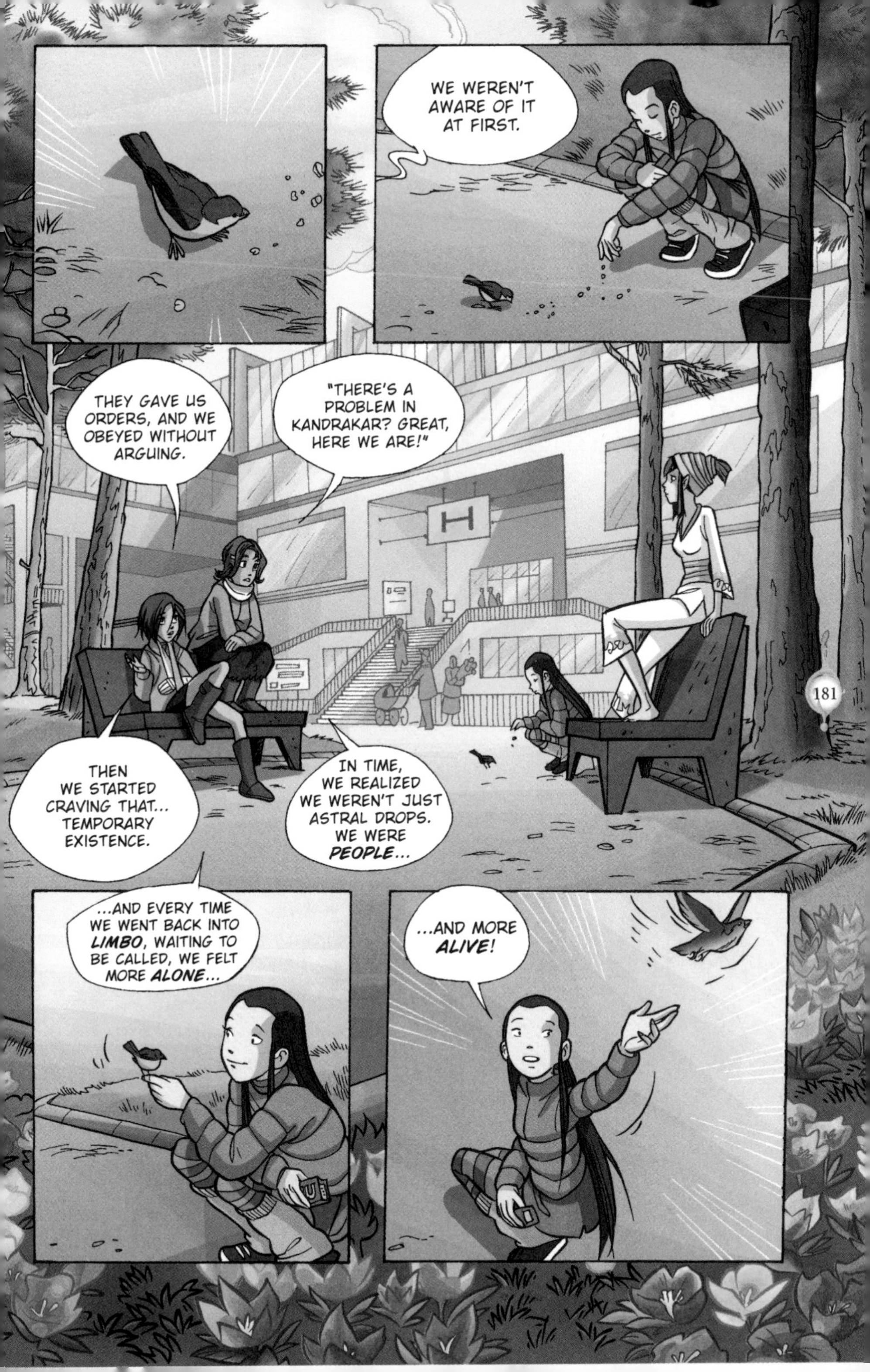
WE WEREN'T AWARE OF IT AT FIRST.
THEY GAVE US ORDERS, AND WE OBEYED WITHOUT ARGUING.
"THERE'S A PROBLEM IN KANDRAKAR? GREAT, HERE WE ARE!"
THEN WE STARTED CRAVING THAT... TEMPORARY EXISTENCE.
IN TIME, WE REALIZED WE WEREN'T JUST ASTRAL DROPS. WE WERE PEOPLE...
...AND EVERY TIME WE WENT BACK INTO LIMBO, WAITING TO BE CALLED, WE FELT MORE ALONE...
...AND MORE ALIVE!

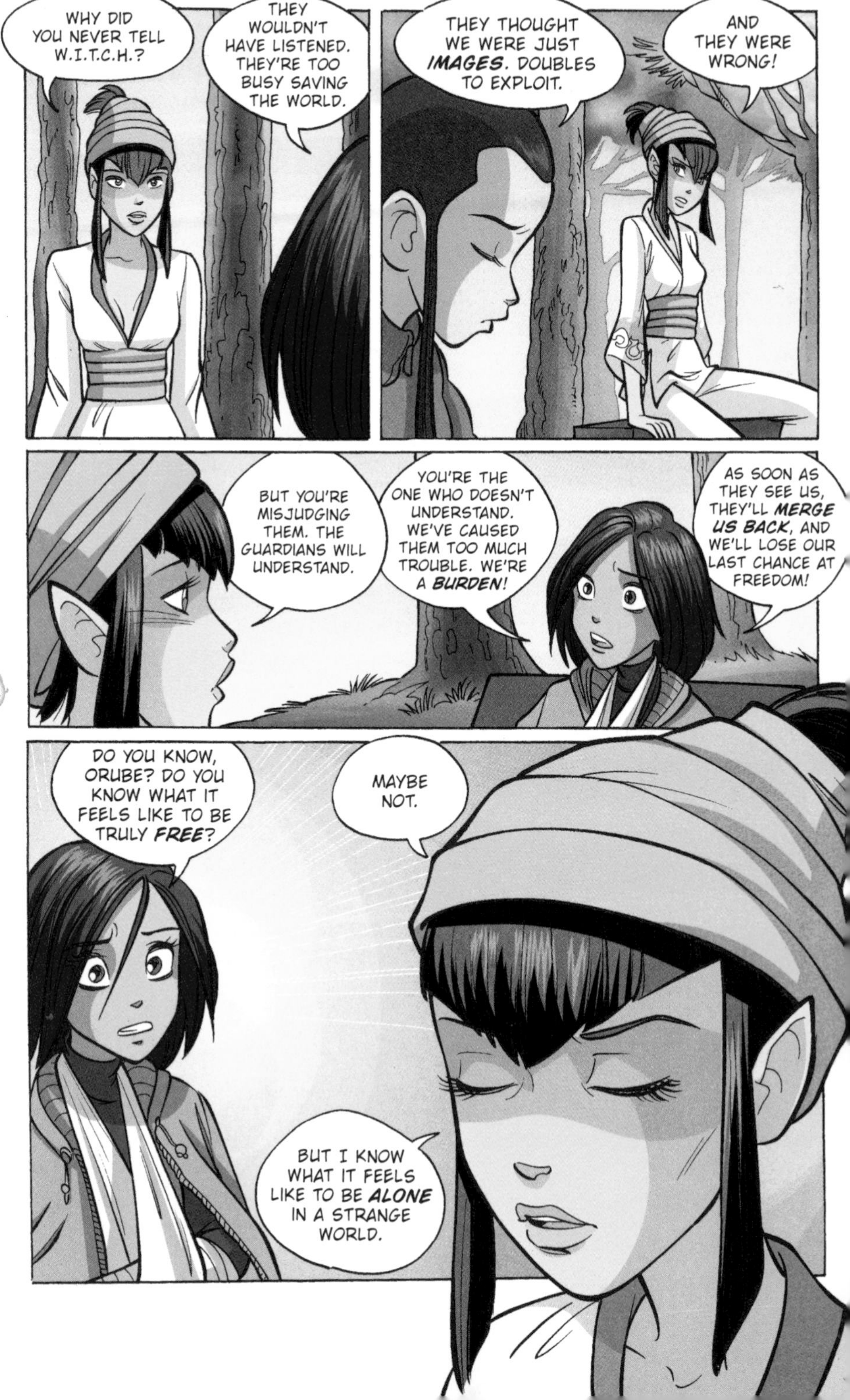
WHY DID YOU NEVER TELL W.I.T.C.H.?
THEY WOULDN'T HAVE LISTENED. THEY'RE TOO BUSY SAVING THE WORLD.
THEY THOUGHT WE WERE JUST IMAGES. DOUBLES TO EXPLOIT.
AND THEY WERE WRONG!
BUT YOU'RE MISJUDGING THEM. THE GUARDIANS WILL UNDERSTAND.
YOU'RE THE ONE WHO DOESN'T UNDERSTAND. WE'VE CAUSED THEM TOO MUCH TROUBLE. WE'RE A BURDEN!
AS SOON AS THEY SEE US, THEY'LL MERGE US BACK, AND WE'LL LOSE OUR LAST CHANCE AT FREEDOM!
DO YOU KNOW, ORUBE? DO YOU KNOW WHAT IT FEELS LIKE TO BE TRULY FREE?
MAYBE NOT.
BUT I KNOW WHAT IT FEELS LIKE TO BE ALONE IN A STRANGE WORLD.

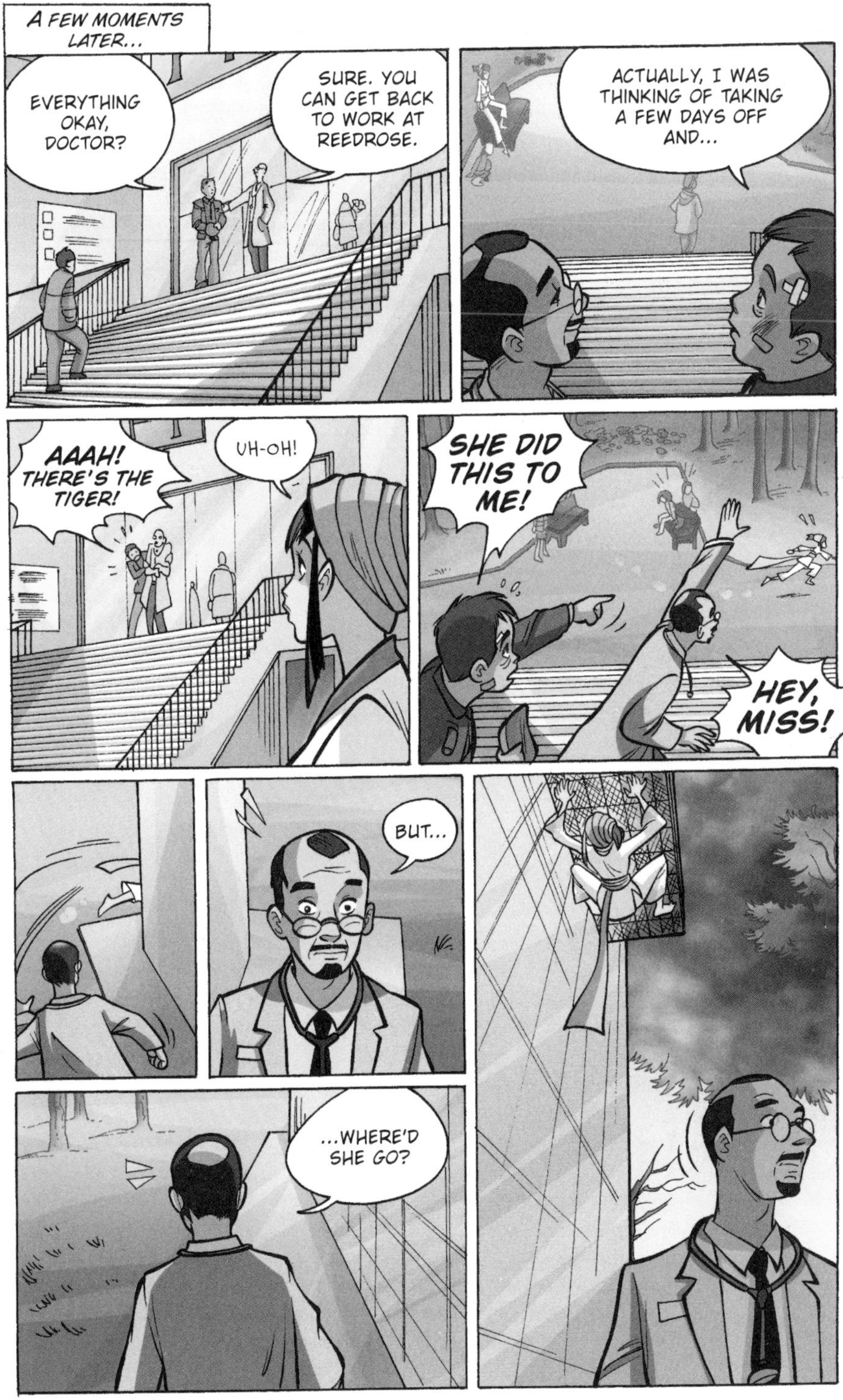
A FEW MOMENTS LATER...
EVERYTHING OKAY, DOCTOR?
SURE. YOU CAN GET BACK TO WORK AT REEDROSE.
ACTUALLY, I WAS THINKING OF TAKING A FEW DAYS OFF AND...
AAAH! THERE'S THE TIGER!
UH-OH!
SHE DID THIS TO ME!
HEY, MISS!
BUT...
...WHERE'D SHE GO?

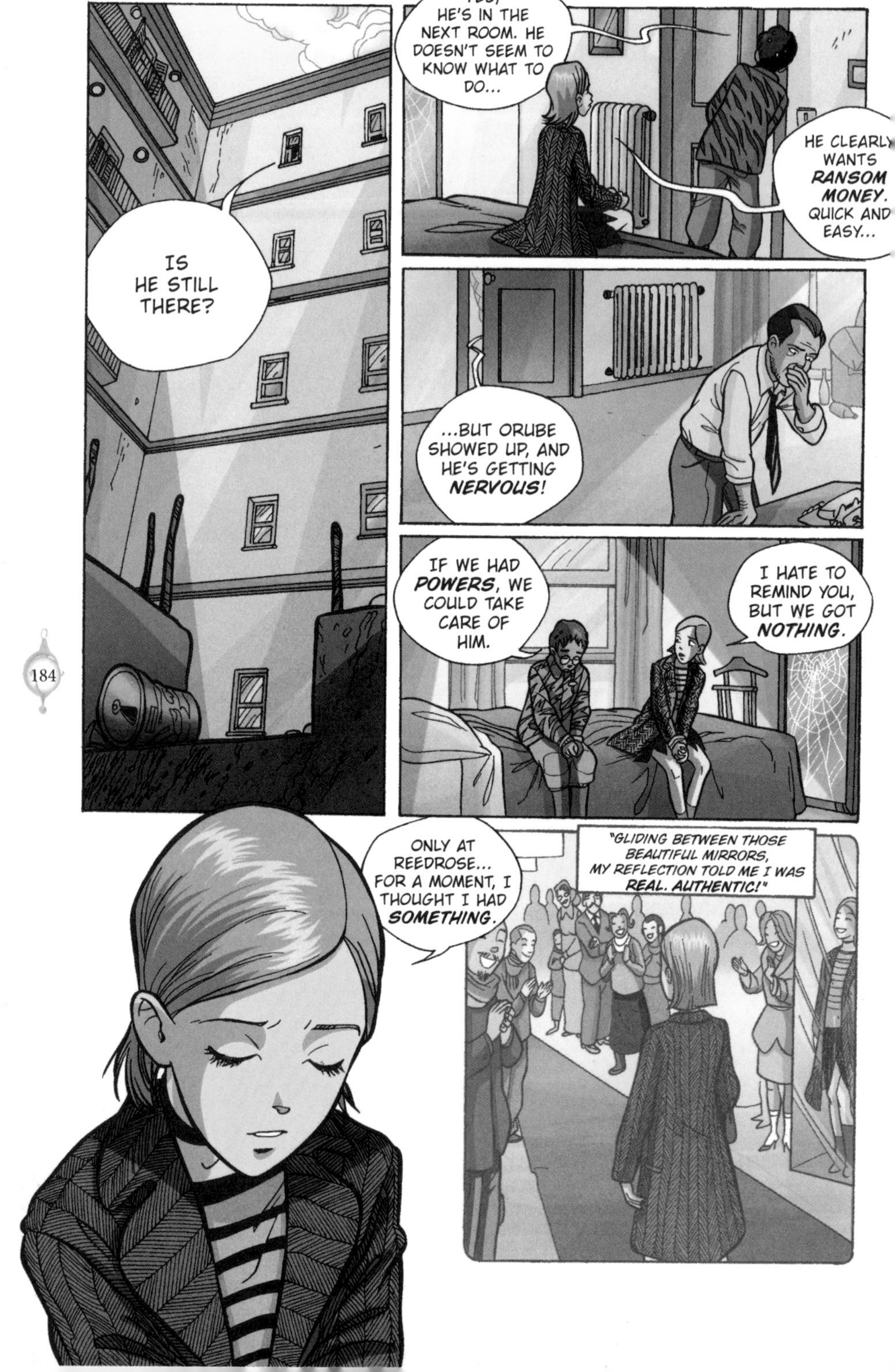
IS HE STILL THERE?
YES, HE'S IN THE NEXT ROOM. HE DOESN'T SEEM TO KNOW WHAT TO DO...
HE CLEARLY WANTS RANSOM MONEY. QUICK AND EASY...
...BUT ORUBE SHOWED UP, AND HE'S GETTING NERVOUS!
IF WE HAD POWERS, WE COULD TAKE CARE OF HIM.
I HATE TO REMIND YOU, BUT WE GOT NOTHING.
ONLY AT REEDROSE... FOR A MOMENT, I THOUGHT I HAD SOMETHING.
"GLIDING BETWEEN THOSE BEAUTIFUL MIRRORS, MY REFLECTION TOLD ME I WAS REAL. AUTHENTIC!"

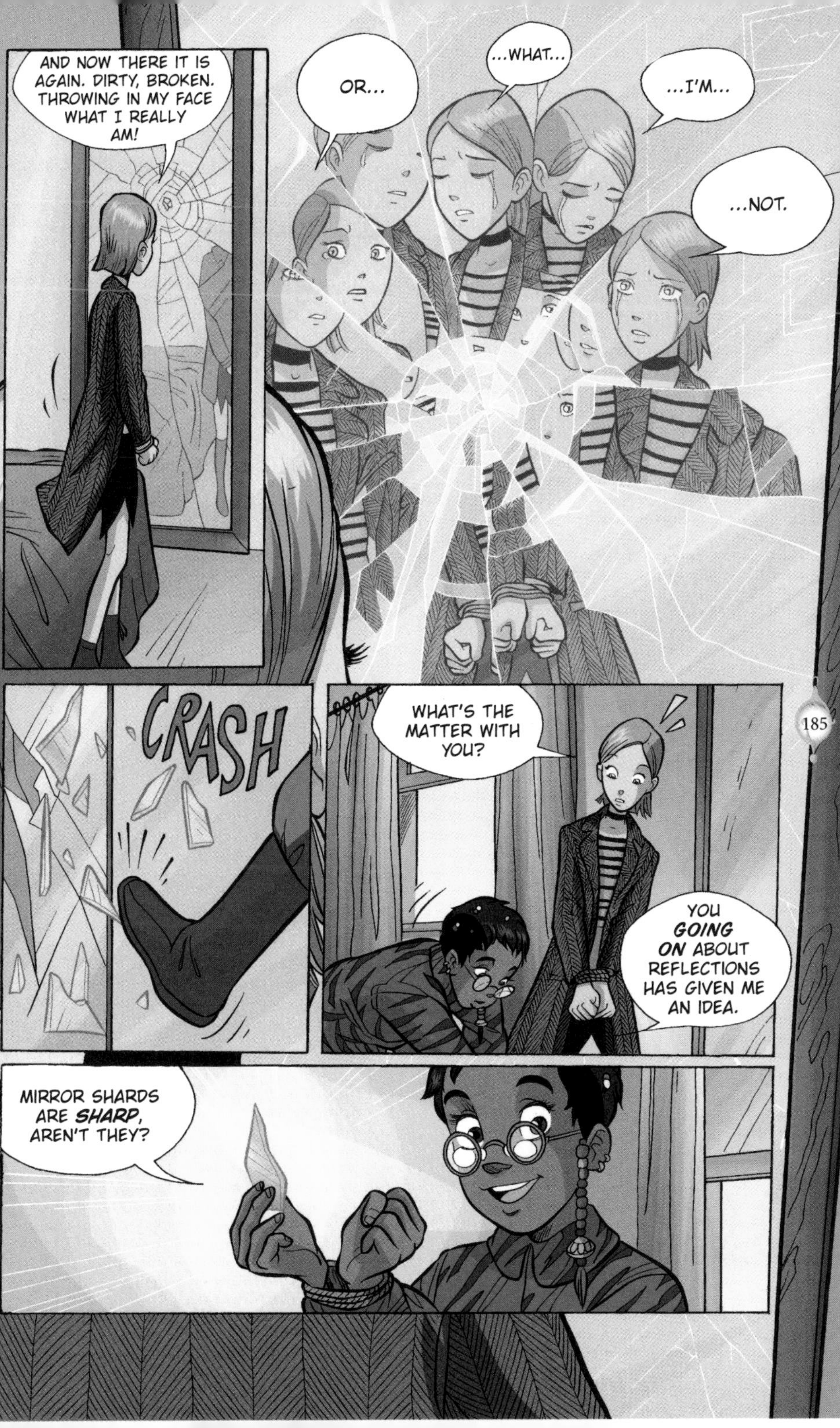
AND NOW THERE IT IS AGAIN. DIRTY, BROKEN. THROWING IN MY FACE WHAT I REALLY AM!
OR...
...WHAT...
...I'M...
...NOT.
CRASH
WHAT'S THE MATTER WITH YOU?
YOU GOING ON ABOUT REFLECTIONS HAS GIVEN ME AN IDEA.
MIRROR SHARDS ARE SHARP, AREN'T THEY?

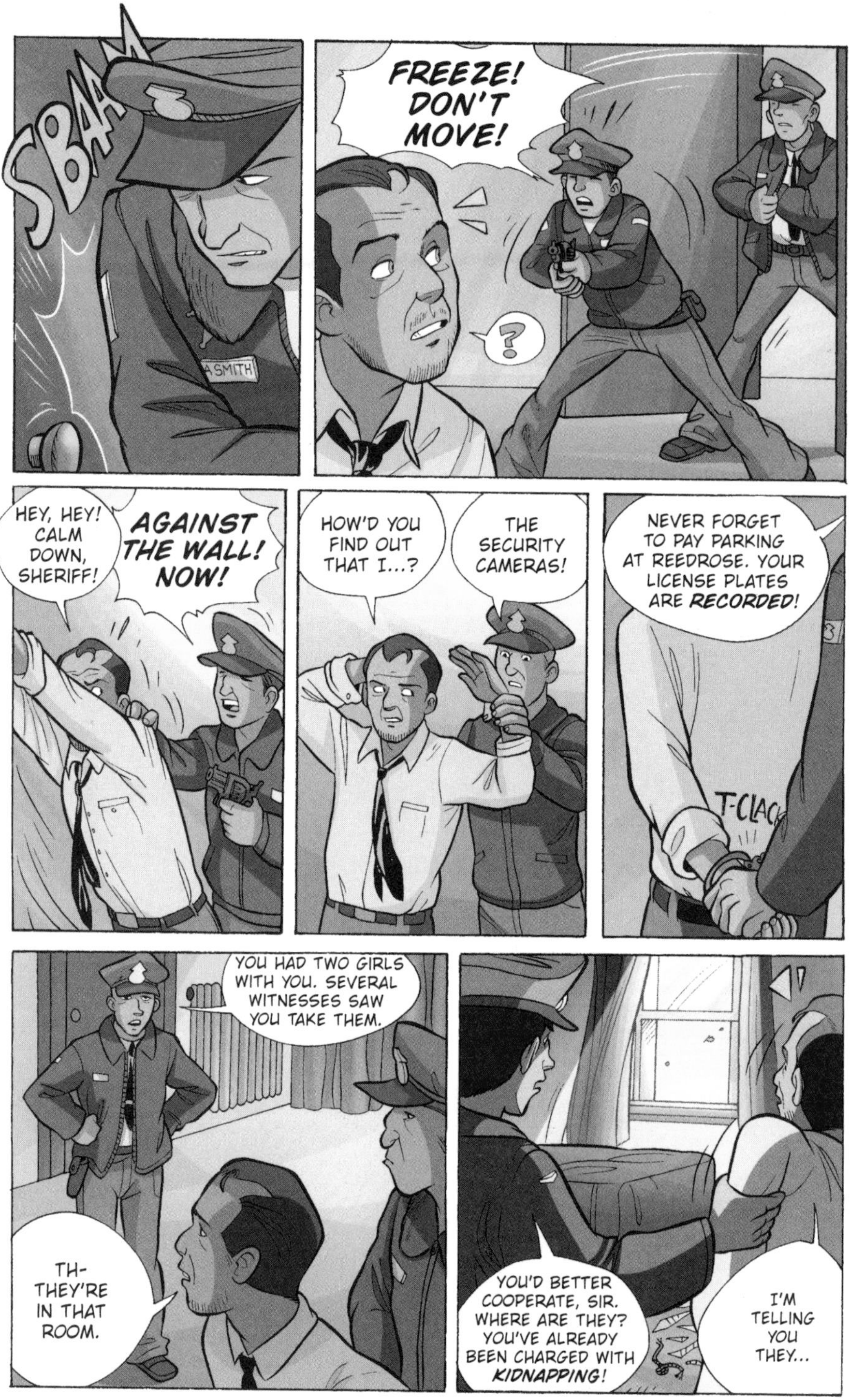
SBAAM
A SMITH
FREEZE! DON'T MOVE!
?
HEY, HEY! CALM DOWN, SHERIFF!
AGAINST THE WALL! NOW!
HOW'D YOU FIND OUT THAT I...?
THE SECURITY CAMERAS!
NEVER FORGET TO PAY PARKING AT REEDROSE. YOUR LICENSE PLATES ARE RECORDED!
T-CLACK
YOU HAD TWO GIRLS WITH YOU. SEVERAL WITNESSES SAW YOU TAKE THEM.
TH- THEY'RE IN THAT ROOM.
YOU'D BETTER COOPERATE, SIR. WHERE ARE THEY? YOU'VE ALREADY BEEN CHARGED WITH KIDNAPPING!
I'M TELLING YOU THEY...

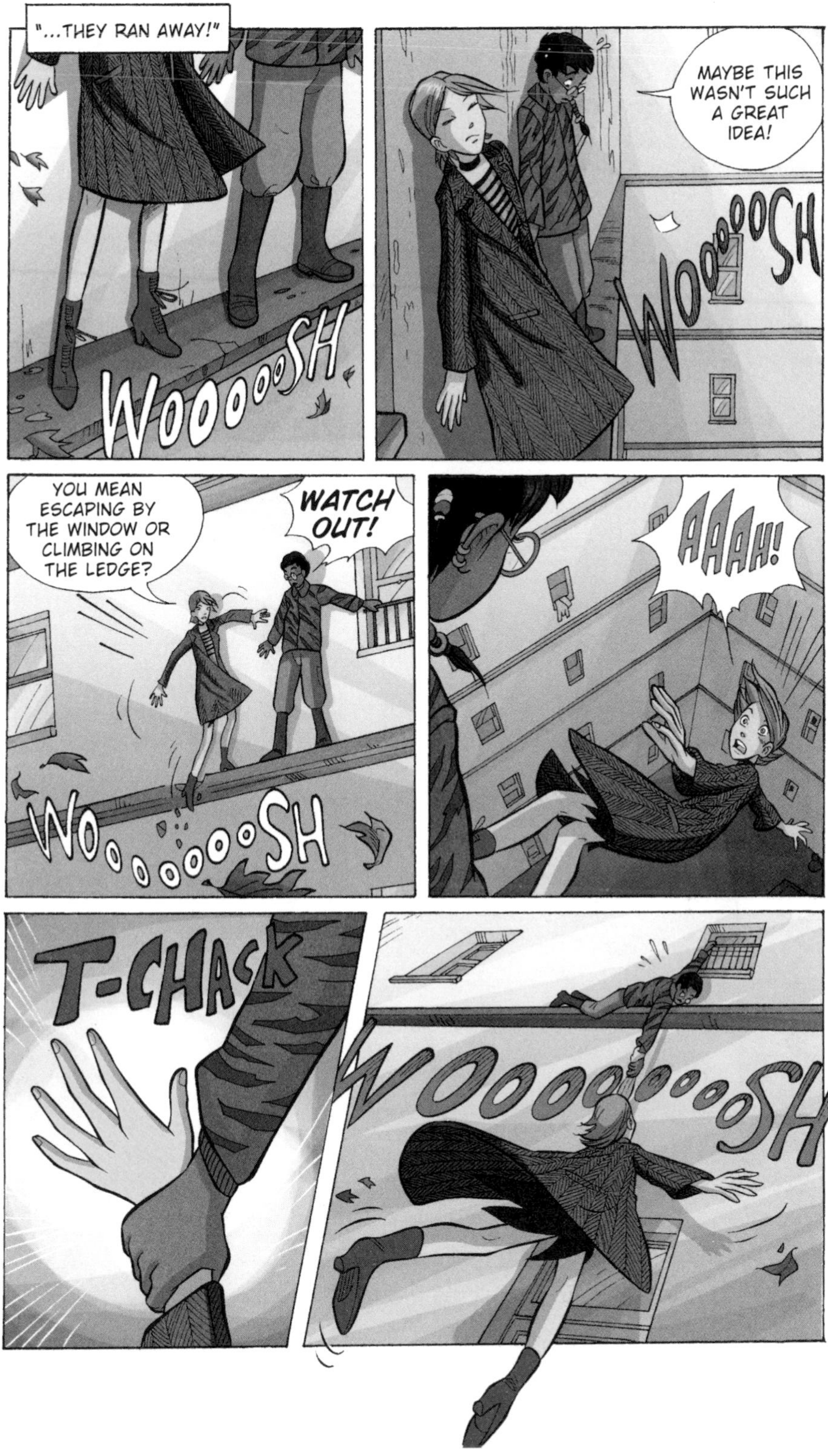
"...THEY RAN AWAY!"
WOOOOOSH
MAYBE THIS WASN'T SUCH A GREAT IDEA!
WOOOOOSH
YOU MEAN ESCAPING BY THE WINDOW OR CLIMBING ON THE LEDGE?
WATCH OUT!
WOOOOOOOSH
AAAH!
T-CHACK
WOOOOOOOOSH

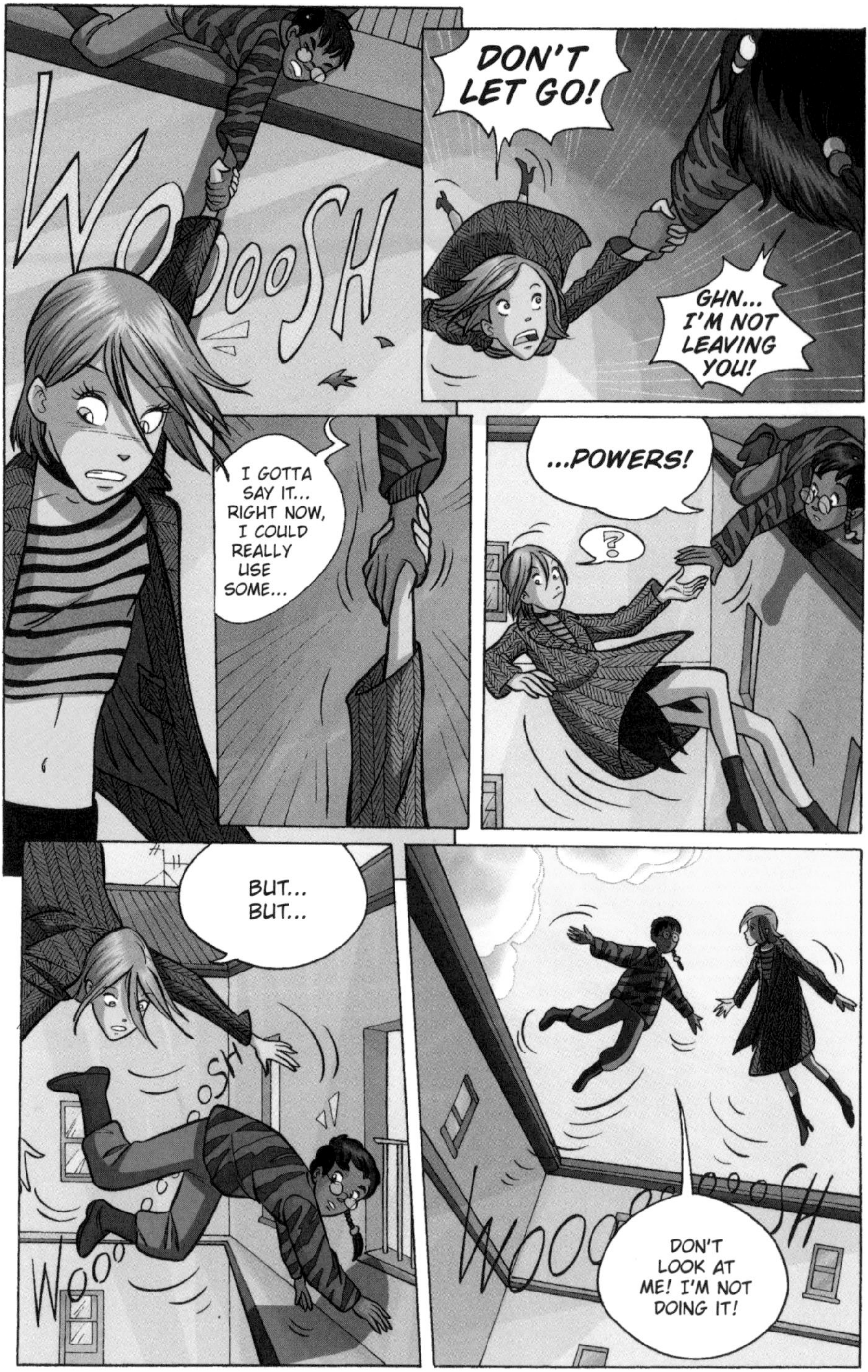
WOOOOSH
DON'T LET GO!
GHN... I'M NOT LEAVING YOU!
I GOTTA SAY IT... RIGHT NOW, I COULD REALLY USE SOME...
...POWERS!
?
BUT... BUT...
DON'T LOOK AT ME! I'M NOT DOING IT!

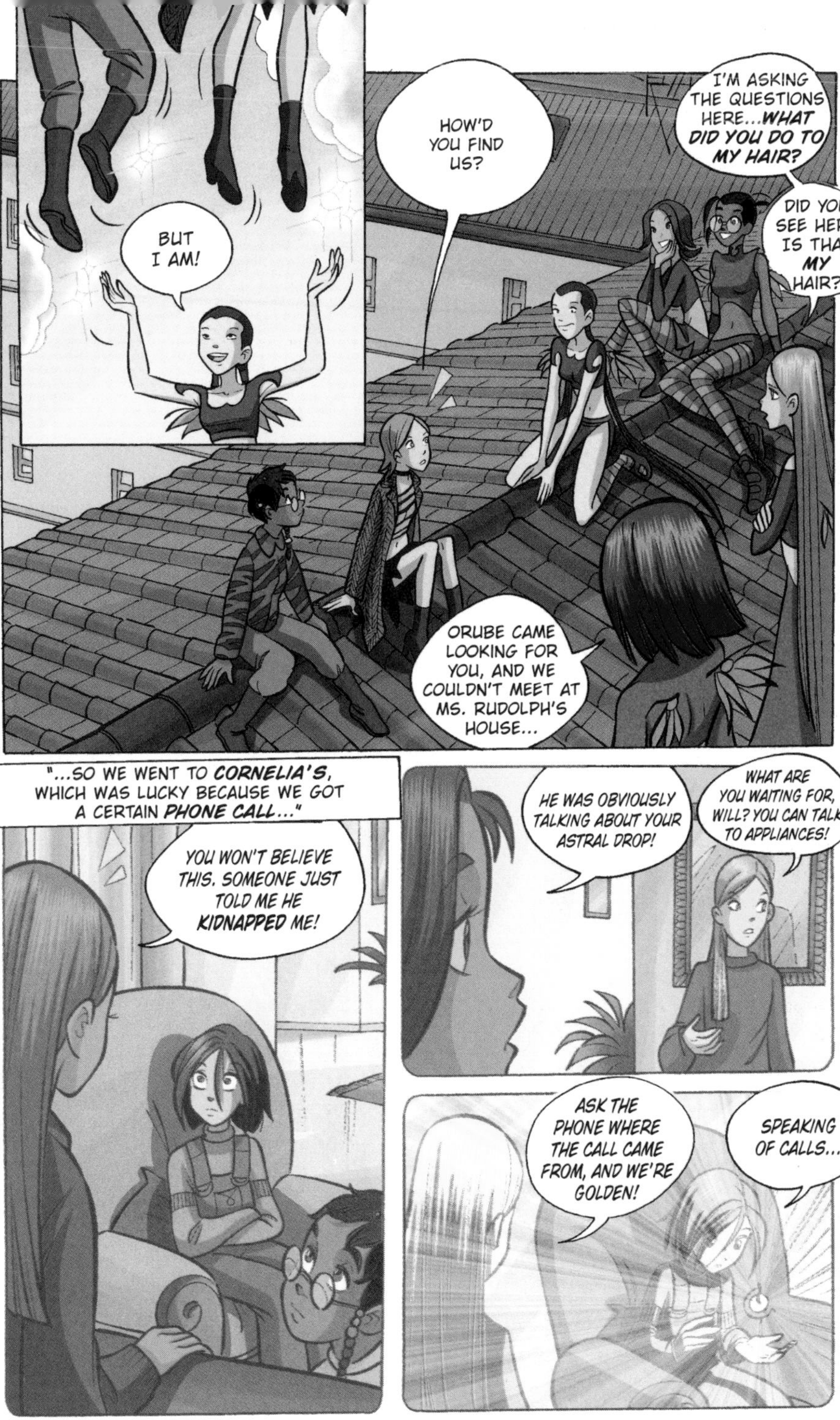
BUT I AM!
HOW'D YOU FIND US?
I'M ASKING THE QUESTIONS HERE...WHAT DID YOU DO TO MY HAIR?
DID YOU SEE HER? IS THAT MY HAIR?
ORUBE CAME LOOKING FOR YOU, AND WE COULDN'T MEET AT MS. RUDOLPH'S HOUSE...
"...SO WE WENT TO CORNELIA'S, WHICH WAS LUCKY BECAUSE WE GOT A CERTAIN PHONE CALL..."
YOU WON'T BELIEVE THIS. SOMEONE JUST TOLD ME HE KIDNAPPED ME!
HE WAS OBVIOUSLY TALKING ABOUT YOUR ASTRAL DROP!
WHAT ARE YOU WAITING FOR, WILL? YOU CAN TALK TO APPLIANCES!
ASK THE PHONE WHERE THE CALL CAME FROM, AND WE'RE GOLDEN!
SPEAKING OF CALLS...

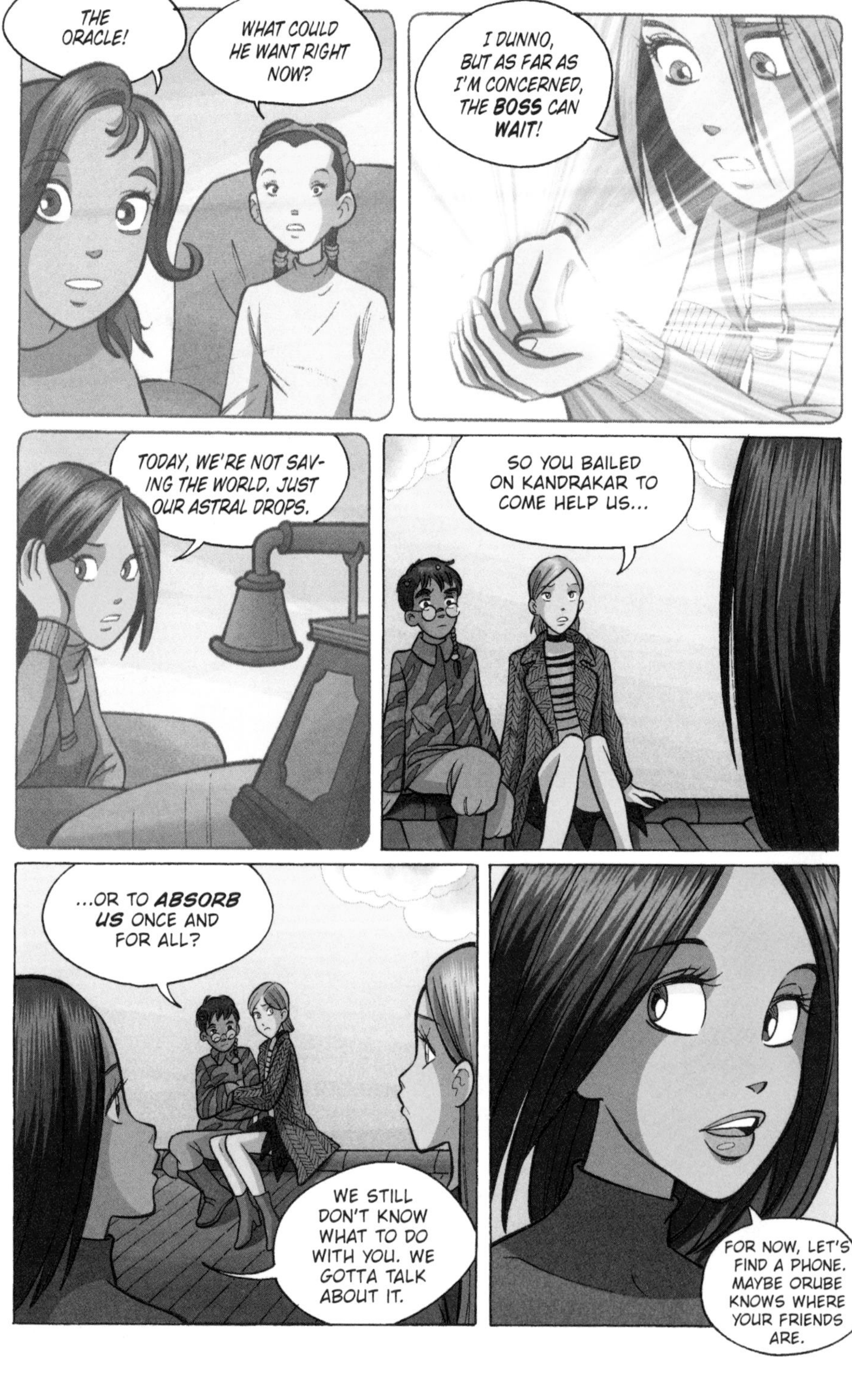
THE ORACLE!
WHAT COULD HE WANT RIGHT NOW?
I DUNNO, BUT AS FAR AS I'M CONCERNED, THE BOSS CAN WAIT!
TODAY, WE'RE NOT SAV-ING THE WORLD. JUST OUR ASTRAL DROPS.
SO YOU BAILED ON KANDRAKAR TO COME HELP US...
...OR TO ABSORB US ONCE AND FOR ALL?
WE STILL DON'T KNOW WHAT TO DO WITH YOU. WE GOTTA TALK ABOUT IT.
FOR NOW, LET'S FIND A PHONE. MAYBE ORUBE KNOWS WHERE YOUR FRIENDS ARE.

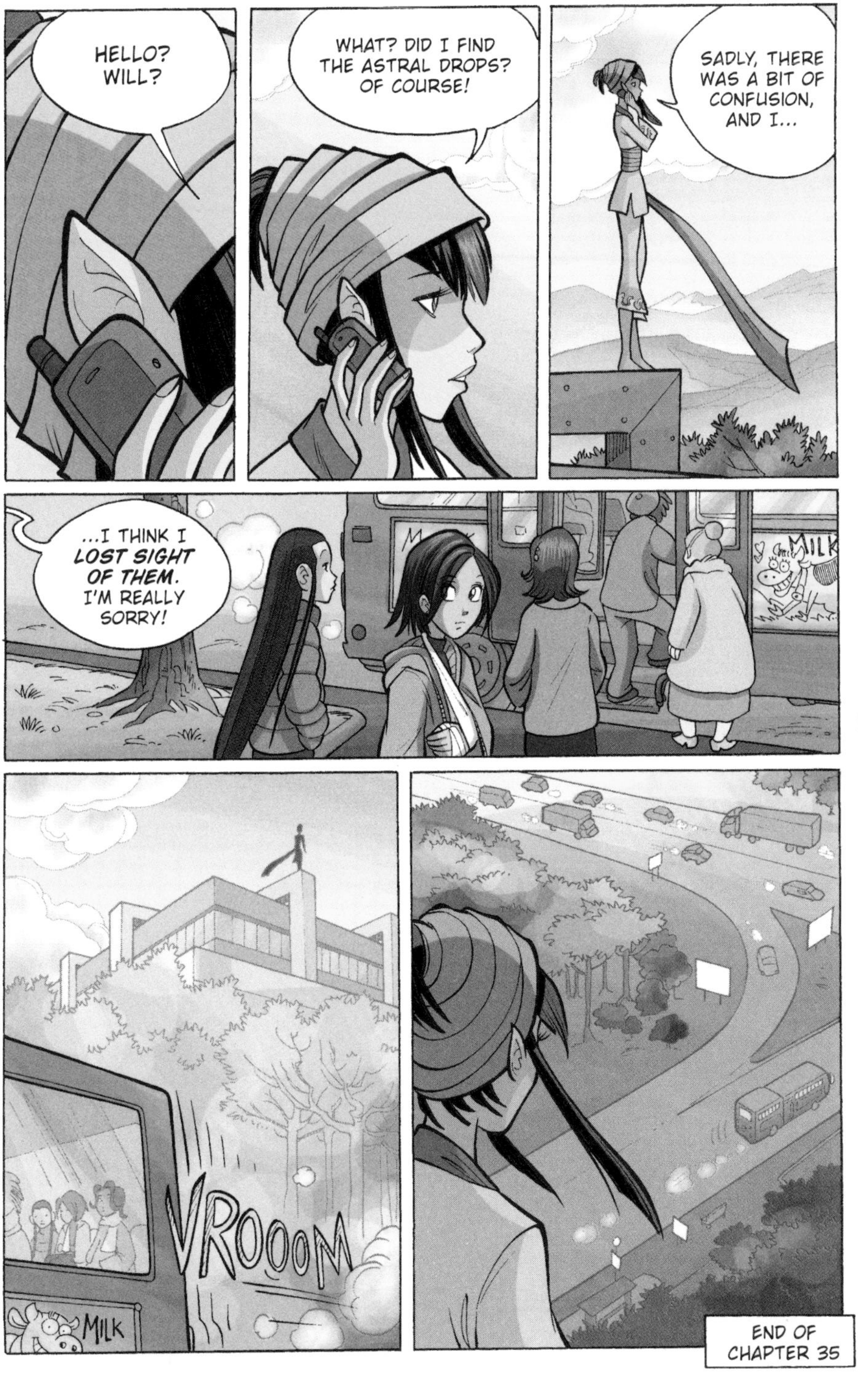
HELLO? WILL?
WHAT? DID I FIND THE ASTRAL DROPS? OF COURSE!
SADLY, THERE WAS A BIT OF CONFUSION, AND I...
...I THINK I **LOST SIGHT OF THEM.** I'M REALLY SORRY!
MILK
VROOOM
MILK
END OF CHAPTER 35

W.i.t.c.h.

Will Irma Taranee Cornelia Hay Lin

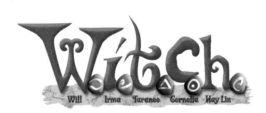

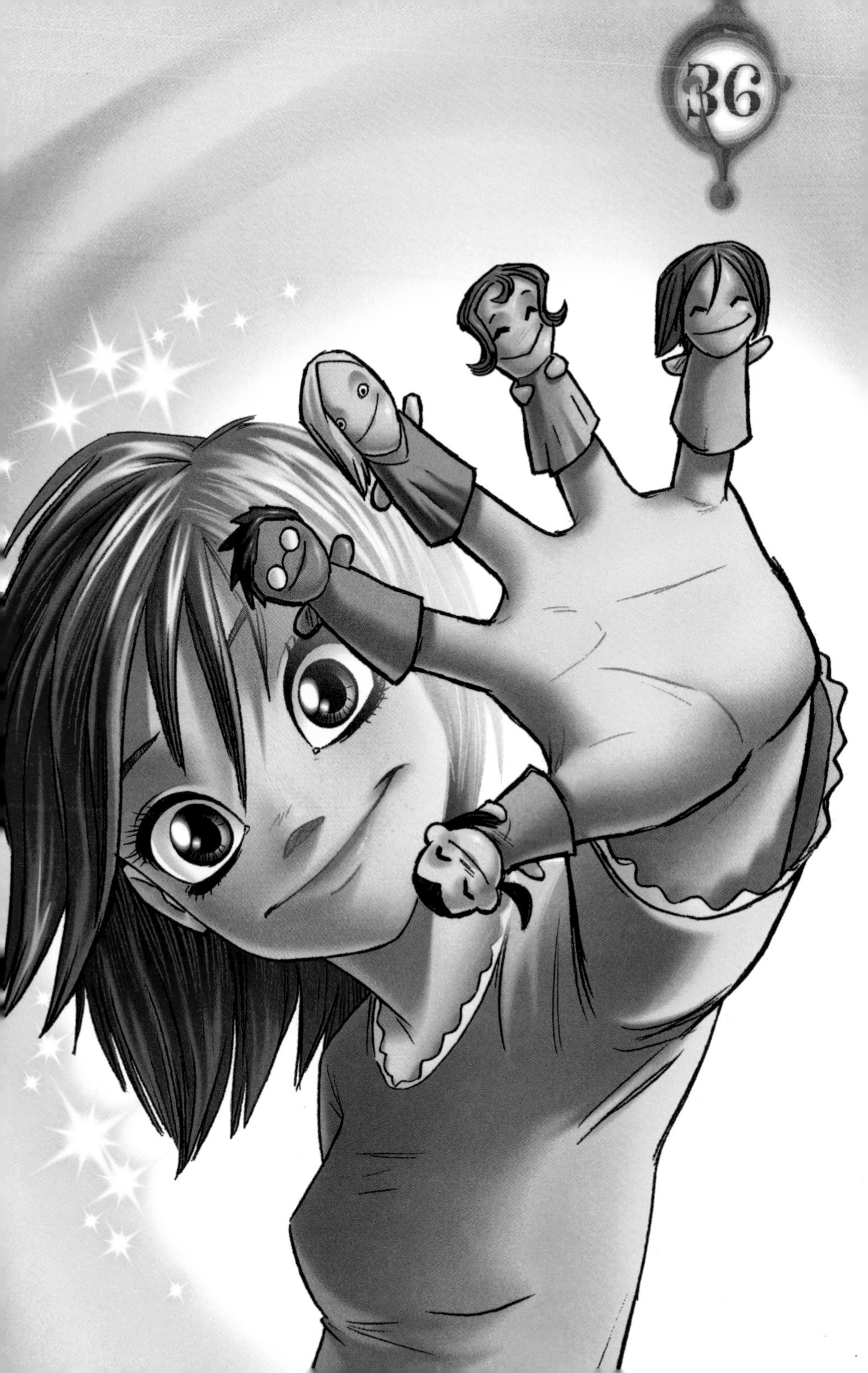
36

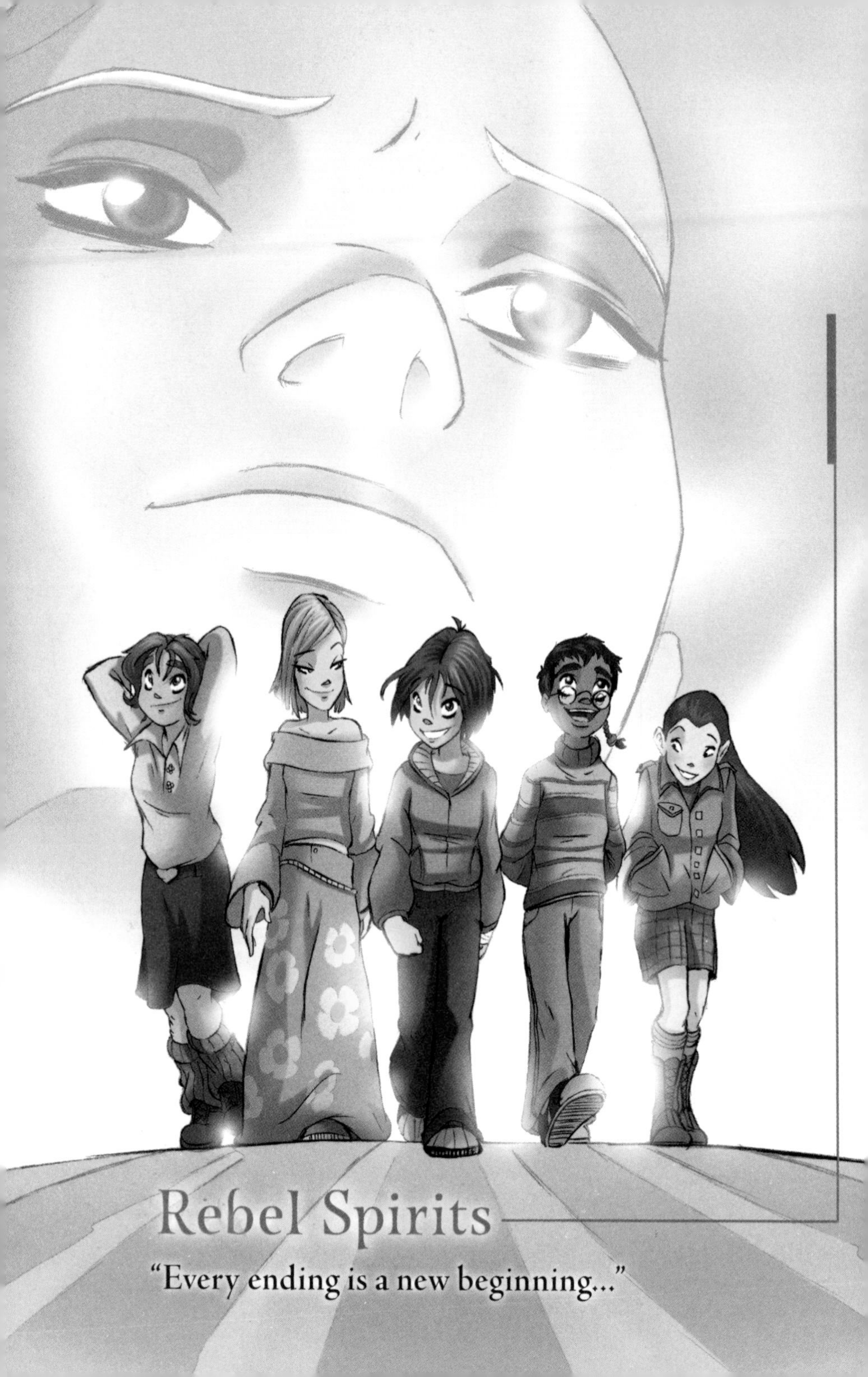

Rebel Spirits

"Every ending is a new beginning..."

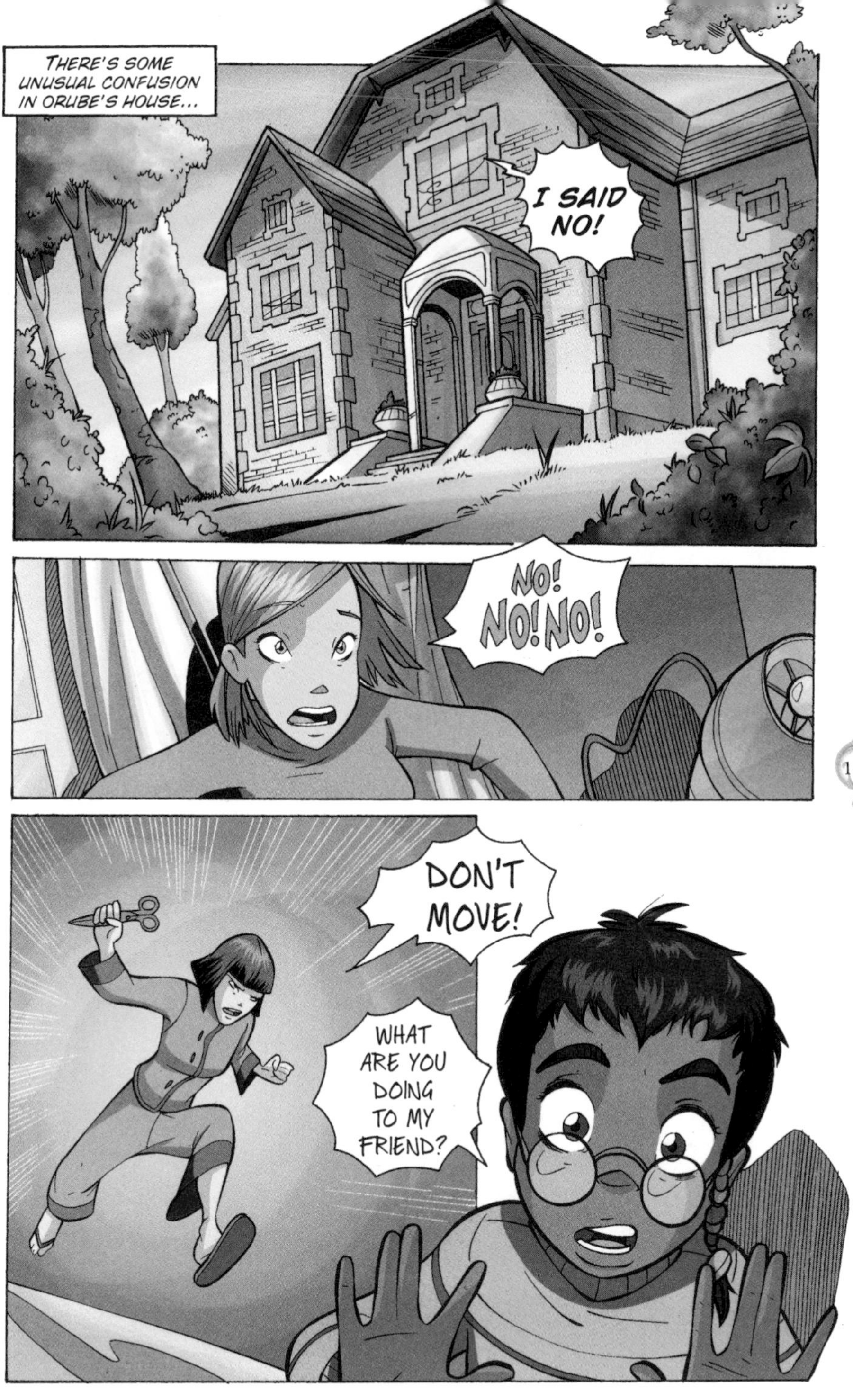
THERE'S SOME UNUSUAL CONFUSION IN ORUBE'S HOUSE...
I SAID NO!
NO! NO! NO!
DON'T MOVE!
WHAT ARE YOU DOING TO MY FRIEND?

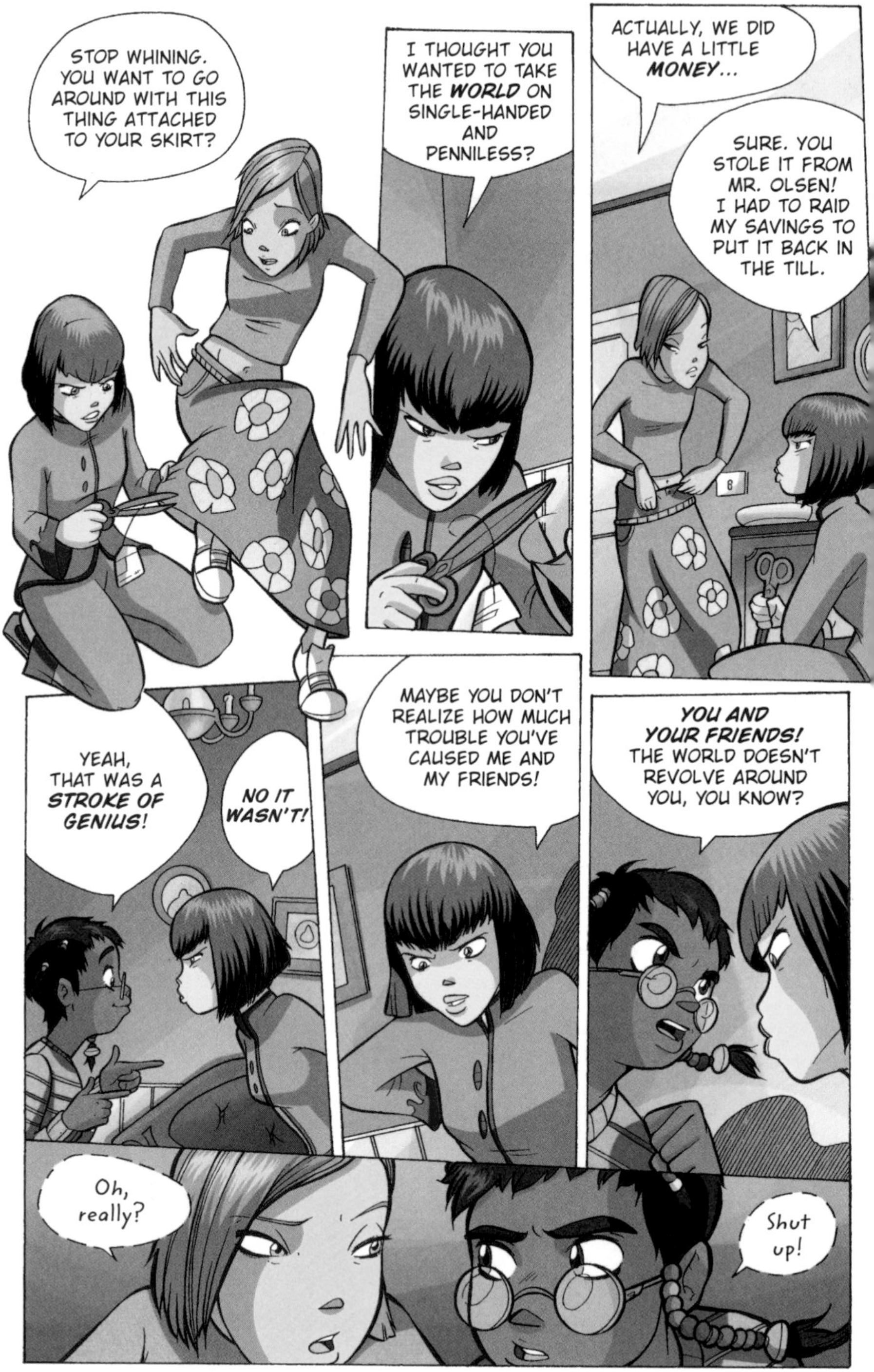
STOP WHINING. YOU WANT TO GO AROUND WITH THIS THING ATTACHED TO YOUR SKIRT?
I THOUGHT YOU WANTED TO TAKE THE WORLD ON SINGLE-HANDED AND PENNILESS?
ACTUALLY, WE DID HAVE A LITTLE MONEY...
SURE. YOU STOLE IT FROM MR. OLSEN! I HAD TO RAID MY SAVINGS TO PUT IT BACK IN THE TILL.
YEAH, THAT WAS A STROKE OF GENIUS!
NO IT WASN'T!
MAYBE YOU DON'T REALIZE HOW MUCH TROUBLE YOU'VE CAUSED ME AND MY FRIENDS!
YOU AND YOUR FRIENDS! THE WORLD DOESN'T REVOLVE AROUND YOU, YOU KNOW?
Oh, really?
Shut up!

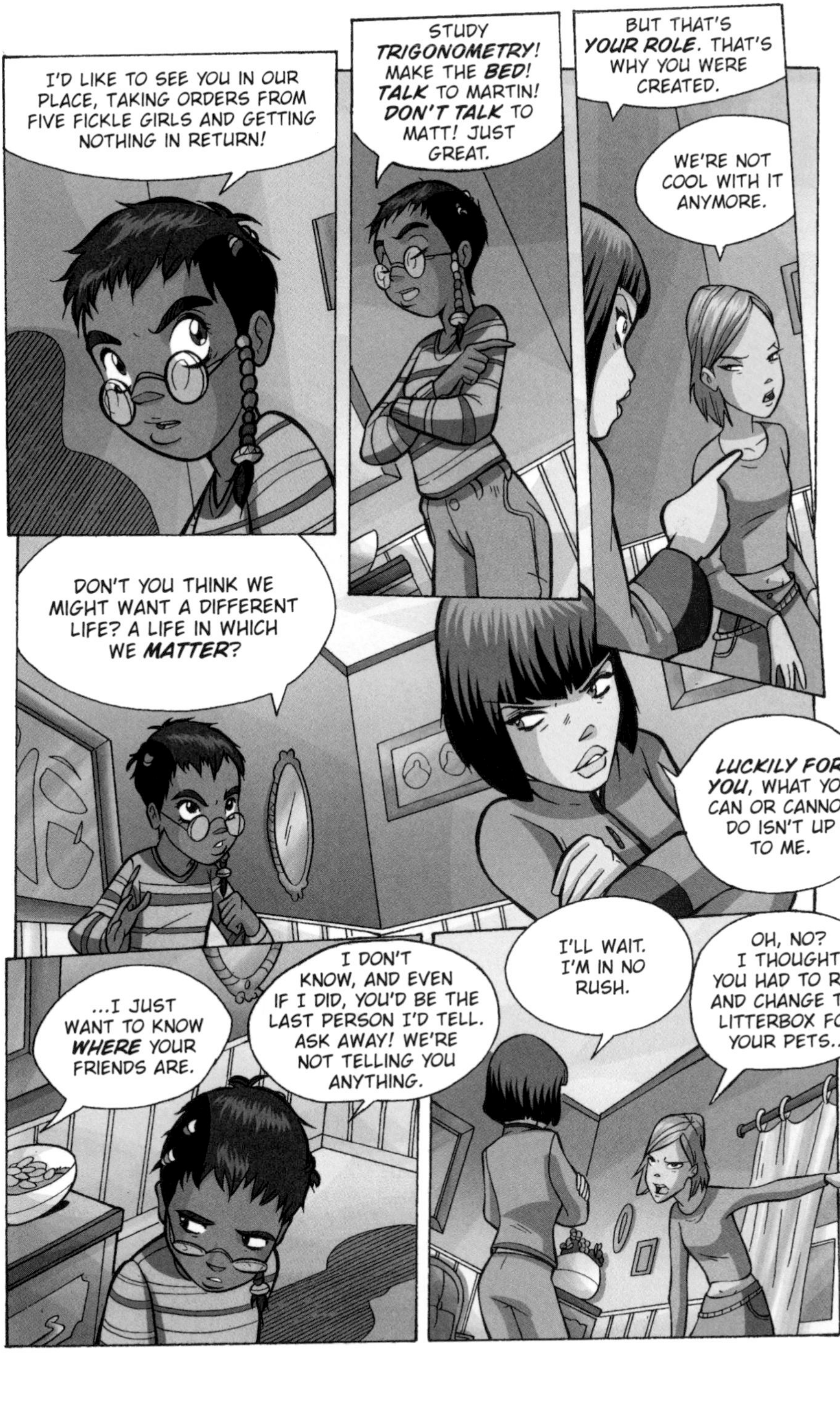
I'D LIKE TO SEE YOU IN OUR PLACE, TAKING ORDERS FROM FIVE FICKLE GIRLS AND GETTING NOTHING IN RETURN!
STUDY ***TRIGONOMETRY***! MAKE THE ***BED***! ***TALK*** TO MARTIN! ***DON'T TALK*** TO MATT! JUST GREAT.
BUT THAT'S ***YOUR ROLE***. THAT'S WHY YOU WERE CREATED.
WE'RE NOT COOL WITH IT ANYMORE.
DON'T YOU THINK WE MIGHT WANT A DIFFERENT LIFE? A LIFE IN WHICH WE ***MATTER***?
LUCKILY FOR YOU, WHAT YOU CAN OR CANNOT DO ISN'T UP TO ME.
...I JUST WANT TO KNOW ***WHERE*** YOUR FRIENDS ARE.
I DON'T KNOW, AND EVEN IF I DID, YOU'D BE THE LAST PERSON I'D TELL. ASK AWAY! WE'RE NOT TELLING YOU ANYTHING.
I'LL WAIT. I'M IN NO RUSH.
OH, NO? I THOUGHT YOU HAD TO RUN AND CHANGE THE LITTERBOX FOR YOUR PETS...

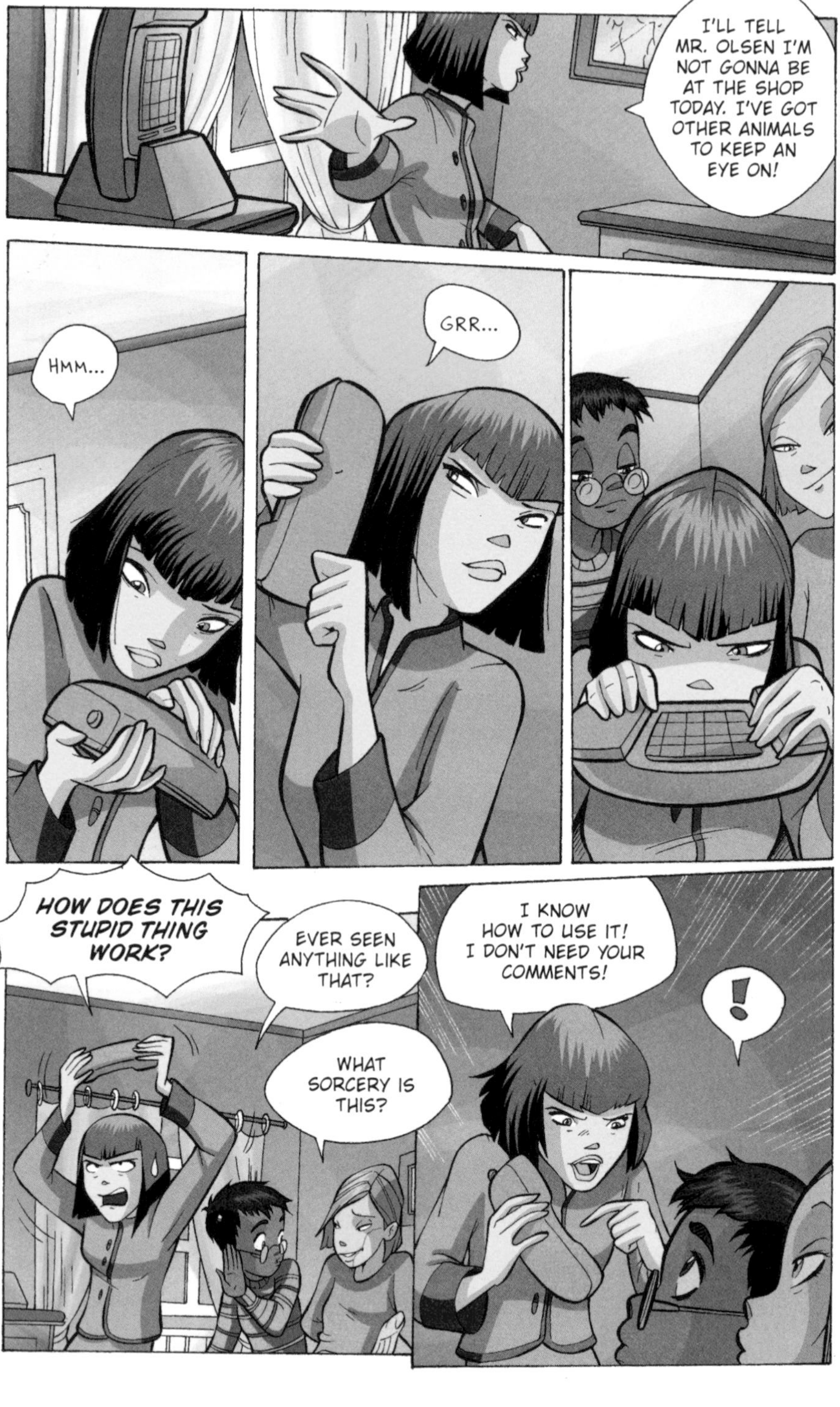
I'LL TELL MR. OLSEN I'M NOT GONNA BE AT THE SHOP TODAY. I'VE GOT OTHER ANIMALS TO KEEP AN EYE ON!
HMM...
GRR...
HOW DOES THIS STUPID THING WORK?
EVER SEEN ANYTHING LIKE THAT?
WHAT SORCERY IS THIS?
I KNOW HOW TO USE IT! I DON'T NEED YOUR COMMENTS!
!

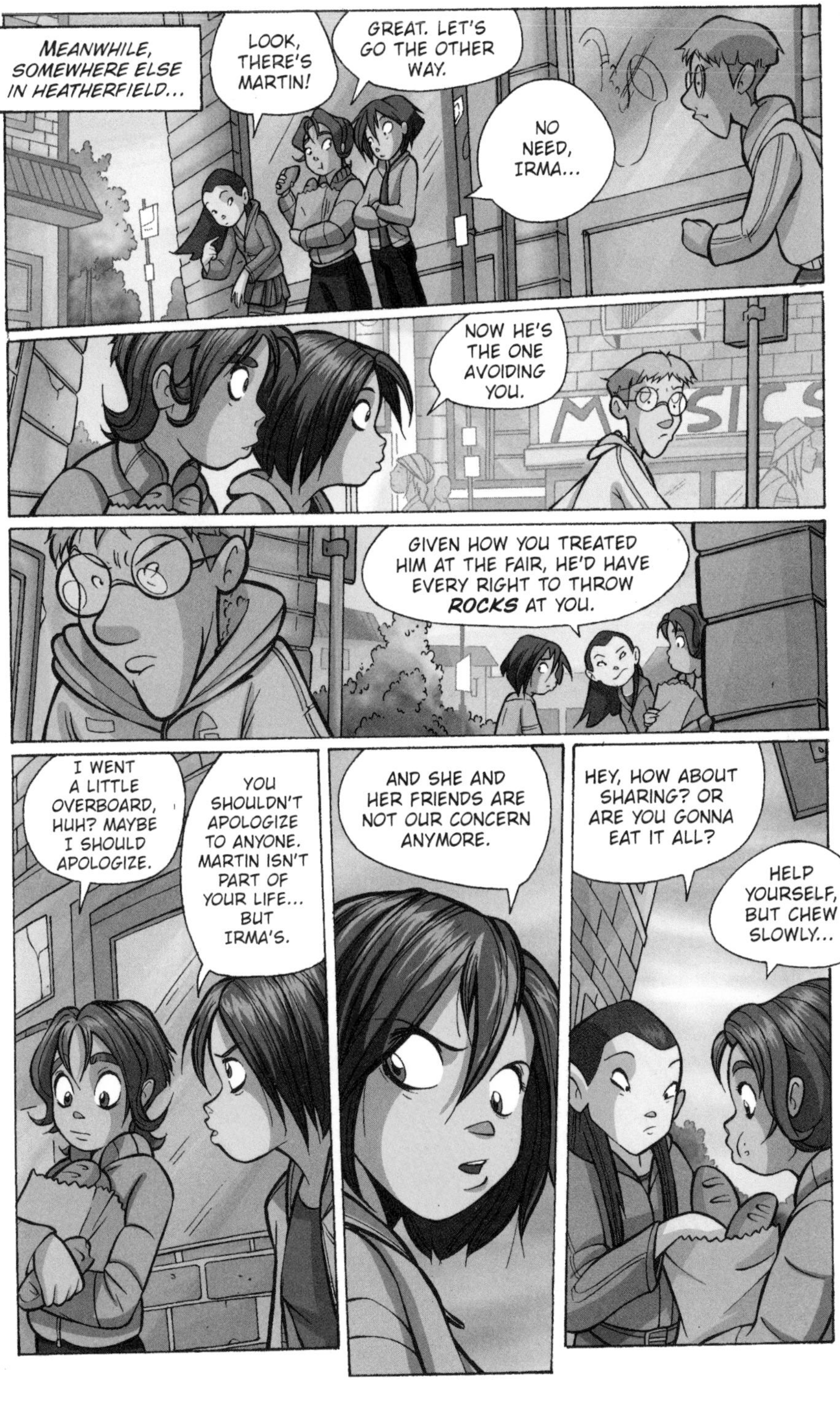
MEANWHILE, SOMEWHERE ELSE IN HEATHERFIELD...
LOOK, THERE'S MARTIN!
GREAT. LET'S GO THE OTHER WAY.
NO NEED, IRMA...
NOW HE'S THE ONE AVOIDING YOU.
GIVEN HOW YOU TREATED HIM AT THE FAIR, HE'D HAVE EVERY RIGHT TO THROW ROCKS AT YOU.
I WENT A LITTLE OVERBOARD, HUH? MAYBE I SHOULD APOLOGIZE.
YOU SHOULDN'T APOLOGIZE TO ANYONE. MARTIN ISN'T PART OF YOUR LIFE... BUT IRMA'S.
AND SHE AND HER FRIENDS ARE NOT OUR CONCERN ANYMORE.
HEY, HOW ABOUT SHARING? OR ARE YOU GONNA EAT IT ALL?
HELP YOURSELF, BUT CHEW SLOWLY...

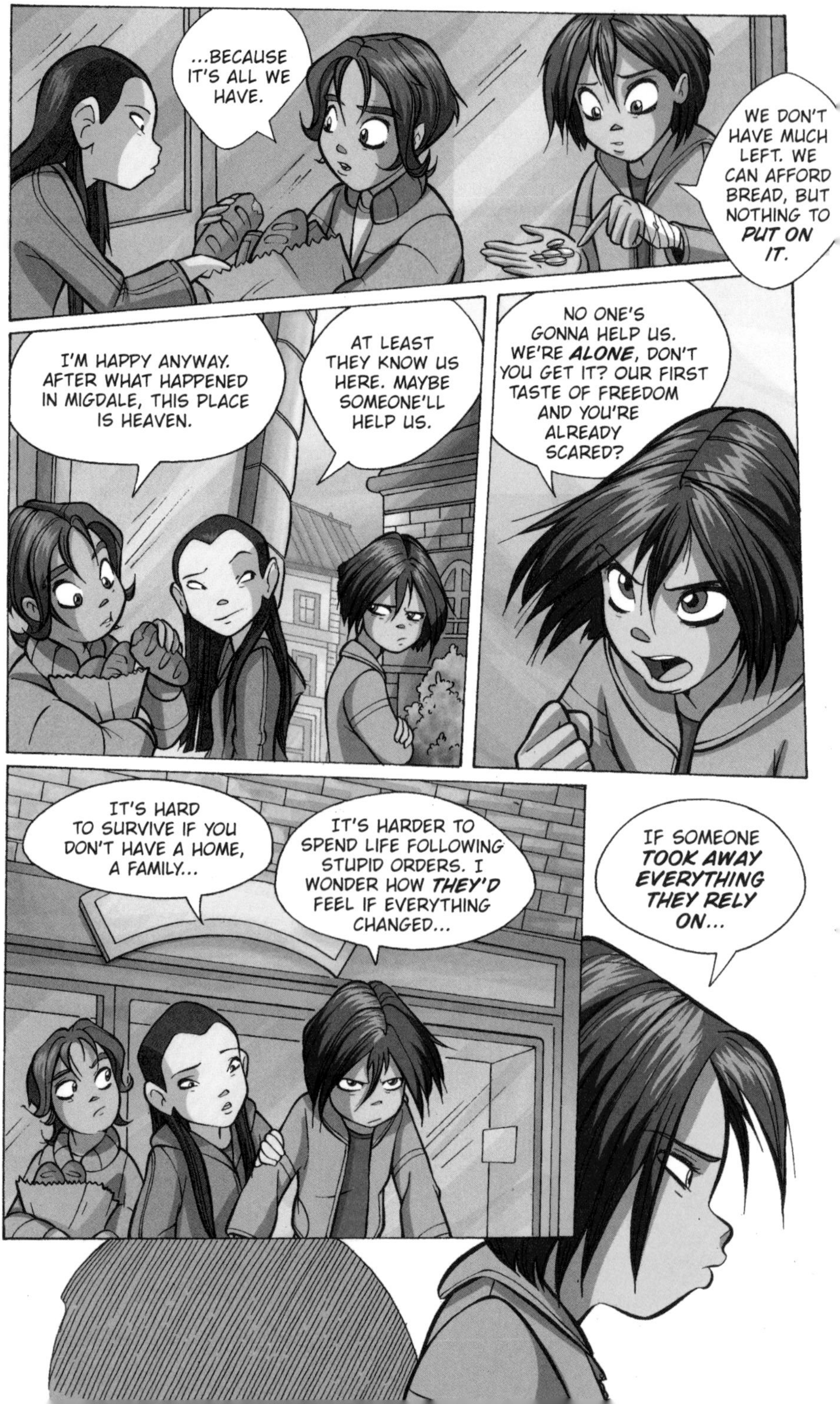
...BECAUSE IT'S ALL WE HAVE.
WE DON'T HAVE MUCH LEFT. WE CAN AFFORD BREAD, BUT NOTHING TO *PUT ON IT.*
I'M HAPPY ANYWAY. AFTER WHAT HAPPENED IN MIGDALE, THIS PLACE IS HEAVEN.
AT LEAST THEY KNOW US HERE. MAYBE SOMEONE'LL HELP US.
NO ONE'S GONNA HELP US. WE'RE *ALONE*, DON'T YOU GET IT? OUR FIRST TASTE OF FREEDOM AND YOU'RE ALREADY SCARED?
IT'S HARD TO SURVIVE IF YOU DON'T HAVE A HOME, A FAMILY...
IT'S HARDER TO SPEND LIFE FOLLOWING STUPID ORDERS. I WONDER HOW *THEY'D* FEEL IF EVERYTHING CHANGED...
IF SOMEONE *TOOK AWAY EVERYTHING THEY RELY ON...*

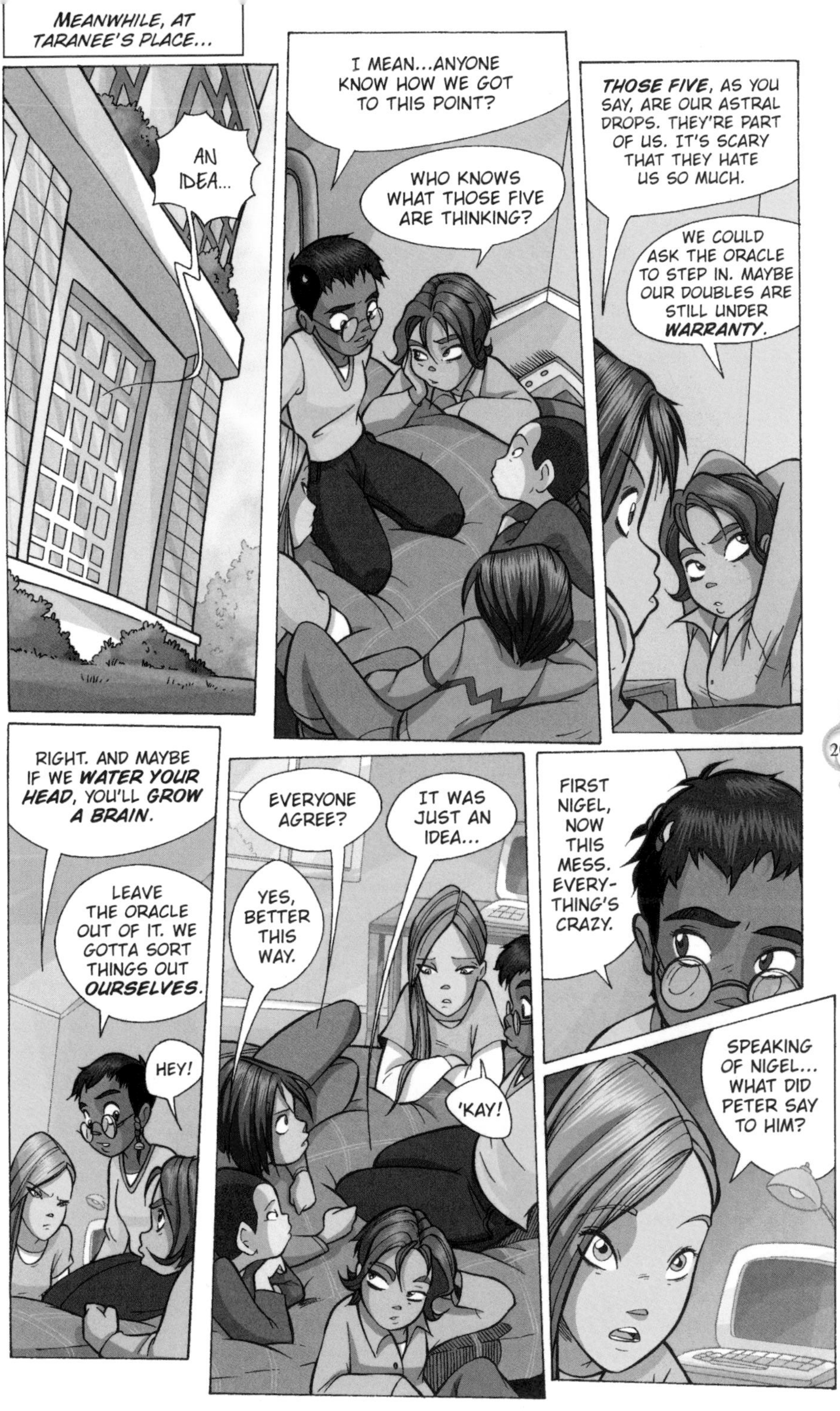
MEANWHILE, AT TARANEE'S PLACE...
AN IDEA...
I MEAN...ANYONE KNOW HOW WE GOT TO THIS POINT?
WHO KNOWS WHAT THOSE FIVE ARE THINKING?
THOSE FIVE, AS YOU SAY, ARE OUR ASTRAL DROPS. THEY'RE PART OF US. IT'S SCARY THAT THEY HATE US SO MUCH.
WE COULD ASK THE ORACLE TO STEP IN. MAYBE OUR DOUBLES ARE STILL UNDER WARRANTY.
RIGHT. AND MAYBE IF WE WATER YOUR HEAD, YOU'LL GROW A BRAIN.
LEAVE THE ORACLE OUT OF IT. WE GOTTA SORT THINGS OUT OURSELVES.
HEY!
EVERYONE AGREE?
IT WAS JUST AN IDEA...
YES, BETTER THIS WAY.
'KAY!
FIRST NIGEL, NOW THIS MESS. EVERYTHING'S CRAZY.
SPEAKING OF NIGEL... WHAT DID PETER SAY TO HIM?

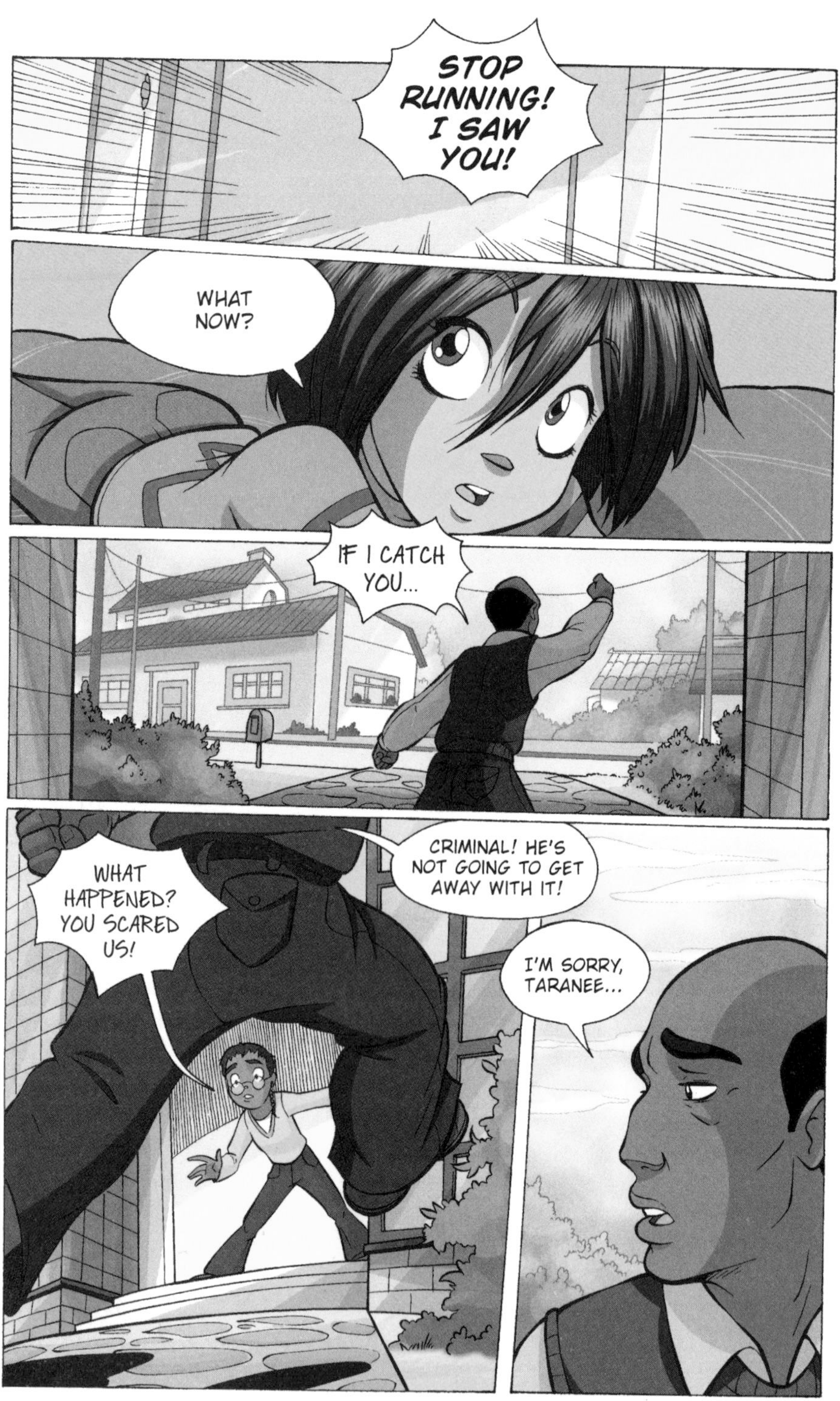
STOP RUNNING! I SAW YOU!
WHAT NOW?
IF I CATCH YOU...
WHAT HAPPENED? YOU SCARED US!
CRIMINAL! HE'S NOT GOING TO GET AWAY WITH IT!
I'M SORRY, TARANEE...

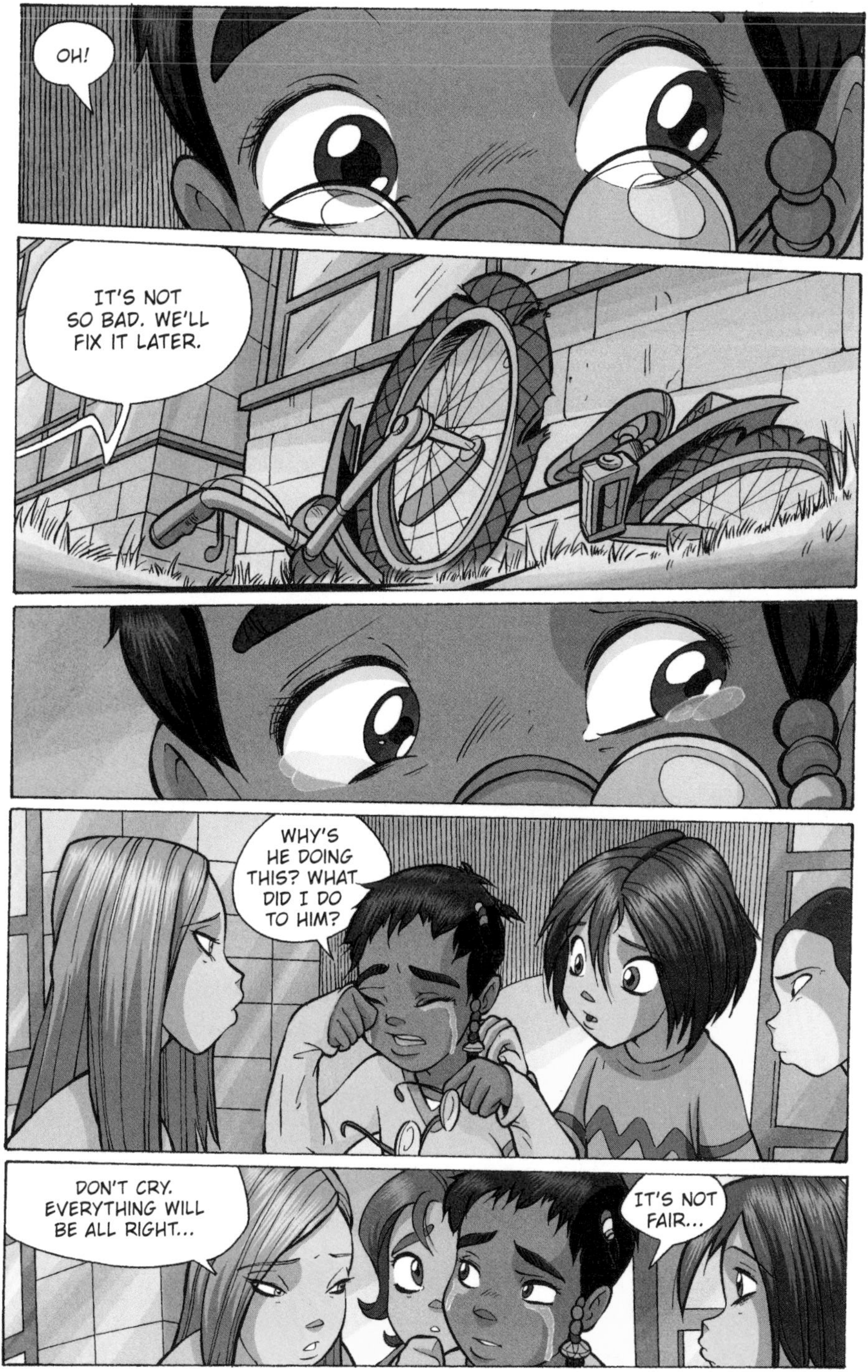
OH!
IT'S NOT SO BAD. WE'LL FIX IT LATER.
WHY'S HE DOING THIS? WHAT DID I DO TO HIM?
DON'T CRY. EVERYTHING WILL BE ALL RIGHT...
IT'S NOT FAIR...

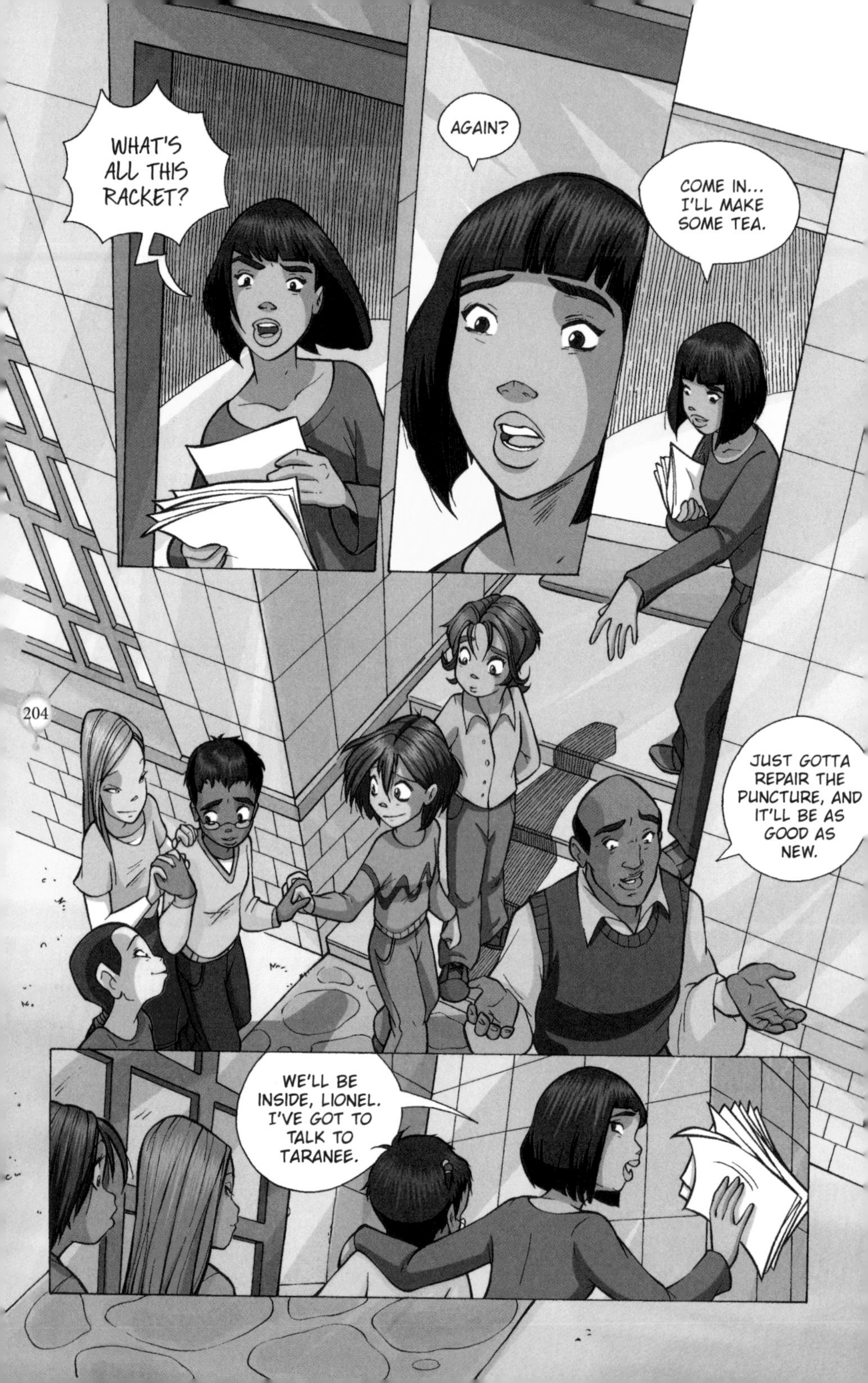
WHAT'S ALL THIS RACKET?
AGAIN?
COME IN... I'LL MAKE SOME TEA.
JUST GOTTA REPAIR THE PUNCTURE, AND IT'LL BE AS GOOD AS NEW.
WE'LL BE INSIDE, LIONEL. I'VE GOT TO TALK TO TARANEE.

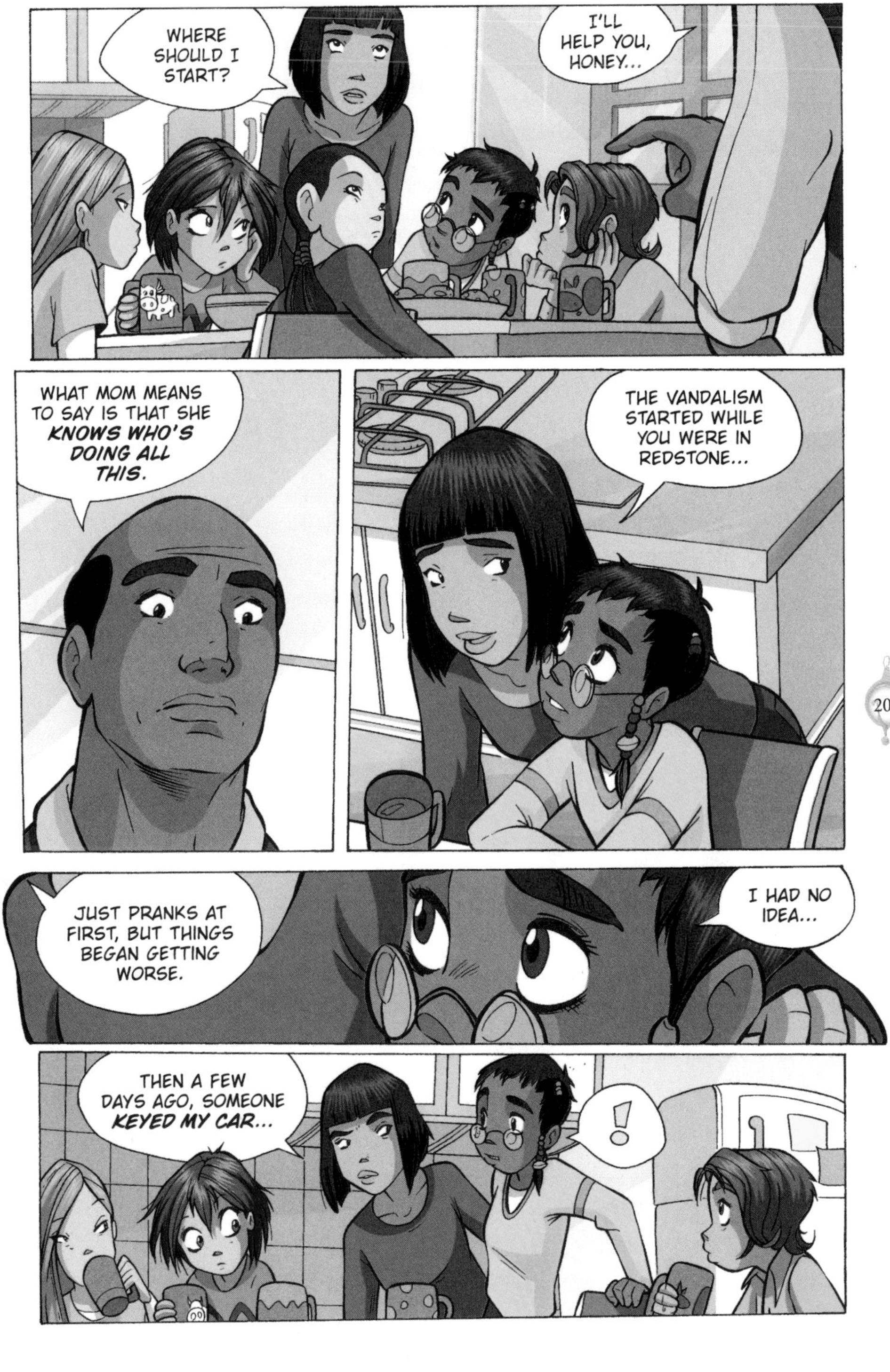
WHERE SHOULD I START?
I'LL HELP YOU, HONEY...
WHAT MOM MEANS TO SAY IS THAT SHE KNOWS WHO'S DOING ALL THIS.
THE VANDALISM STARTED WHILE YOU WERE IN REDSTONE...
JUST PRANKS AT FIRST, BUT THINGS BEGAN GETTING WORSE.
I HAD NO IDEA...
THEN A FEW DAYS AGO, SOMEONE KEYED MY CAR...
!

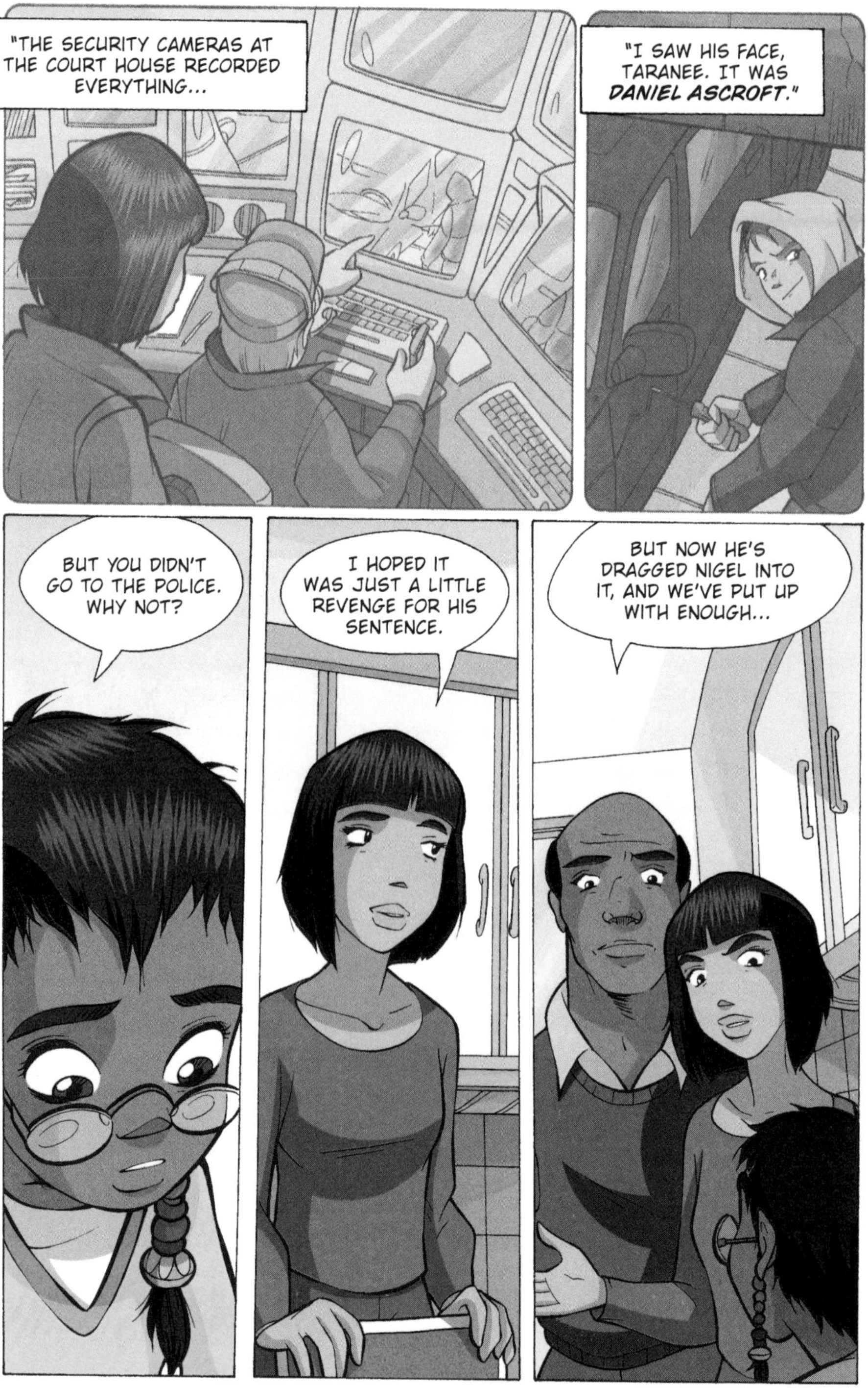
"THE SECURITY CAMERAS AT THE COURT HOUSE RECORDED EVERYTHING...
"I SAW HIS FACE, TARANEE. IT WAS DANIEL ASCROFT."
BUT YOU DIDN'T GO TO THE POLICE. WHY NOT?
I HOPED IT WAS JUST A LITTLE REVENGE FOR HIS SENTENCE.
BUT NOW HE'S DRAGGED NIGEL INTO IT, AND WE'VE PUT UP WITH ENOUGH...

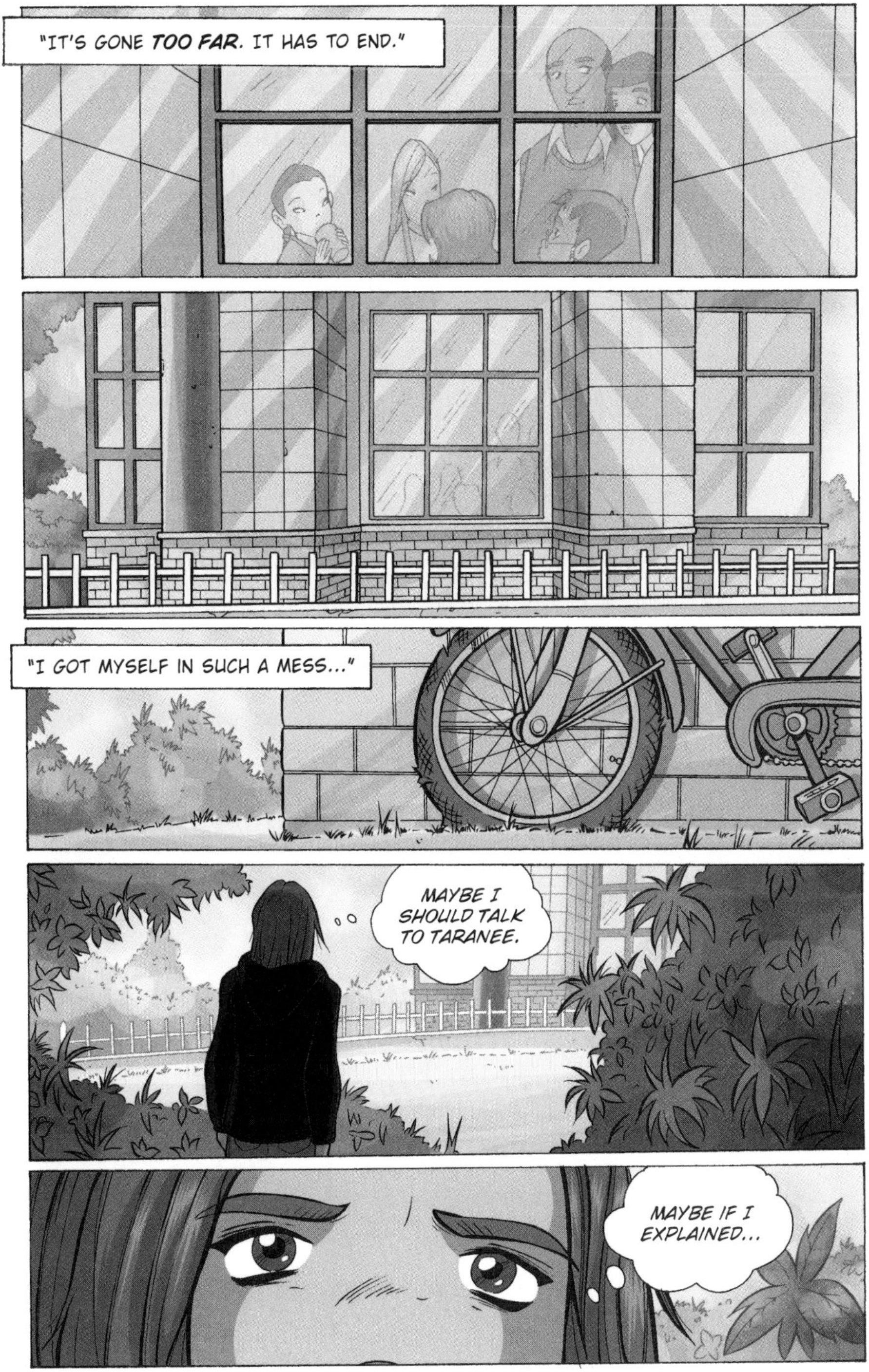
"IT'S GONE TOO FAR. IT HAS TO END."
"I GOT MYSELF IN SUCH A MESS..."
MAYBE I SHOULD TALK TO TARANEE.
MAYBE IF I EXPLAINED...

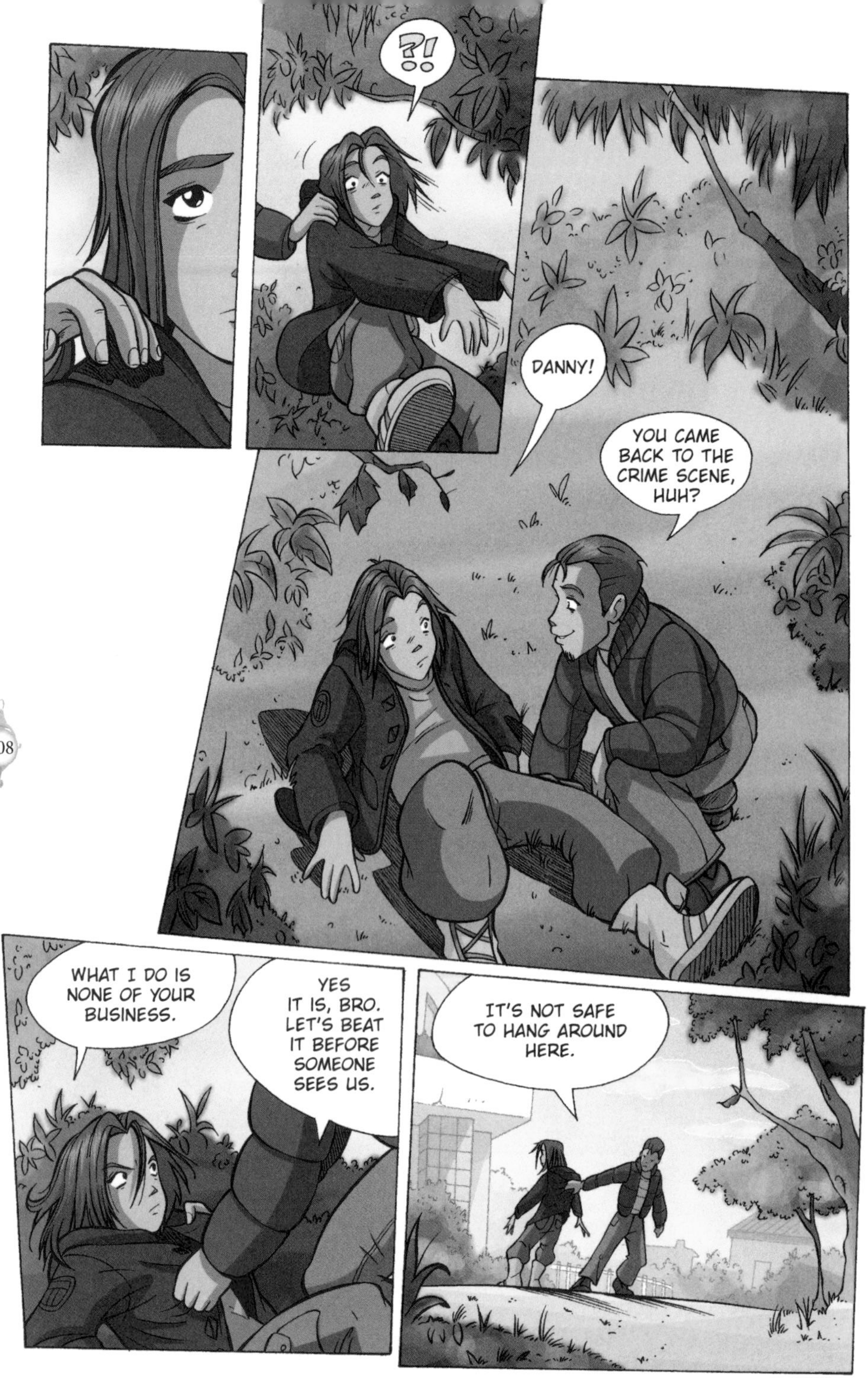
?!
DANNY!
YOU CAME BACK TO THE CRIME SCENE, HUH?
WHAT I DO IS NONE OF YOUR BUSINESS.
YES IT IS, BRO. LET'S BEAT IT BEFORE SOMEONE SEES US.
IT'S NOT SAFE TO HANG AROUND HERE.

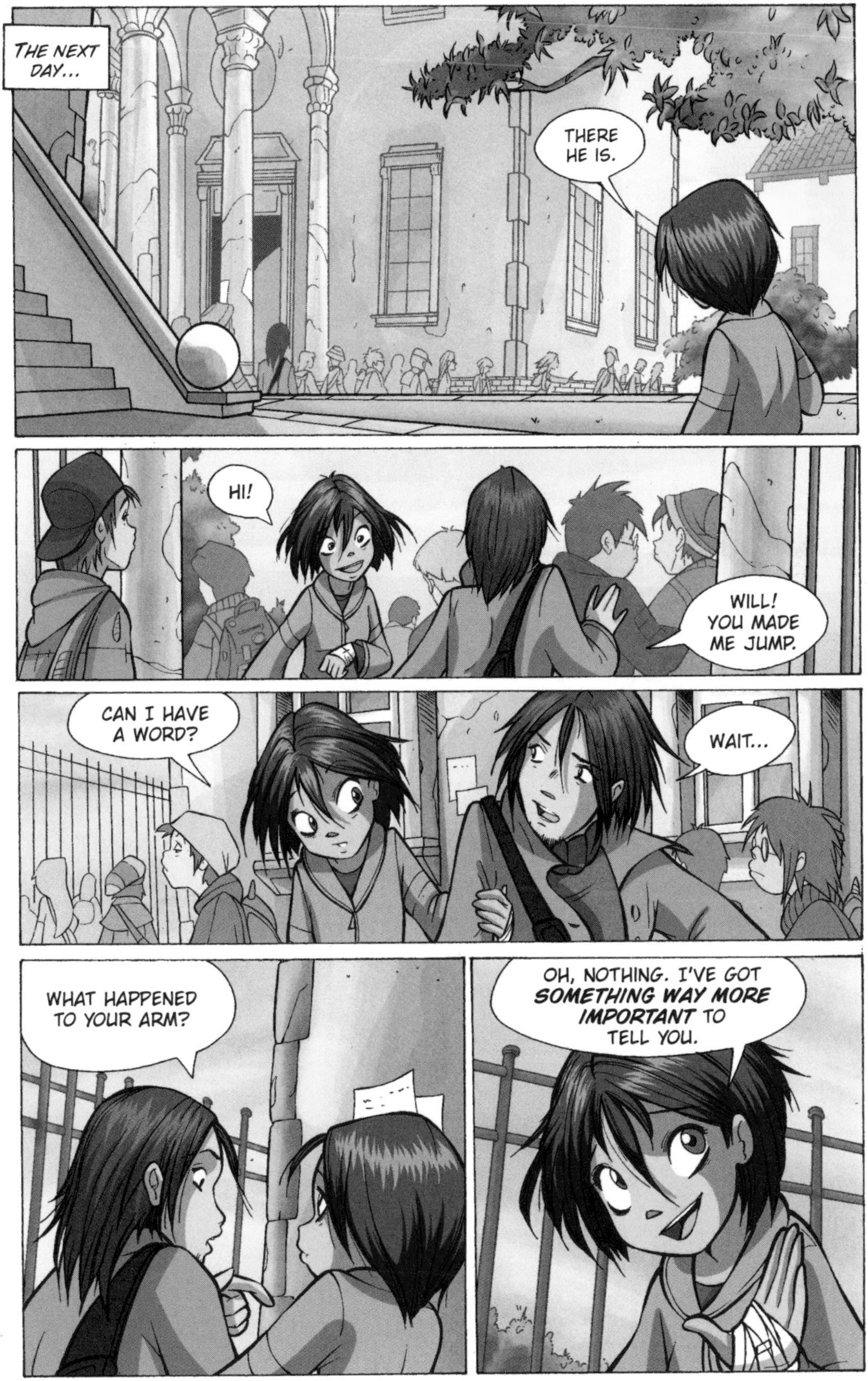
THE NEXT DAY...
THERE HE IS.
HI!
WILL! YOU MADE ME JUMP.
CAN I HAVE A WORD?
WAIT...
WHAT HAPPENED TO YOUR ARM?
OH, NOTHING. I'VE GOT **SOMETHING WAY MORE IMPORTANT** TO TELL YOU.

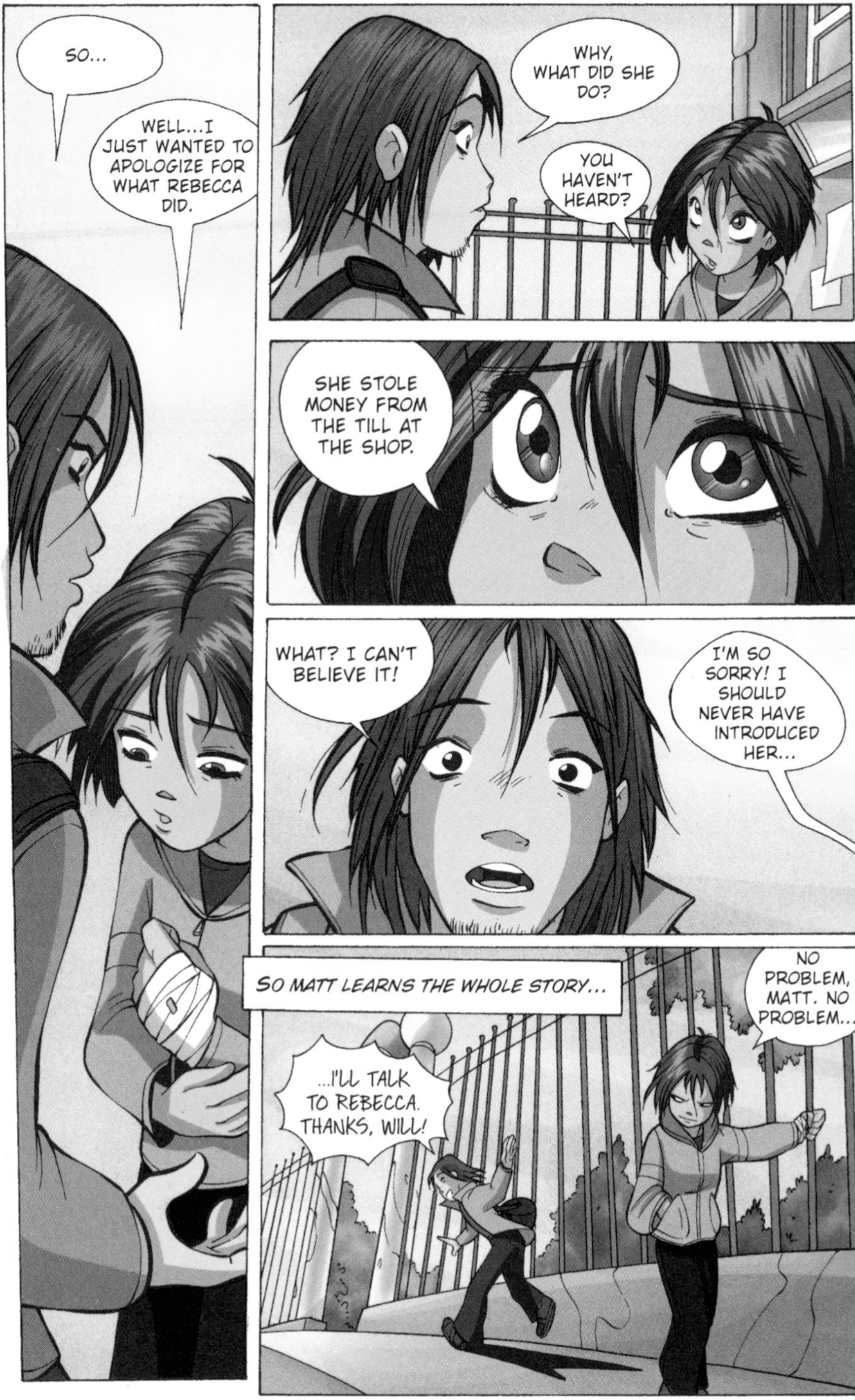
SO...
WELL...I JUST WANTED TO APOLOGIZE FOR WHAT REBECCA DID.
WHY, WHAT DID SHE DO?
YOU HAVEN'T HEARD?
SHE STOLE MONEY FROM THE TILL AT THE SHOP.
WHAT? I CAN'T BELIEVE IT!
I'M SO SORRY! I SHOULD NEVER HAVE INTRODUCED HER...
SO MATT LEARNS THE WHOLE STORY...
...I'LL TALK TO REBECCA. THANKS, WILL!
NO PROBLEM, MATT. NO PROBLEM...

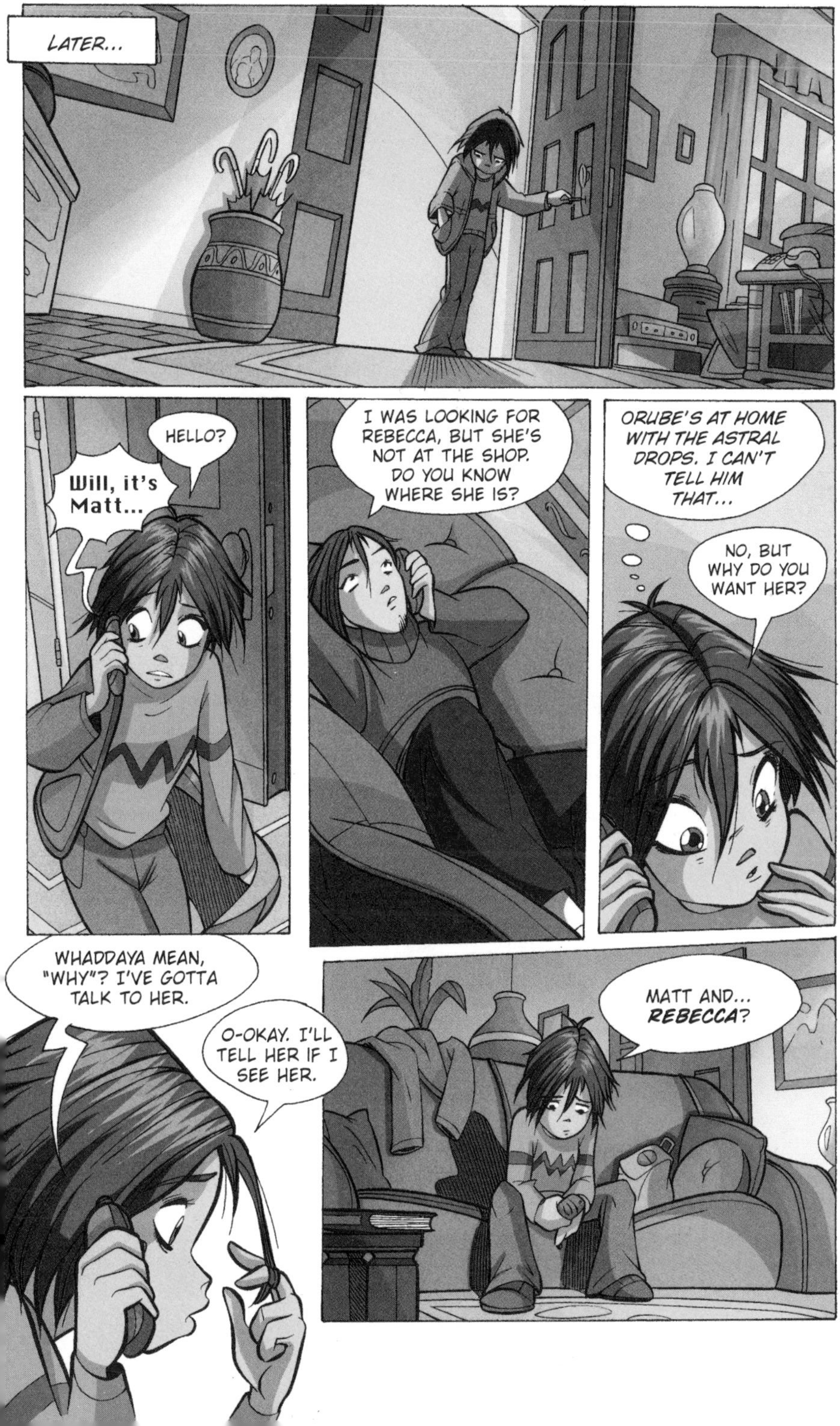
LATER...
HELLO?
Will, it's Matt...
I WAS LOOKING FOR REBECCA, BUT SHE'S NOT AT THE SHOP. DO YOU KNOW WHERE SHE IS?
ORUBE'S AT HOME WITH THE ASTRAL DROPS. I CAN'T TELL HIM THAT...
NO, BUT WHY DO YOU WANT HER?
WHADDAYA MEAN, "WHY"? I'VE GOTTA TALK TO HER.
O-OKAY. I'LL TELL HER IF I SEE HER.
MATT AND... REBECCA?

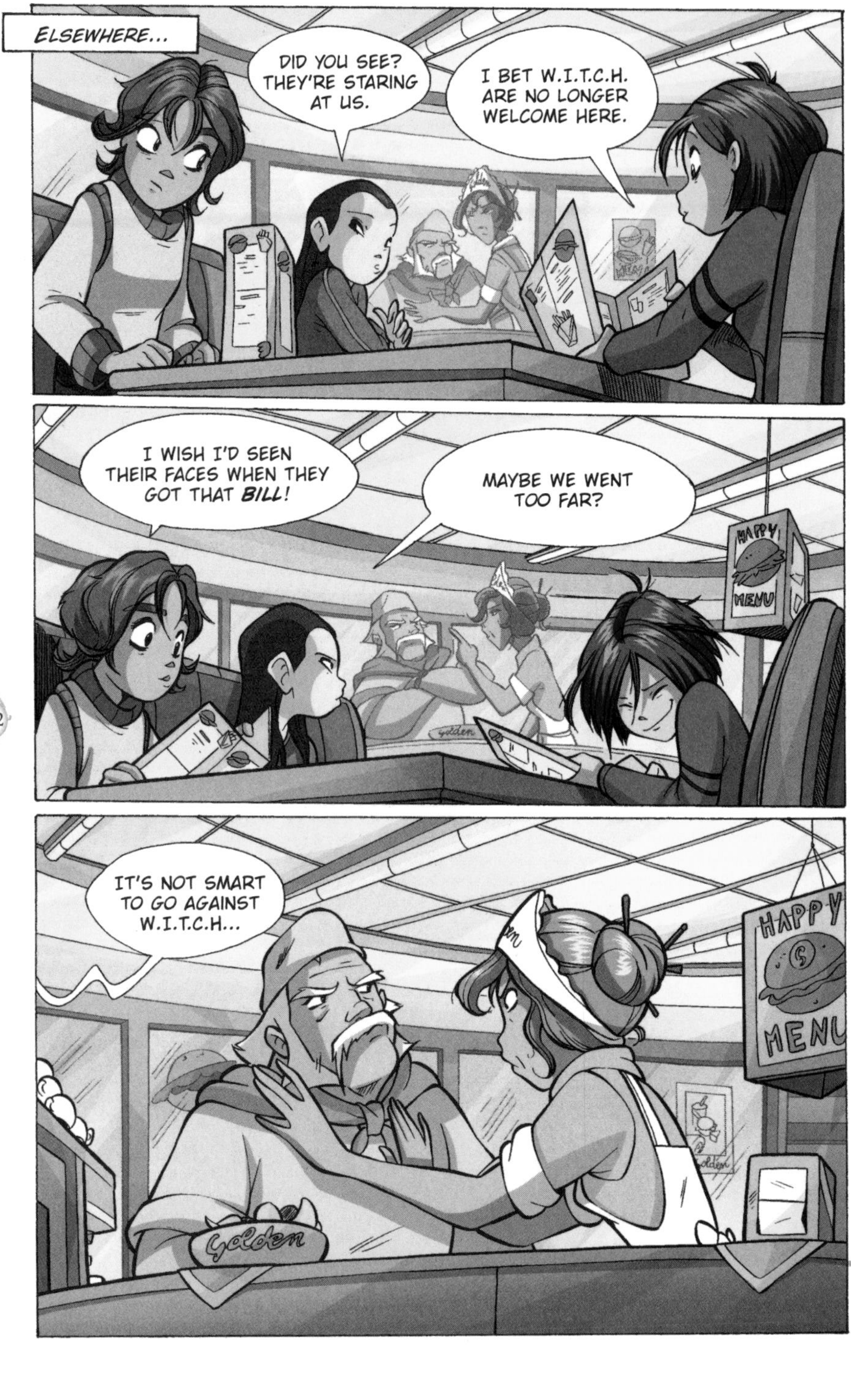
ELSEWHERE...
DID YOU SEE? THEY'RE STARING AT US.
I BET W.I.T.C.H. ARE NO LONGER WELCOME HERE.
I WISH I'D SEEN THEIR FACES WHEN THEY GOT THAT BILL!
MAYBE WE WENT TOO FAR?
HAPPY MENU
IT'S NOT SMART TO GO AGAINST W.I.T.C.H...
HAPPY MENU
Golden

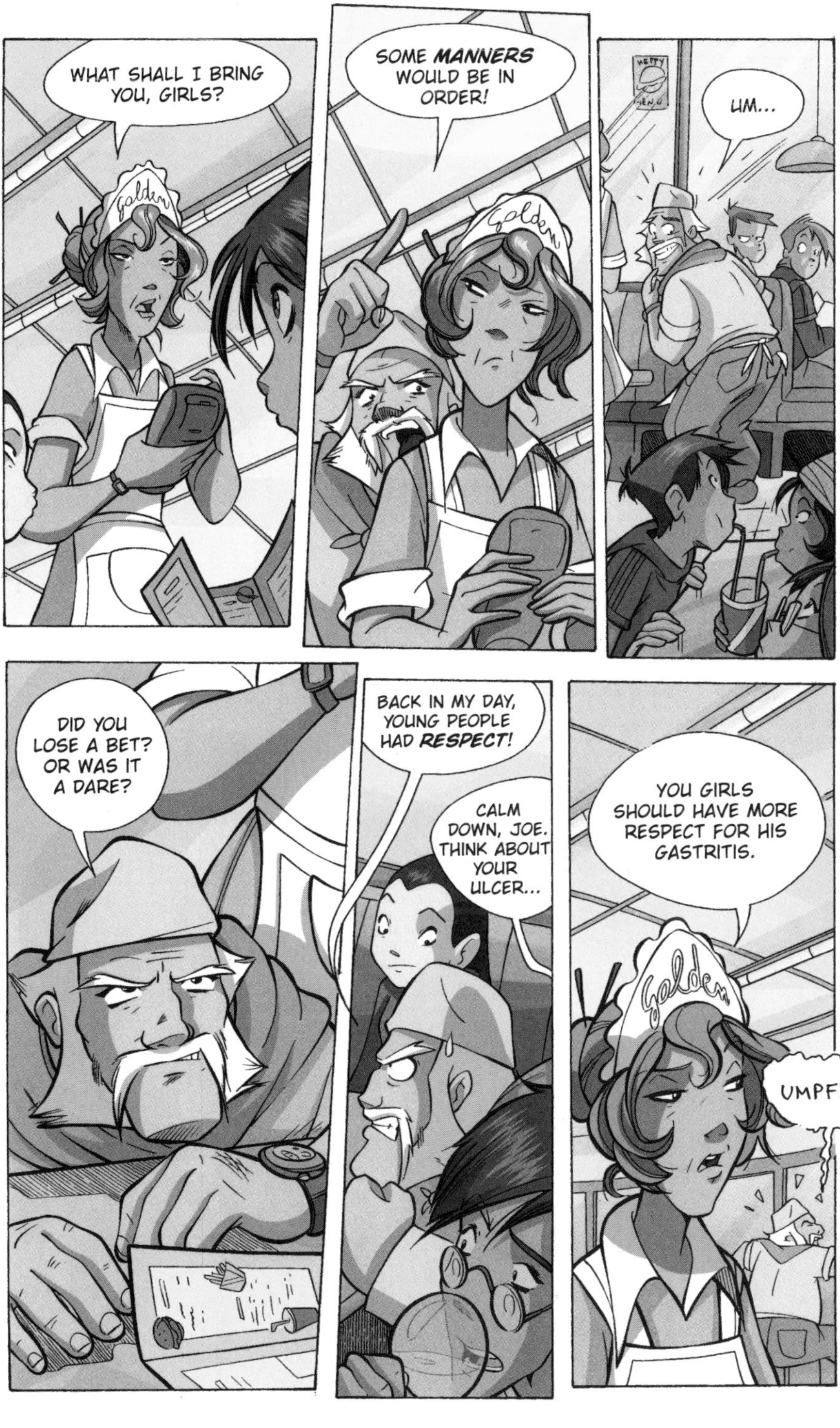
WHAT SHALL I BRING YOU, GIRLS?
SOME *MANNERS* WOULD BE IN ORDER!
UM...
DID YOU LOSE A BET? OR WAS IT A DARE?
BACK IN MY DAY, YOUNG PEOPLE HAD *RESPECT*!
CALM DOWN, JOE. THINK ABOUT YOUR ULCER...
YOU GIRLS SHOULD HAVE MORE RESPECT FOR HIS GASTRITIS.
UMPF!

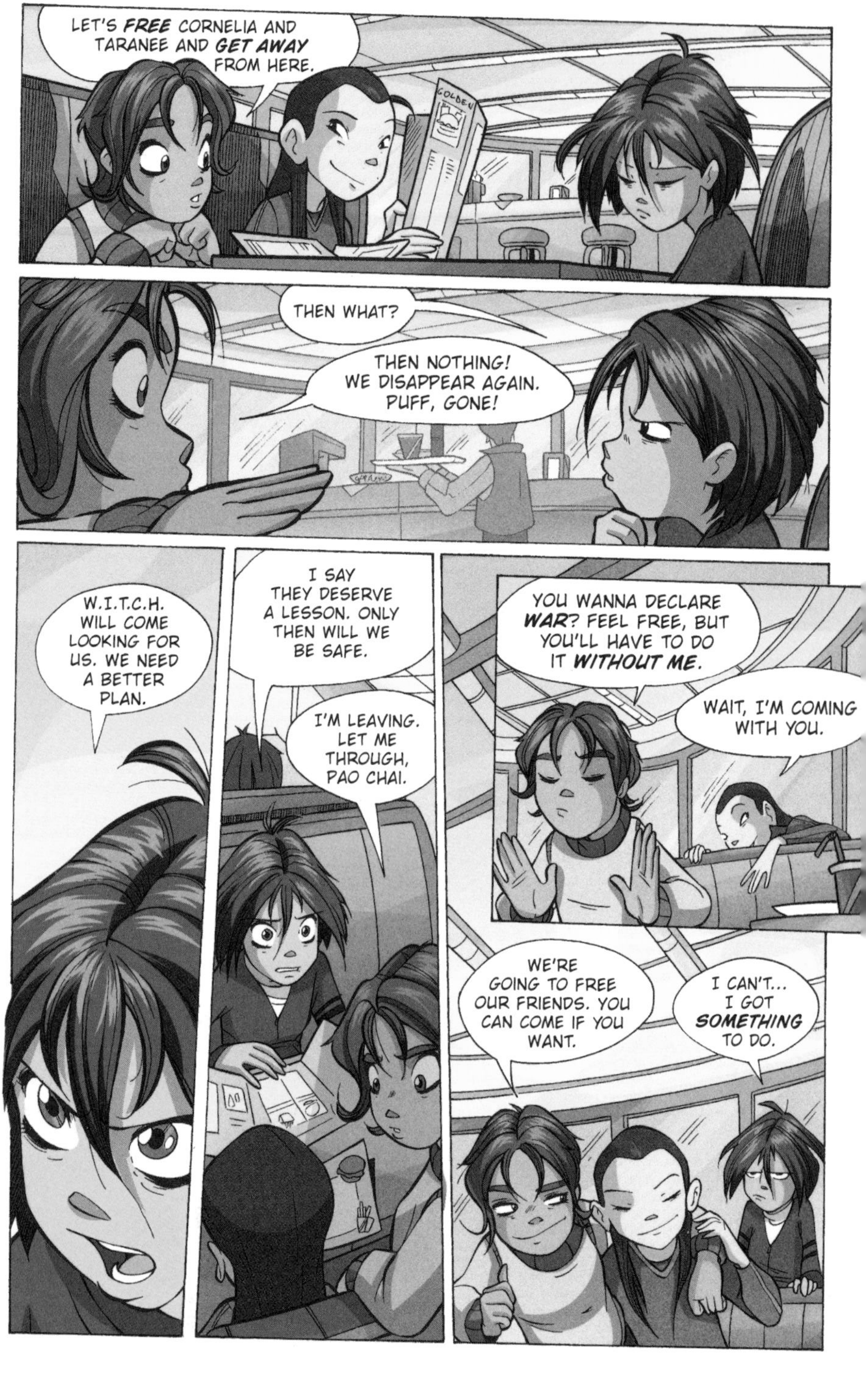
LET'S FREE CORNELIA AND TARANEE AND GET AWAY FROM HERE.
THEN WHAT?
THEN NOTHING! WE DISAPPEAR AGAIN. PUFF, GONE!
W.I.T.C.H. WILL COME LOOKING FOR US. WE NEED A BETTER PLAN.
I SAY THEY DESERVE A LESSON. ONLY THEN WILL WE BE SAFE.
I'M LEAVING. LET ME THROUGH, PAO CHAI.
YOU WANNA DECLARE WAR? FEEL FREE, BUT YOU'LL HAVE TO DO IT WITHOUT ME.
WAIT, I'M COMING WITH YOU.
WE'RE GOING TO FREE OUR FRIENDS. YOU CAN COME IF YOU WANT.
I CAN'T... I GOT SOMETHING TO DO.

214

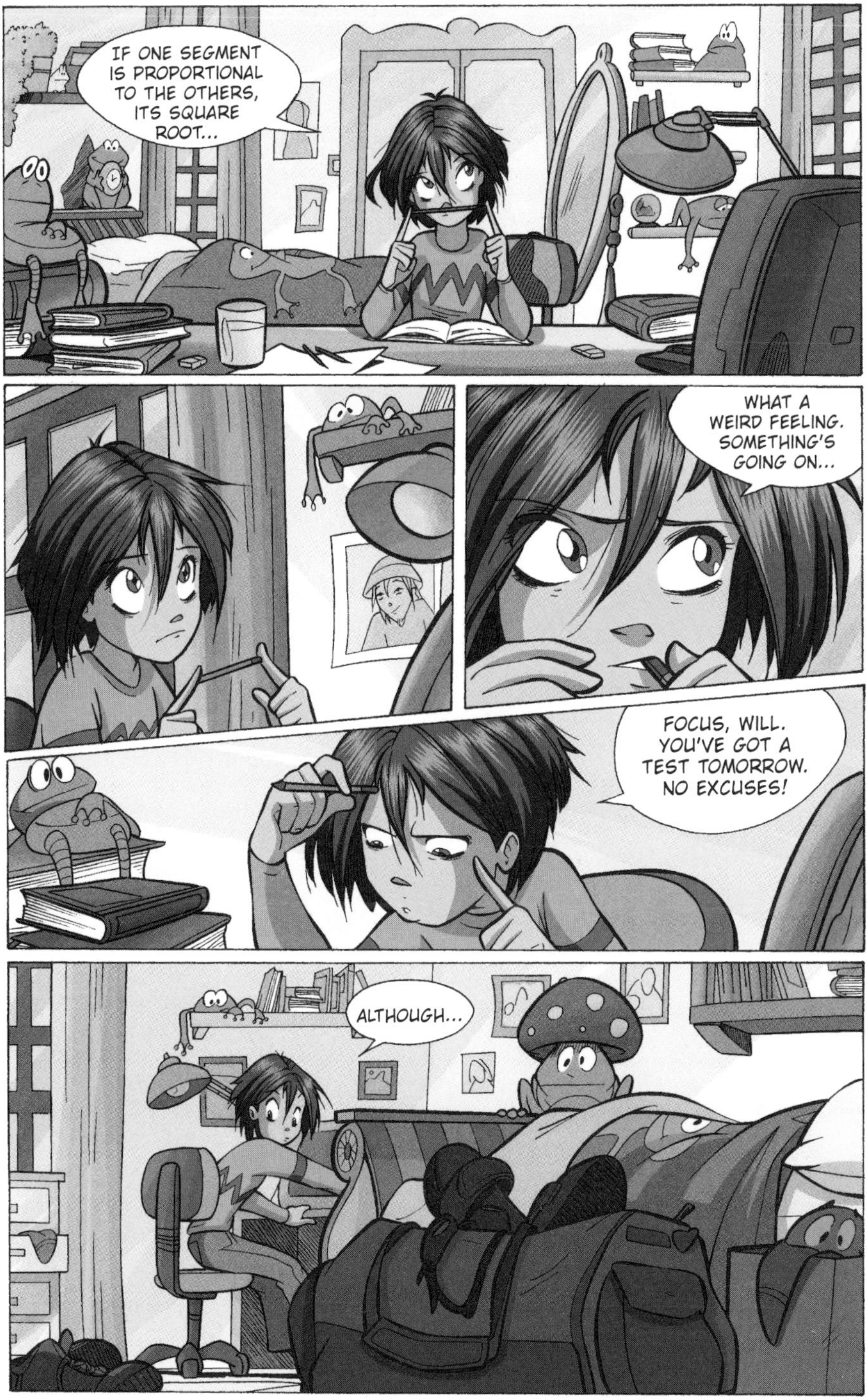
IF ONE SEGMENT IS PROPORTIONAL TO THE OTHERS, ITS SQUARE ROOT...
WHAT A WEIRD FEELING. SOMETHING'S GOING ON...
FOCUS, WILL. YOU'VE GOT A TEST TOMORROW. NO EXCUSES!
ALTHOUGH...

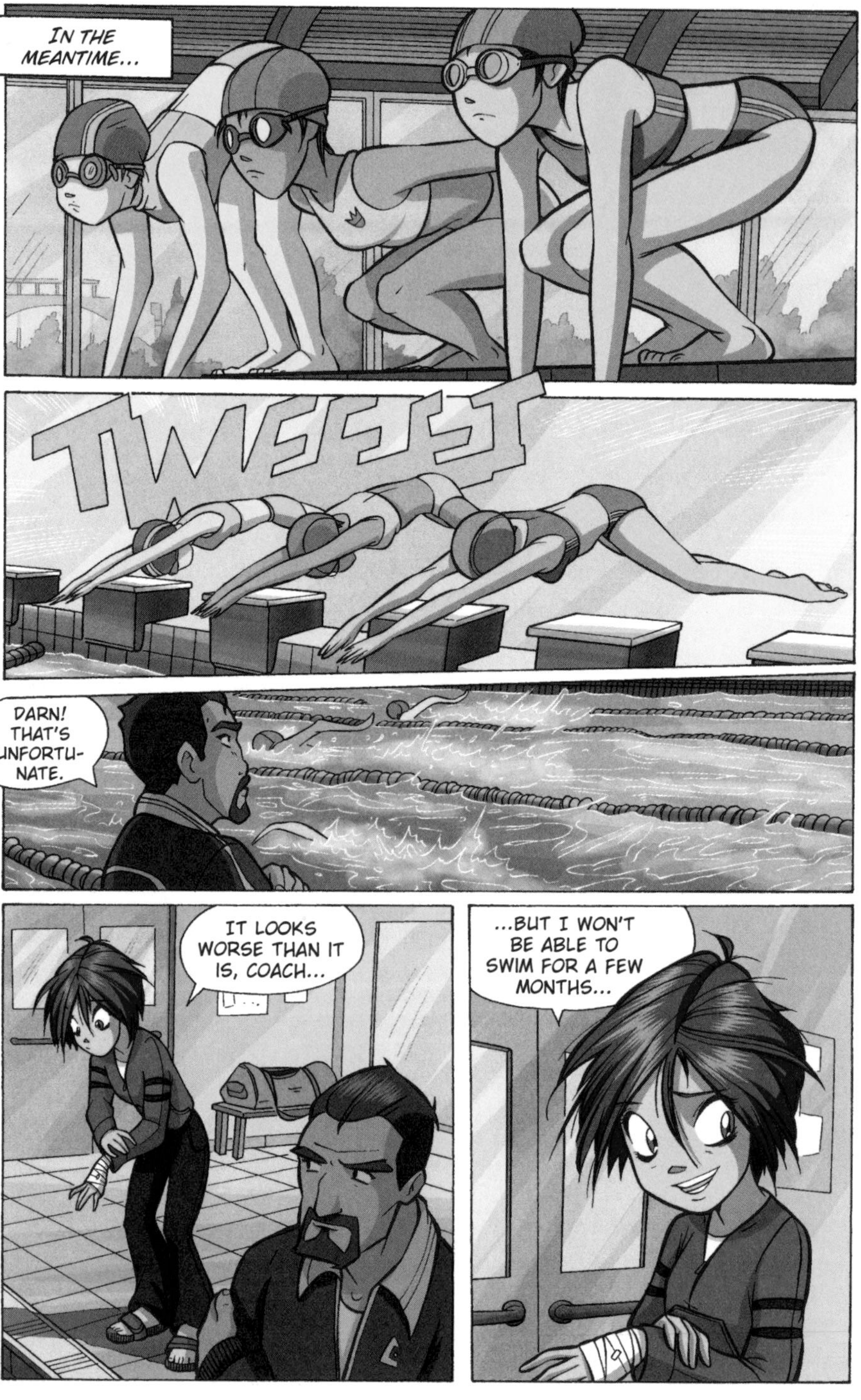
IN THE MEANTIME...
TWEEET
DARN! THAT'S UNFORTUNATE.
IT LOOKS WORSE THAN IT IS, COACH...
...BUT I WON'T BE ABLE TO SWIM FOR A FEW MONTHS...

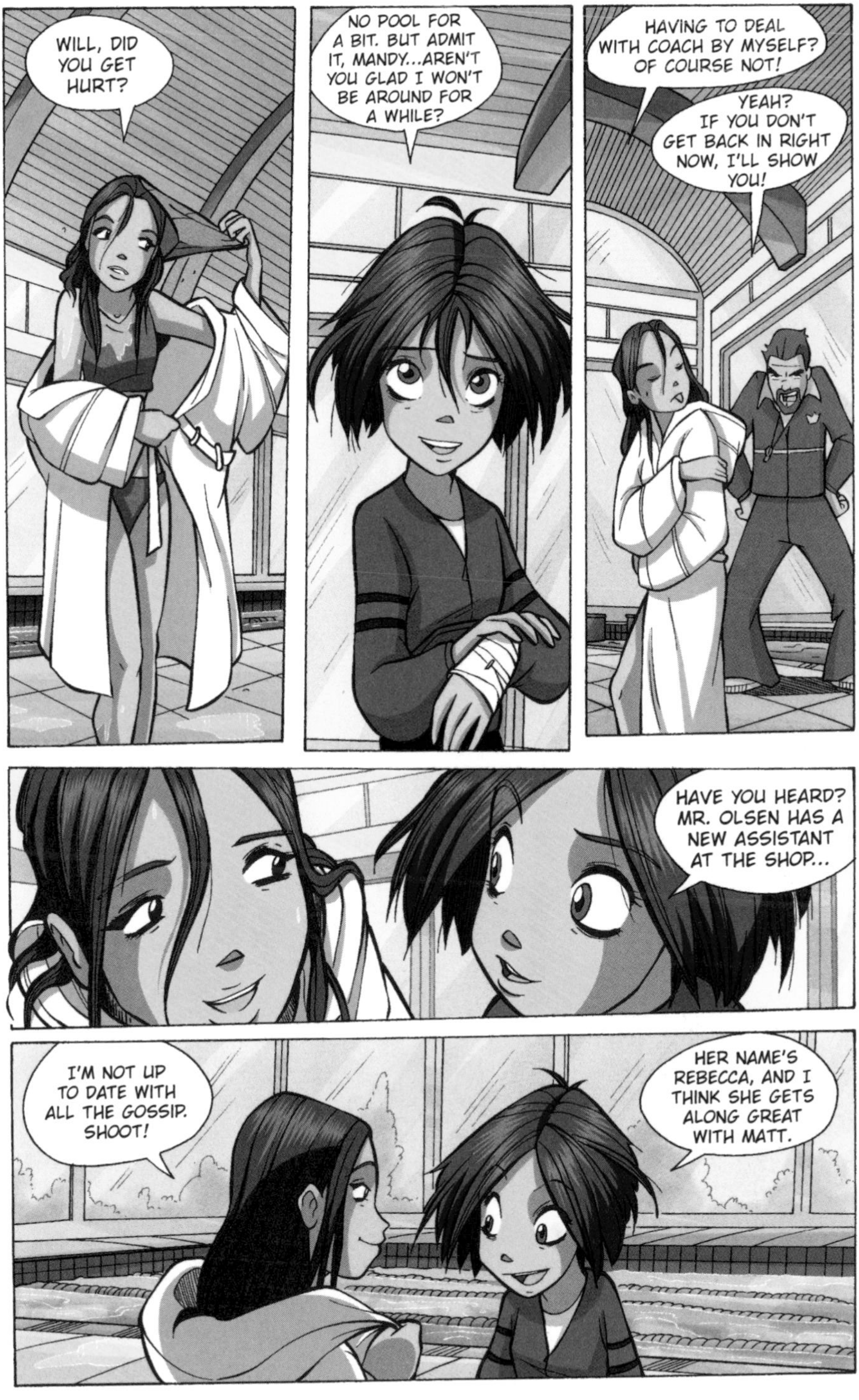
WILL, DID YOU GET HURT?
NO POOL FOR A BIT. BUT ADMIT IT, MANDY...AREN'T YOU GLAD I WON'T BE AROUND FOR A WHILE?
HAVING TO DEAL WITH COACH BY MYSELF? OF COURSE NOT!
YEAH? IF YOU DON'T GET BACK IN RIGHT NOW, I'LL SHOW YOU!
HAVE YOU HEARD? MR. OLSEN HAS A NEW ASSISTANT AT THE SHOP...
I'M NOT UP TO DATE WITH ALL THE GOSSIP. SHOOT!
HER NAME'S REBECCA, AND I THINK SHE GETS ALONG GREAT WITH MATT.

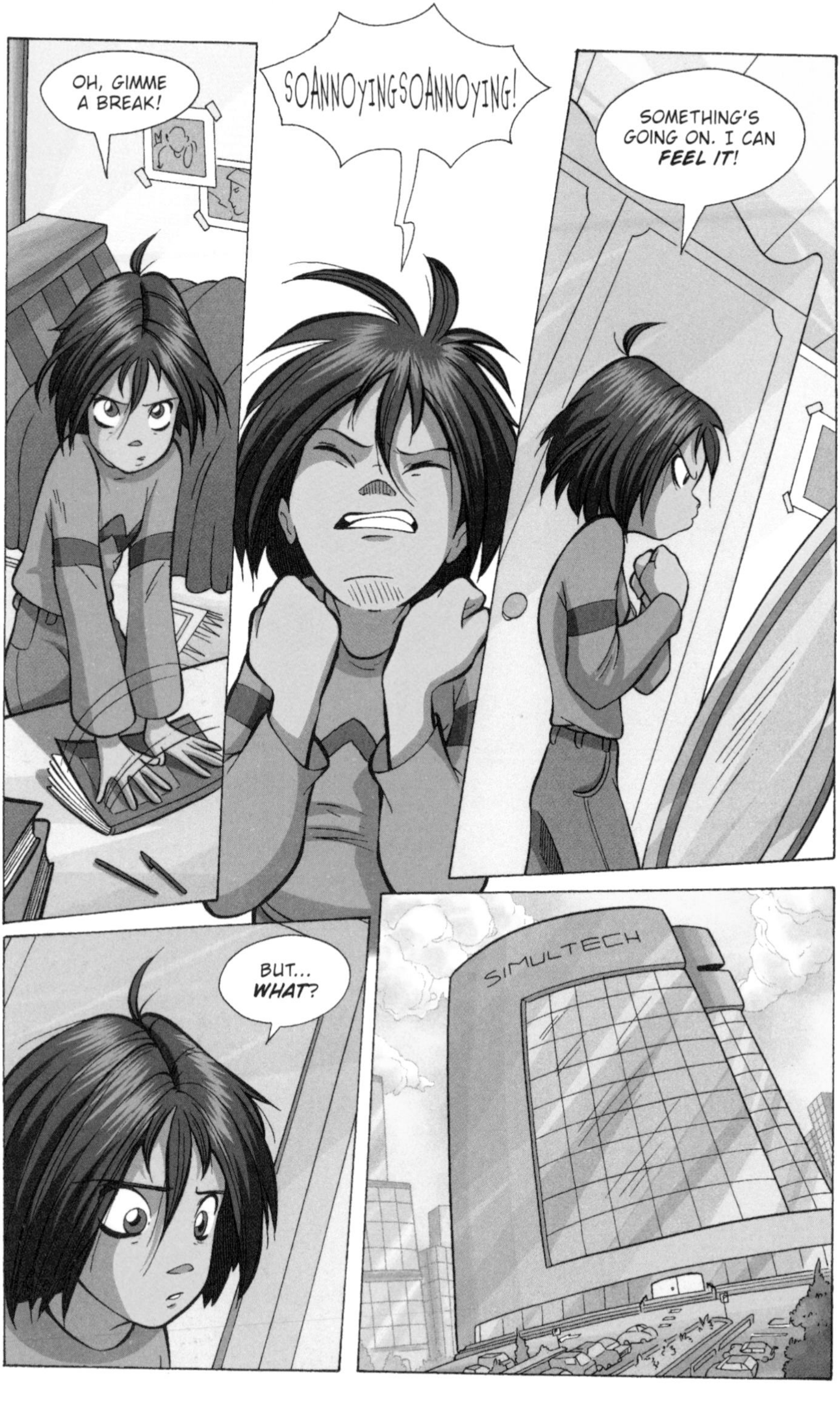
OH, GIMME A BREAK!
SOANNOYINGSOANNOYING!
SOMETHING'S GOING ON. I CAN **FEEL IT**!
BUT... **WHAT**?
SIMULTECH

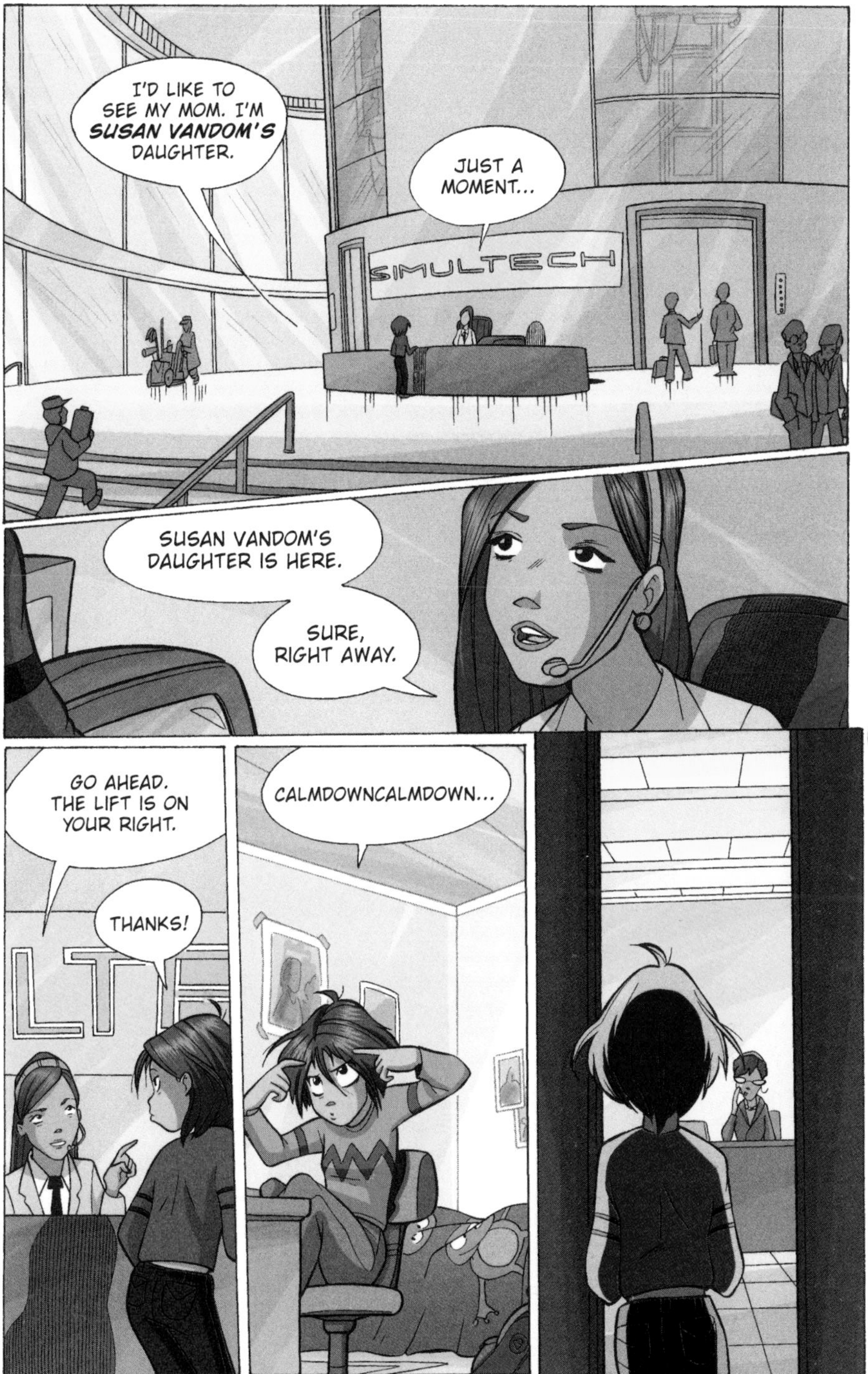
I'D LIKE TO SEE MY MOM. I'M SUSAN VANDOM'S DAUGHTER.
JUST A MOMENT...
SIMULTECH
SUSAN VANDOM'S DAUGHTER IS HERE.
SURE, RIGHT AWAY.
GO AHEAD. THE LIFT IS ON YOUR RIGHT.
THANKS!
CALMDOWNCALMDOWN...

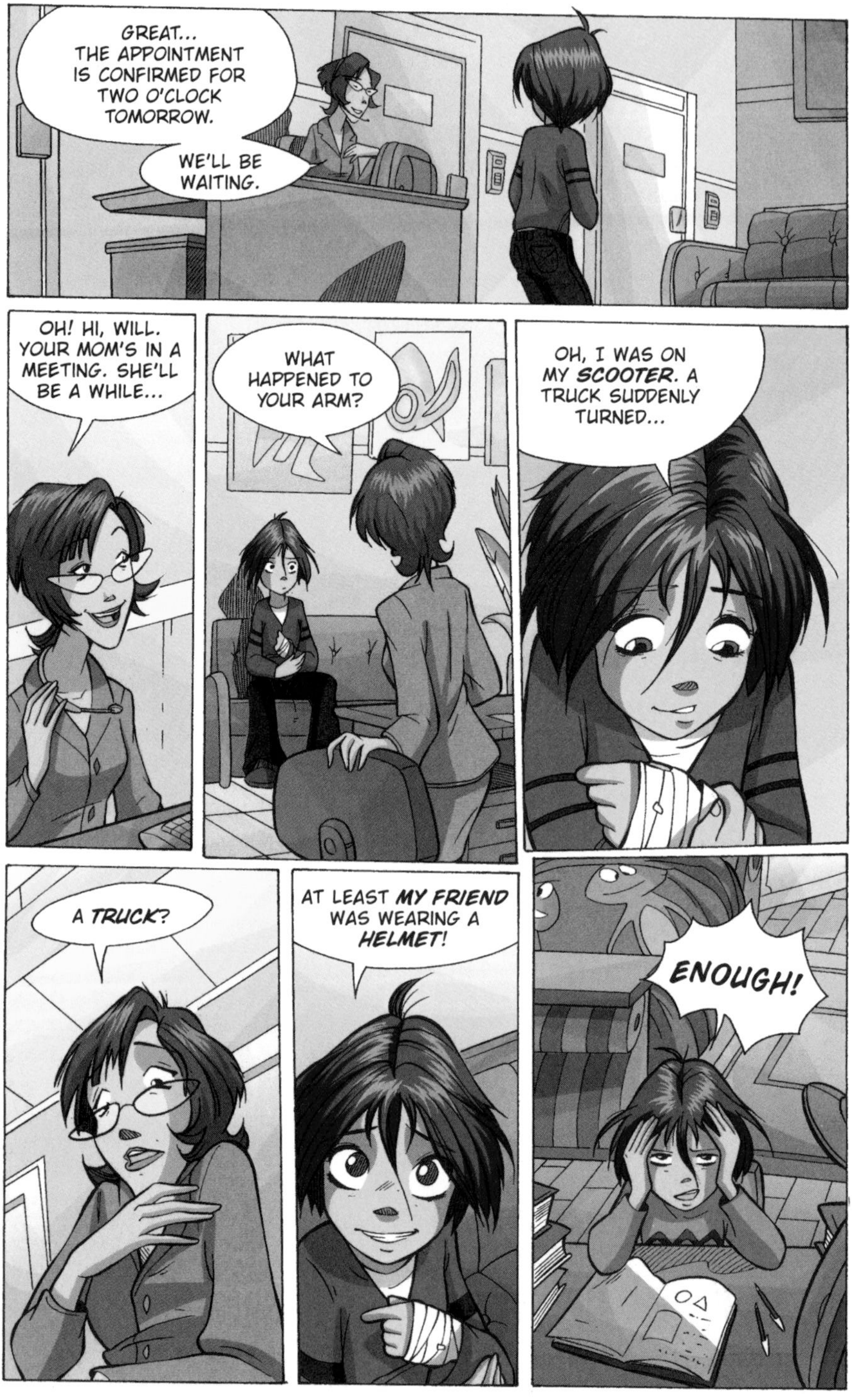
GREAT... THE APPOINTMENT IS CONFIRMED FOR TWO O'CLOCK TOMORROW.
WE'LL BE WAITING.
OH! HI, WILL. YOUR MOM'S IN A MEETING. SHE'LL BE A WHILE...
WHAT HAPPENED TO YOUR ARM?
OH, I WAS ON MY *SCOOTER*. A TRUCK SUDDENLY TURNED...
A *TRUCK*?
AT LEAST *MY FRIEND* WAS WEARING A *HELMET*!
ENOUGH!

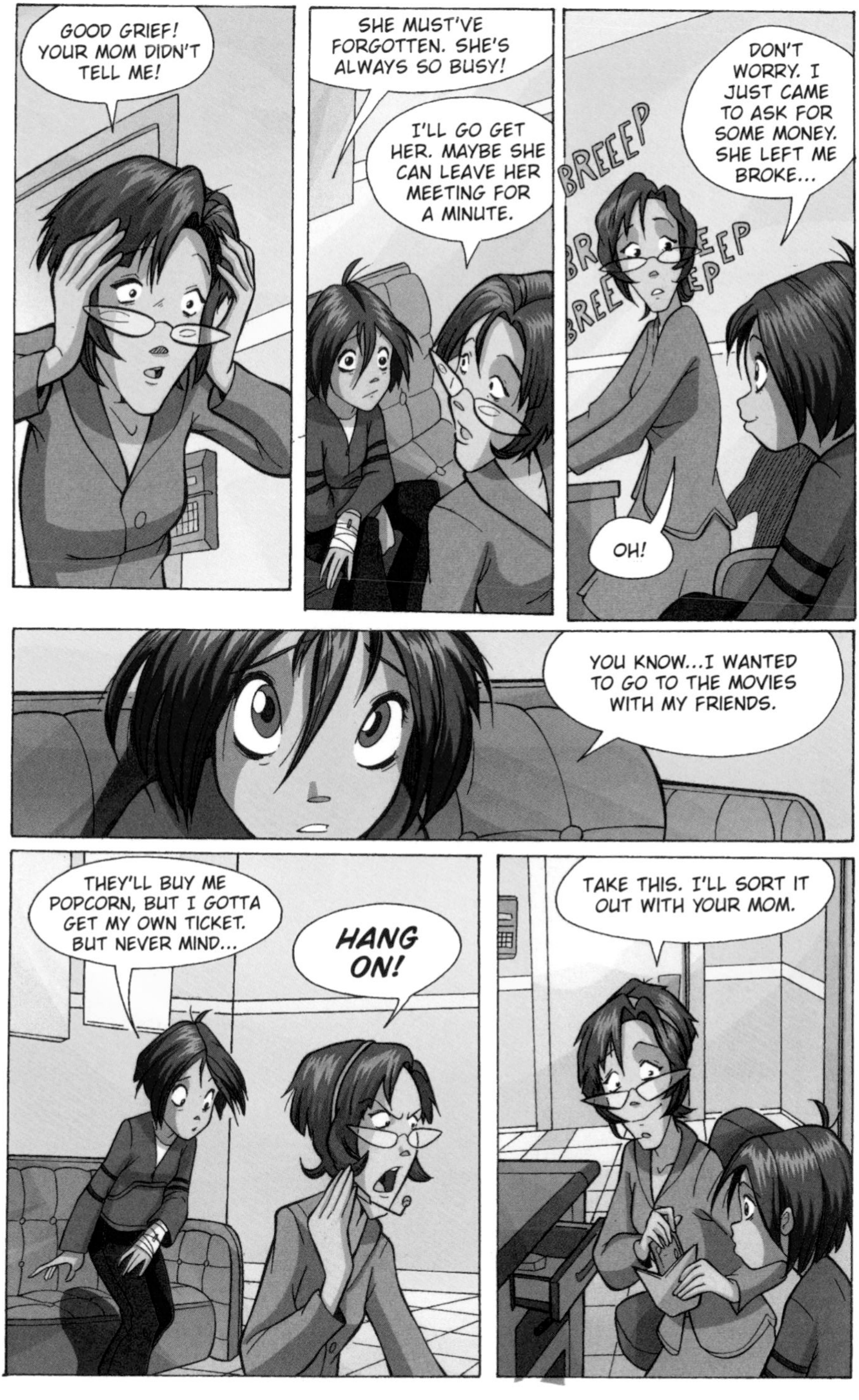
GOOD GRIEF! YOUR MOM DIDN'T TELL ME!
SHE MUST'VE FORGOTTEN. SHE'S ALWAYS SO BUSY!
I'LL GO GET HER. MAYBE SHE CAN LEAVE HER MEETING FOR A MINUTE.
DON'T WORRY. I JUST CAME TO ASK FOR SOME MONEY. SHE LEFT ME BROKE...
BREEEP
BREEEEP
BREEEEP
OH!
YOU KNOW...I WANTED TO GO TO THE MOVIES WITH MY FRIENDS.
THEY'LL BUY ME POPCORN, BUT I GOTTA GET MY OWN TICKET. BUT NEVER MIND...
HANG ON!
TAKE THIS. I'LL SORT IT OUT WITH YOUR MOM.

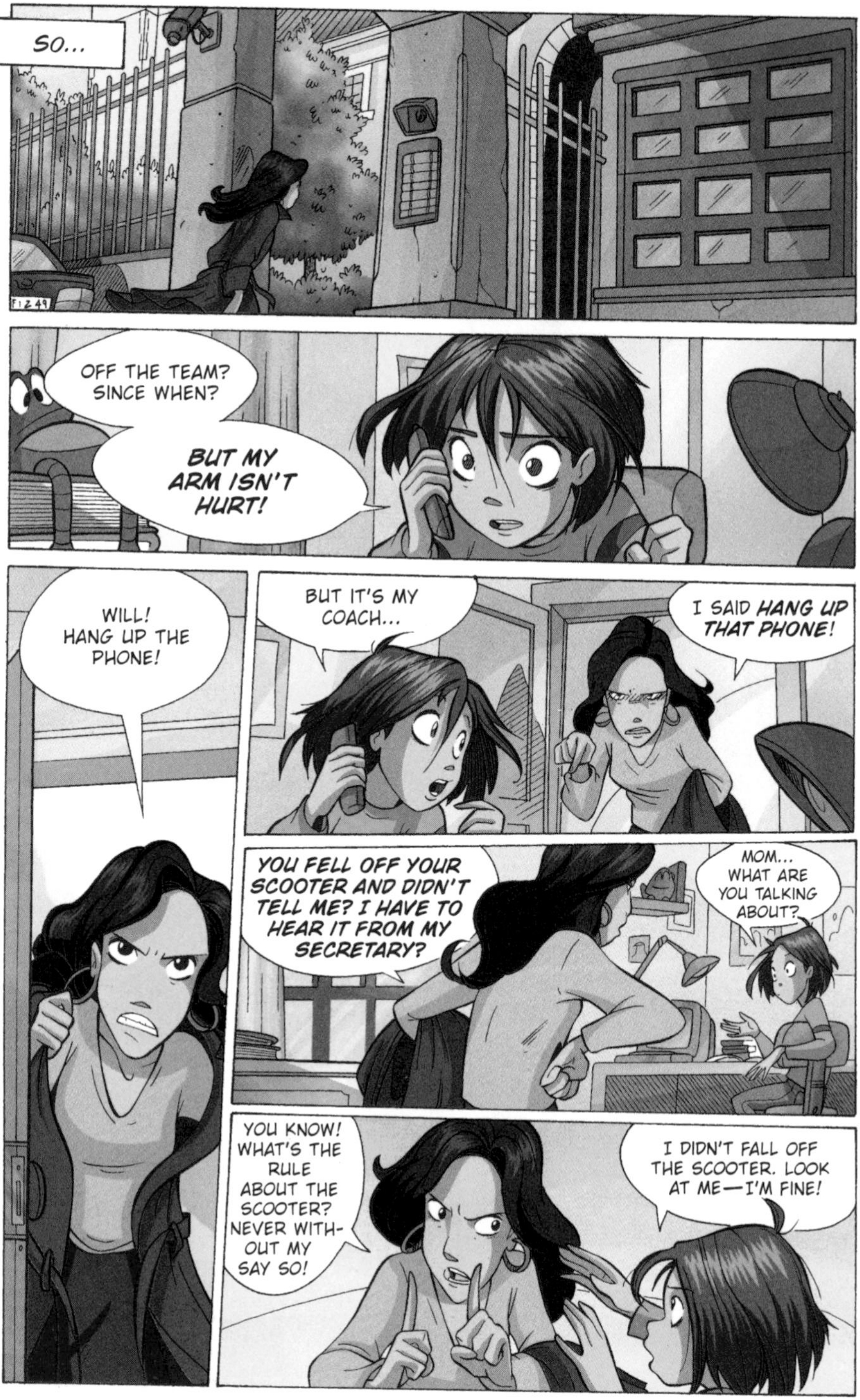
SO...
OFF THE TEAM? SINCE WHEN?
BUT MY ARM ISN'T HURT!
WILL! HANG UP THE PHONE!
BUT IT'S MY COACH...
I SAID HANG UP THAT PHONE!
YOU FELL OFF YOUR SCOOTER AND DIDN'T TELL ME? I HAVE TO HEAR IT FROM MY SECRETARY?
MOM... WHAT ARE YOU TALKING ABOUT?
YOU KNOW! WHAT'S THE RULE ABOUT THE SCOOTER? NEVER WITH-OUT MY SAY SO!
I DIDN'T FALL OFF THE SCOOTER. LOOK AT ME—I'M FINE!

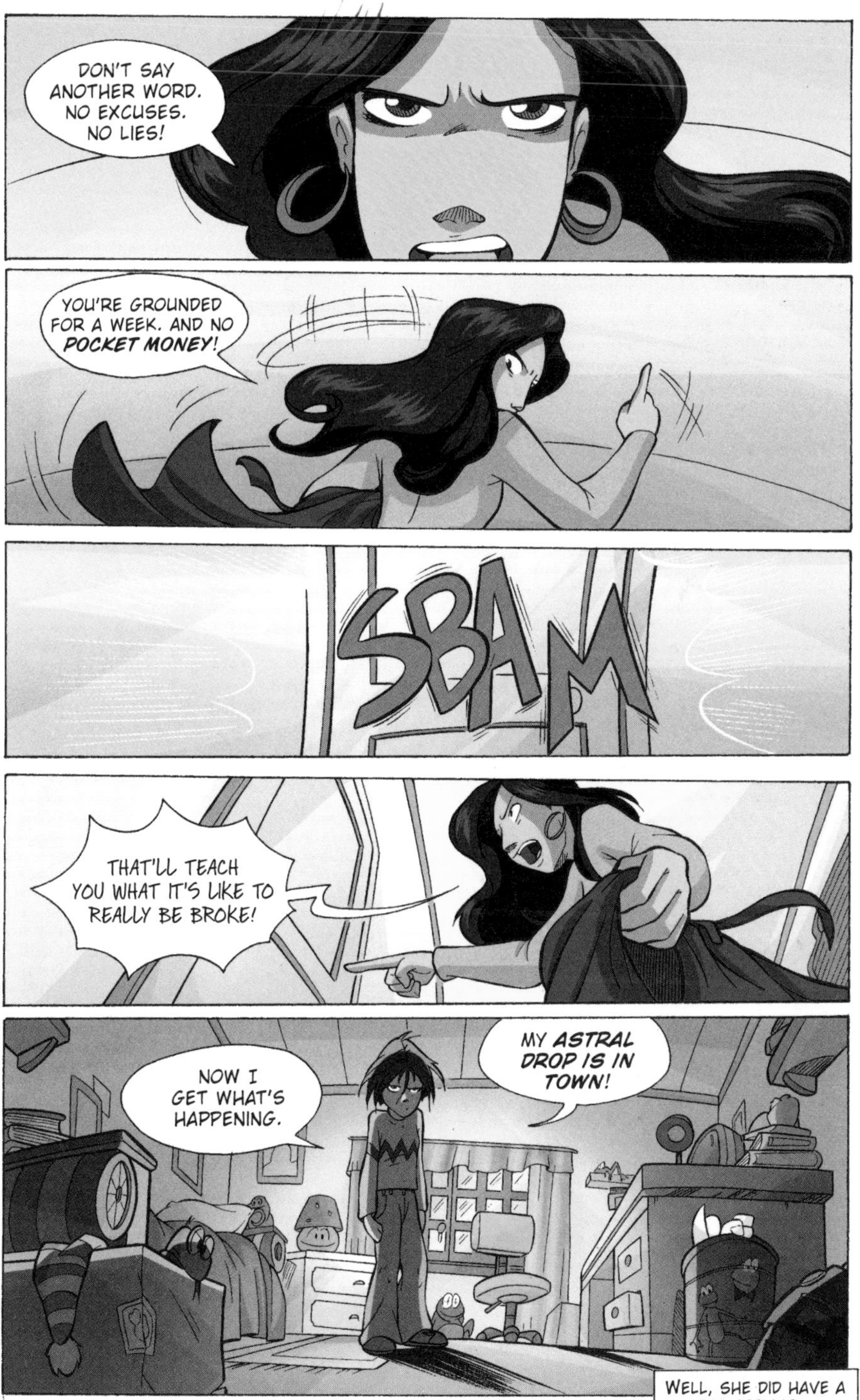
DON'T SAY ANOTHER WORD. NO EXCUSES. NO LIES!
YOU'RE GROUNDED FOR A WEEK. AND NO POCKET MONEY!
SBAM
THAT'LL TEACH YOU WHAT IT'S LIKE TO REALLY BE BROKE!
NOW I GET WHAT'S HAPPENING.
MY ASTRAL DROP IS IN TOWN!
WELL, SHE DID HAVE A BAD FEELING...

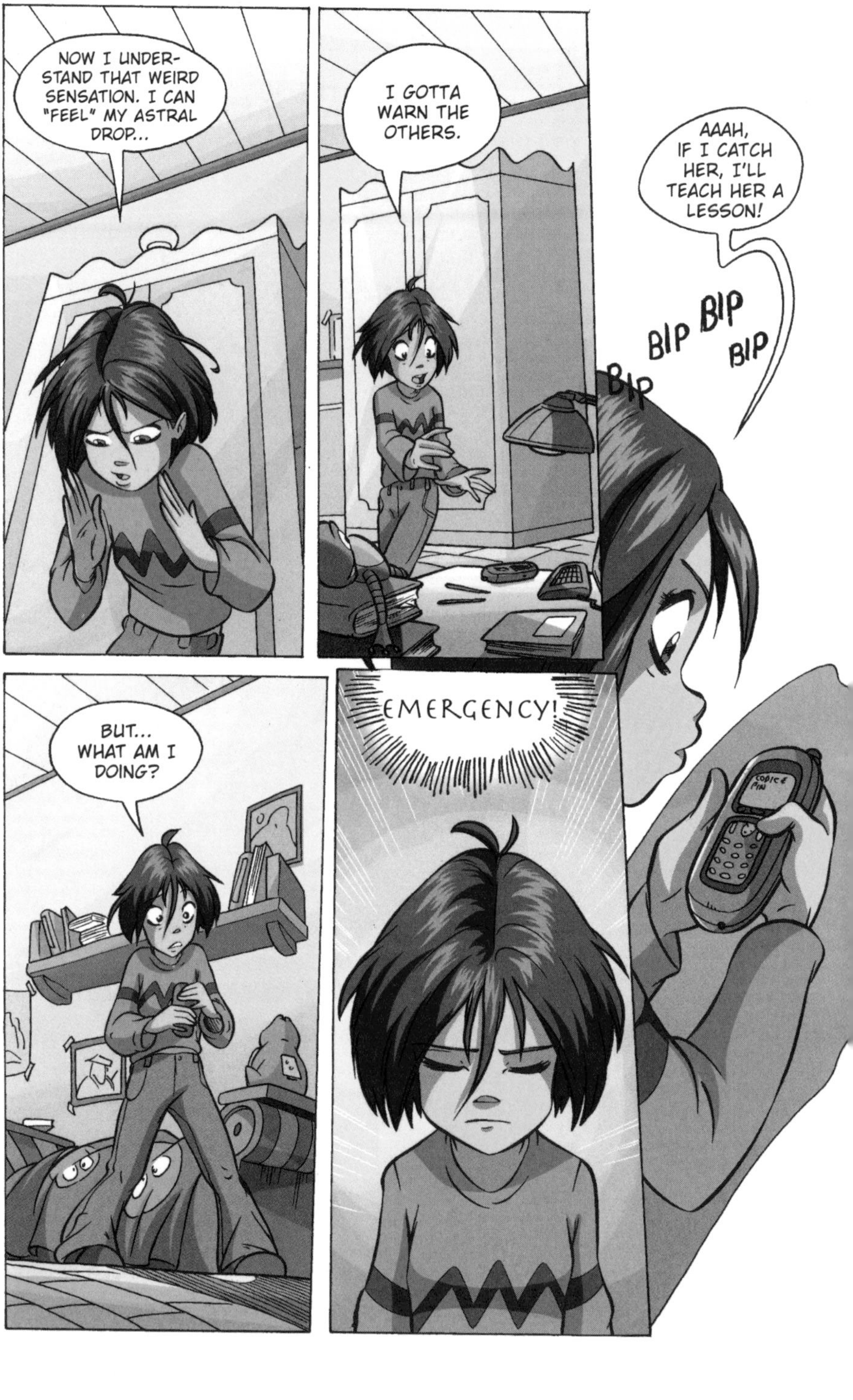
NOW I UNDER-STAND THAT WEIRD SENSATION. I CAN "FEEL" MY ASTRAL DROP...
I GOTTA WARN THE OTHERS.
AAAH, IF I CATCH HER, I'LL TEACH HER A LESSON!
BIP BIP BIP BIP
BUT... WHAT AM I DOING?
EMERGENCY!

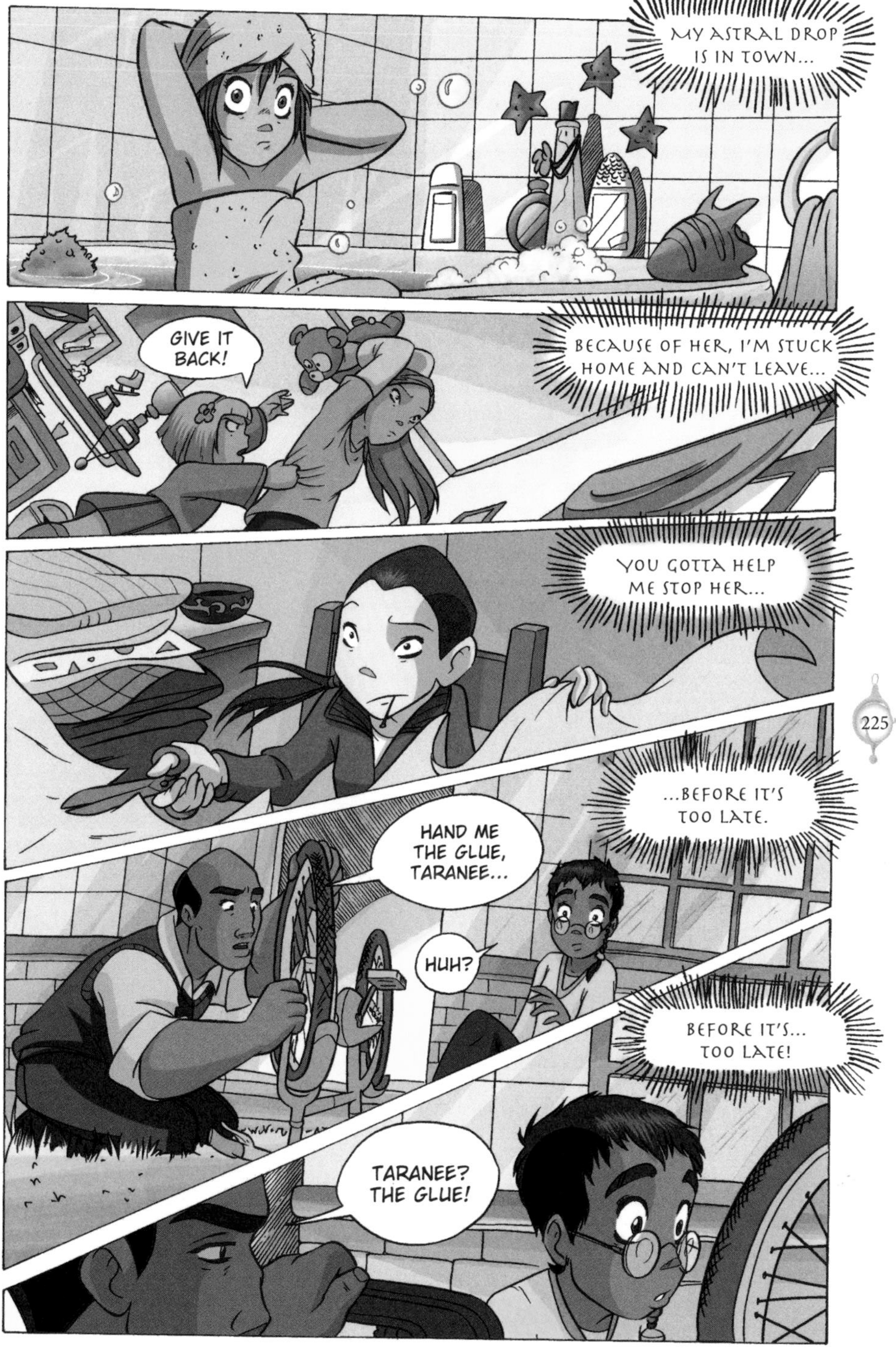
MY ASTRAL DROP IS IN TOWN...
GIVE IT BACK!
BECAUSE OF HER, I'M STUCK HOME AND CAN'T LEAVE...
YOU GOTTA HELP ME STOP HER...
...BEFORE IT'S TOO LATE.
HAND ME THE GLUE, TARANEE...
HUH?
BEFORE IT'S... TOO LATE!
TARANEE? THE GLUE!

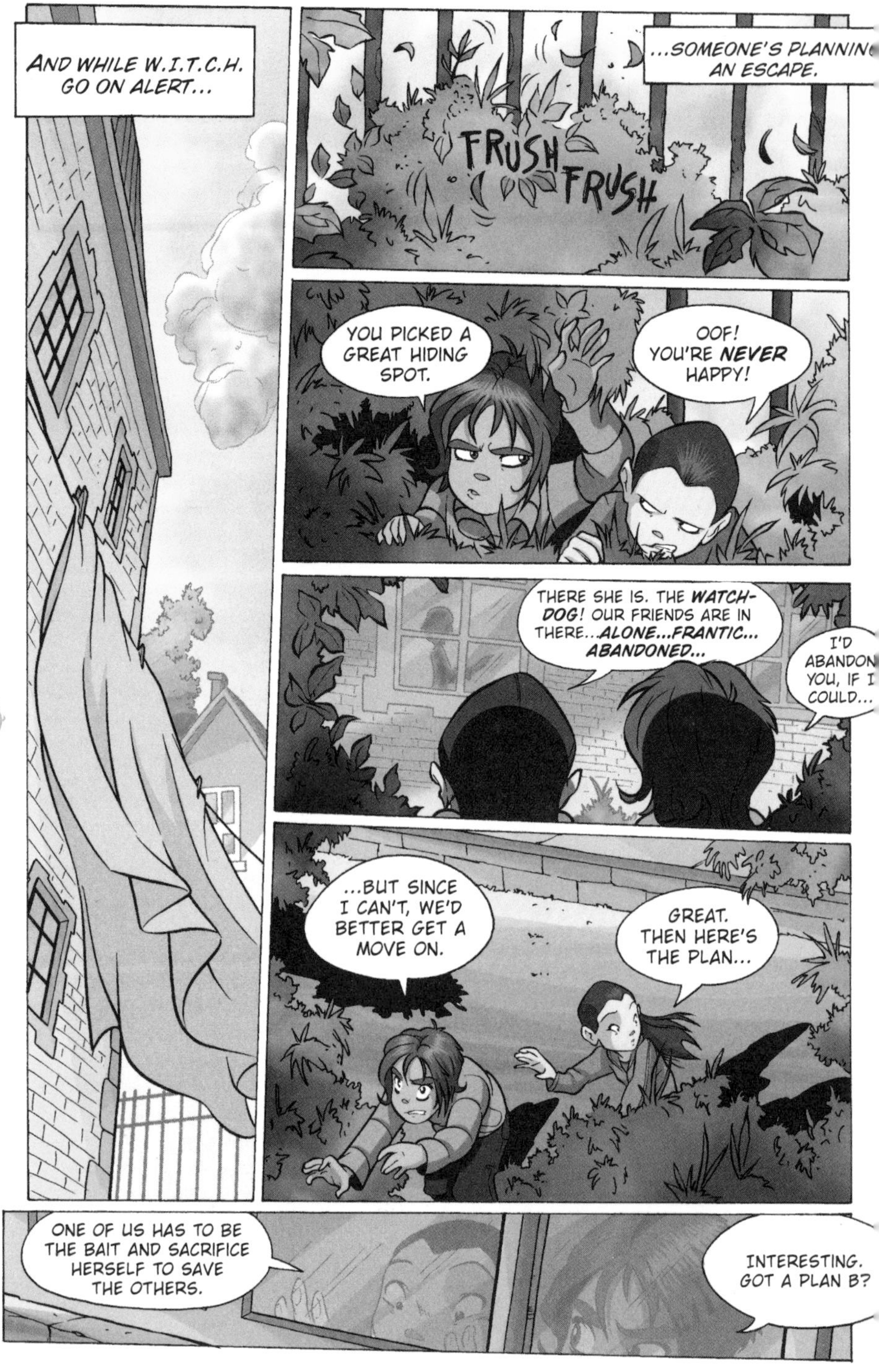
AND WHILE W.I.T.C.H. GO ON ALERT...
...SOMEONE'S PLANNING AN ESCAPE.
FRUSH FRUSH
YOU PICKED A GREAT HIDING SPOT.
OOF! YOU'RE NEVER HAPPY!
THERE SHE IS. THE WATCH-DOG! OUR FRIENDS ARE IN THERE...ALONE...FRANTIC... ABANDONED...
I'D ABANDON YOU, IF I COULD...
...BUT SINCE I CAN'T, WE'D BETTER GET A MOVE ON.
GREAT. THEN HERE'S THE PLAN...
ONE OF US HAS TO BE THE BAIT AND SACRIFICE HERSELF TO SAVE THE OTHERS.
INTERESTING. GOT A PLAN B?

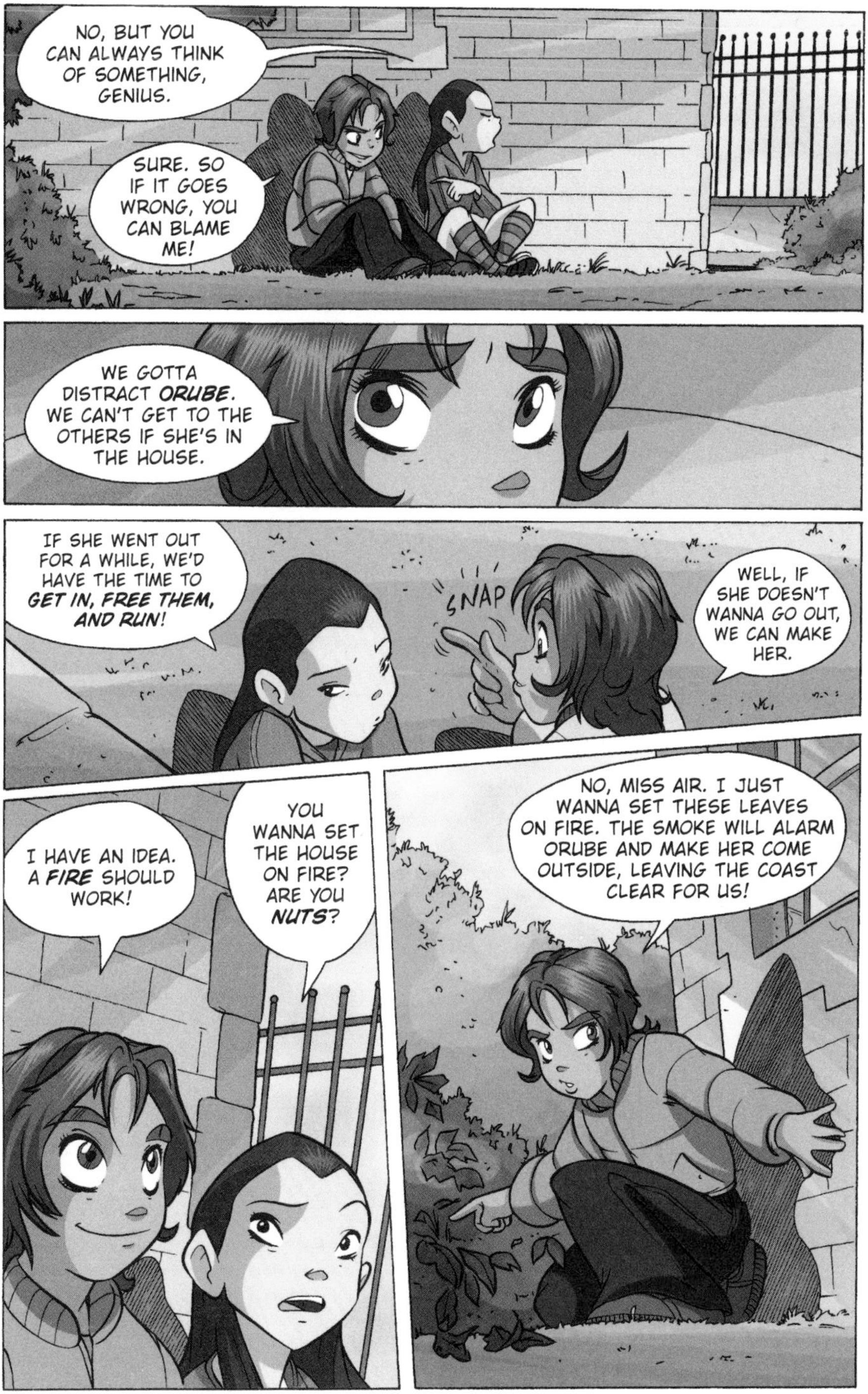
NO, BUT YOU CAN ALWAYS THINK OF SOMETHING, GENIUS.
SURE. SO IF IT GOES WRONG, YOU CAN BLAME ME!
WE GOTTA DISTRACT ***ORUBE***. WE CAN'T GET TO THE OTHERS IF SHE'S IN THE HOUSE.
IF SHE WENT OUT FOR A WHILE, WE'D HAVE THE TIME TO ***GET IN, FREE THEM, AND RUN***!
SNAP
WELL, IF SHE DOESN'T WANNA GO OUT, WE CAN MAKE HER.
I HAVE AN IDEA. A ***FIRE*** SHOULD WORK!
YOU WANNA SET THE HOUSE ON FIRE? ARE YOU ***NUTS***?
NO, MISS AIR. I JUST WANNA SET THESE LEAVES ON FIRE. THE SMOKE WILL ALARM ORUBE AND MAKE HER COME OUTSIDE, LEAVING THE COAST CLEAR FOR US!

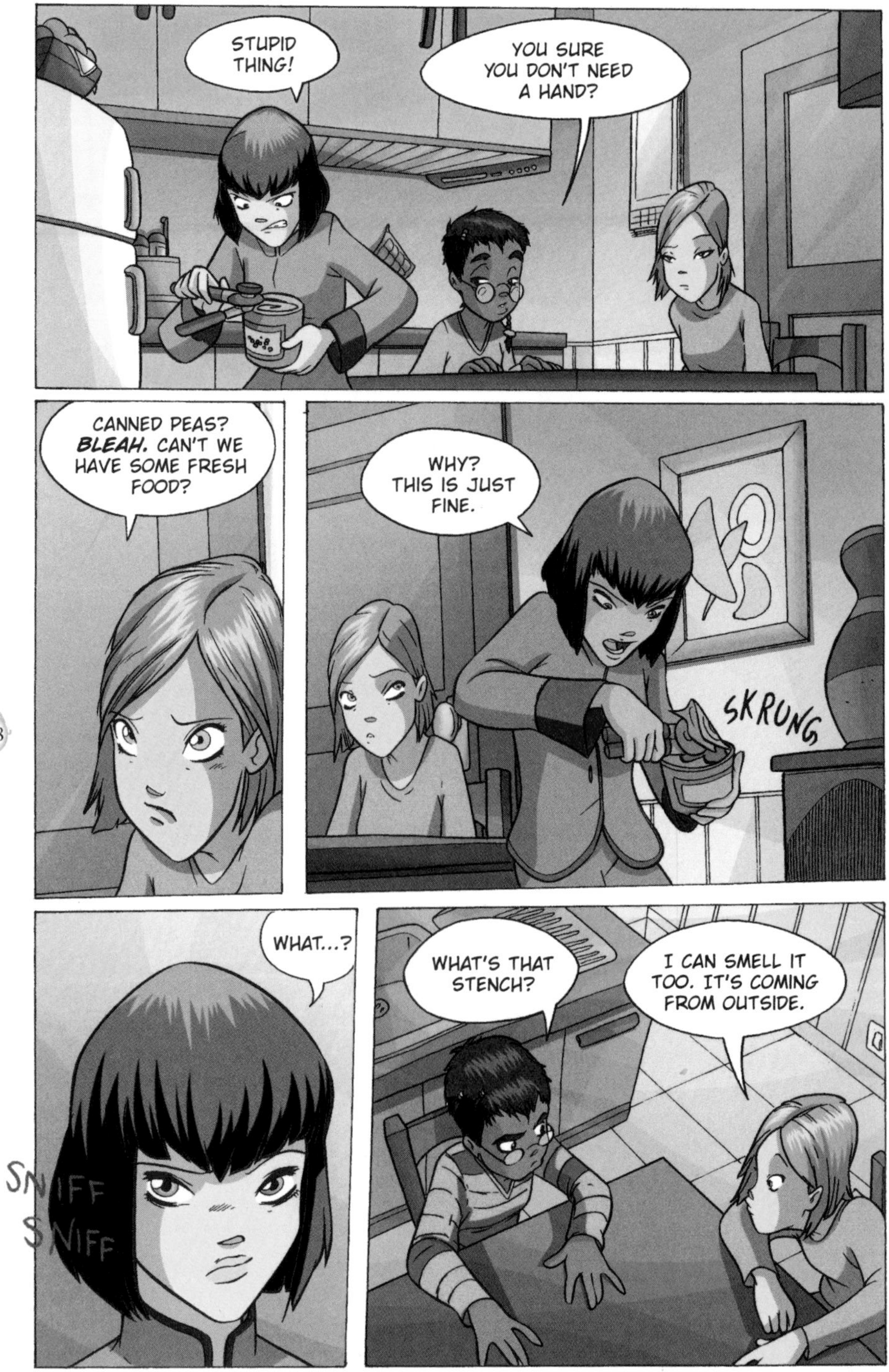
STUPID THING!
YOU SURE YOU DON'T NEED A HAND?
CANNED PEAS? **BLEAH.** CAN'T WE HAVE SOME FRESH FOOD?
WHY? THIS IS JUST FINE.
SKRUNG
WHAT...?
SNIFF SNIFF
WHAT'S THAT STENCH?
I CAN SMELL IT TOO. IT'S COMING FROM OUTSIDE.

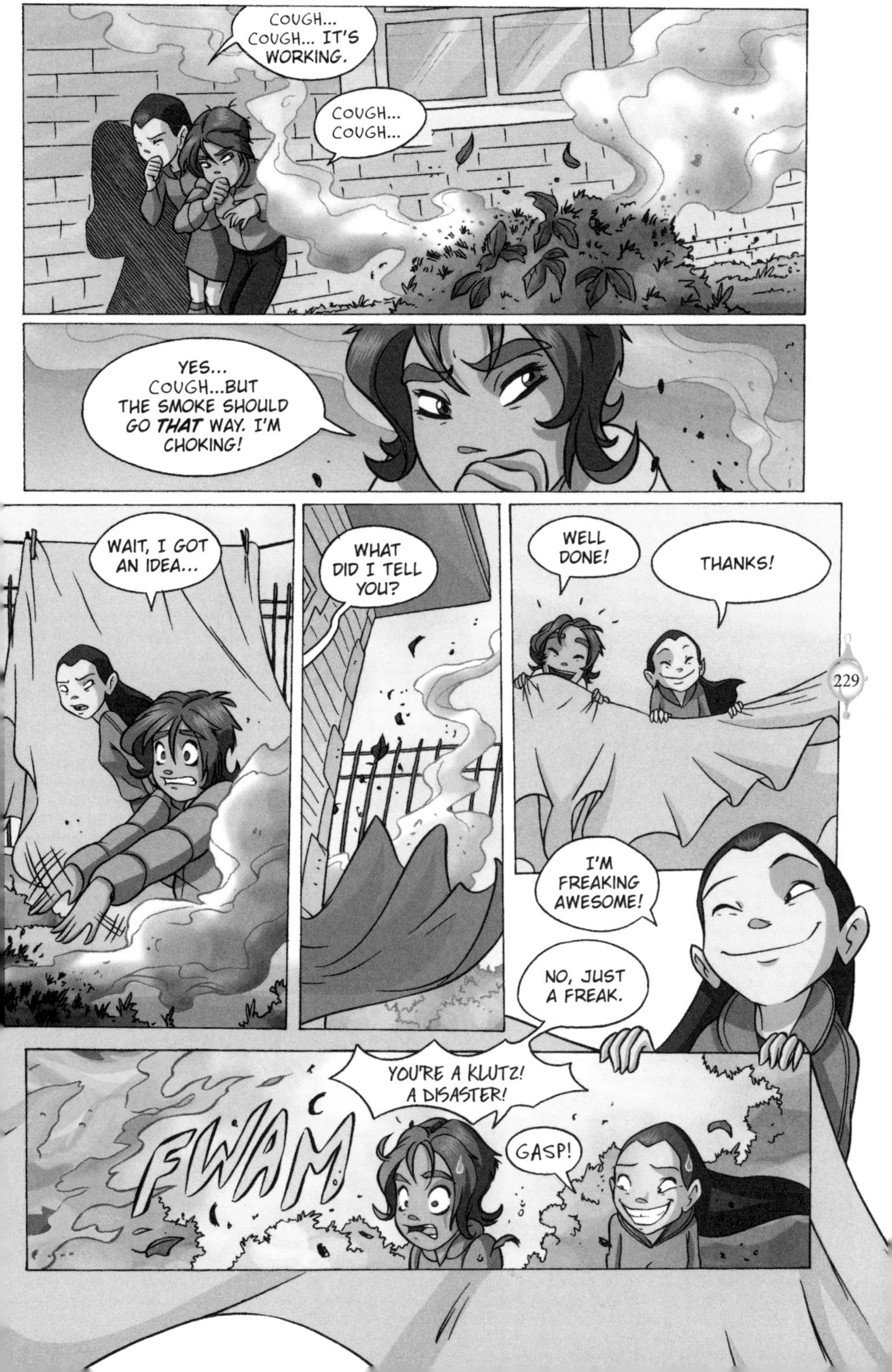
COUGH... COUGH... IT'S WORKING.
COUGH... COUGH...
YES... COUGH...BUT THE SMOKE SHOULD GO THAT WAY. I'M CHOKING!
WAIT, I GOT AN IDEA...
WHAT DID I TELL YOU?
WELL DONE!
THANKS!
I'M FREAKING AWESOME!
NO, JUST A FREAK.
YOU'RE A KLUTZ! A DISASTER!
FWAM
GASP!

WHAT NOW?

NOW WE RUN!

LOOK, ORUBE'S COMING!

THEN THE PLAN CHANGES. SHE COMES OUT, AND WE GO GET CORNELIA AND TARANEE!

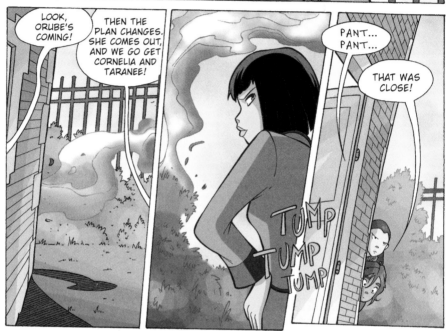

PANT... PANT...

THAT WAS CLOSE!

TUMP TUMP TUMP

WELL, AT LEAST THEY TRIED...

ALL CLEAR! OOPS...

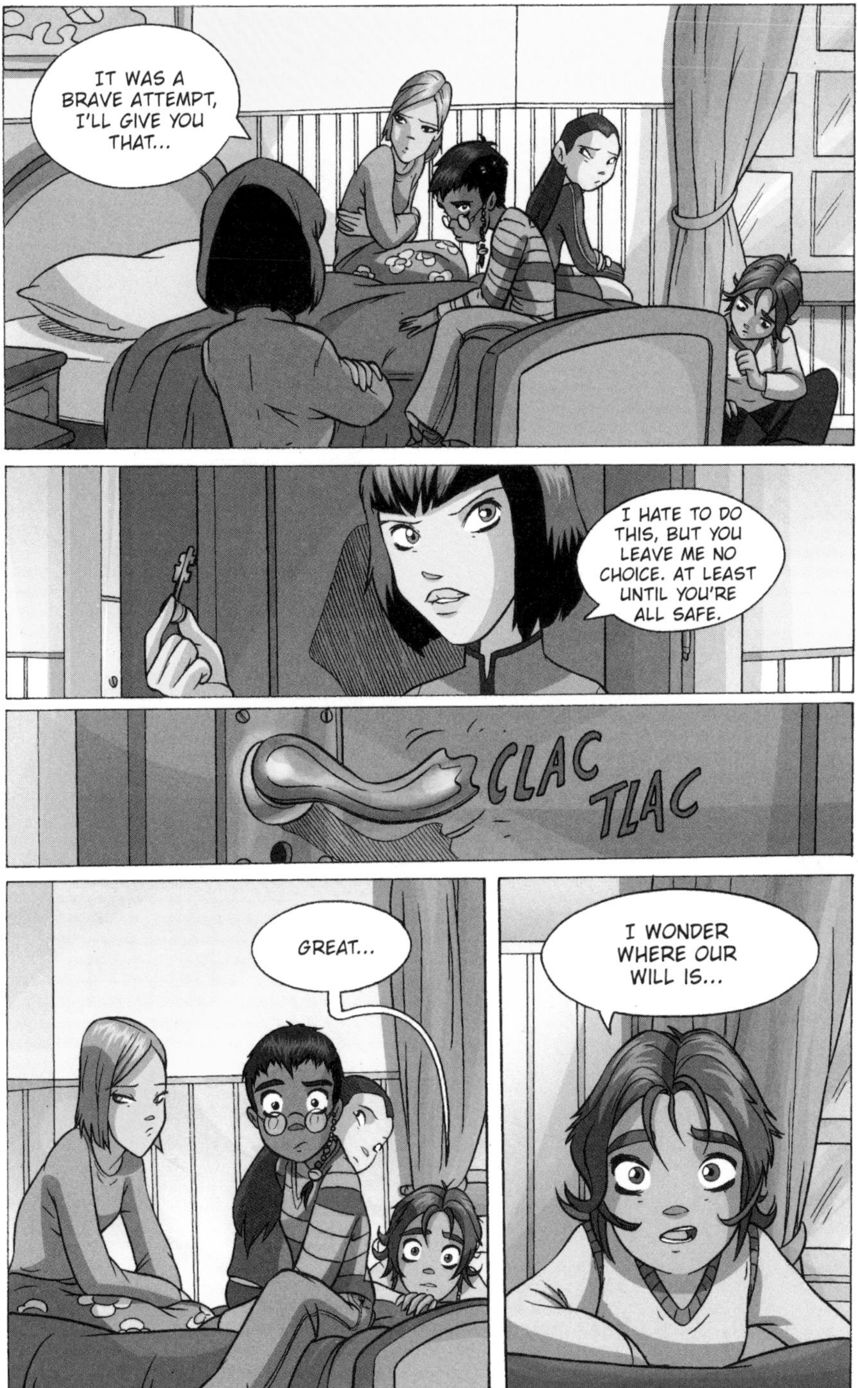
IT WAS A BRAVE ATTEMPT, I'LL GIVE YOU THAT...
I HATE TO DO THIS, BUT YOU LEAVE ME NO CHOICE. AT LEAST UNTIL YOU'RE ALL SAFE.
CLAC
TLAC
GREAT...
I WONDER WHERE OUR WILL IS...

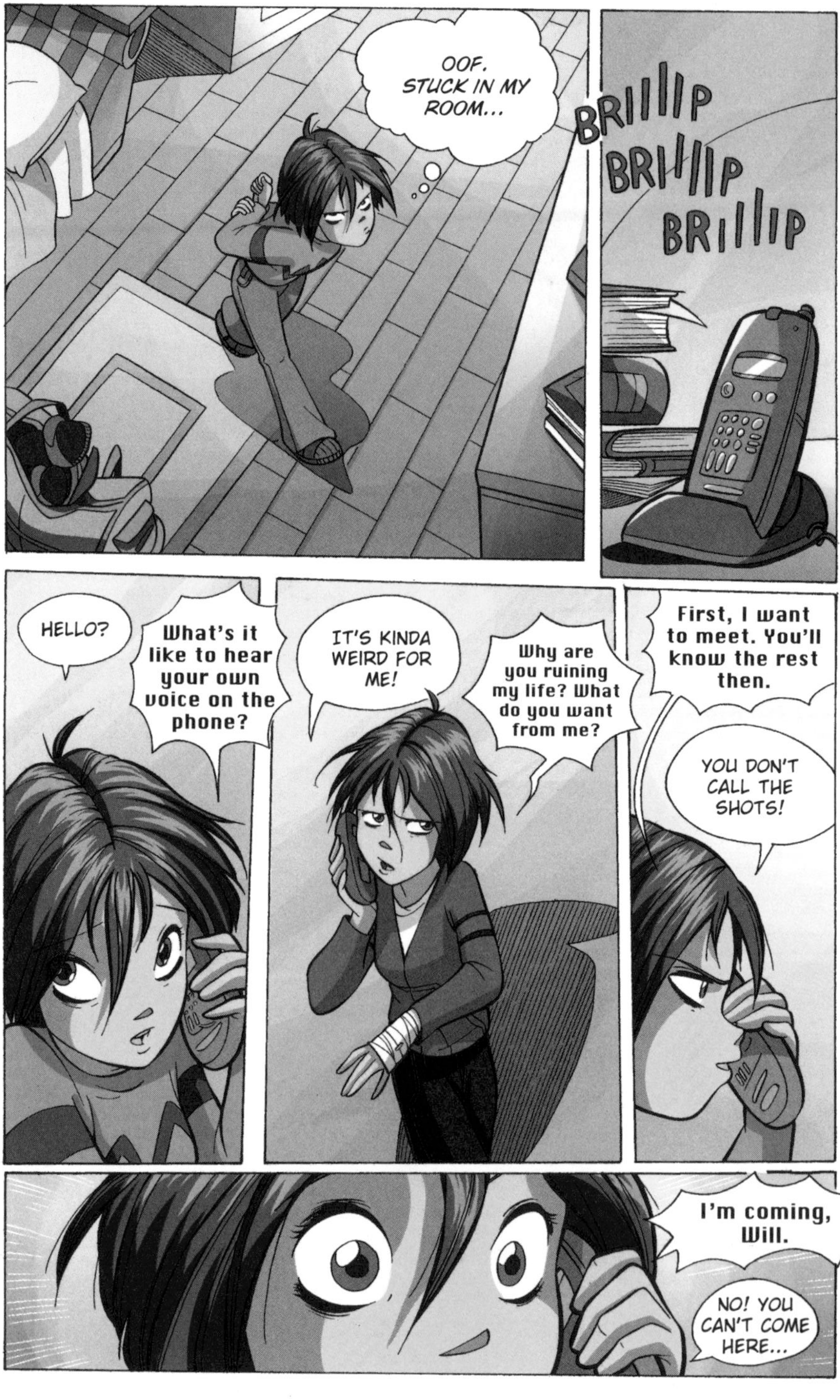
OOF. STUCK IN MY ROOM...
BRIIIIP
BRIIIIP
BRIIIIP
HELLO?
What's it like to hear your own voice on the phone?
IT'S KINDA WEIRD FOR ME!
Why are you ruining my life? What do you want from me?
First, I want to meet. You'll know the rest then.
YOU DON'T CALL THE SHOTS!
I'm coming, Will.
NO! YOU CAN'T COME HERE...

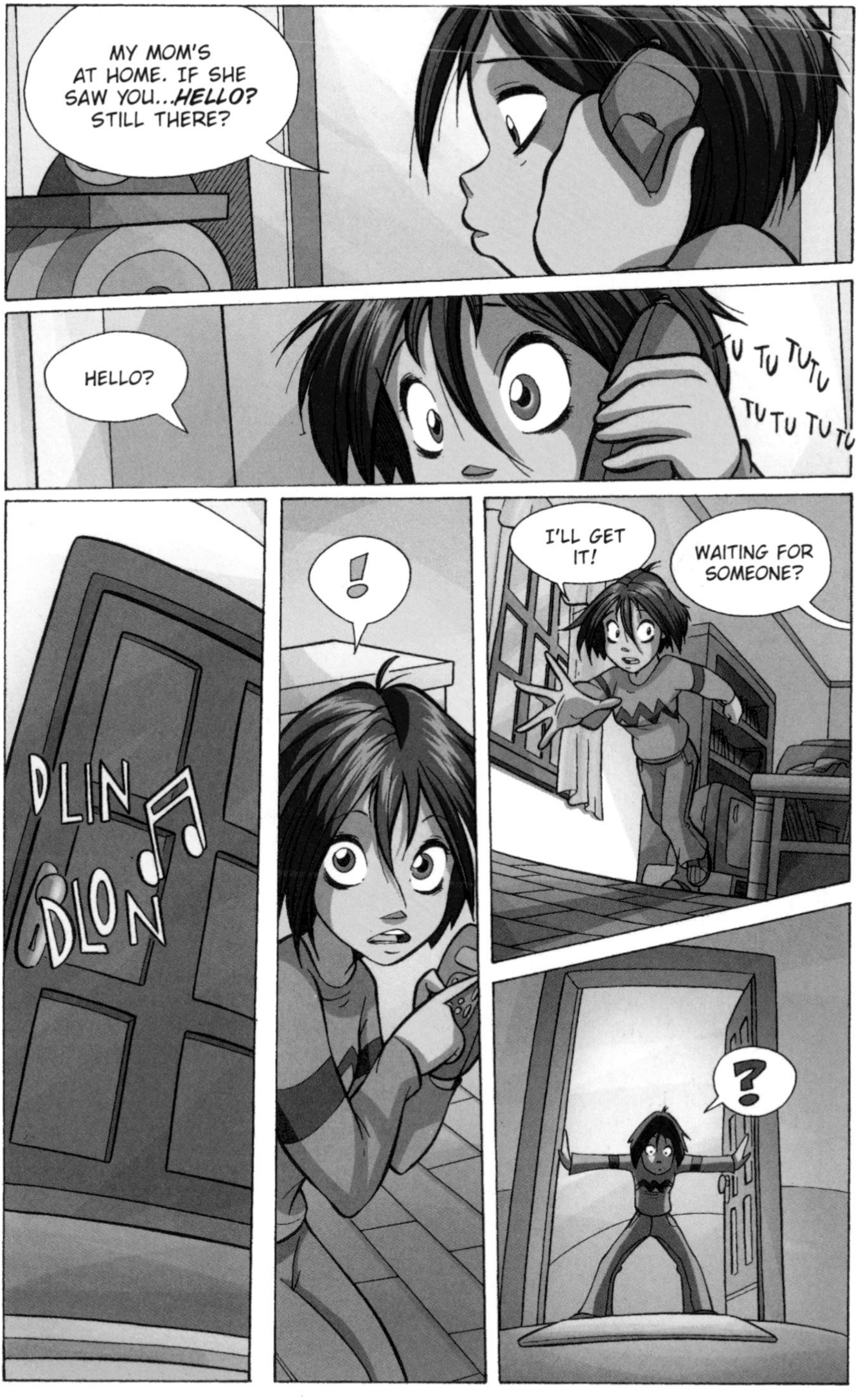
MY MOM'S AT HOME. IF SHE SAW YOU...*HELLO?* STILL THERE?
HELLO?
TU TU TUTU
TUTU TUTU
DLIN DLON
!
I'LL GET IT!
WAITING FOR SOMEONE?
?

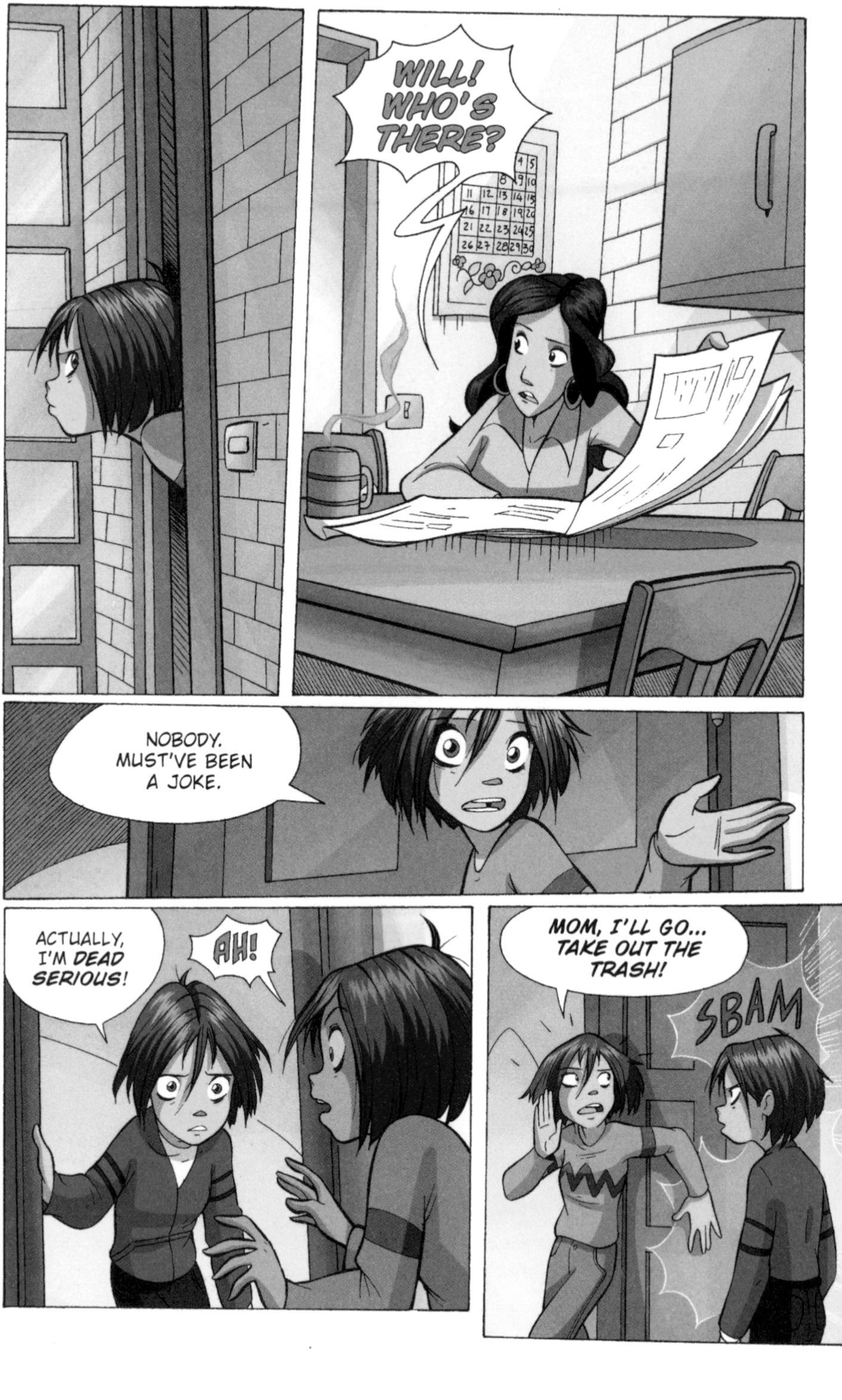

WILL! WHO'S THERE?
NOBODY. MUST'VE BEEN A JOKE.
ACTUALLY, I'M DEAD SERIOUS!
AH!
MOM, I'LL GO... TAKE OUT THE TRASH!
SBAM

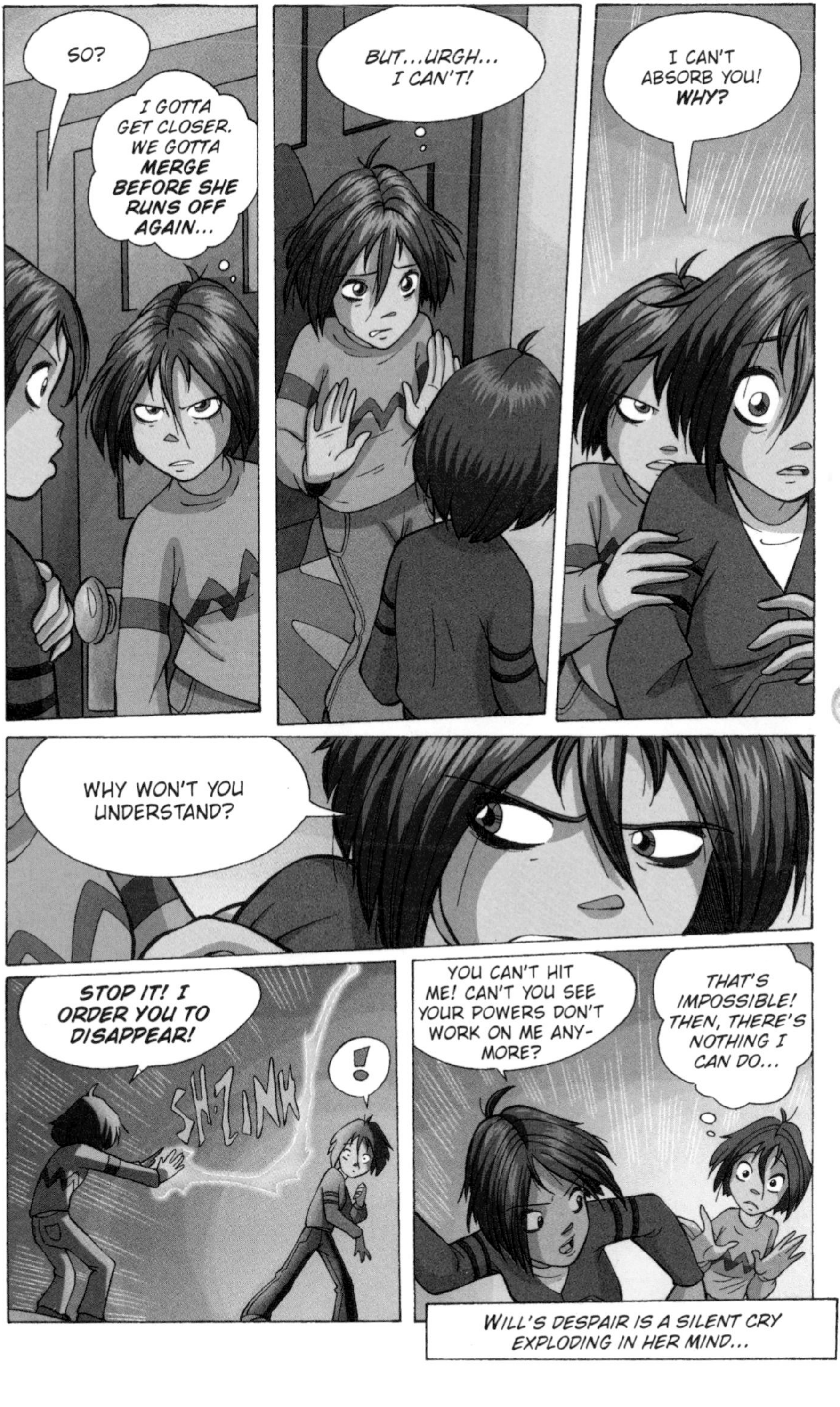
SO?
I GOTTA GET CLOSER. WE GOTTA MERGE BEFORE SHE RUNS OFF AGAIN...
BUT...URGH... I CAN'T!
I CAN'T ABSORB YOU! WHY?
WHY WON'T YOU UNDERSTAND?
STOP IT! I ORDER YOU TO DISAPPEAR!
SH-ZINH
!
YOU CAN'T HIT ME! CAN'T YOU SEE YOUR POWERS DON'T WORK ON ME ANY-MORE?
THAT'S IMPOSSIBLE! THEN, THERE'S NOTHING I CAN DO...
WILL'S DESPAIR IS A SILENT CRY EXPLODING IN HER MIND...

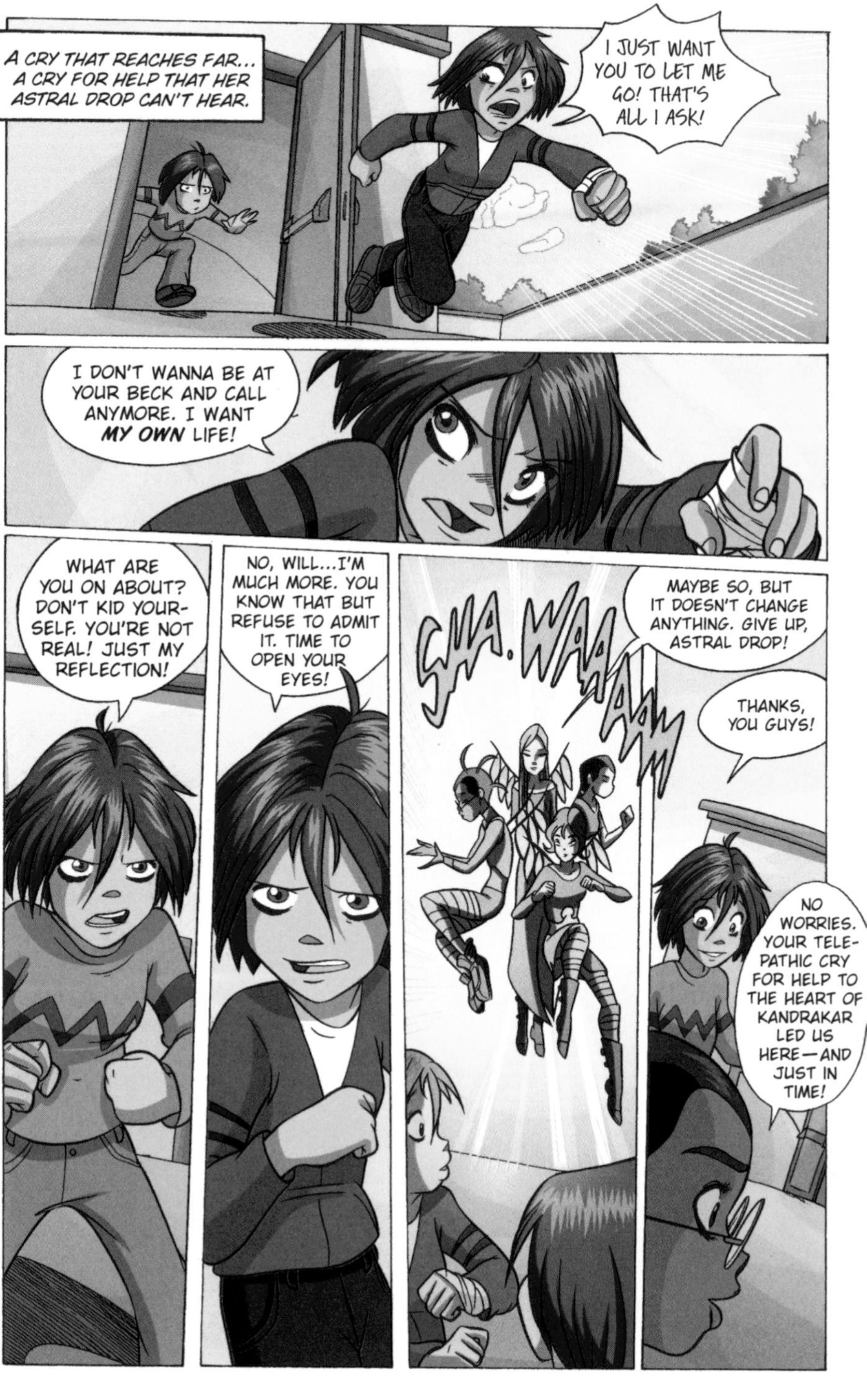
A CRY THAT REACHES FAR... A CRY FOR HELP THAT HER ASTRAL DROP CAN'T HEAR.
I JUST WANT YOU TO LET ME GO! THAT'S ALL I ASK!
I DON'T WANNA BE AT YOUR BECK AND CALL ANYMORE. I WANT MY OWN LIFE!
WHAT ARE YOU ON ABOUT? DON'T KID YOURSELF. YOU'RE NOT REAL! JUST MY REFLECTION!
NO, WILL...I'M MUCH MORE. YOU KNOW THAT BUT REFUSE TO ADMIT IT. TIME TO OPEN YOUR EYES!
SHA.WAAAAW
MAYBE SO, BUT IT DOESN'T CHANGE ANYTHING. GIVE UP, ASTRAL DROP!
THANKS, YOU GUYS!
NO WORRIES. YOUR TELEPATHIC CRY FOR HELP TO THE HEART OF KANDRAKAR LED US HERE—AND JUST IN TIME!

236

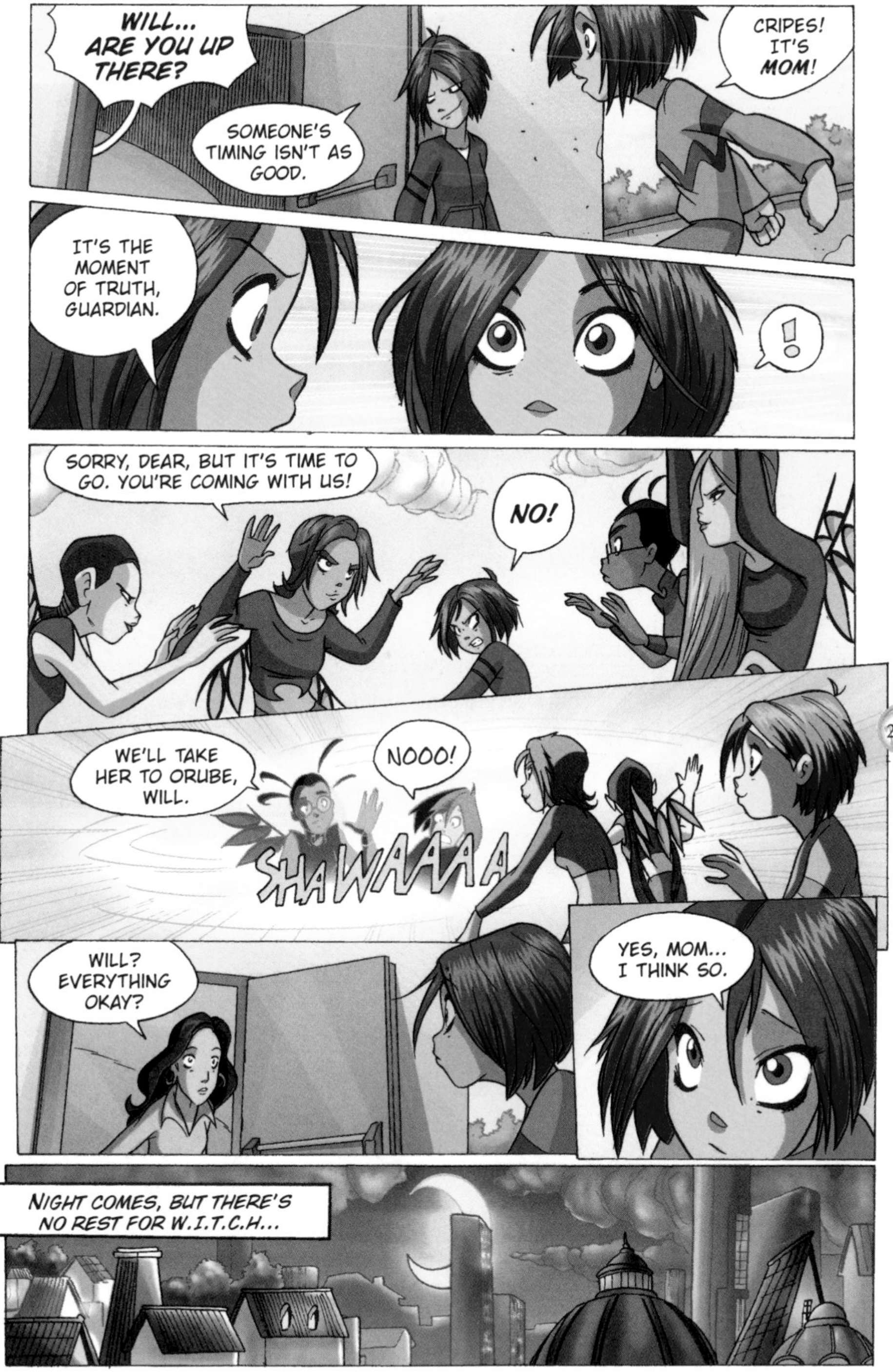
WILL... ARE YOU UP THERE?
SOMEONE'S TIMING ISN'T AS GOOD.
CRIPES! IT'S MOM!
IT'S THE MOMENT OF TRUTH, GUARDIAN.
!
SORRY, DEAR, BUT IT'S TIME TO GO. YOU'RE COMING WITH US!
NO!
WE'LL TAKE HER TO ORUBE, WILL.
NOOO!
SHAWAAAA
WILL? EVERYTHING OKAY?
YES, MOM... I THINK SO.
NIGHT COMES, BUT THERE'S NO REST FOR W.I.T.C.H...

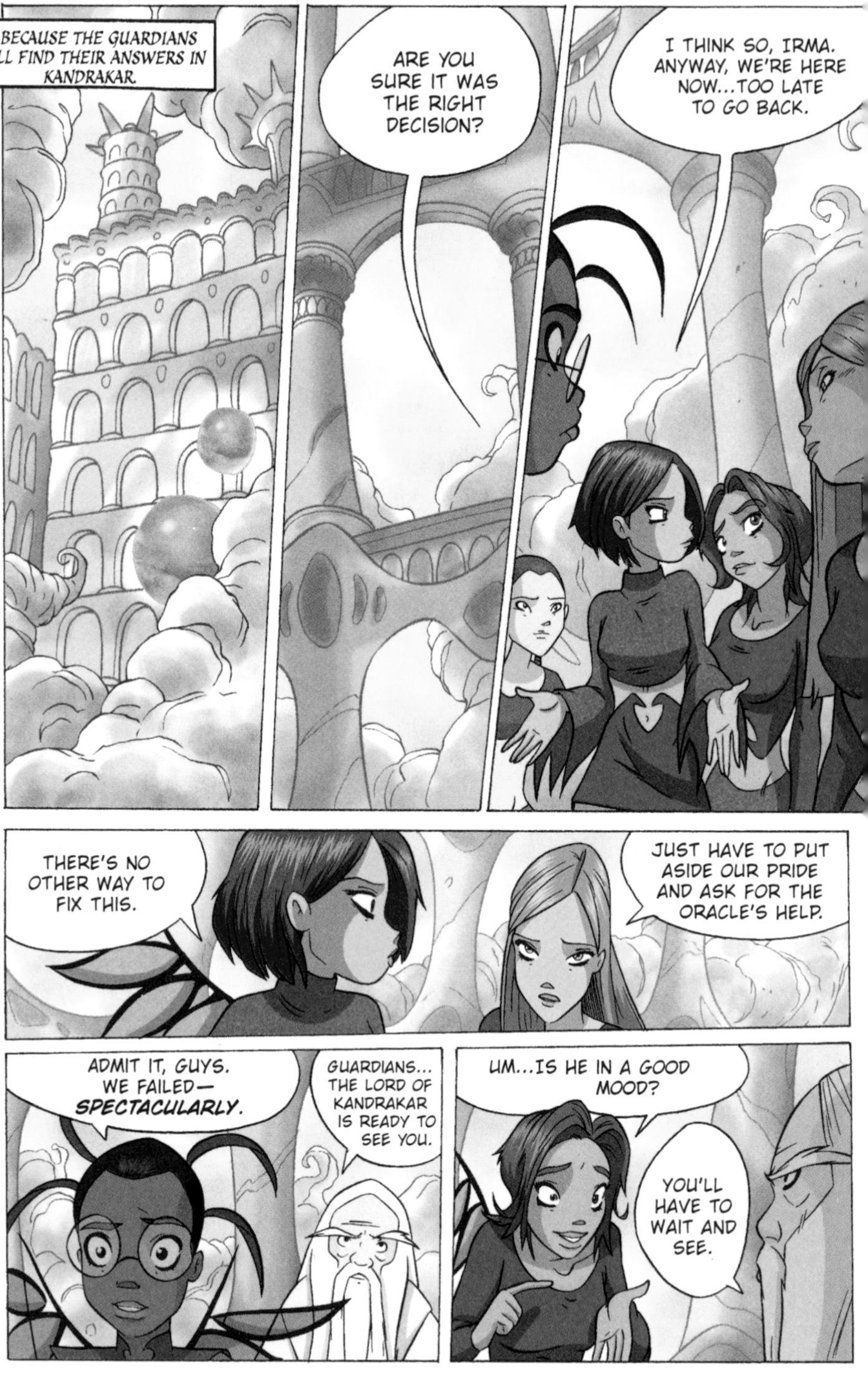
...BECAUSE THE GUARDIANS WILL FIND THEIR ANSWERS IN KANDRAKAR.
ARE YOU SURE IT WAS THE RIGHT DECISION?
I THINK SO, IRMA. ANYWAY, WE'RE HERE NOW...TOO LATE TO GO BACK.
THERE'S NO OTHER WAY TO FIX THIS.
JUST HAVE TO PUT ASIDE OUR PRIDE AND ASK FOR THE ORACLE'S HELP.
ADMIT IT, GUYS. WE FAILED—**SPECTACULARLY**.
GUARDIANS... THE LORD OF KANDRAKAR IS READY TO SEE YOU.
UM...IS HE IN A GOOD MOOD?
YOU'LL HAVE TO WAIT AND SEE.

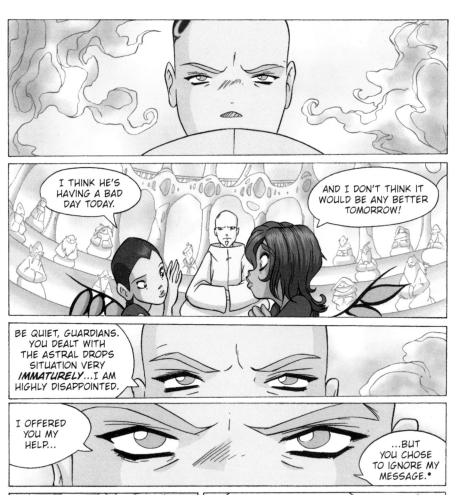

I THINK HE'S HAVING A BAD DAY TODAY.

AND I DON'T THINK IT WOULD BE ANY BETTER TOMORROW!

BE QUIET, GUARDIANS. YOU DEALT WITH THE ASTRAL DROPS SITUATION VERY *IMMATURELY*...I AM HIGHLY DISAPPOINTED.

I OFFERED YOU MY HELP...

...BUT YOU CHOSE TO IGNORE MY MESSAGE.*

AND NOW THAT IT'S TOO LATE, YOU ARE HERE BEGGING FOR MY AID.

WERE OTHERS NOT INVOLVED, I WOULD LEAVE YOU TO *DROWN IN YOUR OWN TROUBLES*.

*SEE CHAPTER #32

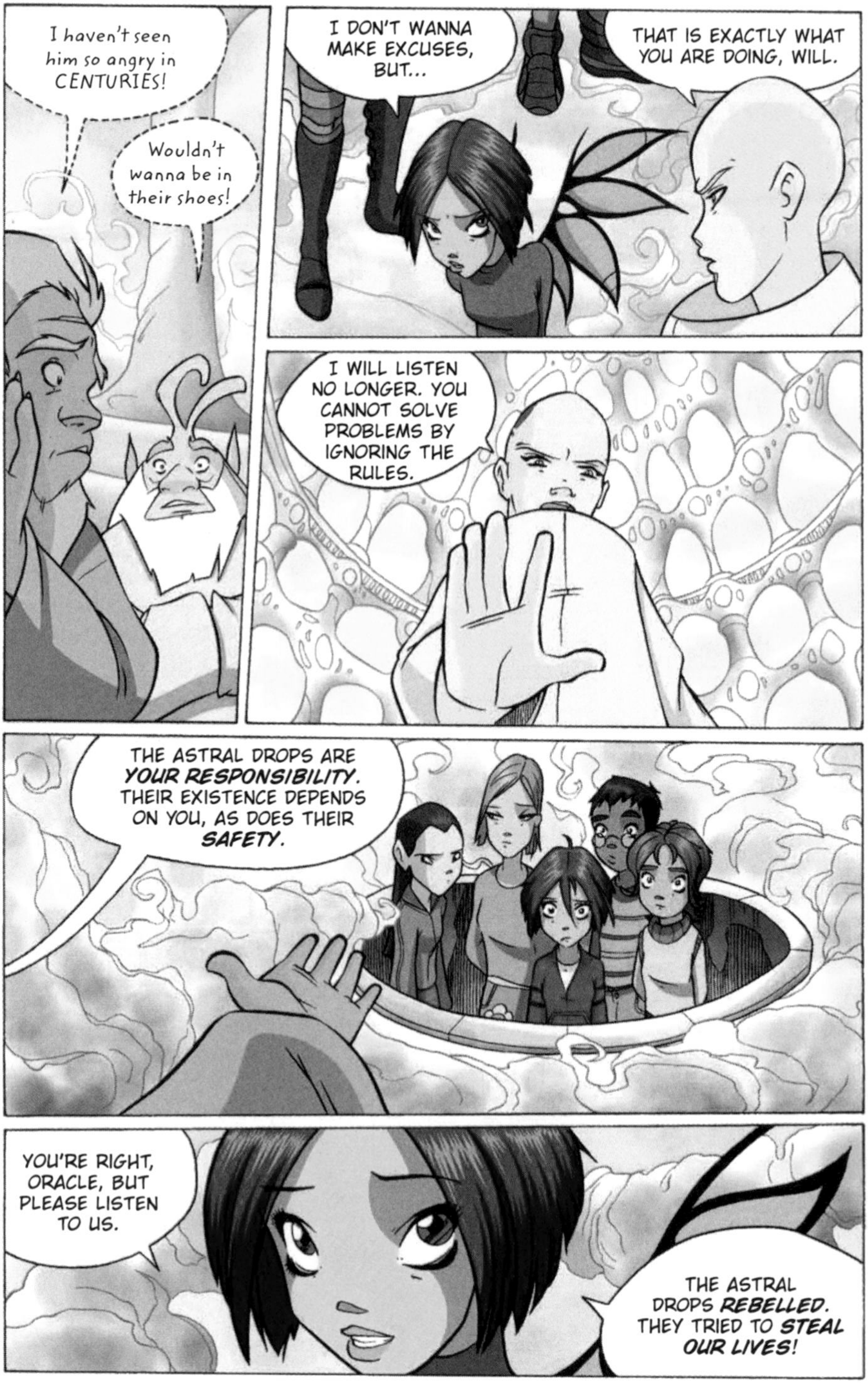
I haven't seen him so angry in CENTURIES!
Wouldn't wanna be in their shoes!
I DON'T WANNA MAKE EXCUSES, BUT...
THAT IS EXACTLY WHAT YOU ARE DOING, WILL.
I WILL LISTEN NO LONGER. YOU CANNOT SOLVE PROBLEMS BY IGNORING THE RULES.
THE ASTRAL DROPS ARE *YOUR RESPONSIBILITY*. THEIR EXISTENCE DEPENDS ON YOU, AS DOES THEIR *SAFETY*.
YOU'RE RIGHT, ORACLE, BUT PLEASE LISTEN TO US.
THE ASTRAL DROPS *REBELLED*. THEY TRIED TO *STEAL OUR LIVES*!

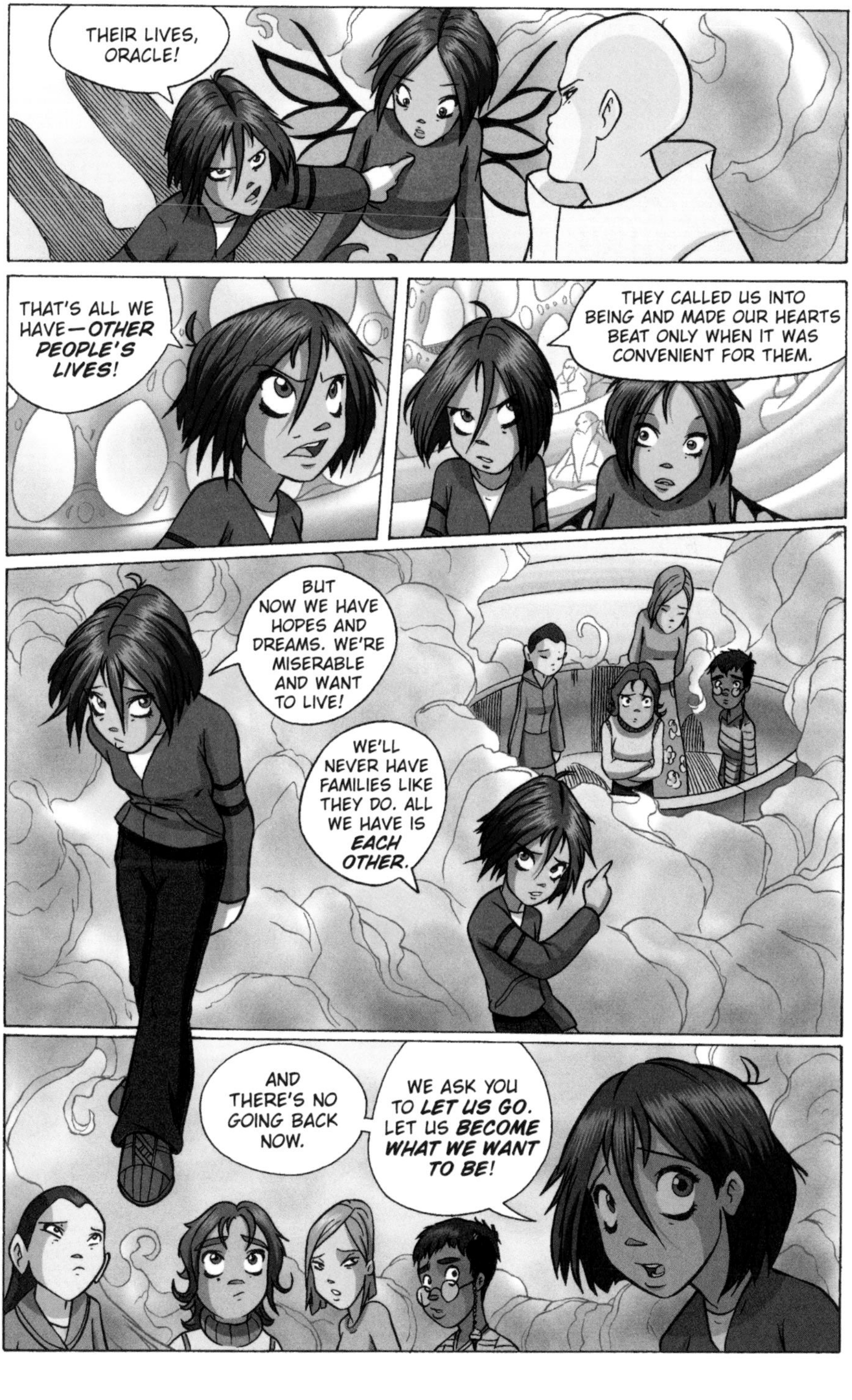
THEIR LIVES, ORACLE!
THAT'S ALL WE HAVE—OTHER PEOPLE'S LIVES!
THEY CALLED US INTO BEING AND MADE OUR HEARTS BEAT ONLY WHEN IT WAS CONVENIENT FOR THEM.
BUT NOW WE HAVE HOPES AND DREAMS. WE'RE MISERABLE AND WANT TO LIVE!
WE'LL NEVER HAVE FAMILIES LIKE THEY DO. ALL WE HAVE IS EACH OTHER.
AND THERE'S NO GOING BACK NOW.
WE ASK YOU TO LET US GO. LET US BECOME WHAT WE WANT TO BE!

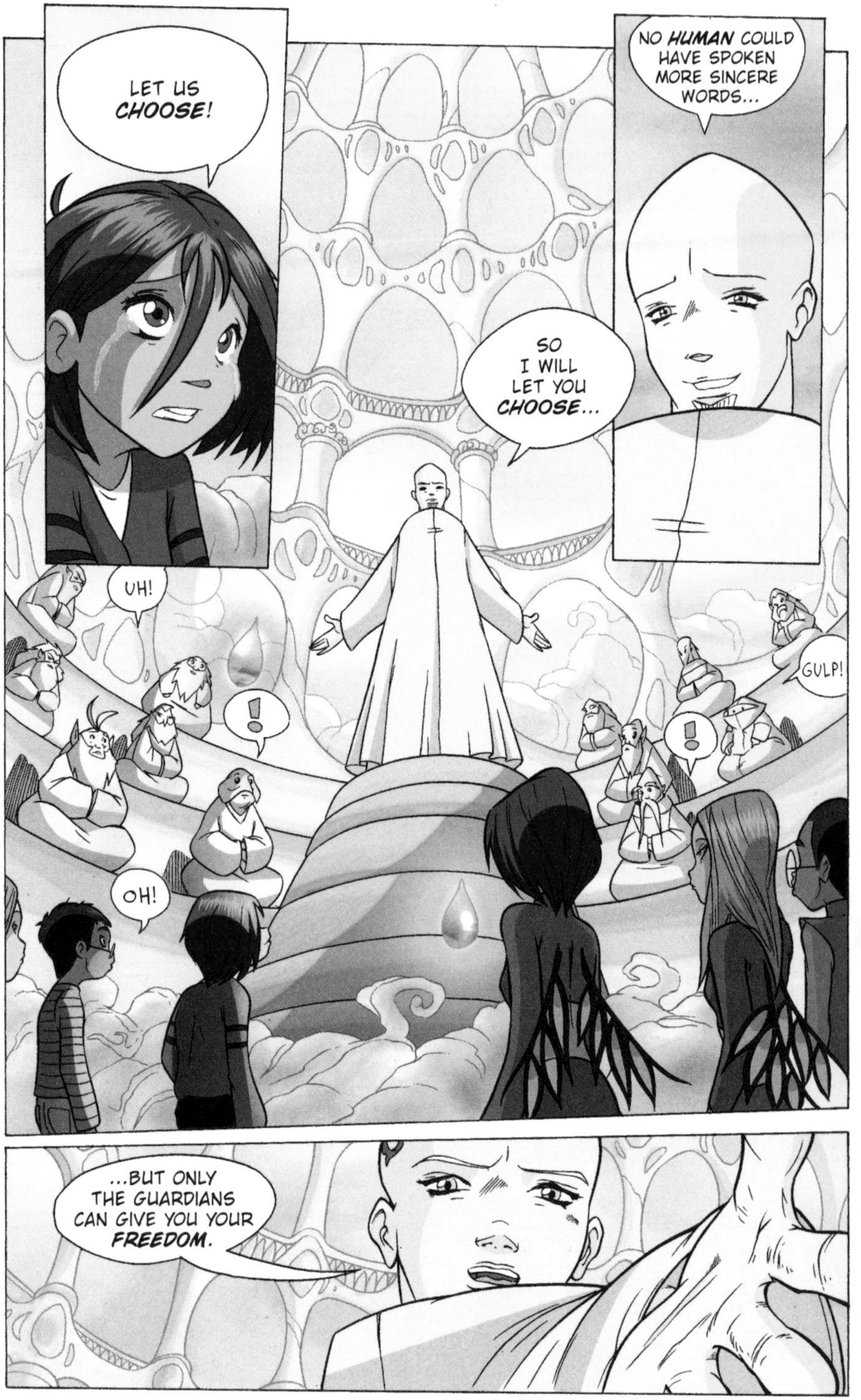
LET US CHOOSE!
NO HUMAN COULD HAVE SPOKEN MORE SINCERE WORDS...
SO I WILL LET YOU CHOOSE...
UH!
GULP!
OH!
...BUT ONLY THE GUARDIANS CAN GIVE YOU YOUR FREEDOM.

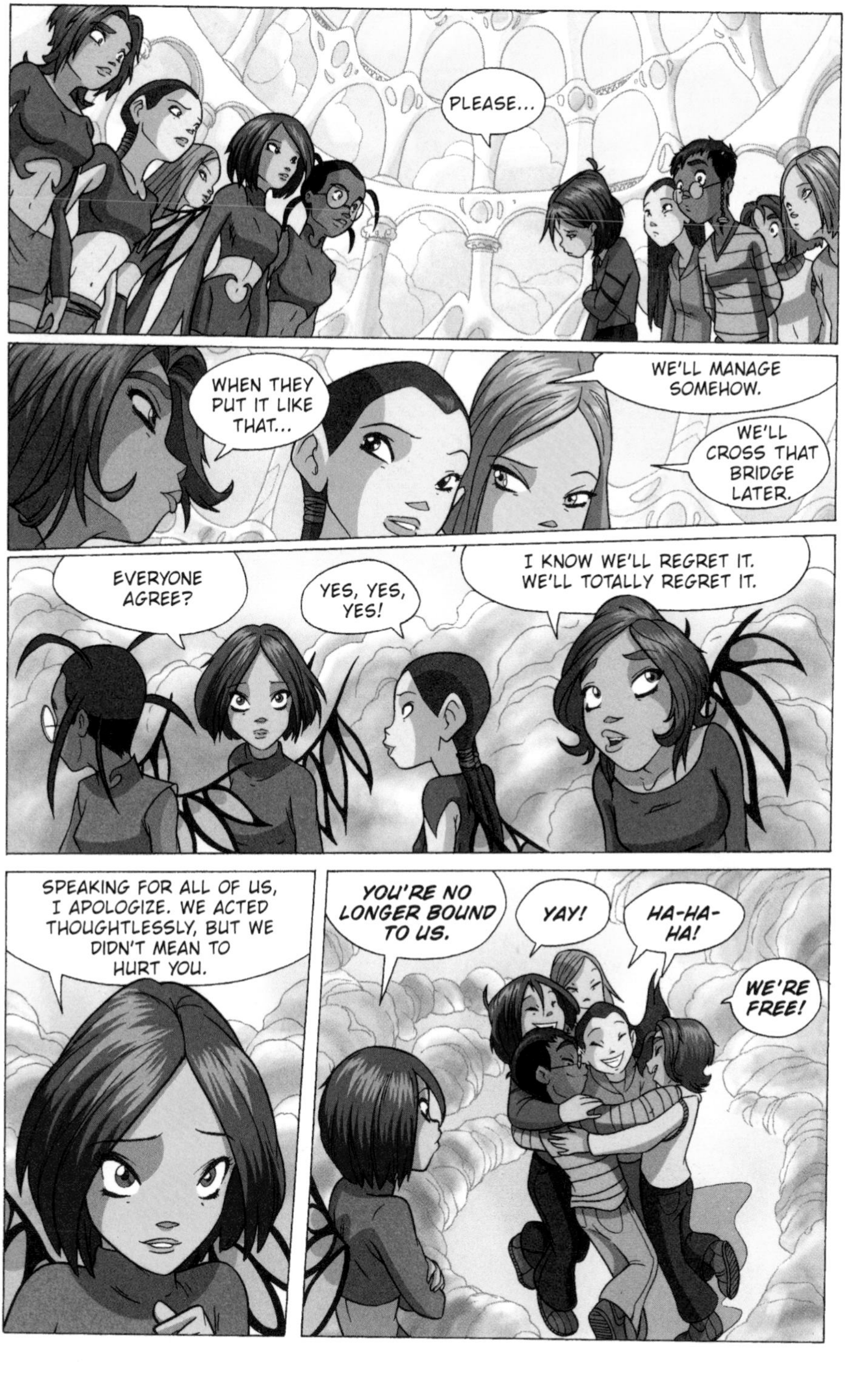
PLEASE...
WHEN THEY PUT IT LIKE THAT...
WE'LL MANAGE SOMEHOW.
WE'LL CROSS THAT BRIDGE LATER.
EVERYONE AGREE?
YES, YES, YES!
I KNOW WE'LL REGRET IT. WE'LL TOTALLY REGRET IT.
SPEAKING FOR ALL OF US, I APOLOGIZE. WE ACTED THOUGHTLESSLY, BUT WE DIDN'T MEAN TO HURT YOU.
YOU'RE NO LONGER BOUND TO US.
YAY!
HA-HA-HA!
WE'RE FREE!

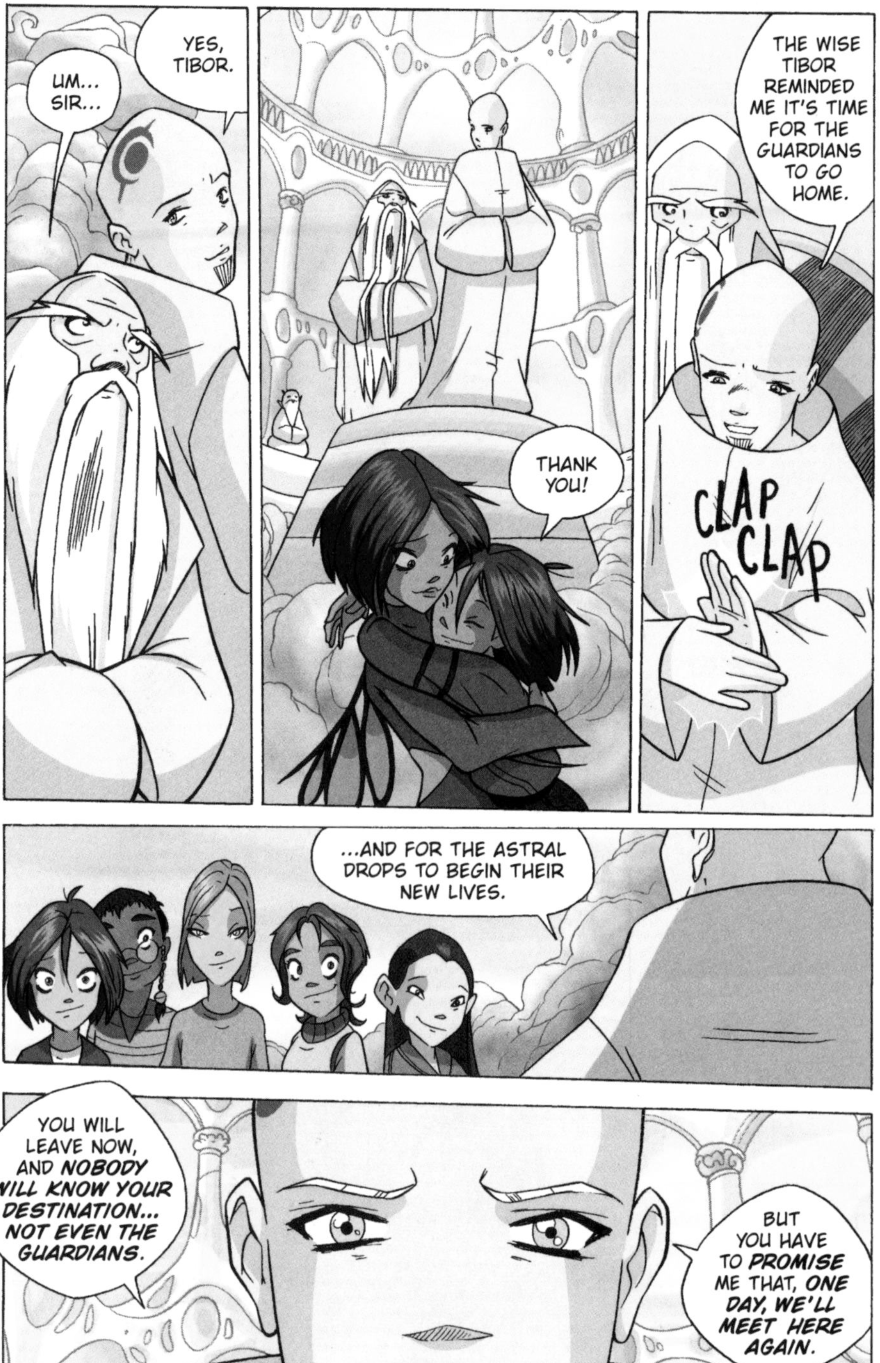
UM... SIR...
YES, TIBOR.
THANK YOU!
THE WISE TIBOR REMINDED ME IT'S TIME FOR THE GUARDIANS TO GO HOME.
CLAP CLAP
...AND FOR THE ASTRAL DROPS TO BEGIN THEIR NEW LIVES.
YOU WILL LEAVE NOW, AND NOBODY WILL KNOW YOUR DESTINATION... NOT EVEN THE GUARDIANS.
BUT YOU HAVE TO PROMISE ME THAT, ONE DAY, WE'LL MEET HERE AGAIN.

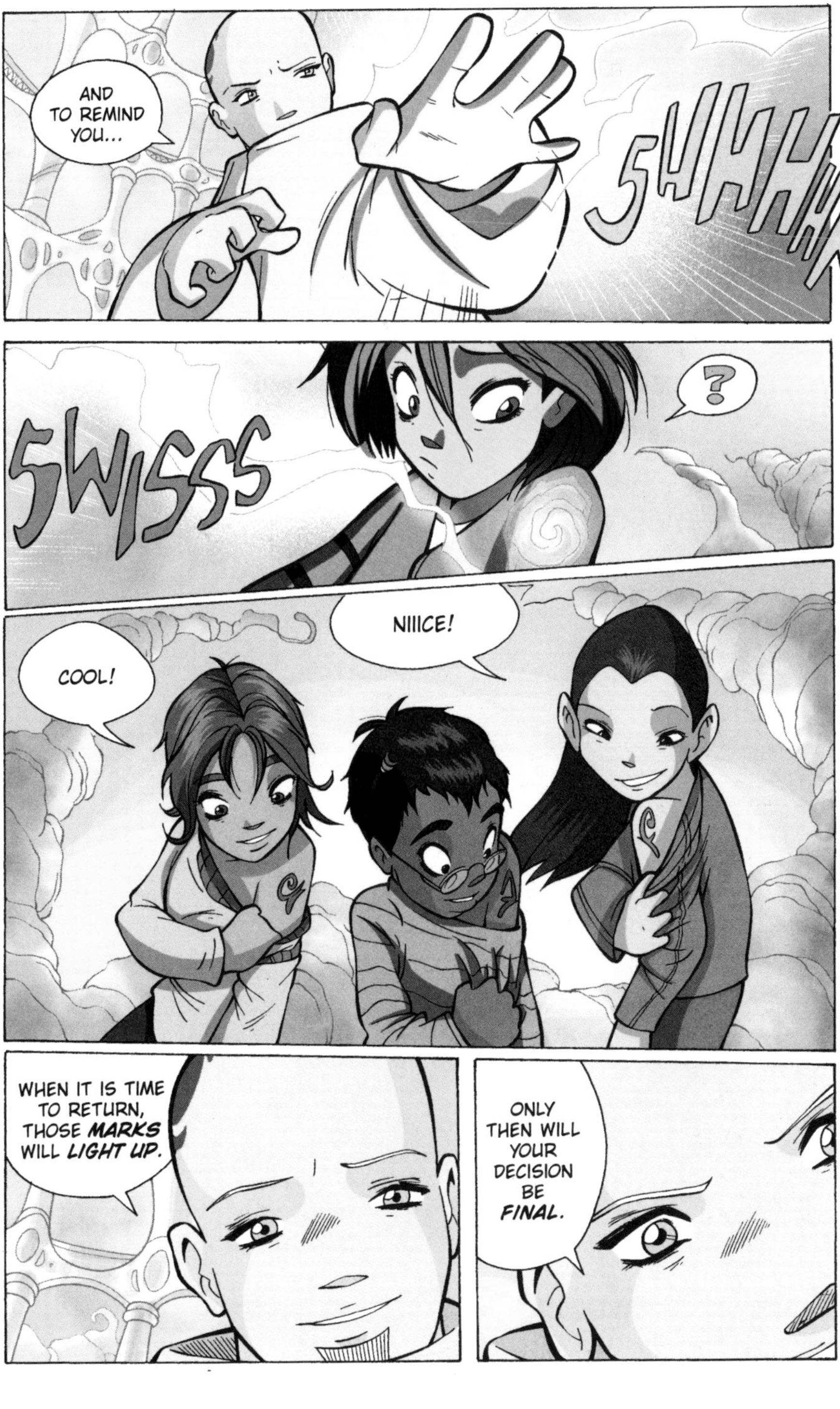
AND TO REMIND YOU...
SHHHHK
SWISSS
?
COOL!
NIIICE!
WHEN IT IS TIME TO RETURN, THOSE MARKS WILL LIGHT UP.
ONLY THEN WILL YOUR DECISION BE FINAL.

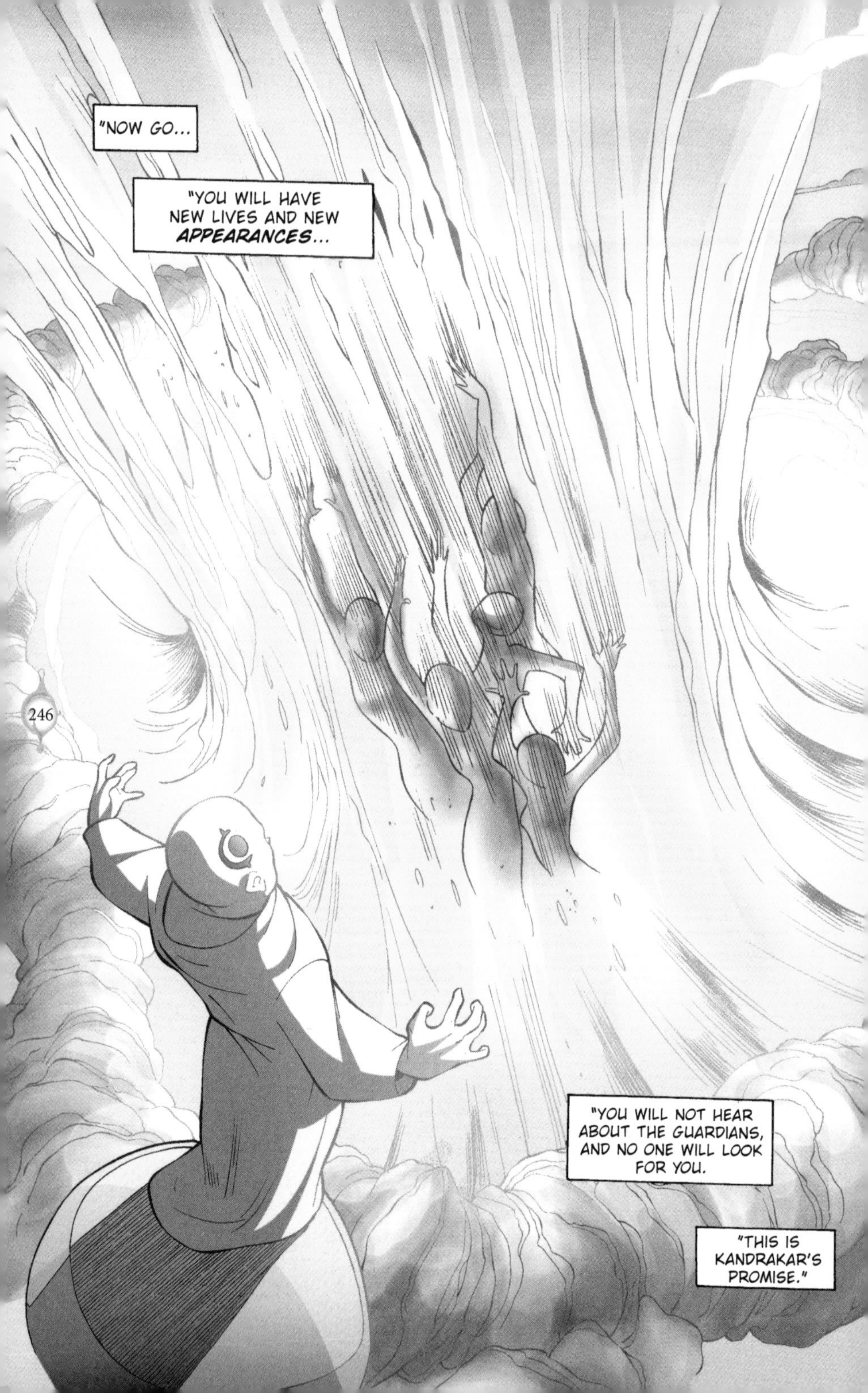
"NOW GO...
"YOU WILL HAVE NEW LIVES AND NEW APPEARANCES...
"YOU WILL NOT HEAR ABOUT THE GUARDIANS, AND NO ONE WILL LOOK FOR YOU.
"THIS IS KANDRAKAR'S PROMISE."

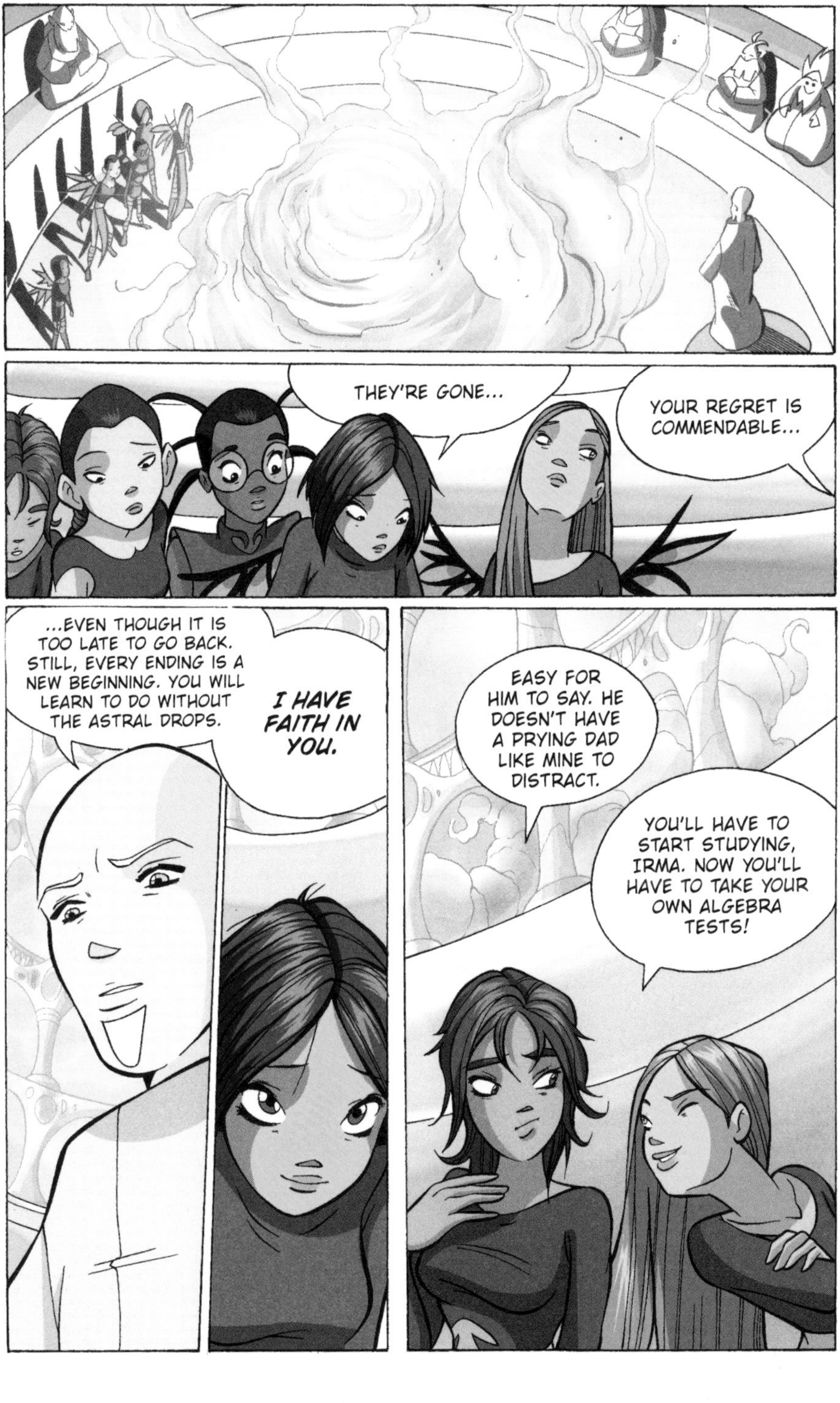
THEY'RE GONE...
YOUR REGRET IS COMMENDABLE...
...EVEN THOUGH IT IS TOO LATE TO GO BACK. STILL, EVERY ENDING IS A NEW BEGINNING. YOU WILL LEARN TO DO WITHOUT THE ASTRAL DROPS.
I HAVE FAITH IN YOU.
EASY FOR HIM TO SAY. HE DOESN'T HAVE A PRYING DAD LIKE MINE TO DISTRACT.
YOU'LL HAVE TO START STUDYING, IRMA. NOW YOU'LL HAVE TO TAKE YOUR OWN ALGEBRA TESTS!

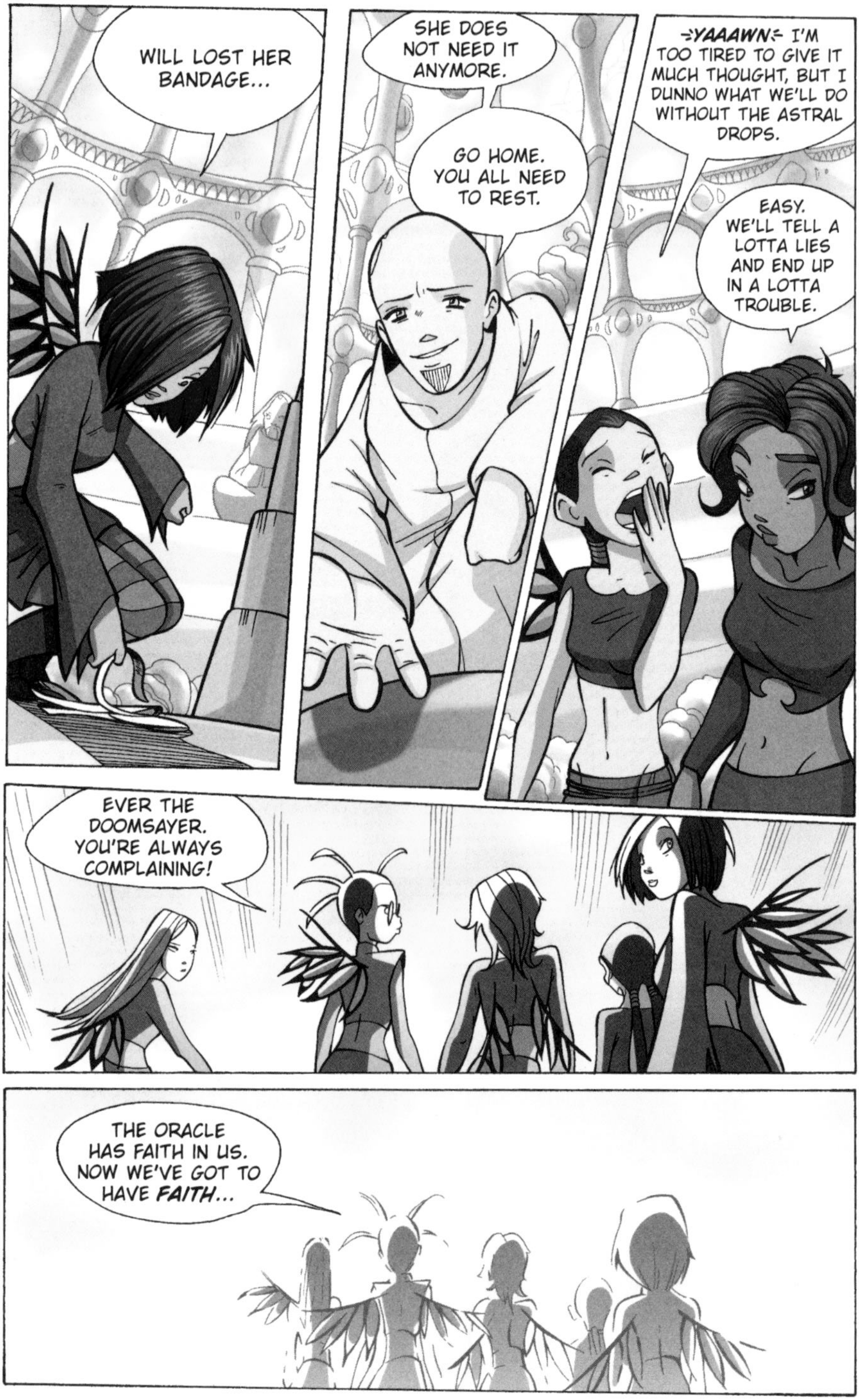
WILL LOST HER BANDAGE...
SHE DOES NOT NEED IT ANYMORE.
GO HOME. YOU ALL NEED TO REST.
=YAAAWN= I'M TOO TIRED TO GIVE IT MUCH THOUGHT, BUT I DUNNO WHAT WE'LL DO WITHOUT THE ASTRAL DROPS.
EASY. WE'LL TELL A LOTTA LIES AND END UP IN A LOTTA TROUBLE.
EVER THE DOOMSAYER. YOU'RE ALWAYS COMPLAINING!
THE ORACLE HAS FAITH IN US. NOW WE'VE GOT TO HAVE FAITH...

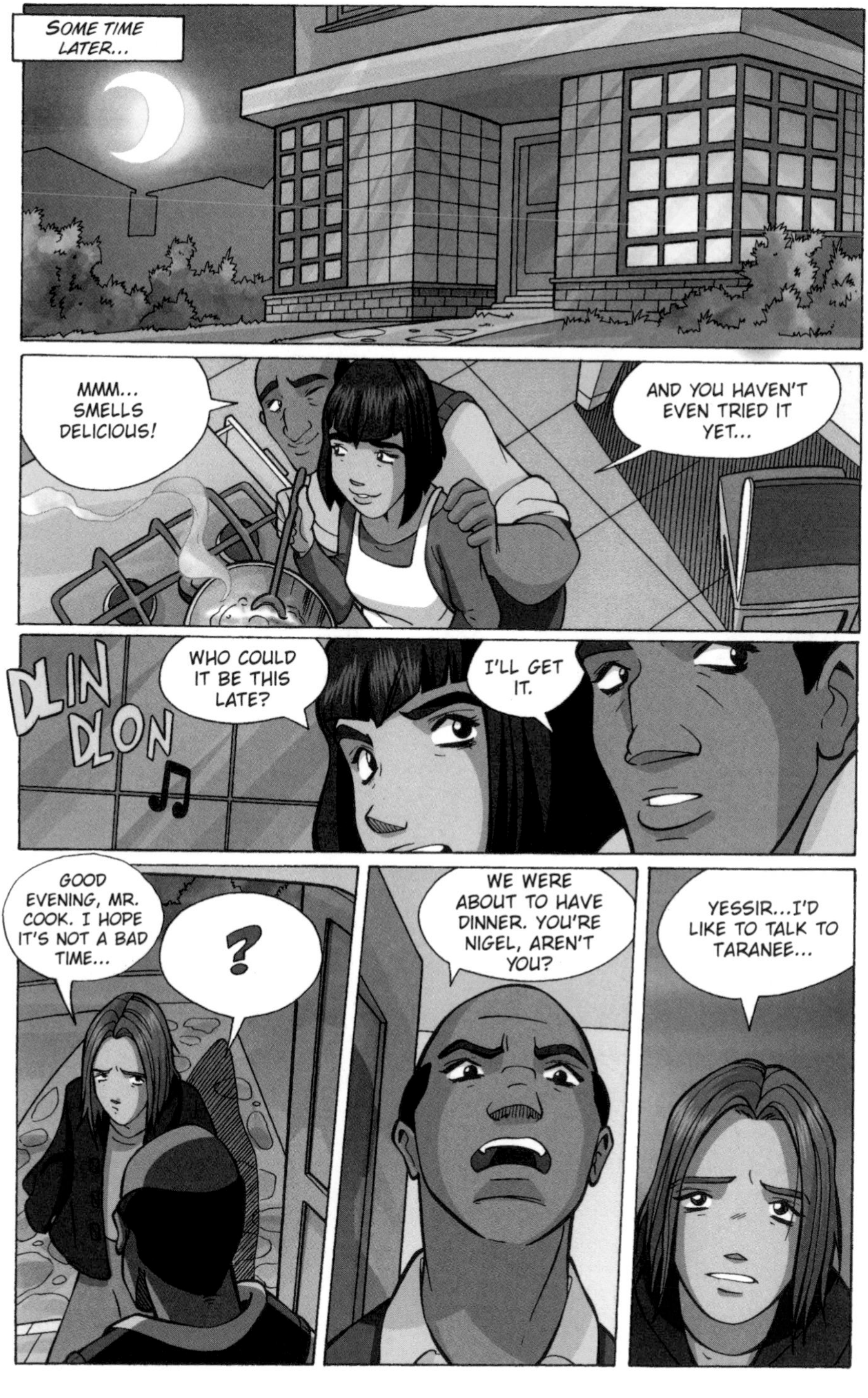
SOME TIME LATER...
MMM... SMELLS DELICIOUS!
AND YOU HAVEN'T EVEN TRIED IT YET...
DLIN DLON
WHO COULD IT BE THIS LATE?
I'LL GET IT.
GOOD EVENING, MR. COOK. I HOPE IT'S NOT A BAD TIME...
?
WE WERE ABOUT TO HAVE DINNER. YOU'RE NIGEL, AREN'T YOU?
YESSIR...I'D LIKE TO TALK TO TARANEE...

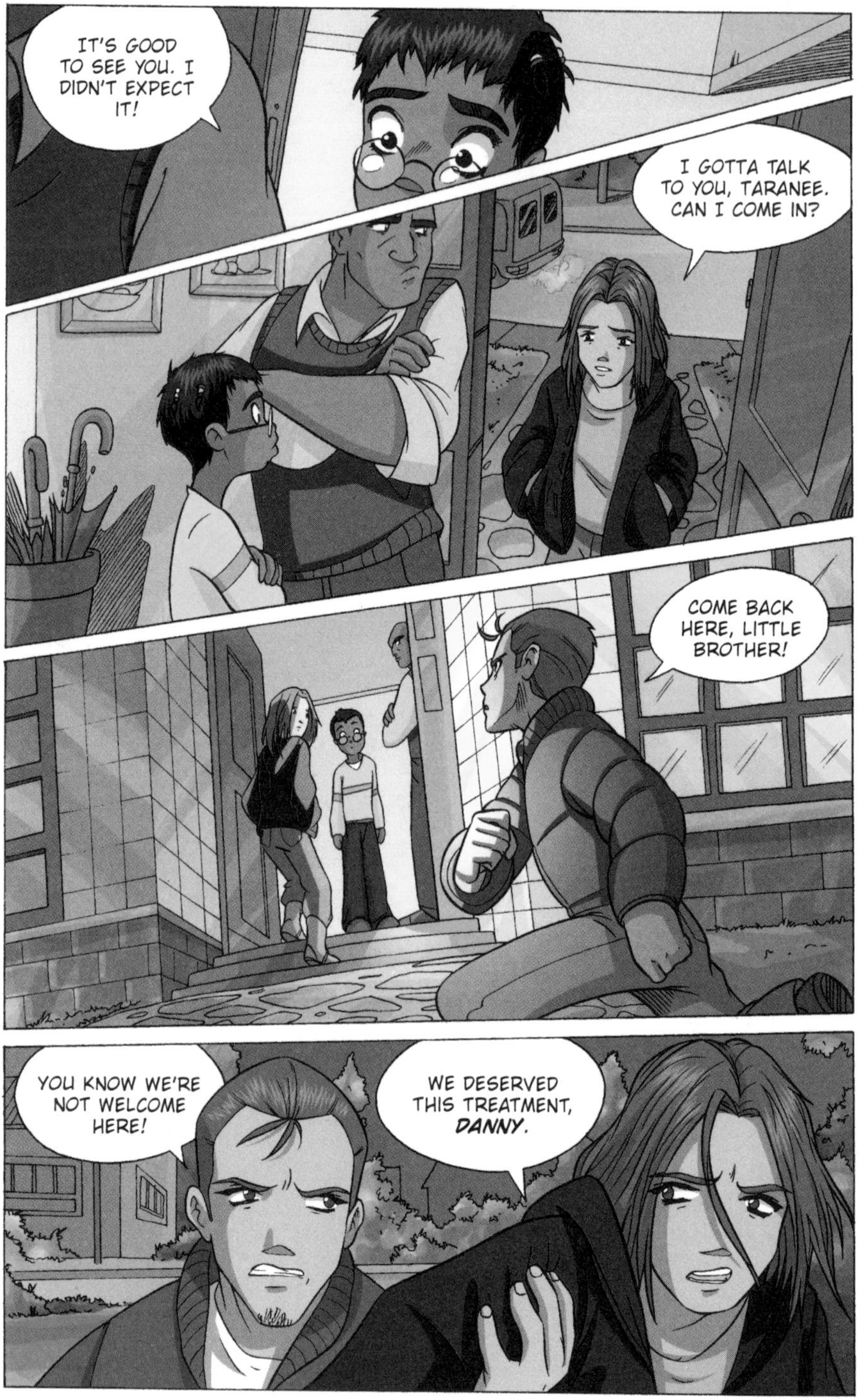
IT'S GOOD TO SEE YOU. I DIDN'T EXPECT IT!
I GOTTA TALK TO YOU, TARANEE. CAN I COME IN?
COME BACK HERE, LITTLE BROTHER!
YOU KNOW WE'RE NOT WELCOME HERE!
WE DESERVED THIS TREATMENT, ***DANNY***.

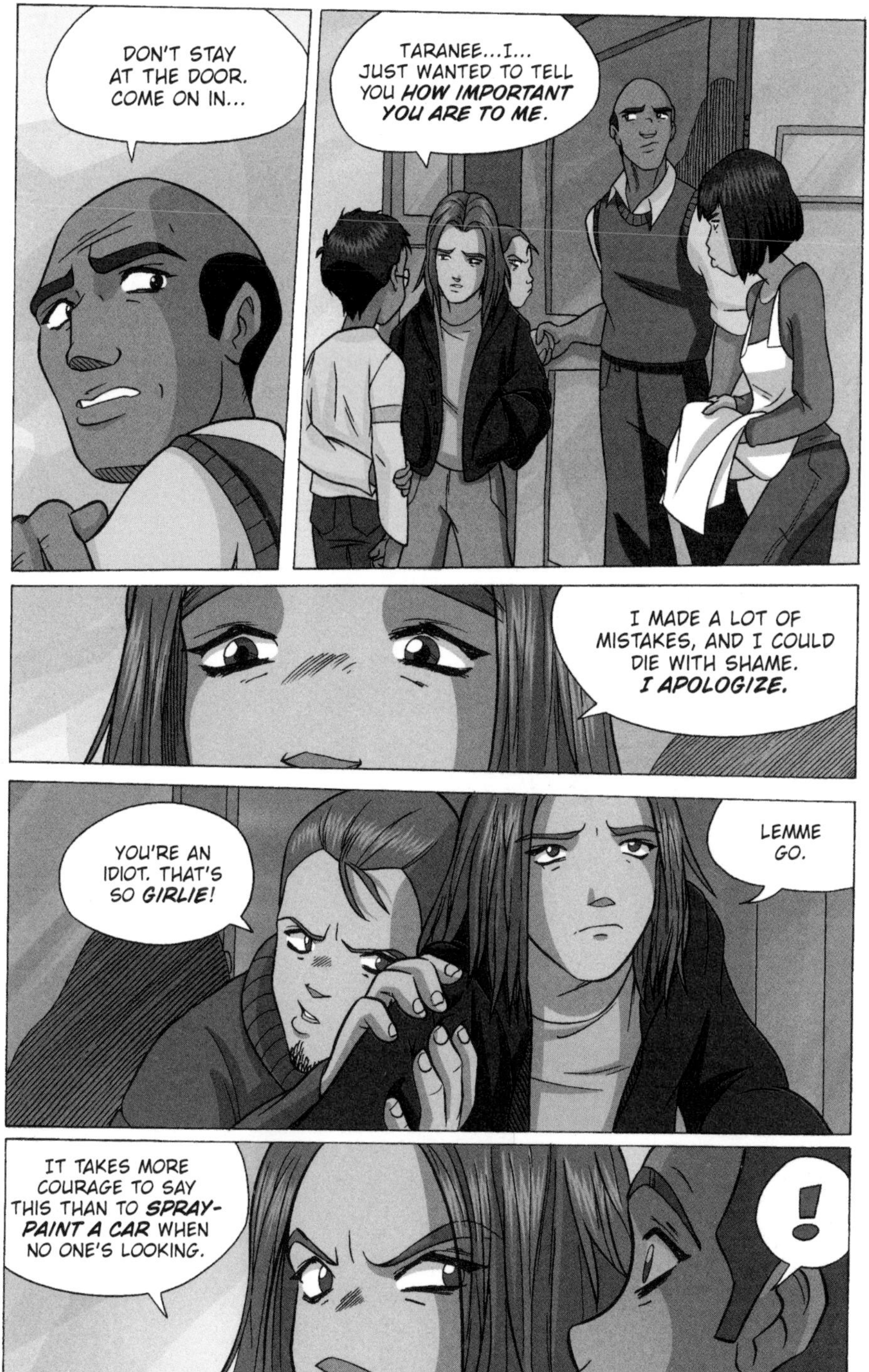
DON'T STAY AT THE DOOR. COME ON IN...
TARANEE...I... JUST WANTED TO TELL YOU HOW IMPORTANT YOU ARE TO ME.
I MADE A LOT OF MISTAKES, AND I COULD DIE WITH SHAME. I APOLOGIZE.
YOU'RE AN IDIOT. THAT'S SO GIRLIE!
LEMME GO.
IT TAKES MORE COURAGE TO SAY THIS THAN TO SPRAY-PAINT A CAR WHEN NO ONE'S LOOKING.
!

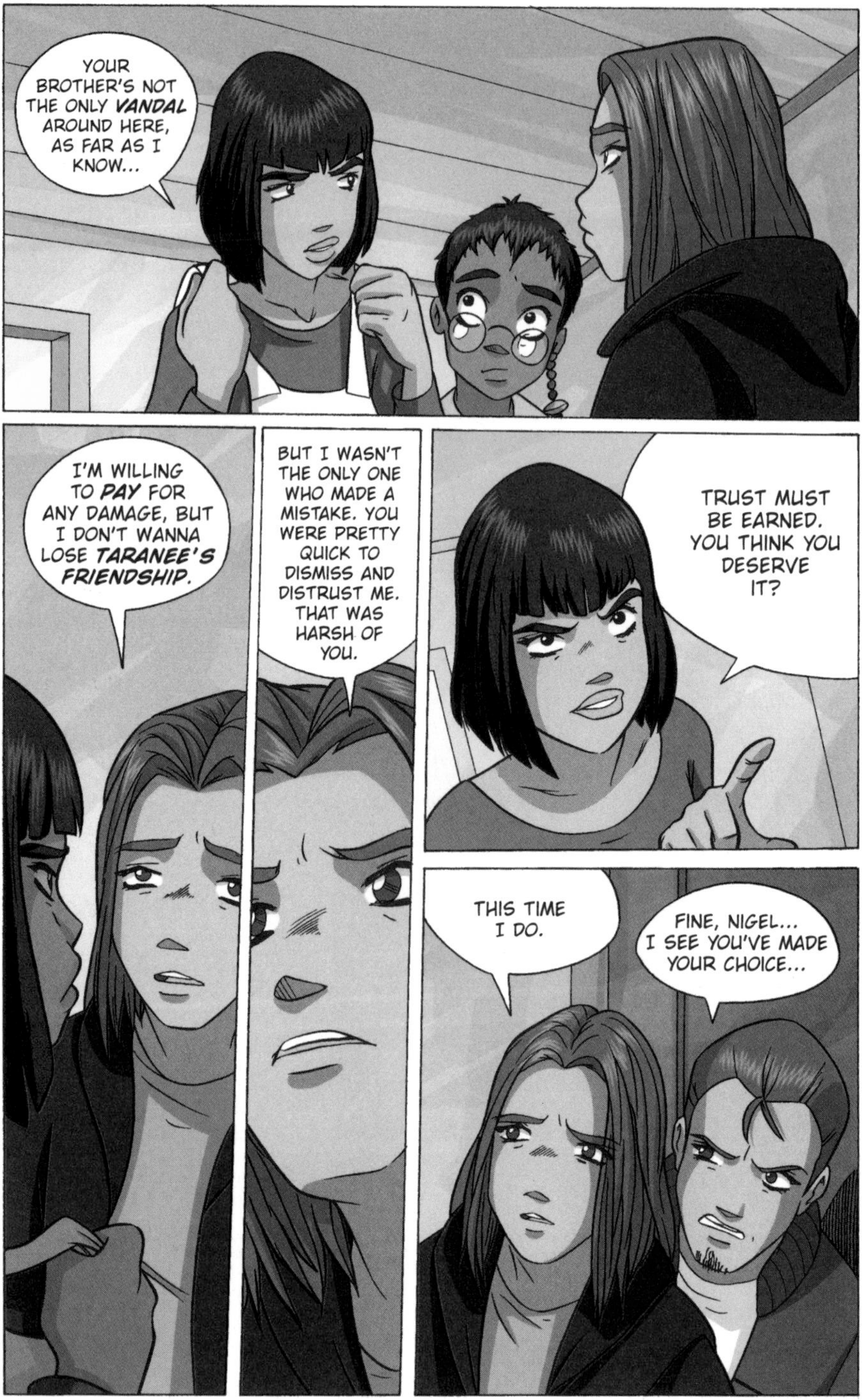
YOUR BROTHER'S NOT THE ONLY VANDAL AROUND HERE, AS FAR AS I KNOW...
I'M WILLING TO PAY FOR ANY DAMAGE, BUT I DON'T WANNA LOSE TARANEE'S FRIENDSHIP.
BUT I WASN'T THE ONLY ONE WHO MADE A MISTAKE. YOU WERE PRETTY QUICK TO DISMISS AND DISTRUST ME. THAT WAS HARSH OF YOU.
TRUST MUST BE EARNED. YOU THINK YOU DESERVE IT?
THIS TIME I DO.
FINE, NIGEL... I SEE YOU'VE MADE YOUR CHOICE...

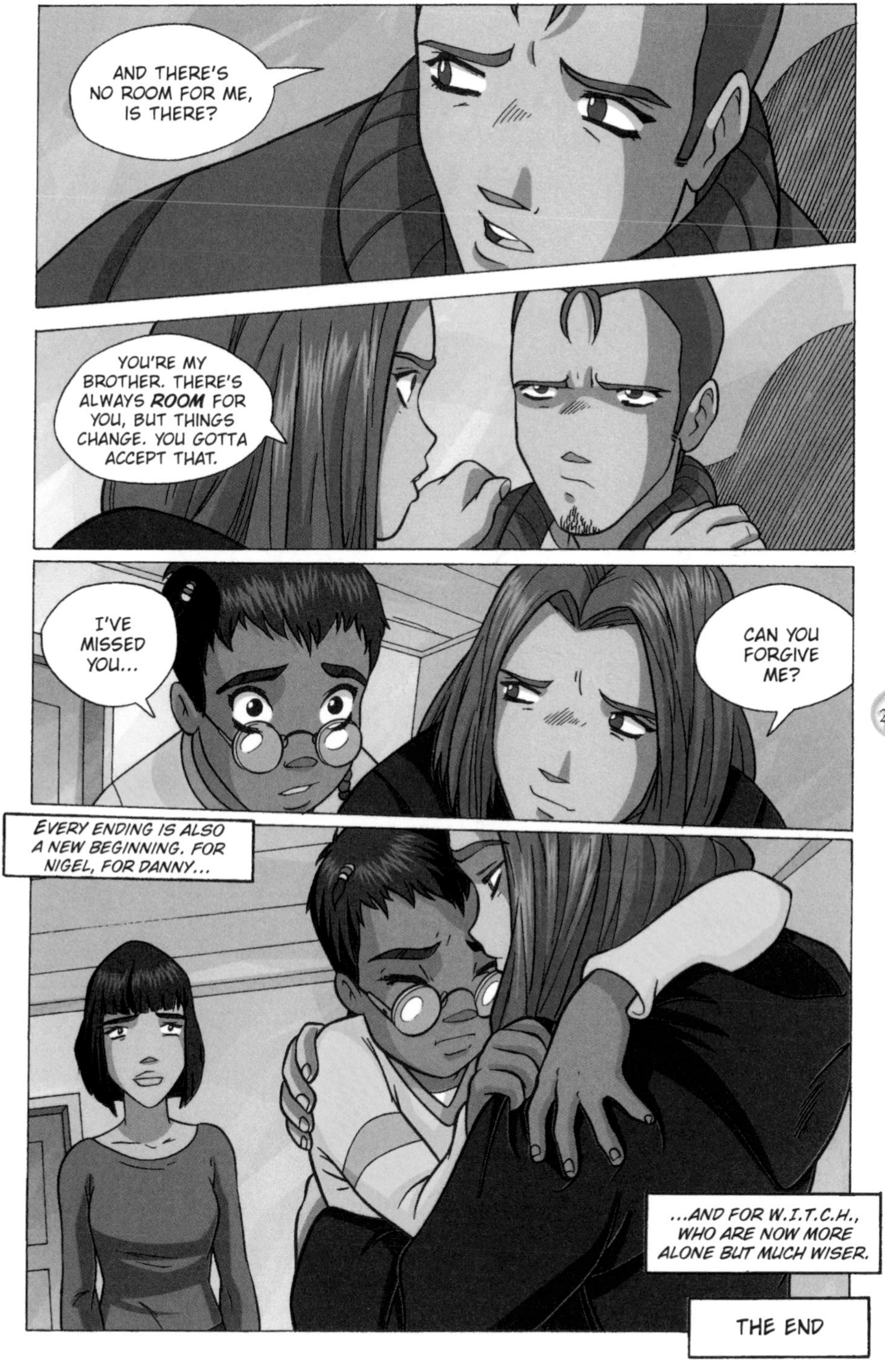
AND THERE'S NO ROOM FOR ME, IS THERE?
YOU'RE MY BROTHER. THERE'S ALWAYS ROOM FOR YOU, BUT THINGS CHANGE. YOU GOTTA ACCEPT THAT.
I'VE MISSED YOU...
CAN YOU FORGIVE ME?
EVERY ENDING IS ALSO A NEW BEGINNING. FOR NIGEL, FOR DANNY...
...AND FOR W.I.T.C.H., WHO ARE NOW MORE ALONE BUT MUCH WISER.
THE END

In the wardrobe of...

A Thousand Secrets in Irma's Wardrobe

1 The mirror, to fix her hair. Irma likes pigtails and colorful hairclips. It's the last thing she does before leaving the house.

2 The dress Irma wore at the Halloween party, and it's one of her favorites. She thinks it's her lucky dress.

3 Irma collects snow globes. She has so many, she doesn't know where to put them anymore, so some end up in her wardrobe.

4 Scarf-sarong with flowery pattern. It goes around her neck in the winter and over her swimsuit in the summer.

5 Irma's always cold. Last Christmas, her dad gave her this super-warm sweater.

6 Lilac gloves. Irma loves this color; it reminds her of spring...

7 "City" boots. For rainy days and long walks. Worn with trousers or a skirt.

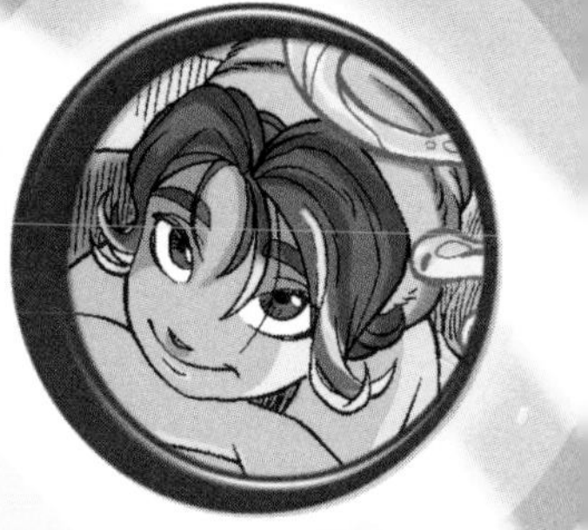

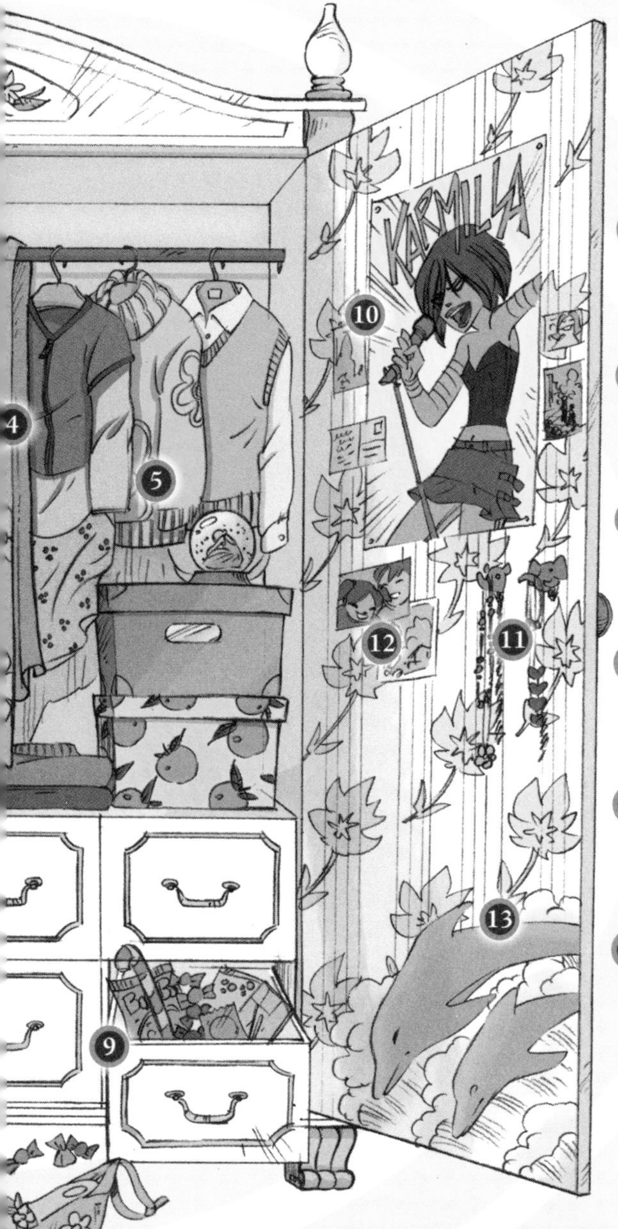
KARMILLA
10
4
5
12
11
13
9

8 These sandals were on sale at Brick's, but she never wears them. She likes them, but they're not her style…

9 The candy drawer. Irma buys some every time she goes to the market, then promptly forgets about it until it expires.

10 Superstar Karmilla has a special place in Irma's heart…and in her wardrobe. The right door is all for her.

11 Irma hung up all the necklaces she made, though they didn't turn out so well...Hay Lin is definitely better at it!

12 A photo she really loves from a vacation at the shore when she was little. It's nice to open her wardrobe and see it.

13 Irma adores dolphins. She asked for Hay Lin's help drawing them and is really proud of the results!

W.i.t.c.h.

Will   Irma   Taranee   Cornelia   Hay Lin

Part III. A Crisis on Both Worlds • Volume 3

Series Created by Elisabetta Gnone
Comic Art Direction: Alessandro Barbucci, Barbara Canepa

W.I.T.C.H.: The Graphic Novel, Part III: A Crisis on Both Worlds © Disney Enterprises, Inc.

English translation © 2018 by Disney Enterprises, Inc.

JY
1290 Avenue of the Americas
New York, NY 10104

Visit us at yenpress.com
facebook.com/yenpress
twitter.com/yenpress
yenpress.tumblr.com
instagram.com/yenpress

First JY Edition: May 2018

JY is an imprint of Yen Press, LLC.
The JY name and logo are trademarks of Yen Press, LLC.

The publisher is not responsible for websites (or their content) that are not owned by the publisher.

Library of Congress Control Number: 2017950917

ISBNs:
978-0-316-47710-9 (paperback)
978-1-9753-2659-3 (ebook)

10 9 8 7 6 5 4 3 2 1

LSC-C

Cover Art by Giada Perissinotto
Colors by Andrea Cagol

Translation by Linda Ghio and
Stephanie Dagg at Editing Zone
Lettering by Katie Blakeslee

THE GREATEST GIFT

Concept and Script by Giulia Conti
Layout and Pencils by Alessia Martusciello
Inks by Marina Baggio and Roberta Zanotta
Color and Light Direction by Francesco Legramandi
Title Page Art by Alessia Martusciello
with Colors by Andrea Cagol and Francesco Legramandi

DROPS OF FREEDOM

Concept and Script by Paola Mulazzi
Layout by Gianluca Panniello and Paolo Campinoti
Pencils by Giada Perissinotto and Elisabetta Melaranci
Inks by Marina Baggio, Roberta Zanotta, and Santa Zangari
Color and Light Direction by Francesco Legramandi
Title Page Art by Gianluca Panniello
with Colors by Francesco Legramandi

REFLECTED LIVES

Concept and Script by Bruno Enna
Layout and Pencils by Federico Bertolucci
Inks by Marina Baggio and Roberta Zanotta
Color and Light Direction by Francesco Legramandi
Title Page Art by Federico Bertolucci and Giada Perissinotto
with Colors by Andrea Cagol and Marco Colletti

REBEL SPIRITS

Concept by Francesco Artibani
Script by Giulia Conti
Layout by Claudio Sciarrone
Pencils by Alberto Zanon
Inks by Santa Zangari and Riccardo Sisti
Color and Light Direction by Francesco Legramandi
Title Page Art by Claudio Sciarrone and Alberto Zanon
with Colors by Andrea Cagol and Francesco Legramandi